THE MINA SCARLETTI SERIES

Books 1-3

Books 1-3

Linda Stratmann

SAPERE
BOOKS

THE MINA SCARLETTI SERIES

Published by Sapere Books.

20 Windermere Drive, Leeds, England, LS17 7UZ,
United Kingdom

saperebooks.com

BOOK ONE: MR SCARLETTI'S GHOST

Chapter One

On a sparkling June day Mina Scarletti gazed out across the dipping waters of the Channel, thinking about ghosts. They were pirates and murderers with the coarse burn of the noose still on their sinewy throats, smugglers endlessly searching for lost cargoes, and lovers driven by grief or shame to seek cold peace below the waves. Their images, scored in wood and glistening with thick black ink on cheap paper, rolled and pocketed, torn and soiled, were, she thought with no trace of regret, the only children she would ever have.

Mina had awoken that morning to find that a narrow line of pain had drawn itself down the right side of her neck, darting over her shoulder and plunging into her back. She was usually free of pain but every so often it would return like an old friend needing to be soothed, and then she would go out and rest her palms on the railings of the King's Road esplanade, and lean there for a while, looking at the sea. Two worlds met and fought here, worlds where life in one meant death in the other, and hungry wavelets hissed as they scrambled for purchase on the pebbled beach where ribbons of black weed gave off a sour rank odour.

Stiffly, awkwardly, Mina turned for home, walking with her odd, limping, lurching gait, like a small dark bird with a broken wing. She was composing a new story about a haunted jewel that had been flung into the sea by a cursed and dying man, but was found again in the maw of a great ugly fish. Mina wondered, not for the first time, what her nervous mother would think if she knew that her daughter occupied her hours with writing not wholesome stories for children, as the family had been led to believe, but tales of almost unimaginable horror.

The quiet season was drawing to a close, and Brighton, freshly painted and varnished, its gardens invitingly in bloom, was awaiting its first flood of visitors. It was the best part of the year, when the town was bathed in a warm, clear, glowing light that glittered off the sea. In a few days the seafront would be crowded with noisy families; women in their gaudy holiday clothes, men chasing hats that had been whipped from their heads by the unaccustomed breeze, children scattered like frilly scuttling crabs over the shingled beach, while overhead, from early to late, clifftop bands boomed and blared under snapping flags. Vehicles of every size and kind would rattle back and forth along the King's Road, which became a kind of Piccadilly-by-the-sea. Contemplative visitors, who read novels or simply wished to gaze at the sea in peace, turned to the old Chain Pier in the east, but fashionable promenaders who had come to see and be seen flocked to the bazaars, exhibitions and wide walking deck of the new West Pier.

Everywhere the smiling, sunny faces of strangers would suddenly darken and turn away when they saw Mina. Sometimes a helpful gentleman, not seeing her face, would hurry up and offer his arm, and as she turned to smile at him he would recoil in alarm to see the head of a woman of twenty-five on what he had assumed to be the body of a shrivelled ancient.

If Mina Scarletti had not had a twisted back she would have stood just over five feet in height, but as it was, her spine, curving treacherously first one way and then the other like a bony snake, had crushed and shrunk her to the size of a child, tilted her hip, forced her shoulder blade and ribcage out of their proper places, and made her into a cruel parody of womanhood. Medical men, after their accustomed fashion had given the affliction a Latin name, *scoliosis*.

Shock, pity and embarrassment were the landscape of Mina's daily life, but the one ghost she never thought of was the ghost of what she might have been.

Mina hobbled up the slope of Montpelier Road, a long narrow street prettily carved with the forms of seashells and ammonites, which lay on the western side of the town where the breezes were kinder than in the gusty east. The Scarlettis had moved there two years ago, when her father's declining health had forced him to retire from his business of publishing stories for the Scarletti Library of Romance, and leave the choking fogs of London. Brighton, he had been assured, was in itself a doctor, and his best hope of recovery. Their new home with its gracefully curving bay windows that welcomed in the healing light was, as everything that is best in Brighton, tall, like a plant reaching for the sun. It was hard enough for the maidservant, Rose, a strong young girl, who tackled the stairs from basement to attic with a permanent unspoken grumble on her lips, but for Mina, every step was a hill.

Henry Scarletti had not expected to die so soon, indeed he had rather expected to live, since the most successful doctors are those who only have good news for their patients. In his last few days, choking on the tumours in his swollen throat, he had been unable to eat or speak, but he knew that Mina was beside him. There were those who claimed to have seen the spirit of a dying person leave the body and rise up to Heaven like a soft transparent wisp of light, but at the moment of her father's passing, Mina saw nothing.

After Henry's death Mina's mother Louisa retired into a state of melancholy and Mina took the entire management of the household upon herself. Her first act had been to engage Miss Simmons, a quiet, dutiful person, as a nurse companion to her mother, and the second was to let the upper floor apartments to a fifty-year-old widow, Mrs Parchment, who had retired to Brighton for her health and pleasure. This energetic lady enjoyed brisk walks, sunshine and sea breezes, and thought nothing of basking in a cold east wind with a cliff-top picnic of bread and cheese or watching gales sweep in from the sea, bringing heavy waves crashing on to the esplanade. Mina hoped that Mrs Parchment might do what she had failed to achieve; take her mother out into the light to breathe sea air and see the moving colours of fashionable visitors, but found to her disappointment that the lady was not disposed to enjoy any company other than her own.

There was a black iron railing by the side of the three tall steps to Mina's front door, which assisted her climb, and she energetically clutched and swayed herself to the top. Many people, seeing her ungainly rocking walk along a flat pavement concluded that she was unable to use a staircase, either up or down, but there were few obstacles she could not negotiate unaided if she set her mind to it.

She was looking forward to a busy afternoon, composing her new story and writing letters to her brothers and sister. Her older brother, Edward, had been preoccupied with business in London since their father's death, and her sister, Enid, the beauty of the family, had escaped the house of mourning to marry a Mr Inskip, the dullest solicitor in England, and became the mother of twins within a year. Enid had once confessed that marriage and motherhood were not all what she had expected them to be, and neither, it appeared, was Mr Inskip. There was always the hope that Mina's younger brother Richard would descend upon Brighton, as she had not seen him in several weeks. Richard, with a cheerful optimistic nature and confidence that the future would somehow take care of itself, was constantly about to make a great fortune in ventures which he was only able to describe in the vaguest terms. It was impossible not to like him, but every time he came home, lifting his mother's spirits with his extravagant promises, and borrowing money, Mina suspected that his generosity was chiefly benefitting his gambling friends.

As she took off her bonnet in the hallway Rose came up from the kitchen, carrying a laden tea tray, which she took into the parlour. No doubt, thought Mina, her mother was entertaining one of her church visitors, ladies whose sole occupations in life were to call on the sick and miserable, and make them even more painfully aware of just how sick and miserable they were. Mrs Bettinson, particularly, was a connoisseur of misery in others — she fed on it and it made her fat. Her visits gave Louisa free rein to dwell on her many reasons for unhappiness, one of which Mina felt sure was herself. When Mrs Bettinson departed, leaving Louisa in an even more melancholy state than before, she always seemed a little fatter. Mina often found that lady sitting like a mountain of black frills with an inhospitable summit, in command of the parlour. She was, like the Queen, in a permanent state of mourning, although in her case it was not for one adored husband, but a series of relatives who had followed one another to the grave with such regularity that she had hardly been able to trim her gown with lilac before the next funeral plunged her once again into night. Unlike Mina's mother, however, Mrs Bettinson was able to manage her grief with equanimity, soothing herself by contemplating the distress of others. In particular she continued to assail Mina with stories of this or that wonderful doctor who had achieved the most marvellous cures. During the last ten years Mina had been subjected to every kind of treatment: deportment classes, shoulder bandages, a plaster of Paris waistcoat, and a steel brace, none of which had assisted her. She had been accused of causing the condition herself through bad habits of sitting and standing, accusations she had always denied even when threatened with surgery to cut or stretch her muscles. The final diagnosis, that the condition was incurable but would not get any worse, had come as a relief. She was four feet eight inches in height and there she would remain.

Louisa made no efforts to contradict Mrs Bettinson's implied and sometimes outright declaration that Mina's refusal to consult yet another medical man was only adding to her mother's unhappiness. Their visitor's latest enthusiasm was for a Dr Hamid, who she said was very handsome-looking, and had come all the way from India with some mysterious herbs, and opened an establishment where he did something unusual with steam. His special baths had helped so many to regain their health that he had been dubbed 'Dr Brighton'. Mina, who had had her fill of medical men, did not want to see Dr Hamid or Dr Brighton or any other doctor, even to please her mother, which it most probably would not, and informed Mrs Bettinson of this with a firmness that only just stopped short of insolence.

That afternoon, Mina, having no wish to spend time in the company of someone who found her defiant contentment so intolerable, decided to retire to her room and pursue her story of the jewel discovered in an ugly fish, a fish which now she thought about it was very fat with glossy black scales. The story had written itself a little further during her walk, and the jewel was now haunted by the ghost of a lovelorn lady, the dead betrothed of the cursed man who had thrown it away in a paroxysm of grief, but it would keep returning to him until he was able to break the curse, and be reunited with his beloved in death. Mina needed to commit the story to paper before she forgot the details, and started to work her way up the stairs.

Rose emerged from the parlour. 'Excuse me, Miss, but Mrs Scarletti says she would like you to take tea with her.'

Mina paused, wondering if she could plead a headache or a backache or any sort of an ache, but the streak of pain that had pinched her into wakefulness that morning had been warmed by the sun and was gone. Rose stood awkwardly shifting from one foot to the other, as if there was something more she wanted to say but dared not.

'Thank you, Rose,' said Mina, accepting that *The Cursed Emerald* would have to wait. Rose looked relieved and hurried away. Mina limped downstairs, opened the door of the parlour, and paused there in some surprise, for she was met with an unusual sight.

Louisa Scarletti was one of those fair, thin, frail-looking women, who always seemed to be on the verge of some terrible illness but was actually in perfect health. She had been favoured with an opalescent skin, vivid blue eyes and a cascade of blonde hair so pale it was almost white. It was now more than a year since Henry had died, sufficient time for most widows to begin participating in at least a few activities in which widowhood was not an essential feature, but she had become enamoured of the life of a semi-invalid, and embraced suffering as if it was in itself a comfort.

Louisa's favoured position from which to take tea was reclining on a sofa surrounded by cushions, a smelling bottle at her fingertips, sipping at barely half a cup of a pale tepid infusion, while weakly declining the temptation of a biscuit. Her lustre gone, she resembled an arrangement of *immortelles*, painted porcelain flowers that lived forever under a glass dome as a tribute to the dead. That afternoon, however, Mina found her mother sitting upright by the tea table wielding the heavy silver pot with energy and aplomb. Her companion, Simmons, with a wary and slightly uneasy look, sat silently by, poised for any duty or emergency.

'Mina, my dear, do take some tea,' said Louisa brightly. 'And I would very much like you to meet Mr Bradley.'

Mina entered the room, and a gentleman who had been seated in an easy chair at once started up. He had obviously been warned to expect someone of Mina's appearance, for he adopted a curious pose, his shoulders hunched forward, his hands clasped in front of him like a clergyman about to confer a blessing on the recently bereaved. He was not a clergyman, but Mina could not be sure what he was. A little below middling height and fleshy but not yet fat, he was aged about forty-five and neatly dressed after the fashion of a moderately well-to-do professional gentleman, with a dark rim of hair wrapped like a glossy, swollen worm about his balding head, and short trimmed side-whiskers. His features were unremarkable, but when he gazed on Mina his eyes opened very wide, his jaw sagged in dismay, and he adopted a look of sympathy that bordered on the grotesque.

'Mr Bradley is recently arrived in Brighton and I am pleased to say that he has joined the congregation at Christ Church,' said Louisa, with a deft application of the milk jug. 'He is a gentleman of unusual perception and you would do well to pay very great attention to what he says.'

'Oh, you are too kind!' exclaimed Bradley, allowing his body to undulate in his hostess's direction while keeping his attention focussed on Mina. 'Miss Scarletti, it is, I must say, the very greatest pleasure to meet you. Your mother, who is in my opinion a lady of the most extraordinary courage, has told me all about you.'

Mina said nothing, but inclined her head in greeting, then crossed the room to a chair and sat down, Mr Bradley observing her gait as if the very sight of her affliction was causing him the most exquisite pain.

Simmons distributed teacups and plates and offered a platter of fancy cakes, and when they were all settled Louisa said, 'Mr Bradley, although he is far too modest to speak of it to any degree, has a rare ability, in fact I do believe I have never met another individual with his gift. He is actually able to perceive the spirit of a living person, in quite the most extraordinary detail. Colours and shapes — just imagine! He can in this way ascertain whether the person, be they man, woman or child, is in poor health, either in body or mind. But more than this, he can offer comfort for the spirit, and even — yes — *cure* what is ill. We are fortunate indeed that he has decided to make his home here.' Louisa, with a rare flush of her pale cheek, took a mouthful of cake.

'Are you a medical man?' asked Mina, feeling sure that their visitor was not, and thinking that his arrival in a town many of whose amenities were devoted to the requirements of invalids was no coincidence.

Mr Bradley smiled and gave a self-deprecating gesture. 'Medical men attempt to cure only what they can see, and are very imperfect judges of what they cannot. No, I am neither a doctor nor a surgeon, and have never professed to be such. I,' he said, pressing his palms to his chest, 'am only the poor conduit of a greater power; and I must reassure you, for I am asked this very often, that such little abilities as I have are not exercised for my own advantage. I exist only to be of help to my fellow creatures.' He paused briefly to enjoy the admiration of his audience, most of which emanated from his hostess. Simmons, who had gone back to her chair, looked more afraid than anything else. Their visitor, sensing perhaps that Mina did not regard him with the degree of respect he was accustomed to command, fixed her with a solemn frown. 'There are those, I know, who are so impudent as to demand payment for what they do, but I am a gentleman of independent means and have no need to make myself rich from the suffering of others. I am visiting members of the Christ Church congregation to advise that I intend to start some prayer meetings where those in need of comfort may seek guidance, and where I will do what I can to assist in the Lord's work of the healing of the sick.'

'I declare,' said Louisa, 'I can feel your influence at work already — simply by being in your presence I am better than I was. But Mr Bradley —' She waved a fragment of cake at Mina — 'is there nothing you can do for my poor daughter?'

Mr Bradley sighed, and again he opened his eyes wide, and they were very large and brown and sad, like those of an aged and weary cow. 'If you will allow me?' he asked.

11

'But of course,' said Louisa, and finishing the cake, gestured to Simmons to bring her another.

Mr Bradley put aside his teacup, dabbed his lips with a napkin, rose to his feet and smiled. 'Do not be afraid, Miss Scarletti,' he said.

'Is there something I should be afraid of?' enquired Mina.

He laughed. 'Oh, no, nothing at all! I merely wish to touch your hand, very lightly. You may or may not know this, but touch is one of what we call our five senses, that tell us all that we need to know. I can use that sense to see and understand what others cannot. When I touch your hand, you will experience an extraordinary feeling, as the divine power, which reaches out through me, a humble vessel, meets your own immortal spirit.' He adopted a more serious look. 'I must first reassure you that we of the church abhor any suggestion that the healing power we are privileged to convey comes from anywhere but on high.'

'Oh, I had never thought it otherwise,' said Louisa. 'Can people be so envious and so cruel as to say such things?'

'I regret that is so,' said Mr Bradley, with the air of a martyr, 'but you, dear lady, are too kind and too perceptive to think other than what is manifestly right.' He gestured to Mina to rise, then as she eased herself from her chair, he gave a little gasp of dismay, darted forward and offered his arm. 'My apologies, dear young lady. Let me assist you. Your spirit is so strong that I had quite forgotten your — er —'

Mina rose to her feet unassisted, declining to complete the sentence, letting the awkward moment hang in the air.

'Mina, dear, you must do whatever Mr Bradley asks of you,' said her mother, sternly. 'I do not want a repetition of your behaviour before those kind doctors who tried so hard to help you.'

Mr Bradley stood facing Mina, offered her his hand with the palm upward, cupped as if it held a gift, and raised his eyebrows and nodded to show that she must place her hand in his. Mina did not care for Mr Bradley's mournful glistening eyes and neither did she relish the thought of touching his skin, but she complied for her mother's sake, going no further than resting her fingertips lightly on his. He smiled, taking her reserve as an expression of modesty. A few moments passed, but Mina did not experience an extraordinary sensation, which was not a matter of great surprise to her.

Mr Bradley, who clearly needed to demonstrate that something very remarkable was taking place, took a deep breath and tilted his head back, allowing his eyelids to flutter closed. Louisa, one hand pressed to her bosom, stared at him with a look of rapt admiration and just a little hint of excitement. She seemed to be holding her breath. There was a brief pause for the better increase of anticipation.

'Oh but this is most wonderful!' exclaimed Mr Bradley — so suddenly that Louisa gave a little start — his face suffused with an expression of great joy. 'Miss Scarletti, I can see your spirit form most clearly — it clothes you in a beautiful glow, soft like the most delicate amber. And I can tell you, my dear young lady, and I know how much this will gladden your heart — that your spirit form, the one that you will wear for eternity after you have passed the veil, is as straight and tall as anyone could desire!'

'But Mr Bradley,' said Mina, with a mischievous smile, 'why would I wish to be other than I am?'

His fingers moved back quite abruptly, and he looked astonished, then he shook his hand, almost as if Mina's touch had stung him.

'Mina, whatever can you mean by that?' demanded her mother. 'This is so like you, to be wilful and impertinent. Really, I hardly know what to do with you sometimes.'

'Oh, please do not fret, dear lady,' said Bradley, recovering his composure, 'and above all, you must not blame yourself. I can see that your unfortunate daughter labours under an affliction of the mind, one that threatens to eat into her very soul. I do believe that she cannot help what she is saying.'

'But can *you* help her?' asked Louisa.

'The bodily —' he paused, 'deformity, I can do nothing for. Only the Almighty will cure her after she has passed. But I can at least intercede with the Lord to ensure that her case becomes no worse.'

Mina's mother gave a sigh of gratitude, as if he was making a promise that had not already been offered by more human agencies.

'While she remains in the flesh, however, there is a disturbance in her spirit which I may be able to ease.'

'Oh, please do try,' exclaimed Louisa. 'I would be so very grateful!'

'I will pray for her,' said Mr Bradley magnanimously, 'but Miss Scarletti must also work to heal herself. I advise her to pray both morning and night, and as often throughout the day as possible. And she must come to my meetings, which I intend to hold every Wednesday afternoon at Christ Church where my little group of the devout will sit and pray and let the healing powers of the Almighty bathe them in delight. You will be there too, I hope, dear lady?'

'Oh, you may count on my attendance,' said Louisa eagerly, 'and Mina will, of course, follow your guidance.'

Mina saw that she was about to be encased again, in a device not of plaster or steel, but no less restraining for that. She was not averse to prayer, and already prayed night and morning; for the ease of her mother's sorrows, for the souls of her father and her sister Marianne who had faded away from consumption ten years ago, for Edward's success and Enid's happiness and for Richard to find whatever his butterfly attention sought. Now it seemed that she must also pray for herself, but she could think of nothing she lacked that she might wish to pray for. She did not look forward to joining Mr Bradley's assemblage of the unhappy matrons of Brighton.

Mina, although she did not consider herself to be worldly, was under no illusions as to why her mother's mood would be lifted by visits from a single gentleman of independent means ten years her junior and of moderately acceptable appearance. If she was honest with herself there was nothing about Mr Bradley to which she could object, especially since in one day he had brought about the improvement that Mina had been attempting unsuccessfully for a year. He was not, as far as she could see, trying to woo her mother, neither was he attempting to extract money from her; he was, she thought, a man of little or no talent who lacked occupation, and was trying to court popularity by telling people what he imagined they wanted to hear.

It transpired later that week that the Reverend Mr Vaughan, Vicar of Christ Church, was not amenable to Mr Bradley holding his devotional meetings on church premises. The Reverend had heard some of the church ladies talk about promises of healing, and despite Mr Bradley's protestations of Christian piety, had detected a potential whiff of brimstone in the arrangement. Mr Bradley was obliged to look for other situations, and so it was decided that the meetings would be held in the Scarletti front parlour, a simple gathering for which the invitations and planning of refreshments occupied Mina's mother for a full three days of perpetual agitation.

Chapter Two

The first meeting was graced by five lady visitors and two gentlemen, who kept Rose and Simmons busy with constant demands for tea, bread and butter, biscuits, sponge cake and fruit, consuming enough to feed a funeral party even before the proceedings had begun. Mr Bradley, bathing in the glow of admiring faces, and thrusting out the suspicion of a developing *embonpoint*, allowed himself to take centre place, and lead the company in prayer.

Having invoked the power of God, and being satisfied that he had not inadvertently summoned a more diabolical spirit, Mr Bradley then proceeded to the healing, which was no more than inviting his little group of devotees to sit in silence and contemplate what infirmity they wished to be cured, while he walked about the circle, allowing his hand to hover over the head of each person. There were a few pitying glances at Mina, the assumption being that she would be asking for divine intervention to straighten her back, something not even Mr Bradley's disciples deemed remotely possible.

Mina was not thinking of herself at all, but was taking advantage of the quiet time to compose a new story about an incubus, which preyed on virtuous widows, and which in her mind's eye looked very like Mr Bradley. Could her mother not see that this man's presence in their house was an insult? Where were Mr Bradley and his pretensions when her father was dying? Where was his healing power when Marianne had lost her fragile hold on life at the age of twelve? It was she for whom Mina had first started writing stories of magic and adventure, stories in which her sister was the golden-haired heroine.

Marianne lived on in print for, unexpectedly, Henry's business partner, Mr Greville, had offered to publish the stories for a new venture, the Scarletti Children's Library. Mina was invited to visit to the office and saw packets of little books piled high on shelves, some of them books that her father had never dared bring home, with stories of brigands and murderers and haunted castles, all illustrated by woodcuts. These appealed to Mina's taste and spirit rather better than pious tales in which the worst sin that anyone might commit was vanity. When Mr Greville suggested that she might like to write him a story about a child who gave her last penny to a ragged boy, Mina was already eagerly perusing *The Goblin's Curse*, and was lost forever to the world of morally-improving literature.

The peace of the little circle was broken only by the gurgling of Mrs Bettinson's stomach and the gentle snores of a Mrs Phipps, an elderly lady who was a regular attendee at gatherings of every kind, and slept through all of them, although she always succeeded in being awake when refreshments were served. Mr Bradley then

15

proceeded to what he announced was 'a special healing' which amounted to no more than his going about the circle again, taking each lady briefly by the hand, and placing his fingertips on the forehead of each gentleman. He then led the company in a final prayer, and suggested that they all needed more tea.

One of the company, a Miss Whinstone, was a lady of Louisa's age, but less well-favoured by the hand of time. Since emerging from the period of mourning appropriate to the loss of her beloved brother, she had invariably dressed in the same unflattering shade of bronze, which was reflected in her skin, giving her cheeks a sickly yellow cast. Her face was drawn into a permanent frown of anxiety, and she always appeared to be flinching from something. Miss Whinstone had arrived with trembling fingers, clutching a copy of the *Brighton Gazette*, which was open at the page of town news, but she did not refer to it until the meeting was drawing to a close.

'Mr Bradley,' she whispered, confidentially, 'if I might seek your advice ...'

'But of course!' he exclaimed. 'How might I assist you?'

She hesitated, then pushed the paper towards him. 'I have read — I have seen—'

'Ah,' said Mrs Bettinson, whose steely gaze missed nothing, 'yes, a most extraordinary thing, but ungodly, I fear.'

'And yet there is the involvement of Professor Gaskin, who I understand is a scientific gentleman of some note,' said Miss Whinstone, meekly.

'He is said to be one of the most scientific men in the world,' Mr Bradley assured her, 'and I am confident that he would not lend his name to anything ungodly.'

Mrs Bettinson looked unconvinced.

'Science,' announced a Mr Conroy, a portly gentleman with a red face, 'is a very remarkable thing.' He hooked his thumbs into his waistcoat pockets, thrust out his lower lip, and stared about the room in case anyone chose to contradict him.

The assembled company agreed to a man and woman that science was indeed remarkable.

Louisa, who did not read newspapers in case they affected her nerves, and had not had one in the house for some years, tried her best to look as though she knew what everyone was talking about, without success. Mina could see the early signs that her mother might be obliged to plead faintness to avoid embarrassment, so she quickly but politely borrowed Miss Whinstone's newspaper, and read the article aloud. The company fell silent. Mina had a sweet, clear reading voice, and no-one felt inclined to do other than listen to her.

Important announcement from William Gaskin, FRS, Professor of Chemistry and Physics

Professor Gaskin is honoured to make it known that the noted spirit medium Miss Hilarie Eustace will shortly be visiting Brighton where she will be pleased to offer demonstrations of her powers entirely gratis. Professor Gaskin, a founder member of the famous Ghost Club once patronised by the late Mr Charles Dickens, has devoted many years to the study of ghostly phenomena, and his experience enables him to state with considerable authority that Miss Eustace is entirely genuine. She has been subjected to numerous rigorous tests all of which prove without a doubt that she is a medium of unusually consistent and convincing ability. Miss Eustace has demonstrated on very many occasions the production of spirit rappings and moving lights, all of which occur while she is in a trance. The agent of these manifestations is her spirit guide, Phoebe, a creature of the most extraordinary and angelic beauty who, when conditions are favourable, appears before astonished onlookers clad in glowing raiment. Professor Gaskin has himself seen this spirit rise from the ground, float through the air, and then melt slowly into nothingness, a sight which can only create the most profound amazement in anyone privileged to witness it. Next week's Gazette will announce details of where Miss Eustace will be conducting her séances, and how the public might apply for tickets.

'It seems,' said Mr Conroy, with a throaty laugh, 'that you have a rival, Mr Bradley.'

'Not at all,' said Mr Bradley, cheerfully. 'If you imagine that I am jealous of this lady's powers or her ability to command the attention of the public then you very much mistake me. If she can indeed perform all that she claims to do, and it appears that Professor Gaskin has proved that she can, then I will gladly add myself to the number of her devoted admirers.'

'Then you have not seen her demonstrations?' asked Mina, and there was a general clamour in the room to the effect that Mr Bradley, if he had not already seen the miraculous Miss Eustace, ought to do so as soon as was practically possible.

He raised a hand to speak and the room at once fell silent again. 'I have not seen the lady, and it might be advisable if I was not to. Imagine, if you will, the consequences that would follow if two persons, both of whom are able to act as receptacles of supernatural power, were in the same room, and one of them was to enter the trance state, which is a most perilous condition.' He paused dramatically to allow his listeners to consider the dreadful results that might stem from that situation. 'Of course, I would do nothing to deliberately harm Miss Eustace, but suppose that by my very presence, I was to quite unintentionally attract forces that were drawn to her in her receptive state, and were more than the delicate frame of a lady could endure.'

'Why, it could kill her!' exclaimed Miss Whinstone, the tea in her cup vibrating like a choppy sea.

'Or at the very least induce catatonia. She might never waken again. Such things have been known.' Bradley shook his head, regretfully. 'No, much as I would wish to witness one of her demonstrations, I dare not, but I can see no objection to anyone else attending. I understand that she created a very great sensation when exhibiting in London only last week. I spoke to a lady who was present on that occasion who was so overcome by powerful emotions when she tried to tell me what she had seen that she was quite unable to find words to describe her experience. You are very fortunate that Miss Eustace comes here now, for if she was here in the autumn season you would not be able to get near her for Dukes and Earls and Countesses.'

'Oh,' said Miss Whinstone, 'but my doctor says that I have a weak heart and a rheumatic stomach — from eating too much, or possibly from eating too little, I forget which — and I think if I was to see Miss Eustace I would catch the most terrible fright. And perhaps it might kill me, so I had really better not go.'

'She wouldn't frighten *me*,' said Mrs Bettinson, and the other ladies suggested that they felt the same, apart from Mrs Phipps who, having finished her tea, had fallen asleep again.

'But isn't it all poppycock and playacting?' said a Mr Jordan, grunting and looking at his watch, something he liked to do every few minutes for no reason that anyone could discern. He was a smartly turned-out gentleman of about thirty who had said very little throughout the afternoon, contenting himself with an expression of deep scepticism.

'If it is, the lady gains no advantage by it,' said Mr Bradley, reasonably. 'Of course, there are persons who pretend to be mediums and attempt to play tricks on the public, but there is one sure way of knowing them. It is really very simple, they will do nothing without first being paid.'

Mina's mother had expressed no opinion about Miss Eustace, and after the meeting only commented that she had to wonder if such a person could be wholly respectable. Nevertheless, she told Mina to arrange for a regular delivery of all the popular Brighton newspapers and was later seen perusing them with interest. In a matter of days the dreadful Miss Eustace passed through a process of metamorphosis in which she became by stages the dangerous Miss Eustace, the alarming Miss Eustace, the uncommon Miss Eustace, the fascinating Miss Eustace, and finally, the astonishing Miss Eustace. One evening, at nine o'clock on the hour, a hired carriage arrived in Montpelier Road and Louisa Scarletti and Mrs Bettinson boarded it in a state of very considerable excitement.

'I do not know why this should be,' said Mina's mother, 'but it has been my observation that men who are very clever and whose words repay the most earnest attention are often very ugly, whereas those who have been favoured with a handsome countenance have nothing in their heads worth speaking of.'

'Perhaps,' said Mina, 'men with attractive faces see no reason to cultivate their minds, and men with good minds exercise them so often they have no time to make themselves handsome. But do you speak of Mr Bradley? He seems to me to have neither good features nor a mind that is out of the ordinary.'

Her mother looked displeased, but Mina did not mind that. It was the morning after the visit to Miss Eustace, and Louisa, in command of the breakfast table, already looked plumper and rosier as if, like Brighton, she had been painted for the summer season. Mina wondered if her mother's year of melancholy widowhood that had followed her husband's death had in recent months been less a genuine affliction than a craving for the solicitude of friends. Now, with other things on her mind, she had turned her natural vitality to other projects.

Simmons sat forlornly by, her manner expressing anxiety, either that her mistress was about to be enlivened to the point of a brainstorm, or that she would be so restored to glowing health that the services of a nurse and companion might no longer be required.

'I do *not* speak of Mr Bradley, who although not a scholarly gentleman has a reasonably good mind and is not displeasing to look at,' said Louisa severely. 'It is Professor Gaskin, who has been instrumental in introducing Miss Eustace to both London and Brighton society. He is a man with a very powerful brain, and a mind that constantly seeks the truth. But he has a bad posture and very large ears. His wife is a respectable sort of person, but she is dreadfully plain, poor creature, and does not dress at all well.' Louisa could not help preening herself.

The previous night's séance had taken place in the parlour of Professor Gaskin's lodgings, and had been attended by eight ladies and gentlemen who were considered to be the very best of the resident Brighton society. Mina's mother said that she felt sure there was a solicitor amongst their number, as well as Dr Hamid, who she thought was a very interesting and intelligent sort of person. The company was comfortably seated in front of a curtain that had been drawn across one corner of the room. The professor had then addressed them on the subject of Miss Eustace's wonderful sensitivity; how he had encountered her first with the attitude of a sceptic, thinking to expose deception. On witnessing her demonstrations, however, not only had he become convinced of her genuineness, but he had also realised that she was worthy of serious scientific study. Miss Eustace, he had told the company, was possessed of powers that the most learned men could not as yet explain.

The professor had reassured everyone present not to be afraid of what they were about to experience, and for greater confidence, he had then led them in a short prayer followed by a rousing hymn. 'I think,' Louisa told Mina, 'that that *fully* answers Reverend Vaughan's objections. There was nothing irreligious in the proceedings, in fact quite the contrary. Professor Gaskin says that the spirits are gladdened by our devotion, since they are pure Christian spirits sent by God to guide those who are receptive to His teachings.'

'What sort of person is Miss Eustace?' asked Mina, who was tempted to ask if this creature of the holy spirits had ridden into the room on a sunbeam, but refrained from a comment that she felt would not have advanced the conversation.

'She is a very proper and modest young lady,' said Louisa. 'I have to confess, I was concerned that I might be confronted by a person of coarse manners and appearance, and then I would have been obliged to leave immediately, but that was not the case. She was most tastefully attired, and behaved throughout with great decorum. She was seated on a chair in front of the curtain, facing us, and I am sure that she did not move from her place, yet all around us we saw lights and heard noises that no living soul in the room could have made. Professor Gaskin showed us a bell and a tambourine behind the curtain, also a pencil and paper. All of us heard the bell ring several times and a good hard rattle on the tambourine, then the sound of the pencil moving. None of us was near enough to touch them.'

'All this was behind the curtain, hidden from view?' asked Mina.

'It was. One of the gentlemen present said he wanted to draw the curtain and see what was happening for himself, but Professor Gaskin explained that any disturbance could injure the medium, and so he refrained, but very unwillingly. He was a bad influence and I think he will not be admitted again.'

Mina thought that had she been present she too might have been tempted to part the curtains, and wondered what she would have seen. A bell suspended in the air ringing itself; a tambourine in the grasp of a ghostly hand? Somehow she doubted it. Surely a more earthly and tangible arrangement of wires and black thread would answer the purpose.

'Then, as if that was not wonderful enough, Professor Gaskin announced that he could feel a hand on his shoulder. Of course we all felt somewhat alarmed, but he reassured us that there was nothing to be afraid of, and if anyone should feel the same thing they should not try and clasp the hand, for it disturbed the energy. And then,' Louisa went on, her eyes glowing with excitement, 'I felt it — very briefly — fingers touching my cheek. It was quite extraordinary!'

'It could not have been anyone in the room?' asked Mina.

'Oh no, most assuredly not. We were all, on the strict instructions of Professor Gaskin, holding hands, so no person in the room could have touched my face, and, of course, Miss Eustace was the furthest away of all. The surprising thing was that I had imagined a spirit hand to be somehow different, less … well … less like a real, solid, warm hand of a living person. But there was nothing insubstantial about it at all. If Miss Eustace can manifest things of this nature she must have very considerable powers.' Louisa waved a hand at Simmons to attend to her plate, and the young woman, anxious to please, scurried to comply.

'So a spirit hand feels just like the hand of a living person,' said Mina, without a change in her expression. 'That is most remarkable. I wonder how Professor Gaskin can explain such a thing.'

'He has many years of study before him,' said her mother who, if she detected irony in Mina's tone, chose to ignore it, 'but he remains hopeful that one day he will be able to reveal to the world how the spirit powers manifest themselves. Miss Eustace was, as you may imagine, quite exhausted, so that was all we were able to experience on that occasion. We all sang another hymn and then when the gas was turned up —'

'The gas?' said Mina. 'The gas had been lowered? That is a detail you omitted. Was there candlelight? Or was the séance conducted in darkness?'

Louisa looked offended at the question. 'Of course there was darkness; you don't suppose we could have seen the little spirit lights otherwise? But I can assure you that Miss Eustace did not move, or we would have heard her. When the gas was turned up she was barely conscious, and had no memory whatsoever of what had occurred. Then Professor Gaskin drew the curtain aside and all was as it had been before — except for the paper.' She poured more tea, exhumed a warm roll from its napkin and applied a salve of butter and honey. 'You, Mina, have a hard, inflexible mind, and will no doubt find this impossible to believe, but there was writing on the paper — clear writing! It can only have been a message from the spirits. It said that all those present would enjoy good fortune.'

Mina had never seen a ghost or experienced anything that suggested the existence of a force outside of the body apart from what was already known to and approved of by science, such as the warmth and light of the sun. The world of paper ghosts she had created from her imagination was, she thought, a great deal more interesting than the commonplace manifestations described by her mother. She was not sure that she even believed in the apparitions of deceased loved ones that fanciful people sometimes reported seeing. Her stories, far from inducing her to credit the possibility of ghosts, did rather the opposite, since they created a vivid impression in her mind that was very different from what she saw around her. Perhaps, she thought, all ghosts, both those in stories and those said to be real, were only the product of the human mind. In her own case she knew they were false and wrote about them to entertain her readers, but for those who did not write, they became not words, but visions.

Still, Mina was obliged to admit that the evening's séance had been considered a success by all present, and her mother said that she would certainly go again, since Professor Gaskin had said that they had only seen a tiny part of what Miss Eustace could do. There were things he had seen with his own eyes that they would not believe until they had seen them for themselves. The professor was intending to write a book about Miss Eustace, which, he was quite sure, would cause a sensation not only amongst the public but all the leading men of science.

'She is undoubtedly genuine,' said Louisa. 'She refuses to take any payment at all for her work, although some of those present did press her with small gifts, but she *asked* for nothing! When I go again I will see if Miss Whinstone can be persuaded to come, as I am sure she will benefit. I did ask Mrs Parchment, but really she is impossible. I do believe she may be an atheist, or even one of those horrid materialists who Professor Gaskin says are even worse. How you could have admitted such a person to the house, I do not know.'

'I did not seek to enquire after her religious observation when I accepted her as a tenant,' said Mina. 'She seems perfectly respectable, paid a month in advance without quibble and has given us no trouble and regular rent ever since.'

'Her husband was little more than a peddler,' said Louisa, shaking a copy of the *Gazette* at Mina. 'Do you see this advertisement? Parchment's Pink Complexion Pills, that was he.' She allowed her fingertips to glide over her cheek, as if to demonstrate that she needed no such thing. 'The man must have been a scoundrel, since I believe they once had a fine house in London with a carriage and servants, but I suppose that is all gone now, and the poor woman has to live in one room and pay rent and entertain herself with long walks and fresh air. What a thing to come to!'

Mina was curious as to the nature of the gifts Miss Eustace had been persuaded to accept, but when she asked, her mother replied dismissively that she didn't know, in a manner that entirely confirmed Mina's suspicion that they took the form of money and that her mother had been one of those to part with a 'gift'. Miss Eustace without doubt made a tidy enough income from her activities but then, Mina thought, the lady had provided a few hours of entertainment as one might do at a musical recital and it seemed harmless enough.

As Mina climbed the stairs to her room, trying to ignore the pain that stitched down her back, its needle-sharp point embedded deep in her hip, she began to have second thoughts. Was this new enthusiasm of her mother's really so unobjectionable? Ought she to be concerned about something that might in time become detrimental, either to health or purse? By the time Mina had reached the top of the stairs her worries had multiplied to the point where she felt she needed sensible advice, and decided to write a letter to her older brother, Edward.

Chapter Three

Mina's room was a quiet place where the ghosts that lived so noisily in her mind were transferred by the medium of her pen to a new life as dark ink bled on to clean paper. Her desk was set before the window where she might take advantage of the clear brilliant daylight to compose, or read, or sometimes just to gaze out on to the street and think. There were few distractions. The northern end of Montpelier Road was far enough from the seafront to avoid the worst clusterings of excited visitors, the flowing movements and gentle sounds of passers-by affording an unobtrusive and pleasing reminder of the life of the town.

Before Mina settled down to write, she tried to stretch her back, reaching around her shoulder with one hand, pushing her fingertips into the sore muscles there, trying to prise the knots apart, then she sat, tucking a cushion under one hip to help straighten her posture. She knew that Edward would not come to Brighton. He rarely left his business, or, more importantly, Miss Hooper, a young lady of good family he was ardently pursuing with a view to marriage. Rival suitors of similar persistence, lesser charm but greater fortune ensured that he dared not be out of the capital for long. Mina started the letter with good news, her mother's improved health and state of mind. She decided not to alarm her brother by revealing that their mother had attended a séance, but wrote instead of the interesting new arrivals in Brighton, Mr Bradley, Professor Gaskin and Miss Eustace, who had recently been in London, and wondered if Edward had heard of them, begging him to tell all he knew.

She could not help but hope that Miss Eustace would prove to be a nine days' wonder, and vanish like one of her own spirits, to be superseded by some other novelty as Brighton, under its surge of summer visitors, blossomed into life.

Two days later, Mina received a small packet from Edward, containing a letter and a booklet, and took them to her room to read. Edward expressed his sincere relief that his mother was so much improved, and reassured Mina that he was in the best of health, although hard-pressed by business. Unhappily, he advised that the loveliest girl in the world was sorely afflicted by a cold in the head, which had thrown him into the most perfect anguish. He ended with a stern warning that it would be as well not to meddle in the affairs of people claiming to be in touch with spirits. Mr Bradley was unknown to him, but Professor Gaskin was a respected man of science, the author of many papers on the subject of chemistry and physics, who had lately espoused the claims of spiritualists and had made himself something of a laughing stock amongst his friends and colleagues. The professor had been advocating the claims of a Miss Eustace who had recently appeared in London, claiming that she had triumphantly proved herself to be a genuine medium, and advertised her as such, but the truth, commented Edward, was less convincing.

There was, he added, a new fashion for spirit mediums in London, and the gullible were willing to pay them any sum for the most ridiculous displays of obvious fakery. Professor Gaskin and his wife, shepherding Miss Eustace, had recently removed to Brighton for the early summer season, where they hoped to have fewer rivals and be more successful. Miss Eustace claimed to accept no money for her séances but it was widely believed that she lived on the hospitality of the Gaskins and accepted payments from her sitters. The enclosed booklet, he added, was a recent publication, and an object lesson, but he felt sorely afraid that it was a lesson many would chose to ignore. He urged Mina to read it carefully and take its message to heart.

The booklet, some sixteen pages long, was called *The Claims of D.D. Home Refuted Containing a Very Full Account of the Lyon Case, and His Disgrace*, by Josiah Rand MD. Mr Home, said the author, had been a very active and celebrated spirit medium for a number of years, including amongst his adherents medical men, scientists, barristers, military men, titled personages, and other notable individuals. He was said by many to be the most powerful medium alive, able to levitate heavy items of furniture, cause musical instruments to play by themselves, and touch hot coals without harm, but his most famous achievement was to rise in the air and hover sometimes several feet above his astounded audience.

Scottish-born Home had lived in America from an early age, and was one of many thousands who, after the widespread publicity given to the spirit rappings of the Fox sisters in Hydesville, New York in 1848, had suddenly discovered that he too had mediumistic powers. The sisters' exhibitions, which, said Dr Rand, most closely resembled the activities of the almost-certainly fraudulent Cock Lane ghost, had themselves attracted allegations of trickery, which had had no deleterious effects on the ladies' continuing fame.

In March 1855, Home had sailed for England, where an ardent believer in his mediumistic powers, who also happened to be a hotelier, had generously granted him free accommodation. The tall, slender youth — he was then only twenty-two — with blue eyes, flowing auburn locks, and the luminous transparency of the consumptive, seemed already to be hovering on the boundary of another world. In repose his face suggested suffering, and this, together with a gentle air of kindliness, was enough to recommend him to ladies, especially those rather older than himself. His natural charm lent him an easy persuasiveness, but it was his undoubted ability to produce powerful spirit manifestations that quickly gained him an entrée into fashionable society and brought many admirers. There were, however, also sceptics who charged him with fraud, and these included the poet Robert Browning, who had openly declared Home to be a charlatan. Browning went so far as to satirise

Home in a poem as 'Mr Sludge, "the Medium"'. Home was not averse to critical examination, and a distinguished scientist, Sir David Brewster, who was an authority on the nature of light, attended Home's séances. While believing that the phenomena were attributable not to the work of spirits but clever conjuring, Brewster was forced to admit that he was unable to explain what he had seen. The controversy only increased Home's fame, and income.

None of this information was especially troubling to Mina, but what followed was alarming to a considerable degree. In 1866, Jane Lyon, a seventy-five-year-old widow, had asked Home if he could manifest the spirit of her dead husband. Home conducted a number of private séances and received gifts of thirty and fifty pounds. Home then discovered that Mrs Lyon, while living in very modest circumstances, was the mistress of a substantial fortune, and had no relatives. He was easily able to persuade her that her late husband wished her to adopt him as her son, and place him in a financial position in life appropriate to his new rank. Eleven days after their first meeting Mrs Lyon accompanied Home to her bank and there arranged to sell a block of bonds for twenty-four thousand pounds which she then transferred to her new 'son'. Home next persuaded Mrs Lyon that her husband wished her to destroy her previous will and make a new one in his favour. He changed his name to Lyon, received a further sum of six thousand pounds, and secured his position by having Mrs Lyon create deeds in his favour, which were stated to be irrevocable.

Gradually, however, Mrs Lyon opened her eyes and saw her terrible folly. She realised that had her husband been living he would never have placed her in such a harmful position, and friends advised her that she was being imposed upon by a fraud. There had been a quarrel between the unhappy woman and her leech, which had not resolved the matter, and she went to law. The court had denounced Home as a cheat and an impostor, and the practice of spiritualism as mischievous nonsense, calculated to delude the vain, the weak, the foolish and the superstitious, and assist the adventurer. The supposedly irrevocable deeds were duly set aside and he was ordered to return her property.

Mina read this dreadful litany of crime with a mounting sense of horror. Messages from the dead, tambourines that played themselves and men who flew about the room she could face with equanimity, but the vile behaviour of a heartless rogue who would use an elderly widow's love for her dead husband to dupe her out of her fortune appalled her.

The extraordinary thing, she learned as she read on, was that Home, so far from having been put in prison, or drummed out of English society with a strong suggestion that he ought to return to America forthwith, was still residing in England and practising as a medium. He continued to enjoy the confidence of the public and basked in the attention of eminent scientists. Even a claim that he had been detected in imposture at a séance had been swept aside by his adherents who stated that the light on that occasion had been so dim that it was impossible to tell one way or the other whether fraud had been used. Spiritualists, it seemed, saw everything as marvellous, but were blind to the mundane.

Mrs Browning, the poet's wife, who had received wreaths of flowers from spirit hands at Home's séances and had been told that there were rays of glory pouring from a crown over her head that only the medium could see, had to the end of her life remained unreservedly convinced. When Home's critics denounced him as morally worthless, she had riposted that even if he *was* morally worthless it would not impugn his being a true medium any more than her dentist's ability as a dentist would be held suspect if he were caught shoplifting. Mina at once saw the fatal flaws in this argument. Dentistry was a demonstrable medical skill based on knowledge and dexterity, whereas mediumship was a matter of trust and belief. The point at issue was not whether Home was skilled, but whether he was trustworthy, and on the evidence before her he clearly was not.

A Professor William Crookes was currently subjecting Home to an impressive array of tests, which Dr Rand earnestly hoped would show the charlatan for what he was, but he was not sanguine that this would be the result. Dr Rand felt, and Mina was obliged to agree, that Professor Crookes's interest was probably aroused by a willingness to believe, which would make him an easy dupe for a fraud of more than twenty years' experience. It was often assumed, declared Rand, that frauds most easily deluded the unintelligent, and that the best witnesses were men of science. In reality, the man of science was often the easiest mark since he thought too much and tried to find a beautiful explanation for what he had observed that could be fashioned into a scholarly paper while ignoring the sordid and simple truth.

Since the damning episode with Mrs Lyon, Home had not to anyone's knowledge perpetrated a scheme on a similar scale, but memories were short and believers many. Dr Rand ended his document by issuing a warning, especially to women, against entering into any financial arrangements with Home. Rumours were afoot that the adventurer, who still had youth and celebrity on his side, was looking for a wealthy wife.

Mina was still digesting this information when a great deal of clattering and loud exclamations from downstairs announced that her brother Richard had made one of his impromptu visits. Wondering what he was up to this time Mina eased herself down the staircase, but had yet to reach the lowest step when she was swept up into his arms and lifted from the ground. 'How is my best girl?' he asked, planting smacking kisses on her cheeks.

The question may have seemed no more than a brotherly greeting, but she knew that there lay underneath it a real concern for her health. She reassured him that she was well, which of course meant that she was no worse, and importantly, no shorter.

Richard had been favoured with the willowy height and fair hair and complexion of his mother, and the frank and somewhat raffish charm of his father. He was only a year younger than Mina, and the proximity of age meant that they had, until he was sent to school — or to be more accurate a series of schools — been brought up in each other's company. He deposited Mina very carefully on her feet, held her at arm's length and gazed at her affectionately, then smiled and nodded as he saw that she was indeed well.

With his usual excellent timing he had arrived just in time to enjoy luncheon, and as they ate, their mother talked with some enthusiasm of the rarefied circle of which she was now a member, and the accomplishments of Miss Eustace, who was, she thought, not above thirty and with good connections. Edward, she said, with a very pointed glance in Richard's direction, was in a fair way to achieving the hand of Miss Hooper, who would be an ornament to the family, and she looked to have some happy news from him in the near future. Richard smiled, but would not be drawn, and turned the conversation to his business interests, which he described as in a flourishing state but in need of liquid capital to ensure that he became an established success. He spoke vaguely of partners and offices, and clerks but in insufficient detail to enable his listeners to determine the exact nature of his enterprise. One certainty that accompanied all of Richard's schemes was that they were in want of investment, and his mother promised to transfer funds to him the next day. Unlike the depredations of the egregious Mr Home, Richard only asked for small sums that their mother could easily afford, and Mina comforted herself with the fact that the funds were at least going to a loved and undoubtedly loving son and not a lying adventurer.

Later that day, Louisa went to take tea with Miss Whinstone and Mrs Bettinson, and Richard and Mina strolled arm-in-arm along the seafront, where gaily-coloured posters were advertising the new attractions on the West Pier. Richard was careful to match his long stride to Mina's short steps, and for a time they were happy just to walk and enjoy the sun and tranquil air.

'Now then,' said Mina after a while, 'you do not deceive me and I want the truth. What is this business for which you need Mother to supply yet another investment? If it is gambling debts I shall be very annoyed.'

'Oh, I have been bitten too many times by that horrid monster,' Richard assured her, 'and have no pleasure in it any more. I am doing what I can to move in the best society and put on a brave show in the hopes of charming myself into a fortune. But it is very costly and dreadful dull work.'

27

'I despair of you sometimes!' Mina exclaimed. 'Do you really intend to cheat some unfortunate lady of her fortune with winning smiles?'

'Oh, as to that, there will be no cheating. If a rich lady wants a young husband to dance attendance on her then she knows what the bargain is. And I would be a model of the type, and act my part to her satisfaction.' He raised his hat and directed his appreciation to two prettily-dressed ladies in a passing carriage, who were unable to resist laughing and blushing in return.

Richard, Mina was obliged to admit, had a curious yet consistent idea of morality. She knew that he would never steal from or blatantly defraud anyone, had never borrowed money without the intention of repaying it, although he invariably failed to do so, and was quite incapable of committing an act of unkindness. 'But you are not yet engaged?' she asked.

'No, and neither is there any prospect of it at present. There are rich enterprises I have in my sights, but I fear that the odds are against me.'

'Have the ladies found you out as an adventurer?' she teased. 'If they are clever they will hold on to their money. If I wanted a handsome face in my drawing room I would purchase a painting. That would be far less trouble than a husband.'

'The London ladies of fortune are like castles moated about with lawyers,' he said gloomily. 'If I have no success there then I might come to Brighton for the high season and lurk around the pavilion, where I might discover a dowager duchess taking the air, and win her hand.'

Mina looked at him carefully and saw that for all the outward show of elegance his garments were not as fresh or as fashionable as they needed to be for such an undertaking. 'I hope you are not in debt for lodgings,' she said, 'or do you remain with Edward?'

'Edward vouchsafes me a corner of his attic,' said Richard. 'He is well, but his talk is all about work. It is a subject for which I feel very little enthusiasm, and I can contribute nothing to the conversation.'

'That does not bode well for Miss Hooper,' said Mina. 'A woman should expect her husband to have more than one subject on which he can talk with some authority, preferably several.'

'I have met the lovely Miss Hooper,' said Richard, 'and I think she will not be very demanding in the area of conversation. I can see why Edward is so much in love with her; her father is really quite rich. But that china doll kind of beauty has never appealed to me. I like the kind of girl who —' He hesitated.

'The kind of girl you could not introduce to Mother?' ventured Mina.

He laughed. 'You have it, my dear.' He squeezed her hand affectionately. 'But Mina, you must be very dull here. Do you really wish to wait on Mother forever? She has Simmons now, and she can do very well without you, you know. You should think of marrying.'

'Oh, come now, who would have me?' said Mina with a smile. 'A miser looking for an unpaid drudge perhaps, who would expect me to be grateful that he has deigned to look at me? No, I shall never marry, and I am perfectly content with that.' She did not say it but sometimes she felt almost fortunate, enjoying unimaginable freedom for a respectable single young lady. No-one, seeing the little woman with the crooked body and curious gait, could suppose her to be anything other than honest. No-one would press her to marry a tedious man or allow children to command her time and absorb her strength. By not being constrained into the narrow sphere of wife and mother she had discovered that she had the choice of being almost anything else she pleased.

They strolled on a little further. There was a long pause in the conversation, and into the cheerful enjoyment of the early summer weather there crept a grey chill. 'What is it, Mina?' said Richard. 'I am not a fool and I can see that something is making you unhappy.'

They stopped walking, and gazed out across the beach to the distant glitter of the sea. Pleasure boats were drawn up on to the shore like the drying carcasses of stranded porpoises, and there was an almost endless line of freshly-painted bathing machines ready to trundle into the water, their large wheels and small bodies making them look like colourful spiders.

Mina looked further, to where the bright water met the soft cloudy horizon, then closed her eyes and thought of sea-spirits and mermaids and kings with green hair and enchanted reefs of pearl and coral.

'Do you still go sea-bathing?' asked Richard. 'I have heard it is very beneficial.'

'So all the medical men say, but I have had my fill of medical men and their opinions,' said Mina. 'I get neither pleasure nor relief from sea-water, warm or cold. There was a time when I bathed once a week when the weather was fine, but that was only to please Mother, and I was able eventually to persuade her not to be too disappointed if I stopped.' She turned to him. 'I am perfectly well, but if you must know I am concerned about Mother's enthusiasm for Miss Eustace. I am far from convinced that she is not a charlatan preying on the superstitious.'

'Oh, I have no doubt that she is,' said Richard, airily. 'These people are all cheats and conjurers, but they provide amusement and I really think they do no harm. There is a new sensation on the West Pier — did you see the posters? Madame Proserpina the fortune teller. Guaranteed genuine. I am sure the crowds will flock to her.'

'But that is a matter of a few pence, and I have no quarrel with that if folk get enjoyment from it,' said Mina. 'If Miss Eustace asks for a shilling or two or even half a guinea at the end of the evening than it is worth it for the improvement in Mother's health and happiness. But there are villains who prey on widows with money, and try to filch their entire fortunes from them.' Mina took the booklet from her pocket and showed Richard the story of Mr Home.

He read it, she thought, with rather greater interest than she might have wished. As he did so Mina watched a few early summer families trudge out on to the beach, the children bringing fistfuls of seaweed as proud offerings to their less than delighted mothers, while distant bells announced the approach of the first caravans of donkeys. The warm, furred flanks of the donkeys and the slippery dark weed could not, she thought, have been more different, yet the weed while it remained wet could live on the beach and the donkeys could tread some way into the water. The land and the sea; life and death. Where did one end and the other start? It was not a simple question. Was there a clear-cut boundary like the line of markers where one might go from Brighton to Hove in a single step, or was there a wide borderland of sea-washed pebbles where two worlds became one? Were they really so incompatible that a fleshless spirit could not co-exist with the living?

'Mrs Lyon had a lucky escape from ruin,' said Richard at last. 'Has Miss Eustace tried to persuade Mother that she can pass on messages from Father or Marianne, or demanded large sums of money?'

'Not as far as I am aware, and she may not; after all, Mother has a family to protect her, and poor Mrs Lyon had none. But there are many ladies in Brighton in Mrs Lyon's position, and they may be in danger.'

He looked serious and thoughtful. 'Have you shown Mother this booklet?'

'No, do you think I should? I am not sure it would do any good.'

'I agree. She would only see it as a criticism of her new favourite. And she would tell you that whatever Mr Home did — and he has many defenders — has nothing to do with Miss Eustace. It would not change her mind.'

'Has Mother ever changed her mind?' asked Mina, although she knew the answer.

'Not by persuasion, no. In order for Mother to change her mind she must come to believe that the view she has just adopted is the one she has always held. Mere printer's ink won't do it.'

Mina sighed. 'I fear you are right.'

'And if you say anything to the detriment of Miss Eustace Mother will have the perfect reply — that you have not seen the lady for yourself and therefore can know nothing about the matter.'

Mina was reluctant to go and see a spirit medium and be ranked with the gullible, but she thought that unless the danger passed it must come to that. She was not, however, as she soon found, the only person in Brighton with doubts. The activities of Miss Eustace had provoked a correspondence in the newspapers in which a number of people who had not been to her séances denounced them as mere conjuring tricks, and others who had been, while unable to explain what they had seen, nevertheless entertained grave suspicions. When Mina's mother read the letters she was scathingly contemptuous about those who talked of what they did not know, or were so closed of mind that they could not see what was before their eyes. There was a strong implication in her tone that she considered Mina to be a member of that offending class. When Mina suggested that she might venture to experience a séance for herself her mother was surprised but not displeased, and said that it would be easy to arrange. All her friends had gone there or were about to go; even the nervous Miss Whinstone, who was hoping for a message from her late brother Archibald, had finally been persuaded.

Chapter Four

Miss Eustace held her séances at the simple lodgings taken by Professor and Mrs Gaskin near Queen's Park. Mina, her mother, Mrs Bettinson and Miss Whinstone travelled there by cab one evening, with Miss Whinstone protesting all the way that she was afraid her heart would stop with fright, and Mrs Bettinson looking as though she rather hoped it would.

They were ushered into a small parlour arranged in an unconventional style. Two rows of five plain chairs had been placed in a semi-circle sufficiently far apart that no seated person could reach out and touch another, but they might, if both extended their arms, hold hands with those on either side. The chairs faced a corner of the room, which was obscured by a pair of curtains of some dark opaque material that hung from a cord fastened to a bracket on the wall at either end, and overlapped in the centre. Mina found herself curiously attracted to the curtains, and had she been alone in the room would undoubtedly have pulled them aside to make a close examination of what lay behind them and determine for herself whether what was supposed to have been moved by spirits showed evidence of a more corporeal hand. The sun had set and the window curtains had been closely drawn, but the light in the room was fairly good from the gas lamps. The only other furniture was a sideboard on which stood a water carafe, a tray of glasses, a candlestick fitted with a new wax candle, and a box of matches.

Louisa introduced her daughter and Miss Whinstone to the Gaskins, who received them with friendly but slightly exaggerated politeness.

The professor was a tall man of about fifty-five, with a cloud of peppery grey hair, eyebrows like the wings of a small bird, and abundant whiskers. One might almost imagine that his head was stuffed full of hair, since it had also sought an exit by bursting through his nostrils and ears, the latter organs being of elephantine construction with undulating edges.

He both walked and stood with a stoop, not, thought Mina, from any fault with his spine, but from a poor habit of posture. It always surprised her to see a person who was blessed with the ability to walk straight but had chosen not to. Either his head was being borne down by the weight of his powerful scientific brain, or he needed to hover over everyone around him the better to impress them with his superior knowledge. Mina's diminutive stature was a particular challenge to him, and he raised his voice as he spoke to her, whether to better cover the distance between them, or because he thought that her bodily deformity meant that she also had some defect of the intellect, she could not determine. His artificially bright, almost simpering smile as he addressed her, drew her towards the latter conclusion. Mina gave him only the most perfunctory greeting, and made no attempt to impress upon him the fact that she was not an imbecile; rather she hoped that he might remain in ignorance of this for as long as possible, as it would give her more freedom to observe the proceedings unimpeded.

Mrs Gaskin, who appeared to be the same age as her husband, was an excessively plain woman, inclining to stoutness and heavily whaleboned. She dressed in an unflattering style suggestive of the most uncompromising virtue and carried herself like a duchess. Her smiles of greeting lacked warmth, and were dispensed by way of charity, serving to enhance her own position. She remained close to the professor, attached by invisible chains of ownership as if his scientific eminence made him a valuable prize amongst husbands. Mina, who thought herself as good as the next person and needed no husband, professorial or otherwise, was unimpressed. More importantly, she had learned long ago that scholarship did not always mean that a man was right in his pronouncements, and neither did it ensure common sense, or knowledge of character.

Two other ladies were also present, Mrs Peasgood and Mrs Mowbray, cheerful widows in search of entertainment, whose confiding manner towards each other suggested that they were sisters. Mrs Phipps, the lady who had slept through most of Mr Bradley's healing circle, arrived leaning heavily on the arm of her nephew who looked highly embarrassed to be there at all, stared at the curtained corner with alarm, and hurried away as soon as he felt able to do so without appearing to be impolite.

The last visitor to be introduced was Dr Hamid, a quiet man of middling height, about forty-five and very gentlemanly, with black hair going grey and a neatly trimmed beard. All Mina knew of him was what her mother had told her, that he was the son of an Indian physician of great distinction and a Scottish mother, and the proprietor of Dr Hamid's Indian medicated vapour bath and shampooing establishment in Brighton, whose customers had spoken very highly of the relief afforded them from his treatments. The oriental 'shampoo', or 'massage' as it was sometimes called, appeared by all accounts to be a frightful ordeal in which the practitioner pressed and rubbed and sometimes twisted or even stood upon the recumbent form of the patient. Mina had heard about travellers to the East who had submitted to the ministrations of large Turkish gentlemen in the bathhouses popular there, and had later written of their clicking joints and spines cracking like pistol shots. As if to remind her of this, her shoulder gave her a savage pinch.

Dr Hamid wore a dark suit and cravat and carried black gloves, and there was a black band around one sleeve and his hat, but Mina saw that this was not the formal fashionable mourning of a man who had slipped easily into an outward show of widowerhood. As they were introduced she saw an ill-concealed pain in his

33

eyes, the look of a man who was searching for a part of himself that had been suddenly and cruelly snatched away, which he had been unable to acknowledge was gone forever. Just as she was crushed in body so he was crushed in spirit and who could know if his prospect of recovery was any better than her own? There was no trace in his expression of the pity or curiosity with which she was often viewed; rather there was interest, and a hint of recognition.

The company was ushered to their seats, but although Professor and Mrs Gaskin secured places on the front row, as might have been expected, they did not sit together but at either end, like sentinels. Mina, her mother and Miss Whinstone made up the centre of the row, but Miss Whinstone, clutching a lace handkerchief and flapping her arms nervously, exclaimed that she did not think she could bear to be so near to the curtain as she dreaded to think what lay behind it, and she really believed that she might faint if she was to see anything at all. Mrs Gaskin did her best to reassure her increasingly agitated guest, but to no avail, and so Miss Whinstone was sent to the back row, and since it was thought best that she be seated with her friends, Mina and her mother were asked to join her, with Dr Hamid and the two widowed sisters taking the seats in front. Mina quietly protested that she was unable to see the proceedings but her mother insisted that she should remain beside Miss Whinstone to attend to her if she should faint. Dr Hamid, overhearing this exchange, at once rose and turned to address them. 'Excuse me, ladies, if I could be of assistance, it would be my pleasure to attend on Miss Whinstone, and Miss Scarletti could then have my place.' It was all done in such a disarming manner that Louisa could do nothing but agree, and Mina returned to the front row.

Before the eagerly expected entrance of Miss Eustace Professor Gaskin rose to address the onlookers.

'My dear friends, it gives me great pleasure not only to see those who have attended our evenings before but also some new faces. I offer a warm welcome to you all. Some of you may have read criticisms in the press of our gatherings, and I do not intend to respond to them directly as I take no note of anything said by persons wholly ignorant of our proceedings here, and indeed ignorant of anything concerning the world of the spirit. It hardly needs to be said that we have avoided criticism throughout these demonstrations by holding them here and not at Miss Eustace's own lodgings, so rendering it impossible for anyone to claim that she has arranged the room to facilitate deception. Everything in this room may be freely and thoroughly examined by anyone present, both before and after the séance, to satisfy themselves that there is nothing that might invite suspicion.'

But not during, thought Mina, who would have liked to go forward and take up that challenge, but realised that to do so would embarrass her mother in front of her friends, and accepted that such an action should be left for another time.

'You may be interested to know,' added the professor, 'that some of the finest minds in the land have been examining the evidence for spiritualism for over a year and will shortly be publishing their conclusions. The gentlemen, and not a few ladies, of the London Dialectical Society have been holding meetings and séances and taking the evidence of interested persons of good reputation. I have been privileged to see a copy of the report, and I can reveal to you all now that it has concluded that there is abundant evidence for the reality of the manifestations which astound us and which we cannot as yet explain.' He paused for vocal expressions of pleasure from his listeners then held up his hand for silence.

'Despite this support from the learned amongst us, there will always be those whose minds remain closed to the truth,' he continued, with a look of great sorrow for those unfortunates. 'It has even been suggested that Miss Eustace carries out her séances under cover of darkness in order to conceal deception, and that the phenomena which many of you have already witnessed are not the work of some force as yet unknown to science but her own hands.'

A little murmur of amused incredulity ran about the room.

'Darkness is certainly essential to our proceedings, but not for the reasons suggested by those cavillers who know nothing of which they speak, but because light can absorb the vital energy of the medium. The phenomena produced by Miss Eustace are not, as we know, the result of any action by her physical hands, but by a force that is as yet beyond our understanding, which extends beyond the periphery of her body and causes vibrations in the ether: a force hitherto unknown to science, the study of which will, I am sure, reveal to us in time a wholly new branch of knowledge.' He paused. 'However, for your further assurance, and the confusion of her critics, I will ensure that before we begin Miss Eustace is secured to her chair so that she is unable to rise from it or carry out any actions with her hands.'

'It is the greatest insult,' said Mrs Gaskin, loudly, 'to call into question such a virtuous lady, and it says much regarding the coarse and ignorant unbelievers who would subject her to such a proceeding. But their downfall will be our victory!'

'And then,' said the professor in a gentler tone than his good lady, 'we may raise them to greater understanding. Let us take a few moments of silent prayer, in which we give thanks to the Lord God for His miracles as His blessing to the holy, and ask Him to give us the power to save and enlighten those who are even now mired in the slough of prejudice.'

'For they are as children,' intoned Mrs Gaskin, 'and we must lead them.'

There were a few moments of quiet reflection after which the professor said, 'Amen!' very firmly, and the company echoed him.

'And now,' said Professor Gaskin, 'I would like to bring before you — Miss Eustace.'

He threw the curtains apart with a brave flourish, as a man might have done who was displaying a marvel of the world, or a performing lion or some such novelty. There was a little gasp of fright from Miss Whinstone, which was soon quelled, for in the dim alcove created by the corner of the room, on a plain wooden chair, there sat a woman, not a spirit, but a real solid breathing woman, in a pose of great humility, her head bowed as if in prayer. She wore a gown of pearl-grey silk, embellished with flounces and velvet ribbons, with deep ruffled cuffs, and the hands that peeped out and lay clasped upon her lap were small and very white. Her face, seen as she slowly raised her head, was serene with the kind of regular features that made it pleasing without being beautiful. Professor Gaskin offered her his hand with a proud and gallant gesture, and she took it, rose to her feet in one graceful movement, and came forward until she stood before the curtains. The gathering murmured appreciation, which she acknowledged with a slight bow. Professor Gaskin brought the chair forward into the room, and she was seated. 'If I might have the assistance of any observer who will attest that the bindings are properly done?' he asked.

Mina would have liked to volunteer but she did not move quickly enough, and the ropes, which had lain coiled on a small table behind the curtains, were taken up by Dr Hamid, clearly a gentleman who always endeavoured to be useful, and Mrs Mowbray, who had been gazing admiringly at Dr Hamid, something to which he seemed oblivious. Professor Gaskin supervised the binding, which attached Miss Eustace by her wrists to the framework of the chair. While this was being done, Mina had the opportunity to see what other articles were behind the curtains. The small light bentwood table was barely a foot across, and had no cloth to cover it, so it was impossible for anything to be hidden underneath. On its surface was a pencil, a sheet of notepaper, a small handbell and a tambourine. As far as Mina could see there was nothing else behind the curtain, and the wall covering at the rear of the enclosure, was the same as the rest of the room. There was certainly insufficient space to conceal another person or an object of any size.

Once Professor Gaskin's two assistants had pronounced themselves satisfied that Miss Eustace was securely bound, and were back in their places, he lit the candle, turned down the gas, and then, carrying the candle, returned to his seat, the yellow flickering light casting deep moving shadows in his eye sockets and cheeks.

'I would now like everyone to take the hand of the person sitting beside them,' he said. 'Those who are seated on the end of a row, please take the hand of the person beside you with both of yours. This is for the assurance of all present that no-one will be able to move about the room during the proceedings, since the energy of the medium must not be disturbed. I will then blow out the candle, and when I have done so, I ask you all to join me in a hymn. We will have *Abide With*

Me.' This was a popular choice at Christ Church and one to which all the assembled company knew the words.

There was a sobbing whimper from Miss Whinstone, as if she constantly needed to remind everyone in the room that she was not only there, but afraid and in need of attention, but she did not faint. Miss Whinstone, Mina recalled, had never, as far as she was aware, ever fainted, although she often said that she was just about to. Mina encountered on one side the cold dry hands of Mrs Gaskin, and on the other, the tight clasp of Mrs Mowbray. The candle was blown out, and then Professor Gaskin began to groan out the hymn at great volume and other voices, of varying degrees of melodiousness, wove around him.

After a minute or two the singing ceased and the company was overtaken by a more pleasing silence, and enveloped in an aura of arrested breath and expectancy. As Mina's eyes grew used to the darkness, she saw only very dimly the shape of Miss Eustace still seated, her head moving first forward then back, then tilting from side to side as might be done by a person in a fit, or in a trance, or pretending to be in either state. She felt no fear, only curiosity, and just a trace of hope that something would occur with even a hint of the drama she put into her tales, but her practical mind told her that she was about to see nothing more than pretty parlour tricks.

As the seconds passed, the mood of the company was wound tighter and tighter into a state of anticipation, and then the silence was abruptly broken by the sound of a quiet rap on the wall behind them. One or two ladies gasped, and there was even a little scream. The rapping sounded again, only louder this time, and developed into a sequence of knocks that speeded up until they became almost a rattle. Mina tried to glance about her, but she was unable to turn sufficiently to look directly behind, and Mrs Gaskin held her fingers fast. She could see nothing to account for the noise and as far as she was aware no-one had moved from his or her seat. Other raps and knocks followed, stouter and louder, and they were travelling about the room, so they came from the side walls, the ceiling, which of course no-one could have reached even if they had tried, and the floor. The vibration of the floorboards beneath their feet was apparent to all. It was not a sound that might have been produced by fingers or even a foot or a fist. If Mina could have likened it to anything, it was as if some mischievous and invisible person armed with a stout rod had walked about the room belabouring every surface in sight.

A perfect torrent of raps sounded against the far wall directly behind the company, and then, quite suddenly, stopped. There was a silence, all the more anxious because of what had just occurred and a nervous apprehension of what might happen next. The next sound was a musical tinkling noise, as if two of the water glasses on the sideboard were knocking gently together. The more Mina thought of it the more she realised that this was exactly what was producing the sound.

She sensed, quite unpleasantly, that there was a presence in the room, something that had not been there when the company had assembled, and it was nothing she could see or hear other than the effects it was producing. She tried to listen for the whisper of feet on the carpet, and the breath of another individual, but Miss Eustace had started sighing and moaning, and the other ladies were giving little excited gasps, and if there were any sounds other than those she could not make them out. Mina, who lived so much in a world of her own creation, was strongly aware of the difference between the things she conjured up in her mind and the real, solid things she saw about her. She trusted her own observation and rejected the idea that there was a spirit in the room that owed its existence solely to her imagination. There was, she felt sure, a being of some kind that was present and apparent to them all, but whether corporeal or not, alive or not, she was unable to tell. More to the point, she wanted very much to find out. Others might be happy to sit holding hands and receive impressions, but for Mina this was not enough.

There was a sudden little squeal from Mrs Mowbray: 'There was a wind on my face!' and a few moments later Mina's mother exclaimed, 'Oh! I felt a hand touch my cheek!'

Mina was just wondering if these experiences were the product of overheated anticipation, when something like a silk handkerchief caressed her throat. She shivered at the sensation, and would have liked to escape Mrs Gaskin's hands and clasp the thing before it was gone, but Mrs Gaskin had a firm, almost bruising grip on her fingers, and any attempt Mina might have made to break free would have caused some disquiet.

After a few moments, there was another period of near silence, and then the bell behind the curtain began to ring, to be followed by the rattle of the tambourine. Whatever was in the alcove was extremely lively, and there were either two hands or two entities, since the ringing and the rattling started to sound together until the noise resembled nothing more than the jangling music of the minstrel bands on the marine parade. If this was an example of the music of the spirits, thought Mina, then heaven promised to be a very clamorous and unmelodic place.

All then fell quiet again, apart from the sound of panting breath and little gasps from the ladies, then they heard the scratch of a pencil moving on paper. There was another long silence followed by a sudden muffled thud, suggesting that the table behind the curtain had fallen or been knocked over, which caused loud exclamations from the company. Mina longed for a swift movement and a sudden blaze of gaslight, but no-one stirred.

The period of silence that followed lasted for a minute or two, and Mina began to wonder if the séance was over. Professor Gaskin must have thought so too, for he was just starting to rise from his chair and say something when he was stopped by the sound of Miss Eustace crying out. Soft moans began to issue from the lips of the medium, and above her head, where her hands could not have reached even had they been free, there appeared a little dancing light. It was not enough to illuminate the room, but very sharp and clear to see, and it hovered above her like a fairy sprite. Another light soon joined it, and then the two danced together about the room, moving about each other, never more than a few feet apart, until first one, and then the other went out.

It was such a pretty display that strange and unaccountable as it was, no-one could be afraid of it, and there was a little sorrowful sigh when the lights vanished. Mina was mystified. These were like no lights she had ever seen; they had neither the yellow flicker of a candle or a spill, nor the sizzling flare of a match, but each was a single bright constant point and they had just appeared without any sign of having been ignited by something else. A professor of chemistry might, though Mina, be able to explain the phenomenon, but then a professor of chemistry was in the room and believed he saw disembodied spirits.

Miss Eustace, who had fallen into a brief silence, began to breathe very heavily and rapidly, with little gasping sounds and groans. Everyone took this as a signal that another marvel was to follow, and there were little murmurs of anticipation and the sound of people shifting in their seats. Mina felt sure that all the onlookers were leaning forward and craning their necks. They were not disappointed, for high above Miss Eustace's head a brightly-glowing form began to issue from between the curtains, which parted in the centre just enough to allow it to intrude into the room. There was an exclamation from the audience, and Mina sensed that what they were seeing was a new exhibition that no-one, quite possibly even the Gaskins, had expected.

The apparition was hovering about six feet from the ground, and as it pushed forward it grew in both size and brilliance, and began to adopt a familiar shape, until it became apparent to everyone that they were seeing a pair of hands, palm to palm in an attitude of prayer, only so far above the floor that they could not be attached to any living thing. The vision remained still for a while, and Mina hoped that it might perform some act appropriate to a pair of hands, or do anything other than remain stiff as a statue's but it seemed that the hands were simply being offered as an object of admiration. Slowly, they rose up almost to the ceiling, and tilted backwards, still in the same attitude. Then they seemed to be shrinking, although Mina thought that this was an illusion created as they withdrew behind the darkness of the curtains, and finally, they vanished.

There were muffled exclamations of pleasurable apprehension as the company waited for what might happen next, and after a few moments, a new shape, veiled in a gauzy glow, peered from the parted curtains. The softness of the outline concealed its form, but as it turned from one side to another there were gasps and cries all around, for it was a face, the face of a man with thick hair clustering on his brow, pools of hollow darkness for eyes and a long black beard. A sudden terrible scream rang out and an exclamation: 'Archibald!' Miss Whinstone rose abruptly to her feet, and there was a loud crash as finally and unequivocally she fainted. There was pandemonium in the room, and someone called for lights and someone called for a doctor, and chairs were pushed back and people dropped hands and stood up. Professor Gaskin pleaded for calm, and relit the candle, and then Dr Hamid tended to the prostrate form of Miss Whinstone, who soon came to her senses and was furnished with a glass of water. Miss Eustace was, saw Mina, still firmly tied to her chair, and appeared to be unconscious, but Mrs Gaskin untied her and dabbed her forehead with a handkerchief, and she raised her head with an exhausted smile.

The disturbance gave Mina the opportunity to go and look behind the curtains, and there was, she had to admit, little enough to see. The table that had fallen was now standing upright with the bell and tambourine in place, and there was an untidy pencilled scrawl on the paper. Mrs Gaskin loomed up beside her. 'Please do look at everything,' she said, triumphantly.

'I didn't intend to intrude, but I am naturally curious,' said Mina. 'I would like to learn more.'

'We are all students,' said Mrs Gaskin, grandiloquently, suggesting that as students went she was at the very least senior in understanding.

Mina picked up the paper on which was inscribed a pious wish for the good health and fortune of those in attendance. 'The spirits have very poor handwriting,' she observed, 'or perhaps they cannot see in the dark.'

'I do not know how the writing is produced,' said Mrs Gaskin. 'It may be that the force exerted by Miss Eustace is as yet insufficiently refined to allow a more elegant hand.'

'Has she given you no clue as to how it is done?'

'None at all. She is always quite unable to recall anything of what has passed, and least of all is she aware of how her powers are exercised.'

Mina, while not wanting to appear to be making an obvious search for trickery, moved about the little alcove, sure that if there were any cords or strings she would encounter them, but she was aware of nothing other than what she could see. 'Miss Eustace is most remarkable,' she said, 'and I profess myself to be full of wonder at what I have seen today.'

Mrs Gaskin smiled indulgently. 'I have seen even more remarkable things, and if you come to us again I am sure that you will see them, too. As our numbers grow and the spirits gain strength from the favourable energies that surround them so they will grant us more powerful manifestations.'

Mina was intrigued by the idea that the spirits were more powerful in the presence of devoted believers. Was Miss Eustace more inclined to perform miracles in front of her most ardent supporters? Or did it mean that believers were more likely to see what they were supposed to see? And what about unbelievers? Supposing someone, a stage magician for example, was to come for the sole purpose of exposing deception? Would he be a source of unfavourable energy, assuming there even to be such a thing? All these were matters Mina felt she ought not to pursue with Mrs Gaskin; she merely offered her gratitude for the invitation and the hope that she might be allowed to come again. Mrs Gaskin's sturdy whalebones creaked and strained with the sincere humility of Mina's appreciation.

The excitement over, the company had in the meantime settled down to tea and conversation. Miss Eustace had withdrawn, or at least Mina assumed she had done so and not vanished in a puff of smoke, and Dr Hamid had arranged for Miss Whinstone to be conveyed to her home in a cab in the company of Mrs Bettinson. As Mrs Gaskin went to join her guests, Mina crossed the room to where the water glasses on the sideboard had been disturbed, but could see nothing to suggest how they might have moved without human agency. That part of the room smelt slightly of the candle and matches, but nothing more.

'You are new to these gatherings,' said Dr Hamid, appearing by her side.

She turned and looked up at him. He was not at all discomfited by recent events and seemed to be the kind of gentleman that one could always rely upon to deal with any emergency without either fuss or self-aggrandisement. 'Yes,' said Mina, 'my mother has taken a very great interest in them and I determined to come and see for myself.'

'This is my third visit,' he said, 'and thus far all we have had was a great deal of noise and a few lights. You have been favoured with some unusual manifestations.'

There was a hint of caution in his voice, a little doubt, perhaps, thought Mina, or at the very least a desire for further enquiry. Hopeful that she had at last met someone capable of exercising a proper sense of proportion, she was emboldened to make a frank declaration, if only to see what would be the result.

'To be truthful, I am not sure of what I have seen and heard today,' she said. 'Certainly nothing I have witnessed has convinced me of the existence of mischievous spirits or of powers that extend beyond the human form, or the necessity of founding a new principle of science. If someone was to come to me and demonstrate that it was all a conjuring trick I would be neither surprised nor disappointed.'

He was a little taken aback at the suggestion, but not repelled. 'Miss Whinstone informed me that she recognised the shade of her late brother,' he observed.

'Miss Whinstone is in such a state of nervousness she would have recognised a mop wearing a false beard as her late brother,' Mina replied, drawing a smile from the doctor. 'And I for one do not accept Professor Gaskin's reasons why the performance had to be held in the dark. If it had occurred in a bright light I would have been more willing to accept that there was something in it. For all his protestations, darkness is the best means of concealing a fraud, though how it was worked, I cannot say.'

'I think you have the strongest nerves of anyone in this room,' said Dr Hamid, 'and as a man of science, I have to confess that I am still unsure of the foundation for these events, although I would not wish to offend our hosts by saying so.' He slid one of the glasses on the sideboard across the polished wooden surface. It moved with barely a touch of his fingers.

'Where there are simple rational explanations, I prefer them,' said Mina, 'and I am suspicious of anyone who professes to be in possession of a new truth for the good of mankind and then uses it to fill their purse or elevate themselves in society.'

'I hope,' he said, with an unforced humility, 'that you will not see me in that light. I offer treatments for the afflicted, but I must also necessarily be a man of business, since we must all earn our bread or starve.'

'You will not be surprised to know,' Mina told him, 'that I view all medical men with suspicion, and that is not from prejudice, but experience. I hope you are not offended but I must speak my mind on that point.'

'Not at all,' he said, gently, 'and I can well understand what events might have led you to that opinion.'

'But thus far,' she admitted, 'I have heard only good of you.'

'You are too kind.' He hesitated. 'Miss Scarletti, if you do not mind my commenting, I can see that you are suffering some pain.'

Mina frowned. She had no objection to anyone mentioning either her appearance or its consequences; the thing she could not abide was the offer of false hope.

'I am sorry if I have distressed you,' he said, 'but I am very familiar with the presentation of *scoliosis*. There is an ache which starts in the shoulder from the strain placed upon the muscles — just — if you will permit me —' He reached out and touched her shoulder with his fingertips — 'just here.'

With some surprise Mina was obliged to acknowledge that he had touched the exact spot from which the pain was spreading.

'I trust you will not be offering me a cure?' she said wryly.

'The man who claims he can correct the curvature in your spine is either ignorant or a charlatan,' he assured her. 'But what I can offer is relief for the pain in your back. My sister Anna attends to the lady patients, and would, I know, wish to see you. I promise you that there will be no metal braces, no plaster of Paris waistcoats, no narcotic mixtures and above all, no knives.'

Mina was not yet willing to admit this to be a serious conversation. 'And she will not tread on my spine and wrap my arms about my head and make my joints crack?'

'Only if she deems it necessary,' he said solemnly, and Mina realised that he was teasing her. He produced a card, wrote something on the back with a pencil, and handed it to her. 'That is my promise that if you present yourself at my establishment, you will receive your first treatment gratis,' he said. 'Please do come, I know you will feel the benefit.'

Mina did not look at the card; she looked at the man. 'I will,' she heard herself say.

Chapter Five

Inevitably, and to a degree monotonously, Mina was often told by well-meaning folk about wonderful 'cures' for her condition. Often, she was not directly addressed; rather the subject was introduced into a general conversation at which she was present, but it was always very clear that the information was being imparted for her benefit. Sometimes these messages would be passed to her mother, who was expected to impose her wishes on Mina as if her daughter was not a sensible adult able to make her own decisions. On other occasions, Mina would be quietly taken aside and advised in an embarrassed whisper to try Brill's tepid sea-water baths for ladies, or drink Dr Struve's German mineral waters. Each of these helpful advisors was under the impression that she — and it was usually a she — was the very first person ever to make that suggestion.

Mina was also regaled with stories of the wonder cures of the past, such as Dr Dean Mahomed's Indian medicated vapour baths and hot and cold douches, which had been vouched for by nobility and even royalty. Dr Mahomed had died almost twenty years ago, and his establishment on the King's Road, whose walls had once been ornamented with murals of richly-dressed Moghul Emperors and displays of the abandoned crutches and spine-stretchers of his delighted customers, had fallen into disuse. Only last year it had been demolished for yet another hotel. It was Dr Hamid who was now considered to be Dr Dean Mahomed's natural successor in the provision of oriental medicine, and Dr Hamid who, with some apprehension, Mina was about to visit.

The doctor did not command a large property, but it occupied a good position on the seafront where Manchester Street met the Marine Parade, close to the site of Mr Brill's original bathhouse, a rounded protuberance that had once encroached on to the Grand Junction Road and had gone by the unflattering name of Brill's Bunion.

There were thankfully no bunions or indeed any unsightly signs and posters on Dr Hamid's bath-house; it was a simple square building that announced itself as 'Hamid's Indian Vapour Bath and Medicated Shampoo.'

Brill's new bath-house on East Street was a large and prominent presence in Brighton society, much favoured for pleasurable warm bathing, while offering the subtle suggestion that its waters induced a health-giving effect on the skin and organs of the body, but Dr Hamid's baths were different. With mysterious unnamed and specially imported Indian herbs infused in its soothing vapours, it was thought of not so much as a fashionable venue for salubrious repose and dismissing the cares of the world, but as a place of resort for the treatment for diseases such as rheumatism. It was therefore much favoured by invalids, the elderly and the afflicted. Mina had been told — another of those private whispers — that if she went to Dr Hamid's she need have no anxiety that she would be required to share a pool or a vapour room with another patient, as all treatments were given in individual compartments. When she had first been told this she had assumed that the confidence was intended to reassure her that she would not come into close proximity with anyone suffering from an unpleasant disease. On reflection she realised that she was actually being comforted with the knowledge that there would, when she undressed, be no-one present who would gaze on her deformity. Mina thought that had she been a person much given to anxiety, which she was not, she would have other things with which to concern herself than whether another lady bather might catch a glimpse of her spine.

As she approached the entrance door, she was surprised to see a familiar figure emerge, Mr Bradley. She was not especially inclined to speak to him, but was somewhat curious as to the reason he patronised Hamid's, since it ran contrary to his claims to be a healer, and did not object when he tipped his hat and stopped for a conversation.

'Miss Scarletti, are you here to take a vapour bath? I did not know you were a patient of Dr Hamid!'

'This is my first visit, Mr Bradley, but I could say the same of you. I trust you are well?'

'Oh, I am in the pink of health,' he assured her, 'but channelling the powers of the spirits at my healing circles can be very exhausting, and I find the vapour quite restores me. You may or may not know this, but herbs are often held to have beneficial properties.'

'Then I must anticipate my bath with some pleasure,' said Mina, politely.

He paused. 'I trust that Miss Whinstone is fully recovered from her recent episode? She spoke to me at church and told me all that had happened. I was quite astonished.'

'Miss Whinstone was so alarmed that she has become an ardent devotee of Miss Eustace and means to go again and have still more experiences that will frighten her from her wits,' said Mina, who had been told this at very great length by her mother.

He smiled. 'And what did *you* think of the demonstration?'

Mina was happy to express her suspicions and anxieties to her brothers and a fellow doubter like Dr Hamid, but if she had wanted to share them with another person, that person would not have been Mr Bradley. 'I found it quite extraordinary,' she said guardedly. 'It was impossible for me to explain what I had seen.'

He nodded knowingly. 'I can see that you are also becoming a devotee; as most of Brighton will soon be, so I have heard.'

'I can safely say that Miss Eustace arouses my very keen interest, and I shall be eager to see more of what she does, and learn more about her,' said Mina.

Mr Bradley seemed not to catch her meaning, but then she did not expect him to. 'Would you be kind enough to advise your charming mother that I will call upon her to conduct the healing circle again tomorrow?'

'I will certainly do so,' said Mina, trying to look as if the prospect was one that promised enjoyment.

They parted with the usual courtesies.

Mina paused in front of the doors of Dr Hamid's baths, but did not yet feel ready to enter. If she tried to explore her feelings she did not really know why she was there. It was not in the hope of a cure; that, she knew, was impossible. Perhaps it was because Dr Hamid had not promised her a cure, or even an improvement in her condition, and she therefore felt more able to trust him than any doctor she had previously consulted. She had also sensed that he had a genuine understanding of the restrictions imposed by her twisted body on her daily life. But perhaps she was there simply because her shoulder ached and she would like it to stop.

She pushed at the door, and in that moment she was decided. Mina often had a struggle with doors, which were inevitably taller, wider and substantially heavier than she, some of them monstrosities of glass and brass and polished wood, which even a man in full health might find a challenge, but this one, for all its imposing appearance, moved at the touch of her fingers. Some beautiful mechanism had been installed, and whether by a system of gliding counterweights or an oiled machine she did not know, but there could be no invalid or elderly frail person who would not be able to open it.

She found herself in a small but tastefully appointed vestibule, and was greeted by a matronly-looking woman to whom she presented Dr Hamid's card. There was a small counter, and behind it a sign listing a scale of charges. A single vapour bath and shampoo was five shillings, but one could purchase six or a dozen at a reduced price, or even an annual subscription. A visitors' book was open inviting customers to enter their comments, and a carved wooden box held a pile of printed leaflets listing Dr Hamid's qualifications, and the treatments offered by his establishment.

Those waiting for attention would not be required to stand, since there were a number of comfortable seats provided for the repose of ladies and gentlemen, at a variety of different heights, so there was something to suit persons of every size, and there was also a selection of cushions of assorted shapes and varying degrees of firmness. A display of dried flowers and seed heads exuded a subtle and slightly exotic perfume.

Mina had expected something of the Oriental about the interior, portraits of richly-dressed and bejewelled potentates, giant decorated urns, painted parasols, or statuettes of elephants and a great deal of gilding, but apart from a colourful frieze that ran around the upper level of the wall, the lover of ornate decoration was doomed to disappointment. Neither was there a poster blaring out in capital letters with fat exclamation marks the wonderful cures that Dr Hamid had effected, or a gruesome display of abandoned crutches. All was peaceful and pleasant, and nothing offended or disturbed the eye.

Three doors led from the vestibule, one for the gentlemen's bathing facilities, one for the use of ladies, and another unmarked door, which was presumably an office.

The lady nodded as she read the card, and operated a bell-pull. 'Please be so good as to follow the signs, and Miss Hamid will be waiting to receive you,' she said.

Mina opened the door to the ladies' baths and found herself at the head of a corridor, where the walls were decorated with prints of tropical plants and birds. A room to her left was a comfortable salon, where some ladies were reposing on couches, sipping mineral water and reading periodicals. A large window faced the sea and the room was golden with sunshine. A lady with a spotless white wrapper over her gown, and undoubtedly from her appearance, Miss Hamid, was arranging a pretty bowl of fresh flowers, but as soon as she saw Mina, she came to greet her.

'You must be Miss Scarletti,' she said. 'I am so pleased that you have decided to come. Daniel — my brother — told me he hoped you would call.'

'I have never experienced a vapour bath before,' said Mina, 'or indeed the shampoo massage, which I think might be more vigorous than is suitable for me.'

'You have nothing to fear,' said Miss Hamid with a comforting smile. 'The vigour or gentleness of the massage is adjusted precisely to the tolerance and the age and health of the patient. Come.'

Miss Hamid was, thought Mina, just a little older than her brother, and as tall, which meant that she was above the common height for a woman. She had a round face with a small chin, and very dark eyes, and her greying hair was simply dressed. Mina, aware that the lady performed the shampoo massage, noticed that Miss Hamid's hands were well formed and looked very strong.

As they walked, Mina looked about her, and was obliged to comment that the establishment, while delightful, was not quite as she had expected. Miss Hamid gave a little laugh. 'You refer to the absence of gilded domes, and portraits of eastern potentates?' Mina was obliged to confess that she did mean something of the kind, but Miss Hamid, so far from being offended as she had feared, was amused. 'We believe,' she said, 'that where it comes to oriental opulence, that Brighton already has a sufficiency.'

By the time they had reached the door of a compartment Mina felt that her companion had somehow seen into and understood the anxieties in her mind, and every discomfort in her body. She was ushered to a small dressing-box where she was to disrobe entirely and wrap herself in a large sheet. A towel fashioned like a turban was provided to cover her hair and there were several pairs of little wooden shoes of different sizes so that she might select the one that would best fit her bare feet.

'Do you require any assistance?' asked Miss Hamid.

'Thank you, but that will not be necessary,' said Mina, who had arranged with her dressmaker to provide gowns specially designed so that she would be able to dress and undress herself.

'When you are ready,' said Miss Hamid, 'enter the next room, where the vapour bath will proceed. After fifteen minutes it will be complete and then I will bring you fresh dry sheets and take you to the massage room. If you require anything at all, please call, I will be nearby.' She left Mina alone.

Mina proceeded to divest herself of her clothing, and then wound the sheet about her body where it was held in place by linen tapes, and arranged the turban on her head. Any resemblance between herself and the wife of a sultan lounging in an eastern harem, was, she felt, undetectable. Not without some awkwardness, she tried the little wooden shoes, found a pair that fitted, and slipped them on to her feet. She discovered with some surprise that they were very comfortable, being moulded so as to cradle her soles, and easy to walk in. Nevertheless she still felt apprehensive as she went into the vapour room. This was a chamber some eight feet square, lined with pretty blue and white tiles, and with an opening at the top, presumably to allow a free circulation of air. There was one high window, but no danger of being observed, since it was of stained glass with panes of green and blue, admitting only a subdued light. She detected a very faint but pleasing scent of flowers or herbs, which she could not readily identify. In the centre of the room was a simple wooden chair draped in a thick soft towel. Mina sat in the chair and looked about her, but could not see where the vapour was to come from. In just a few moments she understood. The floor of the room, which was tiled in a latticework design, was not a continuous surface but admitted little diamond-shaped gaps, and it was from these gaps that a vapour began to arise. It rose around her like a soft perfumed cloud and gradually began to fill the room. Any apprehension she might have felt was quickly dispelled by the deliciousness of the scent, and the feeling of warmth that stole over her. She closed her eyes, wondering where the vapour, which must already be condensing to spangle the cooler walls, must be going, since she hardly expected to find the room awash with water when she was finished. Wherever the vapour went, she felt sure that there was some ingenious method for its efficient removal. Even the floor had been specially designed so as not to offer a slippery surface underfoot. Dr Hamid seemed to think of everything.

These enquiring thoughts were set aside, as she inhaled the sweet medicated cloud, inducing a delightful sense of tranquillity, while a pleasing perspiration bathed her body. The sheet around her became warm and moist; it clung to her skin, infusing her with its own heat and scent. Pain, indeed the concept that pain might even exist, was somehow washed away, time was washed away, and she felt at peace. It was with some regret that she noticed after a while, that Anna Hamid had entered the room and the vapour was dispersing. The last threads of moisture were beading the walls and running down into a narrow tiled gully around the perimeter.

'Stand very slowly and I will help you,' said Miss Hamid, and there was nothing in her voice to suggest that Mina might need any more help than another person whose body had acquired a beautiful soft suppleness from the medicinal steam. She wrapped Mina in a warm fresh sheet, and drew her to the next room, which was a haven of scented and soothing heat, and laid her on a couch, then oiled her hands and with the most exquisite care, ran her fingers over the contours of Mina's back. Miss Hamid was a strong woman with powerful shoulders, but years of applying her hands to the work of untying the knots in strained muscles had given her a perfectly directed firmness and an understanding delicacy of touch. Her hands exerted a gentle pressure on Mina's back, further warming the already relaxed muscles, and her thumbs located the seat of the shoulder pain and began to smooth it away.

'You seem to know exactly where the discomfort lies,' said Mina. 'You must have other patients with a similar condition.'

'There have been some,' said Miss Hamid, 'but the chief of those is my sister, Eliza.'

'Oh!' said Mina, startled. 'I have not seen any lady in Brighton who is like myself.'

'Eliza rarely goes from home,' said Miss Hamid, sadly. 'Her case is far more advanced than yours. Her spine became curved when she was a very small child, when her bones were weaker and more pliable, and there was no opportunity for her to obtain the help that a child would certainly receive now.'

'I am sorry to hear it,' said Mina.

'It was her predicament that led Daniel and me to make a special study of *scoliosis* and other conditions affecting the spine, and devise our own methods of helping patients. Perhaps,' said Miss Hamid, diffidently, 'I could prevail upon you to call on Eliza. I know that she would appreciate your company.'

'Of course,' said Mina. 'I am only surprised that when I met your brother he did not mention her to me.'

'You encountered him at the salon held by Professor Gaskin, I believe?' asked Miss Hamid, her fingers exerting a delicate tapping and fluttering like tiny feet running up and down Mina's back.

'I did. That was a very curious evening.'

'Do you believe that Miss Eustace's powers are genuine?' asked Miss Hamid, with a note of caution in her voice that inspired Mina to take her into her confidence.

'I saw nothing that convinced me I had witnessed anything more than a clever magician,' she said, boldly, 'and I fear that people are being duped, but I cannot prove it.'

'Daniel has told me that he is not entirely convinced that Miss Eustace's demonstrations are genuine,' said Miss Hamid. 'If you do not mind the question — what drew you to visit her?'

'I think that is a very important question,' said Mina, 'and I have no objection to answering. I went because my mother goes and I do not want her to be exposed to the machinations of a charlatan. My mother goes because she was widowed a year ago and seeks solace, and, I rather think, novelty.'

Miss Hamid began to explore the muscles in the soft angle between Mina's neck and shoulders. 'I think Daniel would not mention Eliza in such company in case they should seize upon her and offer her false hope of a cure,' she said. 'He knows of the terrible machines and even worse operations that a well-meaning doctor will recommend, but someone who claims to be in concert with the spirits can do as much evil.'

'I do not seek a cure,' said Mina, 'since none exists. I am content with that because I must be. Neither do I believe in the kind of spirits that Miss Eustace purports to show us. The world of the spirit is closed to the living; we will meet it soon enough.'

Miss Hamid gently drew Mina's arm across her back to raise her shoulder blade and used her fingertips to seek out clenched and sore muscles with a firm but not unpleasant pressure that made her patient gasp.

'Although Daniel is a man of science, he nevertheless feels some hope, as all of us must do, which induces in him a need to explore and enquire,' said Miss Hamid. 'He is, of course, aware that there are many things we understand today to have a foundation in fact which only a hundred years ago would have seemed to be impossible. I expect you know that he is not long a widower. He and his dear wife Jane were very devoted to each other. She died three months ago after a painful but mercifully short illness. They had been married for twenty-two years and he feels her loss very keenly.'

'What does he seek?' asked Mina. 'Surely he does not hope to communicate with her spirit?'

'I think,' said Miss Hamid reflectively, 'that he looks only for some sign, some certainty that the spirit, the intelligence, the soul, call it what you will of an individual will survive entire, and if he can be assured of this, he will be content, because he will know that one day they will be reunited.'

Mina thought of her father and Marianne. 'We all hope to be reunited with our loved ones in Heaven,' she said. 'But I do not think the Bible said anything about the dead speaking to the living, or playing on tambourines.'

'The Bible teaches us that we all sleep until the Day of Judgement and then and only then do we rise again,' said Miss Hamid. 'I see no reason to doubt it.'

'Then perhaps,' said Mina cautiously, 'your brother should comfort himself with that. Miss Eustace's demonstrations are little more than a sideshow on the pier, like Madame Proserpina the fortune teller, only I fear, very much more expensive.'

'I can see that this worries you greatly,' said Miss Hamid. 'Your neck and shoulders grow more tense under my fingers as you think about it. But now I would beg you to have only pleasurable thoughts.' She anointed her hands with more scented oil and smoothed them over Mina's back. Mina sighed and gave herself up to the sensation. When the massage was done she felt more supple than she could remember ever having felt, with a lightness and freedom from pain that she would have thought impossible.

When Mina was dressed, Miss Hamid brought her a cushion shaped like a door wedge, which she could put underneath one hip to right her posture as she sat, and asked if she had ever been prescribed exercises.

'Only deportment classes,' said Mina. 'I was required to walk in a circle with a bag of shot on my head while juggling oranges. I was not their best student.'

Miss Hamid smiled. 'I believe that oranges are better when the flesh is eaten and the peel dried for its scent. I would like you to undertake some suitable exercises, but I do not wish you to attempt them alone, not yet. Some of the movements known as callisthenics would be very beneficial to you, but only if performed correctly. Others, however, are best avoided. If you would like, then the next time you come here I will show you what to do. You need to strengthen your weaker side, but take care not to neglect the other, and also work on expanding the chest to help your lungs and heart. We will begin slowly. You must be patient and avoid over-exertion which can be harmful.'

Mina smiled, because Miss Hamid knew, and she also knew, that she would return. 'I would like that,' she said.

'Young women are often dissuaded from exercising, as if weakness was a desirable state,' said Miss Hamid. 'But it is not. You can be strong; stronger than you might imagine, stronger than anyone would expect of you. Your mind is already very strong, but your body can be as well.'

Mina had never thought of herself as a creature of the body, but began to see that she had spent the last nine years merely trying to exist with her condition, and find an occupation for her mind that would distract her from it. Miss Hamid had offered her not a cure, which was not within her powers, but a means of alleviating the symptoms, and perhaps also making herself into something better than she was.

With an agreement that she would call on Eliza Hamid in two days' time, Mina departed for her home. As she stepped into the open air she felt that she took with her some of the scent of herbs and flowers in which she had bathed and whose delicious savour she had inhaled. The sun seemed brighter, the sky more glowing, the air softer, the people more colourful, the season more charming than they had been before.

She returned to find that an important package, which she had requested by letter from Mr Greville had arrived. It was an unbound advance copy of the report of the special committee of the London Dialectical Society regarding their investigation into the question of spiritualism, the report that Professor Gaskin had spoken of in such exultant terms.

Chapter Six

Fortunately, Mina's mother, nesting in the parlour in an array of periodicals and pamphlets, was too preoccupied with her own concerns to be curious about the delivery, which did not excite any comment. Mina passed on the message she had been given by Mr Bradley, and Louisa received the news with pleasure and informed Mina that she expected her to attend the healing circle on the following day. It would be a meeting of important and fashionable individuals and quite the most glittering event of the season to date. Mina, expecting no more than the usual gathering of bored widows, quickly agreed and took the parcel up to her room as soon as she was able. The size and weight of the package had suggested to her that it might contain other works, too, since she had expected the report to be a slim bundle of papers, but on unwrapping it she was astonished to find only the report, a work that ran to almost four hundred pages.

It did not, however, take very long for Mina to discover that Professor Gaskin, who claimed to have read the report, had made two very significant errors of judgement. Professor and man of science he might be, but he was as vulnerable to bias as anyone else. He had first of all chosen only to see those areas of evidence that might favour his own viewpoint, interpreting them in a manner that supported his contentions, while ignoring not only the other possible and indeed more probable interpretations of events, but also additional evidence and points of view which were not favourable to his cause. The man who pitied the closed minds of others did so, thought Mina, with a mind that was in itself closed. He had also made the fatally dangerous assumption that no-one present at Miss Eustace's séance would take the trouble to read the report and compare its findings with his description.

Mina settled herself at her desk, raising her hip with the new cushion, which was a wonderful improvement on the old one, and started to read.

Even a small and seemingly harmless falsehood invited suspicion from the outset. Professor Gaskin had implied that the report was to be published by the Dialectical Society, but this, Mina saw at once, was not the case. The Society had appointed a committee to investigate spirit phenomena in January 1869, which had reported its findings in July 1870, in the hopes that the Society would publish them. The Society had noted the committee's report but had declined to publish, a refusal that suggested to Mina a lack of trust in either the conduct of the investigation or its conclusions. The committee members had therefore taken the decision to publish the report themselves.

During the course of the enquiry six subcommittees had been created, each of which had held meetings and séances. The committee had also collected statements from non-members all of whom were believers in supernatural phenomena, having failed, for reasons it was unable to explain, to obtain evidence from anyone who attributed the phenomena to fraud and delusion.

Mina was less interested in opinions than results and so studied the reports of the six subcommittees with especial interest.

Two of the subcommittees reported that no phenomena at all had occurred during their meetings, and another was conducting séances with Mr Home, who, since he was a cheat with money, was in Mina's opinion likely to be a cheat in other things, too. She decided that these three subcommittees had failed to prove anything.

Two subcommittees had heard rappings and witnessed the movement of a table, but this occurred only when certain individuals were taking part. The presence of these persons was undoubtedly essential to the results but whether this was due to their supernatural powers or the ability to deceive was not, in Mina's mind, established beyond doubt.

The most extraordinary performances were at meetings that took place at the houses of two members of the Dialectical Society where, to avoid any suspicion of fraud, the gatherings did not include anyone claiming to have mediumistic powers. Not only did rapping and table moving occur but by giving the meanings 'yes' or 'no' to numbers of raps, or even spelling out words when one of the party named a letter of the alphabet it was possible to establish a free communication with the spirits who had produced the manifestations. These cheerful entities expressed a friendly regard for those present and were able to provide correct answers to questions and personal information. The subcommittee members had no doubt that they had been in communication with spirit intelligences, but reported that they had inevitably failed to obtain any manifestations without the presence in the party of the wives of the two members of the Dialectical Society. Mina was left weighing up two possibilities, one being that the party had been conversing with the spirits of the dead and the other that the two ladies had been mischievously providing their friends with some novel entertainment.

The conclusion drawn by the committee from these mixed results was that sounds and movement of objects did occur without having been produced by muscular or mechanical action, and the ability to spell out answers to questions showed that the phenomena were directed by an intelligence.

Further reports revealed that while many members of the society suspected fraud they had been unable to offer any proof. This was unsurprising since once an observer was suspected of being a sceptic who was bent on exposing imposture, the false medium, on being alerted to the danger, quickly arranged matters so as to avoid detection. This was done in a number of ways, the simplest being to produce no phenomena at the séance and then announce that his or her powers were exhausted that day, or that the spirits were being capricious, or even attributing the failure to a hostile influence in the circle. The hostile influence was of course the sceptic, who was thereafter persona non grata in the company, since both the medium and the circle of believers would not want that person disrupting their sittings in future.

It was with particular interest, and some amusement that Mina read a letter written by the chairman of the Dialectical Society's special committee, a Dr James Edmunds. Fending off earnest attempts by spiritualists to persuade him that he himself could be a powerful medium if he would only open his eyes and recognise the fact, he remained unconvinced by the committee's conclusions, and had submitted his personal observations.

In May 1868, Dr Edmunds had attended a public exhibition at St George's Hall, London, given by the Davenport brothers, Americans who were touring England giving demonstrations of phenomena which they attributed to spirits but which many who had seen their performances had denounced as little more than clever, albeit entertaining, conjuring. Mina recalled the Davenports' tour, which had been widely reported and discussed in the London newspapers. The two young men had a large wooden cabinet specially constructed for their performances, which they carried about with them on their tour. Volunteers from the audience were first invited to make a thorough examination of the apparatus, after which two chairs were placed inside the cabinet, to which the brothers were securely bound. A collection of musical instruments such as tambourines, bells, violins and guitars, joined them in the cabinet and the door was closed. Almost at once the instruments produced a perfect babel of sound, while spirit arms and hands were seen protruding through an overhead aperture. Every so often the door of the cabinet burst violently open and an instrument was tossed out on to the floor. Their most remarkable feat used a coat borrowed from a member of the audience which was placed inside the cabinet and was later found on the person of one of the brothers, yet when they were examined after the performance the knots and ligatures were found to be as sound and tight as before.

Dr Edmunds was unable to explain away what he had seen that night, which had involved flying violins and the use of his own coat in the famous trick. Later the same month he was invited to attend a private séance, which was to be followed by the Davenports giving their acclaimed cabinet performance. Edmunds, though a natural sceptic, determined to approach the evening with an open mind, anticipating that in a private room he would have a better opportunity to observe and investigate the phenomena. Perhaps his reputation had preceded him, or the company was wary of any newcomer, for when the sitters were conducted to their places he found himself at a large round table that had been pushed close to a corner of the room so trapping him in his place. Had he been inclined to slip off his shoes and creep silently about the darkened room looking for evidence of imposture, something he had thought of doing, he would have been quite unable to do so. The part of the table towards the centre of the room, and thus allowing sitters free movement, was, he noticed, occupied by avowed spiritualists. Edmunds wisely decided not to protest about this arrangement in case he was held to be hostile, in which case he felt sure that no phenomena would occur.

The sitting proceeded in complete darkness for some little time. A few raps were heard but nothing of note occurred, and the company was finding the occasion somewhat disappointing, when it was decided to try and obtain a spirit drawing. The gas was re-lit and a portfolio case was placed on the table and opened to demonstrate that it contained nothing but a sheet of plain paper, then the case was closed again and a pencil placed nearby. The gas was about to be turned out when Edmunds suggested to a friend who was also a newcomer to the gathering that as a further test they should first initial the paper. He opened the case and saw that the paper was not as he had at first supposed a plain quarto sheet but a much larger sheet that had been folded. On unfolding it he saw on the interior of one flap a detailed pencil drawing of an angel. He tore off the portion with the drawing and he and his friend wrote on the remaining part of the sheet, which was returned to the case. The gas was turned off and he heard the sound of loud rustling, which led him to suspect that one of the spiritualists at the table had opened the case, and was handling the paper. When the gas was relit there were only a few ambiguous marks on the sheet and the test was declared to be a failure. The spirits, it was explained, were 'capricious'. The sitters were not wholly disappointed by the séance, however, for a basket of fresh flowers was then produced under cover of darkness which a Mrs Guppy claimed had flown through the walls but which Edmunds thought had travelled from no greater distance than the sideboard. Dr Edmunds was by now finding himself unable to conceal the fact that he thought the whole performance was a deception and was unsurprised to be told soon afterwards that the Davenports would not be performing their miracles as they had no spiritual power that evening.

A Mr Samuel Guppy had later written to the committee to deny that Dr Edmunds's account was correct, but a diligent search through the papers enabled Mina to establish not only that Mr Guppy was the husband of Mrs Guppy but that he was an ardent spiritualist, and his wife professed to be a powerful medium who could shower her devotees with fresh flowers, and even rise up and fly about the room.

Other exhibitions carefully observed by the tireless Dr Edmunds had attributed the sound of spirit raps to nothing more supernatural than the medium's foot. He concluded that during all his investigations he had never seen anything that could not be accounted for by unconscious action, delusion or imposture.

There were other statements in the report, some from gentlemen convinced of the reality of what they had observed, and some from those who felt sure that they had observed something of note but did not believe that spirits of the dead were directing events. The consensus, if such a mixture of differing opinions could be termed such, was that there was something occurring which was worthy of further cautious investigation, a conclusion with which Mina could only agree. She would not wish to prejudge the outcome of such an investigation, but her own feeling was that she was more inclined to believe that a bunch of flowers could be carried across a room by human hands than fly through a wall by spirit power. If that made her a sceptic or even a materialist then so be it.

The difficult question was what she should do next. On the one hand, she could not begrudge her mother the pleasure and diversion she gained from the gatherings with Miss Eustace, but on the other, it seemed to her that there was a very real possibility that Miss Eustace was a criminal who made money from deceiving the vulnerable. She determined after some thought to discuss the question with the one person she knew who had attended the séances and appeared to have some doubts — Dr Hamid.

Louisa Scarletti was now, in her own estimation at least, well on her way to becoming the hostess of a fashionable *salon*, and all her talk was of who she might invite to Mr Bradley's healing circle in future, and, more importantly, who should not be invited, and who had attended in the past who ought never to be invited again. She spent much of her time studying the newspapers and directories of Brighton, making lists of her approved guests, and giving orders to the cook.

In one area, however, she remained sorely disappointed. Her efforts, even combined with those of Mr Bradley, to persuade Reverend Vaughan of Christ Church that the healing circle was not irreligious had met with a greater failure than even they might have anticipated. On the Sunday after the first gathering the Reverend had taken as his text Matthew 24.11: 'And many false prophets shall rise, and shall deceive many.' While he did not mention Mr Bradley by name, his meaning could not have been clearer, and during his sermon, the Reverend cast some very severe looks not only at that gentleman, but Louisa, Mina and any others whom he had been informed might be members of the circle. Mr Bradley sat throughout with a fixed smile on his face and pretended that the sermon was nothing to do with him, but Louisa made no secret of her increasing fury. According to St Matthew, the false prophets would arrive in sheep's clothing and perform great signs and miracles, but inwardly, they would be ravening wolves. Mina did not think either Mr Bradley or Miss Eustace looked like ravening wolves, but then, on reflection, she realised that this was the very point that St Matthew was making.

When Mr Bradley's healing circle met again, the sceptical Mr Jordan was not present, whether by his own intention or Louisa's Mina did not know, but the two widowed sisters Mina had met at the séance, Mrs Mowbray and Mrs Peasgood, had been added to the company. Mrs Bettinson, Miss Whinstone, Mrs Phipps and Mr Conroy were early arrivals, and to Mina's surprise when she entered the parlour, she saw her tenant, the normally energetic Mrs Parchment, sitting there looking very stiff and uncomfortable, and staring at a platter of iced cakes with extreme disfavour. How Louisa had persuaded her to attend, Mina could not imagine and why she would have wanted her there was an even greater mystery. Mrs Parchment appeared to be labouring under a similar sense of amazement.

Before the proceedings commenced, several more ladies and two gentlemen crowded into the parlour, which was starting to resemble a crush at a society drawing room. Mr Bradley started by greeting all those present with an equal distribution of his charm, although he swiftly moved on to an oleaginous appreciation of his hostess, and an especial welcome to those new to the circle. The ladies and gentlemen present, he declared, might or might not know this, but it was to Mrs Scarletti that he owed the great success of the little circle, which he anticipated might even in time become a very large circle, or even several circles. Throughout the encomium to her mother Mina could only feel grateful that his attention was thereby diverted from herself. All then proceeded as before, with Mina allowing the peaceful atmosphere devoid of all interruptions to concentrate her mind on completing the composition of her tale of the jewel in the fish.

It was as Mr Bradley conducted the individual healing that Mina's mind came back to what was before her, for when he paused in front of Mrs Parchment he did not, as he had done with the other ladies, touch her hand. Instead he knelt, and rested his palm on her right foot. She started, and almost withdrew the foot, then submitted to the touch with a faint frown.

Mina looked at her mother, and saw her lips curve knowingly. It was too transparent, of course. Mina deduced that the reason Mrs Parchment had not gone on her usual brisk walk that day was because she had some small injury to her foot, something that her mother knew about, and had doubtless communicated privately to Mr Bradley. There was no point in Mina suggesting that there had been any complicity since there was no proof, and both parties would deny it vehemently. The point of the dissimulation was clearly to add to Mr Bradley's fame by demonstrating that his knowledge of Mrs Parchment's injury should be attributed to his special insight. Mina felt disgusted at the imposture, but it appeared trivial enough. If her mother and Mr Bradley thereby felt some enhancement of their status they should be left to enjoy their shallow delights, and if Mrs Parchment imagined her foot to feel better, why then she had received a benefit. Mr Bradley's healing touch was no worse than the coloured water sold by quack doctors, which so many of their patients declared had cured them.

When Mrs Parchment had limped back to her room, Louisa announced to the remaining company that Mr Bradley had not seen the lady walk before he had arrived, and had not known about the injury to her foot. Nevertheless, he had sensed at once that she required a healing and also the precise location of the pain. It was a wonderful proof of his astonishing perception. She also confided that her tenant had barely been able to move at all before the healing, and was therefore now almost cured. Everyone agreed that they had been most privileged to witness the demonstration.

No sooner had the last guest departed than Louisa was busy drawing up a new list of names. Mina had earlier advised her mother that her visit to Dr Hamid's baths had brought her some relief from her accustomed discomfort, and Louisa had initially shown no great interest in this fact, but now she asked Mina if at the next gathering she might take a turn about the room, and say how her pain had diminished.

'But the company will surely form the impression that any benefit I gained was due not to Dr Hamid's establishment but Mr Bradley,' Mina protested.

'Really, Mina, how can you even know that that is not the case?' said her mother dismissively. 'And I do not ask you to do it for Mr Bradley, I ask you to do it for *me*. Is that too great a trouble for you? It seems so.'

'Of course, I will do as you ask,' said Mina, resignedly, wondering how she could possibly avoid it.

'And if Dr Hamid is so very clever,' added Louisa, 'then how has he not healed his own sister, who is, so I have been informed, in a great state? Perhaps I should send Mr Bradley to see *her*.'

Mina clamped her lips shut before she said anything unwise and decided not to mention her invitation to take tea with the Hamids on the following day.

Chapter Seven

Dr Hamid and his family lived in a pleasant villa in Charles Street, not far from the Marine Parade. A maid conducted Mina to a parlour where she was greeted by Anna and her brother. It was a house of mourning, but there was a tasteful restraint about the display, which Mina thought was not about outward show or fashion but deep and privately held feeling. The mantelpiece was simply draped in black, and a framed memorial card was placed beside a black-bordered portrait of a lady, undoubtedly the late Jane Hamid, who looked out across the room with a serene and intelligent expression. Other pictures, also in black frames, showed a venerable gentleman of Indian extraction, with a round face and kindly eyes, and an elderly lady, dignified and handsome; undoubtedly Dr Hamid's parents.

On a small table was a collection of pictures in pretty silver frames of three young people at various ages, the most recent one being of two fine-looking youths and a girl.

'I see you are admiring our portraits,' said Anna with a smile, when the usual politenesses had been exchanged, and refreshments served.

'These are very charming young people,' said Mina.

'Jacob is twenty, now,' said Dr Hamid. 'He is in Edinburgh studying to be a surgeon. My two youngest are at school in London. Nathan is eighteen and will soon join his brother in the study of medicine. My daughter Davina is fifteen and if her wishes can be met, she will also take a medical degree at Edinburgh. There is at present a most unwarranted prejudice in England against women practising medicine, which I hope will be overcome in time.' He looked proudly at the pictures, his eyes naturally moving on to cloud over as they gazed at the portrait of his late wife.

'You are very advanced in your thinking,' said Mina.

He smiled. 'How could I not be with such examples before me? My mother was a very wise and educated lady, as was my late wife, as are both my sisters. I cannot ignore what is plain to see.'

'I am very happy that you have agreed to call on Eliza,' said Anna, warmly. 'She is normally solitary although she will protest that she prefers to be so. I am not altogether convinced of it. She hardly ever ventures downstairs but keeps to her room. Of course, we spend as much time as we can with her, and there is a maid to see to her wants, but she really has no friends.'

Mina put her teacup down. 'I would be delighted to see her.'

'She has just taken her afternoon nap, and is now expecting you. I will take you to her.' Anna conducted Mina upstairs, and knocked on a door. 'Eliza, here is Miss Scarletti to see you.'

There was a brief wait then the door opened. Mina had prepared herself with a determination to show neither pity nor cloying kindness, both of which she abhorred, guessing that any sister of Dr and Anna Hamid would feel the same. In a moment she realised that whatever the expression on her face, it would have made no difference to the woman who stood before her. Eliza, leaning heavily upon a stout stick, was the only adult Mina had ever seen who was smaller than herself. The little woman's body was so distorted that the curve of her spine had lifted her right shoulder higher than her head, which was forced forward on a downward sloping neck so that its normal position was with the face looking down to the floor. The left shoulder was rotated so that it rested several inches below the right and while the necessarily loose and shapeless gown concealed it, Mina knew that the left side of Eliza's body must be collapsed and atrophied to a degree that she herself would hopefully never experience. The unfortunate woman's ribs were almost certainly pressing into her lungs and possibly even constricting the action of her heart. Suddenly Mina saw that her own body, her young strong body in which she could achieve all that she wanted to do in life, was a wonderful blessing to her, and that her inconsequential S of a spine could only mock with its comparatively mild displacement the crushed form of Eliza Hamid. Mina had never intended it, but tears started in her eyes. Anna glanced at her, concerned, and Mina knew that if she faltered now she had failed everyone. She took a deep breath. 'Miss Hamid, I am most delighted to meet you.'

Eliza lifted her head with an effort, and for several moments a searching gaze took in the person before her. 'Please, do come in,' she said. 'Anna, please ask Mary to send up some refreshments. I do so hope there are almond biscuits.'

'Of course,' said Anna.

Mina followed Eliza into a sitting room, where a small couch, heaped with quilts and pillows was undoubtedly the only location where the occupant could sleep in comfort. There was a low easy chair, which was provided with a special cushion, angled so that when Eliza was seated her body tilted back and she could see the person who was with her, without having to strain her neck. Even so, Mina could see that it would be hard for Eliza to maintain her position without assistance, since her head was of normal size, and the neck not strong enough to support it for long. As she wondered at this, Eliza indicated where she should sit, and prodding the tip of her stick into a groove on the side of the chair, and placing one foot on a low stool, stepped neatly, almost nimbly, into position. When she was comfortably settled she placed a padded collar around her neck, and rested her chin on it. Mina could only admire her hostess's independence, the confidence with which she inhabited her confined yet comfortable world.

From the portraits in the parlour below Mina could see that Anna most closely resembled her father, whereas Dr Hamid and Eliza both had the oval face and sculpted cheekbones of their mother. Mina had been told that Eliza was fifty, twice her own age, but pain and the constant fight to draw breath had drawn savage lines in her otherwise youthful skin.

'And now,' said Eliza, 'let us talk, and I hope there will be no mention of joints or spines or bones, or any discomfort at all.'

'I agree,' said Mina. 'That can be so tedious.' She looked about her. The room was well supplied with books, and there was a table at Eliza's elbow with an open volume, a pile of newspapers, and a pair of spectacles. 'But I can see that you are a great reader, and we will not want for interesting subjects for our conversation.'

Eliza, it transpired, was an avid devourer of novels, histories and memoirs, and although she rarely stirred from her room, took a keen interest in the world and all its doings. By the time the maid arrived with the almond biscuits there was the unaccustomed sound of laughter in the room. Mina even revealed that she wrote stories of mystery and adventure, which excited Eliza to great admiration.

Eliza tired quickly. Talking and laughing were nourishment to her mind but a strain on her body. Mina had just begun to wonder how she might retire gracefully and leave Eliza to rest, when Anna arrived, announcing that it was time for her sister's massage.

'Please do come again,' said Eliza, eagerly. 'And you must entertain me with your stories, you really must!'

Mina promised that she would, wondering what she might have written that would be suitable. 'If Dr Hamid is not too busy, I would very much like to speak with him before I go,' she mentioned.

'But of course,' said Anna. 'He is still in the parlour, and you may even find there is a sandwich left, although I very much doubt it.'

There were no sandwiches left, but Mina did not mind that. She found Dr Hamid draining the last of the tea, and looking quietly thoughtful. His was a gentle melancholy, with no room for self-pity, only a contemplation of loss and its meaning.

He looked up as she entered, and rose to his feet until she was seated. 'I am grateful for your visit,' he said. 'I know that Eliza will benefit from your company.'

'It has been my privilege,' said Mina. 'We had so many things to talk about, and I would very much like to call on her again. But if I may, there is a subject that concerns us both which I would like to discuss with you.'

'Please do,' he said, surprised. He offered to ring for more refreshments, but Mina said that was not necessary.

'The subject is Miss Eustace,' she said.

'Ah,' said Dr Hamid. He picked up his empty teacup, contemplated its interior and put it down again.

'You know my opinion of these manifestations,' said Mina. 'I believe them to be nothing more than conjuring, and if that was my only concern I would not be so troubled. If the lady can provide a diversion for idle minds or comfort for the bereaved, then I cannot blame her any more than if she was a fortune teller or played the piano. But what if the lady is a dangerous and calculating criminal? Some of those who profess to be mediums are really thieves. They ask for large sums of money in return for supposedly bringing messages from deceased loved ones and their poor dupes are so deep in their power that they give them all they own. Those who go to séances simply to be entertained will not be vulnerable; no, it is the lonely and unhappy and recently bereaved who will fall victim. Is that not cruel and evil?'

'Of course,' he agreed readily, 'and I believe that Miss Eustace does receive payment in the form of gifts, but these are small and voluntarily given. Do you have any evidence that she is demanding large sums of money?'

'No,' Mina admitted. 'But then if someone is being gulled out of their fortune they are not going to discuss it in company. It might happen secretly and not be discovered until it is too late. And small gifts may over time become large demands.'

He looked unconvinced. 'I cannot imagine that *you* would ever be gulled. Are you perhaps concerned for your mother?'

Mina paused. 'I confess that that was my first thought, and I am sure that she does make payments to Miss Eustace, although she will not admit it to me. But outrageous villains such as Mr Home, the medium who defrauded an elderly widow of thirty thousand pounds, do not prey on ladies who have families to watch over their concerns. My mother may hand over her few guineas but she will not be asked for all her fortune. And if she should suddenly decide to transfer her funds outside the family, our solicitor or our bank will let me know, since I have dealt with the family finances since my father died. There are other ladies, however, who attend Miss Eustace's séances, who have no relatives and manage their own affairs. I am thinking of Miss Whinstone, for example, who was in a highly nervous state even before she had heard of Miss Eustace. Her brother was all her family and he died two years ago, leaving her very comfortably provided for. She undoubtedly believes that she has seen his ghost, and who knows what that might lead to.'

Mina could see that Dr Hamid, while not sharing her anxieties, clearly recognised that she was in great earnest and was giving her words serious consideration. 'You are presumably asking for my advice?'

'I ask for advice, or observations, or any comment that might assist me,' said Mina, with some energy. 'I wish I did not have to trouble you with this, but my brothers are rarely here for me to consult and, of course, they have not seen Miss Eustace for themselves or formed an opinion of her.'

'I will endeavour to be worthy of your trust,' said Dr Hamid, very solemnly, 'but I find it difficult to imagine what you might do without clear evidence of wrongdoing. You cannot accuse someone of a crime, either to their face or to another person, or, more difficult still, of the intention to commit a crime, without proof. An accusation without foundation is in itself a crime.'

'Yes,' Mina agreed, 'and I am not in a position to acquire evidence, especially without knowing the intended victim.'

'Even supposing there to be one,' said Dr Hamid. 'You must consider the possibility that your fears are unfounded.'

In the face of such undeniable good sense, Mina did consider. 'You are right, of course,' she said at last, in a calmer frame of mind. 'I have been too alarmed by reading about undoubted frauds and have concluded that Miss Eustace is of their number. But as you rightly say, I have no evidence. She may be no more than a sixpenny sideshow after all, and harmless enough. From what I have read it is private séances with a single client where mediums bent on extortion may practise their designs on an unprotected individual, and Miss Eustace does not conduct those.' There was a long thoughtful pause. Dr Hamid looked worried, and Mina, seeing his expression, understood. 'Or does she? If she does, you must tell me.'

'I think,' he said, hesitantly, 'I think it is possible that she may, or at least might do so if asked. There was some talk following an earlier séance; Mrs Gaskin said that Miss Eustace could do a great deal more than produce rappings and lights; she could bring personal messages from loved ones who have passed, but it was harder to do so where a crowd was gathered together, because the energy of many in once place was confusing to the spirits.'

'Did she say that Miss Eustace was willing to conduct private consultations?'

'She did not suggest it herself, but one of the ladies asked if such a thing was possible, and she said it might be.'

'They are subtler than I thought,' said Mina, 'letting the dupes carve their own path. Did anyone actually ask her to arrange such a consultation?'

Dr Hamid looked uncomfortable. 'No, it was just a general conversation, but the information did arouse considerable interest. It did cross my mind that …' He shook his head. 'No matter.'

Mina could only pity the unhappy man before her. 'I don't suppose there was any mention of payment?' she said gently. 'There so rarely is.'

'Not in so many words.' Dr Hamid peered into the empty teapot, and gazed thoughtfully at the crumbs on the sandwich plate, as though considering whether or not to ring for more after all.

'You must tell me everything you can remember,' Mina demanded.. 'A hint, a glance, an allegorical tale, there must have been *some* communication.'

He was surprised, but did his best. 'There was a suggestion that only serious enquirers would benefit.'

'By serious I suppose they mean those able to pay more than a guinea, perhaps much more,' said Mina. 'Of course, the Gaskins may be as much dupes as anyone else, lured by the promise of celebrity. At present, Miss Eustace feeds off them, but the professor hopes one day to publish his book, and give lectures, or even found a chair at a university.'

'Professor and Mrs Gaskin will not be amenable to any suggestion that Miss Eustace is a trickster,' said Dr Hamid, 'and those of her devotees who choose to pay large sums for consultations may pronounce themselves satisfied with what they receive.'

'Until they find their bank accounts empty and see what fools they have been,' said Mina, 'and then, of course, it will be too late, and I for one will regret having stood by and allowed it.' She opened her reticule and drew out the booklet about Mr Home, and the pages of the Dialectical Society report which included Dr Edmunds's statement. 'Please borrow these and read them,' she said. 'It will show you that the dangers are very real, and also how a clever man, a medical man, was not deceived by performances which fooled others. In the case of Mr Home, the law did take his victim's part, but it was only after she herself accused him, and she was fortunate in that she acted quickly and was able to recover her funds. Others might not be so prompt, and what consolation would it be to them if they saw the criminals put in prison but were themselves left destitute? Once you have read this, we will speak again and decide what to do.'

He raised his eyebrows, possibly at the word 'we', but took the pages from her. 'I am really not sure what can be done,' he said. 'You cannot force a victim of a crime to take action if they do not believe there has been a crime. They would undoubtedly defend Miss Eustace against any allegations, and the only person to suffer would be you.'

'You are right, of course,' said Mina, 'and I do appreciate that to accuse someone of a felony without evidence is a serious matter. But what I might perhaps be able to do is demonstrate that Miss Eustace is a false medium. If I succeeded then her dupes would abandon her and she would not be able to part innocent victims from their money.'

'And if her powers prove to be genuine?' Dr Hamid pointed out. 'We must not have closed minds.'

'If she is genuine,' said Mina, 'then she should delight in having her powers put to the test. She should welcome all and every test that there is; she should *ask* to be tested, *demand* it. If she is proven to be true it can only add to her fame, and increase the numbers of her devotees. I would follow her myself.'

'But Professor Gaskin has already been testing her powers and is satisfied that they are genuine,' Dr Hamid objected, 'and he has a world of experience and special apparatus. Could you carry out a test that would be any better than he could perform?'

'Yes, I could,' said Mina, 'because he seeks to measure the phenomena and not to question them. I suppose I could ask if I might move about the room during the proceedings, but I feel quite certain that that would never be allowed. In fact, the arrangement of the room and the conduct of the séance, the holding of hands, the positioning of Professor and Mrs Gaskin — all these things are designed to ensure that no-one can rise from their seat, or even turn and look about them without anyone else knowing about it.'

'Miss Eustace would no doubt protest that such movement would disturb her energy,' said Dr Hamid.

'No doubt,' said Mina, dryly. 'But can you not see that we are tied to our seats as much as she? The conditions she demands are supposedly to ensure that she is best able to produce phenomena, but do they not also aid deception and prevent us from applying unwanted tests?'

He looked down at the papers in his hands.

'The full document is some four hundred pages,' said Mina.

'Which I am sure you have read in its entirety,' he said. 'This will suffice me for the present. Was there anything in the report to suggest how you might proceed?'

'No, only because the authors were too trusting or lacked boldness. I only know that we must expose the fraud in a manner that cannot be denied; act quickly and decisively; give her no warning of what we mean to do.' Mina gave the matter some thought while Dr Hamid looked on silently, his expression suggesting mounting disquiet, if not for the fate of the widows of Brighton then for Mina.

'I think,' she said at last, 'that if there is another apparition we must find some means of seizing it before it disappears. If it is truly the ghost of Archibald Whinstone then it will melt into mist. If it is a mop with a false beard then we will show it to the company for what it is, and Miss Eustace will be quite exploded.'

'But if it *was* a mop with a false beard, which it may have been, it was wielded by no hand that we could see, appeared from nowhere and then vanished again,' Dr Hamid reminded her. 'Can you explain that?'

'I can explain nothing as yet,' said Mina. 'There are too many things that we are not allowed to see or touch. If we were to take matters into our own hands, however, the explanation may become apparent.'

'I think we ought to proceed very carefully,' said Dr Hamid, cautiously. 'I do not wish to insult a lady. Perhaps we might ask her — in the interests of science — if she would submit to a test.'

'Which she would either refuse, or else, since she has warning of our intentions, arrange matters to her own liking,' said Mina, frustrated that he did not share the urgency of her concern. 'We *must* surprise her.'

He shook his head. 'Even if I was willing to consent to such a thing, which, I must make it clear, I am not, since from what you say it seems to involve committing an assault, I think it is impossible to make a plan as we have no means of knowing what we might be presented with. So far each of Miss Eustace's demonstrations has differed from the others. The phenomena we saw on the last occasion were unlike anything I have seen before.'

Mina realised that, while interested in the issue as an intellectual question, he was not as determinedly sceptical as she and quite unwilling to take the bull by the horns. He, of course, as a professional man, had far more to lose by making a public demonstration. 'Do you agree,' she said, 'that the matter is of some importance, and that at the very least we should continue to attend Miss Eustace's séances and keep our eyes and ears open and see what more we can learn?'

To that he was more than happy to agree. Mina realised that she had quite a task in hand if she was to bring Dr Hamid unreservedly on to her side. To expose trickery might need a capability for rapid action, and a measure of size and strength, all of which were beyond her. Dr Hamid had these attributes but he lacked her conviction and recklessness.

It was with this in mind that the very next day Mina went to see Anna Hamid at the baths and asked if she might be shown how to do the strengthening exercises. Anna, detecting a fresh and possibly dangerous determination in her visitor was careful to warn Mina not to try to do too much at once. She demonstrated some simple movements that required no apparatus, the raising and lowering of the arms, or extending and holding them out to the sides. Some further exercises could be carried out while holding a light staff, such as a broom handle. She told Mina that she must not on any account twist her body or make jumps, and if any exercise caused her a moment's discomfort she should stop at once. Only when Mina had mastered these simple callisthenics and could perform them properly and without pain should she take the next step. Mina asked what the next step might be and Anna declined to reveal this in case Mina decided to press ahead with it before she was ready. It was, of course, exactly what Mina had in mind, but she was obliged to accept the inevitable and do as Anna directed her. One day, she promised herself, she would be strong.

Chapter Eight

Mina returned home to find her mother with a sour and angry expression, drinking hot tea and stabbing at a currant cake as if it had mortally offended her. Louisa's ruse to excite the cream of Brighton society with the accomplishments of Mr Bradley had worked rather too well. The clamour for his healing circle had become so great that he had been obliged to inform her that the Scarletti parlour was now quite inadequate to accommodate all the attendees and he had instead hired a nearby meeting room for his next gathering. Louisa, who had hoped that Mr Bradley's popularity would result in further fashionable salons *chez* Scarletti, was understandably annoyed. Mina tried to soothe her mother by suggesting that she could still hold elegant social events at home, a literary or musical circle perhaps. She was a little mollified, and Mina, to her immense relief, soon saw her engaged with new plans that did not involve Mr Bradley.

Mina had learned enough to understand that the next step in her campaign to discover more about Miss Eustace must be to establish a reputation as an unquestioning believer in that lady's mediumistic powers. Her ability not only to be admitted to a séance, but to be placed in a position most advantageous for exposing fraud, depended entirely on her convincing everyone concerned that she was a true adherent, one who could with confidence be positioned in a place of trust where she could be relied upon to protect the medium from prying, suspicious folk. Since so much of what mediums and supposed healers did was to tell people what they wished to hear, Mina found it amusing that she was making Miss Eustace a victim of her own methods.

Even her mother would not be fooled by such a sudden conversion, so Mina began with a careful and humble approach, explaining that ever since attending the séance she had thought long and deeply about what she had seen, had found herself quite unable to explain it away by any natural arguments, and was eager to see more. Louisa looked pleased. She said that Miss Eustace was increasingly in demand, and as well as the séances at the Gaskins' rooms she was also being called upon to give demonstrations in other houses, including some of the most elegant in Brighton. Tickets were hard to come by, but she thought they would always be available to sincere persons. Mina tried her hardest to look sincere, and Louisa melted and said she was sure to be able to get tickets.

Mina was extremely grateful to learn that her mother, who had not forgiven Mr Bradley for deserting her parlour for the bleak space of a meeting hall that could accommodate a hundred invalids, did not think she would be troubling herself to attend any more of the healing circles. In any case, the forthcoming meeting was to take place on the same evening as Miss Eustace's next séance at the Gaskins' and she could hardly attend both.

There was one very important piece of information about Miss Eustace which was, felt Mina, being withheld. Whether this was deliberate or not she could not be sure, so she essayed a gentle probe to test the water.

'I understand that Miss Eustace does not lodge with Professor and Mrs Gaskin?' she asked.

'No,' said her mother, 'and that is to avoid any suggestion that she is able to arrange the room in advance. I think that is very sensible. Sceptical people will seize on the smallest thing and make some great difficulty out of it, so she has quite done away with that.'

Mina thought that since the Gaskins were such devotees there would be no difficulty in Miss Eustace asking them to arrange the séance room exactly as she would wish, but she did not mention this.

'I wonder where she *does* lodge?' she asked, with the air of the idly curious to whom the precise answer was not of any importance. 'These sceptical persons would surely complain if they thought that she was living in grand style somewhere. But she does not strike me as someone who would do so. She seems to be a very quiet and modest lady.'

'No, luxury and outward show are not at all to her taste,' her mother assured her. 'Miss Eustace's needs are very few. I believe she has a small and simple apartment where she can retire alone in order to rest and restore her energy.'

'Her peace and privacy are of the utmost importance,' said Mina. 'She must be quite exhausted after her demonstrations, and I am sure she would not want curious persons intruding on her rest.'

'Coarse newspapermen making a great noise, and sceptical persons with their bad thoughts,' said Louisa, with a shudder. 'She must stay well away from them or it upsets her. Professor Gaskin, who of course knows about such things, says that she reminds him of a delicate balance that needs to be perfectly aligned if it is to be true. That is why he and Mrs Gaskin care for her and ensure she is protected at all times.'

It was a small matter but another little clue, thought Mina. Miss Eustace was keeping her address a secret. There might be any number of perfectly understandable reasons why that was the case, but it was also very possible that the lady had something to hide. Quite what it was she might be hiding Mina did not know, but she was now determined that some at least of the lady's secrets would be revealed at the next séance.

Mina had no plan in mind when she attended her second séance, but she had resolved to watch carefully for any opportunity to learn more about Miss Eustace. All she knew was that great wonders were about to be performed in front of her eyes that would convince even the most sceptical person of the divine truth of spiritualism. Either that or there would be a demonstration of blatant trickery that would only fool the gullible. Mina, as a sceptic pretending to be gullible, felt that she was there in disguise, like a spy sent to a foreign court to learn secrets. She was a deceiver, appearing to be of the shining faithful but harbouring deep in her bosom the dark seeds of doubt. It was quite an adventure. She tried at first to conceal her feelings of excitement beneath a calm exterior, but then saw that this was unnecessary. Her keen anticipation would be interpreted by believers as a quasi-religious ecstasy wholly appropriate to the situation.

Dr Hamid was there, and greeted Mina and her mother with a look of deep concern it was impossible for him to conceal.

'Poor man,' said Mina's mother, when they were out of earshot. 'I do so hope Miss Eustace can bring him comfort.' Mina felt sure, however, that the doctor's glance was not an expression of inner suffering, but an unspoken warning that she should not commit an indiscretion. Mina had never committed an indiscretion, but when she came to think about it she was twenty-five and single and independent and might therefore do as she liked. Perhaps indiscretion was something she lacked in her daily life and she ought to try it at least once. She knew that unless something very remarkable was to occur she could not count on Dr Hamid to assist her. Nevertheless, his presence as a level-headed scientific observer was of considerable value.

The Gaskins' parlour had been rearranged since Mina's earlier visit. No longer were there two rows of chairs, but a large round table had been brought in and dining chairs in sufficient numbers for the company arranged around it. At least the table had not been pushed close to a wall to trap doubters as the Dialectical Society's Dr Edmunds had been trapped at the Davenports' failed séance; there was more than enough room for a person or disembodied spirit lights or flying violins to proceed about its perimeter. The table was bare, and Mina wondered if this was to prevent breakages in case it was to suddenly tip and tilt, which she knew from her reading that they were, in the right company, prone to do.

Besides Mina's mother and her party of ladies, and Dr Hamid, the others in attendance were a young gentleman called Mr Clee, and the two widowed sisters, of whom the younger, Mrs Mowbray, a lady nearing fifty with a very prominent bust, was making her interest in Dr Hamid increasingly obvious, eyeing him as if he was something she might like to purchase and take home. Her face bore unmistakable traces of paint.

Miss Whinstone was making sure, both noisily and repeatedly, that everyone knew she was braving the dangers of heart failure yet again. Mrs Bettinson was almost welded to her side, holding her up with a firm grasp on her arm, as if she had been a life-sized puppet. As Mrs Bettinson moved, so Miss Whinstone moved, and they walked together like a pair of comedy dancers on a stage. Every so often the legs of the puppet seemed to fail and the lady threatened to collapse, or at least claimed that she was about to collapse, and Mrs Bettinson's hand tightened. Mrs Gaskin sailed up with some kind words for Miss Whinstone, assuring her that she was a very important member of the gathering, and expressing the hope that she would not think of going since her presence was an inspiration to the spirits. She must not think, said Mrs Gaskin with a smile like medicinal syrup, that the dear spirits meant any harm; they were a benevolent influence and could do only good. Miss Whinstone, fortified by Mrs Gaskin's praise and a small glass of sherry, decided to remain. Louisa, meanwhile, was watching Mrs Gaskin very closely, and with an unfriendly air. For a moment Mina thought hopefully that she was beginning to have reservations about the séances, and then she realised that her mother, with her nose still very firmly out of joint after losing the opportunity to preside over Mr Bradley's healing salon, was jealous.

The dark curtains that had enclosed one corner of the room had been drawn back and Professor Gaskin was eagerly bustling about and encouraging everyone present to take a look at everything in the recess for reassurance that no trickery of any kind was involved. He spoke mournfully of letters recently published in the *Gazette* written by ignorant, hypercritical and ill-mannered persons. Such people could only serve to upset refined individuals such as Miss Eustace, and he had taken great care that these destructive influences should not be permitted to attend until such time as they became humble enough to receive the truth. Only the other day, he revealed, a man from the *Gazette* had applied for a ticket and had been very firmly refused. The company murmured approbation for this sensible precaution.

Mina joined those who dared to look into the space behind the curtains, but saw and felt nothing out of the ordinary. It might have aroused suspicion of her intentions had she passed her hands over the walls but a pretended loss of balance, which she was sure would have appeared excusable in one such as herself, seemed to force her to put one palm to the wall. She found it solid, with nothing to suggest any recent alterations, and no secret doors or cavities. The little table with the hand bell, tambourine, paper and pencil had been pushed into the corner, and Mina was able unobtrusively to satisfy herself that the paper was a single unfolded, unmarked sheet. The only other item in the space was the chair. The carpeting of the room ran right to the edges of the floor, and looked to be well bedded into place.

Mina rejoined the general throng in the room. 'The cabinet is, as you have seen, no more than it appears to be,' observed Mrs Gaskin with slightly narrowed eyes.

'But it is a place of great wonders,' said Mina, with a bright happy smile. 'I confess to entertaining some hope that if I stand there long enough I might benefit from the power of the spirits which must surely be very concentrated on that spot.' She touched her hand to her shoulder as if it pained her, which that evening, thanks to Anna Hamid's ministrations, it did not. 'Is that too much to expect?' she asked plaintively.

'Not at all,' said Mrs Gaskin, in a more kindly tone. 'Dear young lady, your faith does you credit. The spirits are our friends and watch over us. If you trust in them,' she added with great assurance, 'you *will* be rewarded.'

Young Mr Clee, however, a trim and active gentleman with a sweep of dark Byronic curls, was a bold, even impudent individual, who had no reservations about making a public display of scepticism. Once the recess was empty of other guests, he strode inside, and examined the walls minutely, first passing his hands over their surface, hitting them soundly with his fists, and closely examining any marks that excited his suspicion. He next stamped upon the floor as if testing for trapdoors, peered under the little table, scrutinised everything on it, and lifted the chair to look underneath. He even attempted to lift the edge of the carpet, but it was too securely fastened to suggest that anything might be hidden beneath it. Finding nothing untoward, he folded his arms and shook his head with a very puzzled look that was almost comical. Perhaps it was his bemused expression that led the Gaskins not to regard him as a serious threat to the proceedings, and he was not asked to leave, but the professor and his wife, after a long and earnest conversation of which he was undoubtedly the subject, kept him under careful observation.

Professor Gaskin started urging the visitors to sit around the table, and the troublesome Mr Clee was so shepherded that he found himself situated at the furthest location from the corner that had so captivated his attention. Once everyone was in place the curtains were drawn to conceal the recess.

The maid came to the door and announced Miss Eustace, which created a surge of excitement, as if the medium was about to walk in with stars and moons and rainbows sparkling about her head. That lady, with her customary demure and humble deportment, entered the room without fuss, and a hush fell as she was conducted to a vacant place at the table, the one nearest the recess, where she reposed, with a Gaskin guarding her on either side.

Mina had expected the gas to be turned off as it had been before, but this time the room remained lit. She was not in an unfavourable place, since she could see the curtains to her right. There was no cloth on the table and Mina laid her hands on its surface and found it very smooth and polished. Had she or anyone else wanted to move the table while their hands were in such a position this would have been quite impossible, as they could not have obtained any purchase. It was not a heavy table by any means, and anyone, even Mina, was capable of effecting some movement, but only by grasping it at the edges in a very pronounced and obvious manner. She determined to watch and see if anyone attempted to grasp the table, but this possibility was immediately removed when the company was asked to hold hands. 'We take hands,' said Professor Gaskin, 'to form a complete circle and concentrate our energy. I beg you all not to release your hands until asked. We will now sing *Praise God From Whom All Blessings Flow.*'

Mina realised that she had omitted to see if the table was upon casters. She would have to do so later. Her mother was holding her right hand very tightly with thin strong fingers like a pair of sugar nippers. Dr Hamid sat to her left, and as he took her hand she sensed a considerable strength from him, but without the crushing muscular pressure that so many gentlemen thoughtlessly inflicted. Perhaps, she concluded, his knowledge of bodily massage applied to both frail and robust had given him this rare sensitivity. She looked at Miss Eustace. The medium's eyes were closed, and she had drawn a shawl over her head, and was bending forward as if she wanted to seal herself away from the world and all its corporeal creatures.

Once the badly-sung hymn had reached its merciful end, all fell silent. Ten pairings of clasped hands rested upon the table. Nothing moved. They were all seated very close to the table's edge, and while hands and arms and the tabletop were all clearly visible to everyone, there was, thought Mina, no method of knowing what feet might freely do.

It was no surprise therefore, to Mina when she heard a few light knocking sounds that vibrated through the wood of the table. These were followed, however, by other sounds which she felt sure did not originate from the table and could have been produced by no-one in the room, as they appeared to come from the wall. These noises were very similar in nature to those that had been heard at the previous séance although softer, more like a sharp tapping with knuckles than a stick. The sounds seemed to travel along the far wall then briefly stopped, and after a few moments appeared to be coming from a side wall. Everyone followed the noises with their eyes but there was nothing to be seen.

'Spirit, make yourself known!' said Miss Eustace. It was the first time that Mina had heard the lady speak, if one discounted the sighing and moaning that had accompanied her previous exhibition, and it was a melodious voice, which, while soft, suggested that it could if required, flow thrillingly through a large space.

Three very loud raps came from the centre of the table, which made everyone start. Mr Clee tried to peer underneath but from his position was not able to see to the table's centre, a situation he clearly found frustrating.

'Archibald, is that you?' asked Miss Whinstone, querulously.

There were three stronger raps. It was hard for Mina to tell, but they appeared to be coming from the underside of the table and not its top.

'This has happened before,' said Professor Gaskin, excitedly. 'The spirits always take three raps to mean yes, and one is no. Miss Whinstone, you may question the spirit if you wish.'

Mina wondered what the spirit of Archibald Whinstone might be doing crouching underneath a dining table, something she felt sure he had not been in the habit of doing while alive.

'Archibald — will we meet again in Heaven?' asked Miss Whinstone.

Three raps sounded very emphatically, and the lady could not withhold a sob.

'And when will that come to pass?' she blurted out.

There was a moment of shocked silence as everyone, including possibly the spirit of Archibald Whinstone, took in the enormity of her question. 'Dear lady, the spirits will not answer such a question,' said Professor Gaskin, gently. 'Some things are known only to God.'

The table gave a curious little motion; Mina might almost have said it twitched. It was not attempting to slide or rise, rather it appeared unsettled and Miss Whinstone gave a little scream of fright. 'The spirit is disturbed,' said the professor, but Mr Clee burst out, 'Oh, take no notice! I am sure that Miss Eustace was making the raps with her foot and now she is obviously moving the table with her knee.' Several of the people around the table gasped.

'Sir!' exclaimed Professor Gaskin. 'That is an insult to a very fine and selfless lady!'

'Well, I'll not see any more of this nonsense!' said Mr Clee. 'It is an outrage to the intelligence! If Miss Eustace can make the table rise up in the air without being near it *and* without touching it, why then I might say I'd seen something.'

Miss Eustace raised her head and gazed on Mr Clee with an expression of great calm. Her mouth curved softly into a smile. Even he, with his contemptuous scowl was taken aback, and said no more. She rose slowly to her feet, her face bearing an expression of sublime and intense concentration. She let go of the Gaskins' hands, and stepped back a pace, her chair sliding back from the table's edge, lifting her arms like the wings of a bird. She had the rapt and astonished attention of everyone in the room. With great deliberation, she let her arms sink downwards, until her palms hovered just above the tabletop, and there she stood, eyes closed for a full minute during which no-one, even Mr Clee, dared speak or move. She then took a deep breath, and her hands trembled as they gradually rose until they were more than four inches above the table. As she did so to everyone's amazement, the table rose with her. She was gasping, and there was a flush of moisture on her forehead.

Miss Whinstone moaned, and Mr Clee who was placed directly opposite Miss Eustace, looked on aghast. He had jumped to his feet, and was holding his hands over the table as if trying to feel the power that was making it rise. Everyone had now taken his or her hands from the tabletop. Mina, still in the circle, could see the table rising before her, but with no idea of how it had been achieved. She was small enough to glance underneath but this only confirmed that all four legs of the table had risen from the floor and there was neither a secret mechanism nor a hidden confederate. The table began to vibrate, and then quite abruptly, it fell back to the floor with a loud crash.

Miss Eustace sat down again. Breathlessly, she took a linen kerchief from her sleeve and dabbed her forehead.

'I don't know what to say!' exclaimed the formerly sceptical Mr Clee. 'I confess that I came here with the express design of proving fraud but now I see that I was wrong — very wrong.' He hurried to the medium's side. 'Miss Eustace, please accept my sincerest apologies.'

She bowed her head. 'Of course.'

'I suggest,' said Professor Gaskin, 'that we all rest for a short while. Miss Eustace, will you be able to continue?'

'I will,' she said. 'I feel a strong connection with my guide this evening, but I need to gather my strength again.'

Miss Eustace was brought a glass of water from which she sipped, then she rose and went to the hidden corner, drew the curtains aside and sat upon the chair leaning forward a little, as one who prayed. There she remained motionless.

Mina and the others left the table and gathered into little knots of eager whisperers to talk of what they had seen. She would have liked to make a close examination of the table, but since she was affecting the manner of an uncritical believer, dared not do anything that might suggest prying. She was able, however, to see with a quick glance that the table was not on casters and its legs were very slender. The amount of force required to move it was no longer an especially relevant question, however, since it had clearly risen while Miss Eustace was not in contact with it.

Mr Clee was in any case doing Mina's work for her, since he started busily examining the table, running his hands over its surface, feeling about its edges, and even getting down on his hands and knees and looking underneath. At last he stood and shook his head. 'I am astonished,' he said at last. 'I had thought I might witness a simple sleight of hand, but I cannot explain it at all, apart that is, from the operation of some supernatural agency.' Mina thought that the gentleman was too easily convinced.

Miss Whinstone was swaying in an alarming fashion, but Mrs Bettinson made sure that she tottered into a seat, and having been prepared for such an emergency, produced a fan, which she used with some energy. 'Dear Archibald!' exclaimed Miss Whinstone. 'I do so hope I didn't offend him!'

'Well, he was a mild enough creature when he was alive so I shouldn't think he'd be easily offended now he's dead,' said Mrs Bettinson.

Mrs Gaskin came and took the suffering Miss Whinstone by the hand. 'Please do not distress yourself,' she said. 'I do not think your brother's spirit was offended at all, rather he was showing a commendable sense of delicacy by not replying to a question of a personal nature while in the company of others.'

'Then — will he answer me while I am alone?' exclaimed Miss Whinstone. 'I have so prayed to hear from him!'

Mrs Gaskin patted her hand. 'His spirit will be directed by Miss Eustace. If you so wish, I will recommend that she make an appointment to call on you. You will be assured then of a result.'

Miss Whinstone burst into tears of gratitude, and even had the strength to wave away Mrs Bettinson's intrusive fan. And now, thought Mina, it was certain; Miss Eustace was offering private consultations, much as Mr Home had done, and the unhappy Miss Whinstone was her dupe. It was useless, of course, to say anything to the lady. Mina could only watch and hope that the comfort of conversation with a deceased brother was not bought too dearly.

After a short while, Professor Gaskin suggested that the next exhibition was about to commence. He could not promise what might occur, perhaps nothing, perhaps a great wonder. He asked Mr Clee to assist him in ensuring that Miss Eustace was securely tied to her chair, and the young man agreed with some enthusiasm. As the knots were tied Mr Clee gazed up into the lady's face with an expression of very pronounced admiration, although her features remained serenely unmoved.

Professor Gaskin asked for volunteers to assure themselves that the knots were securely tied and that it was impossible for Miss Eustace to rise from her chair. Dr Hamid came forward for this duty and Mrs Mowbray almost elbowed her sister aside in her eagerness to assist him. This done, the curtains were drawn, concealing Miss Eustace from view, the candle lit, and the gas turned down, and everyone repaired to the now motionless table, and held hands in a circle. Professor Gaskin blew out the candle, and they were all plunged into the dark.

There was another round of hymn singing, and another silence, but barely a minute later the bell and the tambourine sounded from behind the curtains. Mina kept her eyes on the shrouded corner, looking for the emergence of stuffed gloves or bearded mops, but to her surprise there was a faint whisper of sound as the curtains parted, and a figure, enveloped in a pearlescent glow, was revealed.

There was an intake of breath from all around her. The figure was quite still, like a statue, or a life-size doll. Mina, who thought it might be a doll, although she could not explain where it had come from, was expecting that after it had attracted the admiration of the onlookers, the curtains would simply close and hide it from view, but then the apparition raised its arm towards the company, very slowly and gracefully, and extended its fingers. Mina was still not convinced that the thing before her was anything more than a manufactured object that would have been better employed in a booth on the West Pier, but then it began to come forward, and emerged completely from behind the curtains. It was covered from head to foot in a fine filmy drapery, which shone with its own luminescence. Its form was female, that much was apparent, but it was rather taller than Miss Eustace. The features were indistinct, as if seen through a cloud, and the arms and hands were bare although covered from shoulder to fingertips in a soft mist of light. It was not clad as a lady might decently be clad, but it was a thing of nature, having hardly more than a layer or two of glowing veils covering its form. Even the shape of its lower limbs could be seen as if through a fine gauze. If it resembled anything it was like a marble statue of a Greek goddess except that this had every appearance of being alive. It walked forward very slowly. It was not, thought Mina, the usual walk of a living creature, and its feet, assuming it had them, made no sound as they traversed the carpeted floor.

'Do not be afraid!' whispered Professor Gaskin. 'But, above all, I beg you not to touch the apparition unless it touches you. It is Miss Eustace's spirit guide, assembled into a form that we can see using energy drawn from the medium's own body. Any attempt to take hold of it would result in Miss Eustace's death, for it would melt the substance of the form in an instant, and it would not then be able to flow back into her.'

'But where is Miss Eustace!' exclaimed Mr Clee.

'She is still behind the curtain, but she must not be disturbed.'

'I must see!' He leapt to his feet.

'Please, no, that would be very dangerous!' cried Professor Gaskin, but before he could do anything, the apparition approached Mr Clee, and extended a hand in a soft fluid movement, laying a light touch upon his arm.

'Oh!' exclaimed Clee. 'It is a wondrous thing!' To his astonishment, the apparition took him by the hand and began drawing him towards the curtained corner, and he, as if mesmerised, followed.

'She approves,' said Professor Gaskin. 'Do not be afraid, but go with her. You may look behind the curtain but you must be very careful and, above all, do not disturb the body of the medium.'

Mr Clee approached the recess, and cautiously drew back the curtain. The most powerful source of light in the room was the glow of the apparition's garments. It did not re-enter the recess but stood to one side and with a gesture indicated that Mr Clee should go in. Everyone craned forward, and it was just possible to see the form of Miss Eustace, her shawl drawn over her head, slumped in her chair. Mr Clee hesitated, then passed through the curtains which closed behind him. A few moments elapsed, during which Mina wondered if he would ever return, then the curtains parted once again and he emerged and faced the company, his face, bathed in the glow of spirit light, pale with awe.

'It is she,' he said, in a voice that trembled with emotion, 'undoubtedly she, living and breathing, but in a trance.'

Gaskin rose and took the astonished and visibly shaken young man by the elbow and led him back to his chair. 'The apparition before us is Phoebe,' he said, 'the creature of radiant light, whose brilliance casts out doubt and ignorance. All who see her must believe.'

'I believe!' exclaimed Miss Whinstone, and there was a general chorus of assent, in which Mina joined.

Phoebe seemed to enjoy this approbation, for she showed no signs of wanting to depart. She was an accommodating spirit, and tripped lightly about the room turning her head this way and that so that all present were favoured with her filmy gaze.

'Does she speak?' asked Mrs Mowbray.

'Yes, ask her to speak!' exclaimed Mrs Bettinson.

'She might at least nod or shake her head in answer to questions,' said Mina's mother. 'Or why else has she come before us?' she added tetchily.

'Tell us, Phoebe,' said Professor Gaskin, 'does the spirit world you inhabit have houses and churches such as this one?'

Phoebe slowly nodded her head.

'And will all of the faithful have homes there?'

Another nod.

'Are all those who dwell there happy?' asked Mrs Gaskin.

Not unexpectedly there was an emphatic nod.

'And do they love and worship the Lord God?'

The graceful spirit held her arms open to them all and nodded again as if to demonstrate that they were all embraced by the great love of God. She moved about them once again, holding a hand over the head of each person present, as if imparting a blessing, then she turned and walked back towards the curtained recess.

'She tires,' said Professor Gaskin. 'Ask no more of her, I beg you. This is the longest she has ever appeared and we are truly favoured today!'

As Phoebe walked past Mina she felt a sudden impulse. She rose stiffly to her feet and sighed and groaned aloud as if in pain. She was easily able to slip her left hand from Dr Hamid's clasp and such was the surprise of her movement that she was even able to escape her mother's hand.

'Mina? What is it? Sit down at once!' urged Louisa, and Dr Hamid started up to assist, but Mina staggered, throwing out her arms, and her weight, such as it was, fell against the glowing apparition. She had been hoping to do no more than gain some sense of how solid or otherwise the thing might be, but to her amazement, while she was careful not to fall to the ground, the radiant Phoebe, unbalanced and surprised, toppled and fell to the floor with an audible thump.

Mrs Gaskin cried out, Miss Whinstone screamed, and more importantly Phoebe gave a gasp that sounded very like 'Ooof!'.

'Oh, I am so very sorry,' Mina exclaimed, 'how clumsy I am! Please allow me to help.' She reached out to the figure on the carpet and offered to assist Phoebe to her feet, but before she could do so, an enraged Mrs Gaskin had seized hold of her by both arms and pulled her roughly away.

'Do not touch her!' she cried. 'Who knows what damage you have done!'

Phoebe appeared unhurt; indeed in her fall she had acquired a new nimbleness to her movements and jumping up, she hurried into the recess before anyone else dared to try and help.

The table had been abandoned and everyone was now on his or her feet. Someone turned up the gas, revealing a great many shocked, flustered and angry faces. 'Please, everyone remain calm!' said Professor Gaskin.

Dr Hamid came forward. 'With your permission, Professor, I would like to tend to Miss Eustace and ensure that she is well.'

Professor Gaskin threw up his arms in despair. 'I dare not permit it, sir, I dare not!' he exclaimed. 'No-one must disturb her now, not by sight or touch. The form of Phoebe is made from Miss Eustace's own body. While it appears, the lady is in a very fragile and weakened condition, hovering between this world and the next. It takes fully two minutes, sometimes more for the substance of Phoebe to be reabsorbed into Miss Eustace's body. If that process is interrupted then Miss Eustace will surely die.'

'Would it help if we all sang a hymn?' asked Mr Clee. 'Only the Lord can help her now.'

'Yes!' exclaimed the professor, seizing upon a straw of comfort. He addressed the company in a voice breaking with emotion. 'Ladies and gentlemen all, we must sing, sing as loud as we can, as if our lives depended on it, as indeed Miss Eustace's very well might.' He began to bellow out, 'Praise my soul the king of heaven,' and everyone quickly joined him.

Dr Hamid, seeing that he was not wanted to attend to Miss Eustace, extricated Mina from the infuriated and painful grasp of Mrs Gaskin and drew her to a seat.

'Was that well done?' he asked quietly when the singing had stopped and Professor Gaskin had sunk into a chair, panting with effort.

'I believe so,' said Mina, calmly. 'Why, even Mrs Gaskin may in time find it in her heart to forgive a poor cripple. My mother will not forgive me, but then she never does. But I know now that Phoebe is as solid as I am, and speaks and breathes.'

'You have taken a very great risk,' he said.

'The greatest risk was damage to myself,' said Mina.

He looked concerned. 'Are you hurt?'

She smiled. 'Only from contact with Mrs Gaskin. I have had worse pain and greater bruises. I will recover without any attention.'

'And what of Miss Eustace? You are not anxious for her?'

'Oh, I am sure she is unharmed and will very soon emerge triumphant.'

Mrs Mowbray hovered nearby. 'That was a very fine thing to do!' she exclaimed, sarcastically, 'but I suppose, poor thing, you could not help it. Now we must hope that Miss Eustace lives, but I daresay even if she does, you will not be invited here again.'

'I fear that may be correct,' said Dr Hamid. Mrs Mowbray tried very hard to place herself where he had no choice but to admire her, but on discovering that there was no position where that might be possible, she scowled at Mina and drifted away. She was soon in conversation with Mr Clee.

Mina, resting under Dr Hamid's watchful eye, saw her mother bearing down upon her, and was bracing herself for the consequences, when she was alerted by a great gasp from the other members of the company as Miss Eustace reappeared from behind the curtains. The medium seemed exhausted, and held her hand to her forehead, staggering as though she might fall. Dr Hamid rose to go to her, but Professor and Mrs Gaskin hurried to offer their support, and shunning all other help, quickly conducted their stricken protégée from the room.

Mr Clee took it upon himself to fully pull back the curtains and reveal to the company that the recess was exactly as it had been before the séance, except for the fact that someone or something had written 'Praise be to God' on the paper.

'Well,' said Louisa, staring down on Mina with barely concealed fury, 'you have not killed Miss Eustace, that is some comfort. You silly girl! I had intended to invite her to our house to conduct a séance there, but she will not come now! It would not even do to send you away, she will be sure to say you are a bad influence and that the spirits will not come.'

'Miss Eustace is, as we have seen, a good and forgiving person,' said Mr Clee, who had a bright and engaging smile when he was not scowling with suspicion. 'Why, I now see that I was most insulting to her when I came here, and yet when I repented she forgave me and granted me the blessing she gives to her most devoted admirers. Perhaps, Miss Scarletti, your sensation of faintness and your fall was only because you were overcome with the power exerted by Miss Eustace, something for which you can scarcely be blamed.'

Louisa gave him a derisive look, but said no more on the subject.

There was a little more desultory conversation, but Mina did not wish to discuss the event with Dr Hamid while others were present, and Mr Clee had taken some of the wind out of her mother's sails. The maid arrived with tea, but the Gaskins did not reappear and shortly afterwards everyone departed.

As they travelled home in the company of Miss Whinstone and Mrs Bettinson, Mina, with the mark of Mrs Gaskin's fingertips still burning on her arms, was enveloped in the thundercloud of her mother's displeasure. Since Louisa did not address Mina directly but spoke exclusively to her friends about her difficult daughter as if she was not there, Mina felt entitled to assume that she was not expected to join in the conversation. She still felt that she could not believe in the reality of what she had seen. It was not that she did not believe in the existence of the immortal soul, but she could not imagine that the souls of the dead would come to earth and play crude tricks. Perhaps there were genuine mediums who received messages from the dead, but Miss Eustace was not, she thought, of their number. Mina was unable to explain how the table had risen, although she thought it to be a trick within the abilities of a good conjurer. She was in no doubt, however, that the radiant Phoebe, as advised by Professor Gaskin was indeed composed of material from the medium's own body, though not in the manner he had implied.

Once home, she avoided her mother's lecture by pleading that she was in pain and needed rest. She took two oranges and went up to her room. There, clasping an orange in each hand, she did her exercises.

Chapter Nine

Mina did not want to upset her mother, and had deliberately made her attempt to unmask the apparition appear to be an accident, as anything else would have been a far greater embarrassment. Her failure — and she could only see it as such — did, however, give her the opportunity of making one task serve two purposes, both soothing Louisa's displeasure and acquiring more information. She arranged to call upon Professor Gaskin the very next day, and informed her mother of her intention. Louisa was astonished, and protesting that Mina was only attempting to cause more trouble, forbade her to go. Mina explained that her purpose was to offer her very sincere apologies for what had occurred and she was hoping that her contrition would smooth the way to Miss Eustace being admitted to their home. Her mother was temporarily mollified.

Mina was unsure if Mrs Gaskin would intrude upon her interview with the professor and wished that she was strong enough to resist future violent assaults upon her person, but as it so happened, that lady was addressing a meeting of a charitable society and could not be present.

Mina was shown into the parlour of the Gaskins' lodgings, which, while not arranged very differently from the way it had been furnished for the séances, nevertheless appeared to be a quite commonplace room. The table was now in the centre and covered by a cloth, and the dark curtains in the corner had been fully drawn back, to reveal that all that had lain behind them had been removed.

The window curtains were open, and since it was a sunny morning, Mina was able for the first time to see the room bathed in a strong natural light that would surely have revealed any imperfections suggestive of trapdoors and the entrances to secret passages. She saw nothing to excite her suspicions, and as she reflected on this she could feel an idea for a new story rapidly forming in her mind.

Mina was not entirely sure how best to present herself, but hoped that all she really needed to do was say little and allow Professor Gaskin to talk freely. He was, she had observed, a gentleman who took enormous satisfaction in imparting his wisdom to others, sometimes at great length, scarcely pausing to allow them to make their own ideas known, since it was with him a predetermined fact that he knew more on his subject than his listeners. He might have allowed another professor to state his opinions, but not a young woman.

They were seated, but Professor Gaskin chose to perch on his chair like a man just about to rise from it, and Mina took this as an indication that their interview would be a short one.

'Delighted as I am to receive you, Miss Scarletti, I can assure you that an apology is not necessary,' he said when Mina had expressed her remorse for the untoward incident. 'I could see that it was merely an unfortunate accident brought on by a paroxysm of emotion to which ladies are so often prone. Mrs Gaskin, I might say, is of the same opinion.'

'You are too kind, professor,' said Mina, who did not believe for a moment that Mrs Gaskin would be so forgiving. 'Might I ask after the health of Miss Eustace? I would be mortified if I have endangered her delicate constitution.'

'She is entirely recovered,' he reassured her, 'and has taken no ill-effects that would prevent her from undertaking further demonstrations.'

'Oh, that is such a great relief to me!' said Mina with an extravagant display of sincerity. 'I would very much like to call upon her to offer my apologies in person. If you could supply me with her address, I will send her a note.'

He smiled, thinly. 'I will make your sentiments known when next I see her, but Miss Eustace does not receive visitors. Even Mrs Gaskin and I do not call on her. The address of her lodgings is therefore not a matter for public information.'

His tone was kindly but firm, and Mina understood that she would receive no further information on that point. 'Please do reassure Miss Eustace that she has in me a most devoted admirer, and one who hopes to be favoured with personal messages from those loved ones who have departed this earthly life. I trust and hope therefore that I will continue to be permitted to attend Miss Eustace's demonstrations?'

The professor's eyes took on a distant look, and he lowered his head so as not to meet her eager gaze. 'Ah, as to that, if it was simply my own wishes I would have no objection at all, but Miss Eustace feels, and my dear lady wife also feels, that in view of what occurred, which, of course, we all accept was the purest accident, that your presence might induce a certain — anxiety, and thereby create a disturbance in the flow of energy, which might prevent any future manifestations.'

'I understand, of course,' said Mina. 'I would not want to be responsible for obstructing the proceedings which would be a great hindrance to the truth being revealed. I know, however, that my mother would be honoured to receive Miss Eustace at our home, and I do hope that she will not be disappointed. If I ask her to write to you on the subject, would be so kind as to pass her letter to Miss Eustace?

'I will certainly do so,' said the professor, who seemed relieved that she had taken the rebuff with such equanimity. He afforded her a hearty smile, and clasped his hands together. 'Is there anything else I can do for you?' he added in a tone that suggested that if there was not, the interview was at an end.

Mina thought quickly, realising that if she was to acquire any more information she must direct the conversation another way.

'If I might ask you a question?'

He had been about to rise from his seat, but sank back again, resuming his position. 'But of course!'

'I know that you have seen Phoebe, Miss Eustace's wonderful spirit guide, on other occasions, but have you ever touched or been touched by her?'

'Well — I —' He puffed out his cheeks with thought. 'She has on one occasion laid her hand on my sleeve, but that is all.'

'I see. And have any other sitters touched her?'

'Er — no — well, Miss Eustace has always said that if any forms should appear it means grave danger to her if they are grasped and so I have always warned the sitters against it in the strongest possible terms. Phoebe does sometimes offer a light touch as she did to Mr Clee, but no more than that.'

'How interesting,' said Mina. 'So it appears that I am the first person to have anything other than the most superficial contact with her.'

He stared at her. 'Well, yes, so it appears.'

'Perhaps,' Mina ventured, 'my experience could be of some value. I have been told that you are making a scientific study of Miss Eustace and her phenomena. I cannot, of course, offer anything more than my humble observations, and you may do with them as you please.'

'I would be most interested to hear them,' said the professor.

'What I felt,' said Mina, 'very fleetingly, was that there was a form underneath the glowing cloud, a form, if you will pardon me, barely clothed, almost in a state of nature, and most undoubtedly female.'

Professor Gaskin's substantial eyebrows gave a noticeable twitch as if they were about to take flight.

'The delineations of the body were quite unmistakable,' Mina assured him. 'A youthful figure, a miracle of both science and art, which I am sure if we were able to see it without its draperies would dazzle us with its beauty. How Miss Eustace was able to produce such a phenomenon in so short a time is quite mysterious to me.'

'Really?' said Professor Gaskin, who was clearly giving the description some very intense thought.

'Now that I have given the events further consideration I can see that despite my interruption, the evening was a success. I attended quite unsure of what was to be revealed and came away with a most profound sense that something of very great importance had occurred. And, of course, Mr Clee, who came hoping to expose a fraud, now seems to be utterly converted!'

'As is so often the case, in my experience,' said Professor Gaskin. 'Even the most hardened sceptics will have their eyes opened to the truth if they were only to stop criticising what others report and go and see for themselves. I have to confess that when I first went to see Miss Eustace in London I was not prepared to be convinced, but I was obliged to conclude against all my previous prejudices, that the phenomena produced by Miss Eustace are genuine, and worthy of serious academic study. I have tried to impress this upon many of my friends in the scientific world, but I am afraid so far without result.'

Mina was about to make an observation concerning the findings of the Dialectical Society but stopped herself just in time. The more ignorant she appeared the more she would learn. 'And are you the *only* man of science studying these phenomena?' she asked.

'There are others, but for the most part they are going about it in quite the wrong way and will not listen to my protests. All they try to do is look for trickery, and since there is no trickery to discover, their work is wasted.' He shook his head despairingly. 'I was able to satisfy myself from the very beginning that I was observing preternormal events under circumstances that absolutely precluded trickery of any kind. Having disposed of that question, I then addressed myself to the important concerns. What I hope to do is discover and describe new laws of science that will explain what we are undoubtedly experiencing. I have been corresponding with Dr William Crookes, a Fellow of the Royal Society, who is as far as I can see the only man of note who is willing to entertain the idea that the phenomena are real and should be studied. In the last year he has been conducting experiments with a Mr Home, but has not thus far published his results. He has recently given me to understand, however, that Mr Home has provided irrefutable evidence of genuine psychic phenomena under rigorous test conditions.' The professor was not as pleased with this result as he might have been, and Mina concluded that he would have been very much happier if the success had not gone to another man.

'I have heard astounding things of Mr Home,' said Mina.

'Oh, I think that Crookes has been very fortunate to secure him,' said Gaskin with a grimace that left Mina in no doubt that it was Crookes's espousal of Home that had led him to seek out a rival exponent.

'If you publish your findings first, then the acclaim will be all yours,' said Mina. 'Are you close to success? I do hope so. If you write a book I should certainly want to purchase a copy.'

'Oh, I would like to say that I have made significant progress, but that, I am afraid, would be overstating my achievements to date. Still, I am well aware that a debate that has been raging for many years will not be resolved in a matter of weeks or even months. I am, after all, asking men of science to entirely remould their ideas. Not, I fear, an easy task. All I can do at present is accumulate evidence, but I am confident that there will come a time when it is so overwhelming that truth will triumph.' He sighed. 'But I believe Mr Crookes will have priority. I am told that the next edition of the *Quarterly Journal of Science* will include an article describing his experiments, with findings that will astonish the world.'

'He must be most gratified that such a highly reputable publication has consented to publish a piece on spiritualism,' observed Mina.

'Ah, well,' said Professor Gaskin with a hint of awkwardness, 'you see, there was no difficulty about that since he is the editor.'

Mina made no comment but resolved to obtain a copy. 'I hope that Mr Crookes has discovered the answer to such mysteries as how Miss Eustace was able to lift the table without touching it. What is your opinion on that point?'

The professor, more comfortable now he saw that he was in the presence of a true enthusiast, leaned back in his chair, rested his hands in his lap and stared at the ceiling. 'I call it vital energy, something the medium is able to exert at a distance from her body. It is quite invisible to most people, of course, and even she is unable to explain it. I imagine it to be like a thread, very fine and strong, that she can throw from her fingertips and use it to grasp and control objects.' He smiled indulgently and leaned forward with a conspiratorial air. 'Would you believe that sceptics who have not, of course, been present at such demonstrations, and therefore have no entitlement to comment on them at all, have declared that all those who claim to have witnessed these phenomena have been labouring under a delusion or a hallucination? But such things been observed times without number by men and women of the best education and highest reputation. The very idea that persons of breeding and intelligence should be suffering from an overheated imagination is patently absurd.'

'Your theory of a fine thread has a great deal to recommend it,' said Mina. 'Has she always been able to do this? I would be interested in learning her history.'

'I have been told,' said the professor, 'that she comes from a respectable family and first discovered her mediumistic powers when she was just fourteen. The phenomena then took the form merely of raps, which appeared not to come from any human intelligence, but as time passed she found that she was able to receive messages and it later became apparent that these came from persons who were in spirit. She did not undertake demonstrations, and her family it seems were ashamed of her and did not court publicity; on the contrary they kept her abilities hidden in case she should be classed as a lunatic and bring shame upon them.'

Mina listened attentively, but did not interrupt the story. If it was true, and even if the rappings had been no more than the product of youthful imagination and a craving for notoriety, she could understand Miss Eustace's wish to escape the displeasure of her family and become greater than she was.

'One day,' the professor went on, '— this was when she was about twenty — a lady who was a stranger to her came and said that she had received a message from a spirit telling her that she should call upon Miss Eustace who she would discover was a very powerful medium, and that the spirit, which was of her late husband, would only fully manifest itself through her agency. Miss Eustace was astonished by this, but the lady entreated her to make the attempt, which was a great success. Even so, Miss Eustace would not go on. She realised that to travel that path would direct her life in a way that she did not wish it to proceed, a way that would be very hard for her. She was then engaged to be married to a young man of good family and felt that her future lay with him. Unfortunately, before they could marry, he passed from this life, and her grief was so profound that her family thought she would soon join her beloved. It was then that Phoebe first came to her, bringing the shade of her intended, who said that she must in future devote herself to opening the eyes of unbelievers.'

'She has certainly opened my eyes,' said Mina, with her sweetest smile.

She returned home feeling almost sorrowful at how simple it was for a young woman of no more than the usual education to deceive a man celebrated for his intelligence and learning. Mina assured her mother that she had humbled herself before Professor Gaskin and that Miss Eustace might yet grace their home. Leaving her mother to write the desired letter, Mina wrote to Edward, expressing her earnest hopes that Miss Hooper was fully recovered from her cold, and asking him to send her the next edition of the *Quarterly Journal of Science*.

After luncheon she returned to Dr Hamid's baths, where she found the proprietor in his office, a neat room adorned with portraits of his wife and children, and beautifully scented with a display of dried herbs. He was not displeased to see her, and quickly pulled up a chair, providing it with a cushion so that she could face him across the desk in comfort.

'You will be pleased to know,' she told him, 'that I have just called upon Professor Gaskin to apologise for my error. Nevertheless I am to be excluded from future séances, rather like a disreputable gentleman who has been expelled from his club for improper behaviour; but I knew I risked that, and I may in time be readmitted if I play my part as a true believer. Will you continue to go?'

'I will,' said Dr Hamid, opening a bottle of mineral water and pouring a glass for them both. 'Do try this flavour; it is very good. I am not so determined a sceptic as you, although I do have my reservations, but I must admit, I also have hope.'

Mina sipped the water, which was pink and tasted of berries and spice. 'My greatest hope is that Mr Home may find himself where he belongs, in prison, instead of as he is at present, deluding another person. This time, it is not a lady being cheated of her fortune but a noted scientist, a Mr Crookes, who is being fleeced of his reputation. He is a Fellow of the Royal Society and editor of a respected journal, and ought to know better.'

'I have read your booklet about Mr Home and can only agree,' Dr Hamid admitted. 'This is not a fellow in whom we can place any trust. But our concern is

Miss Eustace. Just because we have reason to suspect one medium of fraud, does that mean they are all dishonest? Can you be sure that Miss Eustace is of Mr Home's ilk?'

'After my adventure last night, I am quite certain,' said Mina. 'It is no wonder to me now why the lady insists that no-one must touch her spirit guide. Oh, I know that it is Professor Gaskin who says so, but I am sure that he takes his orders from Miss Eustace, who he thinks will make his name as a great innovator. I can assure you that the lovely Phoebe is no more of the other world than I am. I cannot explain the glowing drapery but I am sure a chemist could do that unless he was, like Professor Gaskin, blindfolded by his own credulity. When I fell against her I knew beyond doubt that what I was encountering was the body of a real, warm, breathing woman.'

'But consider,' said Dr Hamid thoughtfully, 'and I am not necessarily disagreeing with your conclusions, but merely offering this observation — there have been many cases where persons attending a séance have been touched by spirit hands and reported that they felt something like a solid human hand. I have experienced this myself. That seems to be very similar to what you have described. Could not Miss Eustace have used the vital energy produced by her body to create something warm and shaped like a woman?'

'Could not Miss Eustace have dressed up in a lot of white muslin and pretended to be a ghost?' replied Mina.

'She could, of course,' said Dr Hamid, 'but from my recollection I am sure that Phoebe was several inches taller than Miss Eustace.'

'She was, but I think that has a simple explanation,' said Mina. 'Miss Eustace tends to adopt a slightly round-shouldered posture. She presents herself as the very essence of humility. As we both know, any bending of the spine will make a person appear to be shorter than they are. In order to become Phoebe she had only to stand up straight and walk on tiptoe. That was probably why she lost her balance and fell. You don't imagine that *I* can easily knock another person to the ground?'

'No, but then you surprise me every day,' said Dr Hamid, with a smile. 'Though if Miss Eustace did indeed transform herself into Phoebe, she was able to change her clothes in just two minutes. Has the lady been born who can do that?'

'We all can,' said Mina. 'It is a matter of finding the right dressmaker.'

He paused. 'I hope you like the mineral water; it is manufactured expressly for me.'

'It is quite delicious. I will place an order for a dozen bottles if you can deliver them.'

They both sipped their drinks. 'I think,' said Dr Hamid after a great deal of thought, 'and I am reluctant to admit it because to do so would be to relinquish hope — that you may be right about Miss Eustace. Hope blinds people to the truth, makes them see only partial reality or even if they do see it all, they offer explanations that conform to their prejudices and ignore the more probable truth.' He put down his glass, opened a drawer, removed the papers that Mina had lent to him and laid them on the desk before him. 'How can you do it, Miss Scarletti?' he said, shaking his head. 'How can you take away hope? Some of us have nothing else; some of us live for it.'

'I have had false hope offered to me and taken away so many times that I am more content to live without it,' said Mina. 'I prefer the possible and the probable to the mysterious and unlikely.'

'Dr Edmunds of the Dialectical Society whose observations I have read with very great interest, is a sensible and forthright man,' said Dr Hamid, 'but he admits in his statement that he was a sceptic from the outset, so it might take a great deal to move him, and I suspect that he is not a widower.'

'I think that he is not a man who would let his feelings affect his judgement, and neither, I believe are you.'

He looked dejected and gazed at the portrait of his wife.

'I have lost a darling sister, and also a father who I loved dearly,' said Mina. 'I miss them every day, but they live on in my heart. Neither of them has ever rapped on walls or tables or rung bells or shaken a tambourine, and it is ludicrous to imagine that they might start doing so now.'

He nodded, wistfully. 'Jane could not abide loud noise; she loved sweet music and harmony.'

'The only reason mediums employ bells and tambourines is that they can be played in the dark with one hand and are not expected to produce a melody,' said Mina. 'Let one play a tune on the trumpet and I might be persuaded to listen.'

'You have an explanation for everything,' he replied, with a smile.

'Not everything; far from it. And now that I am an outcast I need your help if I am to expose the fraud. I can see all too clearly that if I simply stood up and said that I did not believe, the opprobrium would fall upon me and not Miss Eustace. We need proof. If you are continuing to attend the séances you must observe them for me and carry back a report. There is no-one else to whom I might appeal. All the others who attend are fervent believers in Miss Eustace with not a critical eye amongst them.'

Dr Hamid rested his fingertips on Dr Rand's scathing denunciation of Mr Home. 'There are very many ladies like Jane Lyon residing in Brighton,' he observed. 'Widows or spinsters of means who are as vulnerable as she and have no-one to advise them. Well, I will see what I can do.'

That was, Mina feared, the best agreement she was likely to have. Before she left she purchased a subscription and enjoyed another vapour bath and massage. Anna was pleased with Mina's report on the exercises, satisfied herself that her patient was making progress without over-straining herself, and suggested that if she might like to try it some light work with dumbbells might be the next step. Mina was eager for the next step. She had hope, a real true hope of something that she could reach out and take with her own efforts, hope that she could build the muscles of her back so that they would support her spine and prevent any risk of further collapse, hope that her lungs and heart would never be crushed by her own ribs. It was agreed that Mina would call to see Eliza again, and bring some of her own stories to read. Mina could see that she was Eliza's hope — not of any change in her body since that was past any possibility of improvement, but the new friendship had opened a door to a new place for Eliza's enquiring mind to explore.

Mina went home and pursued her exercises relentlessly. She spent the rest of the day at her desk. She had completed the tale of the cursed emerald, and her next composition was a story about a haunted castle. Its master was a tall, stooping man with elephantine ears who had the command of a whole orchestra of ghosts able to entertain him with the most delightful music. The heroine of the tale, who had been kidnapped for her sweet singing voice, was trying to escape through a maze of tunnels she had discovered by finding a trapdoor hidden under a carpet in a curtained recess. Chased by ghosts she had turned and seized one, only to find that it was made of airy nothing and melted away in her arms.

Chapter Ten

Miss Whinstone, when she called next morning for a conversation over the teacups with Louisa, was labouring under a fresh burden of barely suppressed excitement, and had made a change in her appearance so substantial that it was hard to know if one should be pleased or alarmed for her. Abandoning the dull bronze gown she had favoured since putting off her mourning, she had found something in light green, which matched the colour of her eyes. It was an old gown, something she had worn before her dear brother Archibald had died and was therefore, she was obliged to admit, dreadfully out of fashion, but she thought that with a little good advice she might have it altered and trimmed and no-one would know that it was not just arrived from Paris. It was time, she said, touching her hair, which had had extra attention given to its dressing that day, to do away with drabness and go out and enjoy the summer months. She knew this because she had consulted Miss Eustace at a private séance the night before, and Archibald had come and told her so.

Louisa had grudgingly permitted Mina to sit with them in the parlour, although not without expressing grave concern that her daughter might commit some solecism or random act of mayhem that would hinder or even prevent Miss Whinstone's recall of events. Mina promised to sit very quietly without stirring from her chair, and say nothing at all unless spoken to. She was perfectly content with this arrangement since all she wished to do was listen, and had no desire to interrupt Miss Whinstone's flow of useful information.

Miss Simmons, who with her employer's restoration to vital good health was less of a nursemaid than someone who could be relied upon to fetch and carry, sat in a corner in a dark drab gown, like a piece of old furniture than no-one had troubled to discard because it was occasionally useful. Whatever her opinions were of her position in the household, she kept them to herself.

Miss Eustace, enthused their visitor, was a good-natured and kindly young woman, who existed only to act as a channel through which the living could speak to their departed loved ones. Unable to resist inserting a touch of drama into the proceedings, Miss Whinstone felt obliged to mention that she had been very nervous to start with, and required a glass of water and the application of a smelling bottle before she could even consent to begin, imploring Miss Eustace not to summon any spirits that she would find frightening. Miss Eustace had gently reassured her that all would be as calm as possible, and she had nothing at all to fear, rather she would be uplifted and cheered by any communications she received.

Miss Whinstone's private séance had taken place not in the Gaskins' parlour but in the lady's own home, which, she believed, was why her brother's spirit had come so readily. Archibald had always had her best interests at heart, and his wise counsel was something she had sorely missed, but through the agency of Miss Eustace, however, she had been able to speak to and even touch him, and had received messages of great comfort.

The proceedings had begun with the medium and her client sitting facing each other across a small table, and after a few minutes of prayer and reflection, Miss Eustace had quietly drifted into a state of trance. Mina would have liked to know if the two women had sat in the dark, but since it was not mentioned she assumed that they had. Her reading on spiritualism had led her to the conclusion that sitters at a séance only made a point of mentioning the available light when there was any. It was not long, said Miss Whinstone, before the spirit of her dearest Archibald made itself known by tapping softly on the table. Miss Eustace had whispered to her, asking that she should place her hands underneath the table, and she had felt, very distinctly, her brother's hand touching hers.

'And it was certainly he,' she gasped. 'I know that there are some who might say it was all in my imagination, or that it was really Miss Eustace's hand I could feel — ' Miss Whinstone cast a very accusing look at Mina — 'but Miss Eustace was sitting much too far away to touch me, and in any case it was undoubtedly a man's hand, in a leather glove, very like the ones Archibald used to wear. Miss Eustace has such small, delicate hands and I could not have made that mistake. And there was no-one else in the room.'

'Did your brother speak to you?' asked Louisa.

'No, although I am told that if I am patient that may happen in time. It would so please me to hear his dear voice again! But he was able to send me messages by knocking on the table. I asked him questions and he could answer yes or no by the number of knocks, or if I spoke the letters of the alphabet out loud he could show his agreement to them and so spell out words.'

'How very wonderful!' exclaimed Louisa, almost quivering with impatient curiosity coloured by a bitter hint of jealousy. 'Did he have anything of importance to convey?'

Miss Whinstone glowed at the recollection. 'He told me that he is very happy and has a fine house to live in, and worships God daily, but I must not think of joining him for a long while yet as I have my life to lead here first, and good and charitable works to perform. I have missed him so, and he misses me, but the pain of separation will be eased now that we can converse. And he assured me that he is in good company, for he sees Mr Scarletti and Mr Bettinson and many others and they are very friendly.'

'Extraordinary!' said Louisa, as well she might, thought Mina. Archibald Whinstone had died not long after the Scarlettis had moved to Brighton. Her father had only met him once, declared him to be a peevish fellow, and had not expressed any great desire to see him again. 'Was your brother friends with Mr Bettinson?' queried Louisa.

'Oh, but that is the marvellous thing!' exclaimed Miss Whinstone. 'They could not abide each other while they lived, and just before Mr Bettinson died they were not on speaking terms. Mr Bettinson, who I cannot say I liked a great deal, was a very quarrelsome man who went to law on the smallest excuse. Archibald wrote a letter to the *Gazette* to complain about a speech that some foolish gentleman had made at a meeting and Mr Bettinson had imagined that Archibald was referring to him. No argument could convince him that he was wrong, and he was on the point of suing poor Archibald when he suddenly fell down and died of apoplexy. But Archibald said that now they are both in the spirit they have quite made up their differences and are the greatest of friends.'

'So the spirit world is a place of harmony where all quarrels may be mended and all wrongs righted,' said Louisa.

'Oh yes,' said Miss Whinstone ecstatically, 'and how happy I am to have been granted even this little sight of its wonders.'

Both women turned to look at Mina as if she might be inclined to say something. Mina was inclined to say a great deal, but was determined to keep to her promise. She smiled politely, took more tea, and was silent.

'I am happy to say that I have now quite lost my fear of the spirits,' announced Miss Whinstone. 'Passing into another phase only makes us better than we were.'

'And — please excuse me for asking this — but you are quite, quite certain, beyond any doubt, that it was your brother to whom you spoke?' asked Louisa.

'I could not be more certain!' exclaimed Miss Whinstone. 'He spoke of his will, which he had signed only days before he died, and how glad he was that he had done so, as it had made matters so much easier for me to manage. He was always so thoughtful.'

'I hope he had good advice for your future,' said Louisa.

'Yes ...' said Miss Whinstone, uncertainly. She paused and her eyes narrowed in concern. 'At least, I think so.' She gave a nervous laugh. 'Of course, some of it was not entirely clear to me, it was all a matter of interpreting the little knockings and I fear that there may have been times when I became confused and misunderstood. But Miss Eustace assures me that if we were to try again then I would become more adept at following what is said.'

'What was it you thought he said?' asked Louisa, quickly urging Simmons to bring more refreshments.

'Oh, it was very private, very —' Miss Whinstone shook her head at the proffered plate, and gulped her tea so quickly she almost choked. The brightness of her mood had faded, and her smile became more brittle and then broke. 'Oh, my dear Mrs Scarletti, I really do not know what to do for the best!' Her hands shook and Simmons removed her teacup to the table before there was an accident.

'If you felt able to confide in me,' said Mina's mother, encouragingly, her eyes glistening at the promise of a secret communication, 'I might be able to advise you; and my dear Harriet, if I may call you that, for we have been friends for some little time, I beg you please to address me as Louisa.' She sipped her tea and savoured the sweet taste of a biscuit.

Miss Whinstone looked relieved, and Louisa gave Mina a sharp look and a nod toward the door to convey the suggestion that she ought to leave the room at once. Another glance at Simmons and a peremptory gesture was a command to remove both the tea tray and her daughter. Mina was preparing to depart, when Miss Whinstone abruptly rose to her feet. 'I think — I should go now. Louisa, you are kindness itself, but —'

'Mina and Simmons are both about to leave us, so we will be quite private,' said Louisa quickly.

'Yes, I understand, and perhaps when I am more composed, I will call on you again, and we will speak further. It may just be that I have made a silly mistake — indeed I hope that I have done — and I would regret it if I spoke too soon.'

No persuasion could induce her to remain, and Miss Whinstone made her goodbyes and hurried away before she was tempted to say more.

Mina avoided her mother's accusing look, since she was in no temper to be blamed for Miss Whinstone's decision to go home, taking her confidences with her. She wondered how well Miss Eustace had been rewarded for that private consultation, a question it would have been improper to discuss. It was no mystery to her why Archibald Whinstone had after his death become by coincidence bosom friends with two men who had disliked him in life and whose widows just happened to be members of Miss Eustace's circle. The deceased men bound the living relatives closer together in sympathy, and accounts of the private séances would pass very rapidly around Brighton, and create a stir of interest that no-one with any pretensions to fashion could afford to ignore.

The reference to Archibald Whinstone's will was, however, unexpected. It was not something that Miss Eustace could have known about; a private family transaction that had taken place almost two years ago, and which was hardly newsworthy. It was a small personal detail that had obviously served to convince Miss Whinstone that she was indeed conversing with her brother, and, Mina was forced to admit, would have weighed somewhat with her had she received similar intelligence from her father.

These thoughts were interrupted by the arrival of two letters, the first of which Louisa read with some astonishment and pleasure. Mina was about to retire to her room, but her mother insisted she remain. 'I wrote to Professor Gaskin as you suggested, begging him to intercede with Miss Eustace about the question of holding a séance here, and would you believe this is a letter from the lady herself. She is extremely generous and says that she does not blame you in any way for what happened, but feels that there may be some disturbance in the vital energy — whatever that might mean — when you are present. At any rate she wishes to pay us a visit, and has also asked that Mr Clee might accompany her as he seems able to bring balance to the energy. Both, it seems are very eager to converse with *you*. That is quite extraordinary! But I am relieved to say that she does not preclude the idea that we may hold a séance here.' Louisa gave Mina a stern look. 'The entire plan will almost certainly stand or fall on your behaviour. I will issue an invitation forthwith, but I must warn you, you must do nothing to upset the vital energy.'

Mina gave her mother her solemn pledge as to her good behaviour. Louisa's mood was further improved by the second letter, which was from Mr Bradley. He stated that she and Mina had been sorely missed at his new enlarged healing circle, and begged them to accept the honour of being his special guests on the next occasion. Louisa, without troubling herself to consult Mina as to her wishes, promptly replied in the affirmative on behalf of them both.

On the following Sunday, Reverend Vaughan showed no lessening of his endeavours to keep his flock on the true path. He took as his text 1 Timothy chapter 4: 'In the latter time some shall depart from the faith giving heed to seducing spirits and the doctrine of devils, speaking lies and hypocrisy … ' It had come to his notice, he said, that some of his flock were in danger of departing from their faith and heeding these lying, seducing spirits. Some had even dared to compare the demonstrations of mediums with the miracles of Jesus Christ. Reverend Vaughan was uncompromising. These so-called 'miracles' performed under the concealing cloak of Stygian darkness could only be the work of fraudulent false prophets living off the gullible who followed them like so many credulous sheep. He reminded the congregation that when the Lord Jesus Christ performed his miracles he did not do so in secrecy and darkness, but in the full light of day, so that all men might witness the glory of God's goodness. Neither did He use the curious paraphernalia that, so he had been informed, these mediums employed. Jesus did not retire behind a curtain to change water into wine, and He preferred healing the sick to playing tambourines.

When the service was over, there was a great deal of amused chatter from the faithful, but Louisa remained tight-lipped.

When Mina next visited Eliza she took with her a gift of two of her stories. One was the tale of a young sailor, who, when he discovered that his shipmates were vicious thieves, refused to join in their depredations and was cruelly murdered, his body thrown overboard into a stormy sea. It sank to the ocean floor, many miles deep, where the handsome corpse was found by a beautiful mermaid, who entombed it in coral, and then fell in love with the sailor's ghost. But she could not speak to him and he could not see her, so their love was doomed. She pined away and died, and after her death they were finally united. The second story concerned malevolent spirits that lived in a wooden chair. It was discovered that the chair had been made from the wood of a tree used to hang murderers and had absorbed their wicked influence at the moment of their deaths. The haunting, once its source was recognised, was quickly resolved with the aid of a sharp axe and a good fire.

Eliza was eager to know what Mina was currently writing and so she described the tale of the ghostly orchestra, which was as yet incomplete. 'I am not sure how to end it,' she admitted. 'I would like the heroine to escape the castle unharmed, but I fear readers may be tired of the device where she simply stumbles across another secret trapdoor, or a hidden passage, and I suppose it would be too much of a coincidence to have a prince or a good fairy arrive to rescue her.'

'If I might suggest something?' asked Eliza, timidly.

'Oh, please do!'

'Why not have the lady meet a friendly ghost who will show her the way?'

'That is an excellent idea!' said Mina.

'Like you, I do not believe that the spirits of those who meant us no harm in life can mean anything but good after death. But the owner of the castle in your story — is that not meant to be Professor Gaskin? I have never seen him, of course, but Daniel has amused me greatly with descriptions of him.'

'You are very perceptive to notice that,' said Mina. 'Yes, the character is inspired by the professor. Fortunately he is unlikely to read my stories, and even if he did I suspect that he would not recognise himself.'

Eliza studied the engraving on the front cover of the mermaid story. The creature was more fish than woman, and what woman there was peered decorously from a waving mass of seaweed. 'I wonder if I might write a story?' she said. 'I do so enjoy tales of the sea, and often wonder what it must be like to be able to swim so freely. If one was half woman and half fish it would be easy. Oh, but I should not steal your story from you, I must think of something else! An octopus man who can fly, perhaps!'

They both laughed.

The conversation turned to the correspondence in the *Gazette*, which Eliza had been following with considerable interest. 'Daniel says he does not know quite what to make of Miss Eustace,' said Eliza, 'that is to say, is the lady a fraud or not? Have you spoken to her?'

'No, but I will soon have the opportunity as she will be visiting us this afternoon with her new acolyte, Mr Clee. He, I think, is one of those energetic young men who like to be at the forefront of everything, and can be neutral about nothing. If he cannot oppose something with all his might then he will propose it with equal force. He seems to admire Miss Eustace; perhaps they will make a match.'

'You must come and tell me all about their visit,' said Eliza, eagerly 'and perhaps I might even prevail upon the lady to call on me.'

'That would be amusing, no doubt,' said Mina, in a cautious tone, 'but the lady must, I fear, be viewed in the light of a travelling conjurer, or as a kind of Madame Proserpina who tells fortunes on the West Pier for sixpence. The difference being that Miss Eustace plays tricks on the imagination and is more expensive.'

'I will write to her,' said Eliza. 'Perhaps she will call on me, too. I have never seen a conjurer, and should very much like to. Do you know where she lives?'

'That is all a part of her mystery,' said Mina. 'I am not sure that anyone knows. If one must write to her then all correspondence should be addressed to Professor Gaskin.'

'Then I will write to him — or better still, would you be so kind as to deliver a note to Miss Eustace this afternoon when she calls?'

Mina hesitated, but knew that if she did not do so then Eliza would find another means of sending a letter to Miss Eustace. 'I will,' she said, reluctantly, 'but only if you promise to heed my warnings, and above all, consult your brother and sister on the matter. If the lady demands large sums of money from you then she is a criminal and should be shown the door.'

Before she left, Mina expressed her concerns to Anna. 'Of course we must protect her,' said Anna, 'and I am very grateful that you have spoken to me, although I did suspect that it would come to this. But she is an adult with a mind of her own, and I would not prevent her from finding a diversion. I will permit a visit, but Eliza has no fortune to lose, so you may rest easy on that point.'

Later that day, Mina completed her new story, and the helpful shade that guided the heroine to freedom took the form of a girl of twelve, called Marianne, with long pale hair.

Chapter Eleven

Just as it had been an interesting exercise to see the Gaskins' parlour in sunlight, so Mina was grateful for the long, bright summer afternoon, which enabled her better to gaze on Miss Eustace.

Soft, shadowed gaslight that could be a friend to the vain had previously made the lady appear to be hardly more than twenty-five, but in Brighton's famous white glare Mina saw that she was older, perhaps by as much as ten years. She had a steady gaze, large grey eyes and expressive hands.

Mr Clee, who conducted her in a respectful manner, was not yet thirty, and determined to be cheerful good company whether this was required or not. He had a winning smile and made constant use of it, as if his entire mission in life was to fascinate ladies of all ages. Unlike so many young men whose opinion of themselves far outweighed the opinion of the world, Mr Clee had every chance of success. Louisa returned his smile prettily, and touched a brooch in her hair to ensure that it was still in place, and even the stony Simmons dared to blush, then quickly turned her head aside as if ashamed of her own susceptibility. Mina was immune to the charm of charming gentlemen, not that she had ever known it to be untrammelled by duty and pity.

Mina had the responsibility of delivering Eliza Hamid's letter to Miss Eustace, which, with some trepidation, she did.

'How grateful I am that you have been so kind as to forgive my poor daughter,' said Louisa. 'The mortification I would have suffered had you experienced the smallest discomfort would have been immeasurable. I was, at the time, on the very point of inviting you here to conduct an evening séance, and I was afraid, as to some extent I still am, that it might prove to be impossible.'

'No-one has anything with which to reproach themselves,' said Miss Eustace, kindly, 'and I see no reason why I cannot conduct a séance here.'

'Then I hope we may agree on a suitable day,' said Louisa eagerly, 'and for your greater confidence, I will ensure that Mina is not present.'

'Oh, that will not be necessary,' said Miss Eustace. She turned her dreamy look towards Mina. 'In fact, Miss Scarletti, I would very much like you to be there.'

'Thank you,' said Mina, surprised.

'But does she not upset the vital energy?' said Louisa, frowning.

'Oh, not at all!' exclaimed Mr Clee, with some alacrity. 'In fact, rather the reverse. After the last séance Miss Eustace observed to me that the figure of Phoebe has never been more brilliant or more clearly displayed or lasted so long. I have given this very careful thought and I believe that what we experienced was an etheric power that acts like electricity. Some individuals can exert either positive or negative forces and if they are placed in the right position they may become a human battery. The great majority of persons exert no force at all, and negatives are quite common, but positives like Miss Eustace are most rare. I have found that I am a very strong negative, and there may have been other negatives present at the last séance, but you, Miss Scarletti,' he beamed, 'you are a positive and you completed the arrangement. The forces that you were subjected to were too powerful for one so inexperienced, and it was this that made you stumble. It is our belief that you may, unknown to yourself, be a medium of most extraordinary power!'

There was a long silence. Mina was not sure how to react, in fact she was not sure how she was expected to react. Should she show fear, modesty, pleasure? Certainly amazement was called for. 'You amaze me,' she said at last.

'Is that all you can say?' snapped her mother.

'You take the news most calmly, if I might say so,' said Miss Eustace with a smile. 'When I was first told I was a medium I refused to believe it at all.'

Disbelief, thought Mina. That was the option she had failed to consider.

'Are you quite sure this is correct?' she said. 'There was nothing suggestive of this at the first séance I attended.'

'I believe,' said Mr Clee, 'that your abilities have stayed hidden, but it was your presence at the first séance that brought them out, only to be displayed at the subsequent event.'

'This is very like what Mr Bradley told me,' said Louisa. 'I don't know if you have met the gentleman, but he conducts meetings for the purposes of prayer and healing, and the spirits make themselves known through him.'

'I have heard him mentioned very often, but we have never met,' said Miss Eustace. 'He has been invited to attend a séance, but declined.'

'Perhaps he is one of these positive people,' said Louisa. 'He is of the opinion that were he even to be in the same room as yourself, the powerful forces that he attracts might harm you, and thus with considerable regret he must stay away.'

'He is a gentleman I would very much like to observe,' said Mr Clee, 'and there can be no harm in *my* attending his healing circle.'

'I am sure it would be possible to arrange that,' said Louisa, patting the brooch in her hair yet again. 'I suppose you are acquainted with what the Reverend Vaughan has been insinuating about Mr Bradley, that the spirits he brings to heal us come not from Heaven but quite another place. Not that we believe that for a moment. If his eyes could only be opened, what a wonderful thing that would be!'

'All will come in time,' said Miss Eustace, gently. 'Those who commune with God will one day come to understand that the spirits are sent by Him as ministering angels.'

Simmons had gone to the refreshment table and picked up a plate of small cakes to offer to the company. No-one had especially noticed her, but she suddenly dropped the plate and gave a little scream, then stepped back with both hands clasped to her face.

'What is it, Simmons?' asked Louisa.

Simmons, trembling with fright, extended a finger. 'The table!' she exclaimed. 'It moved!'

Everyone turned and stared at the table, which looked disinclined to repeat the demonstration.

'Nonsense, Simmons, you have got yourself overexcited by all this talk of séances and probably knocked it with your foot,' said Louisa. 'And now you have made such a mess of crumbs!'

'But it moved! I promise you it did!' insisted Simmons.

'If I might comment,' said Mr Clee. 'It is possible, since we know we have two positives and one negative in this room, that Miss Simmons might be another negative and thus complete the circle.'

Louisa was about to ring for Rose, but turned to Mr Clee in astonishment. 'What can you mean?'

'Miss Simmons, if you could return to your place, and sit very quietly I will see if I can detect any disturbance in the ether,' said Miss Eustace.

Simmons crept back to her chair in the corner, but could not avoid glancing at the table as if afraid of it.

'Ah,' said Miss Eustace after a brief interlude, 'yes, I do feel it! Mr Clee, I believe you are correct.'

Louisa seemed very taken aback by this, and not best pleased, since, thought Mina, her mother undoubtedly believed that anything remarkable in the household should repose in herself, not Mina, and most certainly not in her companion.

'With your permission, Mrs Scarletti,' said Miss Eustace, 'we might try to conduct a test. Scientists nowadays are so insistent on tests for everything, and I am sure that I don't mind that at all.'

'Professor Gaskin would be most interested in the result,' said Mr Clee. 'Of course, if you are concerned that you might offend Mrs Gaskin by our making important discoveries here and not within her circle —'

'I am sure that Mrs Gaskin will be happy for the cause of science and is not looking for any credit for herself,' said Louisa quickly. 'What must we do?'

It was soon arranged that for the sake of safety the table should be cleared of any moveables. Louisa rang for Rose who tidied up the spilled cakes and removed the tray. Everyone watched her very carefully as she did so, and there was a tangible sense of relief when she had departed.

'Your maid is neither positive nor negative and she has not therefore created any disturbance in the energy,' said Mr Clee, approvingly. 'I suggest now that the four of us gather around the table.' Louisa stood, but he smiled regretfully and said, 'My apologies, Mrs Scarletti, but in this instance you can only be an observer and not a participant.'

Louisa sat down. 'Very well,' she said, concealing her ill grace as best she could.

Mr Clee jumped up and began arranging chairs so that four persons might sit around the little table, then with a gesture he invited Mina, Miss Eustace and Simmons to be seated.

'Will we need to turn out the lights?' enquired Louisa.

'We will try it in the light first,' said Miss Eustace. 'We should begin by all placing both hands palm down on the table top.'

Mina complied. She was seated opposite Simmons who was staring down at her hands afraid, as if they might jump up and do something she could not control. 'If we close our eyes it will assist concentration,' said Miss Eustace.

Simmons's eyes snapped tightly shut, but Mina simply lowered her eyelids to give the impression that they were closed. The table was so small that she could see from between her lashes not only her own hands but the left hand of Miss Eustace and the right of Mr Clee on either side of her.

'What must we do now?' asked Simmons tremulously.

'We need only wait and pray silently,' said Miss Eustace. 'No-one must move, and our hands must touch the table only very lightly so that we cannot unconsciously influence it by muscular pressure.'

Mina feared that her mother was not much given to silence. When not the centre of attention she tended to fidget until she was, and there was a very real risk that she would pretend some spirit visitation in order to prove her credentials and enter the thus far forbidden circle. Fortunately there was not long to wait. The table, which was not at all heavy, gave a little shudder, and then rocked gently from side to side. There were some soft tapping sounds, like little clicks.

'Are you there?' asked Mr Clee, eagerly. 'If you are, dear friends, give three taps for yes.'

There were three soft clicks.

'Do you recognise a powerful medium in the room? You may give three taps for yes and one for no.'

Three clicks and then a pause and three more.

'Is that to mean that there are two?'

Three clicks.

'Is one of them Miss Scarletti?'

Three clicks.

'Miss Scarletti,' said Mr Clee, 'you may ask the spirit a question if you wish.'

'I hardly know what to ask,' said Mina. 'Does the spirit know everything?'

'It does, but it may choose what is right to impart to the living,' said Miss Eustace.

'I would like to know who the spirit was when alive,' said Mina.

'Then ask.'

Mina paused. 'Are you the spirit of my sister?'

One click.

'Are you the spirit of my father?'

Three clicks.

Despite herself, Mina found that she was trembling. Whether this was from the renewed sharp awareness of her loss, or anger that she was being so manipulated, or even the foolish hope that somehow her father was really in the room with her, she could not say.

'Ask him if he is with God,' said Louisa. Her voice was muffled as if she was holding a handkerchief to her face.

'I need no séance to tell me that,' said Mina. 'But how do I know if this is indeed my father and not some false spirit come to delude me?'

'You are too strong for false spirits to work through you,' said Miss Eustace, 'as am I.'

'I cannot be so sure of that,' said Mina. 'And whatever question I was to ask would tell me nothing, since both a true and a false spirit would know the answer.' But not, she thought, a fraud. 'Father dear,' she said, after a pause, 'can you tell me the last words you spoke to me on the day that you passed into spirit?'

The table was obstinately still. Several minutes elapsed, but there was no more.

'Oh, I am so sorry, but the spirit has gone,' said Miss Eustace. 'Do not be downcast, Miss Scarletti, if you try again I know he will come, and better and stronger than before!'

The séance, thought Mina, angrily, had been a charade from start to finish with the table acting under the slender fingertips of Miss Eustace. No doubt the lady had first undertaken to frighten Simmons by somehow moving it with her foot, easily done under the cover of her heavy skirts, or even a carefully laid black thread. The medium dared not answer Mina's question as she did not know the answer, and had employed the pretence that the spirit had left. Henry Scarletti, had he been present, would undoubtedly have seen the bleak humour of Mina's question, and either chided his daughter or made something up. Only Mina and her mother of all those in the room knew that for the last week of his life Henry Scarletti had been unable to speak. There were no words on his last day alive.

'Oh,' exclaimed Louisa, 'it is just too much to bear! Henry was such a dear man and Mina has frightened him away with her silly questions. Miss Eustace, would you consent to see me privately one evening as you did Miss Whinstone?'

'Of course I will,' said Miss Eustace, reassuringly. 'And very soon.'

Mr Clee put the table and chairs back in their accustomed places, conducted Miss Simmons back to the safety of her corner, and then turned his attention to Mina with all the extravagant passion of the recent convert. His new devotion to the cult of Miss Eustace was, she thought, like that of a man who had once been addicted to drink, and had become overnight a champion of, and learned authority upon, temperance.

'You cannot fail to be curious as to what the spirit world has to offer,' he said. 'So many others with only a small part of your natural ability have been ambitious for advancement, and sought it, yes, and achieved it too. They have striven night and day for knowledge and perfection and purity. They have conquered their basest instincts and become as creatures of the light. You, Miss Scarletti, have hidden faculties that others can only dream of, which have hitherto lain dormant in your soul. Only liberate and develop them, and you will have powers that will grant you unimaginable freedom. You will soar to the dazzling heights, and find true happiness and contentment in the service of the Lord. The path is there before you! Will you follow it?'

In the face of this exhortation, it would have seemed churlish for Mina to make the reply that immediately sprang to her lips which was 'No.'

'I am overwhelmed with wonder,' she said, carefully. 'There is so much for me to learn and understand. Do you really think I am equal to it?'

'I have no doubts! Oh *please* say that you will!' His eyes were very compelling, and the colour of sea mist. She wondered if he was entirely sane.

'I will pray,' she said firmly, 'that is what I will do, I will pray for guidance. I am sure that the good Lord will give me the answers I need. And I will hope also that the spirit of my father will come to me again, perhaps when I am alone with my thoughts, and he will speak to me and tell me what I must do. When he does, I promise that I will listen to him.'

'But will he come again?' said her mother, uncertainly. 'Do we not need all these positives and negatives Mr Clee has told us about?'

'Oh, but I may do it alone, now; the power has awakened in me, Mother, I can feel it!' said Mina, with her sunniest expression.

Louisa looked alarmed. 'Please don't go tipping tables, or you will break everything in the house,' she said. 'And if Henry should come again, ask him what I ought to do about Mrs Parchment, who I think is an ungodly influence.'

'Our tenant, who my mother suspects of atheism or worse,' Mina explained to Miss Eustace with a smile, 'but she is I believe merely a lady who enjoys her own company and walking in all weathers.'

More refreshments were offered, but Miss Eustace and Mr Clee, saying they had other important calls to make in the town, took their leave.

'That was a nonsense question you asked,' said Louisa, before Mina could escape back to her room. 'There could have been no answer as you well know.'

'And there was none,' said Mina.

'I am not a fool,' said her mother, 'although you sometimes appear to think me one. The question was a test, was it not?'

'It was,' Mina admitted, 'but no medium who offers herself as genuine would object to that. Miss Eustace herself said she welcomed tests.'

'I did not mean a test of Miss Eustace who is undoubtedly genuine, but a test of the spirit, to see whether it was Henry's or some imposter. And now I come to think of it, we have our confirmation.'

'We do?' queried Mina.

'Of course we do! Henry was unable to speak. His silence was the reply.'

In the face of her mother's air of triumph there was nothing Mina could say. She was left with the most profound regret that she had chosen to deliver Eliza's letter at the start of the afternoon, for had she left it until later she might very well not have delivered it at all.

Chapter Twelve

Mina hoped that by invoking a powerful devotion to prayer she could stave off any repeated attempts by Miss Eustace to turn her into a medium. If pressed she could always announce that the spirit of her father had appeared to her and warned her not to attempt it, as she was too frail for the work. Whether Miss Eustace would renew her campaign in the light of this unassailable supernatural authority Mina did not know, but she hoped that the lady would be perceptive enough to know when she was beaten.

The visit and its curious developments left Mina wondering why Miss Eustace had attempted to make her into a rival for her business, but she could only conclude that what the medium sought was not a rival but a partner, and had lighted on Mina because she thought that her deformity made her vulnerable. So many things, thought Mina, made people vulnerable to this kind of persuasion — grief, illness, loneliness, vanity, greed, boredom, failing mental faculties or the lure of undeserved fame, and who was there who had not suffered from or been guilty of at least one of these?

In the middle of her new concerns she was grateful for a visit from Richard, to whom she could unburden herself freely. He burst in with his usual energy and was discovered in the hallway, inspecting a large oriental vase of indifferent attractions, usually employed as a receptacle for umbrellas, which had never excited his interest before. Their mother was out visiting, taking Simmons with her under the pretence that her biddable companion was really that more fashionable appendage, a ladies' maid, so Mina and her brother had the parlour to themselves. Mina regaled him at some length with accounts of the séances she had attended, her actions and observations, and the conclusions she had drawn, while Richard lounged at his ease, in a manner he would never have dared adopt in front of his mother, looking very comfortable and more amused than disturbed at recent events. His scheme to find a wealthy wife had not, he admitted, advanced since their last conversation. The ladies he had approached with protestations of love had had the temerity to compare notes, and discovered that he had addressed the identical words to them all. 'I have no more widows in my sights and must turn to spinsters, or all is lost,' he said, 'but there are few of that number who do not have a kind brother or watchful parents.'

'I hope you will not think of wooing Miss Whinstone,' said Mina. 'She has trimmed her old green dress and gilded her hair. Were you the cause of that?'

He shuddered. 'Oh no, I need to have *some* affection for the lady I marry, and Miss Whinstone is quite beyond me, I am afraid, unless she becomes suddenly very much richer than she is, in which case I might be able to feel a little love for her. But what of Miss Eustace? You say she is young and charming, which promises well. Is she also wealthy?'

'I know nothing of her means,' said Mina, 'but I suspect that if she is not already wealthy then she soon will be. I have asked Mother how much she asks for a private séance but she refused to tell me.'

'I see two courses of action,' said Richard, thoughtfully, 'and they are not incompatible, so both may be undertaken at once. The first is that I woo Miss Eustace and make her and her fortune mine, and then she will devote herself entirely to me and abandon her pretence of communing with the spirit world, and the second is that *you* take up the trade of raising ghosts, which will be far less danger to Mother than anything Miss Eustace can do.'

'As to the first I believe you have at least one rival,' said Mina, 'a Mr Clee, who since she converted him to her cause is rarely from her side; and I refuse to do the second.'

Richard took a case of cigars from his pocket but Mina gave him a warning look and he sighed and put it away again. 'Oh, can't you be persuaded, Mina? I'm sure that with practice you could do it very well. It's a good business to get into, it's all the rage and it can only get better. Brighton is a big enough town to stand two mediums, or even more in the high season; why, there are dozens in London. If you start now you would make your name before everyone else sees the opportunity. Then when the notables and the fashionables come in you could name your price.'

'I am glad that I know you are teasing me,' said Mina, maintaining her good humour, 'or I would be very annoyed. It's a dishonest trade and I want no part of it.'

'But everyone knows it's all trickery, don't they?' he said airily. 'A little simple conjuring that wouldn't fool a baby unless it wanted to be.'

'It preys upon the grief-stricken,' she reminded him.

'And it makes them feel happier,' said Richard. 'What can be wrong with that? Would you rather the widows of Brighton turned to drink?'

'That is not the only alternative, and you know it,' said Mina severely. 'Of all the places in the world there are few that can rival Brighton for variety of amusements and worthy causes to pursue.'

He lowered his head, then tilted it and gazed up at her coyly, like a schoolboy who had been caught stealing a bun. 'You will be very angry with me, then.'

'I am always angry with you; only the subject matter changes. What have you done now? I hope you have not come to ask Mother for more money?'

'I only want to borrow twenty pounds' he said, lightly.

'I will *give* you twenty pounds if you tell me why you want it.'

His face brightened.

'*And* if it does not involve gambling, fraud or immorality.'

His face fell.

'Oh, come now, Richard, tell me everything.'

'Must I?' he complained.

'Yes, you must, or I cannot save you if you come to grief.'

'You can't blame me,' he protested, 'it was you who suggested the idea.'

'I did?'

'Well, not exactly suggested, but it was all through you that I thought of it. You showed me the booklet about Mr Home, and I thought, well, here is a fine conjurer and no mistake; now, where can I find one like him and bring him on, so to speak.'

'Are you encouraging someone to emulate Mr Home?' demanded Mina, appalled.

'Oh, not the stealing from old ladies,' said Richard, quickly. 'I draw the line at that, but I have some friends who know all the secrets of sleight of hand, illusion, mechanical and optical contrivances and even the art of chemistry, and can dress them up into a magnificent display.'

'I see,' said Mina, 'so you are hoping to employ some conjurer to pretend to be a medium?'

'That's more or less the idea, although the individual who I hope will become the star of the Brighton firmament is a lady — well, near enough a lady; at least she can act the part, I've seen her do it many a time.'

'An actress?' said Mina, to whom this came as very little surprise.

'Actress, singer, dancer, you name it, she will do it,' said Richard, enthusiastically. 'Game for almost anything.'

'Doubtless,' said Mina. 'But why here in Brighton and not London?'

'Ah, well, you see, Mother asked Edward to keep an eye on me, keep me off the primrose path, so to speak, and unless he invents a better telescope he won't be able to do it without leaving the delightful Miss Hooper which I know he won't do. And Nellie — that's Nellie Gilden, and the most sporting girl you ever saw — is too well known to London audiences. Also — now, this is in the strictest confidence, you understand — for some years she has been the trusted assistant to the famous magician M. Baptiste who claims to have been a student of the renowned M. Houdin, professor of legerdemain and presenter of theatrical *soirées fantastiques*. She knows all her master's secrets, but he, it has to be said, has not yet discovered the secret of being kind to his assistant, so keeping her happy. So Nellie has been looking for another situation, but since M. Baptiste knows every conjurer in the business he would soon find her out if she took up with another man. When she told me her difficulty, I thought of the answer at once: Nellie Gilden of London, artiste and conjurer's assistant, is in the process of transforming herself into Miss Kate Foxton, spirit medium of Brighton.'

He took a card from his pocket and showed it to Mina. 'There! Isn't she the loveliest girl?' It was a photographic portrait of a young woman with a pretty face, a voluptuous figure which the tightness of her costume served only to accentuate, and a great mass of lustrous hair which tumbled past her shoulders to frame a notable décolletage.

'I can certainly see why you find her interesting,' said Mina. 'And this is why you need the money, to set up your — friend with costumes and everything she needs to dupe people.'

'It's only what she did before, on stage,' said Richard, reasonably. 'And it will be the most wonderful entertainment! With all the tricks Nellie knows there won't be a soul who doesn't think they have had value for money.'

'You make it sound almost honest,' said Mina dryly.

'And respectable,' said Richard.

'Oh, I wouldn't go that far. So, what is your plan? I am sure you have one.'

'Of course! I will arrange for lodgings and bring Nellie down here and then advertise her as the wonder of the world. The rest will follow.' He took the portrait, looked at it fondly, tucked it in his pocket, which he patted, and then leaned back again with a smile of supreme confidence.

'And what are you going to tell Mother?' said Mina practically. 'If you are living in Brighton she will want to see you often and know what you are doing.'

'Oh, Mina dear, don't make it hard for me,' he sighed. 'All I want to do is earn my living, as Mother has always told me I must. She should be delighted that I am complying with her wishes at last. I am sure I will think of something to say.'

'Well, assuming that you are successful we will either have to find some kind of plausible fiction that will not leave her mortified beyond endurance, or you will have to move on quickly to some more acceptable occupation. Whatever happens, I do not think it wise that Nellie and Mother should ever meet.'

'Nellie is really the best girl in the world; *you* should meet her, I hope you will.'

'I mean to.' Mina had a new, more worrying thought. 'I don't suppose you intend to marry her?'

He twisted his hands together and gazed at the floor, as his father used to do when admitting to an indiscretion. 'No, that would be difficult.'

'Difficult as well as unwise?' asked Mina.

'Yes, because of M. Baptiste.'

'He is hoping to marry her himself?' she ventured.

'Not — precisely,' said Richard awkwardly.

'He is her husband,' said Mina.

'Well — yes — in a manner of speaking.'

'What manner is that?' she demanded. 'In the manner of holding hands and jumping over a log, or in the manner of going to church and having a wedding service and signing a marriage certificate?'

'Er — the latter,' he admitted, 'although it hardly counts,' he added quickly, 'because he has not loved and honoured her as a husband should. But that is another reason I would rather he didn't discover where Nellie is. He has a very bad temper when crossed, and there is a trick he does with swords. It's really quite alarming, and Nellie says the swords are quite genuine and very sharp indeed.'

Mina shook her head despairingly. 'Well, Richard, because I am so fond of you I shall reluctantly keep your secret, if only to preserve your life. But tell me, since Nellie is such an adept at the magical arts, if she were to attend one of Miss Eustace's séances would she be able to see how her tricks are done?'

'Oh, undoubtedly,' said Richard with a laugh, 'and then do them better herself!'

'Splendid,' said Mina, 'then I am more than ever eager to make her acquaintance.'

'Oh, but you misunderstand my meaning,' said Richard. 'She will, of course, know the secrets and be able to demonstrate them, but unless you are of the magical trade yourself, she will not impart them to another living soul. What if all magicians were to go about revealing each other's secrets? There would be quarrels and murder done, and business would collapse, and all would be chaos.'

'Well, how interesting,' said Mina, surmising that the world of the theatre was a topsy-turvy place with its own laws and morality quite foreign to what was expected in the parlours of Brighton. Despite this setback she thought Nellie Gilden might yet prove useful, if she could win her confidence.

'I don't suppose you could make that twenty-five pounds?' asked Richard.

Mr Bradley had secured a meeting room at a nearby hotel for his next healing circle, accommodation that could comfortably seat a hundred persons, and was being called upon to do so. There was a small charge for admission, a contribution towards the cost of hire, and simple refreshments. Many of those in attendance were known to Mina: Miss Whinstone, whose green gown had been styled and embellished to her satisfaction, and who, mistakenly believing that she now looked fully ten years younger, had taken to preening herself; Mrs Phipps, accompanied by her nephew, whose main purpose was to prevent her falling out of her chair when she enjoyed her accustomed doze; and Mrs Bettinson, who looked discomfited by the fact that her friends had thrown off their melancholy and was looking around the room in the hope of espying a new project to which to devote her energies. Louisa had brought not only Mina but Simmons, who seemed to be there only so that her drabness could provide a sombre backdrop to her mistress's finery, and Mrs Parchment, whose foot still required Mr Bradley's ministrations.

Some of the assembled throng had, Mina was sure, come simply for entertainment and gossip, but others, as evidenced by the line of bath chairs outside whose occupants, disabled either by old age or injury, were being assisted indoors by attendants, felt in need of Mr Bradley's healing hands. A few eyes were cast in Mina's direction, some of those present perhaps hoping that they were about to witness a miracle, in which her back would straighten and she would announce herself cured, others pitying her inevitable disappointment.

They had hardly taken their seats before Louisa was greeted by an enthusiastic Mr Clee, who quickly attached himself to her party, and declared himself to be bereft of all happiness if he was not permitted to make himself useful.

Louisa was content to accommodate his wishes, and enquired after the health of Miss Eustace. The medium, said Mr Clee, was very tired after all her work, but she fully expected to be restored following a short rest. 'Miss Eustace is so often called upon in the afternoons and evenings that she likes to spend her mornings in perfect quiet and solitude,' he explained.

'She does not seem to go about in society a great deal,' Louisa observed.

'No, she prefers small gatherings if any. I do believe that if she was not called to the service of society she would retreat into some cloistered community of religious and charitable ladies.'

'You do not think she intends to marry?' asked Louisa. 'There are rumours in town that she may soon be betrothed.'

He looked amused at the question. 'Oh no, I cannot think she would ever do so. I have heard the gossip, and I know that there are some who say that I am attached to the lady. I do hold her in great esteem, but as one would a great teacher or a mystic.'

'How interesting,' said Louisa, smoothing the lace on her collar. She had recently emerged from the full, deep black mourning appropriate to a widow, and ignoring the slightly less restricted period that would normally have been expected to last until winter, had leaped instead into half-mourning which allowed more elaborate trimming and jewellery and would soon usher her into brighter colours.

For reasons that Mina dreaded to think about, all the ladies present seemed heartened to learn that Mr Clee was not in love with Miss Eustace.

'Miss Scarletti,' he said, 'I trust you have not suffered any ill-effects from your experience of table tipping?'

'I am well, thank you,' said Mina, 'although I am not sure that my being present was in any way responsible for what occurred.'

'Miss Eustace feels very strongly that it was,' replied Mr Clee. 'But if you are uncertain, then perhaps we might make another attempt? I would be delighted to assist. You have only to ask, and it will be arranged!'

'Thank you,' said Mina, preferring not to elaborate on her true preferences while her mother was present. 'I am still hoping to hear more from my father on the subject.'

'Or if Mrs Parchment might like to try?' he said, turning his irrepressible smile to that lady.

'For what purpose?' said Mrs Parchment, with a determinedly unfriendly expression. 'I believe I exhausted all possible subjects of conversation with my husband when he was living, and have nothing further I wish to say to him now.'

'I understand that your husband was a great benefactor to society,' said Mr Clee. 'Was he not the inventor of Parchment's Pills?'

'Oh, yes, that and many other things. He could cure anything and anyone — except for himself.'

The conversation ended when Mr Bradley appeared before the company, and welcomed everyone to the gathering. He was, he said, honoured to see before him the very cream of Brighton society, the most revered and respectable of its inhabitants, who would, he knew, oppose the wholly unfounded suggestions that his humble efforts were in any way irreligious. He made special mention of his honoured guests, and Louisa looked thoroughly displeased to discover that what she had imagined to be her exclusive status was shared with a great many others.

The meeting started with prayers, in which the Reverend Vaughan of Christ Church was especially mentioned, hopes being expressed that the respected gentleman would soon come to appreciate the godliness of Mr Bradley's mission.

He then proceeded to the formal healing. Since the faithful were too numerous to be in a circle, but were seated in rows, Mr Bradley, in order to spread his restorative influence, was obliged to walk back and forth along each row in turn, one arm flung out to hover over the head of each person in the room. 'For the power of the Lord is infinite,' he intoned as he proceeded, 'and I am but his humble vessel. Through me he shows his healing power, and such is his goodness that it will soothe and calm the affliction not only of all those present but their loved ones, too; parents and children, husbands and wives, brothers and sisters, even to the husbands, wives and children of their brothers and sisters, all, all will be healed by the grace of the Almighty.'

There was the sound of sighing and even weeping in the room, and it came from all around, as some of the sitters thought about those in their families who were ill and without hope of recovery.

Quite suddenly, and without any warning, Miss Whinstone leaned forward with a cry, and began to gulp and sob convulsively. Everyone around her tried to comfort her, but her body heaved and shuddered uncontrollably as deep groans of misery were torn from her. Someone went to get a glass of water, and someone else suggested she be laid on the floor, and any number of people wanted to call for a

111

doctor, but Mr Bradley stopped and turned to her, laying a hand upon her head. 'Oh, my sister in God,' he said, 'be at peace. Only do as the Lord commands you and your conscience guides you and all will be well.' Gradually, the sobbing slowed, and her gasping breaths calmed to the point where she could speak.

'Thank you,' she said, gratefully, wiping her eyes with a handkerchief. 'I must do all that a Christian woman should.'

He smiled at her and passed on.

Miss Whinstone reassured her friends that she was recovered, but despite Louisa's most forceful efforts she would tell no-one of the reason for her distress, and it was thought best to take her home.

When Mina next went to Dr Hamid's baths she found Anna anxious to speak with her, and they retired to the privacy of the office. 'I was intending to call, but I am very glad you have come,' she said. 'I am concerned about Eliza.'

Mina was seized with a sudden dread. She and Eliza had formed a bond not only of sympathy but of similar tastes in their two meetings, and she feared that the new friendship was about to be snatched away. 'Oh, I do hope she is not unwell! May I call on her?'

'She is well enough, have no fear on that point, and we hope that she may live contentedly for many years yet, and enjoy your company, but it is another matter I need to discuss. The last time we met we spoke of Eliza's wish to meet Miss Eustace. Daniel and I considered the request and decided that it was unlikely to be of any harm. She has very few visitors, and we thought that a new face would do her good.'

'Did Miss Eustace call on her?' asked Mina, apprehensively.

'Yes, and a Mr Clee. They stayed for some considerable time.'

'Oh, I think I know what you are about to tell me,' said Mina, unhappily. 'And I blame myself, now. I should have seen the danger. I suppose Miss Eustace has tried to persuade your sister that she is a powerful spirit medium?'

'You are right, she has!' exclaimed Anna. 'How did you guess? Has she tried to persuade you, also?'

'Yes, she has, and I am sorry to say it occurred after I delivered your sister's note, and I would have done anything then to have taken it back.'

'I assume that she did not succeed with you,' said Anna.

'No — she cannot — will not!' Mina assured her with some energy.

'I wish Eliza was of the same mind as you,' said Anna, 'but I fear that Miss Eustace has prevailed. Please do not blame yourself, Eliza is our responsibility, and the decision to allow the visit was ours.'

They were both silent and thoughtful for a few moments. 'Would you like me to go and see your sister and tell her that Miss Eustace tries these tricks on everyone?' suggested Mina, although she was not hopeful that this would be of any use.

Anna sighed. 'I hardly know what to do. You see, Eliza is happy, happier than I have seen her in many years. She feels newly favoured, instead of at a disadvantage. Ought I to take that away from her? Even if it is an illusion it seems harmless enough.'

'I entirely understand,' said Mina, 'and it is the seeming harmless that is, I believe, the real danger, the thin end of what may be a long and subtle wedge with a bad conclusion. Does your sister propose to go to séances now? Or have them come to her?'

'No, and this is what I meant to discuss. Eliza wants to conduct a séance herself at our house tomorrow evening. There would be only Daniel and myself, but could I ask you to be there also? And if you have a kind friend with a critical eye then by all means bring that friend with you.'

'Of course I will come,' said Mina, 'and if my brother Richard is not otherwise engaged I will ask him to accompany me. Is Miss Eustace to be there as well?'

'No, Eliza asked her to attend, but she has another appointment.'

'That is something,' said Mina with considerable relief. 'If we are fortunate then we will all sit in the dark and nothing will happen and she will give up the idea.'

'Thank you for that comfort,' said Anna.

Once Mina's bath and massage were done she went to see Dr Hamid, who had concluded his treatment of a patient and returned to his office. He glanced up at her with some concern as she entered.

'Please, I know what you are going to say, but Eliza knows her own mind,' he said defensively. 'I can't treat her like a child. The best thing I can do to protect her is let her have her enjoyment but be on hand to keep a watch against any dangers.'

'Of course you can't forbid her to hold a séance,' said Mina. 'At least, you could, but I have given this some thought, and I can see that it would be unwise. If she is determined enough she will do it whatever you say, so it would be best if she did it while you were there. Miss Hamid has asked me to come to your house tomorrow, and my brother Richard, too, who is the most pronounced sceptic, and we will all keep our eyes open.'

'At least Eliza is no Jane Lyon,' said Dr Hamid. 'The man who tries to steal her fortune will have little to tempt him. My father always feared that she could be the target of an adventurer, and ensured in his will that her capital cannot be touched and she has only the income for her lifetime.'

'I am relieved to hear it,' said Mina. She sat down, and they faced each other across the desk, both feeling worried and helpless. 'Something is happening, but I am not sure what,' she said. 'Miss Eustace has tried to make me into a medium and failed. Now she is playing her tricks on your sister. My mother is about to throw off her mourning six months too soon, Miss Whinstone is beside herself but won't say why, and Mr Clee went from sceptic to believer in five minutes. It is as if a disease is rampaging through the town.'

'Sometimes all we can do in these instances is mop the patient's brow and allow the fever to burn itself out,' said Dr Hamid.

'Are we immune to this plague?' asked Mina.

He smiled. 'I think so. I know you are, and Anna is too.'

'But you, I think, like to hope just a little.'

'Just a little,' he admitted. 'And you do not?'

'Oh, I don't deny the existence of the soul,' said Mina. 'We all have to hope for something, but when I die I will not choose to converse with my family through a mountebank.'

He said nothing but his gaze drifted as it so often did, to the portrait of his wife.

'My brother,' said Mina, 'who has a closer acquaintance with the theatrical profession than he would like my mother to know about, tells me it is all done by conjuring, but unfortunately he refuses to give up his sacred secrets.' She shook her head. 'If I was brave enough I would enter Miss Eustace's fold and dare her to do her worst, and then I would find out all about her, but if I did that and then turned around and tried to expose her for what she is, I would only look like a jealous rival, and then she would be more famous than ever.'

'I only want to do what is best for Eliza, but I hardly know what that is,' said Dr Hamid.

'If we all take care of her tomorrow night,' said Mina hopefully, 'she will have a little pleasure followed by a disappointment, but that will soon pass, and she will then be more used to company and so we might find her willing to try another form of entertainment. A ride in the fresh air; views of the sea; a tour of the flower gardens. There is a grand new aquarium being built. I mean to go to it as soon as it opens, and I will ask her to accompany me. She will need a bath chair of course, but she would not be the only person in Brighton to do so; they are a very common sight on the esplanade, so she would not attract the curious.'

'You are a kind friend,' he said, with a sad smile.

'Only promise me that you will not falter in our bid to expose Miss Eustace. There are some who think it is foolish old ladies who are the most easily persuaded, but in reality it is men of education who understand the world and want to understand it better who are the greatest fools.'

He was thoughtful for a moment, then he nodded. 'I promise,' he said.

Chapter Thirteen

When Mina next saw her new friend she felt ashamed of herself for even having thought of trying to persuade her that she was being duped. Eliza's shining eyes, her animated nature and sense of anticipation were all too obvious, and if they were doomed to be dulled by failure then Mina promised herself that she would help to avert the worst of the blow and quickly suggest some alternative interest that would be a better direction for this new and otherwise laudable energy.

The tiny woman had been brought downstairs, and was perched on a padded chair in the parlour, enveloped with pretty shawls, in such a way that it was not obvious that her twisted body was being carefully supported so that she could sit upright. There she held court, and graciously and intelligently conversed with all the company. Richard was his usual handsome, charming self, the Hamids were perfect hosts, and the evening would, thought Mina, have been wholly delightful had there been no thought of holding a séance.

'But Mr Scarletti,' said Eliza, to Richard, 'I have not told you or dear Mina — I know we have not known each other long, but I do hope I may address you so — of what transpired when Miss Eustace and Mr Clee called on me.'

'I am all ears,' said Richard, affably. 'I have not, so far, met these fascinating people, but hope to do so very soon.'

'Oh, they have the nicest manners, and are very kind,' said Eliza. 'Of course, we talked at great length about how Miss Eustace was achieving remarkable things with the spirit world and she said that you, Mina, are the most wonderful medium yourself, but you do not know it yet.'

'I am certainly not aware of having any abilities in that direction,' said Mina. 'However, I promise faithfully to use no mediumistic powers at all tonight. The only influence exerted will be yours. That you can depend upon.'

'We dared to hold a little séance ourselves, just the three of us,' said Eliza, 'but at first nothing at all happened. Miss Eustace told me that she was very weary that evening and when she tires all her powers desert her for a day or two and will not come back until she has rested. Then they saw that I was disappointed so they agreed to try once more, and this time there were the most extraordinary raps and knocks, and all coming from a spirit called Joey, who I think is a child and quite a mischievous little fellow. I thought, of course, that he had come through Miss Eustace, but he said he had not, because she had no energy he might use, and it was all my doing!' She beamed with pleasure and excitement, and her breath laboured under the emotion.

Anna and her brother, who had undoubtedly heard this account before, looked at each other sorrowfully, but said nothing.

'And did Joey have any messages?' asked Richard.

'Only that he liked very much to play on the tambourine, and he asked if I could procure one for him so that he could play it for me, and if I did then he promised that he would give me some flowers. Is that not extraordinary?'

'If he is a little scamp you must take care he does not steal them from an honest tradesman,' said Richard, 'or pick them from a public garden.'

'Oh, I hadn't thought of that!' exclaimed Eliza. 'Well, perhaps since he is a spirit he can just conjure them up out of nothing; Miss Eustace says that spirits can bring wonderful gifts sometimes. She had a basket of strawberries only the other day.'

'I do not think,' said Dr Hamid, gently, 'that even a spirit may make something like a flower or a strawberry where there was nothing at all before. Think of how long it takes for them to grow in nature.'

'Well, we must try it and see,' said Eliza, with a touch of defiance in her voice. 'Science does not know everything, and if Joey *does* bring me flowers tonight you may have hard work to explain it.'

'You must not be disappointed if he doesn't come,' said Mina.

'Oh no, I won't be,' said Eliza, brightly, 'I don't suppose the spirits come every time, and if he does not then we will try again another day. But let us begin. Anna, please be so kind as to arrange the table for me.'

The table was brought to the centre of the room, and positioned so that Eliza could rest her hands on its surface; chairs were put in place around it, and a tambourine was set in its centre. 'Now where are we to sit?' asked Anna. 'You direct us, Eliza, and we will do whatever you wish.'

'Oh, I suppose we just sit and hold hands,' said Eliza. 'Is there a special way we should be ordered?' She looked enquiringly at Mina.

'I am not aware of any,' said Mina.

'I believe,' said Dr Hamid, 'that Miss Eustace likes to alternate ladies and gentlemen, but due to the preponderance of ladies it has never yet proved possible.'

'Then there are those positive and negative influences that Mr Clee is so clever about,' said Eliza. 'And they must be alternated too.' She looked thoughtful. 'Mina, you and I are both positive, so we must be facing, and not joined. Daniel?'

'Oh, I think we can assume that I have no ability in either direction,' said Dr Hamid.

'And, of course, we can know nothing of Anna or Mr Scarletti,' said Eliza. 'What a quandary! If Mr Clee was here he would know at once. I did ask if he could attend, but I fear he cannot come.' She shook her head regretfully, an emotion which was not shared by her companions.

No-one moved and all attention was fixed on Eliza as she considered the difficulty. 'Very well,' she said at last, 'I will have Daniel and Mr Scarletti on either side of me, and then Mina you may take your brother's hand to your left and Anna's to the right.' Everyone immediately complied with her wishes. 'That is perfect!' she said happily, when everyone was seated. 'I am sure that this is the best arrangement; in fact I can feel the power in me already. Daniel, if you would be so kind as to turn the light out, and resume your place.'

'You wish there to be no light at all?' he asked.

'I do; it is best,' she said authoritatively. 'Light can absorb all the power of the medium and then nothing is possible.'

Mina recalled that the dreadful Mr Home was one of the few mediums said to scorn darkness, which served to explain the devotion of his adherents. Nevertheless, she felt sure that there were some tricks equally well performed in the light. A conjurer who demonstrated his tricks on the variety stage but would only work in the dark would not, she thought, enjoy a long and successful career.

Dr Hamid obediently extinguished the gas and made his way carefully back to his seat. The curtains had been closely drawn and not a single thread of light intruded into the room. Everyone clasped hands. 'And now,' said Eliza, the tension evident in her voice, 'I entreat you all to complete silence. Sometimes when the spirits come they are very quiet.'

Silence fell, or what counted for silence in a room occupied by breathing people, and they all sat very still. There would be no trickery this time. Mina had made Richard promise on pain of her great displeasure and a cessation of money supplies that he would only observe and not influence events, and she knew that Dr Hamid and Anna would not want to encourage Eliza into believing she was a medium any more than she did herself. Eliza's belief seemed genuine, in that she truly thought that spirits would come through her supposed supernatural powers, and it seemed unlikely that she would play tricks to convince her companions.

There was a very faint squeaking noise.

Eliza gave a little gasp. 'Joey? Is that you?'

'I am truly sorry,' said Richard, 'I moved and my chair creaked.'

'Was it not the spirit that made you do it?' she asked, hopefully.

'I regret, no.'

The breathing stillness fell again, a calm in which Mina almost thought she could drift into a dream. There in her curious inner life were the stories she found — she never really felt that she constructed them, but that they existed already like gems to be mined, and she lifted out them whole and brought them into the light and polished them. Time passed, five, ten, fifteen minutes or more, she could not tell, maybe as much as half an hour, and she discovered a new story of a gathering such as this, in which everyone waited in the dark silence and nothing came, until, with the company on the point of giving up, there came a ghostly tapping at the door.

She was so lost in her tale, that she did not realise at first that the tapping was real.

'Who can that be I wonder?' said Anna.

'Well, we will find out soon enough, and it seems the spirits will do nothing tonight, Eliza,' said Dr Hamid. 'So let us end the attempt there.'

He turned up the light, and the maid announced that the visitor was Mr Clee.

'Oh!' exclaimed Eliza, clapping her hands, 'that is wonderful! Please show him in, I had thought he was engaged elsewhere. Perhaps we will have some success, now.'

Mr Clee appeared, and was very apologetic. 'Please excuse my lateness,' he said. 'Miss Eustace had asked me to usher the visitors at her séance tonight, and I thought I would not be able to come here, but she has a slight headache and will not be appearing after all; so here I am. I hope I have not inconvenienced you.'

'Not at all!' exclaimed Eliza. 'You are just the man I was most hoping to see.' He beamed delightedly and sat beside her. 'We have been sitting here in the dark holding hands for ever so long, and I am afraid Joey could not come, and we are all very disappointed,' she confessed.

'How were the sitters arranged?' he asked. Eliza described the order of seating and he nodded. 'There was not a great deal wrong in that, but you see the numbers were odd and for the better flow of energy they should be even.'

She gave a little gasp. 'Oh! I was not aware of that — but, of course, now you are here the numbers *are* even and we may try again!'

'I hope you won't tire yourself, Eliza,' said Dr Hamid, anxiously.

'When I am tired, I will be sure to let you know,' said Eliza with a hint of reproach. 'Oh, Daniel, can we not try just one more time?'

He relented. 'Very well, but a few minutes only, and then I must insist you rest.'

'Oh, we will see if I need rest or not!' she exclaimed, laughing. 'Mr Clee, please advise us on where we are to sit.'

'But of course!' said Mr Clee. 'I recommend that I, as a negative, sit between the two positives.' He took Eliza's right hand and indicated that Mina sit on his other side. 'And everyone else must simply alternate male and female.' Mina took Richard's hand and then Anna and Dr Hamid completed the circle. 'That is an excellent arrangement, I doubt that it could be bettered.'

The lights were lowered again. The air was close and still like ink. Mina could hear Eliza's breath as her constricted lungs struggled under the excitement. Richard to her right was unmoving, but a tremor began in Mr Clee's grasp to her left. It was hard to tell, but it felt as though his entire body had started to shake.

'Do you feel that, Miss Hamid, like a spark or a flame of electricity? It is most pronounced!' said Clee.

118

'Yes! I do!' Eliza exclaimed. 'Do you feel it Mina?'

'I feel — something,' said Mina, cautiously, 'but I am not sure what it is.'

'Are we all holding hands?' asked Mr Clee. 'No-one must let go!'

Everyone assured him that they were holding tight.

Several moments passed during which the quivering and shaking of Mr Clee's body intensified. 'It is the power!' he exclaimed 'I have none myself, but it moves through me!'

'It grows stronger,' said Eliza. 'I can hardly hold on to your hand!'

'You must not let go!' he cried, and Mina for her part was determined not to release her grip on Mr Clee.

The shaking continued for a full minute, then there were three loud knocks on the centre of the table.

'Oh — it is Joey!' said Eliza, joyously. 'He is here! He is here!' There were three more knocks. 'Can you play the tambourine, Joey? I bought one especially for you.'

High above their heads there appeared a glowing light, not the solid brightness of the little dancing fairy points that had appeared at Miss Eustace's séance, but something softer, a little cloud, that hovered over the table, and turned and twisted and revolved, and as it did so, grew slowly larger.

'Oh Joey, my dear, is that you?' gasped Eliza. 'Will you show me your face? I should so like to see your face!'

The cloud changed, as clouds do, and gradually attained a shape that could almost be called a face. There were no eyes or even a mouth, but something like a nose was at its centre and there was a straggly fluff around it that could have been hair. It hovered in front of Eliza, and seemed to nod, as if bowing to acknowledge her, then it swirled about, circling the table.

'Oh Joey, can you speak? Please speak to me!' asked Eliza.

The face danced in an odd jerky pattern, still hovering high above the table, and there were two loud raps.

'Two?' said Eliza, mystified, 'Oh — that was not a yes or a no — perhaps it means that he cannot.'

There were three raps.

'Joey, can you play the tambourine? Oh, please do!'

The face bowed again and there was the sound of the tambourine being lifted off the table, and a soft rustling like the wind stirring through metal leaves.

Eliza laughed with joy to hear it. 'Oh Joey, I wish I could reach out and touch your dear face — will you let me?'

There was a louder rattle on the tambourine. 'Do not think of it,' said Mr Clee, nervously, through clenched teeth. 'Keep tight hold of my hand, or all will disappear! Remember it is your own energy that creates the substance of this apparition and plays the instrument. It must not be disturbed!'

In a few more moments the tambourine started a good clattering rhythm, which it seemed to be doing while hanging in mid-air quite unaided by the cloudy shape, which shook itself, and sailed about over the heads of the sitters like a veil caught in a breeze, and there was an eerie sound like the wailing of a whistle.

Eliza gasped and cried aloud, and even with all the noises that surrounded them Mina could detect a new and disturbing rhythm to her friend's breathing, as if she was finding it hard and painful to inhale. 'Dr Hamid,' said Mina, 'I am concerned for Eliza.'

'As am I,' he said. The scraping of his chair showed that he had jumped to his feet. 'Enough! This is enough! She cannot endure any more! I will not allow it!' His footsteps sounded across the room. There was a loud crash as the tambourine fell to the tabletop, a final strangled scream from the whistle, and the glowing cloud vanished in a trice. As the gas illuminated the scene, Mina saw that no-one had moved from the table apart from Dr Hamid, and all other hands were still securely clasped. The tambourine lay on the table, and beside it was a small scattering of fresh flowers. Eliza was pale and struggling for breath. Her sister and brother ran to her at once. Water was fetched, her brow was bathed, and her bent back gently but firmly stroked.

Mr Clee had the good grace to look worried. 'I do hope the lady has taken no harm,' he said. 'The materialisation though a small one was constructed from her own vital energy and it needed at least a full minute to recombine with the substance of her body. The interruption gave it only a few moments. It will have shocked her, like being struck a blow.' He shook his head.

'She was already in danger,' said Dr Hamid, sternly, 'and I would suggest that this is never attempted again.'

'Oh, but it was so beautiful,' exclaimed Eliza breathlessly. 'Please, don't blame Mr Clee! And look — Joey brought me the flowers he promised!'

'I blame myself for permitting this,' said Dr Hamid. 'Come now, Eliza, I will take you to your room.' She was too weak to protest. He lifted her effortlessly, and it looked as though it was a child and not an older sister that he held in his arms, then he strode from the parlour.

'There was really no danger,' Mr Clee protested, 'if only —'

'I tell you what,' said Richard, standing up, suddenly, and leaning menacingly over the seated man, 'if you were to leave this house immediately there would be no danger of my striking you.'

Mr Clee took the hint and departed very quickly.

Anna sank into a chair, and Richard, seeing a carafe on the side table, poured a glass of water, which she took, gratefully. 'There was trickery here, tonight, as I am sure you suspect, and Mr Clee was the trickster,' said Richard. 'Miss Eustace has made him her creature, and he is a vile being to prey on your sister in this way.'

'But how was it done?' said Mina. 'I assume he brought the flowers in his pocket, and he could have thrown them on the table at the end, but I had hold of his right hand throughout the sitting, I did not let go for even a moment, all the time the light appeared and the tambourine played, and Eliza had his left, indeed he exhorted her to keep constant hold.'

'Oh, these people have their methods,' said Richard. 'It is surprising what can be achieved with a little practice.' He picked up the tambourine and examined it.

'Well, at least Eliza will be safe, now,' said Mina. 'I do not know what they wanted of her, but I am sure that they will not be permitted near her again. And if she tries to hold séances alone she will find that the power has gone.'

Dr Hamid returned, to say that Eliza was resting, but asking for her sister, and also the flowers. Reluctantly Anna put the flowers in a little dish with some water and went up to Eliza.

'We will not intrude on you further,' said Mina, 'but let me know when Eliza is well enough to receive visitors, and if she would like to see me, then, of course, I will come at once.'

'I am expected at Miss Eustace's séance in two days' time,' said Dr Hamid. 'Should I go? Or would it be better to sever all relations with that circle?'

Richard raised his eyebrows. 'Miss Scarletti asked me to watch carefully at these meetings to see if the sitters were being duped,' Dr Hamid explained.

'I leave the choice to you,' said Mina. 'Of course, your sister is your first concern, I understand that.'

'Oh, I think if you need a spy, Mina, that can be arranged,' said Richard. He was thoughtful as they made their way home. 'So is that the summit of these charlatans' achievements so far? Rappings, tambourines, flowers, a shape that could be almost anything and Miss Eustace in glowing draperies?'

'As far as I am aware.'

He was still carrying the tambourine which Dr Hamid, who was glad to see it gone, had presented to him.

'Then I do not think Nellie has anything to learn from her, rather Miss Eustace must look to her reputation.'

'I fear that we must both now be deemed an unacceptable presence at Miss Eustace's performances,' said Mina.

'Oh, I shall find a way around that,' said Richard. 'Leave it to me.'

The following day there were two pieces of news, which were brought to Louisa by Mrs Bettinson. Miss Eustace, she said, was suffering from a bad cold and had decided not to hold any further séances until her health was improved. Mina wondered if that was true, or simply an excuse to avoid possible detection. For all she knew Miss Eustace was even now packing her bags to leave Brighton, something that would happily resolve the difficulty. The second communication was more unsettling. Miss Whinstone, who had refused to tell even her closest friends what was troubling her, had been briefly absent from home on a number of occasions for reasons she would not divulge, and had, according to her servant, recently gone away, her destination, purpose and date of return unknown.

Richard had also departed, and Mina found herself for a time bereft of company. She wrote to Edward, saying as little as possible about Richard's visit, and expressing her hopes that Miss Eustace would not trouble her further.

Miss Whinstone did not appear in church on the Sunday and neither did Mr Bradley. Mrs Bettinson, in a towering mood of frustration, revealed that she still had no idea of Miss Whinstone's whereabouts, although she had called again and been told by the servant that a letter had been received from her employer, giving her instructions and promising to return very shortly. The servant had, to Mrs Bettinson's extreme annoyance, refused to divulge the contents of Miss Whinstone's confidential missive. Mina thought that had such an incident occurred in one of her stories then Miss Whinstone would by now have been murdered for her money, her body, probably headless, hidden in a cellar, and a letter forged to conceal the crime, but she doubted that this was really the case. Mr Bradley's absence was more easily explained. Mrs Bettinson said that he had had an interview with the Reverend Vaughan and as a result had decided to attend another place of worship. She had also been making enquiries after Miss Eustace, and learned that the lady was in better health and hoped to resume her séances later in the week. Mr Clee, she added significantly, was also said to be slightly indisposed.

When Mina returned from church a very troubling note awaited her. Anna Hamid had written to say that although Eliza had recovered from her shock, she had since fallen ill. A heavy cold had settled on her lungs; she was too unwell to receive visitors, and was being nursed night and day. Mina sent a note to express her concern, enclosing one of her stories, which she hoped Anna might like to read to Eliza. The next day she received a reply from Anna who said that Eliza had enjoyed hearing the story and sent her kind wishes to Mina, hoping she would be well enough to see her soon.

Mina's mother had received information that Miss Eustace hoped to be sufficiently recovered to hold another séance in four days' time, and Miss Whinstone was expected home that evening. Mina had heard nothing more from Richard, and was unwilling to rely upon him, since that course of action was more likely to result in disappointment than anything else. For all she knew the delightful Nellie Gilden had decided to return to M. Baptiste, or Richard had thought of another scheme to make his fortune. Dr Hamid and Anna would be devoting themselves to their own concerns and she was left to pursue her worries alone.

Mina wondered if there was, unknown to her, another possible ally. Perhaps one of the ladies who attended Miss Eustace's séances was a sceptic like herself, but had been nervous of speaking out. While she might have visited all the ladies concerned, she decided on a faster and simpler method of interview. It took very little prompting for Mina to achieve her aim, and two days later, Mrs Bettinson, the two widowed sisters, Mrs Mowbray and Mrs Peasgood, and Mrs Phipps all came to take tea with her mother.

Their first and it seemed main subject of conversation was Miss Whinstone, who had suddenly taken it into her head to adopt two orphaned children, a boy and a girl, aged about seven and nine. Even the usually sleepy Mrs Phipps was wide awake during that startling revelation. Only Mrs Bettinson had seen the children, and said that they were clean and well behaved. They did not, she said, rather too pointedly for politeness, resemble Miss Whinstone. Her friend had refused to divulge her reasons for the adoption, except to say that she had been very selfish of late, and felt that she ought to do some good in the world. The children were to live with her during the summer under the care of a nursemaid, and would shortly be found good schools.

The general feeling of the ladies present, at least the opinion that they chose to speak aloud, was that Miss Whinstone had felt lonely since her brother had died, and was entitled to spend her income as she pleased if it brought her consolation.

Mina was able to introduce the subject of Miss Eustace without difficulty by making an enquiry as to that lady's state of health. All the visitors were pleased to hear that the séances were soon to resume, something they were eagerly anticipating. 'I would not miss one for anything!' said Mrs Mowbray. 'Such a good company there, too! That handsome Dr Hamid is a very fine gentleman, and a great favourite! I went for a vapour bath last week, and I had thought to see him, but the ladies are all attended to by his sister, who is very clever lady, and I hope to be better acquainted with her.'

Mina thought it best to make no mention of Eliza's illness or Mrs Mowbray would be sure to hurry round and attempt to see her. She did her best to direct the conversation back to the success, or otherwise, of Miss Eustace's séances.

'All that flim-flam with bells and knockings are one thing,' said Mrs Bettinson, 'and if I hadn't had a private sitting I would be starting to wonder if the lady had any means of speaking to the spirits at all, but when I did, why, that decided me. I heard things she could not have known about. Miss Eustace has never in her life met my brother-in-law, or anyone in my family, but she knew where and when he died and what of. He was always a great one for worrying about his business even when he didn't need to, and through Miss Eustace he told me how happy he was it did so well, and how pleased he was with his partners and how they used their funds. *And* he said he liked the way my sister had arranged the drawing room, but told her not to wind the clock too strong because that made it stop. He was always fussing about that clock. If that wasn't him talking I don't know who it was.'

'It was the same for me,' said Mrs Peasgood. 'Mrs Scarletti, you really ought to consult her when she starts the séances again. I had such good advice from my dear Charles at the private sitting that it was almost as if he stood in the room with me.'

'I have already done so,' said Louisa, 'and I had no doubt that it was Henry who addressed me.' She paused, and sat very straight with a proud look. 'In fact, I saw him, standing before me, as clearly as I see you all now, and we conversed, and he kissed me. I would not have permitted such a familiarity had I not been quite sure that it was my own beloved husband.'

This was the first that Mina had known that her mother had attended a private sitting with Miss Eustace. The nature of the revelation left her momentarily speechless, but her silence was not noticed since her mother was assailed by a battery of questions from her friends, which she fended off with a quiet smile. Mina, full of her own concerns, decided that the matter was too personal, too intimate, to be aired in company and would have to wait.

'I would like to attend a private sitting with Miss Eustace if I am permitted,' said Mina, when she was able to join the conversation. 'Does the lady give of her time gratis or does she ask for a charitable contribution?'

'You know very well, Mina,' said her mother, 'that the lady does not ask for anything for herself and it is left entirely to the person who consults her if they wish to make their appreciation known.'

'I had thought to consult her, but Ronald is quite against it,' said Mrs Phipps. 'He says that if I want advice I should ask him.'

'You are fortunate in having such a kind nephew,' observed Mrs Mowbray, 'and one who works in the law. We do not all have living relatives to guide us.'

Mrs Bettinson gave a very significant look in the direction of Mrs Phipps. The lady was about sixty-five and had been a widow for so long that no-one of her acquaintance could recall a Mr Phipps. Mrs Bettinson had, without any evidence, decided in her own mind that there never had been a Mr Phipps and that Ronald, her supposed nephew, was a son. The idea had become so established that she had convinced herself that it was a demonstrable truth, an opinion from which she was unshakeable.

'But you will continue to attend the séances?' asked Mrs Mowbray.

'I may not go to her again,' said Mrs Phipps. 'According to Ronald she caused a great scandal in London when she held séances there.'

'Surely not,' said Louisa, 'or Professor and Mrs Gaskin would not be so certain of her. They first encountered her in London and if there ever was a scandal, which I doubt, they must have heard of it.'

'Well, they might not know about it, because she was using another name then,' said Mrs Phipps, obstinately.

'And what name would that be?' demanded Louisa.

'Oh, I'm sure I don't know! But it was not Miss Eustace.'

'Then how can he know it was she?' said Louisa, reasonably. 'If the name was not the same then it was probably another woman entirely, and your nephew has made a mistake.'

'Well, I don't think I shall go, all the same,' said Mrs Phipps, firmly. 'Ronald said that she asks two guineas for an evening, and still more if people choose to believe in her. He says that if I want my fortune told I would do better spending sixpence visiting Madame Proserpina on the pier.' She had nothing more to say on the subject, and the other ladies looked on her pityingly as she settled down to her afternoon doze.

When the visitors had finally departed Mina attempted to draw her mother on the subject of her private séance with Miss Eustace, saying that she was eager to learn how her father had appeared and what he had communicated. Louisa was unusually reticent. 'He is happy, of course, and sees Marianne every day,' she said, contentedly. 'He says that her dear spirit was by his side as he passed over and has guided him in his new existence.'

'And you saw him?' asked Mina. 'Really truly saw him? I ask because no-one else has made such a claim. Not just a face, or a hand, but a man standing before you?'

'I did,' said her mother calmly. 'Why would you doubt it?'

'You saw his face?'

'Yes.' Her mother grew irritable. 'Why all these questions, Mina? You will make my head ache if you are not careful.'

'Because I am seeking truth and understanding. Was the room in darkness?'

'At first, it was, but when Henry appeared his spirit was bright almost as day.'

'And Miss Eustace was there and you saw them both in the room at once?'

'But of course. I was only grateful that she was in a trance as certain of Henry's communications were of a tender, romantic nature. There are some things, my dear, that must remain forever between a man and his wife, things that no other person may know.'

As her mother reclined with a self-satisfied expression and took another biscuit, Mina could only stare at her, appalled and confused.

Chapter Fourteen

It was only a matter of time, thought Mina, before everyone she knew, perhaps everyone in Brighton, took leave of their senses and saw ghosts everywhere. Spectres would stroll freely down the marine parade, drive past in carriages, crowd on to the piers, and even sit down to dine with the living.

With no will to try and investigate the source of her mother's new madness, Mina directed her attention instead to the more tangible fact that her vulnerable parent was being drawn into Miss Eustace's grasp, if only so that she might hand over two guineas or even more for an evening of private revelations and dubious visions. Eager to make some progress, and seizing on the clues revealed by Mrs Phipps, Mina quickly secured an interview with that lady's nephew.

Mr Ronald Phipps was a minor variety of the profession of solicitor, a young gentleman dedicated to making his way in the world through hard work, study and maintaining a spotless reputation. The newest and most junior partner in a larger firm, he occupied an office barely larger than a cupboard and sat behind a small desk, which he had made his own by having everything on it arranged as if by a foot rule. Not having an attractive face, he had compensated for this disadvantage by a dignified bearing and the exercise of perfect grooming.

'Thank you for agreeing to see me,' said Mina, perching awkwardly on a chair and wishing she had brought her wedge-shaped cushion with her. 'I wish to speak to you on the subject of Miss Eustace, the spirit medium.'

Deep, distrustful furrows appeared on the brow of young Mr Phipps. 'I sincerely hope that you have not come here in order to arrange for the transfer of finances to that person,' he said, sternly. 'If you have, then not only am I unwilling to assist you but I must warn you in the strongest possible terms against such a course of action.'

'I can assure you,' said Mina, hardly able to conceal her delight that she had discovered another ally, 'that I have no intention of transferring a single farthing to Miss Eustace. But I assume from your comments that other clients have come to you with that request.'

'I cannot discuss the private affairs of others,' he said, with some small softening of his expression, 'only your own, but I am relieved that you have no wish to allow Miss Eustace to command your purse. How may I help you?'

'It is my belief,' said Mina, 'that Miss Eustace is a fraud, exercising her profession in order to dupe the bereaved out of their fortunes. I admit that there are many things she does which I cannot explain, but these are surely just conjuring tricks made to appear as if performed by supernatural means.'

His eyebrows jumped almost to his hairline. 'I cannot, of course, comment, except to say that you would do well not to make your opinions public unless you can prove that what you say is true,' he said.

'That is my intention,' said Mina, 'and I am assembling information for that very purpose. Your aunt recently called to take tea with my mother and I gathered from what she said that you warned her against Miss Eustace on the grounds that she had been involved in some scandal in London, but under another name. I was hoping that you might be able to enlighten me on the circumstances. How did you come by this knowledge, and do you believe it to be trustworthy? Did you learn what other name Miss Eustace had been known under?'

'Ah,' he said, nodding, 'I am afraid this is a little awkward. I do know the origin of this story and I was obliged to warn my aunt before she did anything unwise, but it was in the strictest confidence, as there was no proof. I had not anticipated that she would tell her friends.'

Mr Phipps, thought Mina, while a professional man, was very young in experience or he would have known that this would happen with little, if any, delay. 'From whom did you hear the story?' she asked. 'You must have given it some credence or you would not have passed it on.'

'That is the difficulty,' he said. 'I heard it from an elderly client who I am not at liberty to name. She told me that she had been to one of Miss Eustace's séances, and was sure that she recognised the lady as a medium she had consulted in London some two or three years previously. Unfortunately she was unable to recall the London medium's name but she felt sure that it was not Eustace.'

'What was the nature of the scandal?'

He hesitated.

'I promise that I will not spread any slanders to the gossips of Brighton,' said Mina. 'I am making these enquiries for the protection of my own family but will not act upon any information until I have proof.'

He gave her request some thought. 'Very well,' he said, at last. 'On that understanding I can advise you that there was a rumour, but a rumour *only*, that Miss Eustace had found herself in prison, and that this was connected in some way with her séances. You must appreciate, of course, that there is a significant possibility that my client was mistaken.'

'I would very much like to interview this lady,' said Mina. 'Can you arrange it?'

He shook his head, regretfully. 'That is impossible, I am afraid.'

'Has she passed away?' asked Mina.

'My client is eighty-six and after a recent fit has become quite moribund,' said Mr Phipps. 'She is not expected to live long.'

'Did she confide this story in anyone other than yourself?' asked Mina.

'Not as far as I have been able to discover. I am sorry but I have no further information.'

Mina, after extracting a promise from Mr Phipps that he would let her know at once if he should learn anything more, was obliged to depart disappointed. Even if the story was true, and this was far from certain, how could she confirm it? She had no date and no name. Supposing she read every copy of the *Times* for the last three years and found a story of a medium who had been sent to prison, how could she even prove that it was the same woman, since the name was different? It was not as if the *Times* carried portraits.

From Mr Phipps's office she went to Dr Hamid's baths, where she learned that he was occupied with a patient. Anna, she was told, was at home looking after her sister. Mina waited in the vestibule, and before long Dr Hamid appeared and greeted her. They went into his office to speak, and he sank heavily into his chair, looking weary and worried.

'Eliza is still very weak,' he said. 'Her lungs are badly affected, and Anna is constantly by her side. She speaks of you often, and says how much she would like to see you but she is afraid that she will make you ill, too, and dares not allow a visit.'

'I am very touched by her concern,' said Mina. 'Please do reassure her that I am well, and say that I will visit her as soon as she feels strong enough. And if you could let Miss Anna Hamid know that I have been most diligent with the exercises and already feel some benefit.'

'I shall certainly do so,' he said.

'I have some news of Miss Eustace,' said Mina, 'although what I might do with it I am unsure. It was told to me in the strictest confidence and I promised faithfully not to spread it to idle gossips. I do not, however, count you as such.'

He smiled and poured some mineral water for them both. 'I, too, have news, but please let me know yours first.'

Mina told him of Mrs Phipps's revelations and the visit to her nephew. 'All I can do is keep my eyes and ears open and hope to learn more,' she said.

'That may not prove to be necessary,' he said. 'Miss Eustace resumed her séances last night and although I chose not to go, a patient of mine did, and he has just regaled me with all the circumstances. We may not see that lady again.'

'I am delighted to hear it,' exclaimed Mina. 'Tell me everything!'

'You understand, of course, that I do not normally discuss my patients, however in this instance …'

'I will be the very soul of discretion. And I need to know nothing as to the reasons he consulted you, or what treatment he received, only what he has to say about Miss Eustace.'

'I think he is intending to make the matter public with a letter to the newspapers, and there were others present too, so what I am about to tell you is no secret,' said Dr Hamid. 'You will just hear it a little before the town does. The gentleman's name was Mr Jordan. I am not sure if you are acquainted with him? He has a habit of rattling his watch.'

'Oh, yes,' said Mina, 'I have met him only once, when he attended Mr Bradley's first healing circle at our house. He made comments of a sceptical nature, I recall, and was not invited back.'

'Mr Jordan informed me that he is a very determined opponent of all things supernatural, and had been trying for some time to gain admission to one of Miss Eustace's séances without success, as his opinions were too well known,' said Dr Hamid. 'He has a friend, however, his business partner Mr Conroy, who is a devoted believer, indeed the two men enjoy nothing more than arguing about the subject at some length. It appears that Mr Jordan made a wager with Mr Conroy that if he could only gain admission to one of Miss Eustace's séances he could prove her to be a fraud, and Mr Conroy obtained a ticket for himself and for Mr Jordan who he introduced as his brother.'

'How wonderful! How admirable!' said Mina.

'There was, I think you must admit, some element of fraud in Mr Jordan's proceedings,' said Dr Hamid, carefully.

'I excuse him,' said Mina. 'But what occurred?'

'The deception was complete. No-one present recognised Mr Jordan for who he was and so he was admitted. He decided to bide his time, and to begin with he simply observed the table tipping and other phenomena, and then Miss Eustace retired to her chair behind the curtains. Mr Jordan and Mr Conroy volunteered to tie her securely, which enabled him to observe the arrangements closely. The ropes provided were thick and the lady's wrists very slight, and he felt sure that it was impossible to tie her tightly enough to secure her, and she was therefore perfectly able to free herself if she wished. The curtains were drawn and very soon afterwards the figure of Phoebe emerged. As she passed by him, Mr Jordan quickly snatched his hands from the grasp of the ladies on either side, and before anyone could prevent him, he rose up, seized the form of Phoebe in his arms, and pulled aside the veils that covered her face. To everyone's great astonishment — at least I feel we may exempt Mr Jordan from that emotion — Phoebe proved to be none other than Miss Eustace wearing little more than her undershift and enfolded in some brightly glowing draperies. Of course, Professor Gaskin and Mr Clee leaped forward at once and tore Mr Jordan from the lady by main force, and she had no alternative but to run behind the curtains and hide. As you may imagine the meeting ended in some disarray. Mr Jordan tried to address the other sitters, but he was prevented from doing so, ejected from the house and told never to return. Mr

Conroy, although he had had no warning of what his friend intended to do, was deemed to be a part of the conspiracy, and also found himself *persona non grata* on the pavement very soon afterwards. I am not at all sure if the two gentlemen remain on speaking terms.'

Mina laughed until she was breathless. 'Oh, I *wish* I had been there to see it! So Miss Eustace is no more?'

'We may hope,' said Dr Hamid, more cheerfully, despite his other concerns, 'that we have seen the last of that lady, at least in Brighton. I imagine that Professor and Mrs Gaskin are now very disappointed in her and will retreat back to London, sadder and wiser for their experience.'

'Of course, there is nothing to prevent Miss Eustace going to another town and promoting herself under another name and finding more dupes, but that is not something I am able to concern myself with,' said Mina, regretfully.

'You cannot be everywhere and be a guardian to the world,' said Dr Hamid. 'We must do all we can to protect our loved ones, keep a careful watch for our friends, and help those in need of charity, but that is all that can be expected of us.'

Mina was obliged to agree. She knew that her mother had not been at the previous night's interrupted séance, but had a ticket for that very evening. It was now, she thought, certain that the planned event would not take place. She decided not to mention to her mother that she knew of Miss Eustace's downfall. She was curious to know whether the news had spread to the faithful who had not witnessed it, and, if so, what the town gossips were saying. Her mother, on learning the truth, would no doubt, inform her that she had always had her suspicions, and deride the idea that she had been taken in. Mina, who did not want to cause an upset, but simply hoped to lay the unhealthy fashion to rest, determined to use her mother's reaction as the cue for her own response.

Mina returned home to spend half an hour in her room with a new purchase, a pair of dumbbells. There was as yet no visible difference in her shoulders, but she was confident that that would come as she gained in strength. She emerged to find her mother locked in close enclave with the two widowed sisters, Mrs Mowbray and Mrs Peasgood, who had in all probability arrived carrying the awful news. When Mina joined them, she was greeted with calm politeness and all the conversation was of the weather. The ladies soon departed to make another call, and Mina's mother said that she was tired and took a short nap.

To Mina's increasing surprise nothing was said on the subject of Miss Eustace either at luncheon or at tea. She surmised that her mother did not wish to admit that she had been made a fool of, and, under the impression that Mina knew nothing about it, had therefore decided to drop the subject entirely. Any discomfort would soon pass, and Mina looked forward to daily life returning to something resembling normality. Later that day, however, Mina was surprised to see her mother preparing to go out and found that she, together with Mrs Bettinson, Miss Whinstone and Mrs Parchment were all going to a séance at the Gaskins' apartments.

'Is that still to happen?' Mina asked cautiously. 'When I went to the baths this morning I overheard someone say that all future séances had been cancelled. In fact, one person advised me that Miss Eustace and Professor and Mrs Gaskin were to leave Brighton. Are you to see another spirit medium?'

'You would do well not to listen to ignorant talk,' said her mother, tying her bonnet. 'They will not be leaving and Miss Eustace will be conducting a séance this very night. We are promised something extraordinary, but the conditions must be exactly right. It is open only to a select few. If you had been more cooperative you might have been of that number, but I am afraid there is no hope for you.'

'Then the rumour about the incident provoked by Mr Jordan is false?' asked Mina. 'It was such a curious story that I could not give it any credit.'

'There was an incident of sorts, although it might better be termed an outrage,' said her mother, angrily.

'Surely not!' said Mina. 'Were Mrs Mowbray and Mrs Peasgood there? What did they say?'

Louisa favoured the hall mirror with an admiring glance. 'If you *must* know, Mr Jordan, who is a highly unpleasant person, obtained entry to the séance by giving a false name. He then nearly killed Miss Eustace by committing a grievous assault on her spirit guide, Phoebe. Everyone there was most disgusted by his behaviour and he was made to leave. It also seems, and I find this astonishing, that Mr Conroy, who has always appeared to be such a sensible gentleman, actually abetted him in this. Professor Gaskin said that Mr Jordan, who may not be in his right mind, suffers from a hatred of all things spiritual. Such is his intolerance that he is unable to see, or even refuses to see, what is obvious to others.'

'I was told,' said Mina, 'that Mr Jordan actually claimed that Phoebe was simply Miss Eustace in disguise.'

'Well, that is exactly what such a man would say! I am sure it was nothing of the sort!' said her mother. The carriage arrived with the other ladies and she departed.

Chapter Fifteen

Mina was consumed with curiosity about what would transpire at the séance, but had to wait until the following morning to find out. She saw now that she had been excluded from discussion of the event because her mother, imagining that it might be a day or two before Mina heard of it, wanted to learn everything she could, so as to be prepared to offer a complete refutation.

The next morning Mina did not need to prompt her mother to tell the tale, for she was regaled at great length across the breakfast table with an account of Miss Eustace's wonderful triumph. The lady had been surrounded with sympathetic well-wishers, who had applauded her and pressed her with many gifts, and Phoebe had later appeared wearing gorgeous robes and a glowing crown studded with jewels. The spirit had spoken to them all, and even kissed Professor Gaskin's hand. Their host, said Louisa, had offered a full explanation for the events of the previous night, which showed that Mr Jordan had been labouring under a delusion as to what had really occurred. Not only had Professor Gaskin written to all the Brighton newspapers with a detailed account of the incident, but he had also composed a small pamphlet, which was being printed as he spoke and would enlighten anyone who had heard the false accusations.

That afternoon, the professor's pamphlet, its ink barely dry, appeared in newsagents, libraries and reading rooms all over Brighton. The title was 'Miss Eustace, vindicated; an explanation of spirit phenomena.'

It was with considerable curiosity and a heavy heart that Mina obtained a copy and took it home to study.

Professor Gaskin commenced his address to the denizens of Brighton by stating that a certain intolerant hostile and ignorant person, whom he declined to name, but whose character was perfectly described by the fact that he did not hesitate to use violence to endanger the life of a virtuous lady, had suggested that Miss Eustace had been exposed as a fraud. Nothing, he declared, could be further from the truth. Jealous persons, persons who perhaps were interested in promoting rivals to Miss Eustace and hoped thereby to make their fortunes, had tried to destroy her reputation by spreading a false rumour to the effect that the materialised form of Phoebe had been found to be Miss Eustace clad in glowing robes. This was not at all what had occurred, and in the interests of scientific enquiry and progress he felt obliged to set the record straight.

Miss Eustace, he advised his readers, had but recently recovered from a severe cold, which had greatly decreased her available energy, but such was her selfless devotion to the world of the spirit, she had, in order to please her many admirers, recommenced her séances a little before her full powers had returned to her.

It had been determined to secure her to a chair before she entered the trance state, a duty that was always carried out by independent volunteers, and had this been properly done, nothing untoward would have occurred, but it now appeared that the men who had tied her had not carried out their task as well as they should have done. Indeed one of the men in question was the same man who later created the horrid disturbance, and Professor Gaskin suspected that the failure to tie the medium properly was not due to ineptitude at all, but was actually deliberate. His studies had led him to the conclusion that it was always best to tie the medium when a materialisation was to take place, not as a test of her veracity but for her own protection, in case she started to wander about the room while in a semi-conscious state.

When Phoebe's form had been produced on previous occasions it had been made wholly out of etheric matter drawn from Miss Eustace's body to create a complete materialisation. On the night in question, however, because of Miss Eustace's fragile state of health, there had been insufficient matter to create the whole figure. It was his belief, although he had never previously witnessed it, that in order to arrive at a full materialisation, the process had to pass through a stage of transition, which was not usually seen by sitters, since it took place in a cabinet or behind a curtain. Miss Eustace, although in a semi-trance, and therefore hardly responsible for or even aware of what she was doing, was anxious to meet the expectations of her circle, and rather than disappoint them, the process had commenced, but due to her weakness, it had paused during the transition stage and never achieved full materialisation. At this point, she had produced only sufficient substance to produce the outward appearance of Phoebe and had used it to drape her own form. This amazing material can usually be instantly moulded to adopt any shape; however, on that occasion, the shape that it adopted most easily as causing the least distress to Miss Eustace was that of the medium herself. The knots about her wrists failing, Miss Eustace had in her unconscious condition emerged from behind the curtains, only to be attacked with great savagery and almost killed.

Professor Gaskin took upon himself the entire responsibility for the unfortunate outcome of the sitting. He had allowed Miss Eustace to conduct a séance when not in full health, had inadvertently admitted to the circle a person of dubious reputation and harmful influence, and had then failed to ensure that the medium was properly secured and protected. The one person who should bear no blame at all for the incident was Miss Eustace herself.

Mina's mother had also obtained a copy of the pamphlet, which she studied with considerable satisfaction. Mr Jordan, so her friends had informed her, was beside himself at this development. Not only had he failed in what was practically an attempt to assassinate Miss Eustace, but the gossip about the incident and the circulation of the pamphlet had only increased that lady's fame, and demand for tickets was more intense than ever.

Mina, in despair over her quarry's triumph, retired to her room to consider what to do next. It was very apparent now that adherents of Miss Eustace and perhaps of all mediums could, in face of the most blatant exposure, explain everything away in terms that would serve to maintain and even reinforce their belief. There was no hope for them, and she could do nothing for them; indeed Dr Hamid was quite right, she had no real obligation to anyone but her own intimate circle as well as the helpless and the needy. It was not her place to save strangers from the consequences of their own foolishness and vanity. She tried to write, but unusually the words would not come. She had thought of composing a new tale, about a medium who turned out to be a thief, but what good would that do? It was after all a story, and anything might happen in a story.

Mina briefly considered asking for a private sitting with Miss Eustace, but even if she could bring herself to part with two guineas to the medium she was sure that any application would be refused, or if accepted, the sitting would have an inconclusive result. It was hardly possible for her to attend a séance in disguise.

Although she had heard nothing from Richard, she soon learned that he had been busy with his new pursuits. An advertisement had been placed in the *Gazette*, in the form of a letter from a satisfied customer of the new sensation Miss Foxton, who had recently, so it was claimed, concluded a successful tour of all the major cities in the land where she had astounded everyone with her supernatural demonstrations. Miss Foxton was shortly to astonish Brighton, and tickets could be procured at very reasonable cost. A box number was given for enquiries. Mina thought that when she finally caught up with Richard she should at least be permitted to see the demonstration as a guest.

Richard soon swept back into her life like a burst of intoxication. He had the ability to both raise her mood and drive her to despair, often at the same time. He laughed heartily at the discomfiture of Mr Jordan, whom he did not see as a danger to himself. 'Let him come and welcome!' he said. 'Let him do his worst! In fact I shall send complimentary tickets to him and his friend Mr Conroy to ensure their attendance.'

'So you feel that you have nothing to conceal?' asked Mina with some surprise.

'Oh, my dear girl, we have *everything* to conceal, but we will make a better job of it than Miss Eustace.'

'I have heard a rumour, the truth of which I have been unable to establish, that the lady has been in prison, though under another name,' said Mina.

He laughed again. 'That would not surprise me in the least.'

'But I am afraid I don't know that name,' said Mina seriously.

He made an airy gesture. 'A woman such as she probably has a dozen.'

'I only wish I could find out some way of discovering that name and if the story of her being in prison is true. Do you have any idea as to how it might be done? You always seem to be full of ideas.'

He gave the question a few moments' thought. 'Well, you might waste your money employing a detective, but even if he found out the whole story and bellowed it from the cliff top, what would be the result? Miss Eustace's tribe of followers would refuse to believe it, or see her as a martyr to the cause of truth and a victim of persecution by the ignorant, and they would cling to her even closer. Those who do not as yet follow her would flock to see her and she would be more famous than ever. Those who want to believe will believe. Those who do not will not.'

'Then what can I do?' she pleaded.

He hugged her. 'Oh, Mina, you cannot save the world from itself! I know you are concerned for Mother and that is very good and right, of course, but you are not Miss Whinstone's keeper, or even her friend.'

'I am Eliza Hamid's friend,' said Mina.

'And she has a loving family to protect her,' said Richard.

'She has been very ill these last few days,' said Mina. 'I believe that she caught a cold from Mr Clee, who is young and well able to shake off such a thing, but it has affected her lungs.'

'Mr Clee will not be allowed near her again,' said Richard, firmly. 'When she is well I will get Nellie to entertain her with some conjuring tricks. Perhaps Miss Hamid can host a salon of magical entertainment that will be amusing but not as tiring as a séance. And she will forget all about Mr Clee's phosphorised handkerchief.'

'Phosphorised?' asked Mina.

He shrugged. 'How else do you think it glowed in the dark? It's an old trick. I am amazed that people are still taken in.'

'Do you recall the Davenport brothers?' she asked, thinking of Dr Edmunds and his mystification at the coat trick. 'They caused a great sensation only two or three years ago. People still talk of their confounding the laws of science.'

'Oh, who can forget the magical Davenports and their cabinet of wonders!' he declared. 'I fear they went to some expense for that. Never trust a medium who has his apparatus specially constructed. Well — never trust a medium. Yes, they had a startling and novel array of tricks, but in the end the whole act boiled down to just the one. Only allow that they had some means of getting their hands free, as any good magician can do very quickly and easily, and all is explained. But I cannot fault them as businessmen.'

'Richard,' pleaded Mina, 'don't you think you should consider some means of income which would be more — well —'

'Respectable?' he asked.

'Yes. And less likely to result in your being put in prison,' she added. 'Mother would never forgive you.'

'Oh, you know she would, and so would you! But prison is an uncomfortable place, and I promise I shall make every effort to avoid it.' He jumped up. 'And now, my dear, I have a dozen things to attend to, and you may be sure to receive your ticket very soon.'

'Where is this event to take place?' asked Mina. 'At Miss Gilden's lodgings?'

'Oh no, the rooms are far too small. But I have made some enquiries and found a little band of spiritually-minded ladies who like to meet and talk ghosts over their sherry and biscuits, and so I smiled prettily at them. One of their number, a Mrs Peasgood, who has a delightful home in Kemp Town, has been kind enough to let me use her drawing room gratis. There is ample space for both guests and performance.'

'Mrs Peasgood, the surgeon's widow?' asked Mina.

'Why, yes, do you know her?'

'She is one of Mother's new friends!' exclaimed Mina, in alarm. 'Will you be there?'

'But of course! I am the master of ceremonies for the evening.'

'Richard, you cannot do this!' said Mina. 'Supposing Mother goes, or Mrs Bettinson or her other friends who all know you, as they very well might! What then? Mother would never be able to hold her head up again, and she would find some reason why it was all my fault.'

Richard was unperturbed, and planted a kiss on the top of her head. 'Have no fear, my darling girl! I have thought of everything!'

It was some hours after he left that Mina noticed that the oriental vase in the front hallway had vanished.

Despite accepting the fact that there was nothing further she could do for Miss Eustace's dupes, Mina was still curious enough to pay a visit to Mr Jordan. A Brighton directory and a few discreet enquiries soon provided the information that he was the proprietor of an emporium supplying suits of clothing to young men of fashion. He and Mr Conroy, who dealt in ties, cravats, cummerbunds and hats, had once had separate establishments and had long glared at each other from across the way, but one day they had met by chance, struck up a crusty sort of friendship and gone into partnership. This had flourished so well that they had recently taken another shop next door for ladies' apparel, the supervising angels being Mr Conroy's wife and Mr Jordan's sister.

Mr Conroy was a bluff uncomplicated gentleman, with a talent for putting his customers at their ease, but Mr Jordan adopted a manner that was both imperious and condescending, as if to suggest that while the customer he was serving was neither noble nor royal there were others who were. He employed a hard-pressed assistant, but was always in evidence, looking on with a hard critical eye and making sure to give the wealthier customers his personal attention. The word in Brighton was that Mr Jordan was little more than a jumped-up tailor, although no-one would have said it to his face.

The shop was redolent with the acrid, nostril-stinging scent of new, freshly-steamed wool, with a citrus hint of gentlemen's cologne. When Mina entered she found Mr Jordan overseeing his assistant, who was showing a gentleman a display of fabrics. His watch was in his palm as if he was timing the exercise, but when he saw Mina he snapped it shut, and put it in his pocket. 'Miss Scarletti, how may I assist you?'

'If you have a moment, Mr Jordan, I would be interested in discussing your encounter with Miss Phoebe — or should I say, Miss Eustace, since I understand that you claim they amount to one and the same person.'

He grunted, and beckoned Mina away to one side of the shop, out of the earshot of his customer. 'You are not one of her acolytes?' he said with an unattractive sneer.

'Not at all,' said Mina, choosing to ignore the rudeness of his manner in the interest of extracting information. 'In fact, I had a recent experience when I stumbled and fell against the spectre, and was thereby convinced that it was a living person, and female. It can only have been Miss Eustace. I understand that you went further than this and deliberately clasped her.'

'I did,' he said with some dignity. 'May I assure you it is far from my nature to treat a lady in such a rough and indelicate fashion, but then Miss Eustace, whatever her pretensions, is not a lady. I cannot be sure quite what she is, or indeed who she is, but honest and selfless as she likes to claim she is most assuredly not.'

'And you were quite certain that Phoebe is just Miss Eustace in draperies?'

'Oh, beyond a doubt,' he assured her, with a short barking laugh. 'The supposed spectre struggled and kicked me most unmercifully as I took hold of her. She has all the good manners of a fishwife. I will admit that I cannot explain the mechanism of the imposture, but that is not my business.'

'Do you intend to take any further action against her?' asked Mina.

'No, none,' he declared. 'I have written to the newspapers, of course, but my efforts are swamped by those of her credulous adherents, and she is now unassailable. Really, if these people wish to be parted from their money I can only leave them to their fate. And now, I understand that there is to be a new sensation in town, a Miss Foxton and her — well, I hesitate to say what he might be — her theatrical manager shall we say, a Mr Ricardo. Are you acquainted with these people?'

'I am not familiar with anyone of that name,' said Mina, truthfully.

'He has sent me a letter today with a free ticket, and I shall attend and they must look to it or I will show them up to be the cheats and charlatans they are, and if I can see them both in prison I will consider my work well done.'

'I may well attend myself, as a matter of curiosity only, of course,' said Mina. 'And what of your partner Mr Conroy? Did your actions convince him that Miss Eustace is a fraud?'

'Mr Conroy prefers not to speak of that night,' said Mr Jordan, shutting his mouth with a snap no less firm than his watch.

Mina was naturally abiding by Eliza's instructions not pay her a visit, although she was anxious for news, and after leaving Mr Jordan's she turned her feet towards Dr Hamid's baths, which was not far distant, hoping that someone would be in attendance who would be able to let her know how her friend was progressing. Although Mina's exercises, which she continued with a dedicated determination, concentrated on developing her shoulders, back and chest, there were some that strengthened her legs and Anna had encouraged her in her usual habit of taking short refreshing walks. Mina still limped, and accepted the fact that she would always do so, but at least she could now limp faster and for longer, and without pain.

As she approached the baths she noticed two gentlemen standing outside the building, peering closely at something in the window, but making no attempt to enter. Initially she supposed that it was an advertisement, but as she drew closer she saw that the interior of the establishment, seen through the glass, was in darkness although it was well within its usual hours of opening. A sensation of cold dread settled over her.

The gentlemen stood aside as she approached and she saw that they were looking at a notice bordered in black. 'It's closed up today,' one of them said, and they turned and walked away. Mina, her eyes clouded with emotion, could barely read the sign, which offered apologies for the fact that the establishment was closed due to a family bereavement, and promised that it would reopen on the following day. For several minutes she leaned against the door, making no attempt to control the tears that were coursing freely down her face, and ruminated on how cruel life could be. She thought of Eliza's sweet face and quick mind, and their lively conversations. She thought of how much she had looked forward to writing stories for her friend and encouraging her to seek new amusements. As she stood there several people came up and read the sign and went away, and some asked her if she was well and needed any assistance, but she said that she would recover, it was due to the shock of the bad news. One kind lady who was a friend of Anna's and had known of Eliza's illness confirmed what Mina had feared, and they talked for a few minutes until Mina felt able to leave.

She did not want to go home unless she could be certain of being able to escape to her room and be alone with her grief, and that was far from sure. She thought it likely that her mother would be entertaining her friends that afternoon and did not feel equal to feigning politeness in the company of Mrs Bettinson and her like; neither did she want to carry the tragedy home as if it was simply another piece of town gossip to be bandied about by chattering ladies. She walked instead towards the seashore, where she could best think about the muddled uncertain line between two worlds, and what might happen when crossing from one to the other.

Brighton was beginning to welcome the first of the new season of visitors, but on the eastern side of the town it was not so busy. A great swathe of building work had cut through the approach to the old Chain Pier and carved it away to make room for the new aquarium, but the new truncated entrance to the pier was not unpleasing. Close by, one could stand and take in the sight of the great iron structure that seemed to power its massive way into the sea like a steam train, and see the waves beating against its supports. In mild weather, as it was that day, the waves appeared to be caressing the pier with a firm but approving affection, but Mina knew that they could suddenly turn to rage and resentment. She saw the figure of a man standing alone and looking out to sea, and recognised him as Dr Hamid. She hesitated, then approached him.

'I have just come from the baths,' she said. 'I saw the notice. I don't know what to say. I am so very sorry.'

'I must apologise for closing the business today,' he said quietly.

'Please, there is no need for any apology,' she reassured him.

'There are patients who rely on us for regular treatment; some are elderly, some in great pain. I have a duty to them.' He sighed. 'Anna is at home making all the arrangements, and I would help her but I think I am not very useful at present; at any rate she suggested I go out and take the air for a while.'

'Do you mind if we talk?' she asked. 'If you would rather be alone, let me know, and I will go at once.'

'No, please stay. You were Eliza's friend, and even in such a short while you came to know her better than most. Towards the end, she said what a comfort you were to her and how she hoped that when she was well you would meet again. She liked the stories you sent her.'

Mina hardly dared look into his eyes, the irises like fractured marble, with splinters of pain. 'I was so looking forward to seeing her. She helped me with a story I was writing, and I thought perhaps we might write one together.'

'When she was a child,' said Dr Hamid, 'my father was told that she would most probably not live past her twentieth birthday, but we gave her the best care we could, and she had a not unpleasant life, filled with interest. She inspired me, she inspired Anna and by her example we became better than we might have been and more able to help others.'

'That is her monument,' said Mina. 'She will live on through you and your sister. Please let me know when it would be appropriate for me to call.'

'Of course. I know Anna would like to see you.' There was a long silence as they both looked out across the rolling sea. Carriages rattled past, like ships full of merriment and the promise of delight.

'Too many losses,' he said with another heavy sigh. 'Too many people taken away before their time. Eliza might have lived another twenty years, Jane another thirty. It is so cruel and unnecessary, when there are evil people in this world who live long and good people who do not. I wish I knew why that was! I can only pray, and ...' For a few moments he looked as though he was biting back tears. Not so long ago they had sat beside each other in a circle and clasped hands, and she felt she wanted to reach out and touch his hand as a friend, but it would not have been right. 'When Jane died it was like a light that had illuminated my life going out,' he said. 'I would like to think that somewhere, somehow, that light is still burning, and that one day I will be able to see it again and go towards it. I need to believe. Surely we all do?'

Mina waited for him to say more but he did not. 'I hope,' she said, 'that you are not considering going to see Miss Eustace again?'

'And why should I not?' he demanded with sudden ferocity.

'You know why not,' said Mina, trying to speak as gently as possible.

He shook his head. 'One of my patients told me that he went to her for a private reading and received information that could have come from no-one other than the deceased.'

'So some people claim,' said Mina, 'but I am not convinced it is so.'

'Well, you can hardly blame me for seeking the truth,' he said obstinately.

'No, I cannot, but this is not the time to do it, when you are in pain and wanting to believe anything that will give you comfort. Please tell me you will wait awhile.'

He closed his eyes as if to shut out the world and be alone with his misery.

'I would like to walk a little way,' she said. 'Will you assist me?'

'Yes, of course.' He offered her his arm, and they turned and walked along the Marine Parade with the sun reflecting off the bright white hotels to their right and the sea crashing like shards of blue-veined jasper to their left.

Chapter Sixteen

Mrs Peasgood was a lady nearer in age to sixty than fifty and nearer in weight to fourteen stones than thirteen. Her late husband had been a well-regarded surgeon and had thus left her in extremely comfortable circumstances, with an annuity, a property, three grown sons, and as many grandchildren as any woman could decently want. She lived in a very pleasant villa in Marine Square, the upper part of which she had converted to make a roomy apartment for her sister Mrs Mowbray, whose husband had left her with neither family nor fortune but a great many attentive callers asking for the urgent settlement of their accounts.

On the ground floor of the villa was a magnificent east-facing drawing room, where twenty-five people might easily assemble in comfort, or thirty if they were more determined and less particular. As if one drawing room was not enough, the house had provided a second smaller one, behind the first, the two rooms being separated by a pair of heavy damask curtains, and both accessible quite separately from the hallway, while the back room led through a set of double doors to a beautifully maintained garden. Mrs Peasgood was a lover of music and often gathered her friends for a recital, the main drawing room serving as a kind of auditorium and the smaller as a stage for the performers, so transforming her home into a theatre in miniature.

It was this enviable space into which Richard had somehow cajoled himself and his protégée, the extraordinary Miss Foxton.

Mina, to her great relief, had discovered that her mother had no intention of attending the new sensation's séance. Not only did Louisa feel that patronising Miss Foxton impugned her loyalty to Miss Eustace, which had become immeasurably stronger since the unfortunate incident with Mr Jordan, but she had heard rumours that Miss Foxton was not all that she seemed, and could not imagine what Mrs Peasgood could be thinking of to admit such a creature to her house.

As the ladies assembled in Mrs Peasgood's drawing room Mina looked anxiously about in case her mother had changed her mind, but fortunately she had not, and neither Mrs Bettinson nor Miss Whinstone were present. Mr Jordan and his friend Mr Conroy were there, and while the ladies were engaged in conversation the gentlemen dedicated themselves to the more business-like task of obtaining the best possible seats. Mina wondered if another wager had been made, and feared that Mr Jordan was planning an assault upon Miss Foxton and an exposure of the dastardly Mr Ricardo. She could not imagine how she might protect Richard from such an attempt, which could well prove violent. If Richard brought disgrace on the family she could quite see her mother packing him off somewhere to manage a ranch or plant tea, and realised that she would miss him dreadfully.

Thus far, Mina felt confident that no-one in the room knew Richard by sight, but then she saw a familiar figure enter discreetly and slip though the crowds to find a seat near the back. It was Mr Clee, and Mina surmised that he was there to see what the other medium in town was doing and report his findings to Miss Eustace. He avoided engaging anyone else in conversation, and seemed anxious not to draw attention to himself. Mina was unable to decide if it was more important to protect Richard from Mr Jordan or Mr Clee, but could not see how either feat could be accomplished. She sat where she could see them both, hoping that she would not find it necessary to create a scene.

At length, Mrs Peasgood suggested that those of the company who had not yet taken their places might like to do so. There was an unexpected difficulty when two ladies discovered that Mr Jordan and Mr Conroy had taken what they considered to be their seats, presumably because they always occupied those places at the musical evenings. Mr Conroy was all for giving up the seats to the ladies but Mr Jordan, claiming priority, was not, and incurred his hostess's grave displeasure by sitting with folded arms and stolidly refusing to move. It took all of Mr Conroy's tact and a promise of silk ribbon to enable the gentlemen to keep their places without a quarrel.

Mr Clee, Mina noticed, was watching Mr Jordan very carefully, although he was also pretending to read Professor Gaskin's pamphlet. She feared that even from the back row of seats Mr Clee would recognise Richard, both by features and voice, as any man might another who had threatened to knock him down. She was uncertain what he might choose to do about it, and hoped she would be able to delay him if he made a sudden rush.

Mrs Peasgood glanced at her maid who turned down the lights. There were little exclamations of nervous anticipation as the room was plunged into semi-darkness, not the deep black demanded by many mediums, but a soft accommodating shadow. A moment or two passed during which the sea of onlookers rippled and settled into a pool, then gradually two hands pushed between the curtains and eased them apart. The draperies made a pointed arch in which stood an enigmatic figure, the faint light to which all eyes were becoming accustomed suggesting the form of a tall man.

'Good evening, ladies and gentlemen!' he announced in an accent that was very nearly Italian. It was Richard, of course, and since no member of his family had ever met the great-grandfather whose surname they bore, the attempt was more theatrical than convincing. 'Allow me to introduce myself. I am Signor Ricardo, and I have come before you to introduce a great wonder, the like of which you will never have seen before.' He stepped into the room, allowing the curtains to fall together behind him. They could now see that he was in evening dress, but around his shoulders there swirled a long cape with something on it that glittered like stars. His hair had been brushed back, its unruly waves smoothed with an oily dressing that made it shine and appear darker than it was, and he sported a false moustache of evil aspect and a half-mask of black velvet edged with gold lace. It was a guise in which he might have personated Mephistopheles on the stage and wanted, thought Mina, only a blood red waistcoat to be complete. She breathed a sigh of relief as he continued to speak.

'Newly arrived in this country from her triumphant tour of the continent of Europe where she appeared before the crowned heads and nobility — soon to be the honoured guest of a Very Exalted Personage — I bring you the beautiful, the astonishing, the unique Miss Kate Foxton!'

He threw his arms wide and gave a deep bow, then drew back the curtains on either side. The space behind them was nearly bare, and appeared to have been darkly draped. All that could be seen was, to the right, a deep armchair, and in the centre of the stage a tall oriental vase, which looked very similar to the one that had until recently stood in the Scarlettis' hallway. Not only similar, reflected Mina, but identical — in fact, it was the one that had stood in their hallway, and she was in no doubt that it was Richard who had, under some pretext or other, managed to abstract it.

Signor Ricardo strode across the stage with an attitude appropriate to a tenor at the opera expressing his undying love for a mature soprano, extending his hand towards the space that lay behind the fall of draperies to his left. He then moved backwards, with the lithe tripping gait of a dancer, leading with him the figure of Miss Foxton, whom he conducted to the centre of the stage for the examination and admiration of the audience.

Miss Nellie Gilden, for it was certainly she, was attired quite differently from the revealing costume in which she had posed for the *carte de scandale* which Mina had seen. She wore a plain, drab-coloured costume so voluminous as to conceal her pronounced womanly form almost entirely, and neat little gloves and boots. Her hair, which the photograph had suggested might be gold with more than a hint of amber, had been transformed into a knot of glossy brown curls heaped high and surmounted by a wide hat trimmed with feathers. Mina, knowing that Nellie was an actress and therefore a woman who had abandoned all claims to respectability, looked in vain for anything in her features that might reveal a disreputable mode of life. The portrait, she was obliged to admit, had not done the lady justice. Miss Gilden might have graced any drawing room, any court even, and carried off the guise of a lady with complete success. The freshness of her complexion, which if painted was done with such subtlety that it appeared to be entirely natural, the brightness of her eyes, the curve of her lips, gave her a discreet yet alluring charm. All around, the audience gave a soft murmur of approval.

'Do not be concerned at this lady's youth,' said Mr Ricardo. 'True, she has not seen eighteen summers, but her abilities have been strong since she was but a small child. When only seven years of age she dreamed of the tragic death of a beloved royal personage. Just over six years ago she was in America and begged to be allowed to send a message to a very great man to say that he should not think of going to the theatre that evening. But the words of a young girl carried no weight — would that they had!' He shook his head sorrowfully.

'But now!' he exclaimed, with a suddenness that make everyone jump, 'to happier thoughts! Miss Foxton will shortly enter a state of trance and I beg you all to strict silence and contemplation.' He escorted Miss Foxton to the armchair and there she was seated, taking more care, thought Mina, than one might expect over the exact arrangement of such a simple costume. He then held his hands over her head, and moved them about in circles, to suggest that he was subjecting her to mesmeric influence. After a minute or so, Miss Foxton's eyelids drooped, then closed, and her head sank forward, so that her face was hidden underneath the brim of her hat and the plume of gently quivering feathers. She appeared to be asleep, yet it was more than that, as he demonstrated, since he carefully raised her hand, and allowed it to fall back limply into her lap.

Mr Ricardo then removed his cloak and after swirling it about his head a number of times, for no apparent reason than to add a touch of drama and perhaps also distract the audience's attention from anything Miss Foxton might be doing, he draped it carefully over the somnolent medium. When he stepped back, all that could be seen of Miss Foxton was a small gloved hand, a tiny foot, and the feathers on her hat.

'The lady is in a trance,' he confided to the audience in a hushed whisper, 'and while she is in this state of unconsciousness the vital energy will begin to flow from her body!'

Mr Ricardo began to make extravagant passes over the recumbent figure, then he stepped away, with gestures suggesting that he was pulling at an invisible cord.

Abruptly, Mr Jordan rose to his feet. 'If I may be permitted,' he said in a voice more suited to a public announcement than controlled reverence, 'I wish to take the lady's pulse.'

'Mr Jordan!' whispered Mrs Peasgood. 'Kindly moderate your voice! And will you please sit down!'

Mr Ricardo paused, and smiled at Mr Jordan, who was standing in a very rigid and determined posture, his hands clenched into fists. 'I understand your concern for the lady's state of health,' he said. 'Do be assured that she is in no danger.'

'That I would like to see for myself,' said Mr Jordan, making no attempt to speak more quietly. 'Or are you one of those charlatans who prevent others from going near to the medium so as to cover imposture?'

'Sir!' insisted Mrs Peasgood, 'do please be seated. I fear you are making a disturbance!'

'I do not intend to cause a painful scene while a guest in your house,' said Mr Jordan with great dignity, clearly recalling his peremptory ejection from the Gaskins' parlour, 'neither do I accuse you of being a part of their confederacy —' There were appalled gasps at the effrontery of even mentioning the idea — 'but I do ask, before we proceed any further, to satisfy myself that the lady is well. You cannot object to that.'

'I have no objection at all,' said Mr Ricardo, generously. 'Please do come forward, sir.'

Mr Jordan had clearly not expected to be so accommodated, but after an involuntary start of surprise he approached the covered figure in the armchair. Mr Ricardo drew back the cloak and then carefully lifted the brim of the hat to reveal the peaceful face of the medium. 'A veritable sleeping beauty in the flesh,' he said.

The sceptic paused, and after a moment, took Miss Foxton's hand in his, drew back the fabric of her glove, and pressed his fingertips to her wrist. There was half a minute of expectant silence.

'Are you satisfied now, sir?' asked Mr Ricardo.

Mr Jordan granted him a strange look. 'Hmm — yes — for the moment.'

The glove, hat and cloak were replaced as they had been before. 'Then if you would be so good as to return to your seat.'

There was nothing more that Mr Jordan could do, and unwillingly he turned back and resumed his place.

'And now,' said Mr Ricardo, addressing the audience, 'you will see before your very eyes, something that has never before appeared on any stage, or in any house in all this land. You will actually witness the stream of vital etheric energy as it flows from the lady's body. Prepare yourselves to be amazed.' He waved his hands over Miss Foxton again, but this time he gradually stepped closer, and at last a small gesture enabled him to catch in his fingertips the end of a bright wisp of something that was so light it was almost nothing at all emerging from underneath the cloak. Slowly, then with increasing speed, he pulled and lifted it away. It was a long strip of delicate transparent material that glowed in the semi-darkness and floated in the air as if it had no substance. He stepped backwards away from the recumbent medium, drawing out the banner of light until it extended for several feet, getting wider and brighter as it flowed, and then he carried it across the room to the vase and guided it inside. More and more it came, ten feet, twenty, it was impossible to measure, until far more had come than would have seemed possible, and still it piled softly into the vase. The audience was utterly silent, and as Mina gazed about her she saw that eyes were wide and lips parted in amazement.

The ethereal production at last glided to a conclusion and all was laid in the vase. Mr Ricardo hurried over to the still figure of the medium and touched her wrist. 'She lives,' he said, in a reassuring tone, and there were some sighs of relief.

Mr Jordan rose to his feet again, 'If you will permit me —' he began.

'Really, sir, I will not permit you!' exclaimed Mrs Peasgood testily. 'You have been given liberty once and pronounced yourself satisfied. Now either be seated or depart.'

Mr Jordan sat down again, but with very ill grace.

Mr Ricardo returned to the vase and walked all around it, allowing his hands to hover over its rim, moving them in circles with great deliberation, then he suddenly stepped back with a gesture as if throwing something inside. There were little sparkles in the air, like a cloud of dust motes reflecting all the light in the room. For a few moments he stood still, both arms extended, and then there appeared underneath his fingers little bright darting blue flashes like tiny flames.

There were gasps from the assembled company: partly wonder but mainly alarm. Several people glanced toward the exit as if calculating how easy it would be to escape if the house caught alight. A few looked pityingly at Mina, convinced that she would be unlikely to survive such a catastrophe. Smoke began to rise from the vase, a column of luminous silver blue mist that ascended to the ceiling like a fountain of fire. Fortunately there were no roaring flames, and Mr Ricardo's confidence so near to the display suggested to the onlookers that there was not, after all, any danger of their being roasted alive.

All eyes were on the shining feathery apparition, when gradually a shape began to form behind it, a shape that seemed to have risen from inside the vase and was coalescing into a figure of human stature. The eyes of the onlookers, which had become accustomed to the semi-darkness, were now partly blinded by the fierce blue glow, and for a time it was hard to determine what was being displayed, but eventually it was possible to make out a figure rising up, until it was above the rim of the vase and hovering in the air. As the smoke gradually dispersed, they saw that the form was female, and it was as well that it was a spirit and not a human creature, or its state of undress might have caused outrage instead of wonder. She was youthful, with a face white as a pearl and a great cascade of yellow gold hair. Her graceful form seemed to be quite naked, although she might have been clothed in a substance that resembled a second skin, glowing brightly and glistening with silver spangles, but revealing the outline of her tiny waist, rounded bust and hips, and long graceful limbs. Some delicate gossamer material that hung from her shoulders and wrists appeared to be wings and the undulation of her arms was all that held her in place. Unlike so many ghostly apparitions it was impossible in the presence of this heavenly creature to feel any fear, and the sighs of pleasure and approbation at the vision spoke of the onlookers' sense of privilege to have been there to witness the sight.

So intent was the gaze of everyone in the room, including Mina, that it was some moments before she realised that Richard had vanished. Not that she imagined anything supernatural had occurred, rather that he had slipped quietly to one side while all eyes were on the lovely Nellie. After some graceful movements of her arms, the beautiful sprite, who might have been thought to have done quite enough to ensure her lasting fame, began to float away from her position above the vase from which she had apparently risen, and fly slowly about the little stage. She might have been merely swaying from one side to another, but the illusion that she was actually circling in the air around the vase, but several feet from the floor, was very compelling. Nothing like it had been seen in Brighton before, or possibly anywhere, and some of the ladies were actually sobbing quietly.

Slowly, the delicate sprite flew down to alight on the floor, and then she turned towards the side of the stage and with all the grace of a ballerina extended one arm. There was a small movement of her fingers, which produced the soft rattle of a tambourine. She beckoned, and from behind the curtains the instrument appeared, bathed in an opalescent light, and hovering in the air. Slowly it rose in an arc, like the sun ascending the heavens, and all the time it quivered and sounded. Higher and higher it rose, as if being guided by her gestures, until it reached a peak, and then declined again, finally disappearing behind the curtain on the other side.

The lovely apparition advanced a little, and stood before Mr Jordan, slowly beating her wings, and fixed him with a very enigmatic expression. Mr Jordan, who, if his eyes had started out from his head any more than they were, would have found himself blind, recoiled in terror. He had had no compunction about roughly clasping the figure of Phoebe in his arms, but as he gazed on the fairy creature before him, he was both struck dumb and too afraid to even think of reaching out to touch her. She laughed, and it was a sound like bells. Then, she began to dance.

It was a sight more appropriate to a gentlemen's private booth at a fairground than the drawing room of a respectable widow; still, since the dancer was not after all a living creature, the display of sinuous movements could be excused as unconscious innocence. Her arms were so like serpents that one expected them to turn into silver snakes and snap and hiss, while the undulating motion of her upper body supported by a supple spine pronounced her at once to be other than human.

Her dance done, she swirled lightly around, and tripped back to stand beside the vase, then turned and faced the throng in all her pale star-like glory. Her fingers moved as though she was casting a spell, and slowly she rose up into the air. The silvery smoke began to flow from the vase again, and she slowly dissolved into it and was gone. Just as everyone thought they had seen enough wonders, so the form of Mr Ricardo appeared on an instant before their eyes.

The audience burst into spontaneous applause, which he received with great humility. When the room was silent once more, their host said, 'And now it only remains for the etheric power to return to the body of Miss Foxton.' He circled about the vase once more, and a little wisp of light appeared in his hand. He guided the glowing trail carefully back across the stage to the sleeping body of the medium, and after urging it back below the covering cloak, he needed to do no more than stand by making encouraging gestures as the material flowed in of its own volition. When the last of it had gone, he went to the vase and, tilting it, demonstrated to the audience that it was empty. He then made what Mina assumed to be counter-mesmeric passes over the form of Miss Foxton, who awoke with a sigh, threw back the cloak, took the hand of her gallant magnetiser and rose to her feet. Both made courteous bows to the company before Mr Ricardo came forward and closed the curtains once more.

As the lights went up the room was awash with conversation and everyone stared accusingly at Mr Jordan, who seemed uncertain as to whether he had received a blessing or a curse, since his face alternated between the pallor of fear and a flush of embarrassment. He utterly declined to describe his feelings — even Mr Conroy could get no words from him — and they hurried away, although Mina saw them pause in the hallway and Mr Jordan take a one-pound note from his pocket book and hand it to his friend. Mr Clee also left the house taking care not to speak to anyone on the way.

Chapter Seventeen

Mina had already told her mother that she would not be dining at home that night. Louisa had probably assumed that there would be sufficient refreshment at Mrs Peasgood's but Mina had other plans, a table she had reserved in a nearby restaurant at which she would entertain Richard and Miss Gilden, an invitation which they had accepted eagerly and for which Mina expected to pay.

She was joined at the table at the appointed time, Richard having doffed the mask and moustache, and scrubbed the oil from his hair, while Miss Gilden, her cascade of amber curls neatly dressed, was wearing a charming costume in a shade of blue that was only a little too bright. Whatever her origins, she was clearly experienced in restaurant etiquette and handled the silver and glassware with delicacy and assurance. Even viewed across the table, and with powder and paint so subtle that it was hard to be sure if she had applied any or not, she was a very lovely young woman, although unlikely to be as young as the claimed seventeen. Richard naturally took command of the table and ordered food and wine like a lord.

'I must congratulate you both on an extraordinary demonstration,' said Mina, as they waited for their soups and beefsteaks to arrive.

'Yes, it went mightily well,' said Richard. 'Mind you, I thought we were in for some trouble at the start when Mr Jordan decided to put his oar in. Nellie had already done what was needed for the next part and had to undo it, if you see what I mean. Fortunately Mrs Peasgood's observations gave her a few moments and all was well. It helped us, too, that he started up so early when we had not yet drawn out the etheric force, or he might have demanded to look into the vase. I think that was what he had in mind the second time he spoke but by then our hostess had had enough of him, as we all had, and put him in his place.'

'About the vase ...' said Mina.

'Oh, I popped in to see Mother and told her it needed repair,' said Richard, helping himself to buttered rolls. 'Don't worry, I'll put it back.'

'I suppose,' said Mina, 'that neither of you will tell me how you achieved such startling effects?'

Miss Gilden sipped wine and smiled sweetly. 'Oh, we like to keep our professional secrets,' she said.

'All I can say,' said Richard with a wink, 'is that I have been at great expense for a large roll of black velvet.'

Mina decided not to remind him of whose expense it had actually been.

'All the other materials and costume we required I already had in my possession,' said Miss Gilden, carefully omitting to mention how they had come into her possession or the opinion of M. Baptiste on the matter.

'We have been engaged for three more evenings,' said Richard, 'and this time, we may command five shillings a ticket. It will be a rather longer display but I am sure we are equal to it. Once we have our funds in place Nellie has some marvellous ideas about new sensations, which will need very little additional expense. In time we may even be able to hire a theatre and see what wonders we can perform in the mode of Professor Pepper.'

'He creates the most beautiful apparitions,' said Miss Gilden, with a dreamy look, as if seeing herself as a veritable ghost.

'But surely people know it is all a trick?' said Mina.

'Professor Pepper makes no secret of it, but there are some who like to hope that it is not a trick at all but real,' said Richard. 'Did you know that there are those who try to expose mediums by performing the same tricks and then explaining how they are done?'

'Do they have any success?' asked Mina eagerly, wondering if she could engage the services of such a person.

'None at all,' said Richard with a cheerful shrug, 'the mediums simply say that their accusers are themselves mediums and hiding their powers either knowingly or unconsciously under the guise of conjuring. And, of course, the dispute only adds to the fame of all concerned.'

'I wish someone would expose Mr Home,' said Mina, with some feeling. 'He is little more than a thief.'

'He is a slippery fellow and no mistake, but a clever one, and therefore very rich,' said Miss Gilden. 'But even if he was shown to be a fraud it would make no difference.'

Plates of hot soup were brought to the table, and they all ate, although Mina had less appetite than her companions.

'Have you ever seen the Davenport brothers?' asked Miss Gilden.

'I have read of them,' said Mina. 'They sit inside a cabinet and make musical instruments fly about and have a trick with a coat.'

'Some five or six years ago a watchmaker called Maskelyne witnessed one of their performances, saw how their tricks were done, and promised that he could do them as well. He and his friend Cooke constructed their own cabinet, advertised an exhibition and did all the Davenports' tricks and more, but in full light. They have since gone into the conjuring business themselves.'

'But the Davenports still command an audience,' said Mina. 'They were in London in 1868.'

'Oh yes, Mr Maskelyne did them no harm at all,' said Nellie. 'Just because their tricks could be performed by conjuring does not prove to the spiritualists that this was how the Davenports actually performed them. And the public wants, indeed prefers, to believe that they are communing with the spirits of the dead. It makes the evening more exciting.'

'Would you be willing,' asked Mina, hesitantly, 'to go to one of Miss Eustace's séances and observe how she carries out her tricks? There are some things I think I can guess. I believe she clothes herself as her spirit guide by untying her hands and having some means of changing her garments very quickly.'

'Undoubtedly,' said Miss Gilden. 'Tell me, is there much hymn singing at her séances?'

'Oh yes, Professor and Mrs Gaskin make a very great thing of it; they wish to be thought of as holy.'

Miss Gilden laughed her little bell-like laugh. 'Religion is no more than another disguise. Remember, everything has two faces. When something is shown to you openly and its purpose explained, it really has another secret one. I am sure that Miss Eustace asked very particularly for the hymn singing, as proof of the godliness of her endeavours. The true effect is of course to create noise, to conceal any sounds she might make such as the rustling of silk as she slips out of her costume.'

'Something you did not require,' said Mina.

'Ah, well,' said Miss Gilden archly, 'I have my own methods, which, of course, I cannot describe. My experience is of the stage, where we do not perform in darkness, and neither does our audience sing hymns. I will certainly attend one of Miss Eustace's assemblies, but I do not feel it would be appropriate for me to reveal how she accomplishes her feats.'

Mina was disappointed, but felt she must accept this. Although Miss Gilden might have regarded Miss Eustace as a rival, she would also have seen her as a member of the same profession. Theatre people living on the borders of respectable society had formed their own circle where they would be freely accepted, and assist fellow members in times of difficulty. To reveal the professional secrets of another would have been an act of betrayal, not only of an individual but a class.

The soup plates were cleared, and their steaks and potatoes arrived. Richard, looking pleased at the free and friendly conversation between his sister and his mistress, attacked his meal heartily while Mina and Miss Gilden ate with more decorum.

'Have you never thought,' said Miss Gilden, 'of going on the stage yourself?'

Mina was shocked by that question, not so much by the idea that she might enter the theatrical profession, but the thought that she might be in demand as some kind of novelty for audiences to stare at. Miss Gilden sawed neatly at her steak with no idea that she might have said anything disturbing, and Mina realised that for her, such displays would not be unusual. 'I am not at all sure what I might do upon the stage,' she said. 'I am certain that no-one would part with money to hear me sing or see me dance.'

'But you may personate a child very convincingly,' said Miss Gilden, 'and you have a good speaking voice. If there is no role already written for you I am sure one could be done. Could you dress as a boy? You would be a great success as Tiny Tim.'

Richard gave a concerned glance at his sister, unsure of how she might react, but Mina could only laugh. Used to the pointing fingers of children, or pitying stares of adults who quickly turned away, or the embarrassed whispers of miraculous cures, she had not encountered anyone who was so bold as to comment unashamedly on the practical applications of her unusual appearance.

'Thank you,' she said, 'but my energies are directed another way.'

'Mina writes stories for children,' said Richard, hastily.

For a moment Mina regretted that she had not yet revealed the nature of her endeavours to her own brother, but reflected that if she did so his lack of caution might lead to unwanted disclosures.

'I accept,' said Mina to Miss Gilden, 'that since I am not of the theatre you will not reveal Miss Eustace's secrets to me, but would you be able to comment on whether what she does is a manifestation of the supernatural or conjuring tricks?'

'I can do that without seeing her,' said Nellie, calmly. 'It is the latter. But I am curious to see her, all the same.'

'The rapping noises for example?' said Mina, hoping that by addressing specifics she might draw out more information. 'I recall that at the first séance I attended Miss Eustace was bound to a chair, but the noises were all about the room; the walls, the floor, even the ceiling.'

'There are a hundred ways in which that can be done,' said Miss Gilden, 'whether the medium is bound or not.'

'Tilting of tables?' Mina persisted.

'One of the easiest tricks there is. A child could do it.'

'And making the table rise up from the ground without touching it? Without anyone touching it. It left the floor, completely, I saw it myself.'

Miss Gilden paused and looked reflective. 'Ah, now that is interesting. Was Miss Eustace alone at the table or was she part of a circle?'

Mina described what she had seen, and Miss Gilden gave it some thought. Richard ordered another bottle of wine and stared at his pretty companion with open admiration. 'You see, Nellie is both beautiful and clever!' he announced. 'All our demonstration was her invention. But my lips are, of course, sealed.'

'Not only did the table trick astound us all, but the effect of it was to turn an avowed sceptic into her devoted acolyte,' said Mina.

'Oh, please explain!' said Miss Gilden eagerly, and Mina told her the story of Mr Clee's conversion, his appearance at her house and his part in the séance at Dr Hamid's.

The steak plates were removed, and Richard called for a list of iced puddings, which he studied with interest.

'I cannot imagine how the trickery at Dr Hamid's was effected,' said Mina. 'Obviously I must suspect that Mr Clee was somehow involved as nothing at all happened before he arrived, but both his hands were held fast the whole time. I had hold of one of them myself.'

'Oh, that would pose no difficulty for an adept in the business,' said Miss Gilden. 'One might easily free a hand to perform tricks while making it appear that both were being held. Everything you have described to me is simplicity itself if the practitioner has had sufficient time to master it.'

'But he is not an adept, unless he achieved mastery of the art in a few days,' Mina said. 'Is that even possible?'

'To learn sleight of hand and have the confidence to carry it off alone, with no confederate, in such a short time?' Miss Gilden shook her head. 'No, that would surprise me.'

'Well, that's a conundrum,' said Richard, beckoning the waiter, but Mina, with a sudden flash of understanding, thought that she had the answer, an answer that would explain not only how the lifting of the table had been done but everything else. It was, however, impossible to prove that her idea was right. Denouncing or even plainly demonstrating fraud was, she now saw, no obstacle to the medium and would not deter passionate supporters who clung to their admired favourites and their beliefs. Miss Eustace and her kind remained unassailable.

On the following afternoon Mina was able to study the most recent edition of the *Quarterly Journal of Science* in which its editor, the notable Mr Crookes FRS, had published his own contribution. She could not help but wonder if any other journal would have been so accommodating. The very title 'Experimental Investigation of a New Force' seemed to tell the whole of the story she needed to know; nevertheless, she read on. Mr Crookes had begun his work fired with a belief in phenomena that he thought were inexplicable by any known natural laws, a position which from the point of view of scientific disinterest seemed to Mina to be a poor one. The most remarkable exponent of this force was, he declared, Mr D.D. Home, and it was on the basis of his extensive work with that gentleman that he was able to affirm so conclusively his belief in that force. The marvels which Mr Home had performed before the astonished eyes of Mr Crookes and other observers, who were friends of his, consisted of extracting a tune from an accordion while holding it in his fingertips at the opposite end to the keys, and later while it was being held by another person, and affecting the weight shown by a spring balance by lightly touching the end of a board to which it was attached.

Mina could not explain how Mr Home performed his tricks, and did not expect to be able to do so. If Mr Home had fooled learned men in front of their faces, she was unlikely to be able to devise an answer. She noticed, however, that Mr Crookes was wont to describe the force as 'capricious' and that even the miraculous Mr Home was subject to its unaccountable ebbs and flows. This was his explanation for a number of earlier failed demonstrations, Mr Home's power being 'very variable and at times entirely absent.'

Mr Crookes, thought Mina, was, like Professor Gaskin, too ready to explain away these difficulties in the light of his own prejudices. How likely was it that this supposed force of nature could be present one day and not the next? Did gravity vary from day to day? Did the tide sometimes choose not to appear? She thought not. Mr Crookes in presenting his own case had also, however, unintentionally pointed out its flaws. Everything, Miss Gilden had said, had two faces. Whatever methods Mr Home had used to produce his results, he must have been unable to perform his tricks or chosen not to attempt them when the conditions, which had nothing to do with any supernatural force, were not right. He might even have used those failed attempts to familiarise himself with the equipment and artefacts provided, and learn how he might achieve success in future.

A gentleman called Cox had been present and he had been sufficiently impressed by the phantom accordion and the beam balance trick to suggest that the force used by Mr Home should be given a name. He proposed to call it 'Psychic Force', and suggested that those in whom it manifested itself should be termed 'Psychics'. Personally Mina preferred the word 'charlatan'.

Chapter Eighteen

Over the next few days Mina's pressing anxiety over her mother was alleviated; that lady had abruptly departed for London to visit her eldest daughter and family, saying that her assistance was needed with a domestic difficulty that she declined to describe. This inevitably created a new anxiety for Mina over her sister Enid, although she could not help wondering if the 'domestic difficulty' was the robust good health of Enid's husband, the desperately dull but worthy Mr Inskip.

With time on her hands, Mina was able to complete her story of the ghostly orchestra, although the helpful shade that had guided the heroine to freedom had transmuted since her first imagining of the tale from a young girl with long pale hair to a very small lady with a sweet face. Her next literary endeavour had as its heroine a mother who was obliged to assist her daughter in disposing of the corpse of her son-in-law, who had succumbed to a dose of arsenic in his soup.

She composed her story as she exercised, or took gentle walks in the gardens and on the promenade and piers. She didn't mind the crowds or the noise, or the quick stares that flickered away, or even the assumption made by worried onlookers, when she looked over the pier rails into the crashing sea, that she was contemplating ending an unbearable existence, rather than trying to calculate how long a man's body would take to be washed up on shore. It was a harsh ending for Mr Inskip, his mouth full of seaweed and teeth battered by pebbles, and dead, dead eyes. If only, she mused, all difficulties could be addressed so easily, but her thoughts brought her no answers, and she was even tempted to waste sixpence on a visit to Madame Proserpina, but decided against it.

She saw nothing of Richard, and assumed that he was busily engaged establishing his new career as an impresario of supernatural entertainment, although she was not sure if she should be glad of this or not. It was, admittedly, a source of income, and provided that he did not squander it, as he seemed to do with every other item of value that came into his hands, might make him independent of their mother. After all, M. Robert-Houdin had made a very respectable living on the stage for many years. Their father would in all probability have thought it a wonderful joke and made eyes at Miss Gilden. One afternoon, while Mina was out having her steam bath, the oriental vase reappeared in the hallway, with only a small crack on its rim that had not been there before.

The arrival of Miss Foxton in Brighton had not, to Mina's great disappointment, created any difficulty for Miss Eustace. Each lady had her own coterie, and as Richard had predicted there was ample room for them both in the town. There was no suggestion in any of the prevailing gossip that the two were rivals. If anything, the excitement regarding Miss Foxton had merely served to increase the general interest in spirit mediums, and while Nellie Gilden quickly acquired a large number of admirers, Miss Eustace's fame also advanced. Mina had not heard a great deal of Mr Bradley, but saw from the newspapers that he was continuing to advertise his healing circles and assumed that he still prospered. While she was prepared under sufferance to accompany her mother to his pious demonstrations, she had no intention of going of her own volition.

With no new scheme in mind with which to end the career of Miss Eustace, Mina could only wait and hope that the craze would end, or that some other opponent more powerful than herself, another Mr Maskelyne perhaps, would appear, or that Miss Gilden's observations might provide some clue that would assist her.

The clue, when it did appear, came, however, from another source.

The newspapers had recently reported the death of a Mrs Apperley, a long-time resident of Brighton who was well known for her charitable work. As Mina read a lengthy appreciation of this selfless paragon, a detail that particularly caught her attention was that the lady had been eighty-six. This was the age mentioned by the young solicitor Ronald Phipps as that of the lady who had denounced Miss Eustace. Could Mrs Apperley have been the lady to whom he had referred? He had been silent as to her name, since she was a client, and Mina wondered how she might discover more. The only obstacle to this lady being the one Mr Phipps mentioned was that the visit to the medium had taken place in London and Mrs Apperley had never, to Mina's knowledge, lived in London.

The next time she visited Dr Hamid's baths Mina mentioned Mrs Apperley and her sad demise, and learned that the lady had been a regular customer. Mina was quite open with Anna Hamid about the reasons for her interest, and found her forthcoming, since none of what she had to say was in any way confidential information or related to her patient's medical condition or treatment. On the last visit before her final illness Mrs Apperley had mentioned Miss Eustace, asking if Anna had ever been to one of her séances, commenting only that she had been once and would not trouble herself to go again. Mrs Apperley had never lived in London, but she did, it transpired, have a niece, a Lady Dunkley, who resided there, and a great-nephew of whom she was very fond.

Following Eliza's death, Anna and her brother had determined to devote themselves wholly to each other, Dr Hamid's children and their patients. Both lived with a grief that was weighty and relentless, but they had been able to take comfort from the fact that what they did for others was inspired by their sister.

The energy that Anna had once directed to the care of Eliza had now been transferred to Mina. There was a new kind of steady and concentrated focus on building Mina's strength and endurance, something with which Mina was more than happy to comply. They often worked together as she learned and refined her exercises, and the benefits were becoming apparent. Mina could see a new firmness in her muscles, which were beginning to achieve a defined shape quite out of keeping with what might have been thought womanly. It was pleasing to have such a secret, to have hidden power in her tiny frame. Anna was also experimenting with new ideas for exercises to benefit scoliosis patients for which Eliza would not have been sufficiently robust and Mina was her willing subject. One room in the bathhouse premises was now devoted to assisting patients with careful exercise, and was furnished with all the items that one might need, including a ladder of wooden bars that had been fastened to the wall. Mina had to perform a set of stretches while holding on to the bars, and under Anna's eyes found the heights that were best for her, sometimes grasping with one hand a little higher than the other to try and align her obstinate spine. In time, said Anna cautiously, she might even progress to lifting her feet from the floor and hanging her full weight from the bar, but not yet, she warned, and not without supervision.

The date and location of Mrs Apperley's funeral had been announced in the newspapers, and at the appointed time Mina joined the large throng who attended the service at St George's Kemp Town to give thanks for a long life spent in the service of others. It was not hard to identify the small grouping of people who were the family of the deceased, and Mina's request to be allowed a brief interview with Lady Dunkley was quickly agreed to, it being assumed from her appearance that she was one of Mrs Apperley's charitable cases who wished to offer her personal appreciation.

'Lady Dunkley,' said Mina humbly, 'it is very kind of you to spare a little of your time to speak to me.'

'Not at all,' replied that lady, who had a ready smile. 'Were you well acquainted with my aunt?'

'It is my great regret that I was not,' Mina admitted, 'but here in Brighton, she was generally famed and revered for her devotion to the poor and afflicted. There was, I have learned recently, another more unusual matter that concerned her, and I hope to be able to continue her work in that area.'

'That is very good of you, and it would be much appreciated,' said Lady Dunkley, supplying a small card. 'Please do let me know if there is any way in which I can assist.'

'Thank you,' said Mina. 'For the moment, I require only one small piece of information. Mrs Apperley very recently expressed her doubts about the activities of spirit mediums here in Brighton, who she felt were preying on the bereaved and doing great harm. In the case of one such lady, whose name it might not be politic to mention, she thought she had encountered her once before, in London. Did she perhaps mention this to you?'

'I am afraid not,' said Lady Dunkley. 'We have been abroad for the last six months and I have not seen my aunt to speak to her in that time. In London, you say?' She shook her head. 'My aunt did not visit London very frequently. After she passed eighty travel was very difficult for her. The last time, to my knowledge, that she was in London was almost two years ago for the christening of my grandson.'

'If I may be so bold,' asked Mina, 'when precisely did that take place?'

Lady Dunkley was clearly a little startled at the way the conversation had turned. She hesitated, and the ready smile faded, but after a few moments, as Mina had anticipated, accommodated the wishes of the little woman with the misshapen body who stood before her. 'It was in the early part of September 1869.'

'Do you think it possible that your aunt did go to a spirit medium during that visit?' Mina asked.

Lady Dunkley was even further taken aback by that question, and Mina feared that her boldness had made her venture too far. 'I can only say,' replied the lady, carefully, 'that it was a subject she did once mention to me as a great curiosity, in that it was a subject of conversation in society, but I am afraid I cannot advise you further.'

Mina thanked the lady warmly, and departed. Once home, she packaged up the manuscript of her recently completed story to send to Mr Greville, and included a letter advising him that she had been reading about spirit mediums with the idea of writing a new story to feature one who was guilty of a terrible crime. She had been told of a scandal in London regarding a lady who had been conducting séances in the capital, most probably in September 1869, and had been detected in fraud and sent to prison. Unfortunately she did not have the lady's name, but hoped Mr Greville might know of, or be able to discover, something about the incident.

Since Eliza's death Mina had not seen a great deal of Dr Hamid, although they occasionally met briefly when she visited the baths. After the confidences they had shared, which had seemed to add warmth to their friendship, he had made no more attempts to initiate a conversation, and she wondered if he had regretted his openness. On her next visit to the baths Mina mentioned this to Anna, saying that she hoped she had said nothing to offend her brother. Anna smiled sadly.

'The fault is not yours,' she said. 'I am sorry to say that Daniel has been receiving visits from Miss Eustace, two so far and I believe another is planned.'

'You mean he has paid her for private consultations?' said Mina, both concerned and disappointed.

'I am afraid so. I would prefer it if he did not, but I could not dissuade him.'

'Do you feel he takes any benefit from these consultations?' asked Mina. 'They may all be fraud, but if he finds some comfort in them then maybe — just for a short while —'

'It is hard to be sure,' said Anna, although her worried expression betrayed her feelings. 'You may imagine how it was for him to lose both a wife and a sister within months of each other. He looks for hope and it is hard to reason with him. He knows I do not approve and declines to speak to me on the subject. I think he knows very well that you would be of the same opinion as I, and it is for that reason he avoids speaking to you.'

'I am pleased to hear it,' said Mina, after some thought. 'It shows that he still retains a healthy doubt in what he is doing. Had he been convinced that he was right he would have been so armoured with certainty as to be impregnable to all argument and would be eager to try and convince me, too.'

'I am wondering if he has been warned that you are a bad influence best avoided,' said Anna, awkwardly.

'Oh, I do hope so!' said Mina. 'What could be more fascinating? I shall see him at once.'

'What will you say?' asked Anna.

'If you will permit me, I will be bold with him and ask what messages he has received,' said Mina. 'Miss Eustace, in her private consultations, convinces people that she is genuine by providing personal details of the departed, things which it would seem only their closest family and friends know. Everything else Miss Eustace does, be it ringing bells or raising tables off the floor, can be put down to conjuring tricks. Even the believers in such phenomena who put them down to a supernatural force are not convinced that there is an actual guiding intelligence causing them; they think it is some form of energy produced by the medium, and not the actual spirits of the dead. The private séances, however, leave us with only two possibilities — that Miss Eustace is genuinely bringing messages from the departed or that she is an outright fraud with some secret means of finding out information. Perhaps there might be something in what your brother has experienced which will help us decide.' She paused. 'I do not wish to add to his burdens; only tell me I am wrong and I will go.'

'You are very welcome to try,' said Anna. 'What you learn may do good. Sometimes people will confide in friends what they will not tell their most intimate family.'

'That is true,' said Mina. 'My mother claims to have seen my father's ghost and received messages from him of a private nature, but will tell me no more than that. Perhaps I should interview her great friend, Mrs Bettinson, or her dressmaker, who will no doubt have all the details.'

When Mina knocked on the door of Dr Hamid's office she was careful not to speak, since if he was avoiding her, hearing her voice would have given him the opportunity to plead some other appointment. She knew that he was kindly and would not thoughtlessly turn anyone away even if he was busy, and as she expected he bade her enter. As soon as she saw him, his little guilty hesitation tainted with poorly concealed dismay showed that her surmise was correct; he was ashamed of himself for consulting Miss Eustace, but was unable to give up the visits, and thought that Mina was there to scold him.

They made the usual polite enquiries after each other's health and Mina asked about purchasing some mineral water. He tried to divert her to the lady at the reception desk, but Mina said, 'I will see about it on my way out, but I have more important matters to discuss.'

'If this is to be a long consultation, then perhaps —' he began.

'No, this cannot wait for another time,' she said. 'You know, I think, some of what I have come here to say, but I beg you to hear me out. I understand that you have attended private consultations with Miss Eustace, and I do not blame you for that, neither do I ask you to do anything other than what you feel will benefit you.'

'But you have a mission in mind, or you would not be here,' he said, folding his arms and leaning back in his chair.

'Of course I do,' said Mina, 'and an important one. You may hold in your hands the whole secret of whether or not Miss Eustace is genuine.'

'But supposing,' he said, 'I do not care whether she is or not?'

'Today you may care nothing at all,' said Mina. 'Today, if someone was to offer you conclusive proof that she is a fraud you would prefer not to know. Another day may be different, and then we may talk of this again. The difference between us is that I care very much, but I promise you that whatever the answer is, whatever the truth may prove to be, I will accept it.'

There was a long pause as he stared at his pen, which he had laid aside when Mina entered. He looked as though he very much wanted to take up the pen again and work on his papers, anything other than engage in the conversation she so earnestly wished for. He needed to choose, thought Mina, between his previous accepted view of the world, untrammelled by emotion, and a comfort that he knew in his heart was really an illusion; but he was not yet ready to make that choice. He seemed on the verge of taking the easy path and saying that he did not want to speak on the subject that so consumed his visitor, but as he gazed on Mina, there was a very slight sad smile, the capitulation of a man who saw his inevitable fate.

'I — received a message from Eliza,' he said at last. 'She said that she was in no pain, and I was grateful for that. I know that any charlatan might have invented such a message, but there was one detail about the seat and the nature of the pain that suggested to me that the message could only have come from Eliza. It was something she only ever spoke of to Anna and myself. What more can I say?'

It was a small point, but a convincing one, and she had to admit it took some of the energy from her campaign. He looked so dejected that she decided not to press him further, and wished him well.

She returned home to study the most recent edition of the *Gazette* and found that the arrival of a new medium in Brighton had encouraged a renewal of correspondence on the subject of spiritualism, some of which was from Professor Gaskin, and some from Mr Bradley, who wholeheartedly supported the world of the spirit as a very real, holy and beneficial phenomenon.

One correspondent, who declined to mention his or her name but hid behind the *nom de plume* of FAIR SPEECH, advanced the theory that only some of the manifestations at séances were honest, but that proving one instance of fakery did not mean the medium concerned was a fraud. Even genuine mediums might find their powers failing them on occasion, and having to meet the expectation of their admiring audiences they were sometimes obliged to resort to a little trickery in order to provide a performance. This, thought Mina, was yet another argument that meant that even a medium caught out in a blatant cheat could escape exposure. The poor, hard-pressed and exhausted medium, anxious to please the public, was thereby transformed from a charlatan to an object of sympathy.

In this curious war between the believers and the sceptics, the medium, she realised, was always bound to win. Even a temporary setback could be overcome and the beloved of the spirits would rise again stronger than before. The reason was obvious — the sceptic was a creature of the intellect, using sense and calm reasoning, whereas the supporters of the mediums were led by their emotions; more than that, their passionate need to believe in a more immediate afterlife than promised by scripture, the continued happy existence of loved ones they had lost, and their own immortality. Attack that, and one attacked the fundamental human desire to deny death, a fortress that appeared unassailable.

The one thing that might weaken the power of the mediums was the thing that Mina had been told would never happen — war within their number, which might lead to incaution and therefore revelations that might not otherwise have been made. But mediums, like conjurers, knew each other's secrets, perhaps even exchanged them, and supported each other when needed, and an attack on one was an attack on them all. A betrayal could easily rebound to the detriment of the accuser. Mina realised that if she wanted a war between the mediums she would have to start one herself.

Chapter Nineteen

It was a difficult path to tread, but after some thought Mina felt she had the answer. It was useless to make accusations of fraud, she could see that now, unless she had some very compelling evidence, which was not as yet in her possession, but there was another course she might take. Mina took up her pen and wrote a letter, which she decided to send to all the Brighton newspapers.

Sir,

I have been a spiritualist for many years and have followed with some interest the correspondence on this subject in your pages. There are, as your readers will be aware, two ladies currently residing in Brighton who have been conducting séances. Both have impressed the populace with their sincerity, and the manifestations produced have been of the very highest order; nevertheless, I feel strongly motivated to express my concerns regarding the demonstrations by the most recent arrival in this town. The medium who has been holding séances during the last few weeks is a lady of unquestionable respectability, who has always conducted herself with great modesty, and there has been nothing in either her deportment or her exhibitions that could arouse concern. The same, however, cannot be said of the lady who is newly arrived. The apparition which comes at her command and flies about the room in such a remarkable way may well be clad in a manner appropriate to the regions of spirit from which she comes, but such a sight is not to be tolerated in a drawing room, especially where there are ladies of quality present. Rumour has it, and I earnestly hope that this is rumour and nothing more, that these demonstrations are largely patronised by single gentlemen, and not a few married gentlemen who ought to know better. Is this true? I hope your readers will enlighten me.

Yours truly,
A SPIRITUALIST
Brighton

Mina thought the letter to be of sufficient interest, provoking without being actually actionable, to be taken up by at least one, if not all, the newspapers in Brighton, but that was only the first part of her plan. She carefully prepared two more letters, which she would send once the first was published.

Sir,

I read with considerable concern the attack upon the character of Miss Foxton, who although not named, was undoubtedly the subject of A SPIRITUALIST's letter in your last issue. The writer claims to have been interested in spiritualism for many years but is quite ignorant of the manifestations that with the natural innocence of the newborn babe may appear. He — or is it a she? — with no understanding of these phenomena, chooses to insult Miss Foxton, who cannot be at fault in this matter. I suggest that A SPIRITUALIST write at once to withdraw the unfounded remarks, which include the vilest of rumours. I do not profess to know who the author might be, but do I perhaps detect a motive for the attack — i.e. professional jealousy?

Yours truly,
BRIGHTONIAN
Kemp Town

Sir,

I feel I must protest in the strongest possible terms against the tone and insinuations of the letter from A SPIRITUALIST published in your recent edition. The identity and motives of the author are no mystery to me. A fawning acolyte of Miss Eustace, seeking to enhance his own fame by attaching himself to the lady, has misguidedly sought to add to her reputation by insulting another medium. Should material of this nature be tolerated in a respectable publication? I do not believe it should.

I have personally attended the séances of both the ladies referred to and consider them to be of equal merit and interest.

Yours truly,
A BELIEVER
Brighton

Mina posted the first letter and awaited developments. She had no concern about mounting an attack on Miss Foxton, which could only add to that young lady's fame, and she might make of it what she could. Miss Eustace, if she read the newspapers, which Mina felt sure she did, if only to be well acquainted with events and personalities in Brighton, would not appreciate until the second letter was published that it was she who was suspected of having written the first. Whether or not Mr Clee would recognise himself as the 'fawning acolyte' of her third letter she did not know. The accusation of indecency had a second purpose for Mina; it ensured that her mother, and quite probably those of her friends who knew Richard by sight, would continue to avoid Miss Foxton's séances.

Mina received a kind letter from Mr Greville, who thanked her for her new story, which he agreed to publish, but could not immediately recall having seen any item of news about the imprisonment of a medium for fraud. It was the kind of event that might have received only a paragraph, if that, in any reputable paper. He promised, however, that when he had the opportunity he would look into it further.

Mina's mother returned home, reporting that Enid was fully recovered from a mild attack of hysteria. Curiously, the natural disappointment that must have followed her daughter's recent discovery that she was not, as she had thought, about to become a mother again, had aided rather than delayed her return to health. Mr Inskip, confident that Enid was now well, had just gone abroad to undertake the negotiation of a property purchase by a reclusive nobleman, a loss which the abandoned wife was facing with commendable fortitude.

By the time Louisa Scarletti was preparing to plunge back into Brighton life, the letter denouncing Miss Foxton had appeared in the *Brighton Herald*, and was read with the triumphant declaration that she had always known there was something not quite right about Miss Foxton.

'I have heard,' said Mina, who was rather enjoying stirring the bubbling pot of suspicion, 'that the two ladies are deadly rivals and dislike each other intensely. I would have thought that there was room enough in Brighton for two spirit mediums, but they do not see it that way. I believe that the letter was written by an admirer of Miss Eustace — not the lady herself, who I am quite certain is above such things — who misguidedly seeks to harm Miss Foxton's reputation in order to elevate his or her favourite. And you may not yet have heard this, since you have not been in town, but there is a rumour being spread about Brighton that Miss Eustace has once been in prison for fraud. It surely cannot be true!'

Mina waited for her mother's shocked reaction to this news, but to her surprise she only said, 'And what if it were? That is just the kind of thing that might be an endorsement rather than proof of fraud.'

It took Mina a moment or two to understand that her mother had already heard the story, and dismissed it. 'Do you mean to say you already knew of it? Is it true?'

Louisa smiled. 'I really have no idea. But why should it matter, in any case? Why should it not be true, and no blemish upon the lady? Just because a martyr has been burned at the stake or torn apart by lions it does not make their cause any the less holy, indeed, it becomes more so. I had heard the story from somewhere, and did not trouble myself to enquire further.'

Mina was content. She knew that the seed she had planted would grow, and perhaps in time bear fruit.

Richard did not trouble himself to write to the newspapers in defence of Miss Foxton, but it was with Mina's second and third letters that interest in the rivalry between the mediums was fully aroused. Professor Gaskin in his role as Miss Eustace's patron wrote to deny in the strongest possible terms that she had written the first letter. Its composer was unknown to him, as was Miss Foxton, and his protégée was too kind and gentle an individual to become embroiled in such unpleasantness. His was not the only letter, however; there were several others supporting A SPIRITUALIST's contention that Miss Foxton's exhibitions were indecent, some who agreed with BRIGHTONIAN that the author of the first letter was undoubtedly from the phrasing, female, and a rival who had chosen to offer anonymous insults, and others who agreed with A BELIEVER that the production was that of the 'fawning acolyte', who was known to creep into the séances held by his favourite's rival. While the debate raged through the mails this was as nothing to the rumours that flowed around Brighton, borne by that most ephemeral and rapid means, the spoken word. Mina soon heard her own rumours return to her, but this time she was told with great certainty that Miss Eustace and Miss Foxton had met in the street and almost come to blows, and that the cause was not so much professional jealousy as the fact that both ladies were in love with Mr Clee.

Her mother felt impelled to add her voice to the general furore, and decided that the best mode of protest was for the adherents of Miss Eustace to compose a joint letter to the newspapers and possibly even present the lady with a memorial to show their appreciation. It was for this purpose that a small assembly was arranged in the Scarletti drawing room, to which all interested parties were invited.

Miss Eustace, being the subject of the meeting, was not present, but the throng included Mrs Bettinson, Miss Whinstone, Mr Clee, Mrs Parchment and Mr Bradley, who, while prevented from attending séances, had expressed himself an admirer of the lady in question. Miss Simmons occupied her usual corner, but instead of the downcast eyes and humble demeanour of a servant, she attended to the proceedings with some interest, as if she was one of the invited guests.

'You may or may not know this,' said Mr Bradley, evoking a strong desire in Mina to take one of her dumbbells and throw it at his head, 'but spirit mediums are often denounced by the ignorant, who envy their abilities and their fame.'

'We cannot educate those whose minds are closed to the truth,' said Mina's mother, 'rather I wish to console Miss Eustace that those of greater understanding support her unreservedly.'

The persons of greater understanding populating the room all nodded with expressions conveying relentless wisdom.

'I hope,' said Mrs Parchment, 'that we will be able to dispose of that foul slander on Mr Clee.'

'Oh indeed!' said that gentleman with a laugh. 'Why, I have never even met Miss Foxton, and you are all aware that my admiration for Miss Eustace is as pure as it is sincere. I have no attachment to either lady.'

'There are also some unpleasant rumours in town concerning an incident in London,' said Mina, 'events which are attributed to Miss Eustace, but which must have concerned another person entirely. I know nothing of the detail but it seems to have involved a spirit medium being sent to prison.'

'Well, I can assure you,' said Mr Bradley, with a broad smile, 'that I have never heard anything to the lady's detriment.'

'Nor I,' said Mr Clee. 'And recall that I have been until recently a most pronounced sceptic concerning mediumistic powers. Why, I used to read everything I could to support that prejudice. I was living in London at the time of that incident, and would most certainly have heard if Miss Eustace had been accused of any wrongdoing.'

'But these rumours will persist,' said Mina, 'and I am concerned that they may do harm to the lady's reputation. It is nothing short of slander, and must be stopped. I would suggest that our best course is to discover all we can about what occurred in London, and then when we know for certain the identity of the person involved we can publish our proof of Miss Eustace's innocence, and demand that the whispering stops.'

There was a slight pause, during which Mr Clee seemed about to say something, but restrained himself.

'That is not an easy thing to do,' said Mr Bradley, maintaining his smile with an effort. 'You may or may not know this, but —'

'Well, since you have both resided in London,' interrupted Mina's mother, 'perhaps you can tell us all if indeed there was any such incident as has been rumoured.'

'I am not aware of it,' said Mr Bradley, firmly.

'Nor I,' said Mr Clee, with equal conviction.

'Then that is our proof,' said Mina's mother. 'There is no need to try and find out more if the thing did not happen at all.'

'I think,' said Mr Clee, 'that anyone who is acquainted with Miss Eustace will know that she is incapable of carrying out a dishonourable act. That, I think, should be the whole tenor of our message.'

This was agreed and the meeting fell to discussing the wording of a letter to the press, and whether there should be a memorial or even a pamphlet.

Mina made no contribution to this, since she had her answer. When spreading the rumour of Miss Eustace's imprisonment she had said nothing about the date of the incident, yet Mr Clee had said he was living in London 'at the time.' It was a significant slip, which showed that he knew more than he was telling.

The next day Mina visited the reading rooms where she knew that a set of post office directories was kept, including those of both Brighton and the capital. Here she was able to discover a listing for the London business of the Theatrical Novelties Company, proprietor Benjamin Clee, costumiers and suppliers to the trade. Mr Benjamin Clee had been in this business for over twenty years and Mina wondered if he could be the father of Miss Eustace's new young admirer.

On her way home she thought carefully about the first séance at which Mr Clee had appeared, and the levitating table, and as soon as she was at her desk she drew a circle representing the table on a sheet of paper and marked on it from memory where all the members of the company had been seated. She thought that a great many conjuring tricks were effected by means of black silk threads and thin wires, but the table trick, because it had risen vertically and not tilted, could not be done by a single person. It followed that Miss Eustace had had an accomplice, and that both of them had come prepared with the apparatus they needed, perhaps hidden in the cuffs of their garments. Mr Clee had been seated exactly opposite Miss Eustace, at the furthest distance from her, supposedly to protect her from the interference of a sceptic, but this had actually positioned him where he needed to be to help her. When the table rose, the other sitters had moved back in alarm, but only Mr Clee, the very person who had suggested the test to begin with, had appeared to be holding his hands over its surface.

Mina was now certain that Mr Clee had never been a sceptic; he had been Miss Eustace's creature from the beginning. The two had probably been acquainted and in compact for some little time. The scepticism and the sudden conversion had been a pretence meant to add a touch of drama to the evening and increase the medium's fame. Mr Clee, Mina felt sure, was an accomplished conjurer, which explained how he had been able to perform all the mysteries that had appeared at Eliza Hamid's séance.

The next morning Mina received a letter from Mr Greville. He had found a small paragraph in a newspaper in October 1869 stating that a spirit medium and her husband had both been imprisoned for three months after claiming to have produced the ghost of a client's deceased child, which had proved to be a real child in white draperies. The fraud had been discovered because the tiny phantom had been unable to maintain the composure proper to such an occasion, gone into a fit of giggles, and dropped the spirit 'baby' he carried, which turned out to be a bundle of cloth. The client, outraged at the cruel deception for which she had parted with the sum of five guineas, would not be mollified by any explanation and had brought a prosecution. The medium had practised under the name Madame Peri, but her real name, the court had been told, was Clee.

Mina was unsure what to do with the new information, but decided, after some thought, to take it to Dr Hamid, whom she hoped had not lost his ability to reason. It was some encouragement to her that after she had described her discoveries and the conclusions she had drawn from them, he thought long and hard and even noted down what she had said.

'So,' he said at last, 'it is your contention that the lady called Clee who was sent to prison, presumably a Mrs Clee since the article states that she is married, is none other than Miss Eustace.'

'Yes,' said Mina. 'And since I can make a convincing case that she was well acquainted with, and in collusion with, Mr Clee long before they went through that theatrical ploy of his conversion to her cause, he must be her husband.'

'You have no portrait of this Mrs Clee,' Dr Hamid pointed out, 'so the identification rests solely on the word of Mrs Apperley, and neither do you have the name of the lady she saw, but if she did see this Mrs Clee, and that is far from certain, she last saw her two years ago. Mrs Apperley was then eighty-four years of age. More recently when she was in a state of failing health that led to her death soon afterwards, she concluded that Mrs Clee and Miss Eustace were one and the same. I cannot see a court accepting evidence of that nature. And, of course, Mrs Apperley cannot now be consulted on the matter.'

Mina was tempted to mention that Mrs Apperley's standing as a recently deceased person ought not in some people's minds be an obstacle to the lady being questioned, but restrained herself from commenting. 'But is it not a remarkable coincidence,' she said, 'that the medium who Mrs Apperley said resembles, indeed is Miss Eustace, was actually called Clee? That is not a common name. And then we have Mr Benjamin Clee of London, who is in the very profession that suggests the family has an intimate knowledge of the stage.'

'It is certainly possible,' admitted Dr Hamid, cautiously, 'that Mr Clee is a member of that family, but the connection may not be a close one. Even if he is the son of Benjamin Clee, that proves nothing. He may well once have been a sceptic but later became convinced. And this Mrs Clee need not be a wife, but a cousin or some other relative, or even not related at all. You don't know if it is her real name.'

'But Mr Clee has lied to us,' said Mina. 'Whatever the connection he has with Miss Eustace, he has concealed it, represented himself as a new acquaintance and colluded with her in a piece of trickery which they had arranged between themselves before he even came to the séance. If he has been engaged in that dishonesty, what else is he hiding from us?'

Dr Hamid nodded, and for a while Mina hoped that her arguments were having some effect. She could see in his face the struggle that was taking place in his mind. 'I can understand what you are saying,' he said. 'If the levitation of the table was done as you suggest, with some apparatus concealed in the cuffs, then it does need two people standing opposite each other to perform it, and we might view it more as a theatrical demonstration than a communion with the spirits.'

'Exactly!' said Mina.

'But,' he continued carefully, 'I would maintain that what we see at the séances performed before an audience is different from what takes place at a private consultation.'

'In what way is it different?' asked Mina. 'We have caught them out in a deception. I know that some people claim that mediums sometimes perform conjuring tricks to please the faithful when their powers temporarily desert them, but do you really believe that?'

'Perhaps,' he suggested, 'we might regard the public séances as if they were only a means of advertising the private ones. Perhaps we cannot blame the medium too much for a little — I would not go so far as to call it fraud —'

'I would,' said Mina. 'The rappings and rattling tambourines and spirit faces made of nothing more than rags dipped in some phosphorus material are all trickery which Miss Eustace wants us to believe proceed from the spirits of the dead.'

He shook his head. 'I don't believe she has ever made that claim,' he said. 'Even Professor Gaskin thinks that these phenomena come not from some spirit intelligence, but are a manifestation of the medium's own powers; some force within her own body which she can mould and use.'

'But the lifting of the table —' Mina protested.

'I can see that it is possible that Mr Clee did assist in that, and you may be correct, he may be a relation, but even if he did help, he might have done no more than augment the powers that were already there. Perhaps Miss Eustace was unable to perform it alone. Mr Clee has said he is a strong negative and he might have been needed there to complete the circle.'

Mina stared helplessly at the unhappy man before her. 'What does Miss Eustace charge for a private séance?' she said at last.

He looked startled. 'She asks for nothing,' he said.

'Not directly, perhaps, but I know that she does receive payment from grateful clients. I have heard the sum of two or even five guineas mentioned. That is a goodly fee for an evening's work. Miss Eustace is on her way to becoming a rich woman. How much do you give her?'

He frowned. 'That is a private matter,' he said.

'Then you do give her money.'

'What I choose to give,' he said, with some annoyance, '— voluntarily you understand — is my concern. Now, if I may, I must return to my work. I have a patient I must see in a few minutes.'

'I don't wish to argue with you,' said Mina, sadly. 'I have had losses too and know how you feel. We may disagree strongly on this matter but let us at least be friends.'

He looked relieved that the questioning was over. 'Yes, of course. I am sorry if I spoke harshly. I did not mean to.'

'After all, Mr Jordan and Mr Conroy can be friends and even business partners despite their differences.'

He gave a faint smile. 'If I might change the subject of our conversation,' he said, 'Anna tells me you have been very diligent in your exercises, and I can see that you move more easily than you did.'

169

'Yes, I shall soon be like an ape who hangs from the branches, or a man in a leotard who lifts weights, and astonishes the crowds. I shall take a booth on the West Pier and charge sixpence a show like Madame Proserpina.'

He laughed, and it was the first time she had seen him do that in some while.

Chapter Twenty

Mina's next call was on Mr Jordan, who, with his watch-cover snapping like a hungry alligator, was bustling with energy, supervising an extended display of fashionable garments and fabrics in the recently opened ladies' emporium. Mr Jordan was as ever a smartly-dressed and perfectly groomed man, but that day Mina detected something more. He had made himself into a walking advertisement for gentleman's summer clothes, and all about him was new and fresh. He wore a flower bud in his buttonhole, a sparkling pin in his cravat, and there was more than a sufficiency of cologne.

'The very latest fashions for the summer months,' he said, proudly. 'French-woven striped silk is all the rage, and there can never be too many bows or flounces. The court train, too, is quite the thing just now; there is nothing better to be had in London!' He drew her quietly to one side. 'I can assure you of our utmost discretion. Our ladies are very highly skilled in fitting every variation of the female form, and I know you will find something to please you. We also have a mourning department and our demi-mourning fabrics are both pleasing and tasteful.'

'That is very kind of you,' said Mina, 'and I will pay great attention to your display. But my visit today was on another matter. May we speak privately?'

He looked surprised, but after another consultation of his watch he agreed to allow her a few moments of his time and conducted her to a small office.

Mina explained to Mr Jordan the discoveries she had recently made about Miss Eustace, and asked what he thought ought to be done. She had expected him to be very interested in what she had to say, excited that his initial suspicions had been borne out, and eager to progress his campaign. To her surprise and disappointment he was none of those things, and instead appeared worried that some action was expected of him that he was unable or unwilling to perform.

'Mr Jordan,' said Mina, 'please tell me that you have not gone over to the spiritualists!'

'Oh no, not at all,' he said hastily, 'but you must know that my business partner Mr Conroy and his lady wife are very firm in their belief, and my opposition has caused some unnecessary friction between us. I have decided therefore to withdraw from the fray, and attend to my business. If people wish to be duped then they must take the consequences. I have done all I can, but I believe nothing can save them from their own folly.'

Mina decided to waste no more time on Mr Jordan and returned home, to find a scene of chaos. Rose met her at the door as soon as she arrived. 'Oh, Miss Scarletti,

I am so glad to see you — I didn't know what to do for the best! Mrs Scarletti rang for me and she is in such a state! She's in the parlour now.'

'Is she unwell?' asked Mina, hurrying as best she could to attend to her mother. 'Where is Simmons? Have you fetched her?'

'I think she is more upset than unwell,' said Rose, 'and Miss Simmons is upstairs packing her bags.'

Mina's mother, whose studied fragility had provoked a dramatic collapse under shock, was draped on the chaise longue like a discarded shawl, while the more robust figure of Mrs Parchment stood over her, alternately flapping a lace kerchief in her face and offering whiffs of smelling salts. 'Oh, Mina!' exclaimed her mother, extending her hand as if the weight of her arm could be supported only with a struggle. 'Where were you when I needed you?' Mrs Parchment, looking even grimmer than usual, stood back and allowed Mina to sit by her mother. A rapid glance showed Mina that there was, thankfully, no black-bordered envelope or telegraph message nearby.

'Whatever is the matter?' asked Mina, with the uncomfortable feeling that her mother's distress was in some way connected with the curious mania for the spirits that had so recently gripped the town. 'Has someone upset you? Have you been to a séance? Please do tell me if there is anything I can do.'

Her mother shook her head as if speech had become difficult, and making little choking sounds in her throat, snatched the kerchief from Mrs Parchment's hands and clasped it to her eyes.

'Mrs Parchment,' said Mina, 'please tell me what has happened. Do I need to send Rose for the doctor?'

'No, no,' murmured her mother, 'it is just —' She gulped — 'I have been so terribly betrayed!'

Rose was standing in the doorway and Mina, seeing that this was an emotional shock rather than the onset of disease, sent the maid to fetch brandy, and set about chafing her mother's cool papery hands. 'Now then, Mother, you mustn't be anxious, I am here now, and if you like I will see if I can find Richard, and bring him here to see you, I know that will cheer you up.' Mina paused, suddenly fearing that that had been the wrong thing to say, and it was Richard and his adventures that had provoked the scene before her. Fortunately there was no reaction from either her mother or Mrs Parchment. 'Only tell me what has occurred and I will do my best to set matters right.'

Mina's calming words seemed to have some effect. 'It is that young person, Simmons,' said Mrs Parchment. 'She seemed such a quiet sensible woman, but I am afraid that she deceived us all. She has had a fit of hysterics, and said some very unkind things to both your mother and myself which I will not repeat.'

'She is to leave at once,' said Mina's mother, pleadingly.

'Of course,' said Mina, firmly. 'She must. Mrs Parchment, please look after my mother and I will go and see to it that Miss Simmons quits the house immediately.'

Before either of those ladies could say another word, Mina left the room and with as much energy as she could muster, took the stairs up to Miss Simmons's room, which was at the top of the house. By the time she had made the climb she was grateful indeed for the exercises she had been doing, as a month or two ago she might not have achieved her object without some pain. The newly developed strength in her grip was both a surprise and a pleasure.

Miss Simmons, who was unusually red-faced, was in her bedroom, throwing unfolded garments into a small trunk, where they lay heaped upon each other in great disarray. She looked around in astonishment when Mina appeared, and while labouring under feelings that seemed to approach anger, had the hard defiant look of someone who thought she was about to be scolded and didn't care.

'Please calm down,' said Mina, 'and tell me all that has happened. Don't worry yourself about the trunk, I will get Rose to come and help pack your things. Do you have anywhere to go?'

Simmons breathed more easily and nodded. 'Yes, I have a sister in Brighton. I can go to her.'

'Well, that is something. Now sit down. Neither my mother nor Mrs Parchment will go into any detail about the reasons behind this upheaval, and since it was I who initially employed you, I feel I should know everything before you leave. You have been very efficient in all your work, and unless there is some compelling reason not to, I am prepared to give you a character so you may find another position.'

Miss Simmons sat on her bed, her eyes sparkling with unshed tears. 'It is Mr Clee,' she said.

'Oh dear!' said Mina. 'What has he done?'

Miss Simmons gave her an anxious look. 'You do not like him?' she said.

'My opinion of him is of no consequence,' said Mina. 'I am only interested in learning what has so upset my mother.'

'He is a very charming and clever and nice-looking young gentleman,' said Miss Simmons defensively.

Mina had a horrible suspicion where the conversation might be tending but said nothing.

'I had never thought for a moment that I might receive the admiration of a young man such as he,' Simmons went on, 'but some weeks ago I chanced to encounter him one afternoon as I was going to see my sister on my half-day, and he engaged me in conversation. We struck up a pleasant acquaintanceship and after that, we used to meet as often as we could. My sister always walked with us for propriety's sake, only she was a little way behind so that that we could talk alone. He never — I mean, there was no — he was always very respectful.'

'I am glad to hear it,' said Mina, 'although my mother would undoubtedly have disapproved, especially as these assignations seem to have been made without her knowledge.'

'That was the reason we could tell no-one,' said Miss Simmons. 'James — Mr Clee — said he wanted very much to meet me more often, but he knew that I might lose my place if it became known.'

'Did he speak of his intentions towards you?' asked Mina.

'Oh, yes, and they are the most honourable possible,' said Simmons, happily. 'Marriage, of course. But he has no fortune and cannot think of it at present. He is, however, the favourite and sole heir of a great-aunt, who is in poor health and unlikely to live long, so he is sure to be a rich man very soon.'

'I suppose my mother found out,' said Mina, certain that the wealthy great-aunt would prove to be as illusory as any ghost. She declined to mention her suspicions that Mr Clee was already a married man, as she felt that Miss Simmons was quite upset enough without that suggestion.

'Yes, and I am sorry to say it was Mrs Parchment who told her. She must have seen us walking together and reported it. I think that is very petty-minded, to so destroy the happiness of another. I am not sure the lady approves of marriage at all. From things she has let slip I have gathered that she disliked her husband, perhaps dislikes all men. When I said that Mr Clee and I were intending to announce our betrothal as soon as he came into his fortune, she was very rude to me. She said I was deluded. She accused me of throwing myself at him, and said that it was quite impossible he could have any affection for me. I am afraid I was not at all polite when I replied, and I said a great many things I ought not to have. Still, it is in the open now, and at least your mother knows the truth behind the séance, though it cannot have pleased her.'

'The séance?' said Mina. 'Do you mean the one that took place here?'

'Yes, James asked if I might help him. He said he feared from some incident that had occurred recently that you had lost your faith in the spirit world and he wanted to restore your belief. He hoped very much that the spirits would be able to do all that was necessary, but sometimes, in the presence of an unbeliever, their powers fade and they need help.'

'So when you said that the table had moved —' said Mina, understanding at last.

'James said that Miss Eustace would try to get the spirits to move a table or a chair if they could, but if not, he would give me a signal and I was to pretend that something had happened. That would increase the energy in the room and after that the spirits could do all that was necessary. And you did hear rappings, which gave you a message from your father. I had no part in that, it was quite genuine.'

174

Mina saw that there was no hope for Miss Simmons, who would have to discover the hard way that Mr Clee had no interest in her, and had only courted her with a view to having an accomplice in the Scarletti household. How many other women he had duped in a similar way for the same purpose she dreaded to think.

It took all afternoon to restore the household to some semblance of calm. Mina dispatched a note to Richard, hired a cab for Miss Simmons and her trunk, and wrote a character for her, but not before obtaining her new address in case she might wish to speak to her again. Her mother was settled in a darkened room with her smelling salts and a carafe of water, and Mrs Parchment, whose foot had been restored to its accustomed strength, went out on one of her long walks.

There was very little point, thought Mina, in discussing the revelations concerning the séance with her mother, especially since Simmons, knowing that some of the events had been trickery, persisted in her belief that the rest were not. She could only hope that her mother, lying alone with her thoughts, would make her own conclusions, and come to her senses.

As Mina exercised alone in her room she reflected on the fact that Mr Clee and Miss Eustace had both been very eager to bring her on to the side of the believers. She recalled that Dr Edmunds in his letter to the Dialectical Society had mentioned that when he had expressed scepticism, the spiritualists had tried to persuade him that he was a medium. It appeared to be a common ploy to convert sceptics into believers by promising special powers, but in this case there had been particularly strenuous efforts to persuade her, and Eliza as well. As she pondered the mystery, Mina suddenly realised why both she and Eliza would have been valuable associates to a fraudulent medium, and it was Miss Gilden who had unknowingly supplied the vital clue. Both Mina and Eliza were adults in child-size bodies. Mrs Clee in London had used a child to represent a child's spirit and as a result had been found out and put in prison. She cannot have wanted to risk such an exposure again, yet the ability to produce the form of a child was one that would add greatly to the demands on her services. An adult who could masquerade as a child, smuggled in under cover of darkness, the sound of hymn-singing masking any tell-tale noises, was a considerable asset.

Now that she thought about it, the smuggled confederate was probably the source of the phenomena at the very first séance she had attended. She had sensed another person in the room, and with good reason; there had been one, a very human presence. A figure cloaked in black, moving silently about on stockinged feet, tapping on walls and clinking glasses, while the onlookers, commanded to stay in their seats, had to clasp hands so they found it impossible to turn and look about them. The confederate, in all probability Mr Clee, had then disappeared behind the curtains to wave the glowing apparitions on the end of sticks. There was nothing he had used that could not be hidden under a cloak or in a pocket or up a sleeve. At the second séance the raps on the walls had been more distant, and must have come from someone knocking from the hallway or the next room, but these had occurred when Mr Clee was in plain sight, so there must have been another confederate, the maidservant, perhaps. Phoebe's voluminous draperies must have been made of some soft gauzy material like the delicate wisps that had formed so many yards of Miss Foxton's etheric powers, something that could be rolled up and made very small and carried under Miss Eustace's skirts.

In the middle of these deliberations, Mina was surprised by the sudden arrival of Mr Bradley, and found that unknown to her, her mother had asked Rose to send for him. Mina was unwilling to allow him to sit with her mother alone, and was obliged to remain in the darkened sickroom and listen to that gentleman's sympathetic and uncontroversial mutterings, which pandered to her mother's sense of outrage and were therefore well received. Mr Bradley said that while having only limited acquaintance with Mr Clee, who had occasionally attended his healing circles, he had been impressed by the young man's sincerity, good taste and intelligence. The entire blame for the upset was therefore laid firmly at Miss Simmons's door, that lady having had her foolish head quite turned by Mr Clee's natural friendliness, which she had misunderstood as protestations of love. It would have been useless for Mina to make any mention of the supposed wealthy great-aunt. Since she had originally employed Miss Simmons she was in no doubt as to how such an intervention would have been received, and for peace and quiet decided to remain silent.

Her reflections led her to the conclusion that Dr Hamid, in their most recent conversation, had been correct in one very important respect; there was a significant difference in what was performed at the public séances and the private ones. While it was easy to provide explanations for the simple phenomena produced in front of a gathering, everyone who had been to private consultations had reported being given personal information that that could been known to no-one but the deceased and their intimates. It was with some reluctance that Mina decided that the only way she might gather more information was to obtain a private consultation with Miss Eustace. The chances that Miss Eustace would agree to such a thing were, she realised, extremely slender, but she felt that she at least had to try. Once Mr Bradley had departed, she wrote a letter to Professor Gaskin asking if she might make an appointment.

Mina remained sure that the Gaskins were as much dupes as anyone else, that the professor had embraced spiritualism as a means to enhance his standing, hoping to make great discoveries in science, while his wife bathed in the sunny glow of celebrity and the knowledge that she held a great truth which it was her duty and pleasure to convey to the ignorant. If the Gaskins' apartments were arranged so as to facilitate Miss Eustace's deceptions then it was done in innocence at her behest.

Mina still did not know where the medium lodged, a location where presumably she stored all the items that were necessary to her performances.

Richard breezed in, and said he thought he could have his mother sitting up and drinking tea in a trice. He had good news; his business was prospering and he had no need to borrow money.

'Please do not tell Mother that you are appearing on stage with an almost-naked actress,' said Mina.

'Oh, I will find some story to tell her, don't fear!' he said, hurrying upstairs.

Richard returned after an hour announcing that their mother was vastly improved, and would almost certainly not need nursing, although she had announced her intention of never employing another companion. 'I am afraid that will be your duty from now on,' he said. 'It is not what you might have wished, but I see no way to avoid it.'

'Nonsense,' said Mina. 'I would gladly tend my mother night and day if she really needed me, but this is no more than one of her airy vapours. Rose shall see to her wants, she has been with us for five years and my mother likes and trusts her, and I will engage a daily woman to take care of the cleaning.'

He smiled. 'You have it all planned. Now then,' he said rubbing his hands together, 'Mother declares that she has no appetite for anything except a little broth, so that means there is a dinner in the house that should not go to waste!'

Mina rang for Rose to order dinner and a suitable tray for her mother.

'I really do think that it will benefit my mother far more if I was free to go about my business and put a stop to Miss Eustace, than sitting chained to her side,' said Mina. 'I don't suppose Mother has mentioned Miss Simmons's confession that she was Mr Clee's accomplice in the séance they performed here?'

'She has not, although that doesn't surprise me. Simmons is a good young person and deserves better than Mr Clee, but unfortunately she can be easily persuaded of the reverse. Plain young ladies with no fortune can be made to do almost anything on a promise of marriage.'

Mina gave him a hard look.

'Oh, no, Mina,' he said hastily, 'whatever I have done, I can assure you that I have never given any lady cause to complain of me. Does Nellie seem unhappy? But I know that other men do not have my scruples.'

'Has Miss Gilden attended one of Miss Eustace's séances?' Mina asked, avoiding any further conversation on the subject of Richard's scruples.

'It has been hard to get tickets,' said Richard 'as the gatherings are so well patronised, but yes, by dint of calling herself Lady Finsbury and having an expensive calling card, not to mention one of Mrs Conroy's new Paris gowns, she was one of the congregation last night, and created quite an impression. She is all bows and lace and fans, and looks quite the thing. I think the Gaskins were very taken with her and, of course, Miss Eustace, who thinks of nothing but money and how she can get it, has noticed her particularly.'

'Was Mr Clee there?' asked Mina, concerned that even from his seat at the back of the room he might have recognised Nellie from the séance at Mrs Peasgood's.

'Not in the flesh, but there were some rappings and knockings that might have been him. And if he had stood before her, he would not have seen the dowdy Miss Foxton in the elegant Lady Finsbury. As to her etheric and finely-shaped friend,' he added with a knowing smile, 'I do not believe there was a man in the room who could have described her face.'

'And what were the noble Lady Finsbury's conclusions?' asked Mina.

'Exactly as we suspected, the effects are purely conjuring and chemistry and not very skilled at that. M. Baptiste is a hundred times better and he performs in full light. But then he does not pretend to be anything other than he is.'

'And you, Richard? What are you pretending to be to please Mother?'

'I am the manager of a theatre,' he said, proudly. 'A large theatre, patronised by Brighton's most fashionable society. Respectable entertainment only, of course. Mother never goes to the theatre so I think she will not demand to know more, although if she asks to be driven past the establishment so she can see my name on the posters I will have to make some excuse.'

'I might have wished you to be a private detective,' said Mina, 'then I could have employed you to discover where Miss Eustace lives.'

'Oh, that shouldn't be difficult!' said Richard.

'Excellent,' said Mina 'then I expect the answer within the week.'

Chapter Twenty-One

Not unexpectedly, Mina's letter to Professor Gaskin was favoured with a prompt reply to the effect that Miss Eustace was unable to grant a private séance, as her energies were fully occupied with her present clients. Miss Eustace, thought Mina, would be occupied for as long as was necessary to prevent her ever having such a consultation.

She also received a letter from Miss Simmons, revealing that Mr Clee, the man who she regarded as her future husband, had somehow omitted to tell her his address. She had only ever met him in the streets or gardens of Brighton, and on each occasion they had made the appointment for their next meeting. It was essential, she wrote, that she should advise him of her new position, but unaccountably, at their most recent rendezvous, he had not appeared. Thinking that there might have been some mistake, she had gone to all their usual haunts, but he was nowhere to be found. Miss Simmons was by now consumed with fear that her betrothed had been taken ill, and was unable to send for help. She had called on Professor Gaskin for information, but he was unable to assist, other than assuring her that when he had last seen Mr Clee a few days previously, he was in perfect health. He promised to pass on a message to Miss Eustace, and shortly afterwards a brief note was received advising that although Miss Eustace understood that Mr Clee was resident in Brighton, she did not know his address. Miss Simmons had then attended one of Mr Bradley's healing circles, which she knew Mr Clee occasionally patronised, but Mr Clee was not there, and no-one at the gathering knew where he lived. She had applied for a ticket to Miss Eustace's next séance, feeling sure that she would see Mr Clee there, but was told that the séances were fully subscribed and would be so for some time to come. In desperation she had taken to standing outside Professor Gaskin's lodgings in case Mr Clee should enter, but without any result.

Miss Simmons begged Mina to tell her if she knew her betrothed's address, but, of course, Mina did not. Mina wondered if Dr Hamid had found anything in Eliza's effects to suggest where Mr Clee lived, but on enquiring there, found that all Eliza's correspondence had been sent via Professor Gaskin, his lodgings being the address on the calling card left by Miss Eustace, and Mr Clee had not been a client of Dr Hamid's baths.

The desperate efforts of Miss Simmons to try and find Mr Clee, who, she was eager to advise anyone who wished to listen, was her intended, did eventually produce one result, a letter, postmarked London, the envelope printed with the name of a firm of solicitors, addressed to Miss Simmons at the Scarletti address, which Mina was obliged to bear to her former employee, now residing with her married sister, Mrs Langley, in Dorset Gardens.

Miss Simmons received the missive with great excitement and relief, for while she had never seen Mr Clee's handwriting she felt convinced that the letter was addressed in his hand, while the stationery he had employed proved that he had been attending to urgent business matters in London. Although she did not state it outright there was more than a hint of hope in her voice that the long and worthy life of his great-aunt might have drawn peacefully to its natural close.

Mrs Langley, a capable-looking young woman, was bearing up admirably under the requirements of a baby whose teeth seemed to erupt every five minutes. There was barely time for Mina to be introduced to her before a squeal of renewed outrage from the nursery sent the attentive mother hurrying away. Mina decided it was best to offer to withdraw so that Miss Simmons might enjoy her letter in private, but was reassured that this was unnecessary. 'You have been a better friend to me than anyone other than my own family, and you must share the good news.' Mina sat at the parlour table, while Miss Simmons went to fetch a letter opener. Even with the aid of the little silver knife, used carefully so as not to harm the precious contents, her hands were trembling so violently that it was a close question as to whether she would tear the envelope or stab herself in the hand.

There were two sheets of paper in the envelope, and although Mina could not see what was written, she observed that they were business notepaper, the top one with a printed heading. Miss Simmons read, at first eagerly, then with her eyes opening wide in disbelief, and by the time she reached the bottom of the first page, she almost fell back into a chair.

'Is it bad news?' asked Mina. 'Would you like me to fetch your sister?'

'I don't understand,' she said. 'There must be some mistake.' She glanced at the letter again, but this time her eyes flooded with tears and she was unable to read it. She held it out to Mina. 'Please, look at this, I can't see.'

The letter was not written by Mr Clee, but by a solicitor employed by Mr Clee. This gentleman had been instructed to advise Miss Simmons that he was aware that she had been spreading the rumour in Brighton that she was affianced to his client, a circumstance which had caused considerable distress and annoyance not only to his client but to the young lady of fortune and good family to whom Mr Clee was actually affianced and whom he was due to marry very soon. Miss Simmons was accordingly instructed to cease at once from spreading the untrue story, with the assurance that if she complied, then no unpleasant consequences would ensue. Should she continue, however, his client would have no alternative but to take further action to force her to desist.

There was nothing for Mina to do but go and fetch Mrs Langley at once, and show her the letter. Mrs Langley's expression as she read revealed that the contents, while unpleasant, were not, to her, wholly unforeseen.

Miss Simmons, heartbroken and wretched, was taken to a darkened room to rest. Mina naturally supposed that she ought to leave, but Mrs Langley asked her to remain. Her sister, she said, had spoken very highly of Mina and she would appreciate her advice.

Mrs Langley was a lady of very strong beliefs as to what was right and what was wrong. Proposing marriage to her sister and then pretending that the event had never occurred was a wrong that was not to be accepted lightly or without compensation. Making threats against her sister, who had done nothing more than tell the truth, was not to be tolerated.

Mr Clee had made a very grave error, said Mrs Langley, with the steely look of someone bent on revenge. He had assumed that when he and Miss Simmons had gone on their romantic perambulations while she had followed at a discreet distance, that his words could not be overheard, but he was mistaken. She had been suspicious of his intentions from the start, and being blessed with unusually sharp hearing, she had been able to remain within earshot the whole time, and had heard every word he spoke. Mr Clee, she confirmed, had made her sister an honourable offer which he claimed could only be realised when he came into his fortune. Whatever his motives might have been, it was clear that he now had no further use for her, but by communicating through a solicitor, he had now supplied an address at which he could be reached. If her sister was willing to bring an action for breach of promise of marriage — and she would strongly encourage her to do so — she was fully prepared to go to court and give evidence of Mr Clee's guilt. It only remained for the family to appoint a legal advisor, and Mina suggested that she approach young Mr Phipps who she thought might be the very man.

Since Mrs Langley was a level-headed lady and not given to attacks of emotion, Mina decided to lay before her everything she had thus far uncovered about the medium who had been committed to prison in 1869. If Mr Clee was already a married man, most probably the husband of Miss Eustace, then unless his claim to be affianced to another lady was a lie to extricate himself from any association with Miss Simmons, he had been planning to commit a very serious crime, and had some questions to answer about his conduct. She saw a fresh light in the lady's eyes, the light of a huntress who had sighted her prey, noted its weaknesses and was in determined pursuit. Young Mr Phipps was about to be presented with a case that would shock and scandalise Brighton, and perhaps even bring a sudden end to the career of Miss Eustace.

Mina and Mrs Langley, seeing that they had a shared concern, promised to keep each other acquainted with developments. A few days later, however, Mina received a somewhat disappointing letter from her new friend.

Mr Clee, she learned, on being confronted with the newspaper report of 1869, had denied that he had any acquaintance with the lady named therein, declared that the newspaper must have made an error in the medium's name, and asserted that he was a single man, had never been married, and anyone who attempted to prove otherwise was free to try it, but would inevitably fail.

The confidence with which he made these denials made Mina pause. Either he knew that no proof of a marriage could be found, or he was gambling that no-one would trouble to make enquiries. Mina did not feel equipped to challenge him on this point, but at least Miss Simmons's suit still remained.

There was better news from Richard, which Mina thought well worth the inevitable price of the dinner and wine she provided for her brother and Nellie. Richard had discovered that Miss Eustace was living in a lodging house in Bloomsbury Place. As he had promised the secret had not been a hard one to uncover; he had simply hired a messenger boy to loiter outside the Gaskins' rooms on the night of a séance and then follow the medium to her lair. The lady, it was reported, on leaving the house had stepped quickly into a cab that had been ordered in advance, and it had been a delicate balance between speed and concealment to keep up with her progress unseen. The cab had not paused to take another person on board and Miss Eustace had completed her journey and slipped into the lodgings alone. A careful watch had been kept for some hours but no-one else entered the premises. The house boasted a basement, a ground floor, and three upper storeys, but how these were divided and how many tenants were accommodated was unknown.

'Perhaps Lady Finsbury might pay her a visit,' suggested Nellie, who was resplendent in another new gown and a necklace that sparkled rainbows like broken glass. She patted the jewels occasionally as if wishing that they were real. 'I am sure Miss Eustace would be very amenable to that. The only slight awkwardness would be explaining how I came by her address which she has clearly been at some pains to conceal.'

'I don't suppose she has thought to try to discover if Lady Finsbury exists,' said Richard, easing open a button on his waistcoat and puffing at a cigar. 'These lying types are so easily taken in, you just have to play them with their own tricks.'

'That's it!' said Mina. 'Her own trick! Of course!'

'Oh, you have a perfectly wicked imagination, Mina,' said Richard, appreciatively. 'We are all ears.'

'All that Lady Finsbury needs to do,' explained Mina, 'is say that she was given the address by a spirit. Miss Eustace can hardly argue with that, as it is her stock in trade. Even if she is a conjurer, there may be some shred of belief in her that the things she pretends are real. I suggest, Miss Gilden, that you go there in your finest gown and best jewels, present Lady Finsbury's card, and insist on an immediate interview. She is bound to see you.'

Nellie nodded, thoughtfully. 'I can carry that off without any trouble; and perhaps I should offer some reason why the interview cannot take place at my hotel; a disapproving or invalid husband, perhaps. But what reason should I give for the urgency of my request?'

'There is only one thing that tempts Miss Eustace and her kind, and that is money,' said Mina. 'Perhaps the spirit has spoken of buried treasure or a hidden will, at any rate something of great value, and has directed you to Miss Eustace as the only means of discovering its location.'

'But would she agree to that?' said Richard dubiously. 'She can produce messages that make sense to the listener, but finding some hidden object would surely be beyond her. She might fear losing her reputation if it is not found.'

'If the customer is eager enough and willing to be duped, she will agree,' said Mina. 'Only make it clear that she will be paid well, whatever the result. All we really want is the opportunity for Miss Gilden to visit Miss Eustace, and note anything in her apartments which might offer us clues as to her mode of life and business.'

Miss Gilden smiled. 'That should be easy enough. I shall even provide her with a picture of the spirit.'

'A picture?' said Mina.

'Oh, I have any number of portraits of theatrical persons. What about Rolly?' said Miss Gilden, turning to Richard.

He laughed. 'Oh yes, Rolly Rollason, the master of mirth. He has this thing he says —' Richard adopted a curious pose with his arms wrapped about his head, and affected a villainous grimace — 'I ain't, though! Ain't I?' he said gruffly, and chuckled. 'Very droll.' He paused. 'Nellie, dear, I didn't know you had his picture?'

'Oh, a great many gentlemen give me their pictures,' said the charming Nellie, without even the hint of a blush. 'Yes, there is a very characterful one of him which would do extremely well. He is in evening dress, wearing a monocle and a full wig and staring at a rose. I shall tell Miss Eustace that he is my late uncle. If she manages to produce his ghost that would be most amusing.'

'You will be very convincing, my dear,' said Richard. 'Perhaps, to demonstrate your grief concerning the deceased relative, your personation from *The Wayward Ghost* would be suitable?'

'Oh yes,' said Nellie with a smile. 'It was a burlesque of the tragedy of Hamlet,' she explained to Mina. 'I played Ophelia and sang and danced and went mad and tore my clothes to ribbons.'

'There were gentlemen in the front row in tears every night,' said Richard. 'I think Lady Finsbury might aspire to a slightly more modest exhibition of distress, but if Miss Eustace hesitates to assist then you might open the floodgates a little. Yes, let us make the attempt tomorrow!' He signalled the waiter and ordered a glass of brandy.

'And what of Miss Foxton; how does she prosper?' asked Mina.

'Well, we have not quite reached the heights of the Theatre Royal or the Dome,' said Richard, almost as if that was a possibility, 'but we have played extensively in some very prestigious drawing rooms, and just lately we have been reaching an altogether wider audience by taking our turn at The New Oxford Music Hall in New Street.'

'We appear just after the Chinese sword-swallower and before the one-legged gymnast,' said Nellie.

'How wonderful!' exclaimed Mina, thankful that her mother was as likely to patronise such an establishment as she would a hospital for infectious diseases.

'Only sixpence for a seat in the gallery and packed to bursting every night,' said Richard. 'We are in place for the whole of the summer but we might look for something more elegant in the high season. Mind-reading, perhaps.'

'Can you do that?' asked Mina.

'Oh yes, I used to be the Ethiopian Wonder when I was with M. Baptiste,' said Nellie. 'I had to be Ethiopian so I could wear paint and wouldn't be recognised. It was a wonderful costume.'

'It is all a trick, though,' said Mina.

'Everything is a trick,' said the former Ethiopian Wonder. 'The secret is making it look as if something is happening before your eyes that you know to be impossible. Of course, in a séance it's still impossible and it's still a trick, only then people believe it. And they pay more to see it.'

'I don't expect you to tell me how these things are done,' said Mina, 'but there are some things that I can't explain, and it is those that trouble me most, the things that Miss Eustace tells people at the private séances. Everyone who has been to one says that they are told things, quite personal things unknown to anyone else, things that Miss Eustace could not possibly have known and which therefore must be messages from the deceased. It is those messages that convince people she is genuine. I applied for a private reading myself, but she will not grant me one. That fact alone tells me she is a fraud. If she was genuine she would have nothing to fear.'

'People who want to believe in the spirits are too ready to dismiss something as impossible by natural means,' said Nellie. 'They say that the medium could not have known this or that, but there is always a way. How many secrets are there that are known to only one or two people?'

'Dr Hamid, whose sister died very recently, claims he has received messages from her that convince him,' said Mina. 'Miss Hamid would not discuss the pain she suffered except with her own family, yet Miss Eustace was able to say where it was.'

'It is like every such trick,' said Nellie. 'When you do not know the secret it is mysterious and inexplicable. Once you know, it seems so simple, so obvious, you would swear that a child could do it. Remember, Miss Eustace does not work alone. She is like a spider with a web, and she spins it all around the town and draws people in. I am sure that if you took a single example of something she has said and found out how she learned about it, you would discover a great deal more about the lady and how she deceives people, and perhaps then some of her followers would see her for what she is.'

'Only some, not all?' asked Mina, although she knew the answer.

'Only some,' said Nellie.

Chapter Twenty-Two

Not for the first time Mina was tempted to put her case before the police but on reflection, realised that she had nothing to go to the police with. She had not been fooled or paid over any money, so had nothing personally to complain about, and anything she said would be opposed by a chorus of voices extolling the virtue and probity of the medium.

The next time Mina exercised at Hamid's she expressed her continuing anxieties to Anna. Anna now had quite a number of lady patients who went to her to exercise, often for diseases of the spine. She did not believe in the wearing of stays during these activities, indeed she confided in Mina that she did not approve of the wearing of stays at all, since she thought that a lady's own body ought to be developed to create and support her shape and not pulled into some distortion dictated by fashion in order to please men. She had therefore devised an exercise costume consisting of a loose blouse and pantaloons which ladies might either purchase or hire. Mina had ordered a set made to her own dimensions, and it was beautifully comfortable. If she had one exercise she especially enjoyed it was a simple side stretch, not so much because it was in itself pleasurable, but because she knew from what she was told that when she placed her left hand on the back of a chair and leaned to one side, raising her right foot from the ground, this was the one position in which, perversely, her spine lay perfectly straight. How she wished she had known that some years before, when, ordered to straighten her back by her mother, she could quite simply have adopted this pose.

The exercises with the dumbbells had in the last few weeks so strengthened her upper arms and the muscles of her chest that Anna had deemed her ready to advance to the next stage, which was hanging by both hands from a bar. Mina first stepped on to a low stool then grasped the bar, and Anna slid the stool away, and carefully supervised her so that the stretches were applied in the correct place. It was too soon, she warned, for Mina to attempt this at home, for an exercise incorrectly done was worse than none at all. The weight of Mina's small body seemed to pull through her arms and shoulders and back, lengthening and warming her muscles, but without pain, although the effort made her want to gasp. As Anna eased Mina to the floor, she looked concerned, and asked if all was well, but Mina's slight breathlessness was a good feeling, and she felt tired yet exhilarated, having achieved more than she had ever thought possible.

Dr Hamid, Mina learned later as they were enjoying a tisane, had been visited by Miss Eustace three times for private séances, and planned another. He had now

186

told Anna about the communication regarding Eliza's pain, and Mina asked if Eliza had ever described this to another person.

'Daniel and I were the only persons she ever spoke to on the subject,' said Anna. 'I believe she did not even talk about it to you.'

'That is true,' Mina admitted. 'But both Miss Eustace and Mr Clee came to see her. Might she not have disclosed something then?'

'I very much doubt it. She preferred not to discuss the subject at all, and had they pressed her on the matter she would not have wanted to see them again.'

'And she has not been examined by any other doctor?'

Anna paused. 'We did receive a visit some months ago from Dr Chenai, who Daniel has known for a number of years. He had been making a study of the spine and asked if he might see Eliza. We persuaded her to allow him to examine her, which I think she did only because she thought that it might help others, but I was there and she did not speak a word all the time. I think she was very relieved when he left, and did not need to tell us that she preferred not to see him again.'

'I suppose,' said Mina, 'that Miss Eustace could have read a book about scoliosis and guessed where the pain might be.'

'I had the impression from Daniel that he was told more than that, something very peculiar to Eliza.' She sighed. 'I shall ask him again and see if he will tell me what it was, but he thinks that I only ask him in order to destroy his belief, which, of course, I do, and he prefers for the moment to cling to it.'

'I am hoping that Mr Clee's fame in Brighton will be of short duration,' said Mina, and revealed the impending suit of Miss Simmons and her own suspicions that he was secretly married to Miss Eustace.

There was a very marked change in Anna's expression. 'I have only encountered that young man three times and was not impressed by him,' she said, almost angrily.

'Three times?' asked Mina. 'The first was when he visited Eliza, and the second was the séance. What was the third?'

Anna put her cup down very deliberately, and on her pale fawn cheeks there was a glow of red. 'He came to offer his condolences after Eliza died, and to express the hope that he was in no way to blame. Of course, he was, in a way, as he brought the infection to the house, although it was hardly deliberate and he may not have had the first symptoms himself, so I reassured him that we did not hold him responsible. He then —'

Mina waited.

'He then attempted to woo me.'

Mina hardly knew what to say and decided to remain silent.

'When I was much younger,' said Anna, after she had taken a moment to calm herself, 'I did, from time to time receive expressions of admiration and even offers of marriage from gentlemen, and I rejected them all. My life is not destined that way, and never has been. I am now forty-eight years of age and well aware that a man who proposes marriage is interested not in me, but in my private fortune, which is of some value. Daniel and I jointly own this property, and any husband I chose would at once acquire half the business as well as all my funds. I have no doubt that Mr Clee has been making enquiries about this and therefore has a proper understanding of my worth.'

'What did you say to him?' asked Mina.

'I told him very plainly that I knew what he was up to and wished never to see him again. I thought it as well to be blunt, and he removed himself at once.'

'I am quite sure,' said Mina, secretly wishing that she had been present at that scene, 'that he had no intention of marrying Miss Simmons and wooed her only in order to gain a confederate. The wealthy great-aunt whose heir he was supposed to be would have been a long time dying. I am only wondering if he was being truthful when he said that he was engaged to another. How many victims can this man have?'

'There are too many adventurers of his kind,' said Anna, bitterly. 'They assume that all a woman wants is marriage, and they seek out the vulnerable: women who they assume have little or no chance of marriage because they are plain or middle-aged, and then they marry them and take all their property and neglect or even abuse them.'

'Well, let us hope that Miss Simmons will stop his game for a while,' said Mina. 'I wish I could prove what I suspect to be the case about Miss Eustace. If she and her acolyte and Mr Bradley could all be drummed out of Brighton I would be very much happier.'

'I do not like Mr Bradley,' said Anna. 'He sometimes comes to inhale the vapours, but spends most of his time lounging in the gentlemen's salon reading the newspapers and telling our other customers how important he is. I don't believe he is here for his own health at all, but to drum up custom from among our clients for his own healing circle. After all, if one wants to find people who might seek his services where better to go? They are all here in one place. For all I know he goes to Brill's Baths as well.'

'Mr Bradley started by offering his services gratis, but now he charges for tickets to the larger meetings,' said Mina. 'He says it is only to pay for the hire of the room, and he takes nothing for himself, but I don't know how true that is.'

'I suspect it is untrue,' said Anna. 'The gentleman whose rooms he uses is a customer here and he is a profound believer in Mr Bradley's healing abilities. I would not be surprised if Mr Bradley used the rooms for nothing and makes a tidy income, while his friend also profits by selling refreshments.'

Mina could only feel grateful that Mr Bradley showed no inclination to woo her mother, although she had an unpleasant suspicion that if he were to do so, he might prove successful.

Richard came to see his mother again, a trying visit, since her sole subject of conversation was the terrible betrayal she had suffered at the hands of Miss Simmons. Louisa Scarletti now spent much of her day reclining in her parlour being fetched morsels of food by Rose. Richard smiled a great deal and patted his unhappy parent's hand, and agreed with everything she said, before she declared herself exhausted and retired to her bed.

'I suppose it is still all my fault,' said Mina, when he came to her room. She was at her desk, where Mr Inskip was busily decomposing. She had not yet decided how to end the story, as it was contrary to popular expectation for a murderer to escape conviction.

'And will be until the end of time,' said Richard. 'We must be content with that, I am afraid. Still, she does admit, albeit reluctantly, to feeling a little better; has the wondrous Mr Bradley been here working his magic?'

'It would appear so. Really I would prefer him not to enter the house at all if it was not for the fact that Mother has taken to him, and seems to improve after his visits. He has not been courting her, has he? She has said nothing to make you think that?'

'No, never a suggestion of it.'

'Well, that is something. And how is Miss Gilden?'

Richard, who usually looked cheery every time his beautiful inamorata was mentioned, appeared instead to be slightly discomfited. 'She is very well, and even now is being fitted for a new gown, something I have been assured will take a whole day. Why do fashions have to change once a week?' he said petulantly. 'I am sure it is only to give ladies something to talk about.'

'Has she been to see Miss Eustace?'

Richard threw himself down on Mina's bed. She wondered what he might say if he saw her dumbbells packed away in a box at the bottom of her wardrobe, although the exercise staff might easily be mistaken for a walking cane.

'She has indeed, and with an interesting result. Miss Eustace was astonished to receive a visitor, but as you correctly anticipated was willing to admit a titled lady. Miss Eustace occupies an apartment on the second floor of the house, which seems to comprise only two rooms, and received Lady Finsbury in a parlour, which did not contain anything exceptional. Lady Finsbury explained that the ghost of her beloved great-uncle, Sir Mortimer Portland, had appeared before her, and implored her most earnestly with tears in its diaphanous eyes to see Miss Eustace without delay. Sir Mortimer, said Lady Finsbury, was reputed to have hidden a fortune in jewels in his mansion, Great Portland Hall, which was about to be torn down, and she thought that he was afraid it would be stolen or destroyed before his great-niece, who is his only heir, could take possession of it. The ghost was struggling to describe where the fortune could be found, and finally it gasped that only Miss Eustace of Bloomsbury Place could enable him to materialise sufficiently to draw the treasure map. Miss Eustace, on being assured by Lady Finsbury that any failure to produce her uncle's spirit would be regarded as evidence only of the natural capriciousness of the etheric force, and that she would be paid generously whatever the result, agreed to make the attempt. Nellie showed Miss Eustace Rolly's character portrait, which she asked to retain, saying that it would help her to concentrate on her task. There the matter was left.'

'You said there was an interesting result,' said Mina.

He sat up. 'Yes, two of them, in fact. When Nellie was shown into the parlour, Miss Eustace was closing the door to the adjoining room, but Nellie was able to catch a brief glimpse inside, and saw several large trunks, the kind theatrical people use to transport costumes and properties. Then part-way through the interview, there was a sound in the next room, and Nellie felt sure that there was another person in there. It was too loud to ignore, and so she commented that there must be a spirit in the house. Miss Eustace agreed, and said that spirits often visited her with messages, but sometimes they were just playful and made noises to say that they wanted company. Nellie decided not to press the matter, or it might arouse suspicion, and it was not thereafter alluded to.'

He patted his pockets for a cigar, but desisted at a look from Mina. 'Are we thinking the same thing?' he said.

'I believe so,' said Mina. 'We need to find out what is inside those trunks, but I cannot imagine how that might be done.'

'I agree.' He adopted the attitude of a consultant, and gave the matter his earnest consideration. 'I am reluctant to engage a burglar to carry out the plan —'

'I am most relieved to hear it,' Mina exclaimed.

'They can be expensive, I understand and not necessarily reliable. And much the same can be said of bribing the maid. After all, we have no intention of taking anything; all we want to do is observe what may be there. A common thief or a maid that will take bribes may not be able to resist helping themselves, and where would we be then?'

'Under arrest as accomplices to a robbery I believe,' said Mina.

'Precisely. So I shall do it myself.'

'Richard! You cannot mean that!' she said, horrified. 'Please tell me this is one of your jokes.'

'No, I have thought it all through,' he said calmly. 'I will find some means of entering Miss Eustace's apartments while she is absent, and simply look for the evidence we need, but take away nothing. Can that be against the law?'

'If you force an entry into the house it is,' said Mina. 'And if you were caught, you would never be able to prove that you were not there to steal. Please, Richard, this is a very foolhardy scheme. You must think of something else.'

'If I am caught, I will just say that I am a devoted admirer of the lady and am there to present her with a gift,' he said, with an easy shrug. 'Perhaps I shall take a little nosegay or sweetmeats or my portrait. I shall appear romantically reckless, perhaps, but that is all. But I shall not be caught, and it will be an adventure.'

'Richard, I would very much rather you did not attempt this,' urged Mina. 'You must find some other method. After all, Lady Finsbury managed to gain entry without committing a crime.'

'And having done so I think Miss Eustace will now be doubly suspicious of a new unexpected visitor,' said Richard. 'Oh, I could try to woo the lady, I suppose, but she is reputedly impervious to any such attempts, so it might take me a week or even a fortnight to win her over. No, my plan is by far the best.'

'I cannot condone this,' said Mina. 'How would you even achieve it? You can hardly slip into the house through either door without being seen by the servants.'

'Oh, it's perfectly simple,' he assured her. 'There is a balcony below the windows on the first floor; I can easily climb up and then get a foothold up to the next one. It shouldn't be hard to get in. Nellie says she thought the window was unlocked, so I shall just prise it open and slip inside. The important thing is to work under cover of darkness, and choose a time when Miss Eustace and her friend or husband, or whatever he might be, are away, and to have the means to depart quickly. Nellie will hire a cab and wait for me nearby, and when I am done, I will just jump aboard and fly away in moments.'

'But if you are seen!' Mina exclaimed.

'Did you see me on stage, when I carried the airy sprite about on my shoulders?' he said with a knowing smile. 'Black velvet, Mina, a wondrous material that can deceive the eye. I will be quite invisible!'

All Mina's entreaties were in vain, and Richard pulled a cigar from his pocket and swaggered away to make the arrangements.

Chapter Twenty-Three

Mina was so preoccupied by this new development that she did not pay great attention when first Mr Bradley then Miss Whinstone and Mrs Bettinson called later that day to commiserate with her mother. She was only thankful that her mother had suitable company and demanded little of her, since she needed to retreat into her own thoughts. Mrs Bettinson was looking remarkably satisfied that the new flourishing Louisa who had not needed her had been replaced with the invalid she had always known her to be, and was busily buttering her charge with sympathy. Miss Whinstone, who was looking faded and unhappy, even in her green gown with its extra flounces, could only speak of the cost of maintaining the two children she had adopted, and the constant demands by their school for the payment of 'extras.'

Mina had no information concerning when Richard might make his foolish attempt at housebreaking, and was half-expecting to hear that he was coming up before the magistrates and needing to be bailed, but the next morning he arrived in a rush.

'Mina dear, I have come to entreat your help,' he exclaimed.

'If you have escaped from the police cells I will not shelter you,' she said severely. 'I must take you straight back there.'

'Oh, it is nothing of the sort, and in any case I have not attempted the enterprise yet, but it must be tonight. Miss Eustace is engaged for a séance at Professor Gaskin's and will be from home, and I have everything I need, but Nellie cannot help me with the cab, so you must do it.'

'I must? Richard, might I remind you that I do not approve of this scheme and want nothing to do with it,' she said, crossly. 'In fact, since it has not yet been attempted, I beg you to abandon it at once.'

'But who else can I trust?' he pleaded. 'Mina, my darling sister, all you have to do is wait for me in the street, and if we are questioned then you can say you have been in my company all evening, so you may save me, too.'

'And what of Miss Gilden? Is she unwell?'

'No, she has gone to London. Have you not seen the newspapers?'

Mina shook her head, dreading to think what she had missed.

'There has been some shocking news,' Richard informed her. 'M. Baptiste, and I think in spite of everything Nellie still retains some affection for him, has been shot and wounded in the street by a madwoman. So, as his wife, and in all probability his sole heir, Nellie has rushed to his side. It's understandable, of course, but my plans are now in disarray, and who knows how long she will have to stay there, mopping his brow, or whatever it is ladies do.'

'And,' Mina observed, 'not only Nellie but Miss Foxton and Lady Finsbury are absent from Brighton.'

'Yes, and the Ethiopian Wonder, and whole host of fascinating ladies besides. But, please, promise me you will help.'

'It is a very dangerous scheme,' said Mina.

'But your help will make it less so,' he said with his most persuasive smile. 'I am asking such a little simple thing, and you will not be in any danger at all. If needs be you can always say that all you did was hire a cab at my request, and knew nothing of my reasons for wanting it.'

'And what of the cabman?' she reminded him. 'Will he also be your alibi? Or a witness for the prosecution?'

'The cab will be at the end of the street, so he will see nothing.' He hugged her. 'Please, Mina, darling Mina, you are the only person clever enough to help me.'

It was with considerable reluctance that Mina, accepting that she could not dissuade her brother, agreed to help, if only to protect him from disgrace, and her mother from shame.

Mina felt bereft of proper advice. She dared not approach anyone connected with the law, but felt that at the very least she should speak to someone sympathetic and sensible. After a great deal of hesitation she decided to speak to Dr Hamid, who, she thought, at least needed to know of the grave doubts that had arisen from Nellie's visit. She felt sure that underneath the grief and the hope there was still a man who remained settled in his appreciation of the world and how it was formed and worked.

It was a fine day and he agreed to take a walk with her on the Chain Pier, where he seemed to be not so much contemplating the land and all that moved on it, or even the cool waters and the constantly changing place where the two met, but gazing instead into the air, as if looking about him for evidence of spirits. They walked slowly, not only due to Mina's preferred speed of gait, but because the gentleness of the stroll pleased them both. They passed under the cast iron arches, which housed little kiosks selling toys, sweetmeats and novelties, going toward the old landing stage at the end, where the packet boats arrived from Dieppe. Being of purely commercial use it was the least attractive part of the pier, and it was no coincidence, thought Mina, that the most popular portraits of the pier seemed either to be facing away from it, or with its slime-blackened supports in the misty distance. They stopped briefly for refreshments, and passers-by looked on the pair with approval, seeing a kind gentleman assisting a poor crippled lady.

'I don't know if you have heard about the scandal regarding Mr Clee,' Mina said.

'No,' said Dr Hamid, 'but nothing would surprise me about that individual. Anna has told me about his attempt to win her, and a more transparent fortune hunter was never known. Anna is a fine, honest and loving woman, and I hope even now that she may find someone worthy of her, who will add to her happiness, but that person is not Mr Clee.'

'He may well be married already,' said Mina, 'and he appears also to be engaged to two other ladies, one of whom, my mother's former companion, Miss Simmons, is taking an action for breach of promise.'

'The scoundrel!' he exclaimed, shaking his head in dismay, 'and this is the creature who has attached himself to Miss Eustace, no doubt with hopes of winning her, too. Thankfully Miss Simmons's action will alert her to his true nature. I, like you, have become convinced that he is simply a conjurer, and his object has been from the start to conjure Miss Eustace from her fortune.'

'The lady has many admirers, yet seems to entertain none of them,' said Mina. They walked on. There was little enough to divert them on the pier, other than the sea and the sky, but that was all to the good. 'My brother, Richard, has recently told me he wishes to court her, but I have told him he is unlikely to be successful.' She looked at Dr Hamid carefully as she spoke, but he seemed unconcerned at the news, and she was reassured that he at least had no tender interest in Miss Eustace. 'But Richard can be impulsive and reckless and I fear that he may do something foolish,' she went on.

'He did recklessly offer to knock down Mr Clee unless he left my house, something which I must admit did commend him to me,' said Dr Hamid, with a smile.

'He wishes to make Miss Eustace a gift to express his admiration, but he disdains to deliver it in the usual way,' said Mina. 'He plans to make a bold gesture by placing it in her apartments without her knowing, so it will seem to have appeared by supernatural means.'

He stopped walking and stared at her. 'Goodness — how does he propose to do that?'

'I am very sorry to say that the means he is adopting may place him in danger of arrest,' said Mina.

Dr Hamid looked shocked. 'You must try to dissuade him!'

'I have done my best, truly I have, but he insists on making the attempt. He has asked me to wait with a cab at the end of the street — Miss Eustace lodges not far from Professor and Mrs Gaskin — and I am to be there to make sure he can make his escape.'

'Oh, this is very wrong!' said Dr Hamid, clapping one hand to his forehead and pacing up and down. 'Not only does he risk his own liberty but he draws you in as an accomplice! But you say that he only wishes to leave something, and intends to take nothing away?'

'Oh, Richard is no thief; I can assure you of that. I only hope that if he is caught it will be put down to a youthful escapade and he will have learned his lesson. What do you think I should do?'

He sighed. 'Is there anyone else whose opinion might sway him?'

'Only Mother, and I prefer her to know nothing of it, in fact, I dread her finding out. She is very unhappy over the business with Miss Simmons and I will not add to her worries.'

He looked at her sympathetically. 'I can see that you are very fond of your brother. You would not have harm come to him and whatever he does you will not abandon him. I can only advise you to do your utmost to dissuade him from this foolhardy plan, and if you cannot then no advice I or anyone else can give will prevent you from assisting him. Of course, if he is only intending to leave a gift then it may take just moments to achieve his aim, and you may then hurry him safely away; only do make him promise faithfully that any future gifts are delivered by more conventional means.'

'I will do as you suggest,' she said. 'Will you be at Miss Eustace's séance tonight?'

'That is my plan, and now I can see where I might be able to help you. On my way home I will look to ensure that you and your brother have departed safely before Miss Eustace returns. Where does she lodge?'

'Bloomsbury Place. I will have the cab wait at the northern end.'

'Then I very much hope that we will not meet there.'

The séance was due to start at eight o clock, although how long it was likely to last was unpredictable. Mina hired the cab for eight, but Richard with his customary sense of urgency arrived late and then insisted on stopping on the way to purchase cigars. It was therefore well after half past the hour when they arrived in Bloomsbury Place, and stopped at the end furthest from the seafront, where the road took a turn into College Place and the cabman would not be able to see where Richard was going. The sun was dipping towards the horizon, and the summer light was fading as Richard drew his black velvet cloak about him.

'Did you bring a gift for Miss Eustace to act as your alibi?' asked Mina.

'Oh, no, I forgot,' said Richard. 'Well, it's too late now, I suppose.'

Mina handed him a lace handkerchief.

'Oh, my wonderful sister!' he exclaimed, pocketing it. 'What would I do without you!'

'Please be as quick as you can,' she urged.

He laughed affectionately at her worried expression, kissed her cheek, and then jumped down from the cab and sauntered down the street, disappearing around the corner. 'Am I to wait here, Miss?' asked the cabman.

'Yes, my brother is just delivering a gift to a friend, he will return soon,' said Mina.

Time passed, and she could imagine Richard climbing up to the balcony, swinging his long legs over the railings, then, more perilously, using the narrow window ledges, ascending higher to Miss Eustace's rooms. She hoped that he would not fall, hoped also that when he reached the second floor that he would find the windows had been securely locked, give up the enterprise, and return to her with a rueful expression. He did not return, and after a while she began to worry that he had indeed fallen and was lying injured in the street, or worse still, had become impaled on the iron railings that surrounded the basement area. Perversely, she thought of a story — the ghost of a man who had died in that horrible way, haunting passers-by with the great iron spike through his chest. It was a dreadful image and she almost disliked herself for thinking of it. She was about to ask the cabman to turn around and move closer when there was a knock on the door. Her first happy thought was that it was Richard, thankfully safe, but to her surprise she saw that it was Dr Hamid.

He climbed in, and though it was now growing dark she could see that his face was grim and drawn.

'Did you walk up Bloomsbury Place?' she asked. 'Did you see anything? I was so worried that Richard had fallen, and I was about to go and look for him.'

He shook his head. 'No, no, I saw nothing.' Suddenly he leaned forward, hid his face in his hands and groaned. 'I have been such a fool!' he said. 'Whatever will you think of me!'

'What has happened?' asked Mina. 'Is the séance over? Is Miss Eustace on her way home?'

He raised his head and his face was a picture of misery. 'No, it is still in progress. I made an excuse and left early. I needed to think about what I had been told.' He made a little gulp that was almost a sob. 'How could I have been so taken in?'

'Because she caught you when your grief and pain were fresh and you would have done anything, grasped at any hope, to relieve them,' said Mina, gently.

He nodded. 'You are right, of course. But at first, it seemed so very real, so full of hope! Tonight, we were just a small circle, receiving messages through rapping noises that spelled out words. Eliza — only I now know it cannot have been Eliza — said she was sorry if she had caused any offence to Dr Chenai when he examined her. He is a friend of mine, and some months ago she agreed with some reluctance to allow him this, but I saw at the time that she regretted it and would not answer his questions. The message stated that she found herself unable to look at or speak to him as she was unsettled by his appearance, something for which she now felt profoundly sorry. Dr Chenai had been stricken with a palsy, and one side of his face was drawn up. But the mere idea that Eliza would have made a comment on a person's appearance could only be entertained by someone who had never met her. And then — and then I recalled that Dr Chenai was not afflicted until some weeks after he examined Eliza. She never saw him again, and his case was not reported in the newspapers and I thought it best not to mention it to her, so she never knew of it.'

'Did you challenge Miss Eustace?' asked Mina.

'No, I needed to walk about in the air and think, so I just pleaded another appointment and left, but even if I had, I am sure that some clever explanation would have been forthcoming.' He peered through the window. 'Where is your brother? He seems to be a long time about his mission.'

'He is,' said Mina anxiously, and ordered the cabman to turn and move around the corner into Bloomsbury Place, stopping a few yards nearer to Miss Eustace's lodgings. She peered down the street, but there was no sign of Richard. They waited in silence for a while, and Mina was wondering if she ought to admit her deception to Dr Hamid and reveal the true nature of her brother's mission, when her companion leaned out of the window.

'There is a carriage approaching,' he said. 'It is stopping and a lady is getting down. It is Miss Eustace! Is your brother still there?'

'He must be!' said Mina. She thought she saw a slight movement at the window of Miss Eustace's apartments. 'I can see him!' she gasped. 'He will be discovered!'

In a moment, Dr Hamid had leaped down from the cab and was running down the street. 'Miss Eustace!' he called out, and she looked up in astonishment.

'Dr Hamid!' she said, 'whatever are you doing? Are you well?'

'Yes, and I must apologise for accosting you in this fashion. I happened to be visiting a patient who lives nearby, but my thoughts have been in some disarray since attending the séance tonight. I could think of nothing else — my poor dear sister! I need to know more! Would you allow me the favour of a few moments conversation? Let us walk down to the seafront and view the sunset.'

'Perhaps it would be better to wait until you are calmer,' she advised.

Mina, trying her best to see, was sure now that it was Richard at the upper window but he was unable to descend without grave risk of Miss Eustace seeing him.

'Oh, but I must speak with you now, or I will never be calm again,' pleaded Dr Hamid. 'One minute only, I beg of you, and we will walk just a little way down the street and then up again, and I know it will refresh me. And I will engage you for another private séance — I will do anything, pay any price if I can hear from my dear sister just once more.'

'Very well,' said Miss Eustace, dismissing her cab, 'let us walk.' Dr Hamid took her arm and they strolled down the street towards the seafront.

As soon as their backs were turned, Richard began his perilous descent, his cloak flowing about him so he looked like a gigantic leathery bat crawling down the wall. 'Do you see that, Miss?' asked the cabman, suddenly. 'On the wall of that house. There's something funny going on there! I think I should get the police!'

Mina peered out of the window. 'I can see nothing,' she said, 'but the lady who lives there is a spirit medium and is often visited by ghosts. Perhaps you are seeing a ghost?'

'Oh my word!' gasped the cabman. 'And you say that you can't see it at all?'

'No, it is quite invisible to me. I think your best course is to turn the cab around, so it cannot see you.'

'Oh! Yes! Right away!' he said, complying with some energy.

'And it might be best if you do not speak of this incident to anyone. You would only be accused of drunkenness which would be very unfortunate.'

'I haven't taken a drop,' he declared, 'but I can see as there are those who wouldn't believe me.'

A minute later, the door of the cab opened and Richard climbed breathlessly inside. 'That was good work by Dr Hamid,' he said.

'Did you deliver the gift?' asked Mina, holding out her hand.

He dug in his pocket for the handkerchief and returned it to her. 'Oh yes, with great success.'

Dr Hamid soon joined them. 'Mr Scarletti, I am pleased to see you are safe, but let that narrow escape serve as a warning never to attempt such a dangerous escapade again.'

'I understand there are men who make a living at it, but the work is too hard for me,' said Richard, as Mina signalled the cab to move off. 'Still, if my business partner fails to return from London I may yet be obliged to take up house-breaking as my new career.'

Dr Hamid frowned, not sure if Richard was joking or not. 'And there is another thing of great importance I must say to you. I am sorry if you will be disappointed in the lady who so commands your affections, but it must be said before another moment passes. My eyes have been opened tonight. I have received evidence that has convinced me she is a fraud.'

'Now, it is strange that you should say that,' said Richard, 'because I have just found out the very same thing. It is no wonder that she tries to keep her address a secret, for she has items hidden in her lodgings that she does not want the world to see.'

'You have searched her rooms?' said Dr Hamid, astonished.

'Oh, one thing led to another and I confess that out of a natural curiosity I did, but very carefully. She will not know that anyone has been there. The lady has boxes of costumes, as well as masks, wigs, false beards, stuffed gloves, rag babies and the like, as well as oil of phosphorous and everything she needs to create her spirits. But there was something else, too, a great many items cut from the newspapers, notebooks with intimate details of the residents of Brighton, culled from who knows where. She is a squirrel for gossip and lays her store aside for when it is needed.'

'I am sure,' said Mina, 'that all the private revelations she passes on will be found there.'

'But there was another thing,' said Richard. 'I saw personal effects and clothing which suggests that she does not live alone, or at least that she is visited by another who sometimes sleeps there. A man.' He smiled. 'Well, that was hungry work, and I can quite fancy a bite of supper!'

'It would be my great pleasure for both of you to be my guests,' said Dr Hamid, directing the cab to his home.

'The question is,' said Mina, 'what can we do with the information we now have? We may express our suspicions to the police but that is all. We have no evidence, no facts with which to persuade them to take action. And Miss Eustace has too many supporters for our voices to carry any weight. We most certainly cannot tell anyone what Richard saw in her lodgings tonight or they will want to know how we came by that information.'

'I suppose we could ask someone to keep watch over the premises and see if Mr Clee slips in of an evening and then departs in the morning, but that would prove nothing,' said Richard.

'In any case, I do not think Mr Clee is even in Brighton at present,' said Mina. 'There is the breach of promise action to be heard, and he has engaged a London solicitor. He may well be staying there until the trial. I suspect he will want to keep well away from Miss Simmons and her sister Mrs Langley who may be tempted to box his ears if she sees him, as might the other ladies he has addressed.'

A gloomy atmosphere descended as the three conspirators pondered the difficulty. It was agreed that if any one of them came up with a plan, then that individual would share his or her thoughts with the other two before taking any action.

The next morning Mina was pleased to see that her mother was feeling a little better. Part of the reason for Louisa's recovery was her recognition of the fact that Miss Whinstone was even more miserable than she was, and she did not enjoy competition. Miss Whinstone's wailings about her expenditure on the two orphans was becoming tiresome. They seemed to need a dozen suits of clothing each, and books and equipment for every activity the school offered, including lessons in riding, sailing and languages. She received letters from them once a week, which usually asked for money, and described the appurtenances of wealth that other pupils enjoyed with the strongest possible implication that they would be desolate if they did not acquire the same. All questions as to how she had selected the children or even why she had suddenly taken the course of adoption were met with silence.

Mina was busy with her writing when there was a knock at her door and she opened it to admit Mrs Parchment. 'Miss Scarletti, if I might have a word?'

'Yes, of course, is there anything the matter?'

'Not at all, I am entirely satisfied with my accommodation here. However, I need to inform you at once that I intend to leave Brighton in the very near future. There is family business I must attend to, and it is such that I might be absent for many months or even be obliged to make my home elsewhere. My rent is paid to the end of the month, and I am content with that arrangement. I will inform you of the date of my departure as soon as I know it myself.'

'Thank you for letting me know,' said Mina. 'I hope you have enjoyed your stay here in Brighton.'

Mrs Parchment gave an uncharacteristic smile. 'I have, thank you.'

'Might I ask one thing?'

'Please do.'

'I hope — I trust — that your departure is not connected in any way with the difficulty concerning Miss Simmons? Her behaviour was unacceptable, as was Mr Clee's. I would not like to think that in making the error of employing her I created some dissatisfaction with the arrangements here.'

Mrs Parchment's back achieved a sudden rigidity. 'I do not blame you in any way, Miss Scarletti. Miss Simmons's masquerade of innocence was skilfully done and would have convinced anyone. When the truth is known, she will be exposed for what she is, a conniving and deceitful woman. I know all about her plans to extort money from Mr Clee under false pretences, but I also happen to know that she and her sister, both of whom have told lies to the police, will fail.'

'May I ask how you know this?' asked Mina. Both Miss Simmons and her sister had struck her as truthful, and she did not like to think she had been so categorically deceived.

'You may, but I am advised that that is a matter best aired in court.'

'Will you be giving evidence?'

'I will, since it was I who observed them and reported what I saw.'

'But did you overhear their conversation?'

'That,' said Mrs Parchment with a smirk, 'remains to be seen.'

Mina saw nothing in Mrs Parchment's manner to shake her trust in the veracity of Miss Simmons and her sister. 'I wonder,' she said, 'if the young lady of fortune to whom Mr Clee is shortly to be married will appear to give witness to his good character. That would cause quite a sensation.'

'It would indeed, if such a lady existed.'

'You think she does not?'

'Do you have any evidence that she does?' said Mrs Parchment confidently. 'I have heard this rumour, of course, but I do not give it any credit.'

'But it is not simply a rumour,' Mina advised her, 'the engagement was mentioned in the letter Mr Clee's solicitor sent to Miss Simmons. She showed it to me. Where can the solicitor have obtained the information except from Mr Clee himself?'

Mrs Parchment gave a curiously brittle laugh. 'Oh, there is nothing in that. Young gentlemen, especially handsome young gentlemen like Mr Clee, always imagine that all the ladies are in love with them. Only wait for the trial and she will not appear.'

She swept out, her nose tilted in the air. Mina was left wondering if the young lady of fortune was a myth for quite another reason, because she had been invented by Mr Clee as a means of escaping the consequences of his engagement to Miss Simmons.

Mrs Parchment was kept very busy over the next two days with her preparations for removal from Brighton, and then, quite abruptly, she announced that she would be away on business until the hearing, packed a small travelling bag, and departed.

Chapter Twenty-Four

Richard in the meantime had been saved from the necessity of undertaking burglary as his new profession by the reappearance in Brighton of Nellie Gilden, bringing with her all her many personalities. M. Baptiste was well on the way to recovering from what had proved to be a trivial flesh wound; however, the lady who had shot him was not after all, as had first been supposed, a mad woman, but his lawful wife. These two states were not, Nellie suggested with some acerbity, entirely incompatible. The would-be murderess, who had arrived in London accompanied by her three small children, had come armed not only with a revolver but a French marriage certificate, which predated the conjurer's nuptials with Nellie by ten years. After some harrowing scenes M. and Madame Baptiste had become reconciled, M. Baptiste had announced that he would not bring any charges, and Nellie had left London, her main regret being that the lady had not been a better shot. Her only consolation was a generous gift from her former employer and supposed husband to ensure that his bigamous marriage was never mentioned. After telling Richard the sad tale, Nellie had gone to Mrs Conroy's emporium to console herself with a new parasol.

Pleased as Mina was that M. Baptiste had survived and been reunited with his devoted, if rather desperate, wife and innocent children, and that Richard could now continue his theatrical career, which was at least preferable to burglary, Mina saw another danger. Nellie was a free woman, a single woman, and it was therefore more than possible that she and Richard might marry. Mina only hoped that if this did occur, Nellie might choose to do so as Lady Finsbury, having presumably first found some acceptable method of disposing of Lord Finsbury.

'You will never guess who I encountered in London,' exclaimed Miss Gilden, as she, Richard and Mina enjoyed a quiet supper after the reappearance of Signor Ricardo and the Mystic Beauty on the Brighton stage. 'None other than Rolly! He was hoping to be at the Gaiety for the season, but is now without employment, and it is such a shame, as he does do such amusing eccentrics. I especially admire his Caledonian Marvel, in which he rides a velocipede while wearing a kilt and playing the bagpipes. So I suggested he comes down here to see what is doing.'

'Why not?' said Richard. 'He can even become Signor Ricardo if he wishes.' Richard looked a little subdued. Mina wondered if he thought Nellie's old friend might be a rival for her hand; either that or his ardour had waned since he had discovered that his mistress was not, after all, a married woman.

Nellie produced some portraits of Mr Rollason in his favourite characterisations, which included the Caledonian as well as the King of Siam and a one-eyed sailor. It was very hard to imagine that all these were one and the same man. As she gazed at them a tiny seed of an idea began to take root in Mina's mind.

Two days later, at Brighton Police Court, Mr Clee appeared to answer the charge of breach of promise, the object being for the magistrates to consider whether he should be committed to take his trial at the assizes. As Mrs Parchment had so confidently predicted, there was no betrothed young lady to give evidence on his behalf. Miss Simmons declared that Mr Clee had paid court to her, and that they were secretly engaged to be married, the event depending only on the inheritance he was due to receive from his great-aunt. Mrs Langley also appeared to testify that she had overheard all the conversation between Mr Clee and her sister and entirely supported the prosecution's evidence. A gentleman then appeared to state that he was Mr Clee's cousin, and told the court that Mr Clee had no great-aunt living, neither did he have any relative wealthy enough to provide any expectation of inheriting a fortune. The replies were couched in such a fashion that it suggested that it was Miss Simmons and her sister who had invented the story.

The final witness was Mrs Parchment, who stated that she had reported Miss Simmons's behaviour to Mrs Scarletti on witnessing the companion walking out with a young man, who she readily identified as Mr Clee. She might not, she said, have revealed what she had seen had the conversation been innocuous. If she had believed for an instant that Mr Clee had been making unwelcome overtures to Miss Simmons she would have stepped in and warned the lady. The situation, however, had been quite different. She had been shocked to hear Miss Simmons throwing herself shamelessly at the young gentleman, who had been trying to persuade her that she was deluded about his intentions.

In vain did Miss Simmons weep and Mrs Langley exclaim angrily. The court, taking the balance between the plain young woman of humble origins demanding compensation from the handsome young man with the Byronic curls and the respectable widow declaring that the claim was founded on lies, dismissed the suit. Miss Simmons, distressed almost to the point of collapse, was half carried from the court by her sister.

'I can well understand Mr Clee's interest in Miss Simmons,' Mina later told Richard. 'She was an intimate of my mother and could provide all kinds of information to establish Miss Eustace's credentials, and of course she was a willing confederate in the séance. If it were not for the fact that Mrs Parchment has no fortune I would almost suspect Mr Clee of making her an offer. As it is, she has appointed herself a moral guardian and that seems to be the basis of her actions.'

'But Mrs Parchment does have a considerable fortune,' said Richard. 'At least, her husband died a wealthy man. She may choose to live simply, but that is no clue to her means.'

'How do you know this?' asked Mina.

'True,' said Richard, 'how do I know it? I have read it somewhere very recently.' He thought for a moment. 'Oh, yes, I recall it now. When I was searching Miss Eustace's rooms I found a notebook recording the names of wealthy residents of Brighton, and their worth. Mrs Parchment's name was there, with an extract from a newspaper showing that her husband's estate was worth above forty thousand pounds.'

'Was Mother's name there?' Mina demanded in alarm.

'I don't know, I didn't have time to read all of it.'

'Should I warn Mrs Parchment?' asked Mina.

'Would the lady be prepared to hear anything to the dishonour of Mr Clee?' asked Richard.

'I don't know, but I should at least make the attempt,' said Mina.

On her return home, however, Rose told her that Mrs Parchment had left the house after taking an early breakfast that morning, and a carrier had later called to remove her effects. She had left no forwarding address. Mina was just pondering what to do when Mrs Bettinson appeared, full of news. Mrs Parchment and Mr Clee, she said, had gone straight from the courtroom to the register office where they were married by special licence.

Mina could do nothing but abandon the lady to her fate and hope that her eyes would be opened to her dreadful situation before too long.

The morning post had brought with it an interesting packet from Mr Greville. His enquiries about the fraudulent medium in London had not ended with his discovery of the brief newspaper account. Realising that the sensational papers might provide better detail, he had obtained a copy of the *Illustrated Police News*, and sent it to Mina, observing that its report was undoubtedly culled from other newspapers, but the quality of its woodcuts was excellent. The artist had chosen to depict the sensational exposure of the medium, and the likeness, taken from a portrait photograph, was unmistakable. 'Mrs Hilarie Clee', whether or not that was the lady's real name, was undoubtedly Miss Eustace. The article corrected an impression that had been given previously, in that the imposture had been detected because of the unruly behaviour of not one child, but two, a boy and a girl, said to be the medium's own children. Both she and her husband, Mr Eustace Clee, had been arrested.

Mina realised that there was no time to lose. She told Rose to summon a cab and went to see Miss Whinstone. That lady was looking most forlorn, and despite the unexpected arrival seemed grateful for the company. She was clutching a handkerchief in one hand and a framed portrait in the other, but on Mina's being admitted to the room, she replaced the portrait on a side table with fingers that trembled so violently that the object fell over. Mina retrieved it for her and replaced it, seeing, and this was no great surprise, that it was a photograph of two children.

'Are these the children you have adopted?' she asked.

Miss Whinstone nodded, miserably. 'They are good children, but I had no idea that it was such an expense keeping them at school.'

'I beg you, Miss Whinstone,' said Mina, very determinedly, 'not to pay another farthing for whatever luxuries they demand. You have been the victim of a callous plot.' She proffered the newspaper. 'Take a look at this picture. Do you recognise the lady?'

Miss Whinstone stared at the illustration. 'Why, it is Miss Eustace! The likeness is very marked.'

'I cannot say what her real name is, but she is married with two children, a boy and a girl, the same ages as the ones that have been foisted upon you.'

'But —' Miss Whinstone looked confused.

'Please, you must be open with me. How were you prevailed upon to adopt them? Was it a spirit message? Where did you fetch them from?'

Miss Whinstone uttered a piteous wail. Mina went and sat close to her. 'Please tell me,' she begged, but the unhappy woman shook her head.

'Were they living in an orphanage, or a boarding school or a charity home?' Mina persisted. 'What are their names? Do you have their birth certificates? What papers have you signed?'

Miss Whinstone flapped her hands in confusion at so many questions. Mina rang for the servant to fetch a glass of water and allowed the distraught woman to calm down enough to speak.

'I don't know where they were living,' she said at last. 'The children were brought to me in the Pavilion Gardens by a lady who was a stranger to me. I do not have their certificates; they are called John and Mary, but I believe the births were never registered.'

'Did the lady tell you who they were?'

'No. Really — I can say nothing about it.' She gulped water so rapidly she almost choked, and it splashed down the front of her dress unheeded.

'What papers have you signed?' asked Mina.

Miss Whinstone shook her head. 'None, it was thought best not to.'

'Why was that?' asked Mina. 'For the sake of secrecy?'

There was a long silence.

'Miss Whinstone,' said Mina. 'I think that you have been told lies, by unscrupulous people determined to part you from your fortune, and then made complicit in your own downfall by being manipulated into keeping a secret.'

'But —' whispered the lady, meekly.

'Yes?'

'But Archibald would not have told me a lie.'

'I have no doubt that your brother was a good and honourable man,' said Mina soothingly, 'but any messages you have received from him through Miss Eustace may have been nothing more than an invention to entrap you.'

Miss Whinstone hesitated, and Mina put the newspaper before her again. 'Only read here about her arrest for fraud. Can you continue to trust her?'

'I — I don't know,' said Miss Whinstone, in a voice that seemed to echo from a deep pit of wretchedness. 'I was so happy when she brought me messages from Archibald, happy, that was, until …'

'Until he demanded that you adopt two children?' said Mina. 'On what pretext? Can your brother who cared so much for you really have intended you to be as unhappy as you clearly are now? I cannot believe it of him!'

Miss Whinstone sobbed, and was for a time incoherent, but was able after a while to say with an effort that good as her brother had been, one could never tell what secrets a man might have.

'I understand,' said Mina. 'You need say no more; I can see that it pains you. But it is my belief that your brother was as virtuous a gentleman as you have always known him to be, and that the real transgressor is Miss Eustace.'

Slowly, Miss Whinstone recovered her composure, and dried her eyes. 'Do you really think so?' she asked, hopefully.

'I am certain of it!'

'But what shall I do? I have been sent an account for another quarter's schooling, and they both need new clothes and books.'

'This is my advice,' said Mina. 'Pay nothing to these criminals. You will not be challenged unless you show weakness. Go to see Mr Phipps, the solicitor, without any delay, and put the whole matter into his hands. Any further demands for money can then be redirected to him. Ask him to make enquiries about the antecedents of the children. Once you have proof of what is suspected then the police can be informed. Will you do that?'

Miss Whinstone was drowning under waves of indecision. On the one hand, there was the shame of admitting that she had been made into a fool, and sucked dry of her income. The shame of her brother's transgression was on the other hand, something that she could bury deep and with it came two children, supposedly of his and therefore her blood, a family she could never have hoped for. She looked at the newspaper again, sighed, and took Mina by the hand. 'Will you accompany me?' she asked. 'I do not think I have the strength to go alone.'

Mr Phipps, though a busy man was happy to find time to see Miss Whinstone and was understandably shocked at what she had to reveal. He promised to commence enquiries immediately.

'Well, here is a to-do!' said Mina's mother on her return. All of Brighton, it seemed, was buzzing with the news of Mrs Parchment's nuptials, and the general view was that she had lied in court to extricate Mr Clee from Miss Simmons's suit, and gained a husband as her price. The happy couple were spending their honeymoon at the Grand Hotel. 'What can the silly woman have been thinking of? And he seems to have got a very poor bargain.'

'He has a wealthy wife,' said Mina, 'and for some men that is all that matters.'

'Nonsense, Mrs Parchment doesn't have a penny to her name. I told you so myself, Mina, but you cannot have been listening to me.'

'I thought — I believed that her late husband died a wealthy man,' said Mina. 'Was I mistaken?'

'No, he had made himself rich on the vanity of others. But he and his wife were on bad terms and had separated long before his death. He left all his fortune to a nephew, who out of charity made a small allowance to his aunt. Now that she is married, I expect that will cease. If Mr Clee expected to live in luxury from the proceeds of Parchment's Pink Complexion Pills he is in for a very unpleasant shock.'

With the possibility that Mr Phipps might take several weeks to obtain firm evidence of the duplicity practised upon Miss Whinstone, and Mr and Mrs Clee about to leave town, Mina realised that she had a very short period of time to put her plan into action. She wrote two notes and the next day there was a meeting.

'The thing that makes it especially difficult to expose fraud is that if it takes place it does so before hardly more than ten people, most of whom are devotees of the medium,' said Mina. 'Whatever happens and whatever is said, the thing that counts is how the event is represented to the wider public. The only advantage we have is the fickleness of popular opinion. Just as people may flock to the latest fashion so we may also expect that they will be as quick to abandon it and find the next sensation to amuse them.'

'But, if what you say is true,' said Dr Hamid, in whose parlour the co-conspirators were assembled over a pot of tea and a large plateful of Eliza's favourite almond biscuits, 'as soon as Mr Phipps has his evidence Miss Eustace will be found out.'

'I cannot help but think that she will find some way to extricate herself,' said Mina. 'There are any number of people who would lie or blind themselves to the truth in order to protect her. And we must catch Mr Clee, too, and soon, or he will disappear. We can't wait for Mr Phipps to complete his enquiries.'

'Then what do you suggest?' asked Richard. 'I suppose I could always break into her apartment again and declare my undying love. That should work. I'd have all her secrets in an hour!'

'Promise me that you will not,' said Mina. 'No, we must engage that great and noble personage, Lady Finsbury.'

Nellie, who had been admiring her new pair of lace gloves, laughed.

'Lady Finsbury,' Mina pointed out, 'is an admirer of Miss Eustace, so much so that she wishes to be her patroness, and use her influence to enhance her protégée's fame. Lady Finsbury will hire a hall, she will engage a man to sell tickets and keep undesirables from the door, pack the room only with the most dedicated believers, guarantee that she will purchase a dozen or more tickets for herself and her fashionable friends, and she will promise Miss Eustace a generous extra payment if she can only produce a full form manifestation of her beloved great uncle, Sir Mortimer Portland.'

'Do you expect Miss Eustace to personate a man?' said Richard.

'Not at all. I expect her to get Mr Clee to personate Sir Mortimer. Mr Clee is well known by sight to all of Miss Eustace's circle. Only unmask him and the imposture will be apparent. Remember, in her previous séances, Miss Eustace, through the Gaskins, had full command of all the circumstances. She will imagine that on this occasion she enjoys not only the approbation but the protection of Lady Finsbury. Miss Eustace will undoubtedly make many conditions for her appearance, and Lady Finsbury will agree to them all, but it will be we who have the control.'

'If she should suspect anything …' said Dr Hamid.

'I know,' said Mina. 'If she does then the event will be a failure. She dare not risk a complete failure before such a large gathering, and will produce some slight effects to please the crowd, but there would be nothing we can use to prove fraud beyond a doubt. She has escaped so many times, she knows what to do. The important thing for our purposes is the production of the spirit form of Sir Mortimer Portland. Lady Finsbury must make a very valuable offer to tempt her to do that.'

'Has she brought out a male spirit before?' asked Richard. 'I mean a whole body that walks about, not just a mask and a false beard on a stick.'

'It seems she has. Mother swears that at a private séance she saw Father actually standing before her in the room, and conversed with him and even touched him. It is my belief that it was Mr Clee, as they are of similar height and build, perhaps with a scarf or shawl around his face, as they do not look very alike, but Mother insists that she saw Father clearly and cannot have been mistaken. Lady Finsbury has provided Miss Eustace with a portrait of her great-uncle, and if asked about his height and build, she should mention something very like Mr Clee. That will be enough to tempt them to try the imposture, if, that is, Mr Clee can bear to leave the arms of his new bride.'

It took several days to make all the arrangements. Mina hired a suitable meeting hall, and hoped that with the sale of tickets, which were deliberately priced at a very reasonable level to encourage the maximum possible attendance, she would not be greatly out of pocket. Fortunately, Miss Eustace's circle was so well known that there was no difficulty in securing considerable interest in the event, which it was promised would be the most astounding séance that the renowned medium had ever conducted, with the added relish that it would be graced by a noble lady celebrated for her beauty and taste, and her glittering entourage.

Mina, though not Miss Eustace's most favoured person, was fully intending to be there to both witness and oversee the course of events, and since Richard was acting as doorkeeper there would be no difficulty over her gaining entry, but she thought it best to conceal herself at the back of the room in case Miss Eustace was to spy her and take alarm, which would give her the opportunity of casting the blame for any failure on Mina's bad influence. Once the room was in darkness, Mina intended to creep forward and secure a better position in a seat reserved for her at the front.

On the day of the event another package arrived from Mr Greville, and Mina was just about to open it when Richard, who had hired the cab to take them to the hall, arrived with a downcast expression.

'What is the matter?' asked Mina. 'Has Miss Eustace taken flight? That would be almost as good a result if we were never to see her again.'

He shook his head. 'No, she is here and Lady Finsbury is fawning on her and promising the most astonishing wealth, but I do not think we will see Sir Mortimer, in fact, without her accomplice it is doubtful that anything of note will happen, and we will have spent our money in vain.'

Mina ignored the suggestion that he had had any share in the financial arrangements. 'Has Mr Clee left Brighton?'

'Oh, he is still in Brighton,' said Richard, 'very much so, and unable to leave it if he wished, but he and his lady wife have had a disagreement which took quite a violent turn. I am surprised that it did not echo all over town. The subject of their dispute was, I believe, which one of them was able to pay the bill at the Grand Hotel, and the only thing they could agree upon was that it was neither of them. Mr Clee has by now discovered that his wealthy bride has not a copper coin to her name. There was a great deal of shouting and epithets and some broken furniture and the manager had no choice but to call the police. The two lovebirds are currently cooling their heels in the cells, and will come before a magistrate tomorrow. What shall we do?'

Brother and sister sat together and considered the sad wreckage of their plans.

'There is nothing we can do,' said Mina, eventually. 'All is arranged and must be paid for, but I think now that we will get little result from it. It is my fault, I am afraid, I have been too ambitious. Well,' she said, folding the unopened package and pushing it into her reticule, 'let us go.'

Chapter Twenty-Five

They arrived at the hall shortly before the main crush was expected. Richard and Dr Hamid, while reserving for themselves seats on the front row, had taken on the role of doorkeepers, supposedly to ensure that press-men and other undesirables were refused admission, but actually only to make Miss Eustace believe that this was taking place. The medium had also been reassured that when a volunteer was asked for from the company to check that all was genuine, the person who would step forward would be a friend of Lady Finsbury who was a firm believer in spiritualism.

Professor and Mrs Gaskin were early arrivals. Although they had relinquished their supervision of Miss Eustace to Lady Finsbury and her agents, they remained close by the medium's side, perhaps hoping that some of the glamour of her noble patron would touch their garments, and brush them with a little glossy stain. Nellie was impeccable in her role; her dress, deportment, manners, and mode of speech were exactly as someone who had never met a titled lady would imagine one to be.

Mina took care to make herself inconspicuous, which for the most part meant sitting behind a person of a larger stature, there being more than sufficient to choose from. As the audience arrived, in a steady but powerful stream, all chattering with excitement, Mina was able to see each individual as they entered; her mother, Mrs Bettinson, Mrs Phipps and her nephew, Mrs Langley, Miss Simmons, Mrs Peasgood and her sister and friends, Mr Jordan and Mr Conroy. The crowd was, she knew, salted with representatives of every leading newspaper in Sussex, and there was a local artist specially hired by the *Illustrated Police News* to record the event, and several plain-clothes detectives. The unfortunate Miss Whinstone had, Mina had recently learned, gone away on a sea trip to recuperate from her upset. Mr Clee and his wife were presumably still incarcerated, and did not make an appearance.

As the room filled she remembered that she had not yet looked at the item she had received in the post from Mr Greville, and so pulled it from her reticule and opened the packet. It was another copy of the *Illustrated Police News* from October 1869, and this one included a small picture of Miss Eustace and her husband on trial. It was cruder than the paper's usual portraits, and the likeness of Miss Eustace was only fair while the man in the dock beside her looked nothing like Mr Clee. Mina wondered if the artist had been in court at all.

A theatrical-looking gentleman with a colourful cravat and a flower in his buttonhole strode into the hall and looked about him with an air of aristocratic confidence. He clearly expected to be and indeed was directed to one of the reserved places. Mina was a little mystified at first as to who he might be, although there was something a little familiar about his appearance. He clearly knew Lady Finsbury for he greeted her in a warm but respectful manner. Mina suddenly realised that this must be Rolly Rollason, the man who had posed for the portrait used for Sir Mortimer Portland. In his own person he was a remarkable looking individual, a giraffe of a man, well above six feet in height, with a long neck and prominent Adam's apple but without the bushy hair and long nose of the character he had portrayed. He seemed to be formed almost entirely of arms and legs with prominent knees and elbows attached to a small body. Mina felt some curiosity to see him as the Caledonian Marvel.

It was time. The hall was filled and the doors closed. Richard and Dr Hamid came forward to take their reserved places, and Richard took Lady Finsbury by her tiny fingertips and drew her to face the assembly. All grew silent in anticipation of her words.

'My dear friends,' she began, in a queenly voice, 'for I do most sincerely believe that we who have come together today to celebrate a great truth are friends; how happy I am to see you all! You may be wondering how it was that I came to meet Miss Eustace, and the truth is quite as astonishing and wonderful as any story you may have heard of her powers. Some days ago I received a visitor in the form of a spirit, the spirit of my dear departed great-uncle, Sir Mortimer Portland. I was not afraid, for in life Sir Mortimer was the dearest, kindest and most generous of men, and one who always had my welfare at heart. He had a message for me, one of very great importance, but since I am no medium it was hard for him to express what he wanted so urgently to say. At last he said that I must go at once to see Miss Eustace, who alone was able to receive his words, and this, at the very first opportunity, I did. I have been privileged to witness her powers myself, privileged too, to become acquainted with Professor and Mrs Gaskin whose intelligence and perceptiveness I must applaud. I ask them now to stand and receive your appreciation.'

The Gaskins both rose and faced the audience and bowed without any attempt at humility. There was a polite ripple of approbation.

'They,' Lady Finsbury continued, 'better than any of us here know the foundation of Miss Eustace's powers, and it is to them that we should be grateful for first bringing her to the notice of the public. I would urge you all to study carefully anything they may say or write on the subject.

'I have now determined to do everything in my power to ensure that the fame of Miss Eustace will spread. Her wonders must not be confined to drawing rooms, and seen only by a fortunate few. All the world must know of Miss Eustace. She has astonished Brighton, and next she will astonish London, and all of Europe. Soon, she will conquer America. But today, I know, she will win all your hearts.'

There was enthusiastic applause for Lady Finsbury as Richard escorted her back to her place.

There was no curtain to conceal a stage, and no cabinet. The hall was generally used for meetings at which a long committee table and chairs were used, but the table, which was draped with a thick dark red cloth, had been moved back against the far wall, and all the chairs but one assimilated into the rows laid out for the audience.

The assembled company therefore sat facing nothing apart from an open space with the table at the back and a single chair on which lay a coiled rope. 'May I please have a volunteer to inspect the arrangements?' asked Richard, and before anyone could move Rolly Rollason had leaped energetically to his feet and darted forward. Rolly was a whirling windmill of activity. He picked up the rope and examined it carefully along its length, then, with the ends wrapped around his fists, tugged it hard and loudly declared it to be unbreakable. He picked up the solitary chair, lifted it above his head and looked underneath it, then he drew back the red cloth and showed everyone that nothing was hidden under the table. He next walked about stamping on the floor and pronounced it solid. He was quite an entertainment on his own, and did everything except dance.

Finally, he spotted that there was a door to one side of the room, and hurried over to it, but after making a great display of trying and failing to open it, he told everyone that it was securely locked.

Richard thanked Rolly warmly for his efforts, and asking him to remain, offered his hand to Miss Eustace, who was sitting at the end of the front row. She rose with her customary gracious manner, and came to sit in the chair, then Richard and Dr Hamid tied her in place, and Rolly inspected the knots and said that it was utterly impossible for the lady to escape. Rolly then returned to his seat while Richard and Dr Hamid went to turn down the lamps, allowing Professor and Mrs Gaskin to lead the company in a hymn.

Mina, having already determined her route, left her seat and crept forward into a better place, covered by the darkness and the sound of singing.

The hymn droned to a close, and everyone waited for wonders. The audience, thought Mina, was not only larger than Miss Eustace was used to, it was also, unknown to her, differently composed, being made up partially of those who had seen Miss Eustace's tricks before and were hoping for something novel, those who had seen Miss Foxton and were unlikely to be impressed by anything Miss Eustace could do, and unbelievers. The atmosphere was therefore less one of expectancy than impatience. Believers, thought Mina, were better able than others to endure a long wait for a manifestation. Time ticking away brought them to a state of heightened emotion, the better to appreciate what loomed out of the darkness. Time ticked, but nothing happened. Someone had a coughing fit, someone else giggled, and there was a silken rustling of people shifting in their seats, a creaking of leather shoes, and even some subdued muttering.

At length, after what seemed like an unusually long wait, there was a rap on the far wall. A few moments later another rap sounded from the right. There followed a soporific silence, and then a rap on the wall to the left. It was an unimpressive performance. The dancing lights were next to appear, but while they were attractive enough, they had been seen before, and were not what people had paid their ticket money to see.

A noticeably disgruntled whispering arose, and Mina caught the words 'Miss Foxton', since it appeared that Miss Eustace was being compared unfavourably to her rival. It was apparent to Mina that Miss Eustace, robbed of Mr Clee who was her usual accomplice, had been obliged in some haste to engage another rather less adept. Mina was tempted to turn up the lights and reveal the imposture, but she knew that Miss Eustace would only claim ignorance of what was being done, and it would be impossible to prove that the medium was directing the fraud. The only result of such an action would be an angry audience demanding a refund of their ticket money, a heavy loss to Mina and the closing of the ranks of the faithful about poor ill-used and maligned Miss Eustace.

Even the appearance of the praying hands and the glowing mask from under the tablecloth did little to pacify the crowd, especially when the mask fell off the end of the stick, and had to be retrieved by an invisible, presumably black-gloved hand. This time there was no Miss Whinstone to claim it as a relative, and the result was a mixture of dismay and amusement.

Mina turned to Richard beside her. 'I think we should call an end to this soon,' she whispered. 'Could you make the announcement, and then stand by the lights with Dr Hamid?'

'Right you are!' said Richard. 'It's all a bit lame, I'd say. Sorry, old girl.'

He was about to creep away, but before he could move there was another development, and this one more promising. Mina put her hand on his arm and he stayed.

From underneath the heavy draped tablecloth there came a little extrusion of light, quite formless, but slowly growing. The audience fell silent, as the cloudy shape pushed forward, and became the size of a large pudding, and then a pillow, and then a hound, and then a chair. Having decided on its preferred width, it started to grow in height, and gradually rose to the size of a man. At last it was unfolded, and raised its head and lowered its arms, and stood before them. It was undoubtedly a male figure, dressed as for a fashionable assembly, but covered all over with pale glowing draperies. Through the phosphorescent gauze few of its features were distinct, but there was a luxuriant shrub of wild hair and the thrust of a long nose. A glassy sheen suggested that a monocle adorned one eye and in an outstretched hand it held a single rose.

Bathed in the phantom's pale radiance, Miss Eustace flung her body back in her chair and uttered a great sigh. 'Spirit!' she cried. 'Identify yourself!'

The form slowly turned to face the assembled crowds, some of whom cowered back, while others leaned forward and peered with interest. There was, from the body of the hall, the scratch of busy pencils. 'I have no name, for I am part of another world,' it intoned, in a guttural voice. 'I live in heaven above with the angels, but when I was alive and walked the earth in fleshly form, I had a name, and a history, and loved ones.'

'What was that name?' demanded Miss Eustace. 'And do you have a message for anyone here present?'

'I was once known as Sir Mortimer Portland,' said the form, sonorously, 'and I was the master of Great Portland Hall. I hid a great treasure there, in gold and jewels, which should by rights belong to my heir, Lady Finsbury. The place where it is to be found I will communicate to the lady privately very soon.'

'Let the lady step forward and say that she knows you for her dear relative,' said Miss Eustace.

'Well, here's a pretty thing and no mistake,' came a man's voice from the front row, speaking very loudly. 'Fancy that, to be so personated! It's a disgrace!'

'Be quiet, sir!' urged Professor Gaskin. 'You must let Lady Finsbury speak!'

'I won't be quiet!' said the new voice. 'I will have my say!' There was the sound of a chair moving back.

'Sit down at once, or you will be removed!' snapped Mrs Gaskin, who had forgotten who was in charge of the proceedings.

There was a great deal of annoyed muttering about the interruption, and Mina seized the opportunity and quickly told Richard and Dr Hamid to turn up the lights.

As the yellow glow of the gas lamps flowed through the hall, it could be seen that Rolly Rollason, for it was he who had called out, had got to his feet, but he was no longer Rolly. Under cover of darkness he had donned the elaborate wig, false nose and monocle of his portrait, and was holding the rose he had removed from his buttonhole. 'You, sir,' he said, pointing the rose at the startled spirit, 'are an impostor! I am Sir Mortimer Portland, and I am very much alive, so you can't be my ghost.'

The spirit, which in the glimmer of gaslight resembled nothing more than a man draped in a grubby grey shawl, hesitated. Miss Eustace did not move. During the commotion she had slumped forward so that her head rested almost on her knees, and in that uncomfortable position, her face hidden from view, she remained, to all appearances unconscious.

Professor Gaskin rose up with a cry. 'Oh, please dim the lights! Do so at once or Miss Eustace will surely die!'

'Turn up the lights?' exclaimed Richard, deliberately mishearing, 'All hands to the lights! Let's have more light, here!'

'More light! The professor wants more light!' called Dr Hamid. Several men in grey suits bustled forward, and all around the hall more lamps jumped into flame.

'No! No!' cried the professor, burying his hands in his hair, and clawing at it in desperation; but he was being ignored, for what was visible was very hard to deny. Mrs Gaskin looked unsure whether she should scream or faint. Neither was a strong item in her repertoire, and instead she looked about for someone to insult.

'This is a trick!' she growled at Lady Finsbury, but the lady faced her with some swift and pointed words that should never have left a lady's lips, and Mrs Gaskin retreated, too shocked to speak.

It was the great final scene in the melodrama, and Nellie played it as only she could. She stepped forward, then looked first at one Sir Mortimer and then at the other, as if making up her mind which was the true one. Since Rolly was a full nine inches taller than his impersonator the choice ought not to have taken as long as it did, but Nellie knew how to create and build rapt anticipation in her audience. Finally with an emotional gesture she flew, sobbing wildly, to Rolly and laid her head on his chest. 'Uncle! Dearest uncle!' she cried, 'I thought you were dead!'

Rolly gave a great smirk to the audience and wrapped his arms about his head. 'I ain't dead, though! Ain't I?'

There was a burst of laughter.

'No, it was just a nasty cold in the head, that's all,' he went on, giving his 'niece' a fond hug. 'You must have had a dream and imagined it. And there's no treasure, I'm sorry to say. Never was any.'

'Then who is this?' exclaimed Nellie, turning to the other Sir Mortimer, who had dropped the rose and was backing away, lifting the shawl to try and cover his face.

It was Mr Jordan who strode forward, and before the figure could protest, he whipped away shawl, wig, false nose and monocle, to reveal the shiny pate of Mr Bradley.

There were gasps of recognition from the audience.

Mina, suddenly realising why the picture in the newspaper of Miss Eustace's husband did not resemble Mr Clee, came forward, while Mr Jordan stood by Mr Bradley preventing his escape, and Richard called on everyone for silence, which was not an easy thing to achieve.

'My friends,' said Mina, as soon as the hubbub had subsided sufficiently that she could be heard. 'Not only are these two persons frauds and deceivers, they are also husband and wife and have been practising their wiles for some years. Both have served a prison term, and the proof of that is in my hand.' She raised the newspaper; although there was no chance that anyone could see the illustration, the distinctive page made it very clear as to which paper it was.

'That is a lie!' exploded Mr Bradley. 'And that newspaper is a rag from the gutter! This person is an unbeliever! An imp! A demon! A monster! Why, just look at her, she has the stamp of the fiend himself in her form!'

Louisa Scarletti marched forward and slapped him hard across the face. 'How dare you! She is my daughter!' She burst into tears and hugged Mina, then inevitably appeared to feel faint, and was rescued by Mrs Bettinson and taken back to her seat where Dr Hamid tended to her.

The next person to emerge from the throng was Mr Phipps, who addressed the audience with a packet of papers in his hand. 'Lady Finsbury, Sir Mortimer, ladies and gentlemen,' he began. 'I can confirm that Miss Scarletti has spoken the truth. Here are some legal documents, received by me only an hour ago. They are proof that Mr Bradley and Miss Eustace are indeed husband and wife, and also the parents of two children, who they foisted on to an unsuspecting lady under false pretences and from whom they have been stealing ever since. They have been plying their fraudulent trade for some years and have both served terms in prison.'

Two men in grey suits appeared on either side of the discomfited spirit healer, and took him firmly by the arms.

'You may or may not know this,' said Mina, to Mr Bradley, 'but you are under arrest.'

Mr Bradley, all defiance vanished like the ghost he had pretended to be, was taken away, to the loud hisses and imprecations of his former acolytes, and with missiles of compressed paper bouncing off his head.

The Gaskins stared after him in grotesque dismay, exchanged horrified glances, and then, very quickly and quietly, left the hall.

There was a sudden movement near Mina. Miss Eustace had decided to give up the pretence that she was asleep and use the distraction caused by her husband's arrest to make her escape. She was free of her bonds in an instant, and that feat alone brought a gasp from the audience as they realised how adept she was at such tricks. Only Mina's slight form lay between her and a free route to the door, and she tried to push the trifling obstacle aside, but Mina dropped the newspaper and seized Miss Eustace by both wrists. For a moment or two they struggled, as the medium tried to break free and amazement spread over Miss Eustace's face as she found herself being immobilised by a tiny, seemingly frail woman who was very much stronger than she looked. Mina knew she could only hold on for a short while before her wrenched shoulder and lesser weight allowed her quarry to prevail, but help was at hand.

'I'll take her, thank you,' said Mrs Bettinson, striding up to grab Miss Eustace from behind, pinning her arms to her sides. 'Now then, Miss Cheat, Miss Hoodwink, let's see if you can melt yourself out of this!'

As Miss Eustace was hauled firmly away to join her husband at the police station, Richard came to stand by Mina. 'What a wonder you are!' he said. 'And the best of it, no-one will be asking for their money back!'

Chapter Twenty-Six

Mr Phipps later advised Mina that he had turned over all his documents to the police, who now had ample material with which to mount a search of Miss Eustace's apartments. The very next day the couple attracted a different audience from the one they had recently entertained, when they appeared before the Brighton magistrates. The case was adjourned for the accumulation of new evidence, but it was thought to be certain that they would in due course be committed to take their trial at the next assizes. The couple had asked for bail, but Mr Phipps had argued strongly against this and won.

Mr and Mrs Clee also appeared before the Brighton magistrates, where they were bound over to keep the peace, ordered to pay costs and released. During the entire proceedings they neither looked at nor spoke to one another. On leaving the court they went their separate ways, but Mr Clee was immediately re-arrested and charged with conspiring with the Bradleys to commit fraud. The new Mrs Clee announced her intention of applying for a legal separation from her spouse, something he did not seem averse to, although he was less delighted by her demand for a regular allowance.

Professor Gaskin and his wife were briefly taken into police custody, and for a time they were strongly suspected of having abetted Miss Eustace in her deceit, but it was eventually accepted that they had been little more than unwitting dupes. They regained their freedom, though not their reputations, and agreed with a singular determination to give evidence for the prosecution.

Over the course of the next week, and at the resumed hearing, new facts were made public.

Mr Clee, it was discovered, was Miss Eustace's brother, and an accomplished stage magician, card sharp and occasional spirit medium. He had been attending Brill's baths and learning all he could about the citizens of Brighton, while Mr Bradley had been doing much the same at Dr Hamid's.

When Dr Hamid's friend Dr Chenai was questioned he admitted that while relaxing after an Indian steam bath he had spoken to Mr Bradley and made some incautious comments that had formed the basis of Miss Eustace's supposed communications from Eliza. While Eliza had never told him of the exact position of the pain in her back, he had learned all he needed to know from his examination. There were a dozen other examples of gossip being passed on in this way, all of which had later been recorded in Miss Eustace's extensive notebooks. There were also articles taken from the newspapers about important Brighton figures: their families, illnesses, accidents, deaths and legacies; even information that had been copied from tombstones.

The committal hearing ended as Mr Phipps had anticipated. While awaiting the trial of Mr and Mrs Bradley, the Gaskins, who were not seen in public after the arrest of their protégée, gave up their apartments in Brighton and returned to London, where Mrs Gaskin founded a girls' school and Professor Gaskin devoted himself to studying the chemistry of radiant matter.

As the summer blossomed and the sun broiled the town and its people to a turn, fashions moved on, and the spirit mediums and mystic healers departed. Even Madame Proserpina no longer told fortunes for sixpence on the West Pier, and it was a curious coincidence that she had vanished on the very same day that Miss Eustace had been taken into custody.

Mina was hopeful that there would be no more work for her to do, but Dr Hamid was not so sure. 'Those who want to believe will never be shaken,' he said. 'It enhances their idea of themselves, and in some individuals it will be central to it. Their belief is everything to them; it can become them. If they abandon it then they will be nothing. Even those who have seen the truth about Miss Eustace and her associates may yet believe that another medium will be the true article, forget how they have been made fools of, and take up the next arrival with just as much enthusiasm.'

'Well, we know all their tricks now, and if they try us again we will be ready for them,' said Mina, confidently.

Dr Hamid looked apprehensive, but whether this was at the prospect of the mediums returning to Brighton or Mina commandeering his assistance to deal with them, he didn't say.

There was a new arrival in town, which brought pleasure and meaning to Louisa Scarletti's life. Enid descended upon her mother with the twins and a nursemaid, saying that she planned to stay for several months. She had received a letter from Mr Inskip saying that the property negotiations in distant Roumania were taking longer than he had anticipated and he might well be absent for another six months; indeed, if the snow on the mountain passes next December was as deep as it had been last winter, he might not be able to come home until the spring. Enid, enduring her husband's absence with a fortitude that approached joy, embraced the pleasures of Brighton like a starving person faced with a laden table, while encouraging her mother in a new pastime that she took to with alacrity — spoiling her grandchildren.

There was more good news for the Scarletti family when Mina's brother Edward arrived, bringing with him the delightful Miss Hooper who had at long last consented to become his bride.

Richard was no longer in the theatrical business. It was not so much that mediums were out of fashion, for what Miss Foxton had to offer the eager eye would never be out of fashion, but he had not, as he had hoped, found it to be profitable. Such money as had come in from sales of tickets for private shows or remuneration from The New Oxford Music Hall had somehow found its way into Mrs Conroy's emporium where it had been transformed as if by a conjuring trick into Paris gowns, and lace gloves fit for a queen.

It was with some hesitation that Richard had suggested to Nellie that the business should be given up, and to his surprise she readily agreed, and they parted as friends. Soon afterwards, there was an elegant society wedding, when Nellie Gilden, in her real name of Hetty Gold, became Mrs John Jordan. The event was only marred by one unhappy incident, when the bride, admiring her new husband's favourite timepiece, accidentally dropped it on the ground and stepped on it.

Only one thing still puzzled Mina: her mother's continued insistence that at a private séance conducted by Miss Eustace, she had seen and conversed with her dear deceased Henry, and even clasped him in her arms. No man, she declared, could ever personate him, and she derided the very idea that she could have been mistaken. Mina recalling that the claim had first been made in front of Mrs Bettinson and Miss Whinstone, could not help but wonder if the entire story had been made up to impress her mother's friends and even make them a little jealous.

'Mother,' said Mina, one day in frustration, as they were alone apart from a beribboned baby bouncing on the proud grandmother's knee, its twin having been removed by the nursemaid for feeding, 'I must know the truth of this. When you were at the private séance hosted by Miss Eustace, did you truly see Father, as solid and real a figure as you see me now? Or was it just a story to tease and amuse? No-one would think the worse of you if it was the latter. Come now, surely you can tell me, and I promise not to breathe a word of what you say.'

Louisa waved a teething ring in front of the baby's chubby fingers. 'Oh Mina, how can you ask such a thing?' she said. 'Would I tell a lie?'

'Of course you would not,' said Mina.

'Well then, that is settled.' She gave a wistful smile. 'Dear Henry, I think of him every day, I miss him every moment. No woman could have had a better husband. Yes, Mina, I saw your father as clear and clear as can be. I saw him as I see him always, as I see him even now: in my mind's eye.'

BOOK TWO: THE ROYAL GHOST

Chapter One

Brighton, 1871

Enveloped in the sweet aroma of perfumed oils, Mina Scarletti lay on warm white towels while skilled fingers smoothed away the tension in her back. Mina understood and accepted that she would never be entirely free from pain. Her spine, twisted like an angry snake, distorted the angle of her ribs and hipbone, crushed her small body and placed awkward stresses on her muscles, which gave frequent pinching reminders of a permanent insult. Islands of peace and pleasure still remained within her reach, however, when, after enjoying a herbal steam bath at Dr Daniel Hamid's popular establishment on the Brighton seafront, his sister Anna applied the 'medicated oriental shampoo' or 'massage' as it was sometimes known. After an hour's treatment, Mina felt as flat, pink and boneless as a starfish washed up on the beach, and the world outside looked a little brighter.

Anna had also, with great care and sensitivity, introduced Mina to the world of callisthenics, with classes held in the bathhouse's own gymnasium. Twice a week Mina donned a light, loose assembly of chemise and bloomers, in which she worked to improve the support for her misshapen torso with the aid of stretching exercises and weights. She had even learned to hang by her hands from a bar like a circus acrobat. Mina had deliberately not mentioned this new skill to her mother, Louisa, who would have been horrified at the idea of her daughter adopting such an outrageous posture while wearing an indecent costume.

In recent weeks relaxation had come more easily to Mina, following the news that a dangerous criminal had been arrested. Serious crime was thankfully a great rarity in Brighton, and the publication of a warning notice by the police that some unknown person was sending fruit and cakes laced with arsenic to prominent residents had sent the whole town into a ferment of terror. The word was about that the days of the Borgias had returned. Louisa had determined that she would be greatly affected by the threat of danger, and it had been Mina's exhausting duty to examine and re-examine every item of foodstuff in the house irrespective of whether it had been delivered or purchased directly from a shop. Urgent meetings had been held at the Scarletti home to which Louisa had invited her closest friends, regaling them with the news that they were all about to be murdered and the anxiety was causing her the most terrible suffering.

Once the fiend in human form was in custody and revealed to be a middle-aged spinster with an unhealthy passion for a married doctor, Brighton could heave a municipal sigh of relief, and the search was soon on for fresher and pleasanter sensations. The latest novelty to excite residents and visitors alike was a pamphlet entitled *An Encounter* in which two fanciful ladies had described how, while engaged in a tour of the Royal Pavilion, they had seen the spectre of the late King George IV at a period of his life when he was the young pleasure-seeking Prince of Wales, and affectionately known as 'Prinny'. Some portions of their account were reputed to be of an indelicate nature — whether this was deliberate or unconscious was not apparent — and therefore wholly unfit for the perusal of the female sex. As a result, the pamphlet was selling by the hundred to ladies of all ages and walks of life, the copies being taken secretly to boudoirs to be enjoyed in private. Mina had not read *An Encounter* and had no great wish to do so. She enjoyed both stories and histories, but a work of fiction that had been dressed up to seem like fact in order to delude the impressionable she found merely annoying, not to mention dishonest.

Mina knew the difference between the real and the imaginary, since she occupied her solitary hours writing stories about ghosts and monsters. Her tales were published under a pseudonym by the Scarletti Library of Romance, a company founded by her late father, Henry. The only person privy to her secret identity was her father's business partner, Mr Greville. Her family, in so much as they took any interest in her writing, remained under the impression that she composed moral tales for children. The ghosts and monsters Mina created existed only in her mind, and while she gave them a kind of life by transferring them to paper, she knew that they would not reach out from the page and become real. She was all too aware, however, that suggestible persons of both sexes could easily persuade themselves that they had seen this or that elemental or supernatural being. In the early summer of that year Mina, with the assistance of Dr Hamid, had been instrumental in exposing the activities of a self-styled medium, Miss Eustace, who had taken Brighton by storm and extorted money from her adherents, impersonating a spirit by donning veils that glowed in the dark from the application of oil of phosphorus, and sending messages supposedly from the deceased by tapping a table leg with her foot. Mina had found the deception as transparent as the veils, but those who needed to believe had done so, gratefully, and had had their purses lightened and bank accounts severely depleted as a result. The adventure had cemented a warm friendship between Mina, Dr Hamid and his sister Anna, who often entertained her at their home or accompanied her as she limped her slow walk along the promenade. She had hoped that the public taste for the wonderful had subsided into something approaching common sense, but judging by the success of *An Encounter*, it seemed it had not.

No one had as yet introduced the subject of the supposed ghostly sighting in the Royal Pavilion in conversation with Mina, presumably to avoid stimulating her curiosity about matters no respectable woman, whether married or single, should ever contemplate. Anna Hamid, however, her hands easing away the soreness in

Mina's back to almost nothing, after discussing issues relating to general healthfulness and the current news of the town, asked, after some hesitation, if she had read *An Encounter*.

'There have been letters denouncing it in the *Gazette*, but I have not actually read the book,' said Mina, 'and I am not sure if I would be either entertained or informed by it. If the authors had admitted from the start that it was an invention then I might find it amusing but I believe that they are quite serious about their subject. I rather thought that your brother and I had frightened away all the ghosts from Brighton.'

'That is the reason I am asking, as you know so much about these things, and I would value your opinion from a woman's point of view,' said Anna. 'I am very concerned that this book is upsetting the constitution of those who read it. Many ladies who come here for treatment have read it, and been over-excited to a dangerous degree. Some might think I would be pleased to have more patients seeking our services, but I do not want to line my purse by perfectly healthy ladies being made unwell. I wish to preserve the health of the town, and that means not only treating those who are in pain and discomfort but also maintaining the wellbeing of those who already enjoy it. Several of the patients I have seen recently complaining of attacks of agitation and nervousness have confessed to me that their symptoms began when they read the book. Certain passages I believe they found especially powerful.'

The massage done, Anna helped Mina to sit up and swathed her tiny angular form in scented linen. Anna's pale fawn cheeks were flushed, but she did not elaborate on what she had learned, and Mina knew her well enough not to enquire further. She was, like Mina, a decided spinster, although Anna, at the age of forty-eight, had chosen to be single, whereas Mina, although twenty-five and still of an age to marry and raise a family, had been told some years ago that it would be unwise for her ever to do so.

'If these susceptible ladies are afraid of encountering the Prince's ghost then surely all they need to do is stay away from those places he customarily visited when in town,' Mina suggested.

'I fear it is not the haunting that troubles them,' sighed Anna. 'Far from it; some have told me that they have actually been holding séances with the explicit design of having him appear before them.'

Mina had once seen a caricature of the late King George IV, a gourmand who had become bloated by excess, and could not imagine anyone wishing to see such an unattractive sight, either living or ghostly. Had he been handsome in his youth? Was that what all the fuss was about? Or was it just the thrill of an exalted connection? A lady might forgive a great deal for royalty. 'I am sorry to hear about these foolish séances, but I suppose they are harmless enough diversions if they are not taken too seriously. Do these ladies employ professional mediums? I hope they are not being cheated any more than they deserve.'

'No, they just sit in the dark and call upon the spirits, I believe. One lady told me the Prince appeared in her parlour and took tea with her, but I think she was merely describing what she wished for, and not what actually occurred.'

'Knowing Brighton society as I do, I have no doubt of it. A story to make her friends jealous.'

Anna brought more towels and pressed their soft warmth around Mina's shoulders. 'Well, since you have not read the book, you cannot comment upon it. In fact, I would suggest for the sake of your health that you avoid it altogether. I have not read it myself and have no intention of doing so.'

In view of this strong advice, Mina decided not to pursue the subject with Anna, but she was already considering how she might use her connection to the business of publishing to make enquiries that could alleviate her friend's concerns.

Chapter Two

Mina had first met Dr Daniel Hamid the previous June at a séance conducted by the celebrated spiritualist and sensation of Brighton, Miss Hilarie Eustace. Mina had attended because she was worried — quite rightly as it was to turn out — that her mother and friends were being made the victims of a charlatan whose hidden purpose was to extort large sums of money from the vulnerable bereaved. Dr Hamid, on the other hand, grieving deeply for the recent loss of his beloved Jane, his wife of twenty years, had been seeking hope and comfort in the assurances of mediums. Both hope and comfort had been cruelly wrenched from him by the discovery that he had been duped by a trickster. Furious with the heartless criminal, he had been angry most of all with himself for being so taken in, especially since he had always liked to believe that he was a rational scientific man. He had at once thrown his energies into helping Mina expose Miss Eustace and her confederates as frauds and thieves, even taking some risks, which brought him close to the boundaries of what might seem appropriate for a doctor of medicine. The lady had demonstrated her selfless sincerity by performing her evening séances without making any charge, receiving only those rewards voluntarily given by the grateful, but it was discovered that she also offered private sittings to suitable individuals for which she charged a substantial fee. Behind closed doors, with only the medium and her dupe present, messages were passed on, supposedly from much-loved deceased relatives, which induced the victim to part with ever-increasing sums of money. Mina's determined campaign had revealed the despicable scheme before an appalled public, and the miscreants were now contemplating the fruits of their villainy at the Lewes House of Correction while awaiting trial at the next Sussex assizes.

Once her treatment was over, Mina, feeling much refreshed, went to see Dr Hamid, who had just completed an interview with a patient and was back in his office. Three years younger than Anna, he was neatly bearded, with sad dark eyes.

'I hope you are well?' he asked anxiously as Mina appeared. Each time he saw her, even on a social occasion, he would appraise her walk and posture to see if there was any change in her condition. Her unexpected visit had clearly given him cause for concern, as he was the only doctor she would trust. No one in Brighton was better acquainted than he with the presentation of scoliosis. His older sister, Eliza, who had passed away that summer, had been afflicted to a far greater degree than Mina, her distorted spine creating an exaggerated twist, lifting one shoulder high while forcing the other down, pushing her neck forward so far that she was unable to raise her head. More seriously, her misshapen ribs had constricted the action of both heart and lungs. Dr Hamid and Anna had been devoted to Eliza's care, and she would have lived longer had she not become over-excited after being drawn into the medium's net of delusion.

'I am very well, thank you,' said Mina reassuringly, taking the seat that faced him across the desk, tucking a cushion under one hip to even her posture. 'Miss Hamid's massages always ease my discomfort and are a great blessing. She did, however, mention something that is causing her some disquiet. It seems that séances have come back into fashion in Brighton, and ladies are being disturbed by a publication in which two visitors to the Pavilion have claimed that they saw the ghost of the late King George. If it was not for the fact that it is upsetting people I would think it quite comical. Do you have any observations?'

Dr Hamid's relief that Mina had not come for a professional consultation evaporated rapidly. He looked decidedly uncomfortable, and took some time to compose his reply. 'It is a difficult subject to discuss with any frankness, especially since you are single. I too have seen patients coming here who have been affected by this publication. All of them are ladies who have started to experience fainting fits and unusual excitement. Their family doctors assume that they are suffering from a variety of hysteria, and prescribe soporific mixtures, but that merely treats the symptoms. Anna has found that steam baths and the oriental shampoo are far more beneficial in that they both calm and restore the system. But the book is an unwise publication and should never have been printed. I suspect that the authors were quite unaware of what they were writing and the effect it would have on the more sensitive reader. Some portions of the narrative can be interpreted in quite a shocking light.'

'Then you have read it?'

He tidied the already tidy pile of papers on his desk, in an effort to conceal his embarrassment. 'I — er — well — I was obliged to read it for professional reasons,' he admitted reluctantly.

Mina could not resist a smile. 'And have you suffered from fainting fits and excitement?'

He stared at her in surprise. 'No, of course not!'

'So are gentlemen immune to its effects?'

Dr Hamid was speechless for a moment. 'Apparently so.'

Mina decided to stop teasing him. 'I have been told that the ladies of Brighton are holding séances in their homes to raise the ghost of the late King. Why they might wish to do so I really can't say. It all seems very foolish and we must hope it is a fashion that will be quickly replaced by the next one.'

He nodded emphatically. 'I entertain the same hope. Brighton is a place of fashion after all, and constantly moves from one novelty to another. In a week this may all be forgotten.'

Mina agreed. In August and September it was usual for the town to be gay with noisy families in search of amusement and diversion, but with the approach of October children returned to school, professional gentlemen came to take their leisure, and a new quieter mood began to settle. Later, in November, all would be different again, as the carriage classes began their winter season.

'I have no wish to attend such gatherings; not that I would be invited to them. After Miss Eustace's fall from grace those Brighton spiritualists who continue to believe in her, and yes I am sorry to say that there are still some who regard her as a martyr to the cause, have stamped me as a hardened unbeliever. It appears that I radiate negative influences which would ensure that any attempt to contact the spirits in my presence will fail.'

'Oh, I am done with séances,' said Dr Hamid, feelingly. 'It is a great deal of money to pay out just to learn that you are a fool.'

'Those who can never learn will remain fools all their lives,' said Mina, gently. 'Without your insight and your assistance, Miss Eustace and her henchmen would not now be facing a trial for fraud.'

'That is very kind of you to say so. We can only hope that they will remain where they can do no more harm for a very long time.'

'That is my hope, too,' agreed Mina, 'however, they will be free again one day, and I suspect that once they are, they will continue their lives of deception, since it is all they know, but I do not think they will dare show their faces here again. If there are people still holding séances in Brighton they are at least doing it on their own account, merely for an evening's amusement, and not paying others to cheat them. Let them go on and take what comfort they can until they tire of it and turn to something else. I am pleased to say that my mother will have no truck with such things again, and, in any case, she has plenty to distract her — my sister Enid and her twins are staying with us and they are keeping the fond grandmother happily occupied.' Mina made a significant pause. 'But just in case mother does succumb to temptation, and reads *An Encounter*, what signs of upset should I look for? Fainting and excitement, you say; mother can produce them both at will when she means to have her way, without recourse to disturbing literature. Is there anything else that might give me cause for concern?'

'Imagined symptoms of illness, headaches, difficulty in sleeping, lack of appetite, overindulgence in stimulants or soporifics. The presentation can be different depending on the individual. Tight lacing can make matters very much worse. But if you should notice this in any lady you know, please do refer her to Anna who has devised a special massage to release the harmful vapours.'

'That is very helpful, thank you.' Mina rose to depart, but did not immediately do so. 'I do have one other request.'

'Oh?' said Dr Hamid warily. He had, Mina noticed, a peculiar tone of voice which he had adopted recently at any suggestion she might make which could, if pursued, lead him into the murky waters of professional embarrassment.

'I would like to borrow your copy of *An Encounter* and study it for myself. From what I have heard booksellers might be chary of selling it to a spinster, and I would prefer it if my mother did not know I was reading it. My purpose is to learn what I can about the book, to see if it can be exposed as a mere work of the imagination.'

Dr Hamid looked understandably alarmed. 'Do you think that is wise?'

'I promise I will try very hard not to be put into a great state by it and if I am, then I already know the symptoms, and I will simply come here and enjoy a steam bath and massage which will surely set me right. In any case, I really cannot believe that *all* the ladies who have read the book suffer unpleasant consequences.'

'That is true,' he admitted. 'The ladies who derive such an unhealthy excitement are, I have observed, those with no occupation to use their natural energies, and husbands who neglect them.'

'I shall never have a husband, neglectful or otherwise, and I think I am the happier for it,' Mina declared. 'When I am not practising my callisthenics, or enjoying the sights of the town, or attending to my mother's many whims, my story writing keeps me fully occupied.'

'And what tale are you currently busy with?'

The question was intended to deflect her purpose and she smiled. 'I am writing about a little lady, one who suffers many bodily afflictions and is shunned by society which sees only outward appearances. She has beautiful visions, because she has a good soul, and becomes surrounded by a glowing light. As a result others are at last able to see the goodness within her, and she is much loved.'

He swallowed back a sudden burst of emotion. 'Is she called Eliza?'

'She is.'

A moment passed between them in which shared sadness and fond memories mingled, as they recalled Eliza's too short, yet defiantly cheerful life, which had, in her last weeks, been enlivened by friendship with Mina and enjoyment of the more amusing and less bloodcurdling stories in her repertoire.

'As I am sure you know,' Mina pointed out, 'I am the last person in Brighton to be worried by a ghost story.'

'I know that you are strong-minded but believe me, it is far worse than that. There is material in the book which is quite unsuitable for a respectable single lady. I do not think,' he added cautiously, 'that you would be put into a great state by it, nevertheless, I cannot risk taking the responsibility of lending you a copy. I really am sorry.'

Mina glanced at his desk, feeling sure that a slim volume lay within her reach in a drawer. 'You are being careful of my health, which I understand and appreciate.

But a lady who uncovered the secrets of an extortioner's plot can certainly obtain a book if she sets her mind to it.'

'I have no doubt of it, but it will not be from me.'

'If I can prove that the story is a fraud dressed up as history then that information could help soothe your patients.'

He wavered, but at last shook his head. 'My answer is still no, and please do not press me further. But there is one thing that I should mention. The book nowhere involves séances or mediums. It describes a vision — one for which the ladies were wholly unprepared.'

'A ghostly sighting — well there are many such stories about.'

'And have been since stories began. Brighton is rife with them. But are they no more than idle tales? I think that if ghosts did not exist at all, then people would not talk or write about them. There must be some small grain of truth in it. In fact — ' He hesitated — 'I know you would not like to believe this but from time to time patients of mine have reported seeing phantoms of the deceased — those they love and sorely miss. These are intelligent people, both men and women, not disordered in their minds apart from suffering the grief of recent bereavement. Their visions are clear and convincing — the individuals appear before them as solid and real as if they stood in the same room.'

'Do these visions occur in daylight or darkness?'

'Both.'

'But only of those friends and relations who are constantly in their thoughts, not celebrated individuals unknown to them.'

'True.'

Mina paused reflectively. 'My mother once told me that she saw my father's ghost, but I am not sure what it was she saw. She does like to embroider a tale. And you — have you experienced anything of the nature you describe?'

He uttered a little sigh of regret. 'No. I often think how pleasant it would be to sit in my parlour with Anna and have my dearest Jane and Eliza there with us, so that we might gaze on their faces again, but it has not come to pass. Perhaps some special talent is required which I do not have, and it may be that the ladies who wrote this highly unwise publication do.'

'So you think it may be genuine and not a fiction?'

'It is not, in my view, impossible.'

Mina gazed on him sadly. He had every reason to want to believe in ghosts, as did she. The passing of her dear sister Marianne ten years ago, dead of consumption at the age of twelve, was still a painful memory, and her father's death in the spring of last year after his long wasting illness was a constant ache in her heart, yet she had never sought to call their spirits to her from the heavenly beyond where they now resided, and which was surely now their natural home. Dr Hamid

231

saw only the void in his life that had once been filled by his wife and sister and his judgement was weakened by a keen sense of loss. She wanted to tell him that time would help heal the wound. There would be a scar, of course, and it would still hurt but it would not be so raw and open. But he had surely been told this by others, and as a fundamentally sensible man he realised it himself. Hesitantly she reached out and patted his arm, in a way that a sister might comfort a brother.

He sighed again and nodded. 'I know,' he said. 'I know.'

Chapter Three

Every day in Mina's life was a battle with the infirmity, which had first become noticeable when she was fifteen. She did not, as others might have done, choose to hide from the world, but was determined to live her life to the very fullest in all ways that were both decent and possible, except those that she had been told were denied to her. By not confining herself to those restricted spheres of endeavour thought to be appropriate for women she was able to embrace eagerly all else that the world had to offer. Some three years ago, Mina and her family had deserted the fogs and chills of London to live in Montpelier Road, Brighton, a location chosen for the invigorating air and bright sunshine, which it was hoped would restore her ailing father's health. Her older brother Edward had remained in the capital, where he helped maintain the successful publishing house founded by their father, and also to stay close by the side of the enchanting Miss Hooper, an heiress who had recently consented to be his bride.

Soon after their father's death, Mina's sister Enid, who was considered to be the beauty of the family, had deserted the house of mourning, which she had found unendurable, to marry a Mr Inskip, the dullest solicitor who ever existed, and they had made their home in London. Enid had been amusing herself by tormenting a shoal of ardent and agreeable admirers, and her impetuous acceptance of Mr Inskip, based solely on his superior financial worth, had, she soon realised, been a terrible mistake. In recent months, important business concerns had demanded her husband's presence in the far reaches of Europe and had placed a sea, a mountain pass and great tracts of barren land between them. Enid had come to Brighton to be with her mother, accompanied by her infant twins and a nursemaid, her state of mind and health exhibiting that glowing perfection of contentment that could only be achieved by the extended absence of Mr Inskip. The boys were a source of endless delight to the doting grandmother, if not the mother, and were constantly and resolutely declared to be the image of their Scarletti grandfather. Mina did not want to contemplate the dismay that might ensue if their baby noses ever sharpened to resemble Mr Inskip's proboscis or their infant blue eyes darkened to the colour of silt.

Enid never spoke of her husband; to her he was in a sense dead, and she clearly wished him to remain so. She and her mother spent their days shopping, admiring the babies and engaging in private conversations to which Mina, as a single woman, could never be admitted.

Mina's days were largely solitary; writing or reading, exercising with the dumbbells she kept hidden in the bottom of her wardrobe, or taking in the sights and scents of the town. There were other worlds in her mind, which she could explore freely — places where ghosts and witches and demons abided, and broke out onto the pages of her books to trouble the heroes and heroines she created. Most of all, Mina enjoyed the random and usually unannounced visits of her younger brother Richard, a charming rapscallion with a heart of gold, who divided his time between London and Brighton, depending on where he was most able to obtain and spend money, an elusive commodity which ran rapidly though his fingers like a glistening stream.

As Mina arrived home the maidservant, Rose, was taking a laden tray into the parlour. The pile of iced fancies and a fat yellow sponge cake filled with jam told Mina at once that the visitor being entertained was her mother's friend Mrs Bettinson, whose favourite delights these were. Not that the word 'delight' was one often associated with Mrs Bettinson, a lady who gloried in her widowhood so much that her relatives obligingly died at regular intervals to afford her fresh opportunities to display her imposing bulk in an excess of jet, bombazine and crape. Above all, Mrs Bettinson relished the discovery and dissemination of gossip, and enjoyed the flavour of misery better than that of the choicest pastry.

As Mina entered the parlour, which was smokily warm from the first substantial coal fire of the season, the two ladies glanced up at her quickly and the conversation, which had been proceeding apace, abruptly stopped.

'Why Mina,' said her mother with a brightness that was too brittle to be convincing, 'we were just discussing —' There was a pause — 'the — er — healthfulness of Dr Hamid's steam baths. I trust you are refreshed?'

'Very much so,' said Mina, cheerfully. She limped to a comfortable seat and sat down, making an effort to maintain as straight a posture as possible. Mrs Bettinson frowned at her disapprovingly. 'I am at the very peak of healthfulness,' she added. Mrs Bettinson frowned harder.

Rose poured tea for Mina, and she sipped it with the contented smile that she knew their visitor deplored. A newspaper, the latest copy of the *Brighton Gazette*, was open on her mother's lap. Louisa, who had entered a profound and lengthy period of melancholy following the death of her husband, had only recently begun to emerge into the light of Brighton society in which she was rapidly becoming an acknowledged ornament. Having once declared that newspapers gave her a headache, she now devoured them for all the news of the town and its personalities, taking little interest in events that lay outside that confined circle. Her favourite study was the Local Fashionable Intelligence, which listed those gentry and other persons of note who had just arrived and which hotel they were favouring with their presence. Her thoughts seemed constantly to be occupied with how she might obtain an entrée to a more rarefied social circle than the one she currently enjoyed.

At fifty-five Louisa still had a youthfully slender figure and almost unlined face, with soft pale skin and golden hair that owed nothing to artifice. Her mourning gowns, which had been sombre black for a year, were now being trimmed with white lace and mauve ribbon in preparation for her future butterfly emergence into brilliant colour. Louisa's fresh glow appeared all the more charming beside Mrs Bettinson, who occupied any room she inhabited like a great dark hill topped by a stony monument.

Mina saw that the newspaper was open at the page of correspondence, but Louisa, noticing her glance, folded it shut so quickly that had it been a book it would have made a loud snap. Mina suspected that the two had been discussing *An Encounter*, which had been the subject of much heated debate in the *Gazette*, in so far as this was possible without the paper actually stating why the work was so objectionable. This led her to consider whether her mother had read the book, something that she would never admit to any member of her family. It was easy enough for Mina to avoid being drawn into the conversation, which dwelt largely on recent deaths and other terrible misfortunes, and she quickly finished her tea, declined a cake, and said she would retire to her room. Mrs Bettinson, assuming that Mina was weary and needed rest, nodded, her lip curling with grim satisfaction.

Mina went upstairs as fast as she was able, using both hands on the rail to assist her. If the amount of tea and cake was anything to judge by she had a full hour alone.

It took only moments to find a copy of *An Encounter* under her mother's pillow, and Mina took it to her room. There she sat at her writing desk, placed her special wedge-shaped cushion under one hip that enabled her to sit up straight, and opened the book.

Chapter Four

An Encounter was a short volume numbering some forty pages. The authors were the Misses Ada and Bertha Bland, which were so obviously invented names that it scarcely seemed necessary to mention, as the title page did, that they had adopted pseudonyms in order to preserve their anonymity. The only information revealed about them was that they were sisters, single ladies, daughters of a respectable clergyman, and lived in London.

The cover was bound in plain brown leather and inside was a portrait, a drawing obviously copied from a painting, of the late King George IV in his princely youth. This was not the bloated gourmand he had become in later life, a man so unpopular in his latter years that he hardly ever went about in public and had even had a tunnel built from the basement rooms of the Pavilion so he could visit his stables unseen. This portrait was of a young, handsome, strongly-made man, with a torrent of wavy hair and a commanding expression. How much of this portrayal was accurate and how much was flattery by the artist Mina did not know, but she could see that, as depicted, he might be thought quite a romantic figure, especially as he was at that period of his life Prince Regent, and therefore King of England in all but name, which was enough to make any female heart flutter.

The book had been published that same year, 1871, although there was no indication as to when it had actually been written, and neither was it stated when the events described within had taken place. There was no publisher listed, the title page simply saying that it had been printed for the authors and giving the name and address of a London printing company, Worple and Co. Mina turned to the text for possible clues.

The Misses Bland, having heard of the health-giving properties of Brighton, had, accompanied by their widowed father, taken the train for a day excursion to that popular location. Their object was to enjoy the invigorating sea air and view the gardens and the Pavilion. Once a royal residence, now an amenity of the town, this building, they had been told, was a wonderful sight to behold. None of the family had visited Brighton before, and, said the ladies, they were quite unacquainted with its history. The sisters had determined before they set out to write quite separate accounts of their adventure since they thought it would be amusing and instructive to compare them afterwards. On arrival, their father had expressed a desire to take a bracing walk in the grounds of the Pavilion. The building itself he hesitated to enter, and was content to observe only its exterior. He did not think it an entirely wholesome place, since the late King George had been known for his scandalous behaviour, which caused great grief to his parents and brought shame to the royal family. The King, said the Reverend Bland, was reputed to have lived like an oriental potentate in more ways than one. Further than this he would not say, but his warnings had inadvertently whetted his daughters' appetites to see the royal luxury promised by the domes and minarets that glistened invitingly in the sunshine.

The ladies had at last succeeded in obtaining their father's permission to enter the Pavilion by saying that there was an entertainment they would like to attend, an exhibition by a conjuror who was donating all his fees to a charity for the support of families affected by a disaster at sea. With some reservations the Reverend Bland agreed to this, and it was settled that they would all meet in one hour at the tea room. The ladies' account went on to provide some slight description of the exterior, the velvet lawns, the rookery, and the music of a military band, but their main delight was in the gleaming white Pavilion itself, the fabulously exotic spires and cupolas that made visitors feel as if they had been transported by a magic carpet to lands of the orient.

When the sisters entered the Pavilion they discovered to their disappointment that the entertainment which they had seen advertised in the newspaper would not be given until later that day, after the time appointed for their departure. They decided instead to take a tour of the building, and paid their sixpences to join a party and be guided by an attendant. The first room they saw on leaving the ticket hall was the vestibule, also known as the Hall of the Worthies. Although they thought the decorative columns and carving very fine, and could not fail to be impressed by a large statue of a handsome young soldier waving a sword, a hero of the Crimean War who had died on the battlefield, neither felt any great attraction to the display of busts depicting stern-faced gentlemen, notabilities of Brighton of whom they had never heard. As the attendant expounded at wearisome length on the many virtues and achievements of the citizens of Brighton, the Misses Bland, by mutual agreement, slipped away and explored on their own.

As they walked it seemed to them that the rooms gradually became darker and the shadows deeper. The sound of visitors' voices and the music of the band that had seeped in from outside slowly faded until they vanished altogether. The ladies suddenly realised that they were quite alone, and each commented to the other that it was very strange that no one else was about, as the day was fine and the whole building ought to be thronged with people. Supposing that they had inadvertently wandered into rooms usually denied to visitors, they decided that it would be best to find their way back to the vestibule and re-join their party. After some further twists and turns, which confused them, they entered a room which they were sure from its dimensions and the construction and positioning of its pillars was the vestibule they sought, but it was decorated quite differently, and there were no busts, no statue, and no people. Miss Ada was becoming quite nervous by now, but her sister reassured her that they had simply lost their way, and if they walked on they would soon find the entrance again. They continued to wander, but it was in a drawing room decorated with blue wallpaper and draperies when they really became afraid. They could hear voices again, but although they were not far away they were muffled, as if invisible persons were standing in the room with them, whispering and laughing softly, and when they tried to find the people who spoke they could not. There was music, too, not of a military band, but the gentle sigh of violins and the sweet note of flutes. They heard the clatter of silverware on porcelain and the clink of glassware as if a feast was in progress, but nowhere could they discover where this entertainment was taking place. The room was all hung about with lanterns that cast a strange, smoky, golden light, quite unlike the gleam of gas that had lit the other portions of the house, and they realised that these beautiful old lamps were lit by oil. The sisters walked on, passing through many more rooms, one of them a long gallery decorated in the Chinese style, with deep niches occupied by life-size statues clad in gorgeous oriental robes.

In one large and magnificent room carved serpents wound themselves sinuously about decorative columns, and the walls were hung with lavishly-painted Chinese scenes, the whole topped by a golden dome from which depended a lamp of glittering glass, shaped like a gigantic flower and guarded by dragons. A wide recess housed a pipe organ of enormous dimensions in the form of a triumphal arch. The sisters, their feet sinking into the luxurious carpet, had been looking about them entranced by the sheer size and opulence of the room and everything in it, when a man had appeared before them with remarkable suddenness. Youthful and handsome, he was dressed very elegantly in the style of the last century. The gentleman hesitated as he saw the ladies, then bowed in a formal manner before passing them by and leaving the room. To the sisters' astonishment, when they tried the door they thought he must have come through they found it impossible to open. Not a little puzzled by this, they retraced their steps. Much later when they compared notes, both agreed they had seen the man but while Bertha had not seen him enter the room Ada confessed that it seemed to her as if he had stepped through the wall.

Walking on, they found a drawing room decorated in deep red, resplendent with gilded mirrors, paintings and ornaments, and saw what they thought was a tableau or perhaps a play being enacted. The air was close and very hot, and before them were two figures, extremely lifelike, but moving slowly as though in a dream. The man was sumptuously dressed in a uniform with glittering accoutrements, and he was strongly built with a noble countenance and fine curling hair. The lady was reclining on a long couch which almost filled a recess that faced windows deeply curtained in rich velvet, and she was dressed in a style that had long gone out of fashion. She resembled a figure in a painting rather than a living woman, yet she moved as though alive. Her gown had a very full skirt of lustrous golden silk, with deep side draperies and a bodice and sleeves in sky blue, adorned with pink silk ribbons and bows. The bodice was very low in front, bordered with a great froth of lace revealing a white bosom that undulated like the waves of a milky sea. Most beautiful, however, was the tumbling mass of light ringleted hair that framed a face at once expressive and intelligent. With a movement of effortless grace the lady, who looked upon her swain with great affection, extended a delicate hand towards him, and he at once seized it, fell upon his knees before her and covered the hand with kisses that spoke soundlessly yet eloquently of a burning passion.

All around them the wallpaper glowed like the flames of a fire, and on it there were coiled figures of dragons and serpents, writhing in the most extraordinary manner, and exotic flowers with large fleshy petals.

The Misses Bland had by now begun to wonder if they had stumbled upon something they were not meant to see, yet the two lovers were oblivious of their presence, and gave so much of the appearance of a dumb-show that the ladies doubted that they were entirely real. They had heard of life-like figures worked by mechanical means and thought that perhaps this was the nature of the sight before them, such things not being beyond what a royal building might contain. The male figure then started to utter great groans and sighs, and suddenly threw himself on the couch beside the lady, who, so far from trying to quell his ardour seemed actually to welcome his violent attentions. Before the sisters' horrified gaze he seized his paramour about the waist with one arm, while the other began to make free with her flowing skirts, and leaning forward, pressed his lips…

Mina shut the book.

It was some time before she dared open it again, and the scene that followed was lavished with descriptions that owed a great deal to horticulture and statuary with some military and sporting allusions. No reader would have been in any doubt as to the amorous nature of the event being alluded to, yet the words themselves were not indecent, and it was this and the innocence of the observers that must have saved the authors from prosecution. Any actual indecency was solely created by the mind of the reader.

The Misses Bland, shocked and amazed, departed the drawing room leaving the two figures in a state imitating the exhaustion of two athletes who had just run a race. Before long, they found the vestibule as they had originally encountered it, and so departed the building. By unspoken agreement the only part of their tour they mentioned to their father was the Hall of the Worthies. Neither had liked to talk freely between themselves about what they had seen, and it was only a week afterwards when they had written their individual accounts of the visit that the sisters compared their impressions. They agreed that they could not have seen actual persons but given what their father had said about the tastes of the late King

George they felt sure that they must have seen some automata meant for his private viewing.

Later in the season the sisters once again made a trip to Brighton, and searched the Pavilion very carefully for the rooms they had seen on their earlier unaccompanied wanderings, but while they found what they thought must be the same rooms, none were decorated in the style they had previously observed. There were no large Chinese statues, no pipe organ in the large music room, and the apartment with the red wallpaper was without ornamentation or its long couch. Subtle enquiries regarding life-size figures were met by assertions that there were currently none in the Pavilion, that of the Crimean hero being too large and all the others too small. All statues were, in any case, quite incapable of movement. The only automaton that had recently been displayed in the Pavilion was a mechanical chess player garbed as a Turk. They were shown a poster portraying this machine, and anything less like the gentleman and lady in the red room could not be imagined. The sisters then enquired if there had been a figure or a portrait resembling the lady they had seen, and described her clothing. At this the attendant had looked surprised and directed them to a booklet that included a picture of the very lady. She was, he said, Mrs Fitzherbert, and the great love of the late King George when he had been Prince of Wales. While she had never resided in the Pavilion the Prince had provided her with a house close by and she had been a frequent visitor until he had been obliged to throw her over in order to marry a princess. Another picture in the book alerted their attention, for it was of the very man they had seen in the Red Drawing Room, King George himself, but before his excesses had made him an object of satire, when he had been a young and dashing Prince.

It was only then that the Misses Bland realised that what they had seen had not been mere automata but the ghostly figures of the Prince and his beloved, locked in the throes of their mutual passion for all eternity, sundered by cruel necessity but together again after death.

It was all nonsense, of course, thought Mina, a romantic tale with more intimate detail than might be thought appropriate. As a work of fiction she had encountered far worse. Still, she had promised Dr Hamid and Anna to discover more, and decided to write a letter to Mr Greville, her father's former partner who now managed the Scarletti publishing business. She explained that this mysterious work had set everyone in Brighton talking, and asked if he knew the real identity of the authors.

The book's text did supply some useful clues as to when the sisters' visit had taken place. While military bands were a regular feature during the season, the conjuror and chess automaton were less usual entertainments that must have been advertised in the newspapers. Surely, Mina thought, she could easily discover for herself when the supposed encounter had taken place.

Mina made some notes and returned the book to her mother's room. It was probably unnecessary but she made sure that it was in exactly the same position as before. Back in her bedroom she waited for the symptoms of hysteria to overcome her, but she waited in vain.

Chapter Five

Her letter written, Mina settled to completing her story about Eliza, the little lady with the twisted body who lit up the lives of all those who met her. The house was quiet, the sound of parlour gossip being too distant to invade her peaceful sanctuary. Few noises from downstairs, apart from the doorbell, or the usual clatter of excitement that announced the arrival of Richard, were loud enough to disturb her concentration. Enid's bedroom was next to her own, and as Mina worked she heard voices in the hallway, and guessed that her sister had returned from her walk. Enid's morning constitutional in the company of the nursemaid, Anderson, and the twins had become a regular event, which enabled her to display her latest adornments and invite the admiration of the town. Unlike the fate of many a matron, Enid's figure had been quickly restored to its customary trimness after the birth of her children, and she took great delight in showing off her fashion plate silhouette in tightly-buttoned gowns that drew the eye to her tiny waist. Mina had no concerns that Enid might come into her room and interrupt her work. It was never explicitly stated, but Enid clearly felt awkward in contemplating Mina's distorted form, and had a horror of accidentally seeing her in a state of undress.

If Louisa was busy admiring the twins, then it was certain that Mrs Bettinson had taken her leave, as she was not fond of babies. Mina worked quietly on, but a few minutes later Rose knocked hesitantly on the door and advised Mina that her mother wished to speak to her. Such a summons never boded well and Mina reluctantly put down her pen. For a moment she wondered if her mother wanted her to inspect the twins for potential scoliosis, but as she worked her way downstairs, she passed Anderson taking her contented charges up to the nursery. Mystified, she pushed open the parlour door and found her mother frowning at the *Brighton Gazette*, which was open at the page advertising public amusements. A less amused look could not be imagined.

'You wished to speak to me, mother?' Mina hoped that she was only wanted on some trivial errand, but prepared herself for a lengthy exposition of her mother's well-worn opinions and general irritation with family, friends, society in general and herself in particular.

'It seems,' announced Louisa with a deeply offended expression, 'that we are all obliged to attend a lecture on the subject of Africa.'

'We are?' queried Mina, since this was a new and unexpected departure in Scarletti family entertainment. She was seized by a sudden fear that her wayward brother Richard was undertaking another of his wild and inevitably doomed moneymaking schemes and was about to pass himself off as an expert on the dark continent or even disguise himself as a native of that far away land, and planned to deliver a public address based on legend, newspapers, and his own imagination. The potential for embarrassment was alarming. Only a few months ago he had taken to the stage of Brighton's New Oxford Music Hall in a spangled cloak, false moustache and black velvet mask, employing the worst Italian accent in the world, as the mysterious Signor Ricardo, presenting the supposed spirit medium Miss Foxton, who in actual fact was his then mistress, Nellie Gilden, a former conjuror's assistant.

Mina eased herself into a comfortable seat. This was going to be a more complicated conversation than most. 'Why this sudden interest in Africa?'

Louisa gave a little snort of a laugh. 'Oh, I have no interest in it at all, only I am instructed to go by Enid. Of course, *my* wishes have not been consulted, but she is very insistent about it.'

'When is the lecture to take place?'

'On Monday evening at the Town Hall. Enid saw the announcement in the newspaper and became very excited by it. She said that the subject exerts a powerful hold over her. I believe she may have attended a similar lecture in London, where it obviously affected her brain. Of course, if it is of interest to society there may be a good company there, which would be some diversion at least. Mina, you must go with us, in case Enid becomes distracted. I only hope there will be no horrid pictures on display.'

Mina knew very little about Africa except that from time to time explorers went there looking for the source of the Nile, and many of them failed to return. In recent months the newspapers had been expressing grave anxiety over the fate of a Dr Livingstone who had not been heard of for some time, and no one knew if he was alive or dead. Mina wondered what the source of a river looked like, and supposing one were to discover it, what would one do with it. The subject was certainly a matter for curiosity and she was quite sure it would provide her with a rich vein of ideas for her stories.

'I really cannot imagine what Enid sees in Africa,' Louisa continued. 'She has never shown any interest in it before. Why would anyone want to visit such a place? No one of any importance lives there. So hot and uncomfortable, and I have heard that dangerous wild animals are simply allowed to roam about as they please.'

Mina picked up the newspaper, which was advertising a lecture by Mr Arthur Wallace Hope, veteran of the Crimea and noted explorer, who would be talking about his expeditions to Africa. The name had a familiar ring to it, and since Richard was far too young to pass himself off as having fought in the Crimea, it was some relief to Mina to see that this was not after all, another of his schemes. Tickets were three shillings apiece, family tickets to admit three persons were eight shillings, and they could be purchased at Mr Smith's bookseller's shop on North

Street, where copies of Mr Hope's recent volume *African Quest* would be on sale. All receipts from the lecture were to go to a special fund for the cost of mounting an expedition to find Dr Livingstone. 'It is for a good cause,' she said.

'I am not so sure of that,' said Louisa tartly. 'In fact it would have been far better for everyone if Dr Livingstone had stayed at home. First there is the cost of sending him there on a wild goose chase, and then he gets lost and we are all supposed to pay to have him brought back. What is so complicated about finding the source of a river? If they had asked my advice I would have told them to take a boat at one end and sail down it until they reached the other. But no one ever listens to me.'

Mina thought that if the answer was as simple as her mother supposed then the source of the Nile would have been found some while ago, but she knew better than to argue. 'Perhaps you could suggest that to Mr Hope on Monday? Or would you prefer not to attend?'

'Oh, we must, or Enid will give me a headache with her complaints. She is already choosing her gown and bonnet. Mina, you must go at once and purchase a family ticket with reserved seats.'

Mina saw that her mother was not, in fact, averse to attending the lecture, but preferred to place the responsibility for their going on Enid's shoulders so she would have someone to blame if it proved to be dull or unsuitable. The idea that she or Enid should be the ones to purchase the tickets seemed not to enter Louisa's head, and it was a task which she would never have entrusted to Rose. Mina said nothing. The autumnal weather was charming; the sky bright and clear, the breezes not too harsh, and the destination of a bookshop was always a pleasure. She would walk.

North Street was not so very far from Mina's home in Montpelier Road. When her back was easy she liked to take gentle strolls in the sunshine and fresh clean air. She was obliged to go carefully, so as not to strain the muscles that protested against her awkward gait, the twist in her obstinate spine and tilt of her hipbone causing her to rock from side to side in a manner that made rude children point and laugh, and polite adults glance at her in surprise and then quickly look away. She had been taught the importance of exercise by Anna Hamid, who said it was essential in order to counteract the hours she spent at her writing desk. Lack of activity would stiffen her, lock her fast into her awkward shape and make it harder for her to move. Idleness was her enemy. Mina was well aware that if she lived long enough, there might well come a time when she would be confined to a bath chair, and wholly reliant on another person if she wished to go out in the town, but should that fate ever come about she wanted to delay it as long as possible. She thought again of her friend Eliza Hamid, dead at fifty, her constricted lungs unable to combat an inflammation that a healthy woman would have survived.

For a devoted reader, W.J. Smith's bookshop was a palace of delight. Its handsome windows were lined from their base to their height with rows of shelves displaying more books than one might have thought could possibly be assembled in the space, and the doorways were flanked with racks that towered over Mina and were filled with a wide variety of periodicals. On that day, half of one window was entirely taken up with copies of *African Quest*, nicely bound in maroon leather, the cover stamped in gold with a map of Africa. The book was priced at 6s and, like the lecture, for which there was a prominent advertisement, all proceeds were to go to the fund for the rescue of Dr Livingstone. While Mina was obliged to agree in part with her mother that the brave doctor was in a plight of his own making she nevertheless felt that this was no reason to abandon him unrescued. She was also far from convinced, as her mother was, that the exploration of Africa was an activity that would never bring rewards. Who could know what riches in terms of crops or minerals might lie at the source of the Nile, or what valuable trade routes might be opened? Dr Livingstone's work might one day add greatly to the sum of human happiness, and then he would no longer be denigrated as misguided, or branded an expensive failure, but praised and lauded as a hero. In the window on prominent display was a photographic portrait of the lost gentleman, staring into the camera with deep-set mournful eyes, his brow furrowed with inexpressible pain. Aged about fifty at the time the portrait was taken, he looked older. Now, after five more years in Africa, it was unlikely, thought Mina that he would look half as well, if he was still alive, which was doubtful. Friends of Dr Livingstone frequently wrote to the newspapers expressing their confidence in his abilities and conviction that he was alive. Other reports had twice declared him dead. The only certain thing was that there had been no news of him at all for the last two years.

There was another portrait in the window, and on seeing it Mina at once understood the reason for Enid's sudden interest in Africa. Arthur Wallace Hope was an impressive figure, in the very prime of his vigorous life, tall, muscular and broad of chest, with flaring dark whiskers, the epitome of bold, healthy masculinity. His expression was that of a man who had looked far over the great plains and lakes and rivers of a foreign land, faced dangers and overcome them, fought and suffered, and come through it all with credit. He was not precisely handsome, but his face inspired confidence, and his physique was as far removed from the slight form of Mr Inskip as could be imagined.

In the shop Mina asked to see the seating plan for the lecture and selected three places at the front of the hall. She was not sure if this was a wise thing to do especially in the light of Enid's fondness for tight lacing, but felt that had she purchased tickets near the back, she would have been endlessly castigated for her poor choice. With any luck the Lord Mayor and other town dignitaries would be present, which would add something to her mother's evening when she became tired of listening to the speaker, undoubtably early in the proceedings. Mina also purchased a copy of *African Quest*. While she was there a number of ladies whose veils were drawn fully about their faces, made a creeping, diffident approach to the counter, and, leaning towards the manager in a confidential fashion, whispered their requests. Some explained that they were servants who had been sent by their mistresses on a mission, others declared that the desired purchase was not for themselves but for a friend. The manager understood their needs exactly and with no alteration in his deferential expression provided each of these shy customers with a slim volume ready-wrapped in brown paper. Mina did not have to guess which book they were purchasing, and only wished that her stories would sell as well then she would be a rich woman. The shop did stock her work, which she published under the name Robert Neil, the pseudonym her father had used for his occasional stories, and they brought in a regular income, which, in addition to the annuity left to her by her father made her financially secure if not actually wealthy.

The bookshop lay very near to the public reading room which boasted a fine collection of informative periodicals, including past copies of the *Gazette*, and Mina thought that by studying the attractions advertised in the newspaper as taking place in the Royal Pavilion, she would be able to identify, if not the exact day, then the year and month at least in which the Misses Bland had paid their first visit. Fortunately the *Gazette* was a weekly, rather than a daily, publication, or her task would have been arduous. Slowly she worked her way back through the issues, and, at last, in the paper dated 6 October 1870, she saw an announcement that the automaton chess player who had created such a sensation at London's Crystal Palace had come to Brighton, and would be seen at work in the chess club room of the Royal Pavilion daily from 2-5pm and 8-10pm. Mina had never seen a chess automaton, but knew that they were machines that played chess games with anyone who wished to challenge them. How they actually worked was a mystery, but Mina thought that if the device was only a cleverly-made machine and not something enclosing a hidden human operator, it would not have needed to take a three-hour rest. In the very next issue there was an announcement that Dr H.S. Lynn, the famous conjuror, who had never previously visited Brighton, would be performing his 'Grande Séance de Physique et Mystères Oriental' in the Banqueting Room of the Royal Pavilion on the following Monday, the proceeds to be given to the widows and children of the drowned crewmen of HMS *Captain*, the vessel which had sunk with the loss of almost five hundred souls in the previous month. Dr Lynn promised 'a number of wondrous mysteries' never before seen in Europe, including the Japanese butterfly illusion, for which he was especially noted, as well as 'top spinning extraordinary on a single thread' and the 'instantaneous growth of flowers'. The band of the Inniskilling Dragoons had also been playing very frequently in Brighton during that season. After careful study of the newspapers Mina was able to satisfy herself that Dr Lynn had only given his performance on the one occasion, and the chess automaton, after a short season in Brighton, had returned to Crystal Palace.

Mina, to her surprise, had determined an exact date. Unless there was a similar coincidence of events, the visit of the two authors of *An Encounter* had taken place a little under a year ago, on Monday, 17 October, 1870.

Chapter Six

As soon as Mina returned home she was pounced upon by Enid, who, enraged at the insupportable delay caused by the reading room visit, demanded to see the tickets immediately, since it would be necessary to go back to the shop at once and exchange them if they were not good enough. Fortunately, they were. 'You will be so close to Mr Hope you will be able to smell the pomade on his whiskers,' Mina reassured her. Enid looked as if she was about to faint.

During the next few days Enid found it impossible to conceal her anticipation of Mr Hope's lecture. Her cheeks flushed whenever she mentioned it, which was often, and from the way they flushed when she did not mention it, Mina deduced that her sister was thinking about it. Enid's agitation and Louisa's simmering disapproval made for a very tense household, and Mina longed for a visit from Richard and his happier nonsense.

On the Monday Enid was too excited to eat, which was just as well as she was laced so tightly that anything she swallowed could never have found its way through her digestive system. Rose had helped her dress, and as this involved several changes of costume, as well as anger and tears, it was a relief to everyone when the cab finally arrived and there was no time for Enid to change her mind again.

The spacious upper room of the Town Hall was crowded with patrons. Lectures were a regular attraction there and covered subjects as diverse as religion, history, literature and geography, with the occasional dissertation on moral issues, the sanitary conditions of Brighton and the electoral disabilities of women. Serious talks on morality or religion were well attended by those eager to wear the badge of respectability. It was not, therefore, necessary to actually listen to the speaker, although many who sought illumination, certainty or simply improvement, did so, and declared that they had been mightily edified by the experience. Others thought that just being seen there was sufficient, and after taking the opportunity to mingle with their friends before the lecture commenced, dozed gently through the earnest address, waking only at the sound of applause. Mina had never attended these lectures, but they were fully reported in the newspapers, and she had read with some amusement of the respected Brighton novelist and literary authority Mr Edward Campbell Tainsh and his denouncement of sensational literature as feverish, contemptible and unhealthy. Books, he said, should be restful, dignified and innocent. Mina, having completed her story of the little lady, had commenced a new one, in which a man was being driven mad by the torment of demons that had arisen from a life devoted to cruelty and vice. She decided not to send a presentation copy to Mr Tainsh for his review.

Enid, clutching her copy of *African Quest* as if it was a religious tract, looked keenly about as they entered the lecture room, but the imposing figure of Mr Hope had not yet appeared. The audience, Mina noticed, was composed of the usual assortment of ladies and gentlemen, with some representatives of the Brighton press, but there were appreciable numbers of young men with eager expressions, who looked ready to volunteer for perilous adventures at the smallest inducement.

Dr Hamid arrived, accompanied by Anna, a rare social engagement for them as they usually liked to stay quietly at home together after a long and busy day. Mina wondered if, following Eliza's death, they had decided to seek more entertainment outside their home, inhabited as it was by the unseen ghosts of those they had recently lost. Louisa, studying the company for friends she could greet and outshine, lighted on Mrs Peasgood and Mrs Mowbray, widowed sisters in their fifties, both of whom were plain of face and comfortably stout, and hurried to speak to them. Mrs Peasgood's late husband, a surgeon, had left her well provided for, and her elegant residence in Marine Square, which she shared with her sister, boasted a large drawing room where she often hosted musical entertainments. An invitation to one of Mrs Peasgood's soirees was a notable stamp of status and she was considered a person of influence in Brighton society. By contrast, the late Mr Mowbray's business as a wine merchant had collapsed in debt due to bad management and excessive consumption of his own stock. While Mrs Peasgood appeared thoroughly contented with her position in life, Mrs Mowbray was constantly casting her eyes at single gentlemen, like a hungry spider waiting for an unsuspecting fly to creep within her grasp. She often looked with great approval at Dr Hamid, who was not merely impervious to her attractions but unaware of her interest. The sisters, like Louisa and Mrs Bettinson, had once been members of the little circle who had attended the séances of Miss Eustace, something that none of them now cared to mention.

There was a brief pause in even Louisa's conversation and several pairs of eyes turned to the door as another friend arrived, Miss Whinstone, who did not come alone. Miss Whinstone was a highly-susceptible and nervous spinster, who ordinarily would never have dreamed of attending a lecture on the subject of bloodcurdling adventures in Africa. The mere idea of leaving Brighton made her feel faint, although she had once dared to visit Hove. It was she who had suffered most from the depredations of Miss Eustace, who had deluded her into believing that her deceased brother was sending her messages requiring her to meet expenses for which he felt responsible. The demands had been increasing in both size and frequency when Mina discovered what was happening and put a stop to it.

Miss Whinstone had recently astonished everyone, especially those who knew her best, by acquiring a gentleman friend, Mr Jellico, a retired schoolmaster with weak legs and a passion for acrostics. Their most recent adventures had included a walk on the West Pier, and a visit to the theatre to see a comedy by Shakespeare, and it was now widely rumoured that they were planning a day excursion to Worthing. On learning this Louisa declared that 'dear Harriet' as she called Miss Whinstone whenever she needed to prise gossip from her, had taken leave of her senses, by which she meant that she had had the effrontery to entertain an admirer when she had none. Not that Louisa envied Miss Whinstone her unsteady and grey-whiskered companion, but she would have liked the opportunity to tell him that his attentions were unwanted.

Miss Whinstone, who was usually so scant of courage, had been able, with the support of Mr Jellico and a great many glasses of water, to tell the story of her cruel deception to the Lewes magistrates, as a result of which Miss Eustace and her co-conspirators had not only been committed for trial but refused bail on the grounds that such slippery creatures would surely escape given the slenderest of chances. That evening, Miss Whinstone and her antiquated swain walked unashamedly arm-in-arm, although it was not apparent to the casual observer which of the two was supporting the other.

Still more arrivals flooded into the room, which soon became full to bursting, and through the buzzing chatter Mina could hear that a great many of those present had read or heard of Arthur Wallace Hope's adventures, and not a few carried recently purchased copies of his book, in the expectation that the author could be prevailed upon to enhance it with his signature. In front of the platform there was a table piled high with more volumes in case anyone had neglected to buy a copy, and pen, ink and blotter lay in readiness. To one side of the hall was a long table, whose contents were covered by a plain cloth. It was being guarded in a strict but courteous fashion by a gentleman aged about sixty, who wore the sombre garb of a senior servant. The platform was already supplied with a number of chairs, and at the back, high on the wall, were two large, furled maps, and a pointing rod.

The first man to appear on the platform was an official of the Town Hall, who begged all the ticket holders to be seated, and once this was achieved, the distinguished visitors, Mr Webb the Lord Mayor, and a number of other dignitaries, were announced and received polite but brief applause, before taking their places. At last, the man himself, Mr Arthur Wallace Hope, appeared. Mina had wondered if Hope in the flesh might be less impressive than the Hope of his portrait but if anything the opposite was the case, as Enid's little gasp testified. A portrait could not convey stature, and he was a tall man, standing some six feet in height, broad-shouldered and with a confident step. He surveyed the gathering with a friendly expression before he sat down, and then the Town Hall official, his faint glory eclipsed by the glittering company, very prudently withdrew and left the remainder of the formalities to Mr Webb. The Mayor made a short address, saying what a pleasure it was to welcome such a distinguished man to Brighton, and indicated, as if Mr Hope was too modest to mention it, that after the talk copies of the book *African Quest* would be available for purchase, and the speaker would be delighted to inscribe them, as well as copies previously bought, with his signature and a suitable dedication.

Enid glowed with anticipation.

The Mayor resumed his seat and there was a breathless silence as Hope stepped forward to speak. His voice, booming from his deep chest, was everything one might have anticipated. 'Mr Lord Mayor, Aldermen, distinguished guests, ladies and gentlemen of Brighton, it is my very great honour to address you today. My journey here has been something of a pilgrimage, since one of the first visits I made on my arrival was to the Royal Pavilion, where I stood in the vestibule admiring the magnificent statue of Captain Pechell, one of the honoured sons of this town. A more valiant man and a better comrade-in-arms has never been known, and I confess that his likeness showing him in an attitude of the greatest heroism as he urged his men forward brought a tear to my eye as I recalled our service together in the Crimea and the terrible tragedy of Sebastopol that took him from us in the prime of his active youth. And yet, as I stood there, I felt that he was still with me, his spirit seemed to stand beside me as he himself had once done, and his bravery remains an inspiration to me now.

'One might think that on my return from the Crimea I would have been happy to consider my duty to my country done, but my days in the army had aroused in me a great hunger for travel, adventure, and yes, I admit it, danger!' A thrill of excitement ran through the audience. 'And where can one find all three in greater abundance than in any corner of the great globe? Why, Africa! The untamed, uncharted land, whose immense size can only inspire us with wonder at what we might discover there. Surely there must be opportunities for valuable trade; furs and ivory, mines yielding gold and precious stones, if, that is, we can learn to navigate the great rivers, the courses of which have been a mystery since the time of the ancients. But I want to assure you of this,' he went on very seriously, 'we British go to Africa not as enemies or plunderers. We have no desire to conquer the land and take it for ourselves. We go in friendship, to bring honest trade to the inhabitants as well as the benefits of Christianity to their souls. However — ' He paused and favoured the audience with a significant stare — ' there is one evil in Africa which must be abolished — I am referring to the cruel and abominable trade in slaves. Ladies and gentlemen, do you not wonder how it is that the ivory of your piano keys and your knife handles reaches you? I will tell you. It is carried overland on the backs of slaves who are treated in the most inhumane fashion, and then murdered when they are no longer able to bear their loads. It was the inspiration of Dr David Livingstone to combat this terrible practice not merely by conversion through Christian preaching but by discovering other trade routes that would pass along the rivers of Africa. With this admirable intention he proposed an expedition to open up the Zambezi. It was a monumental and ambitious task and I was at once fired with a great desire to go with him.

'When I volunteered for my first expedition to Africa in 1858 I knew nothing of what it might hold for me, I went as a young man eager for adventure. I thought it would be a fine thing indeed to chart new lands, to discover unknown civilisations, to tread paths that no white man had ever seen, and indeed it was, but I could never have known that with the elation, the achievement and the comradeship there would also be the pain and the loss, disappointment and disease and the savage murderous attacks of slavers. I will take you now, ladies and gentlemen to the shores of the great Zambezi River!'

Hope strode to the back of the platform and unfurled the first of the maps. It illustrated the whole of the continent of Africa, and was easily large enough for the audience to see the rivers and lakes. It was not these, however, that drew the eye, but two blank areas, one to the north, labelled 'Great Desert' and another in the centre described more tantalisingly as 'Unexplored Region'. From the corner of her eye Mina saw some of the youths in the audience lean forward to gaze on the chart that held such promise of adventure, and thought how the hearts of those young men had been stirred and how they must long to go to that unknown place and unlock its mysteries.

The tales told by Mr Hope were undoubtedly thrilling, although Mina felt that some of the details had been tempered by the knowledge that there were ladies in the audience. His descriptions of the ravages of deadly disease were confined to generalisations, and the stories of his encounters with slavers ended at a point where the tragic outcome could be left to the hearer's imagination, nevertheless they were more than exciting enough for Brightonian tastes. Hope knew his audience and steered a careful path, neither boastful nor tainted by false modesty. He had done all that a man might do. He had shot and eaten elephants, hippopotami and giraffes. He had befriended great chieftains. He had suffered from mysterious fevers, and the bites of poisonous insects and snakes. Twice he had almost drowned in swollen rivers, and he had once been stabbed with a spear. It was a tale of desperate privation and suffering such that it seemed impossible for any man to survive. Although the journey had added substantially to the sum of geographical and botanical knowledge, it had ultimately ended by failing in its main purpose, since the Zambezi river had been found to be not fully navigable after all, due to its cataracts and rapids. Dr Livingstone's dream of great steamers passing along the river, laden with produce, had vanished. The survivors of the expedition, stricken with fever and disappointed, yet bracing themselves to be ready for new challenges, had returned to the coast to recuperate and await the arrival of a new steamship with much-needed provisions. There Hope had received a message telling him of the death of his older brother, a tragedy that had necessitated his return to England to settle family business. He did not, however, forget his comrades in Africa, but worked hard to raise further funds to assist the Zambezi party. He had done so in vain, since the expedition, now denounced and even derided in the press as an expensive failure, was recalled.

'But men of courage never despair for long,' said Hope, 'rather they gather their strength and return to the fight afresh! Yes, the idea of the Zambezi as a trade route had perforce to be abandoned as impractical, but now a new object was in sight, or rather an ancient object risen to new prominence, one that has long captured the hearts and minds of men as the greatest adventure the world has to offer — discovering the source of the Nile.'

Even Louisa looked enraptured.

Chapter Seven

The ultimate source of the great river of Africa was, explained Mr Hope, a destination which offered all the allure and excitement of making a flight to the moon and back, and was a prize that had been coveted by men of daring and enterprise for thousands of years. Even modern explorers failed to agree on where the great river rose, and it behoved those men who had the courage, spirit and dedication to answer the great question.

While his sudden and unexpected elevation to master of the family estates should have required him to reside permanently in England, he had felt the call of Africa once more, and fortunately found in his younger brother a man who was not only well able, but content to manage affairs at home. The money raised for the abandoned Zambezi expedition had accordingly been employed to fund another, this one starting at Zanzibar and heading west overland to find the elusive source of the Nile.

Hope then unfurled the second map, this one showing the lake systems of East Africa as far as they had been charted. His previous exploits, he said, made him, without question, the obvious candidate to lead the new venture. His companions were selected with care; some were naturally men of experience, those who had travelled widely and showed that they could endure hardship, but there were others who, though lacking any specific qualification, were hungry for adventure, robust and of the right stalwart character. These latter companions, who were hardly more than boys, brought with them the promise that they could be fashioned into the hardened explorers and leaders of the future.

All preparations had been made, supplies purchased and guides engaged, but only a few weeks into their journey disaster had struck. The party had been attacked by slavers, who had assumed that the travellers were rivals for their evil trade. Both men and boys had fought bravely, but of all the Europeans, only Hope and one of his experienced men, who like himself was a veteran of the Crimea, were not killed outright, and they made a narrow escape. After surviving many dangers and privations they at last reached safety, but his noble-hearted companion, exhausted and suffering from malaria, died soon afterwards. It was to his comrades in adversity, both the courageous Englishmen and their loyal African guides, that *African Quest* was dedicated.

Mina glanced at the youths who were so eager to follow the deadly path to the Nile, and saw not one whit of dismay. Their desires were plain in in their unbearded faces. Others might have perished but to them, surely, would be the glory.

Following Hope's return to England it had taken a year for him to return to full health, during which he had written his book, and he now travelled and lectured about the importance of abolishing the slave trade, opening Africa to lawful commerce, creating riverboat routes for the conveyance of goods, encouraging cultivation of the tracts of fertile land, and extending to the population the great benefits and blessings of Christianity. Whether he would ever return to Africa he did not know. Even now, Dr Livingstone was seeking the source of the Nile, which he believed flowed from Lake Tanganyika, although there were other explorers, notably the late Mr Speke, who would disagree, saying that Lake Victoria was the source. But nothing had been heard from Dr Livingstone for some time and if he was still alive he would be sorely in need of supplies. Hope reiterated that he would take not one penny piece from the lecture fee or the sale of his book, all would be dedicated to the cause of finding and relieving Dr Livingstone.

'But what conclusions can I draw from my many travels and adventures?' he went on. 'First, that we are all God's creatures, wherever we may live and whatever the colour of our skin. Secondly, that cruelty to one's fellow beings is a great abomination. I have witnessed the loss of so many good men; I have seen them on the field of battle, mown down by fusillades, blown to pieces or expiring from the great curse of cholera; in Africa they died from malaria or dysentery, drowned in rapids or were murdered by slavers. These deaths cannot, must not, have happened in vain. We who remain must gain from their sacrifice. We must learn courage, humility and kindness. Ask yourselves, when we contemplate these apparently senseless tragedies, what message comes to us from the Almighty? I can tell you this now, that we are all of us souls looking for salvation. We will only find it by understanding and accepting a great truth. We cannot turn away from it. It is a power that is all around us, but which many seek to deny. It is a power that has an intense focus right here in this very town. I am speaking of spiritualism.' There was a ripple of unease in the audience.

Arthur Wallace Hope looked around him at faces that had suddenly begun to frown, and his mouth curved into a knowing smile. 'Oh, I am well aware that there have been events here in the recent past that have strengthened the convictions of materialists, those who believe only in science and the things they can see and touch, and who dare to deny the existence of the soul. What a terrible hopeless life they must lead, to reject all the many proofs we have of survival after death, to have no faith! I implore you, do not be deceived by these empty and unhappy men and women. We must work together to bring them to a proper understanding, lead them away from the darkness of their bigotry and towards the light of knowledge. I see here the start of a new movement, a new church, even. Brighton, with its healing air and light, and the invigorating power of the sea can only attract beneficial forces. Nothing evil can thrive here! The greatest and most inspiring mediums will come to be nourished by the energy that exists in this blessed place. In the very near future I will be giving a talk at this same location on the revivification of spiritualism in Brighton. Tickets will be free of charge, but donations will be accepted towards the fund for the relief of Dr Livingstone. And now, my dear friends, I bring this talk to a close. You will see at the side of the hall a table with a display of some items I brought back from Africa, which I hope you will find of interest; cloth and beads which are to the Africans as paper money is to us. I will be available to inscribe your books in just a few moments, but before then I will be happy to take any questions from the floor.'

There was the usual polite hesitation that always arose in such situations as no one ever wished to be the first to speak, but finally a gentleman raised his hand.

'Mr Hope, since you believe so strongly in the world of the spirit, would you be willing to express your opinion on a certain book that has attracted a considerable amount of attention here in Brighton.'

There was a stir in the audience as a number of ladies tried unsuccessfully to look as if they had no idea to what the speaker was referring. One or two stifled an embarrassed titter, but several, with stern faces, actually rose to leave.

'Please, ladies and gentlemen,' said Hope in a placatory tone that at once commanded attention, 'I have no intention of offending anyone here. Sir, I am aware of the volume and have indeed read it. Not only that, but I can reveal to you that I have recently been privileged to meet and speak to the two authors.'

This statement aroused a babble of comment, and the sound of busily scribbling pencils in the notebooks of newspapermen. 'Can you tell us who they really are?' called out one correspondent.

'That I cannot do since they preserve their anonymity most carefully. I was introduced to them as the Misses Bland, and did not seek to know more. But I can tell you that I found them to be modest young ladies and was utterly convinced by their assurances that they come from an extremely respectable family and have thus far led very sheltered lives. Their intention in writing the book was simply to give an honest account of their adventures and observations. In doing so, they revealed their innocence and ignorance of the world. Certain passages would appear shocking to the more knowledgeable individual, but the authors only show their pure and childlike understanding, as they wrote without really knowing what they described. But let us put aside the question of delicacy and address ourselves instead to the real importance of that extraordinary event in the Pavilion. These two young ladies actually witnessed persons of the royal court at the time when the late King George was Prince of Wales. It is a wonderful mystery! Did they perhaps witness the ghosts of the Prince and his court, in which case we must bethink ourselves how it was that these spirits appeared not as they were when they left this life, but in the full health and vigour of their youth. Or — and this has been suggested by persons more knowledgeable than I am on such matters — did the sisters actually see into a past age — see not ghosts at all, but the living? And if they did, did they do so by looking through a window in the ether that showed them the past — or did they actually step into the past themselves? These questions are of the utmost importance and must be studied by science. But I promise to speak further on this at my forthcoming talk.'

There was resounding applause, during which Mina saw her expectation that *An Encounter* would quickly lose its novelty value vanish like a phantom. There would be queues outside Mr Smith's bookshop tomorrow. Since there were no more questions from the floor, Hope bowed and left the platform to take his place at the table where copies of *African Quest* were piled. The Lord Mayor stepped forward and asked the members of the audience not to crowd too heavily about the distinguished speaker, but to form queues one row at a time. Since Mina and her party were on the front row, they were called first and Enid, her eyes shining with excitement, almost ran to have her book signed. Louisa accompanied her, not, thought Mina, as unwillingly as she might have done before hearing the author speak. Mina had no wish to stand in a great crush of people, so stayed back and waited for their return.

'That was an unexpected end to the lecture,' said Dr Hamid, appearing with Anna at Mina's side. 'I am glad I decided to come, as it is always advisable to keep informed as to what is upsetting my patients.'

'Will you go to his talk on spiritualism?'

'I fear it may be necessary for the same reason. I hope he will not be in town too long.'

'I know that kind of man all too well,' said Anna grimly. 'He has authority and confidence, and the ability to draw people to him and make them believe what he believes. The more one warns against him the more one seems to be the person who is deluded.'

Miss Whinstone, with a very troubled expression on her face, was being led away and gently comforted by Mr Jellico.

'Poor lady, she has suffered quite enough,' said Mina. 'It will take all her determination to speak at the trial, and now she must fear a revival of the very cause that injured her.'

All around them small chattering groups were forming and none of the talk was of the River Nile.

Dr Hamid and Anna took their leave, and Mina, seeing that Enid had seized the opportunity to tell Mr Hope at great length all about her love of Africa, went to the display table to look at the items on show there. The manservant had removed the plain cover to reveal a rainbow of delights. There were rolls of cotton fabric, some in subtle shades of blue, others in golden beige, dark red and deep brown, either striped or patterned in squares. A printed card told her that the cloth was woven on handlooms and were valuable trading commodities, essential for the traveller in Africa who wished to purchase food and obtain permission to pass through tribal lands. There were also glass trading beads, some strung on twisted cord, others displayed singly, cylinders in a wide variety of glowing hues, some plain but many of them banded and streaked with colour. Mina tried to imagine what a lady of Brighton would look like dressed in garments of that richly-dyed cotton and wearing those beads; bright yellow like the summer sun, blue as the sky, green as parklands, red as roses. A new idea for a story occurred to her, one in which a lady put on some mysterious garments she had discovered in a curio shop and was magically transported back to the land of their origin. The possibilities for adventure were endless.

It was as she stood engrossed in thought, that the gentleman servant approached her.

'Excuse me, but I presume you are Miss Scarletti?'

Mina did not have to ask how he had identified her. 'I am.'

He proffered a card. 'Mr Arthur Wallace Hope presents his compliments. He would like, with your permission, to call on you at your earliest convenience for a private conversation on a highly sensitive matter.'

Mina took the card, which was printed with Hope's London address, a handwritten note adding the name of the Royal Albion Hotel where he might be contacted in Brighton. 'This is quite surprising, of course, but if he would like to call I will be at home at eleven o'clock tomorrow morning.' Mina always carried cards advertising the Scarletti Library of Romance and she wrote her address upon one and handed it to the servant.

He accepted it with a deferential smile and withdrew. Mina's specified time was carefully chosen. Her mother and Enid would be out that morning, exploring the new arrivals at Jordan, Conroy and Co.'s fashionable emporium, where Paris came to Brighton in the form of silk, fans and lace. As she gazed at the card, Mina speculated on what such a notable man might wish to discuss with her, since she was not a person of importance in the community. Why a private conversation? What was sensitive about the subject matter? Mina was left with the uncomfortable feeling that the religious, noble and philanthropic Mr Hope could actually be a very dangerous man, if crossed.

Chapter Eight

Single young women would not normally be expected to receive male visitors to whom they were not related at home alone, and in the case of Mr Arthur Wallace Hope, neither did Mina wish to. She wondered if she should ask Rose to stay with her during the interview, and should Mr Hope object to this arrangement she would be obliged to inform him that the conversation could not take place under any other circumstances. Not that anyone would suspect that some impropriety might take place — that was one advantage of Mina's deformity; it was assumed that she was beyond any man's appetites.

After giving the question some careful thought, Mina dismissed the idea of appointing a chaperone. Whatever it was Mr Hope wanted to say to her it was unlikely to be either romantic or indecent, and she did not want him to be inhibited in his expressions by seeing Rose standing in the corner of the parlour with her sullen stare. Rose, who was both general maidservant and personal maid to Louisa, had, despite the fact that the heavy work of the house was assigned to a charlady, a great deal to complain about, but she did so wordlessly, albeit at great volume. Mina might have ordered the maid to secrecy about the meeting with Mr Hope, but the probability of the visit being mentioned to Louisa at the earliest opportunity was close to a certainty. The best way of limiting the inevitable repercussions was for Rose to know as little about the visit as possible.

Louisa and Enid departed after breakfast, chattering with excitement, and later that morning the nursemaid, Anderson, took the twins out to bathe in the sea air, secure in their perambulator, a four-wheeled carriage like a battle wagon in miniature, with matching compartments and parasols. It was only then that Mina informed Rose that a gentleman might call to discuss a charitable donation, and she was to show him into the parlour and bring tea.

Mr Arthur Wallace Hope arrived true to the hour. As Mina entered the parlour, she found him standing to greet her with the confident posture of a man whose presence in any house bestowed upon it a great favour, and who knew it well. He reminded her of a bear at the zoo risen up on its hind legs, darkly furred, massive and threatening. As he thanked Mina for her kindness in agreeing to see him, his manner was both cordial and respectful, but there was, she saw, a sharp, cool determination lurking behind his smile. Once they were both seated, facing each other at a discreet distance, Mina said, 'I assume that the purpose of your visit is to request a donation to the fund for the relief of Dr Livingstone?'

He looked surprised. 'No, not at all, although if you wish to make a donation I can supply you with the address where it is to be sent.'

'Then I am at a loss to imagine why you have requested to see me.' Mina smiled in the way ladies did when they wished to convey that they did not understand what was being asked of them. Those who did not know her often assumed that her small tilted body was the outward sign of a deficient mind. This misapprehension was usually corrected quickly but sometimes she allowed them to go on with the error for as long as it served her purpose. It was not a mistake anyone made twice.

'I have come,' he said, as if making a grand announcement at a prize giving, 'because I believe that it is in your power to right a terrible wrong.'

Mina was mystified, but had the strong impression that she was being offered something disguised as an honour that would ultimately prove to be quite different in nature. 'That is very flattering. To what are you referring?'

'Can you not guess? I refer to the pitiful plight of the spirit medium, Miss Eustace, who is even now incarcerated in Lewes House of Correction, awaiting trial for crimes of which she is wholly innocent.'

Mina paused. She realised that she would have to tread very carefully with Mr Hope. As far as she was concerned Miss Eustace was a criminal who was exactly where she richly deserved to be, but it would not do to say so at this juncture. Open opposition to her visitor's wishes was not the best policy if she was to learn more of his thoughts and intentions. 'I am given to understand that that is not the lady's real name,' she said cautiously.

Hope dismissed this observation with an indulgent smile. 'Her *nom de théâtre*. Some of the most prominent and sought-after mediums choose to adopt a public name to protect their true identities so that when they are in private they can live a calm and untroubled life. Mediums, by the nature of their work, often require peace and rest after communication with the spirits, especially if a manifestation has been produced, in order to fully restore their exhausted energies.'

Rose arrived with the tea tray and an unreadable expression. After pouring the tea she stood waiting for further instructions. 'That will be all, Rose. I will ring when you are needed again,' said Mina. Rose paused only to cast a glance at Mr Hope before she retreated.

Mina sipped her tea. 'I really do not see how it may be in my power to influence Miss Eustace's situation.'

Hope cradled his teacup in his large hands, where it resembled a porcelain thimble. 'You have, have you not, attended several séances conducted by Miss Eustace?'

'I have, yes.'

'One of which, I am reliably informed, you attempted to disrupt.'

Mina saw that he was referring to an incident in which, after pretending to stumble, she had fallen against the figure of Phoebe, a radiant manifestation produced by Miss Eustace, which she had proved to her satisfaction was the medium herself clad in glowing draperies. Such was the devoted gullibility of the lady's adherents that the exposure had not, as it ought to have done, ended her career. Mina might have protested to Mr Hope that her fall was an accident, but thought it unlikely that she would convince him, and to lie would be a blunder. She remained silent.

'Despite this,' Hope went on, still maintaining his outward air of affability, 'Miss Eustace was kind enough to pay you a visit, and on that occasion she sensed that you yourself are, without knowing it, a powerful medium, who only needed to develop your abilities, something she offered to assist you in doing, however, you rejected her generosity.'

Mina felt suddenly chilled. The incident at the séance was well known in town, but the details of Miss Eustace's visit to her home had not been broadcast. If her visitor knew so much then he had heard it from the lady herself, or her associates. She could only conclude that Mr Hope was no distant admirer of the fascinating fraudster, but one of her intimates. Still she said nothing.

He drained his cup with relish and put it down. 'There followed an event,' he went on, further emboldened by Mina's reticence, 'the one at which Miss Eustace was apprehended. I will not call it a séance, since it was more of a charade, and had been deliberately and carefully designed with the sole object of entrapping Miss Eustace; an attempt to demonstrate to the world that she was a false medium. This shameless mockery was supposedly held at the behest of a new patroness, a Lady Finsbury, who made a very pretty little speech before she revealed her true colours. I must inform you that I have made careful enquiries and have established that no such person as Lady Finsbury exists.' He paused and fixed Mina with an intense and knowing stare. 'You do not seem to find that information surprising.'

Mina was not at all surprised, since the part of 'Lady Finsbury' had been performed with skill and panache by her brother Richard's then mistress, conjuror's assistant Nellie Gilden.

'I believe that you played a significant role in that disgraceful affair; in fact, I think that you devised, financed and orchestrated it. Lady Finsbury, I am convinced, was an actress hired by you in order to lure an innocent lady, one who has been a great comfort to the bereaved, into a dangerous situation. Whatever crimes were committed on that occasion, they were not perpetrated by Miss Eustace, who is the most accomplished and powerful medium in the country. As anyone with a knowledge of spiritualism would have known, such a travesty could never have resulted in a proper display of spiritualism, as it was arranged in such a manner that it could only have ended in failure. Not only that,' he went on, his voice increasing in both force and severity of tone, 'but you arranged for the event to be attended by many of the leading citizens of Brighton, as well as representatives of the press. Do you deny it?' This last was almost a shout, a challenge meant to disturb and rattle her into a confession.

Mina, unused to such treatment, was outraged that her guest thought he could use his position in society and masculine authority to intimidate her in her own home. An angry retort sprang to her lips but was stifled. She was obliged to gather all her resolve in an effort to keep her head and maintain the calmness and dignity that the situation required. 'I will neither confirm nor deny anything,' she informed him, quietly but steadily. 'You have come here to request my assistance, yet thus far have requested nothing, only raised your voice to level accusations. If that is all your message then I require you to leave now.' She made to ring for Rose, but he raised a placatory hand.

'Miss Scarletti, please, I do not mean to offend you, and I apologise if I have done so. My strong feelings on the matter ran away with me and I beg your forgiveness. All I wished to do was establish the facts, which I think I have done to my satisfaction. You need say nothing; your silence on the subject is answer enough. You must admit, however, that as regards Miss Eustace's current unpleasant situation it is very clear to any observer that all roads lead to you. Many prominent ladies and gentlemen in Brighton have described you as the person responsible, with, I am sorry to say, approval. But please, I entreat you, allow me to speak further.'

'Very well,' said Mina reluctantly, staying her hand, thankful that it was she alone who was his focus, and that neither Richard nor Dr Hamid, who had also played a part in the exposure of the fraud, had been identified as her confederates. She was also relieved that Mr Hope, having concluded that the elegant Lady Finsbury was a mere actress, had not therefore thought it necessary to make further enquiries to discover her identity.

Hope had calmed himself and now gazed on her sadly. 'Can I not persuade you to reconsider your opposition to the spirits? I have wide experience of these things and I have found that those who are the strongest mediums are often so fearful of their abilities that at first they reject the spirit world altogether until the time comes when they finally, joyfully, embrace it.'

'There has been no joy for me in the spirit world as presented by mediums,' Mina replied. 'There has been upset and distress, not only to myself but also to my family and my friends. Please do not mistake me. I do not deny the existence of the spirit. I attend church, I read the bible and I pray. But some things are hidden from us during our life on earth and only become apparent after our passing. I am content to wait for that knowledge until my proper time comes.'

'But that is because you have not opened your mind to the brightness that surrounds you!' exclaimed Hope, his face lit up by emotion like that of an evangelical preacher. For a moment Mina was reminded of the expression of Miss

Eustace's horrid acolyte, young Mr Clee, with his Byronic curls and mad, sea-mist eyes as he tried to draw her into the fold. 'Do you not hunger for knowledge and certainty?' Hope went on. 'Miss Eustace can lead you towards that understanding if you will only allow it.'

'Not, I think, where she is presently situated,' said Mina drily.

If he detected a tone of satire in her voice he ignored it. 'No. She is surrounded by negative influences that drain her powers. She is quite unable to manifest even the smallest apparition.'

Since Miss Eustace was presumably without her supplies of transparent draperies and phosphorised oil Mina did not find this situation surprising. She had read of mediums who claimed to be able to pass through solid walls, but decided that it would not be helpful to mention that Miss Eustace was clearly not one of their number. 'You have interviewed her I take it?'

'I have. She is in a most dejected state. She now realises that she allowed herself to fall under the influence of men who did not have her interests at heart but merely wished to exploit her undoubted abilities. They too await trial, and we may safely leave them to their fate. It is she alone who concerns me. I will be open with you, Miss Scarletti. This is what I intend to do. My first object is to see Miss Eustace acquitted of the trumped-up charges against her and, once that is achieved, I will do everything in my power to restore her to her rightful position as one of the leading spirit mediums of our day. She still has many devoted followers here in Brighton and will return in triumph. As I said in my lecture, Brighton is a focus of spiritual power and nowhere, I believe, is it stronger than in the Royal Pavilion. I intend to take a room there — the banqueting hall will be ideal for the purpose — to enable Miss Eustace to conduct her séances in the most favourable possible conditions.'

Mina was shocked that Miss Eustace had the effrontery to want to show her face in Brighton again, whatever the financial lure. 'Do you really think that advisable? If she must hold séances, and I certainly cannot stop her from doing so, would it not be better to try some other location, where there are no people she has cheated? There would be uproar if she came here again.' As soon as the words were out of her mouth, however, Mina understood. Miss Eustace wished to capitalise on the current excitement about the royal ghost. With her abilities she could create a sensation. 'I suppose Brighton would be very receptive to mediums at present,' she admitted.

'Exactly,' beamed Hope, 'and we will soon see what will happen to those suggestions of cheating. Blown away in a sea breeze to be replaced by the warmth of spiritual light.'

'But I still do not see what it is I am being asked to do. Supposing Miss Eustace was acquitted, which I think highly unlikely, am I expected to attend her séances? I rather think she would not permit me under any circumstances to attend a demonstration she might give, for fear that I would show her up as a humbug.'

Hope adopted his friendliest smile, one that Mina was learning to distrust. 'Since it is well known in Brighton that you were the instrument of Miss Eustace's temporary reversal, your opinion on her mediumship does carry some weight here. What I am earnestly requesting, therefore, is that you reconsider your position. When you have done so, and can fully appreciate your former error, I would like you to issue a statement to the press to the effect that you now accept that the lady is a genuine spirit medium.'

Mr Hope, still smiling, sat back in his chair and viewed Mina's dismay with evident satisfaction.

Chapter Nine

Mina was momentarily too amazed to speak, since she had seen with her own eyes the evidence of Miss Eustace's falsity. Richard, who had been foolhardy enough to climb through the window of the medium's lodgings and search her possessions, had found trunks packed with all the paraphernalia of a conjuror, and information she had collected about the residents of Brighton to give verisimilitude to the supposed messages from beyond, material which was now in the hands of the police. The case against Miss Eustace had been made very clear before the Lewes magistrates and Mr Hope could not be ignorant of the facts. An outright refusal was the obvious response, but again she bit back the instinct and stayed calm.

'I am sure you must be aware that the evidence against her is very strong.'

He shrugged. 'There may be evidence as you call it, but these things can be viewed in more ways than one, and I believe that if there proves to be a case of any sort it will not be against the lady, only the men who controlled her.'

'Mr Hope, you must know that I have experienced her trickery myself.'

He gazed on her as one might a child or a simpleton. 'Oh, I know what it is you speak of, your very tangible contact with Phoebe, a dangerous experiment that threatened the lives of you both. I have heard similar statements from so many who close their minds to the great truth. But allow me to explain. What few people appreciate is that the power of a medium is a very delicate thing — it may be well one day and drained the next, yet the public, who rarely understand these things, expect it to be always there in strength. A mere mountebank may perform his tricks at any time, since that is what they are — tricks. For the medium, on the other hand, under certain conditions, and most especially when surrounded by harsh unbelievers, the ability to commune with the spirit world may fail altogether, and yet a convincing display is still expected. On those rare occasions, the medium who does not wish to disappoint those who take such comfort from communication with the spirits, will oblige by employing non-spiritual means to produce the effects desired.'

'So you are saying that mediums do cheat?'

'I would not call it cheating.'

'I would.'

'I reiterate,' he said very patiently, 'this happens only rarely, and it is not done for the advantage of the medium, but in order to give consolation to the bereaved. And that inevitably is exactly when the accusations of fraud arise. Most of the time the apparitions seen and communications received at séances are entirely genuine. Can you not acknowledge that?'

Mina thought carefully. 'Irrespective of what I might think about Miss Eustace's abilities, or all mediums for that matter, there is an important issue which you have not addressed. Miss Eustace is not about to stand trial for fraudulent mediumship; her case is far more serious. She is accused, quite rightly in my opinion, of extorting large sums of money from an unsuspecting lady under false pretences by passing on messages supposedly from the spirit of her late brother, messages which were later proven by documentary evidence to be untrue.'

Hope shook his head emphatically. 'I do not believe that Miss Eustace is guilty of any crime. As to the spirit messages, well, we only have the word of her accuser, Miss Whinstone, as to what words actually passed. There was an arrangement that was made between the parties in good faith, and the lady completely understood its provisions, but she later discovered that it was a greater drain on her resources than anticipated. She could, had she wished, have approached Miss Eustace and asked for some variation, or even requested to cancel the arrangement by mutual agreement, but unfortunately she chose instead to try and extricate herself from her difficulty by claiming that she had been duped.'

Mina was now sufficiently annoyed by this nonsense to state her position clearly. 'That is ridiculous. I suppose it is what Miss Eustace has told you. You should know that Miss Whinstone is a friend of my family. She is a good, kind lady who would never stoop to the action you have described, or indeed any dishonesty. If Miss Eustace wishes to malign her in this way then I certainly cannot offer her any support.'

Mr Hope did not appear discomfited by this. 'You may wish to reconsider. I should mention that in the forthcoming trial it will be a part of Miss Eustace's defence that her accuser did not tell the truth before the magistrates. If Miss Whinstone tells the same tale at the assizes and Miss Eustace is acquitted then your friend will be open to a charge of perjury.'

It was said calmly but it was clearly intended to shock, and it did. Mina knew that it had taken nervous Miss Whinstone all her scant courage to make a public confession to the cruel delusion in which she had been trapped, and could not imagine what additional harm this fresh ordeal would wreak on the lady's fragile constitution.

'And you believe Miss Eustace?'

'I do.'

'That is unpardonable! It is nothing short of slander!'

As Mina's anger mounted, so Hope's satisfaction increased. 'I can see you feel very strongly about what you see as an injustice to your friend. As strongly as I feel about the injustice being done to Miss Eustace. But there is something you can do to mend the situation. Miss Eustace might be persuaded, out of the goodness of her heart, to make some slight changes to her defence. She might, for example, decide to claim simply that she is the innocent victim of a mistake. Miss Whinstone will not, therefore, be shown to have deliberately lied, but simply to have been confused. Under such circumstances there would be no criminal charges for her to answer.'

'How might I —?' Mina stopped. She understood it all now. She was being blackmailed.

Arthur Wallace Hope smiled at her.

She took a deep breath. Her back hurt, her shoulder hurt and her chest hurt. 'You place me in a very difficult position, since if I was to make the statement you ask for it would be a lie. Do you expect me to put my name to a lie?'

'No, Miss Scarletti, I expect you to acknowledge the truth. One day all the world will recognise it. Eyes will be opened, and the cavillers and bigots who deny the world of the spirit will finally see what is so plain and obvious to others. Their refusal to admit to the true way is a great curse on mankind. It is like the folly of the unlawful whom God punished by sending his flood allowing only the righteous to live.'

'I cannot see that this is the same thing at all. Surely you cannot be claiming that unbelievers will be washed away by another flood?'

'It is already happening! It has happened! I have seen it with my own eyes on the battlefields of the Crimea. War is the new flood — it is God's warning to mankind! I know it may seem harsh but it was necessary, like the flood, to sweep away materialism and bring humanity to glory!'

Mina stared at him. He was noble, intelligent, and fiercely driven by the certainty that he was right. Nothing would or could ever shake him from that position. Not only that, but he had the power to convince others, and he knew it.

Mina examined the teapot while she was wondering what to say. She offered to refresh his teacup, but he declined. 'Mr Hope, you have given me a great deal to think about. I cannot give you an answer today. Would you allow me some time to consider what you have said?'

'Of course I will!'

'Please could you assure me that for the time being, Miss Eustace will not be making any accusations of perjury against Miss Whinstone, which would only distress her unnecessarily.'

'You have my promise.'

Mina poured more tea for herself, but its murky depths looked uninviting, and a few dusty leaves had escaped the strainer. She wished she did have the powers he attributed to her, then she could have divined what to do next. As she reflected on what he had said at his lecture, however, a new idea did come to her. She put the cup down. 'Perhaps it would assist me in my deliberations if you were to tell me more about your belief that the Royal Pavilion is a focus of spiritual energy. You mentioned at the lecture that you had actually met the Misses Bland, authors of *An Encounter*?'

'Yes, very recently. I found them modest and virtuous, and quite unconscious of having any powers of their own, although I am sure that they do and would take only a little development. In view of their position in life and retiring natures they do not, however, wish to undertake any séances, which I think is a great pity.'

'How did you encounter them?'

'I wrote to Mr Worple, the printer of the volume, who informed me that, because of the unexpected interest in the book and the timidity of its authors, he had been advised that the ladies would not consent to meet with anyone except for a select few individuals. He was kind enough to ask them if I might be introduced and they were happy to allow it. Our meeting took place at his office in London about two weeks ago, and we had a very pleasant afternoon.'

'So if I wished to meet them I could apply to Mr Worple in the same way?'

'You might try, but in view of your opposition to spiritualism, it would be most unlikely that your application would succeed. You may not write to them directly. The ladies wish to preserve their true identity to save embarrassment to their father, who is a clergyman. They are, I might say, quite astonished at the excitement caused by their book. They wrote it for the purposes of information and had it printed at their own expense, not expecting to achieve fame and fortune. I think the supposed indecency is very much inflated. To the innocent all things are innocent.'

Mina decided that it would not be wise to reveal that she had not only read the book but also discovered the date of the Pavilion visit. Her main concern now was preventing Miss Eustace from defaming Miss Whinstone and also, if at all possible, ensuring that she never returned to ply her fraudulent trade in Brighton. Since the recent surge of interest in the Pavilion as a focus of spiritualism was solely due to *An Encounter* she thought that if she could reveal the work to be a fiction then that interest, even if it did not evaporate since such things rarely did in their entirety, would be weakened to the point where Miss Eustace was no longer able to capitalise on it.

'Very well,' she said. 'I think that I shall pay a visit to the Pavilion and see if I can feel the power of the spirits working there. You may think it strange that I have never been there, but I have lived in Brighton for less than three years, during the first of which I was helping care for my father who was an invalid, and after his death for my mother, who was deeply affected by his loss.'

'I understand, and I very much hope that when you sense the working of the spirits they will bring peace to you and your family. I will leave you now to your thoughts, but if I might be permitted to call again?'

'Of course.' She rose.

'Incidentally, I have heard tell of another medium in Brighton, somewhat different from Miss Eustace, but still one I should like to meet. A Miss Foxton?'

'Yes, I have seen one of her performances, but I believe she is no longer in town. If I should hear of her return I will let you know.'

At this moment, to Mina's concern she heard the front door open. Could it be her brother who was now about to discover her in close compact with a man? But chattering voices in the hallway told her it was far worse than that; her mother and Enid had returned early. Mina hoped desperately that they would hurry upstairs and she could persuade Mr Hope to leave without their seeing him, but instead they burst into the parlour, laughing, and halted in astonishment. Enid did not know whether to be delighted or furious, but Mr Hope favoured them with one of his most pleasing smiles. 'Why Miss Scarletti, these must be your charming sisters!'

Mina made the introductions, while Enid went red in the face and Louisa simpered at the blatant flattery. 'Mrs Scarletti!' Hope exclaimed as he bowed to Louisa, 'why, surely not, you are far too young to have grown daughters! But now I recognise you both as you came to my lecture and I believe I inscribed a book.' He turned the full power of his gaze onto Enid, who looked ready to melt like a jelly left in the sun.

'Oh, I do hope you are not going so soon — please do stay and have some refreshment!' exclaimed Louisa.

'Yes, please do!' Enid begged. 'I should so much like to hear more about Africa!'

'Ladies, I am sorely tempted to accept your kindness, but I regret that I am already engaged for luncheon with the Lord Mayor who expects me to regale him with my experiences in the Crimea. But I promise that we will meet again.' He supplied his card. 'I can be reached here.'

Once the visitor had gone, Enid turned upon Mina with a look of fury. 'Well, what can you mean by it? Why did he call? I can't believe he was here to see you! Was there no mistake?'

'He wished to engage my support for the publication *An Encounter*,' said Mina, which was part of the truth at least. 'He knows what I think of spirit mediums and thought that if I was to say something in favour of the book it might lend some weight to his arguments.' She decided to say nothing about Miss Eustace as that was a sore point with her mother.

'I hope you have not agreed to his wishes,' said Louisa, frowning. 'He is a man of the world and therefore we must excuse him from not thinking the book indecent, but it is quite unsuitable for the female sex.'

'I have not, but I suggested he might like to call again, something I think you would both wish for,' said Mina. 'If you like I will keep him in suspense as to my reply until you tire of his company.'

From Enid's expression Mina thought that situation would be a very long time coming.

Chapter Ten

Mina decided that before she took any further action she should learn as much as she could about Arthur Wallace Hope, and so after luncheon she retired to her room to read *African Quest*. There was a brief tribute to the author in a foreword by none other than Sir Roderick Murchison, the distinguished geologist, president of the Royal Geographical Society and friend of Dr Livingstone. The editor of the *Brighton Gazette* had also, when advertising the recent lecture, published some extremely complimentary words about Mr Hope, from which Mina assumed that neither of these authors had ever had the occasion to oppose his wishes.

Arthur Wallace Hope had been born in 1830, and was the second son of Viscount Hope. Determining on a military career he had joined the 77th East Middlesex Regiment of Foot and served in the Crimea with courage and distinction. He had returned, saddened at the terrible waste of human life, to find that his father had died while he was away. Seeking a purpose and challenge not offered to him by his new status of younger brother and heir presumptive of a Viscount, he soon volunteered for his first trip to Africa. His brother's untimely death, without male issue, had elevated him to the family title, although he preferred to be known as plain Mr Hope.

Mina could easily see why Arthur Wallace Hope had become so convinced of spiritualism. He had been surrounded by death from an early age. Not only had he lost his father and older brother while still in his twenties, but he had witnessed young men dying on the battlefield in their thousands. Seeking adventure in Africa he had been appalled by wars and massacres and seen his own party of gallant friends hacked to death, drowned in surging rapids or ravaged by tropical diseases. It had been impossible for him to accept that the loss of so much promising youth had been for nothing, and that those bright souls were not somewhere close by enjoying a tranquil afterlife where he would one day meet them again.

After some thought, Mina decided that what she most needed was sensible advice, and since this was not available at home, she sent a note to Dr Hamid.

Later that day, her brother Richard arrived unannounced in time for the family to sit down together for dinner. Although not normally the best of timekeepers, his ability to put in an appearance just as food was due to be served was unwaveringly accurate. He was, as ever, buoyantly optimistic about a brand new business undertaking that was going to make his fortune, but predictably, was unable to provide any significant detail concerning its nature. The only certainty was that a small amount of capital would be required, which through some dreadful bad luck he was unable to lay his hands on. His brother Edward was allowing him board and lodgings at his home in London but was being a terrible bore over money. As usual, Louisa smiled indulgently at Richard, said how happy she was to help him make his way in the world, and agreed to provide what was needed.

To Mina's knowledge Richard's last three enterprises, in all of which he had failed to become rich, had been the gaming table, trying to acquire a wealthy wife, and appearing on stage with Nellie, and she dreaded to think what his next venture might be. In due course she would doubtless be burdened with the information and expected to provide an investment. The main subject of conversation, however, once the question of Richard's assured success, Mina's health, the twins' progress, Enid's new gown and Louisa's headaches had been rapidly disposed of, was the visit to their home of the renowned and heroic Arthur Wallace Hope. Both Louisa and Enid thought it obvious to the point where no discussion was required that the distinguished visitor had not wished to see Mina at all, and there had been an innocent error in which she had foolishly encouraged the great man. There, however, their opinions diverged, since Louisa, commenting that Hope must have asked to see Mrs Scarletti and not Miss, was convinced that she had been the object of his interest, whereas Enid who had been a Miss Scarletti not so very long ago was of another viewpoint. Enid, however, as did everyone in the house, knew better than to contradict her mother once she had arrived at a fixed opinion, and only let her opposition be known with very pointed glances at Mina and Richard.

'I suppose,' said Louisa, with a careful lightness of tone, 'that Mr Hope is not a married man? If he is then his poor wife must be very unhappy with him spending all his time travelling.'

'Oh, he has not had the time to marry, surely,' said Enid.

'He might have married while he was in Africa,' suggested Mina.

'What nonsense you talk sometimes,' said Louisa. 'There is no one in Africa for him *to* marry.'

'Unless he has a secret wife who is quite mad and he has her locked up in a tower at his castle!' giggled Enid, who seemed to find this idea quite exciting.

Once dinner was done, Mina suggested that she would like to take a refreshing walk to the seafront and asked Richard if he would go with her, to which he at once agreed. Enid and Louisa, saying they had seen the sea quite recently and did not need to see it again so soon, remained at home to examine their recent purchases and give instructions to Rose as to their care.

'Both Enid and mother are in better health than they have been for some while,' said Richard, as he walked with Mina down Montpelier Road to the inviting vista of the shining ocean. Mina leaned on Richard's arm, which reduced the awkward seesawing of her gait, and therefore the strain on her muscles, and he was happy to amble slowly at her side. Brighton was glowing in its autumn beauty, the sky of that intense clear blue that seems to go on forever, an unusually kind breeze doing no more than rustle garments and make the ribbons of ladies' bonnets flutter. 'I was careful not to mention Mr Inskip in case Enid had a relapse into melancholy. Do we know if that gentleman is alive or dead? Or perhaps he is a little of both? He never seemed to me to be perfectly alive even at the wedding.'

'Enid receives the occasional letter from him, usually to say he is very occupied with business and may not be home for some months. That always seems to cheer her.'

'And before you say it, my dear girl, it is obvious to me that Mr Arthur Wallace Hope came to see you and none other.'

'He did,' said Mina, and was relieved to regale her brother with the full import of the conversation.

'The scoundrel!' exclaimed Richard. 'How dare he! I am sorry I was not here to deal with him.'

'It was a difficult interview,' Mina admitted, 'but I do think I would not have learned all that I did had there been another person present.'

'Do you want me to call him out? I would, you know.'

'No, Richard, I don't want you to do anything except watch and listen if he visits again. And not a word to mother or Enid, who would never believe me in any case.'

'What will you do about his demands?'

'I am not sure. I am only happy that the trial date has not yet been set, so I do have time to decide. The good news is that he seems not to have realised that you and Dr Hamid were part of the business, and I hope he never finds out.'

'You must speak with the good doctor, of course.'

'I have sent him a note, and will call as soon as convenient.'

'And while it might be hard on Miss Whinstone, she must be apprised of the danger to herself.'

'I agree. I cannot leave her unprepared. But she is such a nervous lady that I suspect she will beg me to comply with Mr Hope's wishes in order to spare her from prosecution.'

'Would you do that for her?'

Mina had already given this fraught matter some very serious consideration and had come to an unhappy conclusion. 'If necessary. I would not give in to blackmail on my own account but I cannot see another lady suffer for my obstinacy. Poor Miss Whinstone has endured quite enough without being threatened with a criminal charge. My thoughts are my own, of course. They will not change and I hope that those who know me will understand. But I would look like a fool to the public, and that will be hard. Still, these things are quickly forgotten.'

'If there is anything you need doing, I am your man, you have only to ask, and meanwhile, I will bend my mind to the problem.'

'Just promise me you will not break the law, and do nothing without consulting me first,' Mina pleaded.

They had reached the promenade, where a sting of salt was in the air, and the pebbled beach lay before them like so many pale brown and cream coloured eggs, streaked here and there with dark weed. In the distance was the cowbell tinkle of the last donkey rides of the day, and pleasure boats were being drawn up to take their rest out of the reach of the hungry sea. In the evening, as the sun sank, dusting the waves with rosy light, Brighton's visitors would throng to the cliff top or gather in rows along the promenade to watch the spectacle. Mina, who saw tales of horror in everything around her, thought that the crimson blush of the sea resembled blood. Supposing, she thought, it was blood, the spectral remembrance of a sea battle in which many men had lost their lives? That would make a good story. 'Ghost Blood' she would call it. Mina decided to purchase a small notebook to carry about with her so she could jot down her story ideas before they vanished.

'And now, Richard,' said Mina, as the sky gradually cooled and they strolled along the promenade past tall white hotels, 'I want to know the reason for your visit.'

'Does one need a reason to visit Brighton?' he said with a smile.

'If it was anyone other than you I would have no need to ask. I love the smell of the sea and the air, and for entertainment I am not sure I would find more to delight me in London. But I am sure that you are not here for your health or even pleasure.'

'Now you can't deny that there has been a great deal happening here, what with poisonings and scandals, it has been in the London papers as well, and I could not wait to come here where life is so much richer in incident than London.'

'Surely living with Edward is not as dull as that?' exclaimed Mina.

'Oh, but it is; he talks of nothing but work and Miss Hooper! He is in a perfect frenzy of excitement at the prospect of making that delightful maiden his bride. He wearies me on the subject incessantly. I only hope that when he is her husband at last the lady does not disappoint.'

'You do not admire her?'

'She is pretty, I admit, but tedious. They will make an admirable couple. And would you believe Edward actually suggested that I join the company as a clerk! A clerk! Imagine me sitting at a desk all day, I would dry up like an Egyptian mummy and have to be put in a museum.'

'I assume that you are here to pursue some more pleasurable and less arduous way of making your fortune. Please let me know what it is; reassure me that nothing illegal or scandalous is involved and you will not need to hide it from mother again.'

He grinned. 'Well there has been a lot of talk just lately about a certain book and the ghostly shade of old George as was, only seen when he was young and virile. Now my thought is this — if one book will make money then two will make twice as much. I did think about writing my own but somehow I can't seem to get properly started. So I thought that as you are an author you could give me some advice. Where do you get your ideas from? What do you do when the words refuse to come? Do you have to force yourself to write? It's all a mystery to me.'

'If you need to ask those questions then I would suggest book writing may not be your forte,' advised Mina.

'Perhaps not, although there are many who do not allow that to stop them. Have you read about the ghostly encounter? It might be a bit fast for you.'

'And not for you? I have been told that only mature men or married persons would not find it shocking. Mother has a copy, only she would never admit it.'

'I have read it. Mother likes to think that I am innocent of the ways of the world, but she knows the truth. All I am innocent of is ready money.' A new thought struck him. 'Tell me — how is Nellie? I haven't seen her since she was married. Is she happy with her new husband? I didn't take to him myself.'

'I believe she is content. If their marriage may be likened to a ship then he is the proud owner, but it is her hand on the wheel.'

'Well if he is ever unkind to her you must let me know at once and I will come and teach him the proper way to treat a lady. But do you see where my thoughts are tending? I might not be able to write a book but a play should be far easier. Yes, that is what I shall do!'

'It may be harder than you think,' warned Mina.

'Oh, I am sure it is very easy; after all, what is a play but people standing on a stage and talking a great deal of nonsense! I have seen enough of the theatre to know that!'

'I am not even sure if it is easy to write a bad play, but a good one will certainly require hard work and some literary ability.'

'Aha,' he exclaimed triumphantly, 'in that case you will write it, Mina!'

'I shall do nothing of the sort, and don't try to persuade me.'

'Really? Well, I should be able to dash it off in a day or two in any case, and I know exactly what the crowds will come to see. It will be the story of the Prince and Mrs Fitzherbert and their doomed love. Good or bad writing doesn't signify since there would only be a few performances and no one would know the truth until we have sold all our tickets.'

'We? Richard — I shall have nothing to do with this project in any capacity!'

'Just a little cash advance, that is all,' he pleaded. 'I have to advertise and have tickets printed and hire a room and costumes. Mother's cheque won't cover all of that if I am to make a fine show. I shall get Nellie to personate Mrs Fitzherbert, I am sure she is pining for the theatre and would jump at it.'

'Would her husband not object?'

'No, Nellie will get around that — she has her ways, you know. And I shall be the Prince of Wales. Prinny was said to be very handsome in his youth.' Richard preened himself with a satisfied pat to his chest then allowed his palm to descend to his stomach. Despite his hearty appetite he remained defiantly slender. 'I shall need padding of course. Perhaps we will get Nellie's old friend Rolly Rollason to take part; he's a good sport. I know! He could be Napoleon!'

'Do you think he will be suitable for the role? I believe Napoleon was quite a short man, and Rolly is well above six feet in height.'

'Then he will personate Napoleon on his knees. It will be a novelty. Yes, I can see it now! Prinny and Napoleon will fight with swords for the love of Mrs Fitzherbert and the honour of England! Or the love of England and the honour of Mrs Fitzherbert, whichever is more appropriate. Prinny will stab the Frenchman through the heart to the wild applause of the groundlings.'

'So it will not be a historical piece.'

'Not at all. It will be much more interesting. Then Mrs Fitzherbert will fall into the Prince's arms in an ecstasy of passion. It will be —'

'Indecent?' Mina suggested.

'Piquant.'

'Richard, you do know that the late King George was a very unpopular figure? Gormandising — drinking — running up debts — gambling — mistresses …' Mina's voice tailed off as she realised that she was cataloguing her own brother's principal faults.

'Oh, but I have been told that he was very well thought of in Brighton, since he brought the fashionables to town. And if not, it is high time he was rehabilitated! I would rather spend five minutes carousing with Prinny than a whole evening's dreary banquet with the Queen. I'm sure that good Prince Albert was a splendid sort, but ten years of mourning is really overdoing it.' Richard looked suddenly thoughtful. 'Did Albert ever come to the Pavilion?'

'It is possible,' said Mina grudgingly. 'Please do not personate him. Treason is still a hanging offence.'

'And, of course, the best place to perform my play will be in the Pavilion! I hope it will not be too expensive to hire a room. I shall go there tomorrow and find out.'

'Then I had better come with you, and make sure that you do not make any unwise arrangements with money you do not have.'

They turned back to Montpelier Road, and Mina, leaning on her brother's arm, did not mind the pitying looks of passers-by as she limped by his side. There was a note waiting for her at home saying that Dr Hamid and Anna would be delighted if she joined them for a light supper that evening. Richard, Mina admitted to herself, had been right about one thing — she must warn Miss Whinstone of the threat from Mr Hope, even if the result was capitulating to his demands. Mina wrote a note to Miss Whinstone asking if she might visit her very soon.

Chapter Eleven

Dr Hamid and his sister Anna lived in a pleasant villa near the seafront not far from their place of business. Only once had they allowed a séance to be held in their home, and it was done not at the desire of either, but at the earnest request of their older sister Eliza, who had been seduced by the charm and promises of Miss Eustace and her acolyte Mr Clee into the belief that she was a medium. As Mina had later learned, adults of restricted stature were valuable allies for a spirit medium, able to appear at séances in the guise of ghostly children, yet with the discipline to maintain the deception for as long as necessary. Mediums who lacked such confederates often resorted to creating the illusion themselves by crouching or kneeling, but in doing so risked an embarrassing exposure if distraught parents attempted to embrace the spirit of their dead offspring.

Mr Clee had also tried to draw Mina into Miss Eustace's fold but he had failed. A young man with a persuasive manner and the looks and address of a hero of romantic adventures, he had worked his wiles on the matrons of Brighton to considerable effect. He had initially presented himself at one of Miss Eustace's séances masquerading as a stranger and a sceptic, but had rapidly undergone a miraculous conversion to a devoted worshipper at her shrine. So ardent was Mr Clee that there had been talk all over the town that he was in love with the medium, a rumour that had saddened many a susceptible female heart before he protested that his admiration of the lady was chaste and pure. Only later had it been revealed that he was not only Miss Eustace's co-conspirator in fraud and confederate in the production of supposed spiritual effects, but her brother. Their father, Mr Benjamin Clee, was a respectable purveyor of materials and equipment for the use of conjurors, and both brother and sister were adept in that art. Mina hoped that any attempt by Mr Clee to use his skills to beguile the warders of the Lewes House of Correction where he was now securely confined would fall upon hearts made stony by long experience.

Miss Eustace had not attended the event at the Hamids' house since she had been suffering from a heavy cold, but that illness, of little consequence to a youthful person in otherwise good health, had been carried to the house on the breath of Mr Clee and found its way into Eliza's cramped and underdeveloped lungs. After her death Dr Hamid, distracted with grief, had consulted Miss Eustace in the hope of making some contact with Eliza's sprit. A simple slip had revealed to him that a message purporting to come from Eliza actually had a more earthly origin. 'Perhaps in a quite different sense it was sent by Eliza,' he had once told Mina. 'Oh, I don't mean that it was actually she, but it was what I knew of my sister and what Miss Eustace did not that revealed to me how woefully I had misplaced my trust. It does not take a medium to tell me that Eliza lives on. She still, as she has always done, inspires Anna and me in our study of the spine and its diseases so that we may help others. One day Eliza and I will meet again and she will be healed in a way that I could never achieve and we will be content. But I no longer believe that I will see or speak to her before we are joined in death. I will be patient.'

With Eliza's loss the house seemed quieter. The room where she had spent her days, supported in a chair made specially for her to be able to sit and sleep in comfort and enjoy reading was as she had left it, the book she had been reading lay open at the last page she had perused, and her spectacles were where she had placed them, just ready to be picked up. It was a house of double mourning, for Jane Hamid, and now for Eliza, both taken to their rest far too young. But the future was there too, in photographic portraits of Dr Hamid's sons and daughter. All were engaged in study and destined for the practice of medicine, although in the case of the daughter she would need double the courage and determination of her brothers as she would have to overcome not just examinations but male opposition to women studying medicine at all, in order to achieve her desires.

The day's work done, brother and sister liked to sit together companionably and Mina often joined them. Her good health and increasing vigour were also, she knew, a part of Eliza's legacy. In the last few months she had seen, thanks to the exercises in which Anna had carefully coached her, the first positive change in her form she had known for many a year; her back and limbs were stronger and there was a curve of muscle on shoulders and upper arms that had not been noticeable before. Many would have thought such development unseemly and unwomanly, but Mina, who had her clothes specially made so that she could dress herself unaided, enjoyed her secret.

She still had to take care not to deplete her energies through incautious exertion, and that evening, Mina hired a cab, delivering her note to Miss Whinstone on the way, and finding a stationer still open where she was able to purchase a pocket book to record her story ideas. Once she was settled by the Hamids' fireside and the maid had brought hot cocoa and sandwiches, the conversation turned to the lecture by Arthur Wallace Hope.

'I cannot deny his bravery, and who knows but the exploration of Africa will benefit us one day, but if he is to be the champion of that indecent book then the sooner he is gone from Brighton the better,' said Anna. 'Some of my patients who attended the lecture are actually taking his words as a recommendation, and reading it when they had previously determined not to.'

'I have already been invited to a séance,' added Dr Hamid with obvious distaste. 'I declined, of course.'

'I am afraid the situation is far more serious than that,' Mina confessed. Brother and sister listened to her with increasing concern as she described her conversation with Arthur Wallace Hope. 'Mother and Enid do not know the true reason for his visit, although I have told Richard who has just arrived to stay with us. My next step will be to speak to Miss Whinstone. I don't want to frighten her, but if she is in danger I would not want her to be unprepared for it when I could have warned her.' Dr Hamid and Anna looked at each other, and Mina could see that they saw the wisdom of her proposal. 'I fear that she will ask me to spare her by doing what Mr Hope asks, and I will have to comply. Perhaps I can find some way of meeting the demands of all parties without shaming myself. And then I will try to forget all about Miss Eustace and her kind and go back to my life as it was. I have, however, written to Mr Greville, my late father's business partner, to see if I can discover more about the book. Not only is it causing such dismay amongst the ladies of Brighton, but it is the stimulus to Miss Eustace's wishes to return here. If I can show it to be a fiction then perhaps she will be less welcome. I will let you know what he can tell me.'

Dr Hamid smiled at Mina. 'Mr Hope is a very clever, wealthy, influential and respected man. I wonder if he knows he has met his match?'

There was a knock at the front door, which caused them all some surprise since no visitor was expected, and the maid brought a letter addressed to Dr Hamid. He, assuming it to be of a medical nature, took it to his study, while Anna and Mina made the most of the remaining refreshments, but before Anna could ring for the plates to be cleared her brother returned with the opened letter in his hand and a deep frown on his face.

'This is quite extraordinary. The letter is from Mr Arthur Wallace Hope. He requests a private meeting with me at my earliest convenience.'

'Does he say what the subject of the interview might be?' asked Mina.

Dr Hamid reread the letter carefully and shook his head. 'No, he gives no indication at all. I doubt that it is a medical matter.'

Mina was thoughtful. 'Since he has spoken to Miss Eustace he most probably knows that you used to attend her séances and engaged her for private consultations. I expect she also recalls your presence at the event where she was arrested, though many of her circle were there as well. I think it very doubtful that Mr Hope knows the part you played in her discovery.'

'And he must never know! Fortunately, I was not asked to give evidence before the magistrates and as far as I am aware I will not be called at the trial.'

'Perhaps he believes that you might be sympathetic to her, and would be willing to act as a character witness?' suggested Anna.

'He may well be seeking out people with professional and social status for that very purpose,' agreed Mina. 'He might ask you to sign a statement attesting to your belief that Miss Eustace is genuine.'

'I shall, of course, do neither,' said Dr Hamid firmly.

'There is another possibility,' Mina added. 'He has been making enquiries about me and therefore might know by now that I am a patient of yours. This message comes just hours after he failed to induce me to sign the statement he wanted. Could he be trying to find out more about me — some new way of forcing my hand?'

'If so, that is deplorable, and I will show him the door at once!'

'I would prefer it if you did not,' said Mina.

Dr Hamid looked wary. 'Miss Scarletti — I know that look — what are you suggesting I do?'

'Mr Hope may be quite unaware that we are of the same mind on the subject of sprit mediums. Perhaps you might simply listen to what he has to say, and neither oppose his wishes nor agree to comply with them. Ask for more time to consider, as I did. He might reveal more to you than he has done to me.'

'Very well. I doubt, in any case, that he is a man who can be put off for long. I will write to him at once and arrange to see him tomorrow.'

Chapter Twelve

Next morning, Mina received a letter from Mr Greville. A letter to her from the office of the Scarletti Library of Romance was not an unusual event and excited no comment at the breakfast table, in fact Mina's literary activities did not usually excite any comment at all in her home. Had her mother actually seen her tales of hauntings and horror there would no doubt have been unceasing comment.

Disappointingly, Mr Greville reported that he had been unable to discover anything further concerning the Misses Bland, authors of the sensational *An Encounter*. The proprietor of the printing firm, Mr Worple, was personally known to him, as there were occasional social gatherings of men in the publishing trade, and the office of Worple and Co. was not far from his own. Mr Greville had obliged Mina by finding a pretext to call on Mr Worple and mentioning to him that he was curious about the authors of the notorious book, and asking who they were. Judging by Mr Worple's reaction, this was a question the printer had been asked very many times. Nevertheless, he was more polite and communicative to a brother in the publishing trade than he might have been to a correspondent of the popular press. Mr Worple had replied that all he had been asked to do was print the book as written. He had no means of contacting the authors, since they had initially made a personal visit to his office, and thereafter the copies had been collected by a servant, who carried messages back to her employers. The servant also brought instructions when a further printing was required, and payment of his invoice, which was made in banknotes. On their initial visit to his office, the ladies had asked, in view of the position of their father, who was a clergyman, that their identity should be protected and Mr Worple had respected their wishes. Both ladies had been veiled. They had made only one subsequent visit, some two weeks previously when they had come to the office for an interview with the distinguished explorer Mr Arthur Russell Hope.

The newspapers had become very exercised by the mystery concealing the true identity of the authors, and correspondents, finding Mr Worple unwilling to divulge what they thought he knew, had offered him bribes, or even sent him false messages purporting to come from the Misses Bland hoping to fool him into a revelation. From time to time articles had published with headlines such as 'Who are the Misses Bland?' or 'The Riddle of *An Encounter*'. One of the more sensational periodicals had asked the authors to visit its office promising that they could do so in the strictest confidence, and hinting that a fee might be payable. Another had offered the public a reward of £20 for information as to their identity. No one had come forward.

Frustrated newsmen eager for a story had even taken to lurking outside Mr Worple's office, hoping to see the Misses Bland arrive. Some lady customers had actually been followed back to their homes. The nuisance had been reported to Mr Worple, as a result of which he had been obliged to call the police who had dispersed the loiterers, most of whom they knew by sight, and made sure that these disgraceful incidents were not repeated.

Mr Greville closed his letter with the comment that Mr Worple, who was enjoying valuable repeat orders, was well aware that since he owned no rights over the manuscript, the authors were fully entitled to take their requirements elsewhere, and was therefore unlikely to renege on his agreement not to pry into the affairs of the Misses Bland.

Mina studied the letter wondering what, if anything, she had learned. The book had attributed authorship to two ladies, and both Mr Hope and Mr Worple had met two ladies. They were said to reside in London and their choice of a London printer and the to-ing and fro-ing of a servant suggested that this was true. All that was known about them otherwise was what they had chosen to impart.

A second message arrived, this one from Miss Whinstone, who said that she was at home that morning and Mina would be very welcome to call.

'Who is writing to you, Mina?' asked her mother.

'An admirer!' said Enid, and laughed.

'Miss Whinstone, she would like me to call on her.'

'Oh?' said Louisa, puzzled. 'What can she want?'

'She doesn't say. Perhaps she was upset by Mr Hope's lecture and would like to discuss it with me.'

'Is she going to marry that dreadful old man?' asked Enid.

'I will let you know. If she does, she might ask you to be matron of honour.'

Enid scowled.

Miss Whinstone occupied a small but comfortably appointed apartment in the western portion of town. She and her late, and much missed, brother, Archibald, had once shared the accommodation, and it was now marked by memories of him. His portraits were a prominent feature, presented in carefully polished frames, and such little honours and badges as he had been awarded in his largely uneventful life, which had been marked by service on local charitable committees, were proudly displayed.

Miss Whinstone greeted Mina with genuine warmth of feeling. 'Miss Scarletti, I am very happy to see you. I feel quite ashamed of myself that I have not asked you to call on me sooner. I am so grateful to you for rescuing me, there can really be no other word, from the clutches of those horrid cheats. I know I shall never see my money again, but if my unhappy story can save others who are less able to endure the loss, I shall be content.'

Miss Whinstone, once her period of mourning for her brother had drawn to its conclusion, had been wont to wear a gown of an unflattering shade of dark bronze, the reflection of the silk on her naturally pale face making her look yellow and ill. The messages she had received supposedly from her beloved Archibald through the mediumship of Miss Eustace had initially been cheering and had caused her to trim up and wear an old light green gown, a colour that matched her eyes. She was the same age as Louisa, but without her claims to beauty, nevertheless, when her face was not creased with anxiety, she was not an unhandsome woman. That morning she wore a new gown, in a warm shade of deep plum, a colour that had by some means or other transmitted itself to her hair.

Miss Whinstone showed Mina to the large room which served as both parlour and drawing room, and where she also dined. As Mina entered, Mr Jellico, who had been seated on a sofa, made some effort to rise to his feet to greet her. Mr Jellico was a gentleman of some seventy years, very sparely made, like a withered tree, that looked as though it might snap in a high wind. His eyes, from behind the thick glass of his spectacles, were moist and bright, his hands misshapen, the fingers contracted like claws. His glance as he looked at Miss Whinstone was admiring, even affectionate.

'I am delighted to make your better acquaintance,' said Mr Jellico. Apart from seeing him in passing at Mr Hope's lecture, Mina had met him only when he had accompanied Miss Whinstone to take tea with her mother, and on those occasions he had merely sat silently by and listened.

'And I yours,' said Mina.

'I have been longing for the two of you to meet and converse, as Mr Jellico has been such a good friend and a great comfort to me in these difficult times,' said Miss Whinstone as her maid brought in a laden tray. 'I know I am not a very brave person, and I really did think I might faint dead away before those frightening magistrates, but Mr Jellico sat there and smiled at me, and do you know, he did make me feel a little stronger. I know the trial will be a far worse ordeal, but I am determined to bear it.'

Once the maid had distributed the refreshments and departed, Mina asked her first cautious question. 'What did you think of Mr Arthur Wallace Hope?'

'Oh, I did not care for him at all,' said Miss Whinstone. 'I know some ladies find him very interesting, but when he speaks about all his so-called adventures, all I can think of is how he goes about shooting things, which surely cannot be right.'

'I believe,' said Mr Jellico carefully, 'that in Africa that may be the only way to obtain food. Of course, he may shoot when he is in England too. Gentlemen of his class often do.'

Miss Whinstone's mouth was set in a firm line. 'Archibald never shot anything. He didn't believe in it.'

'My family attended the lecture because of an interest in geography, as I imagine most people did,' said Mina, 'but I was not prepared for Mr Hope's comments about spiritualism.'

'Nor I,' said Miss Whinstone, feelingly, helping Mr Jellico raise a teacup to his lips. 'What a nasty surprise. And to think he is in favour of that dreadful book, something I promise you I will never read.'

Mina took as deep a breath as she could manage. 'The reason I have asked to see you is that Mr Hope called on me yesterday, and your name came up in our conversation.'

Miss Whinstone could only stare at her, and Mr Jellico almost dropped the cup.

'I am afraid that what he had to say you may find alarming, but I cannot in all conscience keep you ignorant of his thoughts and intentions.' Mina glanced at Mr Jellico, and Miss Whinstone understood her hesitation.

'You may speak freely before Mr Jellico. He knows all; both the best and the worst.'

Mr Jellico smiled. 'The worst of it is only that Miss Whinstone has a warm heart.' He put his cup down and prepared himself for Mina's story.

Mina described in as much detail as she could remember the conversation with Mr Hope, holding nothing back, and, as anticipated, her revelations were met with shock and dismay.

'Might I ask,' said Mr Jellico thoughtfully, 'was this interview entirely private? Was there no one there to witness what was said?'

'I am afraid not. He requested a private discussion on a sensitive issue but he did not reveal in advance any clue as to what he might say. Even knowing his belief in the Bland sisters, I was amazed to find him a champion of Miss Eustace, and appalled to hear what he required of me.'

Jellico nodded and Mina sensed that though he was frail of body, his mind was keen and vigorous. 'You are right that you are being unfairly coerced into complying with his request, but if you were to accuse him of this, there is only your word against his, and I expect that he would deny any such intention. Given his position in society and the regard in which he is held, his word will weigh more heavily than yours, and if it came to a dispute you would be in some difficulty. If he should ask to speak to you again, I advise you to ensure that you have a respectable witness to the conversation.'

'That is sound advice. But now I am not sure what to do. On the one hand, I am reluctant to make a statement I know to be untrue, something Mr Hope wishes me to send to the public press, but at the same time I have no wish to place Miss Whinstone in danger. I have given this a great deal of thought, and the only way out I can suggest is for me to prepare and sign a statement for Mr Hope, but somehow find a form of words that would satisfy everyone, although I cannot at present think what they might be.'

'Oh, please,' Miss Whinstone exclaimed with unusual energy, 'I beg of you Miss Scarletti — I beg you most earnestly — do not, whatever you do, comply with this horrid man's request. Let them put me in prison if they must!' She started to tremble and Mr Jellico patted her hand.

'They would not put you in prison, I am sure of that,' he reassured her gently.

This was an unexpected turn of events. 'Miss Whinstone,' asked Mina, 'am I to understand that you do not want me to sign any kind of a statement for Mr Hope?'

'Yes. On no account must you do so. You, who have shown others the truth cannot put your name to a lie, even to save me!'

'Miss Whinstone is right,' agreed Mr Jellico, 'and the danger to you, Miss Scarletti, could be far greater than you might imagine. To begin with, I suspect that if you were to agree to make a statement, you might well find that you could not make a free choice of the words. Supposing he provided you with something to sign which stated that it was made of your own free will and for no consideration? That would not be an unusual requirement. Supposing he had it witnessed and then presented it in court in Miss Eustace's defence?'

'But she is not being tried for fraudulent mediumship. That was all the statement was intended to cover.'

'No, but she is accused of extorting money from Miss Whinstone on the basis of false messages communicated during private séances. The nature of those messages cannot be proven, and we only have Miss Whinstone's word that they did not accord with the evidence that was later produced. If we have a statement from you, and quite possibly other residents of Brighton, that Miss Eustace is genuine, what then becomes of the contention that she told falsehoods? Even if you try to take this middle way you have suggested, and agree to sign something of your own composition, and then later refuse to sign a paper he has drawn up in his own words, just that initial agreement could be held against you and presented in Miss Eustace's favour. As a truthful lady you would not deny it. If there is any doubt at the trial, and her appearance and demeanour excite the sympathy of the jurors, then she might be acquitted.'

Mina could only agree. 'She might, indeed, and if Mr Hope has his way she will be brought to the Pavilion in triumph and produce any number of illustrious ghosts. Of course, if she puts on a great show in the manner of a conjuror and entertains the crowds for a few shillings then I have no objection to that. But if she cannot mend her ways she will fleece some of her adherents of their fortunes and they might not be as brave as Miss Whinstone and speak out.'

'Miss Eustace is not the only danger, I am afraid,' said Mr Jellico with a wheezy sigh. 'There have been other séances held in Brighton just lately. We have both been invited to them and refused, despite the promise that Henry VIII and all his wives will appear and take tea with us. All of it is informal for now, no more than an evening's amusement, but the professional mediums will be sure to hear of it and before long they will descend upon the vulnerable like wolves.'

'But you will save us, Miss Scarletti,' said Miss Whinstone, her voice shaking, her eyes bright. 'I know you will.'

Mina returned home with the weight of the world on her aching shoulders.

Chapter Thirteen

Later that day, Richard and Mina passed through the southern gate into the grounds of the Royal Pavilion. He had suggested taking a carriage, which would have driven them directly up to the entrance porch, but since the day was fine, Mina, despite the effort it cost her, chose to walk her slow way so as to better see everything around her. Thus, they were able to enjoy the luxuriant gardens, which were so well sheltered and tended that trees grew there better than in any part of the town. The lawns were bright with visitors, some of whom were playing croquet. Mina had never played croquet, and no one had ever suggested she try it, since it was a pastime that required the player to swing a large mallet. She was not sure if she would be adept at it, but thought that if she ever took it up, she might at least be able to surprise everyone with her ability to lift the mallet at all, let alone strike a croquet ball.

Mina was not especially well acquainted with the history of the Pavilion; she knew only that it was acquired in the last century by the then Prince of Wales, who later acceded to the throne as George IV, had been remodelled so many times that it no longer resembled the house it had once been, and was now the property of the town. As they approached the domed entrance porch, which itself resembled a palace in miniature, she thought that an entire book could be written about each portion of this astounding building, so detailed and fantastical was the design of every part.

Even though inevitably its apartments were reduced from their once royal grandeur, there was nothing about the Pavilion that could disappoint. Just walking under the first arch was like stepping into another world. Was this, thought Mina, what it would be like to enter paradise — or was it just what the spiritualists hoped it would be like?

The octagonal entrance hall, lit by a Chinese lantern, had once offered the fashionable visitor to the royal apartments their first real view of the wonders that lay in store in its gilded interior, but it now had the humbler duty of an office, where attendants greeted new arrivals and offered to conduct them around the public rooms for the price of sixpence. Mina bought two tickets, and she and Richard joined a party of visitors waiting to embark on a tour. They were soon assigned an attendant, who commenced to point out features of interest. His manner was rather stiff and serious, like an automaton operated by the insertion of a coin, and he did very little to engage his listeners. Mina found herself wondering how many rooms there were in the Pavilion, and how many features each contained, and therefore how long the visit was to take. No wonder the Misses Bland had slipped away to amuse themselves.

The next room, their guide told them, was the vestibule and on entering it Mina found it hard to contain her excitement, since this was without a doubt the Hall of the Worthies, the very room that the Misses Bland had described as the first one they had entered on their great adventure and from where they had escaped their stuffy guide. Mina suspected that theirs had been the same guide. In the centre, and dominating the space, was the statue of the military hero. Greater than life-size, it stood high on a plinth, towering several feet above even the tallest visitor. William Henry Cecil George Pechell, said the inscription, of Her Majesty's 77th had died heroically aged just twenty-five at the siege of Sebastopol on 3 September 1855. The son of a Member of Parliament for Brighton his death had led to a period of public mourning in the town. His statue, depicting him in full uniform, urging on his men with valiantly drawn sword, had been erected by subscription in 1859. Displayed along the sides of the room, and considerably less impressive, were the busts of the notabilities of Brighton, which had been placed there after the building was acquired by the corporation. The whole was lit by an array of hexagonal lanterns embellished by a fantasy of dragons and serpents, while the sage green walls were similarly decorated. Mina at once conceived an idea for a new story in which a visitor to the Pavilion was pursued by mythical beasts that had emerged from the wallpaper. She made a note in her little pocket book, which she now carried everywhere with her. Unfortunately, the attendant, imagining that her note-taking was evidence of her keen interest in what he had to say, was kind enough to describe each of the busts in very great detail.

At this point the attendant mentioned very discreetly that a nearby door lead to an apartment which had once been the King's breakfast room, and was now a cloakroom and retiring room for ladies, while another doorway led to the gentlemen's cloakrooms.

'May I ask a question, please?' Mina interrupted.

'But of course, I will do my best to answer any question you may have about the Pavilion.'

'Would you be able to conduct us to the location where the ghost of the late King George was seen?'

The attendant was too polite to laugh out loud but it was clearly an effort for him not to. 'Oh, dear me, I am afraid that all the ladies ask me the same question and it is the very one I cannot answer. There is no room in the Pavilion which matches the description in that — unfortunate book.'

'You have not seen the ghost yourself?'

'I have never in my ten years as an attendant here seen anything of the kind, or heard of anything of that sort occurring.'

'Well, that is very disappointing,' said Mina.

They proceeded to the Chinese gallery, which, said their guide, was famed for the beauty and delicacy of its design, and was said by those who had seen it in the days of the old King to be one of the most superb apartments that Art and Fancy could produce. While still glorious to the eye, like a visual garden of bamboo and peonies, it contained only a few of the original ornaments, since so much had been removed when the Queen had decided to no longer favour the Pavilion with her presence. Later refurbishments carried out at the town's expense had, however, maintained the essential oriental flavour. 'Am I correct,' asked Mina, 'in thinking that there were once, in the time of the late King, life-sized statues standing in the niches, clad in Chinese costume?'

The guide paused with a look of surprise. 'That is correct.' This scenario was deliciously rife with potential for a tale of horror and Mina again made a note.

The next wonder they beheld was the enormous banqueting room, dominated by a cut crystal chandelier said to weigh more than a ton. Mina could only worry at the safety of such an item, despite the robustness of the gold chains by which it was suspended. When she commented on this, the attendant revealed that Queen Adelaide, the consort of King William IV, had actually had nightmares in which it had fallen, crushing members of the court. This prospect had so terrified her that she had prevailed upon the King to have it removed, and it had not been replaced until the time of the present Queen. Mina again wrote in her notebook: 'Chandelier falling — banquet? ballroom? theatre?' This, she was reminded, was the very room that Mr Hope had said he would hire for the performance of a séance by Miss Eustace. Mina glanced up at the giant chandelier again, but thought it was too much to wish for that it might descend at the very moment that Miss Eustace was underneath it.

The examination of the South Drawing Room, once known as the Green Drawing Room due to the prevailing hue of its draperies, alerted Mina to a passage in *An Encounter* when the ladies had been confused at entering a room they had once thought to be green but now found it had a peculiar blueish coloration. While feeling sure it was the same room, due to its dimensions and the positioning of the columns, they also saw that it was no longer lit by crystal gas standards but a large number of Chinese lanterns. Their account had simply suggested to Mina that since every room in the Pavilion was different in character the ladies had wandered into another room and become confused, but comparing their description with the room she was standing in, she began to wonder.

'These valances are a delightful shade of green,' she commented.

'The only remnant of its former glory,' agreed the attendant with a sigh. 'It was once a very elegant apartment, but little remains to suggest it. Note, however, the fine painting of the ceiling panels, and the beautiful gas lamps and ceiling flowers which were installed by the town authorities and have greatly improved the illumination and ventilation.'

'How was it formerly lit?'

'I believe by oil lanterns as so many of the apartments were.'

'And was it always green?'

'Well, now you mention it, no. It was once known as the Blue Drawing Room but that was very many years ago. This whole suite of rooms has undergone substantial changes mainly dating from the time of King George.'

They moved on through the apartments, and although these were splendid to the eye, the party was assured that what they saw was as nothing to the original beauties of the interior, which had been most dazzling. It had once been the pinnacle of luxury and taste, but with most of the original furniture and decorations having been distributed to other palaces one could only wish that by some magic it might all be restored. Mina was especially curious to see the King's Apartments, assuming that these would be extremely opulent, but discovered that they were no longer so, and the rooms were now available to be hired for private meetings of local societies.

'It all looks rather too grand for me,' said Richard, regretfully. 'A room large enough to hold a play would be an expensive proposition.'

'You may be right,' agreed Mina, but she asked the attendant about hire fees all the same, and he advised her to contact the Pavilion committee.

Their tour done Mina purchased a slim guidebook, which gave a little of the Pavilion's history and what the modern visitor might expect to see, but she was troubled. She had expected to find that the authors of *An Encounter* had simply described the Pavilion into which they had wandered during their ghostly experience, either as they had seen it, or as it was described in the guidebook, but they had done neither. Nowhere in the guidebook was there mention of the life-size Chinese figures or the South Drawing Room being blue and not green.

Their guide had gone on to greet the next party, one of whom was a very voluble lady with a loud voice. It was impossible not to hear her demanding to be shown the 'ghost room'. The guide was apologetic but told her the same as he had told Mina. 'Are you sure?' bellowed the lady in surprise. 'You have never seen the ghost? But you must have done, surely; my mother told me it is not the first such sighting in the Pavilion, and she is never mistaken about such things.'

Mina looked around.

'Careful my dear,' murmured Richard, 'your ears are waving so much that I will catch a chill in the breeze.'

'Take me for a walk,' said Mina, putting her hand on his arm, and they approached the lady and her group a little closer.

'I assure you, Madam,' the guide was protesting, 'I have been an attendant here for ten years and no such matter has ever been reported.'

'Oh, it was far longer ago than that,' insisted the visitor, 'I believe it was a single lady who saw the Prince. It was the subject of some gossip at the time, but I do not know if she wrote a book about it.'

'There are royal ghosts everywhere in Brighton, just now,' chimed in another lady visitor. 'We held a séance at my house only last night, and Mrs Fitzherbert herself made the table tilt and then she wrote a message on a piece of paper.'

'She peered from behind a curtain in my house,' said another, 'and she looked exactly as she does in the portraits.'

'Oh dear,' sighed Mina. 'Let us go home.'

'You are not about to try and persuade all these people that they are imagining things?' asked Richard.

'No, for I would fail.' As with her earlier conflict with the mediums, Mina knew that she could not save everyone from themselves, and if someone was determined to be duped against every argument there was nothing she could do. 'All I wish to do is prove that the supposed encounter was either a mistake or a fraud. That would calm the concerns of Dr and Miss Hamid and help them with their patients, and knock some of the ground from under Mr Hope's campaign to free Miss Eustace.'

'The ladies said they saw the Prince and his inamorata in the costume of their youth,' said Richard, thoughtfully. 'Was no one performing or rehearsing a play at that time?'

'No, I have studied the newspapers and the only entertainment taking place in the Pavilion which required a special costume of any kind was a series of concerts by the band of the Inniskilling Dragoons.'

'A set of fine fellows no doubt,' said Richard. 'I am sure that many of them could be mistaken for bold young Prinny, and who knows, one or two might even be mistaken for Mrs Fitzherbert.'

Once home Mina began drafting ideas for some new stories, called 'The Golden Dragon', 'A Chinese Mystery' and 'The Crystal Phantom', then, when she was sure she would not be disturbed, she took up the dumbbells and worked until her muscles felt warm and ached pleasantly. She was hoping that as she did so some inspiration would appear and show her a way out of her dilemma, but when at last she rested, she remained unenlightened.

Chapter Fourteen

Mina was not expecting a second letter from Mr Greville quite so soon, so when one arrived the next morning she opened it with curiosity.

Dear Miss Scarletti,

I was not anticipating having to write to you again on the question of the book 'An Encounter', which you mentioned to me recently, but circumstances have changed quite unexpectedly and now it is I who must ask if you know any more of the matter. Mr Worple, the printer, who was so very satisfied with the situation only a few days ago has, in view of the enquiries I made on your behalf, just come to see me in a very anxious state. He has been approached by a Brighton solicitor who demanded to know the real names and address of the authors of 'An Encounter', and refused to believe that he does not have that information or is unable to obtain it. Mr Worple has been given to understand that an action is being contemplated against the Misses Bland for plagiarism. It is beyond him to know what publication it is claimed is being plagiarised and my enquiries have come to nothing. Unfortunately, the solicitor has not chosen to reveal his hand at present.

I should mention that Mr Worple is of the opinion that nothing will come of this action. The book has been extremely successful and in his experience when that occurs jealous persons who see some slight similarity between a popular work and one of their own which has not enjoyed the same number of sales make threats of court action hoping to achieve a quick settlement with little trouble and some profit to themselves.

If there is any information you have which might clarify the mystery I would very much appreciate your advising me, assuring you of course of my complete confidentiality.

Mina composed a letter to Mr Greville. She was obliged to tell him that she had no further insights as to the identity of the authors, but had recently learned that Mr Arthur Wallace Hope fervently believed that they were powerful but undeveloped mediums. She also advised him that the Misses Bland's tour of the Pavilion must have taken place on 17 October 1870, giving her reasons behind that opinion. She described her own visit and the fact that an attendant with ten years' service had been adamant that no ghosts had ever been sighted there. Without warning, however, Mina, whose pen seemed to be taking on a life of its own, found herself promising Mr Greville that she would do her best to discover more.

As she sealed the letter Mina reflected on her experience of the Pavilion, and recalled the lady visitor who had been so stridently insistent that the royal ghost had appeared there before. The guide had said he had heard nothing of it in the last ten years, but the lady had countered this argument by declaring that the earlier haunting was longer ago than that, citing her mother as the authority. Mina had thought at the time that this was no more than a piece of town gossip, but now she had to wonder — what if the gossip was based not on mere rumour but an actual publication? If it was, then perhaps this publication was the very same one that had stimulated the legal action?

There was the faintest possible chance that the two events were actually connected but Mina decided to amuse herself by imagining that they were, and considered what she might deduce from that position. First, it meant that the supposedly pirated account had been published more than ten years ago. She doubted that it was written by a noble or royal visitor to the Pavilion during the time it was owned by the Crown. The Queen, she saw in her guidebook, had effectively abandoned the Pavilion in 1845. A book written by a titled individual would have been prominent in the library and widely read — no one would have dared plagiarise it, and the last royal person to write a book about the supernatural was King James I, although his chosen subject was witchcraft. If the author was a member of the public then the work must have been written after 1850, when the building, then in the process of being acquired by Brighton Corporation, was first opened for viewing.

Mina knew that she could not assume that the publication was a book. It might have been a chapter included in a collection of essays, an unbound pamphlet, or a contribution to a journal or magazine. It was not an unpublished letter or no action for plagiarism was possible. Nothing had been said about it before now, which suggested that it had not enjoyed a wide distribution, and few if any copies remained. With no title, no date, no author, no place of publication, and no guarantee that what she sought even existed, Mina needed more clues. How she wished she had taken more notice of the lady, and would be able to find her again and recognise her, but there had been nothing distinctive about her appearance that she could recall.

Mina wondered if Mr Hope knew about the action for plagiarism, and suspected that he did not. He had had only one meeting with the authors, which must have taken place before the accusation. If neither Mr Worple nor Mr Hope knew the identity of the authors and the plaintiff's solicitor had been unable to trace them, then it was possible that the authors did not know of the action either. The solicitor would have to advertise for the information, and employ detectives, and in the meantime Mr Worple, if he had any sense, would print no more copies of *An Encounter*.

That morning's edition of the *Gazette* included a review of Mr Hope's recent lecture, which Mina read with interest, though she did not know how well the newspaper reflected the views of the town. The portion of the lecture describing his adventures in Africa was dealt with very fairly and the writer said many appreciative things about Mr Hope's undoubted courage and spirit of philanthropy.

Addresses were provided to enable readers to send donations to the Viscount Hope funds for the relief of Dr Livingstone and assistance for disabled veterans of the Crimea. On the question of spiritualism, however, the writer took a sterner tone. It was to be regretted that the noble explorer had ventured away from matters in which he was undeniably an expert into areas that were still with good reason unpopular in Brighton. Many of those in the audience were shocked to learn that Mr Hope was an advocate of a certain book, which featured unseemly events in the Royal Pavilion, and had even sought to interview its authors. He had also intimated that he planned to give a lecture on spiritualism in the near future, a subject the *Gazette* suggested he would be best advised to leave well alone until a certain trial was concluded.

Mina looked forward to reading what the paper would write when it received news of the action for plagiarism. She had hardly finished reading when Enid came fresh from her morning *toilette* eager for glowing words of her new hero. As she read the *Gazette's* reservations, so her expression of pleasure darkened and finally she threw the paper down saying that the writer didn't know what he was talking about. She made a great performance out of settling to read *African Quest*, which she had been making valiant efforts to enjoy, but it was not to her usual taste and it was hard work for her to conceal the fact that she found it tedious.

Mina decided that the best place for her to seek more information about the previous ghostly sighting was the Royal Pavilion itself. Richard was nowhere to be found, so she decided to venture there alone, posting her letter to Mr Greville on the way. Someone, she hoped, would have more information than the stuffy attendant she had spoken to regarding both the haunting and the publication she sought, and would be more forthcoming. The more she thought about her tour, the more she became convinced that something in the guide's manner suggested that he knew more than he was willing to say.

Chapter Fifteen

Mina began her enquiries at the Pavilion by spending some time at the bookstall to see if there was anything that recommended itself to her as a possible source of the Misses Bland's story, but all the books and pamphlets had been published in the last ten years, and were either histories of Brighton and the Pavilion or studies of art and design. None of them mentioned a royal spectre. There were, unsurprisingly, no copies of *An Encounter* on display.

'May I assist you?' asked the lady attendant, seeing Mina hesitating over the array of publications. She looked too young to be able to offer advice on old hauntings.

'There are almost too many books to choose from,' said Mina, with a little sigh. 'I will return later to decide which one to purchase.'

'Are you here for a tour?'

'I enjoyed a very interesting tour of the Pavilion quite recently and my guide was very helpful and informative. He told me that he had acted in that capacity for ten years. I suppose he must be the longest serving gentleman here.'

'Very nearly so. But our Mr Merridew has been here rather longer, I believe.'

'Then I would very much like to speak to him. Where can he be found?'

'He should be in the ticket hall if he is not conducting a tour at present. He is very distinguished looking, and you will know him at once by his bald head.'

Mina thanked the lady and returned to the octagonal hall, where she lingered for a while until the gentleman she sought came into view. He was bidding his tour party farewell with extravagantly polite gestures when she approached.

'Mr Merridew?'

He turned to her. She knew how she must look, with her tiny lopsided body, tilted hip, and shoulders at a peculiar angle, but she saw in his eyes neither repulsion nor pity, only welcome. 'That is I,' he announced, as if speaking to a great crowd, the voice rich and resonant. 'Marcus Merridew at your service.' He made a dignified obeisance. 'How might I assist you?'

Merridew was, thought Mina, in his fifties, with an elegant carriage and smiling blue eyes. His face was adorned by an iron-grey beard, trimmed to a perfect point, and his head was domed, quite hairless, and smooth as an egg. Although he was much taller than she, he did not, as so many tall persons did, try to tower over her in an intimidating fashion, but adjusted his posture so they could converse more comfortably.

'I am very interested in anything I might learn from you concerning the Pavilion, since I have been told that you are the most knowledgeable attendant here.'

'You flatter me, dear lady, but that may well be true, I will not deny it. Some of the gentlemen have only been here a short while, whereas I —' He placed his fingertips to his chest with an expression of quiet pride — 'I was born and bred in Brighton.'

'How long have you been an attendant here?'

'I believe I first trod these royal paths some sixteen years ago. But I have not served here continuously all that time.' He gave her an enquiring look. 'You do not know my name?'

It was clear that he expected her to do so, and Mina feared that her ignorance on that point was in danger of causing him some offence. 'I regret, sir, I do not. But my family has not lived here very long. I have spent much of my time in the service of invalids, and have not therefore been able to move in society.'

He nodded understandingly. 'Ah, of course, that would explain it.'

'Allow me to introduce myself. My name is Mina Scarletti.'

Mr Merridew's eyebrows lifted in surprise. 'Then it seems I have the advantage of you, since that name is known to me. Are you by any chance connected with the Scarletti publications company?'

'I am, sir. My father was the manager, Henry Scarletti, who sadly passed away last year.'

'Indeed? May I offer you my deepest condolences for such a sad loss.'

'Thank you, sir. I assume you are a great reader?'

'Not — precisely. But the Scarletti company publishes play texts of which I have studied many.'

Mina was not sure how to respond, and he smiled. 'Allow me to enlighten you. I am an actor, a performer on the legitimate stage. Comedies and tragedies are all one to me; Seneca cannot be too heavy nor Plautus too light. I have toured all the major cities of England, from Manchester to Exeter. My Hamlet was the toast of Bolton. But, I digress. Please let me know how I might assist you.'

'When I was last here I asked an attendant to direct me to the room where the ghost of the late King George was seen, but he said he knew nothing about such a room, and denied that there had been a sighting. I hoped that you might be able to tell me something.'

He stared at her in astonishment. 'But surely you do not believe in that story? It's all nonsense, you know.'

'I think so too, but I should like to try and prove it.'

'Well now, you *do* interest me. How might you go about it?'

'When I was here last I overheard a lady say that there had been a previous rumour about a royal ghost, but it had been many years ago; more than ten. It occurred to me that if such was the case then the book *An Encounter* might simply be a reprinting of an earlier publication, or a retelling of an old story. Do you know anything about this rumour?'

Merridew looked thoughtful. 'Now that you mention it, yes, I do recall something of the sort. When I first became an attendant here someone did tell me of a supposed haunting, but it was only in a very general way.'

'So you don't know if the previous haunting was said to have taken place in the same room?'

'I am afraid not.'

'Would you be able to show me the ghost room? I am surprised that the other attendant didn't know of it. I am sure that you do.'

Merridew hesitated, then he offered her his arm and drew her aside so they were not overheard by the other visitors and guides. 'I will let you into a secret. All the attendants here have been asked by their tour parties to be taken to see the ghost room. But we have been expressly instructed by the Pavilion management committee to say that there is no such place. This is not so. The room is, I am sure, judging by the description, the King's former breakfast room, the one that has been assigned as a cloakroom for ladies. There is an alcove, but not, nowadays, a long couch as described so very dramatically in the book. After Her Majesty decided not to use the Pavilion as a royal residence, the original furnishings were removed.'

'So the description of the room in *An Encounter* is the interior not as it is today, but as it appeared in the days of the late King George?'

'Precisely, which is why the book is obvious nonsense.'

Mina was reflecting on this information when a man who, from his deportment, appeared to be a senior attendant, approached them. 'Mr Merridew, a tour party is ready for you.'

'Ah, if you will excuse me, I must go about my duties. We will speak later I hope?'

'Oh yes, I will wait here for you. But I wish to study a good book on the history of the Pavilion. What would be your recommendation?'

'*The Royal Pavilion in the Days of King George IV*. You will find it very interesting.'

Mina returned to the shop where she purchased the book in question and then found the ladies' cloakroom, which was a large apartment, graced by slender columns, with a door leading to the usual conveniences. Opposite the windows, which afforded a view of the gardens, there was a long recess, filled by a row of chairs. The most striking feature of the room, however, was the wallpaper, of a pronounced oriental design, in a vibrant shade of red. The authors of *An Encounter* had allowed their imaginations to take hold of them, since the dragons and other creatures depicted thereon were noble in aspect and did not appear to be writhing in any pronounced or scandalous fashion. Here, however, with a little embellishment, since there were only a few small paintings and ornaments, and not the costly trappings of King George's day, was undoubtedly the room where the ghosts of the young Prince and his inamorata had supposedly disported themselves.

Mina sat down and studied the book. From time to time, ladies arrived to avail themselves of the facilities, but there were several who made keen studies of the patterned wallpaper, or gazed at the long recess and surreptitiously consulted a publication they kept well hidden from the general gaze.

It soon became clear to Mina that the authors of *An Encounter* had used the very history she had just purchased as the foundation of their description of the interior of the Pavilion in a former age. It even mentioned the warm atmosphere, as the Prince had kept the rooms heated to a degree that many of his visitors found uncomfortable, the large Chinese statues and the formerly blue draperies of the South Drawing Room. Since the book was widely sold, the Misses Bland had not dared to copy actual phrases, but the facts spoke for themselves and Mina, with the eye of an author, could easily spot those fragments of language that had nudged plagiarism without overstepping the mark.

Mina returned to the vestibule and when Mr Merridew had completed his duties he announced himself finished for the day and ready for a pot of tea. They retired to the tearoom, which was filled with thirsty visitors. No places were to be had, but a kind gentleman, seeing Mina approach, picked up his hat and umbrella, rose, bowed, and vacated his table.

'I see you have been making good use of my absence to study that very interesting work,' said Merridew, as the waitress whisked away used chinaware and dusted crumbs from the cloth. Mina ordered tea and scones for two.

'Yes. I believe now that while the ladies who wrote *An Encounter* must have visited the Pavilion they would have been aware that in the days of the Prince the interior was different to today's, and so used the description in this book to make their tale more convincing.'

He laughed. 'It would have been better for them if they had not. They tried too hard and so exposed their deficiencies.'

Mina sensed a valuable clue. 'What do you mean?'

'Well, to understand that you need to know the history of the young Prince and Mrs Fitzherbert.'

The tea arrived, piping hot, with white, delicately gilded scones, like the domes of the Pavilion. Mr Merridew beamed in pleasurable anticipation and helped himself liberally to butter and jam. 'I am all ears,' said Mina.

'When they first met the Prince was a handsome young gallant, and she an enchantingly beautiful widow. He fell most violently in love with her. Nothing would content him but she must be his; he wept, he stormed, he threatened to stab himself, he *did* stab himself; but all to no avail. His royal father, who was quite sane at the time, would never consent to a marriage, since Mrs Fitzherbert was a

Catholic. She was also a virtuous lady, and could not be persuaded to become a royal mistress. Finally, the Prince and Mrs Fitzherbert conducted a secret wedding. This satisfied the lady's scruples, but not the law of the land, which stated that the Prince could not marry without the permission of his father. The marriage was strictly no marriage at all.'

There was a brief interlude for the consumption of tea and scones. 'When was this?' asked Mina.

'In the year 1785. Soon after that the Prince took a house in Brighton, which by a number of transformations over time became the extraordinary edifice you see today. Mrs Fitzherbert lived separately but close by, and their connection was an open secret in town. As a gay young Prince holding fashionable assemblies he brought many illustrious and wealthy visitors to Brighton. Trade prospered and he was most popular. For a time the lovers were as merry as could be, but the Prince spent lavishly and without restraint, and his debts increased with each passing day. His had only one means of extricating himself from this predicament. If he married into a royal house, his father would consent to pay his debts.'

Merridew sipped his tea and gave a sad shake of his head before helping himself to another scone. 'Poor Mrs Fitzherbert, imagine her terrible distress when her lover — the man she thought of as her dearest husband — dismissed her; not face-to-face, but with a letter. How cruel! How heartless! How cowardly! The year was then 1794. The Prince married Princess Caroline of Brunswick and his debts were paid, but he was miserably unhappy as his wife was a shameless hussy who did not wash, and he could hardly bear to look at her. They did not live together long. By 1800 the Prince and Mrs Fitzherbert were reconciled. By then neither were the youthful, handsome and relatively slender persons they had once been but they were content. As the years went by, however, the fickle Prince became enamoured of new, younger mistresses and Mrs Fitzherbert, unable to tolerate the many slights she was forced to endure when in his presence, declined to accept any further invitations to his assemblies. It is doubtful that they met again after 1811. She certainly did not visit the Pavilion. He came to the throne as King George IV in 1820. The next time Mrs Fitzherbert entered the Pavilion it was after King George's death and it was so changed that she did not recognise it as the place where she had once been such a frequent guest. Most of the truly elaborate work, the exterior remodelling and the interior decoration, was done after the Prince and Mrs Fitzherbert parted.'

Mina nodded. This was important information. 'The red wallpaper in what is now the ladies' retiring room — was that there in the time of Mrs Fitzherbert's association with the Prince?'

'It was not.'

'I see. So what you are telling me is that the authors of the book tried too hard to make their story convincing by placing youthful ghosts from the last century against a background that is not as the Pavilion is today, but in so doing they made a mistake. They described a room that was not decorated in that style until after the couple had parted, and which, therefore, they could never have occupied.'

'Exactly!' said Merridew with hearty approval.

'That is a good argument to show up the story as false. Tell me, has anyone tried to hold séances in the Pavilion?'

'No. Several have asked, but all have been refused. The Pavilion management committee will not countenance it, and we are instructed to prevent any such thing occurring. I believe that a number of committee members had their fingers burnt and their pockets emptied during the last eruption of mediums.'

'But I understand that they are happy to allow magicians and other entertainers of a similar kind?'

'Oh, yes, but then they are not pretending to be something they are not.'

'Do you remember a Dr Lynn who gave a charity performance here last year? I have heard he is very skilled. Did you see him perform the Japanese butterfly illusion? I should have liked to have seen that.'

'He is very highly regarded and I had hoped to see him, but he gave only the one performance and I was not in town; I had a theatrical engagement that day.'

'And was there not a chess automaton? He was here for at least a week I believe.'

'Oh, who shall ever forget the Wondrous Ajeeb? A Turk in full costume who sat on a kind of pedestal and beat all-comers at chess. It was quite entertaining to see it at work. Mr Mott of the Brighton chess club, who is champion of all Sussex, was so fascinated by it that he came to see it every day.'

'Because it was on the very day that both Dr Lynn and the Wondrous Ajeeb performed here that the authors of *An Encounter* visited, since they mention them both in their book. It was last October. Do you recall any unusual occurrences being reported during that time?'

Merridew thought carefully, not allowing this to hinder his paying diligent attention to the last of the scones. 'No, nothing springs to mind, and I am sure that if any ladies had claimed to have seen a ghost, even as long ago as last October, I would remember it. Several have claimed to have seen ghosts in the last few weeks, but never when they are in the company of another person. I think you understand my meaning.'

Mina was only a little disappointed since she had not anticipated that the visit of the two ladies would have made a mark on anyone's memory at the time, or it would have been the talk of Brighton.

'If you remember anything, you will let me know?' said Mina, handing him her card.

'I will, dear lady, I will!'

'On another subject, do you think the committee would approve the presentation of a play which includes characterisations of the Prince and Mrs Fitzherbert?'

'My goodness, that is adventurous! Is it a new piece?'

'Yes, my brother is writing it, and plans to appear in it with some of his friends.'

'Is it a drama or a comedy?'

'He intends it to be a drama but I fear it might turn out to be a comedy in the performance.'

Merridew laughed heartily. 'Given the subject matter he might be obliged to submit the text to the committee in advance so they can reassure themselves that the play is suitable, even should it receive the approval of the Lord Chamberlain. I would like to meet your brother! I would be able to pass on the benefit of my many years of experience.'

'I will introduce you as long as you make sure not to lend him any money.'

'I promise most faithfully that I will not. Investment in the theatre is an occupation only for the wealthy who have money they can afford to lose.'

'Are you appearing on stage at present? If so, I will obtain tickets.'

He drained his teacup. 'Er, no, I am currently between engagements. But you may see me nightly at the Dome where I am employed as an usher. One must do what one can.'

Chapter Sixteen

On Mina's return home there was a note waiting for her from Dr Hamid asking her to call and see him as soon as possible. This could only concern his recent interview with Arthur Wallace Hope and such an urgent summons was worrying. The baths were still open and she went there at once, hoping that her anxiety was misplaced. It was clear, however, when she entered Dr Hamid's office that he was a very troubled man.

'I am glad that you were able to come so promptly as I fear that what I have to tell you may involve you directly,' he said, drawing up a comfortable seat for Mina and pouring glasses of his spiced fruit mineral water for them both before slumping heavily back into his chair in most uncharacteristic style. 'Mr Hope came to see me as arranged, and as I am sure you have already observed he is polite and sociable, with a devious manner and a will of iron. He informed me that he has been going about Brighton meeting all the prominent residents who have been clients of Miss Eustace in order to obtain signed statements from them declaring that they believe her to be genuine. I am very glad that you spoke to me on that subject before I met him or I would simply have refused his request and shown him the door. Instead I behaved in a more cautious manner, and as you correctly anticipated, the result was that I learned more of his intentions. I told him that a man in my position needed to give such an undertaking serious thought before it could be performed, and asked him to allow me some time to consider the professional consequences. He seemed easy enough in his mind about that, although he said that it was precisely because of my status as a man of science that he would value my commendation. However —'

Mina sipped her drink and waited.

Dr Hamid took a deep breath and continued — 'he then went on to say that he had spoken to you and he was confident that you would agree to sign a similar statement. Given your recent actions your approval is clearly of some importance to him. I did not, of course, reveal our conversations on the subject.'

Mina was sorry that Mr Hope would stoop to such a deception, but found she was unsurprised. 'I neither refused nor agreed, so his confidence is misplaced,' she said. 'However, I can understand that he might have overstated his case in order to persuade you. I wonder how many other people he has visited and what he has told them? We need to be on our guard.'

'I know,' said Hamid, gloomily. 'He could be out and about even now spreading the word that I am a true believer in Miss Eustace. Some people might be swayed

303

into signing papers in the belief that they are joining a general movement. Has he approached you again?'

'No, but it is only a matter of time before he does.'

'Have you spoken to Miss Whinstone?'

'I have, and it might surprise you to know that she has exhorted me in the strongest possible terms not to sign any such paper.'

'She has? You are right, I am surprised.'

'Yes, she has been strengthened in her resolve by her new friend Mr Jellico, who I have found to be a very astute gentleman.' Mina went on to recount Mr Jellico's observations. 'I had imagined that if I was obliged to sign a paper to help Miss Whinstone, then that would be an end of the matter, but he has opened my eyes. It would only be the beginning. And it would be so much worse for you.'

Dr Hamid shook his head, wonderingly. 'An astute man indeed. It amazes me what the legal mind can make of these things. How glad I am that my father put me in for medicine and not the law.'

'I imagine that fraudulent mediumship in general terms is very hard to prove in court without palpable evidence, and the only spiritualistic fraud relevant to this trial is the one practised on Miss Whinstone when only she and Miss Eustace were present. That is why character witnesses are being sought. I can live better with myself if I do not sign a paper for Mr Hope, but he strikes me as a man who will not go away if I refuse.'

'No indeed.' Dr Hamid drank deeply of the mineral water. 'In that connection, there is another matter I should tell you about. During the course of my conversation with Mr Hope he evinced a general curiosity about scoliosis. He asked me if I was an expert in the condition and I said I had devoted a great deal of my of adult life to its study and treatment. He then went on to ask, since he understood that there were nerves in the spine, whether the condition affected the brain. This is a question I have been asked before, since there are many who believe that the outer presentation of the body is an indication of mental capacity or character. I assured him that those who suffer from scoliosis do not, as a result, suffer from any mental incapacity. He said he was pleased to hear it, although I have to say I sensed from his manner that he was not. He then asked if such conditions could lead to other complaints, such as nervousness or hysteria, or whether persons with scoliosis might be unusually credulous or suggestible. I could see where these questions were tending, so I asked him why he wanted to know and he just brushed it aside and said it was only his curiosity. I told him that, as a general principle, my observation of the many patients I have treated suggests that there is no relationship whatsoever between scoliosis and mental affliction or weakness of any kind. As you may imagine, the line of questioning made me feel extremely uncomfortable and it was transparently obvious that he was looking for some way of attacking your view if you did not comply with his wishes.'

Mina was reminded of the doctors who had been consulted when her condition first became apparent, particularly those who had blamed it on the way she habitually stood or walked, or carried things, and refused to accept any denial that upset their favoured theories. Now she had a new battle on her hands. 'I am sure he could easily find doctors who would support his assumptions. One only has to look at the way experts called upon to give evidence at trials can hold completely opposing opinions, when logically one might suppose they ought to agree. I can see that I shall have to be very careful. Your warning is much appreciated. And on the subject of trials, there has been a recent development concerning the book we discussed, *An Encounter*. Since Mr Hope is a champion of this volume and its authors, any doubts about it or the Misses Bland may provide us with a means of opposing him. I trust you will treat this information as confidential?'

'Of course.'

Mina told him of the allegation of plagiarism. He received the news with surprise and not a little pleasure. 'This is far from being determined,' she added cautiously, 'but I wonder what the consequences might be if it was proved?'

'They could be very serious. It is not a criminal offence, but it can give rise to substantial damages. Some accused might wish to preserve their reputations by settling the matter out of court by a payment of compensation, but if they decided to refute the charge it would be necessary to take it further. I do recall reading in the newspapers of a case of that sort not so long ago, a work on anthropology I believe. No one has a monopoly on facts, but neither does anyone have the right to take another's work and publish it as his own.'

Although all of Mina's work was original, she found the question quite interesting. 'To trouble the law would it have to be the whole of the work that has been copied, or just a portion?'

'Not necessarily the whole, but a material part. If the plaintiff was to succeed, then an order would be made to prevent any future publication of the offending work.'

'But what of the copies previously sold? The culprit would already have profited from them.'

Dr Hamid searched his memory. 'As I recall in that case, the defendant was ordered to pay the plaintiff damages calculated as all the profits made from the sale of the pirated publication as if they had been sales of the plaintiff's original work. He also had to pay all the legal costs. I would not be surprised if the costs in that instance far exceeded any damages, and the plaintiff had mainly to be satisfied with protecting his honour.'

'But that would probably not be so in the case of *An Encounter*. Who knows how many copies have been sold?'

'Sadly, I think a great many. The last time we spoke of this I had hoped that the book would be a foolish fashion, soon gone, but I have been making a few discreet enquiries and also listening more carefully to what my acquaintances and patients have told me and now I fear that may not be the case. The book has been mentioned quite recently in *The Times* editorial column, admittedly in a satirical vein, but that would never stop people from purchasing it, rather the reverse. And I am told that the popular weekly magazines have actually published reviews, while there are engravings of quite a fanciful nature in the illustrated periodicals. It has even been the subject of a cartoon in *Punch*. I don't know what the profits on sales might be, but the plaintiff might well think them worth having and the defendant would be loath to hand them over.'

'So, as I understand it, this legal action is less a matter of literary pique than money. I am not sure which excites more passion. I suppose that must depend on the individual.'

'Miss Scarletti,' said Dr Hamid, leaning forward on his desk with an intense and serious stare, 'I know that you think of the needs of others before your own, but for once, I beg you to think of yourself. You are being blackmailed into making a declaration that will be used to support a criminal by someone who is prepared to attack you personally if you do not comply. You have warned Miss Whinstone of her danger and now I must warn you. Do not keep this to yourself. You must seek legal advice.'

'I agree I must,' said Mina reluctantly. 'And I know the very man. I shall consult young Mr Phipps.'

An exchange of letters secured for Mina a meeting on the following morning with Mr Ronald Phipps. He was a junior member of a prominent firm of Brighton solicitors: Phipps, Laidlaw and Phipps, although since he was not yet deemed ready for a partnership he was not one of the aforementioned Phippses, who were respectively his uncle and cousin.

He was, as always, meticulously groomed in a manner that must have cost him both considerable time and effort. He doubtless enjoyed a healthy cold bath every morning, wherein he scoured himself to pinkness. He had a chilly stare and formal manner, which could edge from unfriendly tolerance to mildly hostile depending on the matter in hand. Nevertheless, he had proved to be an excellent ally, having been instrumental in providing the information that had led to the arrest of Miss Eustace and her associates for the fraud committed on Miss Whinstone. As a result, he and Mina regarded each other with respect, and he had let it be known that his office door would always be open to her if she ever needed his assistance again.

As Mina described her interviews with Arthur Wallace Hope, and the enquiries he had been making about her, Mr Phipps' expression, beginning with a frown of concern, soon developed into alarm to be followed by frank distaste. He clasped his hands together and gave the question some very solemn thought. 'I am sorry to say this, but you have made an extremely dangerous enemy. I do not think Mr Hope is a wicked man, but he is single-minded and determined. He has influence, wealth and respect. If you challenge him directly you cannot win. What you have already done — asked for more time to make your decision — was wise, but he will not wait long, especially in view of the impending trial. Mr Hope can and will destroy those in his path, believing it is the right thing to do for his higher purpose. He will sacrifice any man, or woman, if need be, in order, as he sees it, to save mankind.'

Young Mr Phipps licked his lips nervously and there was a small flicker of fear in his eyes. Mina knew that it was rumoured that he was not as was generally said, the nephew of her mother's friend, Mrs Phipps, a lady of advanced years he escorted to many a social gathering. The lady's late husband was so long deceased that no one could recall him, and gossips liked to believe that he had never existed, Mr Ronald being more closely related to the venerable lady than he liked to say. Mina neither knew nor cared if this was the case, but a man like Arthur Wallace Hope had the ability to find out such secrets and no hesitation in making use of them. For a young solicitor aspiring to add a third 'Phipps' to the firm's title, this threat was of some moment. It was unlikely that Hope would discover that Mina was the author of a series of ghost stories under a *nom de plume*, a fact of which he would undoubtedly make much capital, and which would greatly shock her mother, but even if he did, Mina thought she could ride out that particular storm.

'What is your advice?'

'He will undoubtedly approach you again, but this time you should not speak to him without a witness, preferably myself. I will make such enquiries as I can and seek advice from the senior partners. Sign nothing — but then I hardly need to tell you that.' A faint glimmer of a smile played briefly about one side of his mouth and was hastily dismissed. 'If Mr Hope wishes to prove you weak and foolish he will have a hard time of it.'

'Mr Hope may have his own weakness. He has publicly expressed his belief in the Misses Bland and their sensational story, but recently when visiting the Pavilion I overheard a lady say that the ghost had walked before and I could not help wondering if *An Encounter* was simply copied from another lady's experience. Do you know if that is so?'

'I do not,' said Mr Phipps, with narrowed eyes, 'but I should very much like to.'

Chapter Seventeen

When Mina returned home, she found the Scarletti household pervaded by a flutter of breathless excitement. The only exception to the general jubilation was Rose, who could see additional work looming before her like a persistent spectre. She did not fear it, but viewed it with unspoken bad grace.

The reason for the excitement was a letter Louisa had received from Arthur Wallace Hope. This was no ordinary formal polite missive, expressing how honoured he was to have met the Scarletti family — it did that, of course, in what Louisa declared with a blush to be the most beautiful and gentlemanly language she had ever read, but it ended with a request for her assistance. Mr Hope revealed that he had recently been approached by a respectable and highly-regarded entertainer, a conjuror, newly arrived from the continent and anxious to establish his reputation in England. He was hoping to find a substantial drawing room in which to host a magical soiree. Could Mrs Scarletti, asked Mr Hope, with her knowledge of Brighton society, suggest a suitable location?

Louisa could, and while she might simply have provided the information he required in the form of a letter this was an opportunity not to be missed. Everyone of note in Brighton must know as soon as possible that she had been favoured with the friendship of the famous Arthur Wallace Hope, and there was a general collection of matrons and spinsters whom she could rely upon to carry the news all over town.

It was a vividly glowing Enid who told Mina of this thrilling development, while Louisa busily dashed off notes to her most intimate friends, inviting them to come for tea, saying that they would thereby be regaled with some very interesting news, and replied to Mr Hope promising that she would make enquiries on his behalf.

Mina could not avoid noticing that her mother believed that the gentleman had taken an interest in her. It was in Louisa's mind impossible that he might favour Enid, who was married, and in any case it was she to whom he had chosen to write. Enid, for her part, made her admiration of Mr Hope all too transparent, and Mr Hope, while according her the decorous gallantry appropriate to her married state, had not attempted to conceal that her admiration was returned. Enid clearly thought that the letter to her mother was merely a subterfuge to conceal which lady actually attracted him.

Mina did not know where any of this might lead, but was well aware that it was she who was his object, and her endorsement of Miss Eustace the desired result, his courtship of the good opinion of her mother and sister only a part of his campaign. It was pointless to reveal this to her mother or Enid, although she did suggest mischievously that they might like to invite Mr Hope to the tea party in order for him to make personal enquiries of the ladies. She was greeted by a thunderous look. There was only one widow lady of appropriate age Louisa wished him to take tea with and that was herself.

On the following afternoon a happy and expectant band of ladies assembled in the cosy confines of the Scarletti parlour to be regaled with tea, cake and gossip. Mrs Phipps was one of the number and would have been a useful secret agent to carry intelligence back to her nephew had she not been in the habit of sleeping through most of her visits, waking only when her teacup and plate needed refreshing.

Louisa commanded the room, the wonderful letter in her hand, and talked at a great pace, with the name 'Mr Hope' appearing prominently in every sentence, saying what a charming and attentive gentleman he was, and how her family had been greatly favoured by a visit from him. Now he had been so kind as to make a request and she was sure that someone amongst her dear friends could suggest how his wishes might be accomplished. Mr Hope wished to promote an entertainment for a select gathering of about twenty ladies and gentlemen, and was looking for a suitable drawing room in town. The evening would be offered gratis to all guests, as the object was to confirm his belief that his protégé's displays were to the refined taste of the leading residents of Brighton. If successful then the gentleman intended to take a room at the Pavilion.

Mrs Peasgood, who, in view of her regular musical soirees was the obvious candidate to offer her home, at once demanded to know the name of the gentleman and the nature of the entertainment.

Louisa made a great performance out of consulting Mr Hope's letter, holding it before her face so it was on display to everyone in the room, just in case they had missed it. 'He is called Mystic Stefan. Mr Hope says that he is believed to be the new Monsieur Robert-Houdin, and *he* has performed for the Queen.'

Mrs Peasgood looked unconvinced. 'If this Robert-Houdin is such a wonder, why can *he* not be brought to Brighton?'

'Oh, I am sure he is very busily engaged, and Mr Hope would be bound to know this.'

Mina, who had read of the distinguished magician's recent death in the national newspapers, said nothing.

'There was Dr Lynn at the Pavilion, last year,' interposed Mrs Mowbray. 'He gave a performance for charity. So other conjurors can be very respectable, too.'

'How interesting,' said Mina. 'Did you see him?'

'Alas no, but I have heard that he demonstrates the Japanese butterfly illusion, which is said to be a very pretty thing to watch.'

'Mr Hope's friend,' interrupted Louisa, who was starting to see the conversation veer away from her, 'will, I am sure, be equally as skilled.'

'I am not sure if I wish to see him,' said Miss Whinstone, who was starting to tremble. 'What if this Mystic Stefan proves to be one of those dreadful mediums?'

'Yes, what is it he does?' asked Mrs Bettinson suspiciously. 'I think we ought to be told.'

Louisa looked embarrassed, as well she might since she had obviously not been provided with so much detail and had never, as far as Mina was aware, actually seen a conjuror. 'I suppose he does tricks — he makes things appear — or disappear — but that isn't really important because Mr Hope says he puts on a highly respectable and interesting entertainment.'

'Just as long as he doesn't send us messages from our grandmothers at five guineas each,' said Mrs Bettinson sourly.

'Or from the ghost of King George,' said Enid, with a titter.

The other ladies tried to pretend they didn't know what she meant by that.

'Do you know, it is a very curious thing,' said Mina in a voice that, though gentle, suddenly engaged the attention of the room, 'but I overheard a lady say the other day that the royal ghost which everyone is talking about has appeared in the Pavilion before.'

Louisa frowned. 'Whatever do you mean by that, Mina?' Quickly she held up a warning hand. 'No! Do not tell me, it is almost certainly not a fit topic for you to be concerning yourself with, and I don't want to know about it.'

'Oh, I am not referring to the book which everyone finds so shocking and which no one admits to having read, but nevertheless they talk about it all the time; no, this is something different. You know what I think of people who produce false ghosts by draping themselves in veils, but it does seem from the discussions in the newspapers that there has been a haunting where no such fakery was involved. The ladies had never attended a séance, have no pretensions to be mediums, and have not experienced such a thing before. Richard and I visited the Pavilion recently from curiosity but I regret we saw no apparitions, although we looked for them very hard indeed.'

'I would never dare go there in case I was to see one,' said Miss Whinstone, 'even in the company of Mr Jellico.'

For once Louisa did not look jealous of Miss Whinstone for her elderly admirer and was unable to hold back a satisfied smile, the pause giving Mina the chance to pursue her theme.

'While we were there we overheard a lady visitor say that the ghost had appeared before, only it was many years ago, perhaps ten or even twenty. Our family is too recently settled in Brighton to know anything about it, but I wondered if any ladies here have ever heard of such a thing?' Mina glanced at the faces of her mother's guests. Mrs Bettinson, with a mouth full of cake, was unreadable, and Mrs Phipps was asleep. Mrs Peasgood looked pained, Miss Whinstone alarmed, and Mrs Mowbray surly. Whether this was because they knew anything about the subject or simply did not wish to discuss it Mina could not say. All the ladies had once been taken in by the séances of Miss Eustace and might not want to be reminded of this. 'Mr Hope is convinced that the recent sighting was genuine,' she went on.

'Then he must be right,' said Enid, 'for he has travelled so much and has seen so much.'

'I'm not so sure of that,' said Mrs Bettinson. 'How do we even know he went all the way to Africa and back? He could have made it all up.'

'Well, he didn't!' exclaimed Enid angrily. 'It was in all the papers, and lots of important people said he was there and did brave things!'

Mrs Bettinson remained unimpressed. 'Wouldn't be much to write about if all he did was go there and walk about and not see anything interesting. I mean, elephants and such like. Not that elephants are all that interesting. If I wanted to see an elephant I could wait for the circus to come again. I don't have to go all the way to Africa.'

'I think we should accept that if Mr Hope says that a thing is so then that alone is sufficient proof that it is,' said Louisa sharply, which made Mina even more relieved that she had not mentioned that gentleman's belief in Miss Eustace. 'As to the strange goings on in the Pavilion, the ladies concerned may have seen something but they most probably had overheated imaginations and did not understand the matter. There, that is all *I* have to say on the subject.'

This effectively put a stop to any discussion about ghosts and over fresh tea and cakes it was agreed that Mrs Peasgood would invite Mystic Stefan to perform his miracles in her drawing room. Mrs Peasgood did not appear entirely happy with the arrangement, but bowed to the majority. She had still not recovered her equilibrium following the extraordinary entertainment of Miss Foxton and her manager Signor Ricardo, and hoped never to see anything like it again.

As the ladies were leaving, Mrs Bettinson hung back, and with a thoughtful look approached Mina for a more private conversation. 'There was something,' she said. 'It was a good while back, but I did hear someone say that there had been a ghost in the Pavilion. I don't know who.'

'Was it ever written about in a book?'

'No, not a book. Not a proper book, just a little pamphlet. I only read part of it, it wasn't all that interesting. Not like —' She stopped and chewed her lip.

'Not like the recent one, I suppose. Well, I can't comment on that. Do you still have it?' added Mina, hopefully.

'I shouldn't think so; I threw out a lot of old rubbish when Mr Bettinson died, and that must have gone with it.'

'Do you remember the name of the pamphlet or the author? Please try.' Mina realised she was sounding a little too eager and tried to restrain the force of her questioning.

Mrs Bettinson squeezed her eyes shut and made the effort, then shook her head. 'No, it was too long ago. It was written by a lady, that's all I can remember.' She gave Mina a searching look. 'Why? What's your interest? After all that bother we had before I can see you're up to something.'

'Perhaps I am.'

'Not that that might be a bad thing, the way the last business turned out. I'd help you if I could, but I don't know much.'

'Can you recall where you obtained the pamphlet? Was it on sale?'

'Not that I remember. I think a friend read it and gave it to me. Don't ask me who, I think it was being passed around.'

A pamphlet, written by a lady; with just those two tiny fragments of clues Mina decided to go to the library.

Chapter Eighteen

At the library Mina was soon painfully aware that although she might have more information than previously, it was still hardly adequate to find the item she wanted. She searched the shelves carefully for publications on the subject of Brighton, but even after a diligent examination found nothing to assist her. At last, and realising that she was about to appear very foolish, she approached the desk where a gentleman librarian was seated. He knew her by sight and she him, but she had never needed to ask for assistance before, having preferred to browse the collection for whatever struck her as interesting, since she liked the pleasure of making a discovery.

'I am looking for a pamphlet on the subject of Brighton,' she began, 'but I am sorry to say that I am hampered in my search by not knowing its name, or that of the author. I don't suppose you can suggest where I might look?'

The librarian tried his very best not to look despondent at this request. 'You are sure it was a pamphlet and not a book?'

'Yes.'

'Was this a specific publication? We do have a collection of pamphlets and monographs of Brighton interest, going back many years.'

'It was a specific one, and I believe it was published between ten and twenty years ago. I have been told that the author was a lady.'

The librarian waited in the hope that some more guidance might be forthcoming, but was doomed to be disappointed. 'I'm afraid that we tend to arrange our catalogue of pamphlets by title and not date of publication. In many cases the author does not divulge his or her name.'

'Oh, I see. I suppose there are a great many of them.'

'There are, yes.'

Mina considered this. 'Then I had better start at the letter A.'

Mina took a seat at a table and after a short wait she was brought a box, which, when she opened it, was piled with pamphlets whose titles began with the letters A to C. She hoped for three things; first that the work she sought was held by the library otherwise her search would be in vain; second, that if it was, the ghostly sighting was the main subject and not buried in more general matter; and third that the title started with a letter near the beginning of the alphabet. Several hours and boxes later Mina, still no nearer to her goal, was more thoroughly acquainted with the history, climate, principal buildings and coach roads of Brighton than she could ever have imagined, and she had gained a wealth of information on the worthies of the town, the notable visitors, the Royal connection and the Pavilion. Even though

313

Mrs Bettinson thought the pamphlet had been written by a lady Mina did not dismiss without a look any item with a named male author in case that information should prove to be incorrect. She had reached the letter S when she found a ten-page work, the author of which had chosen to remain anonymous, entitled *Some Confidential Observations by a Lady of Quality*. It was dated 1850 and had been privately printed for the author in Brighton.

The author, who described herself as a single lady resident in Brighton, had been interested in the mysterious Pavilion which had been left empty after the Queen had decided not to visit the town again. When it was mooted that the building and its gardens should be purchased by the corporation, tickets had gone on sale so that residents could see it for themselves. She and her father had purchased tickets and made their way there. The interior had impressed them with the dimensions of its magnificent apartments, but all had been emptied of furniture, ornaments and carpets. In some rooms even the wallpaper had been torn down and taken away. The large echoing spaces of the abandoned building gave it the eerie air of a ruined castle.

It was inevitable, thought Mina, that two accounts of a visit to the same place even at twenty years' distance would have some similarities, but as she read on, some uncanny resemblances started to emerge between *Confidential Observations* and *An Encounter*.

As with the Misses Bland, there had been a prior agreement between family members to write separate accounts of the visit. The author in her wanderings had become separated from her father and got lost in the many rooms and corridors. All sounds of the other visitors had faded, but then she, as had the Misses Bland, became aware of the music of a violin and a flute coming from she knew not where, for although she could hear the musicians as if they were very close to her, she could see no one.

Despite making efforts to follow the sound, it remained elusive, the players invisible. Finding herself alone in a magnificent room with a high domed ceiling, she began to wonder what it must have been like in the time of the Kings George and William, when splendid entertainments had been given there. Slowly, she turned in a circle to look all about her, imagining herself in the centre of a glittering company. It was as she completed the turn that she saw the figure of a man standing in the room, a man who had not been there when she had entered. So sudden was the sight that it seemed to her that he had appeared from nowhere while her back had been turned. He was dressed in an elegant costume, which she thought resembled that of a past age, and on seeing her he paused, and bowed in a very respectful and old-fashioned manner, then walked on, passing from the room using the same door through which she had entered. For a moment she stood there mystified by what she had seen, then decided to examine the far doors of the room, the only ones that had not been in her sight when the man arrived, to see if it was possible for them to open silently, but was nonplussed to find them sealed and impossible to open. The only doors that could open were the ones directly opposite, those the man could not have entered by. She decided to follow the figure and speak to him, but on leaving the room she became confused as to her direction and the man was now nowhere to be seen.

The music began again and she followed the sound, eventually arriving at an apartment with red wallpaper much decorated with dragons and serpents, flowers and foliage. There she saw the man again, and this time there was a lady, beautifully dressed in a gown with flowing skirts of golden silk with blue flounces and pink bows, and two musicians, one playing a violin the other a flute. As she observed them, the gentleman took the lady's hand and made a respectful obeisance, then the pair engaged in a courtly dance. She watched them, enraptured with the sight, and when they were done, they bowed to her, and glided from the room. It was a most beautiful scene, yet an unexpected one, since she had not been told of any entertainment being provided for visitors. Once again she looked for her father and eventually found him, but neither he nor any of the other visitors had seen anything of the lady and gentleman and the musicians.

She asked the attendant who had been collecting tickets at the door about the surprise diversion, but he said there had been none, neither had he seen any such persons in the Pavilion as she described.

Once they were home, both the author and her father wrote a description of their visit to the Pavilion. Her father had declared himself very impressed and thought the corporation should make every effort to acquire the building for the town as it had wonderful possibilities as a place of entertainment. He had seen no strangely dressed persons and heard no music, although the latter circumstance was not altogether surprising as he was hard of hearing. The author had written of her experience as honestly as possible, even though she knew many would not believe her. She had tried to describe the appearance of the gentleman as best she could. He was handsome, with curling hair, and she thought he resembled the portraits of King George IV in his youth. The lady had been beautiful with long flowing locks. The author made sketches of the lady and gentleman and the musicians and their costumes, and later perused a number of books of fashion, and had become convinced that she had seen none other than the late King George IV in his days as the youthful Prince of Wales, and his inamorata, Mrs Fitzherbert. The mystery of the sealed doors was therefore, as far as she was concerned, solved. If they had been in use in the time of the young Prince, then his ghost would simply have passed through them.

As Mina read she felt increasingly sure that the similarities between this work and *An Encounter* were no coincidence. While it was just possible that two similar events might have taken place, some of the expressions and descriptions in the Lady of Quality's account reminded her very strongly of the more recent book. She therefore obtained some sheets of paper and began to make a copy of some of the more memorable portions of the pamphlet, a work that took her some little time. Before she realised it the library was about to close for the day and her body had grown stiff from the prolonged immobility, her back aching as the muscles protested. It was with some difficulty that she rose to her feet and proceeded home.

Comparing her notes with her mother's copy of *An Encounter* Mina saw that the resemblance was, as she had thought, not chance, but blatant and deliberate. The entire incident in the recent work had been copied from the earlier one, in some places with identical words, the main difference being the addition of some sensational material.

Mina, accordingly, wrote at once to Mr Greville imparting to him the nature of her discovery and supplying some extracts from *Confidential Observations* in support of her argument. She also advised Mr Phipps. Surely, she thought, her work was done.

Chapter Nineteen

There was a new burst of excitement in the Scarletti household since Mr Hope was due to call again, and this time he had accepted Louisa's invitation to take dinner with the family. Despite his modest entreaties that they should not go to any great trouble over him, Louisa and Enid were determined to do their utmost to see that their honoured guest was royally entertained, but were uncertain of what such a remarkable man might want to eat. The dilemma was the subject of intense debate.

'Perhaps we should try and make him feel at home,' suggested Enid, 'and give him African food?'

'I doubt that the butcher will be able to supply elephant's foot and even if he could our oven would be quite inadequate to roast it,' said Mina. 'But, I believe that when in Africa Mr Hope was obliged to eat what was there, whether or not it was to his taste, and probably pined for the food of his native land. I am sure Mr Inskip would delight in an English beef dinner at this very moment.'

Enid gave her a sour look, but said nothing.

Richard, on being given the news, pronounced himself delighted and said he was looking forward to it with keen anticipation. His private comment to Mina was, 'It will be an education to meet the blackguard who threatened my sister.'

In the absence of elephant's foot the gathering around the dinner table was provided with beefsteaks, which was thought to be the most appropriate and manly foodstuff for a bold adventurer, and a bottle of good red wine. Louisa and Enid detested beefsteaks, but pretended to like them and Rose, knowing this, brought the dishes in with the triumphant air of one who hoped there would be good pickings later, if it was not all to be turned into pies and rissoles. Richard and Mr Hope demolished their steaks with hearty appetites, and made free with the wine, which the ladies declined. Mina ate sparingly, but that was expected of her.

Mr Hope was all beaming geniality. 'I am most grateful to you, Mrs Scarletti, for proposing the home of Mrs Peasgood as suitable for Mystic Stefan's demonstration. I have paid her a visit and was delighted with the drawing room, and the lady herself received me with great cordiality and was very obliging.' Louisa smiled thinly, but since Mrs Peasgood was approaching sixty, had long given up any pretensions to beauty, and had never shown any inclination to replace the late and much lamented Mr Peasgood, this was not a serious difficulty. 'I believe she is sending invitations to all the members of her music circle, who will be sure to be as refined an assembly as any in Brighton.'

Mina said nothing, but a thought had occurred to her, one that she determined to pursue.

Louisa, between dainty nibbles from the tip of her fork, was all attention to the visitor. 'Mr Hope, I do beg you to tell us all about Mr Stefan, who has not, I think, been to Brighton before? All my friends are clamouring to know more of him, and I found I could tell them almost nothing.'

Hope speared an extra potato with the dexterity of a hunter. 'He is a native of Hungary, I believe, and this is his first visit to these shores. But he has earned some fame abroad, and thought to come and entertain us here. He speaks very little English, however, and that little he does with an accent so thick that he finds it hard to make himself understood. He cannot, therefore, perform as other magical gentlemen do, but works in silence.'

'If his illusions please the eye then he hardly needs to speak. They should speak for themselves,' Mina observed.

'I agree,' said Mr Hope wholeheartedly, and Louisa and Enid who had been about to protest, closed their mouths. 'So many of these conjurors rely on taking the audience into their confidence, telling them what they might expect to see and then surprising them. Mystic Stefan needs none of this, and is in my opinion altogether superior.'

'How did you come to meet him?' asked Mina.

'He brought me a letter of introduction from the celebrated Dr Lynn, who has exhibited here before, but is currently touring abroad. Did you chance to see Dr Lynn when he was here last year?'

'I am very sorry to say we did not,' said Louisa, with a brave attempt at sincerity.

'Oh, he demonstrates with great skill, and has many highly amusing and astounding novelties. His forte is the Japanese butterfly illusion, which few men have truly mastered, but in which Mystic Stefan is also adept.'

Enid had abandoned all attempts at eating her dinner, but maintained the pretence by sawing her steak into fine shreds and giving the contents of her plate the occasional stir with her fork. 'I do look forward to seeing that, it sounds so pretty. Can you say what else he will do?'

Hope fastened her with a look implying mystery and deep knowledge. His eyes, which were dark brown, took on the glow of amber and Enid flushed under their warmth. 'As to that it is best that it should come as a pleasant surprise, but there is one thing I do need to advise you of before you see him. Mystic Stefan has a means of answering all questions that anyone in the audience might ask. His replies are just a "yes" or a "no", but I am told that he is wonderfully accurate. So you must have your questions prepared beforehand. You may speak them aloud if you wish, but most persons prefer to write them on slips of paper.'

A faint frown of disquiet troubled Louisa's brow. 'I hope he has not become entangled with spirit mediums? After recent events in Brighton we have learned to distrust such people.'

Hope met the question with a disarming smile, but there was something cold and forced in his expression. 'Mystic Stefan makes no claims one way or another. He seeks only to entertain. We all may have our opinions as to how he performs his miracles, but only he knows the truth.'

'Well, I know what I shall ask him,' said Enid, lowering her eyelashes.

'I think we can all guess your question,' said Richard. 'What we would like to know is what answer you are hoping for.'

'Perhaps, since he is so adept, and knows so much, he can conjure up the real names of the ladies who wrote that curious book,' said Mina mischievously. 'It would be interesting to discover how they came to write it.'

'Mina!' her mother snapped with a frown.

Richard finished his second glass of wine and poured another. 'My dear sister is far too modest to admit it, but she is herself an author.'

'Mina writes stories for children,' Enid explained quickly. 'Not at all the same thing as proper books.'

'I should hope not!' said Louisa.

'I have never yet written, but I think I may have a talent for it,' Richard went on, 'so I have determined to write a play, something noble and high-minded, with a monumental subject. It will be like Shakespeare — or — those other fellows who are like Shakespeare.'

'That is an admirable ambition,' said Hope, 'and when it is completed I would like to read it.'

Mina smiled, and he caught the look and returned it in a strange moment of mutual understanding. Both had guessed that the chances of Mr Hope being obliged to meet that promise were slim.

Rose was summoned to clear the plates, and at Louisa's direction moved the wine bottle out of Richard's reach. Mr Hope complimented Louisa on the beefsteaks, saying that a good English dinner was the best in the world, and an excellent butcher a treasure beyond price. Dessert was brought, a moulded blancmange decorated with fruit.

'I would be very interested to learn more of your meeting with the Misses Bland,' said Mina, timing her question at the point when her mother was too preoccupied with dessert to interrupt. 'Was it very recent?'

'Yes, about two or three weeks ago. I was very impressed with how modest they are, and their simple and wholly natural sincerity.'

'If I understand correctly from your lecture, the ladies claim to have seen the ghost of the late King, not as he appeared at the time of his passing, but when he was the young Prince of Wales, together with members of his court.'

'Extraordinary, I know, but that is the case,' said Hope. Louisa gave him a worried look, but he did not offer further detail.

'I have recently paid a visit to the Royal Pavilion, and made a study of its history, and I would deduce that the room in which this encounter took place was once the King's breakfast room, but is nowadays a select retiring room for lady visitors. The wallpaper is a beautiful shade of red and with a very distinctive pattern. It is part of King George's oriental redesign, the work of Mr Nash, and most probably dates from about 1820.'

'How very interesting,' said Hope politely, but he gave Mina a searching look. Enid and Louisa clearly thought the subject not at all interesting, but since their guest did they said nothing to deter Mina from further observations. Richard smiled the smile he always gave when he knew Mina was up to something.

'But here is the thing that mystified me,' Mina went on, and from the corner of her eye she saw Richard's smile broaden, 'I would have expected that if the ladies had seen ghosts then the figures would have appeared before them in the room as it is now. I hardly ever read ghost stories myself, but when I have that always seems to be the way of things. But in this case it was not, since the furnishings were not the same. Also, in these ghost stories, the figures always appear as they were in their last moments of life, which these did not. Supposing, however, that the figures were not ghosts at all, and the ladies had, as I believe you yourself suggested, looked or even stepped back by some means or other into the days of the King's youth, then they would have seen him and his court in the room as it was then, perhaps in 1790 or thereabouts, before he parted from the lady he loved, but many years before the red wallpaper was placed there. Instead, the figures, which looked as they did in the last century, were in a room furnished as it was some thirty or more years later, a room they could never have occupied. I am afraid that it struck me then that the Misses Bland have done no more than compose a story for their own amusement, basing it on some histories imperfectly studied, and have found against all expectation that their readers believed that they were describing a real incident. If I write a story about a child meeting a pretty fairy, it is no more than a story, and I know it. A young child might believe it to be real, but I do not think an adult would. Adults do not, as a rule, believe in fairies.'

There was a very distinct silence around the dinner table. Louisa was annoyed, but clearly did not know how to respond, and Enid was simply bewildered. Mina dared not glance at Richard or she could never have maintained a serious expression.

Mr Hope, however, was obviously well used to having his beliefs questioned, something that amused rather than offended him. He gave Mina's comments only a moment's thought before he smiled indulgently. 'The ways of such events are still a mystery to us, but your concerns do not, as you think, show that the ladies invented the story. On the contrary, it proves to me the very high order of their mediumship, something of which they themselves are quite unaware. Please be assured, Mrs Scarletti,' he went on, turning the heat of his gaze towards Louisa, whose concerns evaporated almost instantly, 'the Misses Bland have no desire to conduct the kind of séances of which you disapprove. They do not seek the admiration of the public.'

He addressed the gathering about the table once more, as sure as a man could be that he had captured his audience. 'Miss Scarletti suggests that what she sees as inconsistencies in the book resulted from imperfect study, but this is not so. The authors informed me that they had never before their remarkable vision visited Brighton or made any study of its history or seen any portraits of the Pavilion's apartments. They knew little about the Pavilion other than that it was very famous and had once been a royal residence. I believe that as they moved about the building they were, without realising it, carried by the influence of spirits to different times in its past. Perhaps a kind of blending of the rooms and the figures took place, created by their own unconscious powers. It is an extraordinary and rare phenomenon, one that is not at all understood, and I hope very much to be able to meet the ladies again and persuade them to submit themselves to scientific study. Just imagine,' he went on with forceful intensity, putting down his spoon to gesture with both hands, 'if we could, as they did, travel into the past. What mysteries we could solve, what wrongs we could make right!'

'Oh, indeed!' breathed Enid, her eyes shining.

Mina could see that whatever objections she made, Mr Hope would somehow turn them about to become proofs of his way of thinking. 'Do you believe that the ladies' experience has revealed a previously unknown branch of science?' she asked, without a change in her expression. Beside her, Richard almost choked on his dessert. It was, as they both recalled, a claim made by those who had once championed Miss Eustace, whose science had consisted of little more than anointing filmy draperies with phosphorised oil.

'I do,' said Hope emphatically, 'and I am so happy that you have hit upon this concept, one that so many of the doubters simply do not understand. They refute anything that does not conform to the way they see the world, and cannot conceive that it can differ in any way from their narrow-minded perception. I compliment you, Miss Scarletti; you are a visionary, you open your mind and in so doing you see into the future.'

Mina wished very much that she could see into the future, but she was less concerned with the world of science or the spirit than the happiness of her family. She pitied Enid, unable to find solace in her children and dreading the return of her husband, and she daily expected to hear that Richard's gadfly adventures had ended with him in a morass of debt, or even under arrest. She was powerless to influence Enid and able only to restrain Richard's wilder exploits. Mr Hope, however, too narrow minded to understand his own position, was a different matter. Once he had taken his leave Mina put her new idea into action and sent a note to her brother's former mistress, the beautiful Nellie, asking if she might pay her a visit.

Chapter Twenty

Next morning Mina received yet another letter from Mr Greville.

Dear Miss Scarletti,
Please find enclosed a cheque for the sales of your most recent publication, 'The Tower of Ghost Musicians'.

Mina winced at the title which she thought clumsily worded and which she had not approved. She had wanted to call the story *The Tower of Music* but Mr Greville had pointed out that one could scarcely have a story about ghosts without the word 'ghost' or 'spectre' in the title, any more than one would publish a story with a title that promised ghosts but did not provide any. The letter continued,

Mr Worple wishes me to pass on to you his grateful thanks for the information you have supplied. As you know, he was initially of the opinion that the action for plagiarism against the authors of 'An Encounter' was motivated solely by greed and would quickly prove to have no foundation. Your revelations have convinced him, however, that there is a case to answer and he has therefore undertaken to cooperate fully with the plaintiff's solicitors. He has just revealed to me the outcome, which you might find interesting.

The Misses Bland had recently ordered another printing of the book, with the usual arrangement that their servant would arrive to collect the copies. Under the circumstances Mr Worple decided not to carry out the commission; instead he advised the plaintiff's solicitors when the servant might be expected to call, and they came to his office and lay in wait with the appropriate documents. I was not present at that confrontation, but Mr Worple was, and I am sure you can imagine the ensuing consternation. The servant was required to reveal the real names and address of her employers and accompany the solicitor to their home to serve the papers. It transpired that the ladies are, as they claim to be, sisters, but they are not called Bland, and the father is not a clergyman, although he is a respectable tradesman who pursues the businesses of undertaker and cabinet maker. He knew nothing of his daughters' adventure in the world of publishing and when he learned of it, it came as a great shock to him. When confronted with the situation, the ladies were sufficiently discomfited that they were unable to say anything on the subject, however, one fact of interest did emerge. Your enquiries showed that the visit to the Pavilion could only have taken place on 17 October last year. Not only have the ladies and their father never been to Brighton, all three were on that date at a family gathering in London, and there are therefore over twenty witnesses to the fact that they could not possibly have been in Brighton on the day in question.

I am not sure what to make of this and neither is Mr Worple, but the ladies have been summoned to Brighton for a formal meeting with the plaintiff's solicitor, should their health permit it, and more information may emerge then.

The only other thing I can tell you is that Mr Worple is quite satisfied that the two ladies are the same two who supplied the original manuscript and who also came to his office for a meeting with Mr Arthur Wallace Hope. You might be interested in his account of them, and I cannot help wondering as I write these words if they will one day be personated in one of your stories. One sister, who we understand to be the elder of the two, is more retiring than the other owing to some defect about her face, which means that she is always very heavily veiled in public. When Mr Worple and the solicitor came to interview her, she at once threw a shawl over her head and was very distressed at the intrusion. The younger, who appears to be aged about thirty, is altogether the bolder and sharper of the two. She reviled the visitors for upsetting her sister and would speak of nothing else but their impertinence. Mr Worple thought this was no more than a cunning means of avoiding questioning.

Their father has declared most emphatically that the manuscript, which he has been shown, is not in the handwriting of either of his daughters and is prepared to employ an expert to testify to that effect. The case may prove to be more than usually complicated.

Mina could only agree. There were, she thought, several disparate elements in the publication of *An Encounter*; there was the matter copied from the original pamphlet, the facts about the Pavilion drawn from the book she had studied, the details of the events taking place in the Pavilion on 17 October 1870, and finally the indecent gloss on the story. She concluded that the ladies must somehow have obtained a copy of *Some Confidential Observations by a Lady of Quality*, perhaps one that had been passed on by a friend or relation. If they were telling the truth when they claimed never to have visited the Pavilion, they must have been told about its delights and presented with *The Royal Pavilion in the Days of King George IV*, perhaps by a different person to the one who had given them the pamphlet, someone who had visited on the day in question and might not have been aware that the entertainments were unique to that day. Handwriting could be disguised, or they might simply have adopted a clearer copy than their usual for the purposes of the printer.

Why, if the sisters were so modest and retiring, they had introduced matter of an indelicate nature into a story that had not been so in the original she could not say. Perhaps it had been introduced by a third party after the manuscript left the ladies' hands, the only possible object being to make money.

Mina paid another visit to the reading room and was able to study the newspaper record of the day in January 1850 when the public had been able to view the interior of the Pavilion for the first time. There was no note of who had been there on that occasion, although it was mentioned that some of the visitors, confused by the unusual layout of the great building, had got lost. Mina thought of what it must have been like to be the very first explorers of that lost and faded grandeur, like finding a sunken wreck on the bed of the sea, and picturing what it had once been in the days of its glory. If she had been there she was sure she would have written about it, too, but it would have been a work of the imagination, and who knows but she might have invented a story of stumbling by chance into the royal court of yesteryear. Could it be, she thought, that *Confidential Observations* had always been, and was always intended to be, taken as a work of fiction?

The company who had printed *Confidential Observations* might conceivably have assisted her enquiries, but on examining some Brighton directories she found that it was long defunct, the sole manager having passed away several years ago.

By now the news that the authors of *An Encounter* had been accused of plagiarism should by rights have set all of Brighton, if not Great Britain, abuzz with gossip, but somehow it had not. Over the next few days Mina carefully studied both local and national newspapers and listened carefully to conversations, but it was not discussed or even faintly alluded to. She visited Mr W.J. Smith's bookshop and found that he was no longer selling copies to eager enquirers, but his excuse was that he was waiting for more to be printed. She began to wonder if powerful interests were suppressing the news. She herself was most reluctant to drop the bombshell into conversation as she would then be roundly attacked with demands to know how she had come by the information, and she had no wish to reveal her private correspondence with Mr Greville. If the case did come to court then the truth would be revealed and Mina determined that she would be present when it was, but it could well be many months before any action was heard, if indeed it ever came to court at all. If Mr Hope took an interest in it, which seemed very probable, or the ladies' father had sufficient resources, the whole affair might be quietly settled before the dispute was made public with no one left any the wiser, and all those in the know well-paid to maintain silence.

Mina decided that it was a dreadful shame that so important a case should be in progress without the local press and interested members of the public knowing anything about it. It was one of her wickedest pleasures to place a metaphorical cat into a no less metaphorical flock of pigeons, and so she composed a letter to the editor of the *Gazette*, suggesting that he might care to look into the matter.

Chapter Twenty-One

The inaugural performance of Mystic Stefan had been set for the following Monday, and Mrs Peasgood's neat little cards distributed to a favoured few. All the Scarletti family was invited, but there was one person above all who Mina most wanted to be present at that event, one with the eye of a professional conjuror, who could see how the illusions were being achieved and comment on the competence or otherwise of Mr Hope's protégé.

The former Nellie Gilden had, before her recent marriage, enjoyed an unusual career. Now aged about twenty-five and admitting to seventeen, she had for some years assisted a Monsieur Baptiste, a highly successful stage magician, and was therefore fully conversant with the secrets of that trade, secrets she would never explicitly divulge. She had also been daubed from head to foot in paint to become the Ethiopian Wonder who could supposedly read minds, danced to near naked madness as Ophelia in a burlesque of *Hamlet*, and appeared on the Brighton stage with Richard as the spirit medium Miss Foxton. Demurely clad Miss Foxton had gone into a trance and by dint of some clever manipulation of her clothing, had transformed via a floating trail of ethereal light into a winged sprite that rose up out of an oriental vase clad in a glowing costume as clinging as a cobweb, a garment that left nothing to the heated imagination of any gentleman in the audience. This brazen attempt to become rich on the fashion for conjuring spirits had failed largely because the expense of Nellie's new gowns had outstripped their income by a substantial margin.

It had been an easy task for a woman of Nellie's unusual and varied talents, arrayed in her best gown and resplendent in paste jewellery, to persuade Miss Eustace that she was the wealthy Lady Finsbury and so lure her into the situation that had exposed the medium as a trickster and a thief.

Richard's association with Nellie had given Mina some disquiet, not because she disapproved of Nellie, who was as charming and clever as she was voluptuously lovely, but because of the explosion that would devastate the Scarletti household should Richard decide to marry her and Louisa discover her origins. In the event, Richard had recognised that Nellie was an expense he could not afford, and they had agreed to be merely good friends. Soon afterwards she had made a marriage that provided her with a respectable position in Brighton society.

Nellie's husband Mr Jordan and his business partner Mr Conroy were purveyors of high class clothing of every description, Mr Jordan attending to the gentlemen, Mr Conroy to drapery and accessories, and Mrs Conroy to the ladies. Nellie had assured her husband that she was the best possible means of showing off new fashions all about Brighton, thus sending the ladies into a frenzy of jealousy and creating an immediate demand. Since Mrs Conroy resembled a short barrel with tight staves, Mr Jordan took the point. Having the pleasure of escorting his wife to public and private events where he was the envy of every man in the room, he was content to grant her every whim. Earlier that year, during the craze for spirit mediums, and the pre-eminence of Miss Eustace in particular, Mr Jordan had made himself most unpopular in Brighton, as an uncompromising sceptic. Since then he had been rather better tolerated, the sudden downfall of Miss Eustace, the company of his delightful wife and her strict admonition that he must never utter the words 'I told you so,' being important aspects of his ascent in the town's estimation. They often attended musical recitals hosted by Mrs Peasgood and, as members of that refined circle, would therefore have been invited to view the continental wonders of Mystic Stefan.

Nellie was not one of those wives who liked to stay at home and manage the household. She and her husband occupied what had once been his bachelor apartments above the shop, but this, she had informed him, was a temporary arrangement. The rooms were quite insufficient to hold fashionable gatherings, there was no suitable boudoir for her personal use, nowhere to decently house a ladies' maid, and far too little space for the wardrobe she wished to acquire. Mr Jordan had been charged with finding a house that would please his wife, and making the profits to pay for it.

Thus Nellie, when not delighting society, was often to be seen riding about the town in her smart little carriage, or taking tea in all the best locations. The weather continued fine and clear, and the little equipage arrived at Montpelier Road where the driver assisted Mina into a seat beside Nellie, who wrapped her in a soft blanket in case the October air was too chill for her fragile bones. Now that Nellie was a travelling advertisement for Parisian fashion, or at least that part of it that came to Brighton, there was something more subtle in her dress. The colours were refined, the taste impeccable, the art used to display her womanly form to its best advantage spoke more of husbandly pride than the theatre, and the jewels were real. Nellie, Mina realised, was the only beautiful woman she knew who had never recoiled from her deformity, but then during her time on the stage she might well have seen worse and stranger sights.

'There is a new teashop open which entices with its lovely aromas and delicate cakes,' said Nellie. 'I have secured a table. We slender ladies must indulge ourselves on mouthfuls of delicious air or lose our waistlines.' They set off at a brisk rate. 'Your brother called on me the other day; has he told you of his grand theatrical scheme?'

'He has, though I am not convinced it will come to anything.'

'I am already appointed to be Mrs Fitzherbert to his Prince of Wales, and he has received a promise from Rolly that once his current engagement is over he will give us his Napoleon. I am pleased to take part as a favour to a friend, but Rolly has a less certain existence and if there are to be many performances he will require a fee or a share of the ticket sales. I hope Richard knows this.'

'I doubt that he has given it a thought.'

Nellie's laugh told Mina that she had already reached that conclusion. 'Well, I am sure some arrangement can be made.'

'I hope that you are happy with Mr Jordan,' Mina asked cautiously.

'I am as happy as it is possible to be with Mr Jordan,' smiled Nellie. 'It is a love match. I love his money and he loves *everything* about me.'

'Have you been invited to view the demonstration of Mystic Stefan at Mrs Peasgood's?'

'We have. Is he highly recommended? I have never see him.'

'Nor I, but I would be so grateful if you could attend and let me know what you think of his performance. He is being promoted by Mr Arthur Wallace Hope. I suppose you know that that gentleman has been a caller at our house.'

'All Brighton down to the very last puppy dog cannot fail to know it.'

'It seems that Mystic Stefan is a friend of Dr Lynn who was at the Pavilion last year, and who has recently introduced him to Mr Hope.'

'The name is not familiar, but some theatrical artists change their names if necessary — usually to avoid creditors. Mr Hope, however, has made quite a name for himself amongst conjurors.'

'Oh?'

'Something between a nuisance and a laughing stock. Did you know that he and Dr Lynn are good friends? They dine together when in London, and disagree on almost everything, but that does not seem to affect their regard for each other. Dr Lynn insists that he is a conjuror pure and simple, working with specially prepared apparatus and practised sleight of hand. When Mr Hope refused to believe this Dr Lynn took the unusual step of demonstrating to Mr Hope how some of his illusions are created. He even revealed the secret of the Japanese butterfly trick, but still Mr Hope would not be persuaded. He believes that Dr Lynn is a medium who, without realising it, performs his miracles with the aid of spirits. Mr Hope has been known to openly decry those conjurors who he believes deliberately and knowingly pervert their great spiritual gifts to make money on the popular stage. He has said as much about Monsieur Baptiste, who offered to place Mr Hope in a cabinet and run him through with swords, but he has not taken up the invitation.'

'Perhaps he believes that Mystic Stefan is also a medium.'

'If he is promoting him I have no doubt of it.'

328

Mina was digesting this observation as their carriage reached the teashop, which had been decorated in a style appropriate to the origins of its tea. She walked in assisted by Nellie, and not for one moment did she feel that her companion was using her as a foil to her own beauty or was displaying her as one might a pet marmoset. Once settled at a table with a cloth that winked white in the sunlight, tea was brought and served in thin cups decorated with peonies, accompanied by tiny meringues dipped in chocolate, and almond-crusted macarons arrayed on a silvery pagoda.

'I can see why Mr Hope is so generous to Mystic Stefan if he believes he is a medium, but I also feel that another purpose is being served with the conjuror as his instrument,' said Mina. She told Nellie of Mr Hope's intention to see Miss Eustace free, his request for a signed paper, and the dangers to herself if she refused. 'Mystic Stefan is a part of Mr Hope's campaign to persuade me to his way of thinking. I had not imagined I was an object worthy of his attention, but it seems that when gossips talk of the exposure of Miss Eustace it is my name that is mentioned. If I was to change my mind about her it would work strongly in her favour. Nothing escapes his attention. He makes eyes at Enid and my mother and has expressed an interest in Richard's play. I should mention that he has heard of Miss Foxton, but so far has not connected her or Lady Finsbury with you.'

Nellie was sufficiently adept at disguise that no one in Brighton had identified her as either the dowdy Miss Foxton or her lustrous sprite, but many of those who had seen the one public appearance of the elegant Lady Finsbury had also met Mrs Jordan, and commented on the resemblance.

'Mr Hope tells me he believes Lady Finsbury does not exist,' Mina continued. 'Part of his action in support of Miss Eustace is a claim that the event hosted by Lady Finsbury which showed Miss Eustace to be a fraud was in itself a fraud. Thus far he has not attempted to discover the lady's true identity, but I am concerned that someone might mention to him that you resemble her.'

Nellie seemed untroubled by this prospect. 'Ah yes, the tangled web of deception. It is true, I am told that I do slightly resemble Lady Finsbury, although I am always at pains to state that we are not related. She and Lord Finsbury are now abroad and will remain there permanently, so comparison will not be possible. Mostly, if one looks the part and acts the part, then it is accepted that one is the part. People believe whatever suits them and even pass it on to their friends without troubling themselves to establish if it is true or a lie. I am not sure why that is, but it is a valuable thing to know.'

'What should we do? So far he has not asked me who Lady Finsbury is, but he is sure that it is I who hired her impersonator. He can easily prove that there is no such title, if he has not already done so, so it is useless to have her return to Brighton. It is only because he still hopes that he can persuade or force me into declaring that Miss Eustace is genuine that he does not attack me outright. I am still being assiduously wooed in that respect, but I know he is gathering resources to fight me if needs be. If you were obliged to admit the imposture would that not threaten your marriage? How much does your husband know of your past?'

'He knows of my part in Miss Eustace's arrest, and applauds it. I have also confessed my association with Monsieur Baptiste and he has forgiven me everything, but we do not speak of my past and he would not have it broadcast in town. We must bide our time and hope that the truth of Lady Finsbury will not be explored. If it is — well, I know Mr Hope and his kind, they think themselves very clever but the cleverer the man the more easily he is duped.'

'He must guess that I and my family would not willingly go to a séance and so has invited us to one by a subterfuge. Who knows what Mystic Stefan might do? Bring messages from my father, perhaps. But you will come to the performance?'

'I would be quite desolated to miss it, although my husband is currently in Paris, buying silk. I doubt that Mystic Stefan will demonstrate anything new, but even if I could say how his tricks are done, it would be useless to inform Mr Hope. Anyone who does so would simply be added to his growing list of potential converts to spiritualism.'

Mina sighed. 'I feel sorry for Mr Hope. He has had terrible losses in his life, seen so much of senseless slaughter and cruel disease; so many young men sacrificed in vain. I have no wish to take away a belief which obviously brings him comfort, but I will not have that extortionist freed from prison unpunished so she can ruin others' lives.'

'Dear Mina,' said Nellie, affectionately. 'Your concern does you credit, as does your generosity to a man who clearly means you no good. Do, I implore you, take care.'

'That is what Dr Hamid says.'

'He is a wise man. Too wise ever to have tempted me, but I admire him as one might admire a finely-bound dictionary.'

'I am very fortunate in my friends,' said Mina. 'I could achieve nothing alone.' She was suddenly reminded of a phrenology head showing which parts of the brain were the seats of the various faculties. If the four friends were part of one brain then Dr Hamid would be wisdom, Richard adventurousness, Nellie imitativeness, and Mina imagination. She hoped that together it would be enough.

Chapter Twenty-Two

Nellie's carriage brought Mina home to her front door. As she turned the key she was greeted by an unexpected sound of laughter, not the little trills that rang out in response to the irresistibly amusing activities of the twins, but fits of helpless merriment. Mina pushed open the parlour door and saw her mother trying unsuccessfully to stifle her peals of mirth with a lace-edged handkerchief, while Enid, also laughing, was being led around the room by Mr Arthur Wallace Hope, his hand tenderly cupping her elbow.

'I do believe you almost have it, Mrs Inskip,' said Hope.

'Yes, yes, you are very near, Enid,' gasped Louisa, dabbing her eyes. 'Oh dear me, I never saw such a thing!'

'There!' said Enid, impulsively, and pointed to a small vase on the mantle shelf. A narrow-waisted confection, like Enid herself, it was as pink as a sweetmeat and decorated with roses. Mina knew that it usually stood as part of a cluster of similar vases, but that morning it had been moved to shelter modestly beside the much larger figure of a porcelain dog.

'Oh, that is well done!' exclaimed Hope, 'a very quick success! You have a singular talent, I congratulate you.'

Enid snatched up the vase, but then seemed uncertain what to do with it and looked about her.

'Allow me,' said Mr Hope and, taking it from her hand, he replaced it on the mantle shelf, very near to where it had been before.

'Whatever is this?' asked Mina.

They had been so wrapped up in the activity that none had seen or heard her enter and all now turned to look at her.

'Why Miss Scarletti, I am delighted you have returned in time for our little diversion,' said Hope. 'We are conducting an exercise in the power of the mind. "The willing game" it is called. And it will be all the more amusing and interesting if there are more players. Please do join us.'

Mina entered the room with some trepidation. Had Mr Hope called expecting to find her home? If he had been disappointed, then he had certainly made good use of his time. Was the willing game an innocent amusement, or did it have another more sinister purpose? Another idea for a story crossed her mind but would have to wait to be committed to paper. 'How is it played?'

'We begin by appointing a game leader.'

'That is Mr Hope!' declared Enid.

'But only for today, as it is the first time of playing,' said Hope, modestly. 'In future games anyone might be appointed. The company generally takes it in turns. Then one of the number is chosen and leaves the room for a few minutes. While that person is absent the other players agree on a task for her to perform. She might be asked to guess an object that is being thought of, or find something that has been hidden, or as you have just observed, moved to a new place. When the chosen person returns to the room, she is told what it is she must do, and then the game leader places a light touch on her arm while the others fill all their thoughts with the agreed task. They "will" her to understand and then complete it.'

And now Mina could see exactly where this was tending. 'So the object of the game is for the idea of the task to flow from the minds of the players into the mind of the person who was absent?'

'Exactly!' said Hope cheerfully. 'How astute you are!'

'But what is the purpose of the game leader?'

'He or she acts as a channel through which the thoughts are conducted.'

'The player might guess the task, of course, without any such communication.'

'That is certainly possible, given enough time and after many false guesses, but if the task is accomplished quickly and easily then we may be sure that some "willing" has taken place. I have always found it goes better and faster when the players are related. This is excellent evidence, which in my opinion amounts to scientific proof, that there has been some transference of thought.'

'Surely if the players know each other well, they will be better able to guess,' Mina pointed out.

Hope gave a slight smile and a casual shrug. 'To guess, or to read thoughts, whatever you prefer to believe. Both are possible.'

'Enid is very adept at the game,' said Louisa, with quiet motherly pride.

'Yes, I nearly always get it right!' Enid exclaimed triumphantly. Mina decided not to cite the pressure of Mr Hope's guiding hand as the most probable reason for this success.

'And you, Mrs Scarletti, have also shown a rare talent for it,' added Hope gallantly.

Louisa simpered, and patted her hair as she always did when enjoying the flattery of a gentleman. The pale blonde waves were still captured in a widow's cap, but it was vanity surely that allowed a lock to escape only to be artfully restrained by a pretty comb. She wore, and would probably wear to the day of her death, an oval locket which housed a greying curl of hair, cut from Henry Scarletti's head as he breathed his last, but she had recently added a small brooch at her throat, silver, decorated with tiny pearls, a treasured gift from Henry on the occasion of their betrothal.

Hope turned to Mina. 'I am sure that you would also be very successful.'

Enid narrowed her eyes and bit her lip.

'Oh, do you think so?' Louisa protested. 'Mina always has her head full of stories and never listens to anything I tell her.'

'I believe that Miss Scarletti listens to you more than you might imagine. A loving daughter always does.' He gazed at Mina imploringly. 'Do try. It would please your mother so.'

Mina felt trapped. She could hardly decline after such a request. Refusal or failure would be an insult to her mother, and if she succeeded in any measure then Hope would use this to try and persuade her that she had mediumistic abilities. For a few moments she considered the advantages of feigning exhaustion, illness or possibly death, but knew that she would not convince Hope that she was doing anything other than avoiding the invitation.

'I am eager to try it,' she said at last. 'Tell me, how long must I remain outside the room?'

'Only a minute or so. I will knock on the door to call you,' said Hope, opening the door for her. It was a courteous gesture, but Mina felt both indulged and subtly controlled. It was not a pleasant sensation.

Standing in the hallway, with the closed door separating her from her family and Mr Hope, Mina was conscious of the whispering that must be happening in the parlour, and wondered what was being planned. How she wished that Richard might arrive at this very moment with his disruptive clatter, but he did not. It occurred to her as she waited that during the turns of the game that had already taken place, Mr Hope had, as a result of the requirement for the brief absence of one player, spent a not insignificant amount of time closeted in the parlour with alternately her mother and her sister, and she wondered what, if anything, had been said on matters that did not involve setting tasks for the absent player to perform. All too soon Mina was summoned back into the room, to be faced by Louisa and Enid with unreadable expressions, and Mr Hope with the kindly smile she had come to know and distrust.

'What happens now?' she asked. 'What is my task?'

'You must find something that has been hidden,' said Hope. 'Mrs Scarletti and Mrs Inskip must think very hard about the object you must find, and where it may be discovered. They are willing you to find it. You must try to receive their ideas, and solve the mystery.'

Mina was in two minds about knowing what Louisa and Enid were thinking about. On the one hand, she was reluctant to enter into their thoughts and on the other they were all too apparent. It was certainly nothing to do with the task she had been set. Enid and her mother made an effort to look as though they were concentrating, both closing their eyes. Enid had spread her fingers and placed her hands over her face but Mina could see that underneath she was on the verge of giggles.

'Now,' said Mr Hope, taking Mina gently by the elbow, 'let me see if I can transmit to your mind a picture of what is being thought of.'

'Please may I have a few moments to concentrate?'

'But of course.'

Mina glanced quickly about the room. Mr Hope would not have committed to memory the precise manner in which the parlour was arranged and Louisa and Enid were too preoccupied with their own requirements to pay much attention to it. Mina, on the other hand, managed the household, and issued instructions to the cook, Rose and the charlady. Nothing seemed to be missing, or out of its usual place apart from the vase which Mr Hope had replaced and was not quite correct. Mr Hope, she reasoned, wanted her to succeed, so her task would not be too difficult, but it would not be so simple that she might easily do it by observation. It was then that she noticed that her mother was no longer wearing the little pearl brooch. Such an item, precious in every sense of the word, would never have been treated with carelessness or disrespect. When her mother was not wearing it, it was on her dressing table in a jewel case that had also been a gift from her father.

'Are you ready to make your guess?' asked Mr Hope. Mina felt a firm pressure on her elbow as his clasp intensified. She was sure that he was about to offer some guidance but she needed none, and if she did accuse him of steering her he would naturally deny it.

'Yes, I am. But I beg of you, Mr Hope, do not try to assist me. It is well meant, I know, but I do not want anyone to imagine that you are directing me, and you might do so by accident.' Hope gave her a cautious glance, and seemed to be on the verge of protesting, but he let go without comment, and she crossed the room unaided, to a side table adorned with trinkets, took up a small decorative box and opened it, finding inside, as she suspected, the pearl brooch.

'Why, I can hardly believe it!' pouted Enid. 'How did you know so quickly? You must have been listening at the door.'

'Surely it is because I can read your mind?' said Mina teasingly. 'Or could there be another reason?'

Hope gazed on Mina with wonder and admiration, like a scientist who had just made a great discovery. 'I doubt it. You are miraculous, Miss Scarletti. I can see that you might have noticed that Mrs Scarletti had removed the brooch, but to know so swiftly and surely exactly where it lay, that is an ability far beyond mere guesswork. I wonder what your secret is? Perhaps you do not know it yourself?'

'I will tell you my secret,' Mina replied. 'I did not need to guess, I did not listen at the door, I did not receive any assistance from another individual and I certainly did not read anyone's mind. This brooch has great sentimental value, and I cannot imagine mother treating it other than with respect and tenderness. This box was purchased by my mother and father while on their honeymoon. Where else could such a treasure be?' She limped over to Louisa and gently helped her replace the brooch. As she did so she saw tears glimmer in her mother's eyes.

Hope nodded knowingly. 'Your claim does not surprise me because I have heard such explanations before. I am sure that you imagine that you deduced the answer in the way you have described, but I urge you to entertain the possibility that the idea was placed there by the efforts of your mother and sister to will you into making the discovery.'

'I was trying very hard indeed,' said Enid. 'Mina, did you not feel my thoughts?'

'I felt them very strongly, but only because they were apparent in your expression.'

'You do not believe, Miss Scarletti, because you do not wish to,' sighed Mr Hope, his manner more gentle than accusing, 'but there are many scientific men who share my opinion. Some of them have proposed that there is an organ of sensation, a part of the brain perhaps currently undiscovered, which can enable thoughts to pass from one person to another. But there are others who go still further — they say that the mind can act upon another mind without the need for any bodily organ, and I am inclined to that latter belief.'

Mina understood. 'You speak of the soul or the spirit, and its existence independently of the physical body.'

'I do. Moreover, I think that what is happening here, and indeed in any kind of mental communication, both with the living and the dead, is a force of nature. In a very few years from now, if enough men put their energy into the work, thought transference will be proven and become an accepted scientific fact, and we will laugh at our former ignorance that we ever doubted it. At present, only those with the most sensitive and developed minds can achieve it, but one day, with proper education and guidance, we might all aspire to it, although there will inevitably be classes of persons whose skills in that direction will never be very advanced.'

'I look forward to that time very much,' said Mina warmly. 'Just imagine the world if we were all able to exercise our brains and discover what everyone else thought of us, or learn each other's secrets.'

Louisa looked shocked. 'It would be impossible to live in society!'

Enid said nothing, but her face flushed.

Hope smiled knowingly. 'I know precisely what Miss Scarletti is thinking. She thinks I am a great fool.'

'How very rude!' snapped Enid angrily. 'Mina, how could you?'

'Oh, I am quite used to that,' he said with a laugh. 'When one speaks of new ideas and new discoveries, there are always doubters. Today, Miss Scarletti, you are a doubter, but I will win you over in time, I am quite certain of it.'

No one showed any inclination to continue the game, and Mr Hope did not press the point; he had clearly, thought Mina, achieved what he had come there to do. Soon afterwards he pleaded another engagement that would, to his great regret, oblige him to depart.

When Mr Hope had left them, Enid turned on Mina. 'Why are you so unpleasant to Mr Hope? He is a great man, a brave man, and it is an honour for us to have him come here. If you are not better tempered he might not call again.'

'But don't you see — he wants to convert me to his way of thinking. If I continue to doubt him then he will only come here again and again to repeat his efforts. If you wish him to continue to visit us I think you are quite safe in that respect.'

Enid said nothing and Louisa patted her hair.

Chapter Twenty-Three

On the evening of Mystic Stefan's demonstration Mr Hope was kind enough to call on the Scarlettis with a carriage to convey Louisa, Enid, Mina and Richard to Mrs Peasgood's. All three ladies were treated with the same warm courtesy and gallant attention, but as he handed Enid into her place there was something about the glance that passed between them that Mina found worrying. She began to hope for the early return of Mr Inskip and a removal of Enid back to London and out of danger. Richard, who had been out until very late the previous night, and then slept through breakfast, was looking uncommonly cheerful, which Mina feared was to do with the absence abroad of Nellie's husband.

'Was there no difficulty about my attending this event?' asked Mina, when they were on their way. 'You know, of course, that after certain incidents I was declared *persona non grata* at séances. Or does Mystic Stefan not know of my reputation for chasing away the spirits?'

Mr Hope chuckled. 'This is not a séance, Miss Scarletti. Mystic Stefan assures me that he does not receive messages from those who have passed, although many of the mysteries he performs are beyond my powers to explain, and quite probably beyond his also. But you are all my very special guests, and while believers in the unexplained are always welcome, doubters are doubly so, for they will one day swell the ranks of the believers.'

Those doubters, Mina knew, would include most members of Mrs Peasgood's select circle. She only hoped that the evening would pass without any upsetting incidents.

Mrs Peasgood was usually the best of hostesses, conducting her gatherings with smooth and practised assurance, but that evening she looked uncomfortable, as if she was already regretting giving in to the entreaties of her friends, and nervous about what Mystic Stefan might do. Mrs Mowbray, however, appeared to have no such reservations, although Mina was sure that it was not the presence of the conjuror but of Dr Hamid that largely occupied her thoughts.

Mrs Mowbray was a large but active lady with a prominent bust, which she believed was her best feature, and a substantial amount of whalebone had been employed to ensure that no one could ignore it. Although the doctor had been widowed for only a few months she had convinced herself that all she had to do was wait out a suitable interval of time and he would one day glance in her direction. She had been heard to say that Dr Hamid was the nicest-looking and cleverest man in all Brighton, and no one had sought to contradict her. The fact that Dr Hamid seemed wholly unconscious of the passion he had aroused she doubtless put down to his still missing his late wife, which, in her estimation, only went to show his loving and devoted nature, and his excellent credentials as a husband.

Nellie arrived wearing an extraordinary hat with a silver grey demi-veil that was sure to be all the rage the following day, and such a torrent of lace that it brought gasps of envy from the ladies and looks of terror from their husbands.

As was usual for Mrs Peasgood's soirees, the front portion of the parlour was arranged with rows of comfortable seating for her guests while the rear, which served as a stage for the performance, was occluded by heavy curtains. Mina's interest was in the lighting, since it was the obvious and easiest way to tell if the entertainment was being presented as conjuring or a séance. Conjurors, as Nellie had attested, make much of the fact that they are hiding nothing from the audience. They are, of course, hiding everything of importance and allowing the audience to see only what they wish them to see; that is the art of the conjuror. But they did it in full light, which made their skill all the more remarkable. No one would go to see a conjuror who worked in the dark. Except of course that people did go to see conjurors who worked shrouded in darkness, only those conjurors called themselves spirit mediums and produced glowing spectres and whirling tambourines and brought baskets of fruit from nowhere and claimed that they would die if the lights were turned on. Sometimes someone did turn on the lights, but this had never resulted in the death of the medium, only his or her exposure as a fraud.

The arrivals all mingled cheerfully, especially Mr Hope, who had appointed himself major-domo for the evening, which suited everyone as he was a very commanding and popular presence. A crowd soon gathered around him, the gentlemen wanting to know how dangerous it was to confront an angry elephant, while the ladies, affecting to be terrified by that question, enquired more timorously after the fashionable dress of an African princess. At last all took their seats except for Hope, who stood before the curtains, beaming at the assembly. 'My good friends,' he began, 'I am happy to see so many of you here for what I can promise will be a treat for the eyes. For some years the Mystic Stefan has been dazzling audiences on the continent of Europe with his displays, but now, for the very first time in England, he is here in Brighton to show you just some of what he can achieve. Should he meet with your approval it is his intention to take a room at the Pavilion where larger illusions can be presented. As you already know from the invitation, he has little facility with our language, and so will perform without speaking. Some of you will have prepared questions for him on slips of paper, to which he can provide an answer, either yes or no. The means by which he does this will become apparent in due course. When the time comes for that part of the performance he will indicate whose question will be answered and then you will either hold the paper to your forehead, or, if you dare, speak the question out loud.' He paused to allow the listeners to absorb the information.

'Mr Hope?' ventured Mrs Peasgood. 'I trust that the gentleman will not ask for the lights to be extinguished?' She gave a brittle smile. 'If he did, it would be very hard for some of us to see the entertainment.'

Hope bowed in response. 'The lights may remain as they are. Ladies and gentlemen, it is my very great pleasure to present to you the Mystic Stefan!' He drew the curtains aside and returned to his seat.

In the centre of the stage there stood a man. Given his *nom de théâtre*, Mina had half been expecting to see someone in elaborate attire, a long colourful robe perhaps, embroidered with mysterious symbols, and fashioned with deep sleeves, the better for concealment. Instead, the gentleman was clad in a plain black evening dress suit, with a snowy shirt and neat bow tie. It was hard to detect his age, since he wore his whiskers long, with a fine, curling moustache and heavy brows, but these and his hair, which was also a little longer than strictly fashionable, were black and glossy, which suggested either that he was a relatively young man or used a great deal of dye. As he stepped forward, however, the ease and lightness of his gait suggested youth. He spread his arms wide, opening his hands so all could see that they were empty and bowed to the audience. There was polite applause, which he acknowledged with a smile.

The only furniture on the stage was two tables — to one side was a long table on which could be seen in neat array the objects of his art, including a top hat and a wand, and in the centre was a small, bare, round table with slender legs. Mystic Stefan took up the hat and the wand and showed the inside of the hat to the audience to assure them that it was empty, using the tip of the wand to explore its interior. He then placed the hat brim up on the round table and waved the wand over it. Carefully and with great deliberation, he pushed back the cuffs of his shirt to reveal a few inches of bare forearm, thus demonstrating that there was nothing concealed in his sleeves. Dipping one hand inside the hat, he began to produce from within a rainbow of ribbons, silk handkerchiefs and paper streamers, which, because of their lightness, ascended into the air as he threw them high, and floated down in a colourful cascade, the very volume of these productions suggesting that it was impossible for them all to have been contained in the hat. Just as it seemed that nothing more could be forthcoming, he again put his hand into the hat and this time, brought out a bunch of fresh flowers, which he lifted to his nose to appreciate the perfume. He then proffered them forward, and Mr Hope kindly took them from him and presented them to Mrs Peasgood. That lady had been mollified from her original concern by the nature of the display and took the gift with good grace.

The conjurer, acknowledging a ripple of polite applause, next took a set of large metal rings from the side table. He lifted one away from the set and then another to demonstrate to the audience that they were separate, then tapped them smartly together. In an instant they had become magically linked as though the metal had somehow dissolved. He spun one ring around on its fellow to show that there were no gaps, then struck them together with the others, and showed that there were now three linked in the same way. Further taps and clashes continued, too fast for the eye to appreciate, so that more and more of the rings were woven together, forming patterns which he held up for inspection, until he opened them up into a single structure, seven in all, combined. He then closed them up, gave them a final tap and showed that they were free again.

There followed numerous other delights. He cut a rope in half with scissors, showed the cut ends to the audience, tied the two pieces in a knot, and then blew on it. The knot was gone, and the rope restored to a single piece. He tore a paper streamer into tiny shreds and then by blowing on the fragments, made it new again. With a wave of the wand, a vase full of ink became a vase of water, and then wine. He pulled fresh eggs from an empty cloth bag, which he then broke into the top hat, from which he brought out a freshly-cooked omelette, a feat that precipitated a round of applause, which redoubled when he showed that the hat was clean inside.

Mr Hope now rose and addressed the audience. 'If a lady or gentleman would be kind enough to lend a ring for the next demonstration, I promise it will be returned quite unharmed.' Mrs Peasgood looked doubtful, but Nellie very charmingly removed a glittering token of her husband's adoration from her finger, and instead of handing it to Mr Hope, as that gentleman clearly anticipated, she approached the stage and put it directly into the open palm of Mystic Stefan, who inclined his head in thanks. When both Nellie and Mr Hope were seated again, the ring was placed in a casket, the lid snapped shut and a key turned. Mystic Stefan then produced an orange out of thin air and tossed it to Mr Hope, who caught it deftly and gave it to Enid to hold. There was now much waving of the wand over the casket, and a light tap, before it was opened and shown to be empty. Nellie obligingly gave an affecting performance lamenting the disappearance of her ring. All was not lost, however, as Mr Hope returned the orange to Mystic Stefan, and was prevailed upon to cut it open. The ring was duly discovered buried in the fruit, and after some polishing with a silk handkerchief, restored to its delighted owner.

Stefan bowed again, but in a manner that suggested he had only just begun to show what he could do. Taking a walking cane, he made passes over it with one hand, then, letting go of it, showed that not only could it stand by itself, but with more passes it could be made to dance, swaying from side to side on its point as he moved first one hand then the other in the air around it. He next took one of the metal rings and placed it over his head so that it rested on his shoulders. Some of the colourful paper streamers he crumpled into a ball, which he placed on the palm of his left hand. He then made circular passes over the paper ball with his right hand, and it rose slowly into the air, wobbling a little, and floated gently between his palms without touching either. He smiled at the audience as if to say: 'I know what you are thinking, you believe the paper ball is suspended by a hidden thread'. He took the metal ring from around his neck and passed it back and forth around the ball, showing that it was unsupported. Putting the ring back around his neck, he made further movements above and below the ball with both hands, then with a snap of his fingers it dropped into one palm, and he stepped forward and tossed it into the audience. Enid caught it and showed it to Louisa, who agreed that it was merely crushed tissue paper. The metal ring was handed to Mr Hope, who passed it around so it could be seen that it was quite solid and unbroken.

Stefan then brought forward what appeared to be a kind of nest made of many folded sheets of paper and placed it on the round table. Mr Hope rose to face the audience once more.

'Ladies and gentlemen, you have all been asked to think of a question you wish to address to the magical divination device of Mystic Stefan. All questions must be capable of being answered by either a "yes" or a "no". You may choose to ask your question aloud, or by writing it on a slip of paper and holding it to your forehead. The answer will be revealed on a paper within the device. So, I wonder, who dares ask their question first?'

There was the usual reluctance of individuals to be the first to venture. Heads were turned to see who might be brave enough, but no one was.

'Now, please don't be shy, I can assure you that no secrets will be revealed.'

'I have a question,' said Mina. In fact, she did not have a question, but was impatient to start this portion of the demonstration. 'Please let me have some paper and I will write it down.' Paper and pencil were provided and Mina tore off a piece, made some meaningless scribbles and folded it.

'You will receive your answer on this paper,' said Hope, showing Mina a blank square. He turned it over so everyone could see that it was clean and unmarked on both sides, then handed it to Stefan, who opened out the nest like a flower and dropped the little slip into its deepest recesses. Quickly and dexterously the papers were turned in on each other until the result was a tight round package. This he handed to Mr Hope who gave it to Mina. 'Just place it on your lap, hold the paper with the question to your forehead, and the answer will be revealed.'

Mina obeyed, and saw that Nellie was looking at the package with a smile. Stefan took up the wand once more and made some elaborate passes in Mina's general direction with an expression of the most profound concentration. Something in his manner told Mina that everything else that had gone before was just a preparation

341

for this moment. Had there been music provided it would have been mysterious, soft and evocative of strange things occurring.

Hope then brought the package back to Stefan who unwrapped it, extracted the previously blank paper and held it up to show that on it was written 'No'. Mrs Peasgood and Mrs Mowbray glanced at Mina with expressions of great pity. They had doubtless assumed that she had asked if she would ever be cured, a question Mina had no need to ask as she already knew the answer.

Mrs Mowbray, with a sly glance at Dr Hamid, her slip of paper already written, raised her hand. 'I have a question.' Another blank paper was provided and the elaborate process repeated.

Mrs Peasgood was beginning to look worried. 'Mr Hope, might I ask where the replies are coming from?'

'Ah, that is a very great question, and one to which I am sure none of us here has the answer.' Mr Hope seemed very satisfied with his own reply, which was more than Mrs Peasgood was.

Mrs Mowbray's paper read 'No', a response that she received with very ill grace.

Mrs Peasgood declined to ask a question, so Nellie was next, receiving the answer 'Yes.'

Now that others had dared, Enid volunteered that she would like to ask a question, and also received the answer 'Yes', which she clearly found disappointing.

Mr Hope rose to his feet. 'I have a question,' he announced, 'a very important one, which I do not hesitate to ask aloud. Is Dr Livingstone alive?'

There was a buzz of whispers around the room as he took the paper package into his hands and Mystic Stefan made his magical passes over it. When the package was unwrapped the slip of paper said 'Yes'.

Hope gave a little gasp of joy. 'Oh, then we may breathe again because the dear, brave, good man is alive and may yet be found and relieved! God and the spirits grant that this great work may be done!'

Mystic Stefan, holding the paper nest, suddenly looked astonished, held it to his ear and shook it as if there was something new inside. Replacing it on the table, he folded back the inner petals, dipped his hand inside and took something out, not a paper, but a small colourful object, which he offered to Hope. Mr Hope reached out and the object was dropped into his cupped hands. He stared momentarily dumbstruck at what lay before him. It was a cylindrical blue glass bead, of a similar kind to the ones Mina had seen on display at the Town Hall.

When Hope regained his powers of speech there was an unmistakable sob in his voice. 'Why, this is extraordinary! Miraculous! Not only is Livingstone alive but he has sent me this to say — what is it he can be saying? That he needs supplies, succour? Yes, that is it! Oh, how I wish I could send it to him now! Food, medicines! The poor fellow must be in sore need.'

Mina watched him carefully, but if he was pretending he was doing it very well.

Mystic Stefan merely smiled and stepped back. He took up his top hat, twirled it between his fingers by the brim and put it on, then with an expression of mock surprise, lifted it to reveal a cake. He put the cake on the table, then bowed to the audience, and drew the curtains so they met in the middle.

The audience applauded as vigorously as was thought polite.

Mrs Peasgood rose to her feet. 'I assume the performance is at an end?' she asked, but Hope was clutching the bead in his fist with an expression of fierce determination. 'Mr Hope?'

He started. 'Oh, yes, forgive me. It is over.'

Mrs Peasgood rang for the maid. 'Ladies and gentlemen, the evening's entertainment is now complete, and I am sure we would all like to thank Mr Hope for arranging it. Refreshments will be served in ten minutes.'

While Enid and Louisa were concerned with Mr Hope and the bead, Richard took Mina by the arm and they went to talk to Nellie, who had risen and was making a tour of the room to show off her gown to the best advantage.

'What do you think of Mystic Stefan?' asked Mina.

'He is a conjuror of some ability, but none of his tricks were new, and he was clearly working with little apparatus. Monsieur Baptiste could perform all of what we saw, but with more drama. Of course, much of his work was more suitable for a stage than a drawing room. The rope trick for example, cutting it in half and then joining it up, he did that with a live chicken, removing its head and then restoring it whole.'

'A live chicken? How can one do that?' Richard exclaimed.

Nellie smiled enigmatically. 'Well, the secret is to start with two chickens.'

'It is obvious to me that the device that answers questions is simply another conjuring trick,' said Mina. 'He must have the answers already hidden inside.'

'Of course,' agreed Nellie. 'Its method of operation lies in its construction and the way the papers are folded and unfolded.'

'Do the answers appear by chance? Or does Mystic Stefan decide if they are yes or no?'

'The operator decides. Usually the questions are personal and secret, so no one dares to say if the answers are right or wrong. In any case, most people don't know the right answer, because they ask about the future or the unknown. The general way of proceeding is to give the answer "yes" to any lady who is young and beautiful, since she always asks about romance, usually whether her admirer truly loves her and will be faithful.'

'And if she is not young and beautiful?'

'Then the answer is "no", for the same reason. A gentleman generally asks about business and the answer given depends on how he is dressed.'

'Enid was most unhappy with her answer,' Mina observed. 'She must have asked if Mr Inskip was alive and well. What was your question?'

'I asked if Mystic Stefan was wearing a false beard,' confided Nellie and they all laughed.

'What about the bead he produced and gave to Mr Hope?'

'Was that what it was? I did wonder.'

'Yes, I think it was an African bead, they are used as currency there. I saw some displayed at the lecture.'

Nellie nodded thoughtfully. 'A sop to his patron perhaps. The bead was never in the paper. He palmed it and made it look as if it came from there.'

'Is it unusual to pretend contact with the living?' asked Richard.

'Not at all; I have known mediums do as much when the person being enquired about is far away, especially as in this case, when they are in danger.'

'I am very glad that we had no ghosts appear,' said Mina. 'I expect Mr Hope was too well acquainted with Mrs Peasgood's opinions on that subject to risk giving offence and losing her good will. I was prepared for an event of some kind designed to turn me into a fervent spiritualist, but there was nothing of that description apart from the Livingstone message, which we can hardly treat as evidence unless the man is found and confirms sending it. But Mr Hope is a subtle man — he may simply be paving the way for wonders to come.' She worried about it all the way home.

Chapter Twenty-Four

There was good news for Mina when she opened the next edition of the *Gazette* and saw that her letter had had the desired effect.

'AN ENCOUNTER': IS IT PLAGIARISED?

All Brighton has been talking about this controversial book, indeed we might say all England. Just as we thought there was no more that could be said on the subject, we have a brand new sensation. When we first heard the news, we could hardly believe it, but our enquiries have shown it to be true. We can now inform our readers that an action is being taken by a Brighton lady for damages against the authors of 'An Encounter'. From what we have been able to discover, the lady, whose name is being carefully withheld, wrote a pamphlet many years ago about a ghostly sighting in the Royal Pavilion. Without commenting on the likelihood of such an event, we must point out that the lady in question is highly respectable, and of a pure and elevated character. Her work contained none of the questionable passages that have made 'An Encounter' so notorious, and describes only seeing the shades of the Prince of Wales' royal assembly and an entertainment consisting of music and a genteel and decorous dance. Nevertheless, the lady alleges that the authors of 'An Encounter' have copied a material part of her publication, representing it as their own, while adding the other, less savoury, portions, which are quite unsuitable to be described in the press. Her legal representatives are demanding the immediate withdrawal and destruction of all copies of 'An Encounter', together with damages, not only for the profits they have already made on it, but also to recompense their client for the great distress this situation has caused. The original book was created by a lady of refined and delicate taste, but she fears that those of her intimates who know of it may be under the impression that she is also the author of the subsequent volume. This anxiety has caused her much suffering, and she has asked not only for a public apology, but substantial damages for the attack on her reputation. We do not know, but rumour has it that some thousands of pounds may be involved.

Louisa read the article and gave a sharp snort of a laugh. 'I knew it! These Bland sisters are wicked conniving women. Mr Hope was wrong to trust them.'

'I am sure there is some mistake,' said Enid, sulkily. 'In any case, you can't blame Mr Hope for being kind-hearted. He is very chivalrous towards ladies and likes to think of himself as their champion. He believes Miss Eustace is innocent and he means to prove it too.'

'What nonsense!' Louisa retorted. 'Enid, you can know nothing of the matter. You were not in Brighton when she was here and have never met the woman.'

'But —'

345

'No! I forbid you to speak of it!'

'You won't forbid Mina,' Enid went on, with a stubborn pout. 'She thinks so too but won't admit it.'

Louisa turned to Mina, wide-eyed in astonishment. 'Mina! Is this true?'

Mina made an effort to remain calm. 'It is not. Mr Hope would like it to be true, and I am afraid he has been carried away into telling people it is.'

Louisa gave the newspaper an angry shake. 'I trust you have undeceived him.'

'I have tried, but it doesn't take. Mr Hope believes he is right and encourages others in that view. Some more than most. He thinks it is only a matter of time before everyone agrees with him. One might as well tell the tide not to come in as expect him to change his mind.'

Louisa's expression hardened with new determination. 'I see that I shall have to have a very firm word with him. He is an excellent man in many respects, but overconfidence is something he must learn to curb.'

It was time for Mina to go for her steam bath and massage, which were more needed than ever, as she had been both active and anxious of late. As she left the house she saw Enid and Anderson with the twins in their perambulator, marching down Montpelier Road towards the sea.

Mina did not know what herbs Dr Hamid used in his therapeutic steam baths, only that there were several recipes depending on the condition being treated, and all of them were secret. Her treatment began when wrapped only in a sheet, she sat at rest in the tiled steam room, and as the hot mist enveloped her she closed her eyes and beads of scented moisture rolled down her face and body. Sometimes Mina drifted into a light sleep, in which her sore back and shoulders eased most deliciously, but today she was too concerned about the pressure being placed upon her to become fully relaxed. She wondered when Mr Hope had told Enid that she believed in Miss Eustace, and supposed it had been confided during the 'willing game' when they were alone together in the parlour. What else had he said? She didn't like to think.

Anna, of course, at once detected Mina's tension during the massage that followed. She had not yet read the article in the *Gazette*, although her brother had, and she was extremely gratified to learn from him that the disgusting book was to be withdrawn. 'But, as I understand it, the earlier book was all about ghosts, too,' she said. 'So my ladies will protest that there is truth in it after all.' She worked firmly and diligently at the knots in Mina's muscles. 'Sometimes I wish I could massage their brains for them.'

Her treatment concluded, Mina, feeling somewhat restored, went to see Dr Hamid, who admitted that he had found the article in the *Gazette* highly amusing.

'Where the *Brighton Gazette* leads so the London daily papers will follow,' she assured him, 'not to mention *Reynolds* and *Lloyds*, and all the others that like a good scandal.'

'I wonder how the *Gazette* came to hear of it?' It was a question to which he seemed to neither need nor expect a reply. 'Do you think the respectable lady author would approve of this article? I am not sure that she intended to have her private business advertised in the press.'

'She seems to be biding her time but will, I think, be happy to admit to the first publication when she has received an apology about the second. I, however, am very curious to know what Mr Hope will make of it, since he believes in the Misses Bland's experience. Knowing his ways, I fear he will find some method of dismissing any truth that threatens to upset his beliefs. This plagiarism case has come as something of a relief to me. Mr Hope has been pressing me to make this declaration, sometimes outright and sometimes more subtly, but however he does it I know what he is about. Now that it is public knowledge I can make use of it. It will give me an excuse to delay any decision.'

Mina's way home took her along the Marine Parade, and with the wind from the sea coming in cool and blustery, she decided to hire a cab. There were some days when high gusts threatened to carry her up into the air, skirts flapping, like a witch who had lost her broomstick, and consequently she could not leave the house unaccompanied, but that day she just needed to be careful. Most of the regular Brighton cab drivers knew her by sight and she never had to wait long to secure a vehicle. Within minutes a cab had drawn up beside her, and she was about to board it when she chanced to see Anderson and the twins on the other side of the road. There was no mistaking the unusual double perambulator, but Enid was not with them. Anderson looked dull and bored as usual, although she took her duties seriously, and made sure to give the twins equal attention. The babies, she had told the approving grandmother, were extraordinarily well behaved, and Mina had to agree that they were remarkably content and placid. Neither had yet threatened to produce a tooth, although that event was undoubtedly imminent, so the situation could well change. Louisa had given orders that her grandchildren were not to be pampered, and then proceeded to pamper them mercilessly.

Mina took her seat in the cab, but told the driver not to move off until directed and part drew the window curtain so she could peer out unnoticed. Had Anderson been waiting outside a shop selling confectionery or novels or millinery, Mina would have been able to guess where Enid was, but the nursemaid was exercising her charges around the gardens of the Old Steine. Enid could surely not be far away, but there were few locations in the immediate vicinity to tempt her. The area was, however, much populated by the surgeries of doctors and dentists and Mina wondered if Enid had arranged a medical consultation that she did not wish to reveal to her family. It was a worry, although Enid, she reflected, had not complained of her teeth, or any indisposition, and her husband had been absent too long for her to be in a delicate condition that was not yet apparent.

Anderson walked on slowly, but then paused, leaned over the twins, made a great show of ensuring that they were warmly wrapped, turned about and walked back the way she had come. There was one other possibility, thought Mina with a horrible pang of dread; they were very close to the stately pile of the Royal Albion Hotel. Mina continued to keep watch for some minutes, and saw Anderson's performance repeated a number of times. Finally, she ordered the cab home, wondering what to do.

'Is Enid not yet home?' said Mina lightly, as she joined her mother, who was toasting her toes before a crackling fire in the parlour. 'Surely she isn't shopping again? Does she not have enough ribbon?'

'Enid has taken very well to the climate here,' said Louisa. She was amusing herself with a dish of sugared almonds and a volume by the famed Brightonian master of literature, Mr Tainsh, although she was quick to cast the book aside as soon as Mina entered. Even Louisa found so much noble virtue grating after a while. 'She says it is good for the complexion, as the air is pure and the breeze stimulates the skin if there is not too much sun, and it is beneficial for the twins, too. They are still out for their walk, and may stop for refreshments before they return.'

Mina said nothing, as there was nothing she could decently say. She could hardly make an accusation without proof. She might almost wish she was able to divine thoughts as Mr Hope believed she could. Retiring to her room, she looked amongst her papers and found the card Mr Hope's manservant had given her, showing that his master was staying at the Royal Albion Hotel. Had Enid really gone in to meet him there? Mina fervently hoped that nothing had occurred beyond smiles across a tea table. Even that was highly indiscreet. If they had spoken, the main subject of their conversation, once they had briefly revisited Enid's great love of Africa, Mr Hope's concerns about the safety of Dr Livingstone, and the new science of mind-reading, would almost certainly have been Mina's intransigent attitude to Miss Eustace. Hope could not parade Miss Eustace in front of Mina and ask her to change her mind, so, thought Mina, he was using the Misses Bland and Mystic Stefan as lesser weapons of persuasion, and engaging both Enid and Louisa as agents and spies in her home.

When Enid finally returned an hour later she announced that the walk had done her a great deal of good, and she did appear undeniably cheerful.

'I hope you did not find the Marine Parade too blustery,' said Mina.

'Why no, the air was most invigorating.' Enid gave a little frown. 'How do you know where we walked?'

'I attended Dr Hamid's establishment — do you know it? It is close by the Royal Albion Hotel. I chanced to see you and Anderson with the twins. At least, I saw Anderson, so I assume that you were shopping nearby, or perhaps sheltering from the breeze. It is a pleasant location, but when the wind blows too fiercely it may be hazardous.'

A variety of emotions flitted across Enid's face.

'I would not wish you to expose yourself to any possible dangers,' Mina went on.

Enid's lips trembled then she threw back her head in defiance. 'I thank you for your concern. Yes, the wind is fierce, but I can endure it.'

Chapter Twenty-Five

The day passed without a visit from Mr Hope. Mina suspected that the public revelation of the plagiarism action had, in view of his pronouncements about *An Encounter*, required some urgent investigation. He had probably tried to arrange another meeting with the Bland sisters to discover what they had to say on the matter. Mr Hope, she realised, the man who could stare a charging elephant in the face without flinching, did have one fear — of being made to look a fool.

Next morning, Enid and her mother went out in each other's company together with Anderson, to show off the twins to one of the few notable residents of Brighton who had not yet been privileged to view them, and Richard left the house for an unknown destination almost as soon as he had breakfasted.

Mina was busy completing her new story about the man pursued by demons. The narrative had changed somewhat since its original conception. When she had started to write, the demons had been real and hounded the sinful victim to his grave, where he discovered that even this gave him no respite from their torments. Now the story ended with the revelation that the demons only existed in his overheated brain. Mina was in two minds as to whether death would bring an end to his sufferings or not. Did one lifetime of sin really deserve an eternity of punishment? She supposed it must depend on the sin. Looking back on the earlier pages she saw that she had only alluded to the man's many foul deeds without describing them, leaving the reader to colour in the picture. She hardly felt qualified to insert more frankness, which in any case would result in an unpublishable manuscript. Instead, Mina delved into her stock of adjectives. A few examples of 'unspeakable', 'heinous' and 'loathsome' would suffice.

She was still debating with herself how to end the narrative when she heard the doorbell. Hoping that the visitor was merely a messenger or an importunate tradesman, a situation that only required Rose to send him away with a snarl, she took no notice until Rose knocked at her door. 'It's Mr Hope,' she said. 'He is asking for you most particularly.'

Mina sighed. She might have asked that he be told to leave, but there would be no use in that, as he would only keep returning until satisfied, and in the light of recent developments she was extremely curious to know what he would say. 'Very well, ask him to wait in the parlour. I will come down and speak to him, but you are to remain in the room throughout. Do not leave us alone together for even a moment.'

Rose gave Mina a surprised look, and a spate of questions trembled on her lips but remained unspoken. 'Yes, Miss.'

As she descended the stairs, Mina reflected on the fact that her visitor had appeared at a time when she was almost alone in the house. Was this mere coincidence, or had he been informed by Enid as to when this might be possible?

Mr Hope looked friendly enough, as he always did, but wore a look of underlying concern. His discomfiture deepened when Rose, instead of dutifully removing herself from the room, as he must have anticipated, went to stand in a corner and remained there like a statue, her gaze fixed firmly on the carpet.

'Miss Scarletti, I apologise for calling on you without notification,' he began.

Mina did not sit, but merely placed a hand on the back of a chair for support, neither did she offer Mr Hope a seat. It was the clearest possible indication that their interview was not to be a long one. For his part, Hope looked too distracted to want to sit. 'I am sure you would not have done so without good reason,' she replied.

Hope glanced at Rose. 'I could not trouble you for a glass of water?' he asked.

'Oh, we can do better than that. Rose, please pour a glass of that lovely mineral water for Mr Hope.'

There was a bottle of Dr Hamid's spiced berry water and some glasses in the room, and Rose obeyed. Hope, who had quite clearly not noticed the presence of the beverage, and had made the request anticipating that Rose would be obliged to leave the parlour to enable him to interview Mina alone, attempted unsuccessfully to conceal his disappointment. He took the glass, but was still too agitated to think of sitting down.

'I assume that refreshment was not the sole object of your visit?' said Mina.

He glanced at Rose again. 'The purpose of my visit is such that I would prefer to speak with you in private.'

'Maybe so, but I am afraid that will not be possible. When we last spoke alone my mother discovered it, and delivered a substantial scolding to me afterwards. She is very strict about these things and thought it most improper. People do gossip. At least let me know your subject. If you wish to make me a proposal of marriage you will need to speak to mother first.'

Mr Hope looked understandably alarmed, and for a few moments was unable to make a coherent reply. 'But, I am sure that is not the purpose of your visit,' Mina continued. 'Let me reassure you that Rose is the soul of discretion and will not discuss your business.' Rose favoured Mr Hope with an unsmiling glance, which he did not appear to find encouraging.

At length he sighed and gave in. He drained the glass and set it down. 'Very well. I have just been advised of the date that Miss Eustace's trial begins; it is only four weeks from now. That might seem like a long time, but it is very little when one considers how much information is still to be gathered, and the number of witnesses to be found and statements assembled. Can you reassure me that you will be providing the signed document we discussed earlier? I was wondering if it would help you to make your decision if you were to pay a visit to Miss Eustace and have some conversation with her. I would be happy to arrange it.'

Mr Hope was a tall man, a broad man. He towered over Mina, he overshadowed her like a leviathan come up from the deep, while she, a tiny frail sprat had only moments to see her doom before she was swallowed.

Mina faced him boldly. He was no charging elephant, but he was just as dangerous. 'I have no intention of seeing Miss Eustace again until she appears in the dock at the Lewes assizes. Neither can I presently see my way to providing you with the statement you require. In fact, I am unable to discuss this matter with you at all. I have been ordered by my solicitor to do no such thing, except in his presence. It follows, of course, that anything we say here without him as a witness has no legal force.'

'I don't understand,' said Hope, with a grim expression.

Mina smiled, a sweet innocent smile. 'Neither do I. The law is such a curious thing, is it not? But I am told that that is the case. What I suggest to you, Mr Hope, is that you make an appointment to see my solicitor and then we may conduct this conversation properly in his presence.'

'Who is your solicitor?'

'Mr Phipps.'

'Of Phipps, Laidlaw and Phipps? Which one is he?'

'Neither, he is Mr Ronald Phipps.'

Hope uttered a groan of despair. 'He is a bad choice. I am sorry to hear it.'

'In the meantime, I suggest you peruse the most recent edition of the *Gazette*, which has some interesting information regarding the authors of *An Encounter*. If you continue to support their cause I can hardly support you.'

He gave a scornful grunt. 'I have seen the article. It was almost to be expected. The newspapers are unfailingly inimical to the world of the spirit. They cannot see the great truth — they only know how to deride it so they may sell more copies to the ignorant and the bigoted. It may interest you to know that the Misses Bland are even now in Brighton; in fact, I have already had a meeting with them. They have a perfect defence to the charge, and, in time, their extraordinary abilities will become apparent to the world.'

'A perfect defence? What can it be?'

It was his turn to smile, and it was not a pleasant sight. 'Oh, I couldn't possibly discuss that with you. It is a legal question.'

'I would very much like to meet these ladies.'

'So would many people, but for now they are reluctant to conduct any private interviews. It is my intention to introduce them gradually into society in small select gatherings, in which the people of Brighton can properly appreciate them. Their book is just a beginning. The Misses Bland are destined to achieve great fame. They will be celebrated all over the world. Jealous people who accuse them of dishonesty will find their efforts rebound upon them and do great harm.'

'Have you read the work which was copied?'

'I dispute the word "copied",' he said quickly.

'But what else could it be, if not copied?'

'That will be apparent in due course.' He offered no further clues, but Mina suddenly saw it all, including, chillingly, the reason why he had involved her and her family in the 'willing game'.

'I think our discussion must end there,' she said. 'Rose, please show Mr Hope out.'

'I can see all his plan,' Mina told Richard later. 'I cannot discuss it with mother, who would not listen in any case, and Enid is half in love with the man.'

'She is entirely in love with him,' said Richard. 'Her husband is a poor forgotten creature, and if he ever comes home she will stamp on him like a rat. But Mr Hope's plan?'

'The Misses Bland have been accused of plagiarism. They deny copying the original work, yet the similarities are too great to plead coincidence. I think they mean to say that they read it from the mind of the writer or something very like it, and wrote it down in all innocence thinking it was their own.'

'Will such a defence help them?'

'I doubt that a judge will be convinced. But what Mr Hope is trying to do now is create witnesses who will attest to their abilities. He wants to introduce the ladies into society where they will no doubt perform the "willing game" with great success in front of the best citizens of Brighton. These people will then all be called upon to add some weight to the claims. He has already tried to convince me, and mother and Enid. If the dispute comes to court and there are men of spiritualist persuasion there, the Misses Bland could be given the benefit of the doubt.'

'What about Mystic Stefan? What is his place in Mr Hope's schemes? I thought Hope was using him to bring you onto the side of the spiritualists, but if that is the case he has made a poor effort of it so far.'

'Mystic Stefan claims to be no more than a conjuror. But he is very skilled. Perhaps in return for Mr Hope's sponsorship he is willing to testify that what Miss Eustace and the Misses Bland do cannot be accounted for by stage trickery.'

It was a reasonable enough explanation, but Mina felt sure that there was something else staring her in the face, something important which she was just not seeing.

Chapter Twenty-Six

The public revelation of the plagiarism case and Mr Hope's visit gave Mina an ideal excuse to see Mr Phipps again. She was also anxious to know if he had discovered anything of value. Young Mr Phipps was with a client when she arrived, but he was willing to conclude his business quickly in order to see Mina and she did not have long to wait.

'Are you acting for the plaintiff?' she asked him, showing him the newspaper.

'Not personally; Mr Laidlaw is undertaking that, and I am not at liberty to divulge the identity of the author.'

'But can you tell me if what the newspapers say is correct?'

He paused. 'I do not know where they got their information, but they have done their work well.'

'Do you know who is acting for the defendants?'

'They have engaged a London man. One of the best.'

'And therefore the most expensive?'

'Indeed. No man of reputation would defend such a case unless he was very well paid.'

'I am not sure if the Misses Bland have revealed this, but I think I know what their defence will be. The sisters will claim to be mediums and say that they obtained the manuscript through the spirits, or by mind-reading, or some such device.'

'Surely not!' exclaimed Phipps derisively.

'Mr Hope visited me unexpectedly this morning. I made sure there was a witness to the conversation, but in any case refused to discuss Miss Eustace. He has been trying to convince me and my family that mind-reading is a fact. He would not tell me what the Misses Bland's defence will be, but if the two works are sufficiently similar, so as not to support a claim of coincidence, as the newspaper reports suggest, I think that it can hardly be anything else.'

'That will not be favourably received in court.'

'Mr Hope also told me that he intends to introduce the ladies to Brighton society. He must be trying to convert respectable citizens by having them observe the sisters reading minds, and thus create witnesses as to their abilities.'

'He might try. I understand your concern. He is a very influential and respected man, and money is no object to him. I suggest, however, that you can safely leave this question in our hands. I will pass all your observations to Mr Laidlaw.'

Mina acquiesced. 'During my conversation with Mr Hope he actually suggested that I visit Miss Eustace in prison.'

Mr Phipps looked startled. 'I sincerely hope you did not agree!'

'I did not, and told him that if he wishes to discuss her forthcoming trial with me, he should do so in your presence. I expect you may be hearing from him soon.'

Mr Phipps winced, indicating how little he was looking forward to this.

'I fear that the case against her will rest solely on what passed at her private sittings with Miss Whinstone. Can she not be tried for fraudulent mediumship? There is abundant evidence of that.'

'There is no law specifically against it, unless one wishes to charge her with pretending to summon spirits under the Witchcraft Act of 1735.'

'And the penalty?' asked Mina hopefully.

'Burning is no longer an option. In fact, such cases rarely end in a custodial sentence.'

'I can see why the more serious charge was preferred,' said Mina, imagining Miss Eustace tied to a ducking stool. She made another note in her pocketbook. 'But she might well escape if Mr Hope has his way.'

Mr Phipps, more than usually glum, could only agree. 'Does the man have no weaknesses?'

'None that I have been able to discover. There is his fanatical devotion to spiritualism, which, since it is apparently well-meaning, is tolerated, and attracts many adherents.'

'I cannot believe he is such a paragon. All men have secrets, and whatever Mr Hope's may be, I will find it out.'

Mina was aware of one of Mr Hope's secrets, but the last thing she wanted was for any indiscretions involving her sister to be exposed to the ruinous air of publicity. From Mr Phipps' comments she deduced that he had been trying to find some way of arming himself against Mr Hope. For all she knew he was having him followed by detectives. She hoped that her warning conversation with Enid had proved sufficient to ensure that no further assignations took place.

Next morning, Mina, Enid and Louisa were discussing Mr Hope's forthcoming talk on the subject of spiritualism, which was due to take place in three days. Enid demanded that they all go, and said that she could hardly wait to hear what Mr Hope would say while Mina, more reserved in her anticipation, thought she ought to go as she might learn something of interest. Louisa, however, was adamant that she did not wish to be seen at such an event, and declared that poor Mr Hope was a very misguided man and it was a pity he did not have a sensible wife who could explain things to him properly.

'Mr Hope says that everyone should go as he has an important message we must all hear,' said Enid. 'He says people who won't listen to him have closed their minds to the truth. Even Mina is going, and Mina is only just beginning to believe.'

'Is that true?' queried Louisa.

'I neither believe nor disbelieve,' said Mina. 'All I can say is that I do not believe in anything I have seen so far. I very much doubt that being exhorted by Mr Hope will change that position.'

'Well at least you are going to hear him,' said Enid, sulkily.

Mina did not say so but she rather wished that Mr Hope might prove to be his own worst enemy, and, carried away by his great enthusiasm, make claims that would invite ridicule and so weaken his influence. If so, she would like to be there to witness it.

The conversation was interrupted by the delivery of a note from Mrs Peasgood, announcing that she wished to call. Her handwriting was not as elegant as usual, suggesting unusual haste in the composition, and there was hardly a decent gap of time between the arrival of the card and its sender. Rose showed Mrs Peasgood into the parlour and it was obvious that the visitor was very upset. There was a moment of hesitation as she saw all three women there together.

'Why, what can have brought you here so urgently?' said Louisa. 'I do hope it is not bad news. Do you wish to speak to me alone?'

Mrs Peasgood dabbed her temples with a cologned handkerchief and shook her head. Louisa gestured her to a seat, and told Rose to pour a glass of mineral water and then leave.

Once refreshed, Mrs Peasgood began to speak.

'I know that Mr Hope is a very important man, and he has such a charming way with him, so he always gets what he wants, but I am afraid that this time he has gone too far. He has just paid me a visit asking if he can hold a drawing room at my house and introduce the Misses Bland to all my friends.' She pressed the cool glass to her forehead. 'Is it true that he is a Viscount?' she asked, faintly.

Louisa and Enid looked at each other and it was left to Mina to say, 'He is, but he does not make a great show of it.'

Mrs Peasgood uttered a sigh that almost became a groan. 'That makes things so much harder! I would like to oblige him in any reasonable request, but I do not want to have the authors of that disgusting book in my home.'

'But you were at his lecture,' protested Enid. 'Surely you must remember — Mr Hope assured us that the authors composed it in all innocence, and cannot be blamed for how others might interpret it.'

'They did not compose it all!' snapped Mrs Peasgood. 'Have you seen the *Gazette?*'

'We have,' said Louisa, 'and it does appear that Mr Hope has been misled.'

'Well *I* don't believe it,' said Enid stubbornly. 'It is a well-known fact that not everything in the newspapers is true. Sometimes they just make it all up.'

'In this case,' said Mina, 'I am inclined to believe the *Gazette*. Such a serious action would never have been taken without some proof. There must be an earlier publication which the Misses Bland copied.'

'Well, even if they did, it wasn't deliberate,' argued Enid. 'You'll see; there will never be a court case and they won't have to pay a penny piece.'

'I don't see how that could be at all,' objected Mrs Peasgood. 'And even if they simply forgot that they had read the other book, the one they have shamelessly stolen — one which I understand was wholly above reproach, to which they have added their own offensive insinuations — they have still committed plagiarism and will have to pay the price!'

'But they did not read it and never have!' exclaimed Enid.

Mrs Peasgood stared at her suspiciously. 'How do you know that? You seem to be unusually well-informed.'

Enid blushed. 'Mr Hope told me. I chanced to meet him in the street when I was out walking with Anderson and the twins, and we conversed on the matter. I mentioned the *Gazette* article and he said to take no notice of it as the accusation would be shown to be all lies.'

'But how could they have copied a book they have never read?' asked Mina.

'Because it came to them in a dream. They have always shared their dreams and one night they found they had both dreamt the same thing, so they wrote it down. Dreams are very important things and we should always pay attention to them.'

Louisa looked misty eyed. 'I often dream of Henry as if he were still alive,' she sighed. 'He was a dear man.'

'I can well understand that you would dream of father,' said Mina, soothingly. 'I dream of him, too, and the wonderful conversations we used to have. But I do not see how anyone could dream of the words of another person's book.'

'Perhaps the person who wrote it dreamed about it?' suggested Enid.

'That is not impossible,' Mina agreed, 'but can one person's dreams enter the head of another?'

'I trust they cannot,' said Louisa, looking alarmed.

'Did Mr Hope, in your fascinating conversation with him, elaborate on how it occurred?' Mina enquired of Enid.

'Not exactly, and I am sure it is a very strange matter, which I would not be able to understand. But I suppose the Misses Bland have special brains, which allow it to happen. You must know about it, Mina, you divined where mother hid her brooch just from her thoughts.'

'I guessed where it was, and explained afterwards exactly how I did so. I can assure you I cannot read minds, whatever Mr Hope might like to imply.'

'Well, he says you can, only you do not like to admit it.'

357

'Mr Hope places a great deal of reliance on what was no more than a simple parlour game,' Mina explained to Mrs Peasgood.

'But you only think that because your mind is closed to the truth!' said Enid accusingly.

'I think,' said Louisa, 'that Mina may have a better appreciation of the truth than you do. No arguments, please.'

Enid frowned hard.

'The fact remains,' went on Mrs Peasgood, 'that nothing will persuade me to have those women in my house, and neither will I enter any house they may be visiting. I have so informed Mr Hope. Anyone with the slightest pretensions to respectability will, I am sure, feel the same and do the same. I believe I make my meaning clear?'

'Abundantly,' said Louisa.

'All of my dear friends are bound to agree with me. Which reminds me, I will be holding a musical and poetry evening a week next Wednesday. I shall very shortly be distributing invitations.'

With that singular threat, Mrs Peasgood departed.

'What a perfectly horrid person that Mrs Peasgood is,' said Enid. 'She thinks herself so grand that she can order other people who they might invite into their homes, and where they can visit.'

'I regret to say that she does hold some power in Brighton society,' said Louisa, 'if only because she has a drawing room ideally suited for entertainment and chooses to use it so. But she has had a great horror of anything that might be deemed suspect ever since she allowed that dreadful Miss Foxton to perform there. I am very pleased that I did not attend that event. I am told that she produced an apparition that was quite naked. Fortunately for the morals of the town, the woman has left Brighton. But our way is clear, I am afraid. If Mr Hope wishes to bring the Misses Bland here, they cannot come.'

It crossed Mina's mind that Mr Hope was not above using a subterfuge, and introducing the sisters under another name. She further realised, although she did not say it, that she had the advantage of almost everyone in Brighton since from her correspondence with Mr Greville she knew something of the appearance and character of the sisters. More importantly, no one else, least of all Mr Hope, knew that she had this information.

Chapter Twenty-Seven

Later that day, at a conference held by Dr Hamid's cosy fireside where Anna was wielding a toasting fork, he told Mina that Mr Hope had called on him once again. 'It is rather like being haunted, only by a living man. I am sure there are ghosts that give far less trouble.'

'He keeps trying to charm me with flattery,' said Anna, 'he thinks he can charm all ladies.' Her expression showed that Mr Hope's efforts had been met with icy distaste. She stabbed a crumpet with more than the usual force.

'Perhaps you could have him exorcised?' Mina suggested with a smile.

'I wish I could, but I am not sure how Reverend Godden would take such a request,' said Dr Hamid. 'It is still a matter of surprise to him that we attend church.' He glanced fondly at a portrait of his parents, the Bengali father and Scottish mother who had raised their children in the Christian faith.

'I assume that Mr Hope is still trying to obtain a statement from you?'

'He is, but at your suggestion I am using the controversy over the Misses Bland to put him off. Of course, no sooner had I mentioned them then Mr Hope, who is quite shameless in his espousal of every halfway plausible charlatan, asked if I would host a small gathering to introduce the Misses Bland to my friends. That, I refused outright. I felt quite safe in doing so, citing the alleged indecency of the book and the accusations of plagiarism, and pointing out that a doctor has to be above reproach. I think no more will be said on that subject. Is it true that they are already in Brighton?'

'It is, and under Mr Hope's protection. But I have some information about them, which Mr Hope does not know I have. I will tell you this in the strictest confidence as I would not want anyone outside this room to know it, but you may need it for your own protection in case he tries to introduce you to them by some subterfuge. I have discovered that one of the ladies in question suffers from a defect in her countenance, such that she will only appear in public if she is heavily veiled. I do not think it is simple modesty or a veil for protection against chills. There is some compelling reason why she does not wish her face to be seen.'

To her surprise Dr Hamid and Anna looked very uncomfortable at this news and glanced sharply at each other.

Mina understood at once. 'Has this lady been to the baths for treatment?'

Anna hesitated, then nodded. 'She has, although she did not use the name Bland, and I did not know it was she. I cannot discuss with you the nature of the medical condition or the treatment she received.'

'I would not embarrass you by asking,' said Mina. 'I would very much like to speak to her. Will she return, do you think?'

'It is very possible that she may do so since she felt some benefit from the treatment.'

'Then I may well chance to see her here. Will you be attending Mr Hope's talk on Monday?'

'We will not,' said Anna, before her brother could speak. 'Given the subject matter it would be very unwise.' Dr Hamid nodded agreement.

'My sister is intent on going and I will accompany her,' said Mina. 'I will let you know if I learn anything of note.'

The audience at the Town Hall for Mr Hope's address on spiritualism was not only far smaller than had assembled for the lecture on Africa, but was differently composed. Many of the worthies of Brighton and their wives who had previously crowded to see the great man were notable by their absence. Louisa had, despite Enid's entreaties, remained firm in her resolve not to attend, but had asked Mina to let her know if the man showed any signs of coming to his senses. She, Miss Whinstone and Mrs Bettinson were going to a recital at the Dome. There was a scattering of young men present, some of whom were probably from the newspapers, while others looked as though they were happy to attend any kind of entertainment that did not include the warblings of a mature soprano. The bulk of the audience was made up of ladies of all ages and classes, many of them veiled, some of them in the company of embarrassed-looking husbands. By some dexterous manipulation, there was a goodly gathering of invalids in bathchairs, or accompanied by medical attendants. Mr Ronald Phipps was there, as was another gentleman with whom he exchanged some words, and who Mina felt sure must be the senior partner interesting himself in the Bland case, Mr Laidlaw. He was accompanied by a plumply pretty lady who, she guessed, was Mrs Laidlaw.

Mina looked about to see if there was any lady in the audience with a more than usually heavy veil, but there was not. Enid was glowing, as if her unspoken happiness was enough to make her rise up and float above the company like an apparition. Even if her meetings with the commanding Mr Hope had been wholly innocent, a reputation could be destroyed in a few whispered words, and more than ever Mina wished there was some way she could remove his influence from their lives.

Hope took the platform and acknowledged the applause, his eyes moving carefully over the audience, nodding and smiling at those he recognised. Always an impressive looking man there was something especially compelling about him that night. His hair, dark with flecks of grey, was shaped like wings to frame a countenance that promised nobility, courage and strength. Everything about him inspired confidence, the very shape of his head implied the possession of a powerful mind, and told the audience, even before he spoke, that here was a man to be listened to, trusted and followed.

'My dear friends,' he began. 'I am happy to see so many of you here tonight. We live in an extraordinary world where almost daily great discoveries are being made which will benefit mankind, and our understanding of the mysteries that surround us is growing faster than we can appreciate. We are emerging from the darkness of ignorance and superstition into a great and glorious light. We have machines that do the work of men, devices that capture light to create pictures, cures for disease. If a hundred years ago you had predicted that we might speak to men on other continents by means of a cable, you would have been derided as a fool, yet now the electrical telegraph beneath the Atlantic Ocean is a fact. What a wealth of knowledge we have, and who knows what marvels the future might bring. But science is only one kind of progress. How empty we would be without spiritual awakening. The good news for you is that we are at this time in a period of intense spiritual advance that has been unknown since the lifetime of Jesus Christ. And just as Christ was initially derided and rejected by all but a blessed few, so the spiritualists who are ushering in this new movement are being attacked and ridiculed, when we should be hanging on their every word. Sad to say those men of science who have pronounced on phenomena that have been proven again and again to be real, have with a few notable exceptions done so from a stance of blind scepticism in which they ignore all the evidence that does not suit them, and then assert that everything is a fraud. Truly, I pity them. The subject on which I wish to speak is too great to cover in one evening, so I will proceed to tell you very briefly something of the history of the movement and its principal exponents.'

Mr Hope then went on to describe the careers of those individuals who had ushered in the new age of spiritual enlightenment. Many of the names were known to Mina from her recent reading. Some of these men and women were undoubtedly sincere — visionaries whose value to mankind would only become apparent with time and who for the present were either viewed as prophets or delusional, depending on the preconceived notions of the listener. Hope reminded his audience of how the great prophets of the bible had been received in their lifetimes and contrasted this with the way that they were now revered. Other individuals he named as the current leaders of the movement were, however, table-tippers or producers of raps and clicks, who Mina felt were less worthy of consideration.

'There is a lady,' he went on, 'whose name I cannot mention, since there is a court case shortly to be determined.' There was a stir of discomfort in the audience, some raised eyebrows, and a few frowns. 'I see that some of you here are gentlemen of the press, if your busy pencils are anything to judge by, and you may well have been present at an event which took place in Brighton a few months ago, which I am certain will soon prove to have been a monstrous misunderstanding. Prepare yourselves in only a few weeks from now for some miraculous revelations. That is all I have to say at present on that subject.

'And now I come to the celebrated Misses Bland. I am sorry to say that many in this town have misjudged them on account of a circumstance that in my opinion only goes to prove their innocence. To the pure, all things are pure and it was beyond their imagination that anything they wrote could be seen in an indelicate light. I appeal to you on their behalf to receive them into your homes at small select gatherings and then you may make your own informed judgment.' Mina glanced about her but saw little enthusiasm for this proposal amongst any but the newspapermen.

He paused. 'Ladies and gentlemen. Let us consider what the message is I am bringing to you. What is my name — my name is Hope and hope is what I bring. Over the years our religious leaders have given us little insight into the world of the spirit. For true knowledge and certainty we must turn to men and women of advanced intelligence, who have been graced with the rare ability to see the wonders that lie in store for us.

'In your earthly lives you may have worked diligently, been virtuous, treated others with consideration, honoured your families, and yet you have suffered reverses which were wholly undeserved, and failed to find the love, the respect and the advancement that are surely due to you. Why this is so, I cannot say; it may be evil influences or unkind chance. What I can tell you is that in the spirit world, all injustices will be mended.'

Mr Hope now had the whole attention of his audience, who were listening to him with increasing interest. 'Those who pass from this earthly life aged, infirm of body, suffering the ravages of disease, will in the world of the spirit be whole again — young, strong, comely, in the perfection of health. They will live in fine houses, reunited with their loved ones who have gone before. Married couples who have not lived harmoniously on earth will be permitted to part and they will then be able to make new spiritual unions, a form of marriage that will lead to eternal happiness. Those who have not met with earthly success will find all that they need to develop their minds and gratify their highest senses, so they will achieve recognition. Children who have passed before their parents will be carefully nurtured until they are reunited with their mothers. But what of the wicked, I hear you ask? Will they not be cast into damnation? No, they will be met with compassion, not burning fire, and will be guided to the ways of righteousness, so, having done their penance, and found a true path, they too will be admitted to the world of blessed spirits. Is this not wonderful?'

All around her Mina saw the enthralled expressions of those who had been offered a miracle, and were eased of man's oldest fear — death. Many of those present were elderly, and several had the grey, shrunken countenances of declining health. There were couples whose postures of formality told of marriages endured but not enjoyed, and humbly garbed young men who had been disappointed in their ambitions. In the wonderful world of the spirit, all wrongs would be righted. And then there was Mina herself, bowed but not broken, cheated of the most fundamental desires of womankind, every day a battle against strain and frustration. She did not know if this world described by the great seers was real or not, but she had no wish to hurry towards her death to find out.

On the way home Enid's eyes were bright with happiness, and Mina did not care to enquire why. Here was proof, if Enid had ever needed it, that her union with Mr Inskip was not a blessed one, but a temporary affair, and that her beloved in eternity would be another. 'I expect you will be a disciple of Mr Hope now!' said Enid. 'He is such a clever man; it quite makes my head spin when he speaks.'

'Mine also,' said Mina.

'Oh, please do say you will sign a paper for him! It is such a small thing to do.'

Mina had no wish to argue with her sister. 'It is a serious matter and I have asked the advice of my solicitor. I can do nothing until I hear from him further.'

'Not that dreadful Mr Phipps. I have heard some very unfortunate things about him. I would not go to him on any matter!'

'If Mr Phipps is being slandered then he really ought to know what is being said and who is saying it. Can you enlighten me?'

Even Enid had the sense to say no more.

Chapter Twenty-Eight

Next morning, as Enid excitedly regaled her family across the breakfast table with the wonders revealed by Mr Hope, a set of beautifully printed invitations arrived, addressed to Louisa. 'They are for all the family,' she said, waving a hand at Enid to stop her chattering, 'for an exhibition at the Royal Pavilion. The Mystic Stefan invites us to a demonstration of conjuring, promising never-before-seen mysteries. All ladies will receive a present.'

'Which room has been hired?' asked Richard.

'The banqueting room. He must be expecting a large crowd.'

Richard looked unusually mournful at this prospect, and took the first opportunity of speaking to Mina alone in her room, flinging himself down on her bed in an altogether casual fashion which he would never have displayed before their mother, while Mina sat at her desk with her little wedge of a cushion supporting her hip.

'Dare I ask why you are so despondent?' asked Mina.

'Well, here is Mr Hope taking the banqueting room which may hold hundreds, and I find even the smaller suites are far beyond my means. Do you know, the Pavilion committee actually wants money in advance! That is most unfair since we have not yet performed the play or sold any tickets. I asked them if they could wait for their money, but they absolutely refused. Is that how people run an enterprise nowadays?'

'Surely that should not pose any difficulty to you as you have just borrowed some money from mother.'

'Yes, but I have had expenses.'

This theme was all too familiar to Mina. 'Please don't tell me you have already spent it!'

'I couldn't help it, there was just one thing after another. You know how it is.' He sat up. 'Mina — I don't suppose —'

'No, Richard, this time I must put my foot down. I have lent you money before, paid your bills, and seen you fritter it all away and waste opportunities. Where is the play? Can I see it? Is it written yet?'

'Not yet, but it will be.'

'Good. When you have it complete, show it to me, and if I think it worthy to be performed and not likely to bring shame and ruin to our family, I will reconsider, but not until then.'

Richard gazed on her with his most imploring look, but she remained adamant. He rested his chin in his hands gloomily. 'Also the Pavilion committee has told me it needs to be submitted to the Lord Chamberlain for his approval. Something about preserving good manners, decorum, and the public peace. What has any of that to do with a play?'

'Well, at least you now know what is expected. If that is all you have to say, I think both of us have some writing to do.'

'Can't I sit here and write?'

'No, because you would be forever interrupting me and then neither of us would finish anything.'

He looked so downhearted that she took pity on him and, getting down from her chair, went to his side and hugged him warmly. 'Richard, I love you dearly, but my best advice for you is to forget all about this play, go back to London, take up Edward's offer and try to make a success of it.' It was not what he wanted to hear.

Once Richard had left her Mina tried to settle to her writing. The story involved a young girl visiting a museum and being enthralled by oriental figures in magnificent costumes, which came alive and acted out a drama of the past. Later the girl discovered that what she had seen solved an ancient mystery of a missing princess. Mina managed to construct the framework of the story but so preoccupied was she with Mr Hope's talk and its effect on the listeners that the detail eluded her, and finally after a struggle, she laid aside her pen. More than anything else she was struck by the ease with which he had swayed his audience, and she could only feel helpless at the thought. She might resist him, and so would Dr Hamid, but that was not enough. She needed more facts, more ammunition.

Some months ago, when Mina had been gathering the information which had resulted in Miss Eustace and her coterie finding themselves behind bars, she had obtained through Mr Greville an advance copy of a report made following an enquiry carried out by the erudite men and women of the Dialectical Society into the claims made by devotees of spiritualism. Mina once again turned to its four hundred or so pages, hoping to find something she might use to oppose Mr Hope.

Mina had first been alerted to the dangers of trust in mediums by the activities of a Mr D.D. Home. This Scottish-born American spiritualist had very nearly succeeded in defrauding a seventy-five-year-old widow, Mrs Lyon, of her entire fortune — some £30,000 — by persuading her that he had received messages from her late husband who wished him to have it. Fortunately, a court action had seen through his villainy, cancelled what he had intended to be irrevocable deeds, and obliged him to restore the lady's property. Extraordinarily to Mina's way of thinking, the egregious criminal had not been cast into prison as he richly deserved or even put on the first ship back to his adopted homeland, but remained free to perform his mediumistic tricks, and had even participated in the Dialectical

Society's enquiry. Mina had never met Mr D.D. Home, but often rehearsed exactly what she would say to him if she ever did.

The Society's report had ultimately been inconclusive, although some members of the committee had strongly suspected that the manifestations produced by the mediums they had witnessed were solely the result of trickery designed to deceive credulous onlookers, and said so. The Davenport brothers, famed American mediums who had made a triumphant tour of England, had been subjected to a close examination by one of the Society's members and been caught out in a blatant deception, disguising a prepared drawing to look like a blank sheet with the object of claiming when the picture was revealed later that it was the work of spirits. Their best known performances, however, were those in which they had been securely bound with ropes inside a large wooden cabinet, which they had had specially constructed for their purposes, and from which they were able to produce spirit sounds, wave spirit arms through apertures, and cause musical instruments to fly through the air. Nellie had explained to Mina that none of this was very amazing if one only assumed that, like the good conjurors they indubitably were, the brothers had some method of freeing their hands, and then retying themselves so they would appear to have been bound all along.

Inevitably, the Society's objections were vigorously opposed by champions of the spiritualists, including a Mr Samuel Guppy, a gentleman of advanced years and strong opinions. Mr Guppy's wife was a famed medium, who claimed to be endowed with more than the usual abilities. Her speciality was making all manner of produce appear on the séance table. She had conjured up a basket of fresh flowers and shrubs at a séance attended by a sceptic from the Society, who was sure that it had come from no further than the nearby sideboard, an easy enough deception to manage in darkness. Mrs Guppy naturally claimed that she had brought them from a distance, and she had assured her enthralled devotees that flowers could travel bodily through walls or window panes or shutters, just as easily as a bird flew through the air. Mina was reminded that at the séance conducted by poor Eliza Hamid, a little posy had appeared on the table, which had surely flown from no further distance than Mr Clee's pocket.

Mrs Guppy had more than one trick, since she had, it was reported, been seen by witnesses at séances actually rising into the air, lifted by some unseen agency that placed her on the table around which the guests were seated. Mina found this unimpressive as evidence of spirit activity, since she had already seen Richard produce exactly the same effect with Nellie using nothing more ghostly than a roll of opaque black fabric. Having said that, Nellie was no great weight and Mrs Guppy was reputed to be a lady of generous dimensions, which suggested that she required not one, but two confederates in the room.

To dispel any lingering doubts as to her close relationship with the spirits, Mrs Guppy, when holding subsequent séances, was happy to agree that the doors of the room should be locked and windows fastened. She then allowed herself to be searched by a lady, and when seated at the table her hands were securely held. Despite these precautions, the sitters were still greeted by cascades of fresh scented flowers.

Last July, however, several newspapers had reported an even more sensational achievement by the miraculous Mrs Guppy, and Mina, out of curiosity, had made a study of the various accounts, which had afforded her a great deal of amusement. A Mr Benjamin Coleman had launched the story by advising a journal called *The Spiritualist* that 'living human bodies may be transported from place to place' and that Mrs Guppy, although 'one of the largest and heaviest women of his acquaintance', had been carried a distance of three miles by some invisible agency 'in an instant of time' to be dropped with a heavy thump on a table around which clustered a number of people seated shoulder to shoulder in a dark séance. The doors of the room in which they sat were locked, the windows fastened, and, given the size of the lady in question Mina wondered why Mr Coleman had thought it necessary to add this, the fireplace was covered in. So unexpected was this journey to the lady that she arrived without bonnet, shawl or shoes, and holding a memorandum book in one hand and a pen, still with the ink wet, in the other. When Mrs Guppy, who appeared to have been in a state of trance, recovered from her ordeal, she said that she had been at her home three miles away writing up her household expenses in the company of a Miss Neyland, when she had suddenly lost consciousness and knew nothing more until she found herself at the centre of the circle.

Mrs Guppy returned home by more conventional means, accompanied by a party of interested gentlemen who questioned Miss Neyland. She confirmed that she had been in the company of Mrs Guppy, who was writing up her household accounts. Miss Neyland had been reading a newspaper, and when she looked up found that the lady had simply vanished. A search had confirmed that Mrs Guppy was not in the house. Miss Neyland naturally informed Mr Guppy of his wife's disappearance, but he seemed not to be troubled by this, and after consulting the spirits to satisfy himself that she was safe, went to have his dinner. This curious lack of concern was explained by the fact that he was not a stranger to such incidents, since a gentleman of his acquaintance, a Mr Hearne, had quite literally dropped in on him one evening by descending from the ceiling after being snatched up by the spirits while out taking a walk. Careful reading, however, told Mina that this event had only been witnessed by Mrs Guppy, who had uttered a loud scream, and when her husband came to see what the matter was, told him that their unexpected visitor had fallen from the ceiling like a large black bundle.

Mr Coleman advised his readers of other wonders, too. The most extraordinary items would arrive on the table at séances conducted by Mrs Guppy as soon as asked for — seawater, snow and ice, even lobsters. The readers of *The Spiritualist* were presumably delighted by these tricks, although other newspapers took a heavily satirical tone, suggesting that if spirit transport of individuals was possible, as suggested, then this would do away with the necessity for railways, the only problem remaining to be resolved being that of arriving in the place one wanted to go. There was a danger that the traveller might end up somewhere quite different, such as an income tax office, or the Court of Chancery.

Following a certain amount of press ridicule, Mr Guppy issued a bold challenge, wagering his wife's diamonds against the Crown Jewels. His wife, he offered, after an examination strict enough to satisfy a jury of matrons, would go either to 'the inmost recesses of the Bank of England' or 'the deepest dungeon of the Tower' and there, behind locked and guarded doors, she would bring to her by spiritualistic means, something she did not take in with her. This item might only be flowers or fruit, but it might also be a dog or cat, or even a lion or tiger or elephant from the Zoological gardens. Mr Guppy asserted that just as an engineer could send a ball through an iron plate leaving a hole where it passed, so spirit power could convey a living organism, whether plant or animal, though iron doors and stone walls, without leaving a mark of its passage.

The press was quick to observe that a wager against the Crown Jewels would never be accepted, and thus Mr Guppy could feel perfectly safe that his suggestion would never be taken up. A more moderate stake, however, hinted the newspapers, would surely be possible, and Mr Guppy's response was awaited with interest. One journal, with tongue very firmly in cheek suggested that Mrs Guppy be taken to the 'inmost recesses' of the nearest lunatic asylum. If Mr Guppy was also there to participate in his wife's joys then it might, it was suggested, do him a great deal of good.

Mina had been unsurprised to discover that Mr Hearne, who had made such a dramatic and unexpected visit to the Guppys, was himself a medium, but it further transpired that both he and another medium of their acquaintance had been at the séance table when Mrs Guppy made her unexpected appearance, and that Miss Neyland was herself being developed as a medium. All of Mrs Guppy's mysteries, which would have been hard for her to achieve alone, would have been simplicity itself with a few confederates and a willing audience.

That, of course, was the difficulty concerning Mr Hope, Mina realised. He did not simply believe, he *needed* to believe. If a medium was comprehensively proven to be a fraud he could easily persuade himself that they had resorted to fakery on just the one occasion to please their needy audience, but were otherwise genuine. If a medium confessed to fraud then Hope would put it down to illness, or alcohol, or insanity, or the harsh pressure and even bribery of those dreadful bigoted unbelievers, and he would trumpet his joy when the confession was retracted. In the remote likelihood that it was possible to prove that a medium was and had always been a fake, then there were numerous others he would be certain were genuine. Mr Hope believed in Miss Eustace, and since he was a man used to getting his own way, it seemed that the more Mina refused to approve her, the more his determination to exonerate the fraudster hardened.

Chapter Twenty-Nine

The banqueting room of the Pavilion, the one with the great chandelier that had so alarmed William IV's consort, Queen Adelaide, was a spacious apartment, much used for public events such as balls and concerts. There was easily room enough for rows of seating to accommodate a substantial crowd. Mina suspected that young Mr Phipps would not be one of the recipients of Mr Hope's free tickets and since she very much wanted him to be there, she had made sure that Phipps, Laidlaw and Phipps knew about the event, as tickets would be bound to be available for paying patrons. While Mr Hope might fail to extend his favour to Mr Phipps, he was, thought Mina, unlikely to cause a disturbance by refusing him admission at the door, and so it proved. Mr Phipps, in any case, arrived in the company of his elderly aunt, who leaned heavily on his arm and required his constant attention. Any intolerance of his presence would therefore have been a gross solecism. The gentleman who Mina had previously surmised was Mr Laidlaw was also present with his lady wife, and the two solicitors sat side by side. They glanced at each other once, and thereafter remained carefully silent.

Mina had thought of a new plan but it was one she could not carry out herself, and required the assistance of Richard. He had promised to attend but when the carriage came to take her family to the Pavilion, he was not at home, so they were obliged to go without him, Louisa commenting that her son must have been delayed by business. On their arrival, Mina saw that Nellie too had chosen not to join the assembly, and she had little doubt that the two were together. She hoped against hope that Nellie was simply helping her brother write his play.

Neither Mrs Peasgood nor Mrs Mowbray were there, but Mina saw other Brightonian notables, including the Mayor and one of the aldermen who had attended the lecture on Africa, and they introduced Mr Hope to three couples whom she did not recognise but ascertained from what she overheard that they were members of the Pavilion committee and their wives. Louisa and Enid, seeing an opportunity, decided to lurk about that distinguished group in the hope of obtaining an introduction. When Mina pleaded weariness and took a seat they did not dissuade her. Mina's object was to place herself where she might best observe the audience, and she would not be able to do this on the front row where her mother and sister intended to be.

Dr Hamid arrived and greeted Mina, saying that Anna was busy with her patients, but that in any case she did not find such entertainments to her taste. For his part, he did not either, but felt he should be there if only to discover what Mr Hope was up to.

'I agree,' said Mina, 'and I am very glad to see you here as there is something I would like you to do for me.'

'Ah,' said Dr Hamid, looking apprehensive.

'Would you be able to follow Mystic Stefan after the performance and discover where he is lodging? There is something about him I find very strange and I would like to learn as much about him as I can. You must be sure not to be seen.'

He glanced quickly about the room. 'Is your brother not on hand to undertake your private detective work?'

'No, he has other calls on his time.'

Dr Hamid gave her a sceptical look, as well he might. 'Do you think this is suitable behaviour for a medical practitioner? What would happen if my quarry realised I was following him and stopped to ask me my business?'

'I am confident that you will be able to think of some excuse,' said Mina. 'I would do it myself only I cannot go quickly enough to be sure of getting a cab in good time.'

'Let me consider it,' he said, but with a lack of enthusiasm that suggested that even she would not be able to persuade him.

The end wall of the room had been prepared as a stage for the performance. Screens had been brought in to create a three-sided enclosed space and they were draped with dense, dark fabric, which fell into sufficiently voluminous folds that there could well have been room for something, or someone, to be concealed behind them. The demonstration promised to be more extensive than the one in Mrs Peasgood's parlour, since a long side table was very generously loaded with the paraphernalia of a magician. At the centre back more screens had been arranged to form a curtained recess in which there stood a square table, and there was a smaller table at the front. Mina looked about her, hoping to ascertain if the Misses Bland were there, but while there were some ladies she did not recognise, none of them was heavily veiled.

When the expectant audience was settled Mr Hope addressed the company and introduced Mystic Stefan, who stepped out lightly from behind the screens and bowed. He was clad as before in full evening dress, with the addition of a short dark cloak. He performed an elegant pirouette, his cloak lifting gently to swirl about him, then, as he faced the audience once more, it was seen that in each hand he held a small glass bowl in which goldfish swam. There were gasps and applause, which he acknowledged with a smile.

The bowls were placed on the side table then he took a tray with a dark bottle, a jug of water, and six glasses, and brought it to the front. With grace in every elaborate gesture, he poured water from the jug into the bottle, then poured it back again. Upending the bottle, he shook it to show that it was empty before replacing it on the tray. He now produced as if from nowhere a magic wand and waved it over the bottle. Taking up the supposedly empty bottle once more he used it to fill the glasses, but even more miraculously, the colour of the liquid in each was different, so that one appeared to be white wine, another red, and the next four pale sherry, milk, whisky and crème de menthe. As if this was not enough he then gave the bottle several smart taps with the wand, which broke it in half, and removed the base, from which he pulled a dry white handkerchief.

The next trick required three identical goblets. Into one he poured water, the next he filled with sweets, and the third was left empty. The goblets were then covered with a large scarlet silk handkerchief. After a tap with the wand the handkerchief was whisked away to show that the water was now in the formerly empty goblet and the sweets too had changed places. Once again the goblets were covered and after another tap with the wand the contents had rearranged themselves.

The amazing Stefan now brought forward a carved box of oriental design from which, after demonstrating that it was empty, he drew a host of items which it could never have contained, little parcels of sweetmeats which an attendant distributed to the ladies, coloured balls, streamers, and a whole host of paper lanterns.

His next demonstration required a Japanese fan, with which he had all the dexterity of a juggler, opening and closing it with a deft flick of the wrist, throwing it up so it rotated in the air, and catching it one-handed. He brought a porcelain bowl, and showed that it was filled with nothing more than multi-coloured pieces of torn tissue paper. With the bowl in one hand and the fan in the other he began to fan the papers. By rights they should have been scattered about the room in disarray, but instead they rose together in a cloud, and the fluttering of the delicate papers made them resemble a swarm of exotic butterflies. Stefan now moved about the stage, fanning gently as he went, and he was followed by the paper butterflies, which first rose, high, then sank low. Sometimes the delicate shreds were only a little apart from each other, sometimes the distance was as much as two feet, but all throughout they formed a moving garland about his head. The effect could not fail to both mystify and enchant the audience who uttered little sighs of appreciation. Mina noticed that Mr Hope was leaning forward and paying special attention to this trick, which was the forte of his friend Dr Lynn. Finally the butterflies gathered themselves into a small cluster, and subsided back neatly into their pretty bowl.

Stefan next brought forward a large shallow silver dish, and cast into it some powders causing a brief flash of fire from which a smoky haze arose. Mr Hope rose to his feet and addressed the audience. 'In this next demonstration, Mystic Stefan requests that members of the audience provide items to be cast into the bowl. If they do so, they will see an image of the person or place or object they are thinking of. Be assured that nothing will come to any harm and all your property will be returned to you safely.' To avoid the usual hesitation in such matters, Mr Hope moved amongst the audience with his most ingratiating smile and collected the items. Many of the onlookers, including Enid, were too embarrassed to have their secret thoughts exposed, and Mr Hope understood this and did not press the unwilling. Neither Mina nor Dr Hamid participated, and Mr Hope moved so quickly past Mr Phipps and his party that they could not have taken part even if they had wanted to.

Louisa provided a lace handkerchief and it was dropped into the bowl, whereupon a cloud of white smoke was seen to arise, and in it appeared the face of a man, which had some passing resemblance to Henry Scarletti. Louisa pressed her fingers to her eyes and Enid was obliged to lend her mother her own handkerchief. One of the ladies supplied a locket, and was shown a face she recognised as her late grandfather. One by one, items were dropped into the bowl, which obligingly provided whatever was expected, a child, a church, a bible, a ring. At last it was Mr Hope's turn, and his contribution was the African trade bead he had received at Mystic Stefan's previous demonstration. The image that arose peering through a greenish mist was recognisably that of Dr Livingstone.

There was no suggestion that the demonstration was anything more than a conjuring trick or that the images were other than pictures, especially since the one of Dr Livingstone was a copy of the well-known portrait Mina had already seen in the window of Mr Smith's bookshop. It was no great surprise to anyone that Mr Hope might be thinking of the man who was his friend and whom he desperately wanted to rescue. Nevertheless, Hope was undoubtedly moved by the occurrence. If Mystic Stefan intended to strengthen his reputation with his promoter then, thought Mina, he was surely succeeding.

Stefan then brought a new item from the side table, a square board bearing an article more than a foot in height, mysteriously draped in black cloth. This he placed on the small table in the curtained recess at the back. On carefully removing the cloth a very strange-looking object was revealed, a white arm and hand, very delicate like that of a lady, rising up out of a shallow plinth, and resembling a model made of wax. Stefan made some elaborate passes with the wand, and the arm began to move, swaying gracefully, the fingers opening and closing, undulating as if stroking the keys of a piano.

There were little gasps from around the room, and a few people even leaned forward for a closer look, as if unable to believe their eyes. Mina, supposing the arm to be a contrivance like the Wondrous Ajeeb or the chess-playing Turk of old, decided to look about the room to see the reactions of those around her. Stefan, of course, was smiling enigmatically from behind his luxuriant beard, and most other persons were staring fixedly at the display, looking amazed or even frightened, but there was one lady in the room who wore the same superior smile as Stefan. She was not one of the Pavilion committee party, and Mina could not recall ever having seen her before. There was nothing unusual about the lady or her dress, and she was aged about thirty, but she had a sharp face and a knowing expression.

Stefan, after making some more passes over the disembodied hand, brought a pen, which, after dipping it in ink, he placed in the pale fingers. He next brought a sheet of paper, which he first showed was blank on both sides, and laid it on the table within reach of the pen. As the enthralled onlookers watched, the hand began to write, and so quiet was the room, with all breaths held, that the sound of the scratching nib was clearly heard.

After a few moments the hand lifted, and Stefan picked up the paper and showed it to the audience. The words were unclear, but words there were, and he offered the paper to Mr Hope, who seemed no less astonished than anyone else. Hope darted forward out of his seat and took up the paper, then read aloud: 'Blessings and good fortune'!

There was a relieved murmur, as if the message could have been motivated by anything other than pious goodwill. Such openly or quasi-religious messages were, Mina knew, an essential feature of the work of mediums, used to convince doubters of the godliness and purity of their work. She was reminded of the words of Reverend Vaughan, Vicar of Christchurch in Montpelier Road, whose sermons often warned the unwary of false prophets, assuring his congregation that the Devil could cite scripture when it suited him. Not that Mystic Stefan was a fiend, but there was something about him she did not trust.

The hand was impatient to write more. Putting down the pen it tapped on the table, as if demanding another paper. Stefan smiled, produced what was required, and re-dipped the pen. The hand began to write again, but this time it moved very rapidly, speeding over the sheet. On and on it wrote, until at last it stopped, dropped the pen and seemed to droop with exhaustion.

Stefan lifted the paper and this time it was his turn to look astonished. He passed it to Mr Hope.

Hope, in an increasingly faltering voice, read aloud: 'Food gone, medicines stolen, companions dead, sustained by prayer, God have mercy on me, the sun burns my eyes, I am wounded and ill … D L.' Hope's hands trembled. 'What is this? Is it for me? Can it be — surely not —' His eyes suddenly blazed. 'It must write more! Make it write again!'

Stefan made a helpless gesture and then turned to indicate the white hand, which still drooped as if all its energy was spent. He took the black cloth and covered the hand, then picked up the tray and replaced it on the side table. Hope went to approach it but Stefan stood with palms out, preventing him and solemnly shook his head. Hope sighed and turned back to his seat with the paper in his hand, his face deeply pained.

Stefan came to the front of the stage area and made a respectful bow. The audience understood that this was the end of the performance and applauded. He then summoned an attendant who helped move his tables and equipment behind the black curtain, and finally made another bow and himself disappeared behind the drapery.

There was a hum of conversation in the room as the guests rose to leave, although Hope remained in his seat.

Dr Hamid looked grim. 'I will secure a cab at once,' he told Mina, and left hurriedly.

Chapter Thirty

Mina went to examine the paper in Mr Hope's hand, something he was more than willing for her to do. 'Can you doubt the spirits now?' he demanded. 'The poor dear good man! How he suffers!'

'You think this is a message from Dr Livingstone?' Mina asked.

'It can be none other! Who else would send me such a message! Imagine him, alone and ill, without succour, in the most terrible danger, probably dying!'

'May I see the first message?'

He thrust it at her distractedly and she was able to compare them. She did not say it, but saw that the handwriting on the second message was very much better than the first. Now that she thought about it, before the first message was written by the white hand, Stefan had shown both sides of the blank paper to the audience, but he had omitted to do so for the second one. While he had apparently dipped the pen in ink again, it was possible for him to have made the motion without actually wetting the pen. He might even have employed a second clean pen and provided a paper with the pre-written message, much like the trickery of the Davenport brothers. To the man who had made water transport itself between goblets, and produced a dry kerchief from a bottle of multi-coloured fluids all things were possible. How clever, also, thought Mina, to engage with the question of the fate of Dr Livingstone, a matter that was constantly in the newspapers and therefore known to everyone, and about which it was impossible for anyone to check the veracity of the message. All these objections, she thought, would make no difference to the fixed opinions of Arthur Wallace Hope.

Mina looked about her and saw again the sharp-faced lady with her secret smile, turning to leave.

'Oh, poor Mr Hope!' said Enid, almost elbowing Mina out of the way in her eagerness to comfort the stricken explorer. 'What a terrible thing! How you must suffer! And poor Dr Livingstone who is such a very saintly man. How brave he is! I promise to pray for him, I will pray very hard indeed!' Enid did not have a large bosom, but what there was of it heaved mightily.

'That is very much appreciated, Mrs Inskip,' said Hope gratefully. 'I too shall pray; indeed, I shall make an appeal to all the gentlemen of the church to include Dr Livingstone in their prayers this Sunday, to grant him the strength to go on until help can reach him.' He rose to his feet, looking unusually weary. 'Will you too include the good doctor in your prayers, Miss Scarletti?'

'Of course I will. I pray for all the afflicted and unfortunate in this world.'

Mina and her mother and sister returned home, Mina wondering whether there would be any result from Dr Hamid's expedition. Now that she gave it some thought, she could not help but feel guilty about asking him to do something so dangerous to his reputation. Without knowing how long his adventure might take she was obliged to wait impatiently for a note, which she felt sure would merely be a request for a visit. He was a cautious man and given the nature of his errand, nothing of any significance would be committed to paper. The following morning, after receiving the expected summons, Mina departed early for the baths, where she found Dr Hamid in his office.

She began by apologising to him for asking him to act in such an unprofessional manner, but he waved it aside. 'The request was yours, but the choice was mine, and after what I saw I knew that something had to be done. I know it is not the kind of thing I ought to be undertaking, but I appear to be acquiring new skills in that department, and I am confident that I was not seen. I went as far as I could by cab but the roads are so narrow in the centre of town I found it easier to abandon it and travel on foot. It was not the most salubrious area. However, I can now tell you that the Mystic Stefan is lodging in rooms above a public house in Trafalgar Street. At any rate he went in through the side entrance avoiding the saloon bar entirely. I did look inside and there are stairs leading up to the next floor. That was where I believe he went. He was carrying two large bags, which must have held the materials he used in the performance. I remained in the street for a short while, pretending to be a traveller who had lost his way, in case he went out again, but he did not. However —' He took a deep breath — 'while I was there I saw a closed cab stop at the end of the street and a lady stepped down and began to walk towards where I stood. She wore a veil, but it was not Miss Bland, nevertheless I recognised her from her garments as a lady we both know, and I had to hide round the corner like a footpad in case she saw me. It was not the most edifying experience and I am reluctant to do anything like it again. Then, to my amazement, she entered the building through the same door Mystic Stefan had used, and I saw her ascend the stairs. I decided it would be highly unwise to remain and see how long she stayed there in case I attracted attention or encountered anyone else who knew me, so I went home.'

'Who was the lady?' asked Mina.

'Mrs Mowbray.'

'Really!' Mina exclaimed.

'Of course, there is no means of knowing if she was actually there to see the man. But what her purpose might otherwise have been I really couldn't say. It is not a place a respectable single lady ought to go unaccompanied, even a lady of matronly aspect like Mrs Mowbray. Had it been a female of another sort — well — ' He let the implication hang.

377

'We could have drawn the obvious conclusion,' finished Mina. 'But I think we may absolve Mrs Mowbray of having an illicit liaison of the romantic kind with the Mystic Stefan.'

'And it is improbable that he is a relative if he is Hungarian and a stranger to England. Unless, of course, he is some distant connection she does not wish to acknowledge openly.'

'Well, I for one cannot believe he is Hungarian at all,' Mina declared. 'That is all part of the cloak of concealment these conjurors like to draw around themselves. I suspect that most of the Chinese magicians in this country have never been east of Margate. It is all costume and wigs and an air of mystery. That is why Mystic Stefan doesn't speak, he wants to preserve the illusion. If I was to step on his toe we would find him very fluent in English.'

Dr Hamid looked worried. 'Are you planning to step on his toe?'

'If the opportunity presents itself. But I can see his value to Mr Hope. He is the instrument Mr Hope is using to try and draw me into a belief in mediums so I can join his campaign to exonerate Miss Eustace. And a patron like Mr Hope is a valuable commodity to a performer, so Mystic Stefan provides Mr Hope with what he wants — messages from Dr Livingstone.'

'I agree. Which leaves us with the worrying question of Mrs Mowbray. I have given this a great deal of thought, but am afraid that there is nothing we can do for her. We cannot warn her, or tell her sister what I observed; if confronted she would only deny everything.'

'Perhaps,' wondered Mina, 'Mystic Stefan holds private séances or tells fortunes. That could be the purpose of the visit. Unwise, of course, but less worrying than other possibilities. Mrs Mowbray is not a wealthy woman, so she has no fortune to tempt an adventurer, which may, in this case, be a good thing. She would not wish him to come to the house for such sittings, since her sister would undoubtedly disapprove.'

Dr Hamid nodded thoughtfully at this new, less scandalous interpretation of events. 'I think you may be right. But Mrs Mowbray is surely content with her lot since she lives with her sister most comfortably, and I never observed her wanting to contact her late husband, who left her so dependent on the family affection of Mrs Peasgood. What can she possibly wish for?'

'What indeed? Oh, I meant to ask you, there was a lady at the performance last night, aged about thirty with sharp features. I have not seen her before. Do you know who she is?'

'There were several people there not known to me. Why are you interested in that lady in particular?'

'Because she was the only person not surprised by what she saw. If any member of the audience was a confederate of Mystic Stefan, it was she.'

Dr Hamid was unable to offer any insight, and Mina determined that if she was to see the lady again she would do her best to study her further.

As Mina was leaving she saw an unfamiliar figure walking towards the entrance to the bathhouse, and suspected at once who she might be, since she was so heavily veiled that no outline of her features was visible. If Mina's guess was correct this was the elder Miss Bland, come for her treatment. Mina was tempted to follow her, but it would look suspicious to turn back into the premises, as she had only that moment emerged, also to do so would reveal that she knew that the elder Miss Bland wore a veil to conceal some defect, something she was not at present supposed to know. Mina resolved to do nothing for the moment except observe, and carefully slowed her pace to give her more time to do so, however, an unexpected thing happened. As the lady approached the building she saw Mina and stopped in her tracks, clearly startled. Mina pretended not to notice this, and the lady, after her hesitation, collected herself and moved on, passing swiftly through the doors. Had Miss Bland — if indeed it was she — merely been taken aback at Mina's appearance? It was not unknown for people to recoil from her. Or was there something more? It was almost as if she was being deliberately avoided.

There was one person who would be able to explain some of the mysteries of the Mystic Stefan's performance. Mina sent an urgent message to Nellie, who indicated by a scented note that she would call on her that afternoon, and convey them both to where they could enjoy light refreshments in the tea room of the Grand Hotel. There, surrounded by elegant glamour with service deferential to a fault and where comestibles appeared on tables in the blink of an eye, Mina told Nellie in as much detail as she could recall of the magic of the strange Hungarian.

'How interesting,' said Nellie, sipping from a pale china tea cup and nibbling bread and butter so thin it was almost transparent. 'It confirms my original opinion that Mystic Stefan is no novice. I have been making some enquiries of my own and I can tell you that none of my friends have heard of a conjuror of that name, from which we must assume that he has previously performed under another.'

'I assume the production of images required a simple apparatus combined with actual portraits?'

'Indeed. In such conditions the portraits need not be very distinct, as people tend to see what they expect to see, and the same male or female pictures will be identified many times over by different persons as deceased relatives. Either that or the portrait, as in the case of the one of Dr Livingstone, will be that of a public figure who is well known and held in esteem.'

'I was hoping you would be able to enlighten me as to how the mysterious hand was effected. I know that you are bound by secrecy and cannot describe exactly how it was done, but you might be able to guide me in some way to coming to my own conclusion.'

Nellie gave one of her inscrutable smiles. 'I am sure you have a theory of your own.'

'Yes, I think it was one of those clockwork automatons, and the machinery had been specially made to actually write the first message we were given. Then for the second message, Mystic Stefan simply substituted a dry pen and a paper that had already been written on. But the arm was so graceful in its movements, I have never seen anything like it. I am familiar with mechanical toys and have seen sideshow exhibits that move so stiffly, one would never imagine that they were anything more than what they are. But this — there was no sound of any machinery and I could see no obvious joints. I could almost be persuaded that it was a real, living, but somehow disembodied arm moving of its own volition. Of course, that was the intention of the trick. I believe from the reactions of the audience that I was not alone in this.'

Nellie poured more tea and added just a whisper of milk to her cup. 'The arm, you say, was resting on a table?'

'Yes, it was carried there from another table on a board covered by a cloth.'

'But you did not know it was an arm until the cloth was taken away?'

'No.' Mina thought about this. 'So what was under the cloth and taken to the table might have been something else, perhaps just a wire or rod that he could have removed. The secret is in the second table.'

'I assume that there was room for someone to hide under the table and put an arm through an aperture?'

'There was room, yes, but the lower part of the table was not hidden from view. We could see right through it to the curtain at the back. There was nothing there.'

Nellie took one of her little calling cards from her reticule, and held it up before Mina's eyes. With a deft gesture it vanished, and then, just as suddenly, it reappeared in her hand. She uttered a little laugh at Mina's gasp of astonishment. 'Oh, I may only have been Monsieur Baptiste's assistant, but I took care to learn a trick or two. Consider this. Your senses tell your mind what you are observing, but sometimes those senses can play you false. You know that a card cannot disappear, but that is still what you see. You see darkness under a table, and assume that you are looking through an empty space at a curtain. People thought that Miss Foxton's heavenly sprite rose up out of a vase in a cloud of smoke and floated through the air, whereas she did no such thing.'

'I think I understand,' said Mina. 'You are saying that the arm was actually that of a real person, and there was a confederate there — from the shape and whiteness of the arm, a lady — only somehow our eyes were tricked into seeing just the arm, and no more.'

'Exactly. It is all a trick. Everything you see on stage or at a séance is a trick. This one is really quite simple. I have seen the same thing done with the head of a Sphinx which sits in a box and answers the questions put to it by the audience.'

'I wonder who the confederate could have been?'

'Magicians who do not work with assistants will often hire individuals for simple tasks and pay them a trifle for the performance.'

Mina wondered if the confederate could have been Mrs Mowbray, and that had been the subject of the secret meeting. But was there room for a lady of her proportions to hide under the square table? Were her hand and arm so white and delicate? She could hardly be so desperate for a few pennies that she could be inveigled into doing something quite so vulgar as crouching under a table and putting her arm though an aperture, even if it was possible for her to adopt such a position and then manage to rise from it unaided. One mystery had been solved only to be replaced by another.

Chapter Thirty-One

Richard's current state of despondency was a rare one for him, a mood that normally only lasted for the short while it took for him to dream up another alarming scheme to make money. Even knowing this, Mina was unprepared for the exuberance of his manner next morning. Breakfast was over, Louisa and Enid were out visiting, and Mina was planning a new tale about a witch undergoing horrible punishments when there was a brisk knock on her door and Richard's cheerfully smiling face peered around it.

'The play will take place after all!' he announced, waving a sheet of paper. 'I have received a letter from the Pavilion committee saying that they have reconsidered their decision and will let me have the music room gallery at no charge.'

'At no charge?' Mina glanced at the letter but there was no mistake. 'I wonder how that came about?'

He shrugged. 'Does it matter? I must seize the chance. I trust the printer will not require a stiff advance for the tickets.'

Mina recalled the room in question from her tour of the Pavilion, a pleasant apartment usually employed for recitals before small audiences. Had there been an unexpected cancellation by another hirer, or — and the more she thought about it the more she felt she was right — had Mr Hope paid for it and used his influence on the committee as another means of winning the support of her family?

'What about the requirements of the Lord Chamberlain?'

'Well, I must get around that one somehow, and very soon, or the fashion will fade before the play can go on. For some reason the rule applies to all plays where one charges for tickets. I can do as I please if I charge nothing, but where is the point in that? Why is the law so inconvenient?'

'It is even more inconvenient if you mean to flout it.' Mina saw that she would get no work done that day and put down her pen. 'I have a suggestion. Why not come with me to the Pavilion and I will introduce you to Mr Merridew, who is one of the guides there. He is an actor with many years' experience, and is sure to offer good advice.'

'What a wonderful idea! Mina, you are the darlingest sister in the world! Let us go at once.'

Due to the inclement weather Mina hired a cab and they rattled off together in good humour.

'So you still mean to be Prinny?' enquired Mina. 'I think you are admirably suited to the role.'

'I do indeed, and I have written to Rolly offering him Napoleon.'

'Nellie tells me she will be happy to portray Mrs Fitzherbert.'

'Ah yes,' said Richard with an expression of great satisfaction, 'the absence of her husband abroad has been *very* convenient.'

It was a comment Mina decided not to explore, although she knew that Richard and Nellie had been playing at Prinny and his wife long before the play had ever been thought of. At least, she thought, one of the pair was adept at the art of concealment. 'I hope that the play text is now complete?'

'Well — not exactly.'

She looked at him accusingly. 'Have you started it?'

He crumpled a little under her gaze. 'Er —'

'Obviously not.'

'I have been very occupied with — with —'

'Richard, I don't wish to know. At any rate, as you have already told me that a play is no more than idle chatter, you ought to be able to write it in no time. I expect to see it finished by this evening. Ideally it should take at least an hour to perform; anything less and the public will feel cheated.'

Richard looked startled. 'An hour? I thought fifteen minutes would be more than enough. After all, how many people do you know who can speak for longer than that without repeating themselves and boring everyone.'

'I think it will need to be of some appreciable length if you expect people to pay for tickets.'

'But an hour would be — oh, I don't know — hundreds of words.'

'Thousands, I expect. But you told me yourself it was easy.'

'And what about the actors — how can they be expected to remember so much?'

'You should ask that of Mr Merridew. He is famed for his Hamlet.'

Richard was lost in thought as they arrived at the Pavilion. They had to wait a while in the entrance hall until Marcus Merridew was free from his duties. Seeing Mina from afar he hurried towards her and took her hand. 'Dear lady, how delightful to see you again!'

'I am likewise delighted. Allow me to introduce you to my brother, Richard, who is writing a play which will shortly be performed here.'

'It is always a very great pleasure to meet a lover of the theatre. What is the subject of the piece?'

'It will be about the great romance of the Prince of Wales and Mrs Fitzherbert, set against the magnificent backdrop of the war with Napoleon.'

'Oh my word! How very exciting! Then there will be a large cast required.'

'Er, no, this is my first play so it will be quite a modest production. I will be the Prince of Wales, and the other two roles will be taken by friends of mine. I have very little in the way of funds, or we might have had more actors.'

'That is always the way,' said Merridew, nodding regretfully.

'The main feature of the piece will be a splendid sword fight between the Prince and Napoleon. The Prince will win, of course.'

'Well that sounds most promising! Are you an accomplished swordsman?'

Richard hesitated. 'I expect to be. I might need to learn. Is it hard?'

Merridew considered the question. 'If you like, I can give you some instruction in the art. In my youth I was considered very adept with the rapier. How many performances will there be?'

'To be determined when we know how much interest there is,' said Richard.

'There is still much to be determined,' added Mina.

'I see. Well, with your permission I would be quite fascinated to see a copy of the play script.'

'That is one of the things still to be determined,' muttered Richard.

To Mina's relief, Merridew laughed heartily. 'Ah, the theatre! I do miss it!'

At that moment Mina chanced to notice a familiar figure in the vestibule. 'Why, that is Mr Arthur Wallace Hope.'

'I see him here quite often,' said Merridew. 'A friend of yours, so I have heard. He occasionally takes a tour, but seems mainly to be fascinated by the statue of Captain Pechell. He likes to stand and gaze at it.'

'Understandably, since they were comrades in arms. He comes here to convene with the Captain's spirit.'

'But you don't believe in all that?' asked Merridew. 'If there was a ghost in the Pavilion I think I would have seen one by now.'

'I am not a convert to spiritualism, although Mr Hope has been doing his best to convince me.'

A new tour party was ready to depart and Merridew was obliged to join them. It was quickly decided that he, Mina, Richard and Nellie would all meet up to dine in two days' time to discuss the forthcoming play, and he bid a cheerful farewell.

'I have had a thought,' said Richard. 'Perhaps I don't need to write anything at all.'

'Your play would be a dumb-show, you mean?'

'No, there would be words, but if the actors are simply told the story, then they could just make up the speeches as they go along.'

'Is that a good idea?'

'It's a wonderful idea! Then we will finish with the sword fight, and that could go on for quite some time. And — here is the clever thing — if there is no play text then it is not a play at all. I will call it a diversion and I need not trouble the Lord Chamberlain with it as there will be nothing to send him. So all difficulties are solved.'

'I suppose you will not need as many rehearsals,' Mina admitted.

'Rehearsals?'

'I believe they are usual.'

'Really? Well, we'll see.' Richard patted his stomach. 'Time for some refreshment, I think. Shall we return home?'

Mina hesitated. 'I would rather like to speak to Mr Hope, as it is always instructive to know what he is thinking, but I have been warned not to do so without a reliable witness.'

'I can be reliable,' Richard declared, 'and I should like to have a far closer acquaintance with Mr Hope. Perhaps when Mr Merridew has instructed me in the art of the rapier I will be able to persuade him to treat you with more respect.'

'I trust that we may find a better way,' Mina said, taking his arm. Together they approached the great statue. Hope stood before it, gazing up at the sandstone face, absorbed in his thoughts.

'Is it a good likeness?' Mina asked.

He turned to her, startled. 'Miss Scarletti! Mr Scarletti! What a pleasure to see you both again. Yes, the statue is a fine likeness, so noble and courageous, although nothing; no words, no image, can capture the essential goodness of the man I knew.'

'I can see that you are very drawn to it.'

He sighed. 'I am not a son of Brighton as he was, but if I had been then by rights it would be my statue there and Pechell, an ornament to his family and the town, would be standing here in my place, feeling keen sadness at the cruel death of a friend.'

'Why by rights? Surely his death was a chance of war?'

'In a sense it was, as so much is chance, but I am sorry to say that I must bear some of the blame. The day before, being young and foolhardy, I took too many risks, and against all pleading, placed myself in danger and received a leg wound. Had I not done so I could well have been where Pechell was and been killed in his stead while he was on another part of the field. He and all the men with him were torn apart by a fusillade.' He breathed a deep sigh, and Mina saw tears start in his eyes. 'This place, yes you are right, I am drawn to it — I can feel Pechell's spirit demanding that I come here — it is such a powerful focus of energy. Dr Lynn, so I have been told, was here on the very day of the extraordinary encounter, and he too attracts spiritual energy, though he does not know it; indeed, he continues to deny it against all the evidence. Mystic Stefan undoubtedly has psychic abilities, too, and he may prove to be, if anything, a more powerful medium than Dr Lynn. The butterfly illusion you saw is almost unique in that form and elegance to the performances of Dr Lynn but Mystic Stefan does it equally as well. If I could only draw together all the things that brought so much energy into one place at the same moment then we might even divine the secret of what the Misses Bland experienced. I thought it might have been possible when Stefan made his wonderful demonstration, but it was not. Perhaps something is missing?'

Mina smiled. 'There was the chess automaton, the Wondrous Ajeeb, but I would not attribute any special powers to what is after all only a child's plaything built large.'

Hope stared at her, his jaw dropping as if seeing a vision appear before his eyes. 'Of course! That is it! The Wondrous Ajeeb! I am so grateful to you, Miss Scarletti. Why did I not think of it!'

'Because it is just a machine, Mr Hope,' she reminded him gently.

'Oh no, he cannot be. He is surely imbued with the spirit of the great Turk, the one who has gone before, but whose outer form has sadly perished. But Ajeeb is no longer here in Brighton, I believe?'

'No, I think he must be back at the Crystal Palace where he continues to exhibit.'

'Then he must return,' said Hope, clenching his fists with a look of unshakable determination. 'And we must be prepared for wonderful things.' He laid his hand on the arm of the statue. 'Pechell, you are here, I can feel it. And I hope that you can forgive me.' He turned to Richard with a more benign look. 'I gather that the Pavilion committee has smoothed the way for your play to be performed?'

'They have,' said Richard. Realisation dawned. 'Was that your influence?'

Hope smiled. 'Oh, one just needs to know whose ear to whisper into. I look forward very much to seeing it. I shall take ten tickets and recommend it to all my friends in Brighton.'

'I owe you my thanks,' murmured Richard awkwardly.

'You owe me nothing,' replied Hope. He glanced at Mina. 'Have you given further thought to my request for a statement? Please say that you have.'

'Now you know we cannot discuss that here. I am under strict orders from Mr Phipps.'

Hope made a gesture of frustration. 'I cannot understand why you fail to see a truth that is so very clear to others and has been proved again and again. Is it because you do not want to? I do so hope you are not secretly one of those materialists who believe in nothing at all and can have no comfort in life. They seem to me to be the saddest of creatures. Some of them even deny God; they certainly deny the spirit, the existence of the immortal soul of mankind. What a terrible empty world they must live in! You have said that you go to church and pray, but I cannot help but wonder if that is only a matter of form.'

'I pray often and most earnestly,' replied Mina. 'But whatever I might believe in my heart, it will not change the truth, a truth I cannot yet know.'

'And are you not hungry for the truth? Do you not seek it?'

'The truth is the truth whether I seek it or not. I am content to apply my energies, such as they are, to living this life as best I can.'

He sighed. 'That is the difference between us. I know that the truth is out there, in the great wide world we inhabit. I need to seize it, and lead others to it.' He stared at her, a deep imploring look. 'I want to lead you to it.'

'But I do not wish to be led. Whatever is there I must see and recognise it for myself, not have it forced on me. But to be blunt with you, the truth that you believe in is one I do not recognise. Miss Eustace and her friends only succeeded in demonstrating to me that the works of spirit mediums are a fraud. Some are merely entertainers, some do bring real comfort to the bereaved, but there are also those who are thieves and must be punished. There may be genuine mediums, but I do not know of any. I have read about the trickery of the Davenport brothers, and the supposed flight of Mrs Guppy and the crimes of Mr D.D. Home, and all I have learned supports my original impression. I ask to see the Misses Bland and they are strangely reluctant to see me. What do they have to hide? Are they afraid I will unmask them as cheats? I think they are.'

'Not a bit of it, but you do have a reputation as someone with a profound negative influence on the delicate constitution of spirit mediums.'

'Well, that is a very convenient excuse, is it not? The perfect reason to avoid me and thus avoid the danger of exposure.'

'That is not the reason they are unwilling to meet you. They are very private persons, timid even, and do not go about in society. Their new powers they find very disturbing and are afraid for their health if they exert them too much or encounter anyone such as yourself while they are still in the process of development.'

'I think that is nonsense. If they are genuine, and as powerful as you say, they should hardly be afraid of me. They should want to meet me, in order to convince me that they are genuine. This avoidance further convinces me that they are tricksters.'

Hope frowned thoughtfully. 'If I could arrange a meeting, would you agree to sign the document regarding Miss Eustace?'

'You know we cannot discuss that here.'

'I only wish I could persuade you to attend a séance conducted by some of the leading practitioners of that art. The Davenports have returned to America, but there are others.'

'Mr Home or Mrs Guppy I suppose?'

'Yes. I have attended their séances, which you have not, and can heartily recommend them both. You would see wonders beyond imagining, and I can promise that you would be received into the fold of believers with great happiness.'

'I would rather not meet Mr Home for fear that he would make an attempt to fleece me of my property.' Hope opened his mouth to protest, but Mina waved him to silence. 'Do not try to defend him, the Lyon case is a matter of court record.

And as for Mrs Guppy —' Mina was suddenly struck by a new thought. 'Do you really believe that she can fly through the air and pass through walls?'

'Yes, I do! There are many competent witnesses who say she can. Educated men and women of the most impeccable reputation were present at that extraordinary event and have signed affidavits to confirm what they saw. Oh, I know the men of the press have greeted the news with insults and ridicule, but they were not there. Had they been, they too would have been convinced.'

'If this lady can really do what she claims, and I for one cannot believe that anyone can fly through walls, but if she and other spiritualists can do this, then why, pray, are men risking their lives going to Africa? Why are they marching through lands infested by flies and deadly disease, facing starvation, and wild animals, dangerous rapids and murderous attacks; why are they doing this and suffering and dying? I can see the importance of finding trade routes, but it comes at such a price — the lives of brave men. Why do the spirits not take pity on us and send a medium to find the source of the Nile and then come back and tell us where it is? Why do they not find Dr Livingstone and rescue him and bring him home, if he is alive, or carry his body back for burial if he is no more?'

'I do believe you are mocking me,' said Hope.

'I am afraid that you open yourself to mockery by telling me that you believe a lady, who I understand is of somewhat generous dimensions, can fly through the air and pass through walls without leaving a sizeable hole.'

'Yet you refuse to see her and witness it for yourself.'

'Not at all. But I am a negative influence. More to the point I am not a credulous believer, and it would be known that I was looking for fraud. I would never be admitted, and even if I were, there would be no wonders to behold that day, as my mere presence drains away whatever powers the medium claims to be using. Everyone would be disappointed, and it would all be my fault.'

Hope sighed and shook his head. 'I am so sorry that your mind is closed to these wonders. I do wish you would reconsider. Please, allow me at least to send you the paper I wish you to sign. Read it through and let me know if you can oblige.'

'I will receive it only if you send a copy to my solicitor.'

'Very well, I will. And since we may not discuss the issue except before him, then I will with some reluctance ask him to arrange a time when that can take place. Good day.'

As Hope bowed and walked away Richard stared after him. 'What a very dangerous man,' he said.

As they stood there contemplating the conversation that had passed, a gentleman, very plainly dressed, who had been paying careful attention to the row of busts of the Brighton worthies, noticed that Hope was leaving the Pavilion and discreetly followed him.

Chapter Thirty-Two

Next day, Mina received a note from Mr Ronald Phipps, saying that he had been supplied with a document by Mr Hope and wished to arrange a meeting at his office at a time convenient to all parties. Mina had also received the document that Hope wanted her to sign, and it was everything she feared. It read:

To whom it may concern,

This is to certify that I, Mina Scarletti, have attended séances conducted by the spirit medium Miss Eustace, and declare that I am convinced of the genuineness of the manifestations and materialisations she has produced in my presence. I also renounce all statements I have made in the past which might suggest that I do not believe that Miss Eustace is wholly genuine and apologise for any distress my words and actions may have caused her.

My signature is appended below in order to establish the truth of my beliefs and I confirm that I have not been offered any inducement of whatever nature to secure that signature.

Mina felt she needed to discuss the document with someone who was already conversant with the circumstances, but Richard was absent once more and Dr Hamid and Anna were busy with patients, so Mina took the paper to the one person she would be sure would advise her — Miss Whinstone.

'Oh, my dear,' said that lady, perusing the document, 'you cannot, must not, sign such a thing.'

Mina had hoped that the report in the *Gazette* of Mr Hope's recent talk on spiritualism would strengthen her case and weaken his, but following the previous adverse comment this new review was more muted in tone, and while not actually praising the speaker, neither did it take a contrary point of view. Mr Hope's address, said the correspondent, had been 'interesting' and 'informative' and suggested that 'further study of the subject might be necessary'. Mina felt that a support had been knocked away from under her, and Enid was jubilant.

She had been giving some thought to her last conversation with Mr Hope in which the Wondrous Ajeeb had been mentioned, and accordingly sent a note to Mr Merridew asking if he would be kind enough to let her know if the great automaton should make a future appearance at the Pavilion. He replied quickly, promising to inform her the instant he had any news, and also, if she was interested, to introduce her to Mr Mott, the chess champion, who might be able to provide some fascinating information as to the working of the mechanism.

Mina arrived at the office of Phipps, Laidlaw and Phipps a few minutes before the time appointed for the meeting and asked if she could be admitted to speak to the young solicitor before Mr Hope was there. She was conducted to Mr Phipps' faultlessly neat domain, where he was already studying his copy of the document. They took the precaution of comparing his copy with the one in Mina's possession, and established that they were identical.

'I do not trust Mr Hope at all,' commented Mr Phipps. 'One must take every precaution.'

'He is not a wicked man,' said Mina, 'but he is driven by the need to be correct. I recently encountered him at the Pavilion when I was accompanied by my brother, who was a witness to our conversation, and Mr Hope revealed that he feels some personal guilt concerning the death of Captain Pechell, which may be one of the keys to his obsession. I do not think the guilt is justified as the Captain's death was a tragedy of war, but Hope clearly thinks that had circumstances been different he and not the Captain would have died that day. His belief in spiritualism is a means of comforting himself, and we can never shake it. But there was one other thing I observed — when Mr Hope left the Pavilion another man, who was standing nearby, followed him. I wondered if that man was a detective, and if so, whether he had been sent by you.'

Mr Phipps went slightly pink in the face. 'It seemed like a wise precaution. For all we know he could be undertaking some unlawful action in the pursuit of his ends, but so far it seems he has not. I know he has met with some members of the Pavilion committee, and he has hired and paid for three apartments, the banqueting room, where we saw the performance by the Mystic Stefan, the chess club room, where he means to exhibit an automaton, and the music room gallery, although I am not sure what that is for.'

'That is on behalf of my brother who means to perform a play there. He did so unasked, and I am sure we understand his purpose.'

'Indeed we do. He is also paying for the Misses Bland to occupy lodgings very near to the Royal Albion Hotel, and he does meet them from time to time, but he is never alone with either. The only thing that I have been able to establish is that he might be conducting an intrigue with another lady. My man has been instructed to discover her identity, as the secrecy of their meetings suggests that she might well be married.'

Mina did not know what to say without giving away what she knew. 'Surely you do not intend to drag a lady's name through the mud in order to attack the character of Mr Hope?'

'That ought not to be necessary, but it could well be a bargaining counter. I am sure he has no wish to be named in an action for divorce.'

'No indeed,' said Mina, appalled at the effect that this would have on her family.

Phipps looked at her anxiously. 'Are you quite well, Miss Scarletti? I hope the journey has not fatigued you.'

She laid a palm against her forehead. 'I may have caught a slight chill, that is all.'

He nodded understandingly. 'Well, we will conduct the meeting as quickly as possible so that you may return home and take care of yourself,' he said with unexpected gentleness.

A clerk knocked on the door and announced the arrival of Mr Hope, who was ushered in. He looked annoyed to see Mina already there, and although he did not voice his suspicions that they were plotting against him, it was obvious from his demeanour.

He sat down, his body tense like a lion about to spring, his deep chest thrust forward aggressively. Mr Phipps was not a large man and the presence of Mr Hope made him seem smaller than he was. It was an uncomfortable meeting since Hope and Phipps clearly disliked each other, and each man eyed the other like two contestants about to fight a duel, not actually wanting to meet, but recognising that the safest place to have one's enemy was where you could actually see him. Phipps looked unusually apprehensive, and Mina realised that neither he nor she really knew how low Mr Hope might stoop in the pursuit of his obsession. Mr Hope might be risking his reputation by his own actions, but Mr Phipps could well be suffering from a sense of shame over something — his true parentage — that was in no way his fault.

'I come here,' began Hope, 'in a spirit of peace and reconciliation. I wish to be good friends with Miss Scarletti. Few ladies of my acquaintance rank higher in my estimation, few have earned so much of my respect in so short a time. It pains me, therefore, to find that Miss Scarletti is so opposed in every way to Miss Eustace, who is a lady of exceptional talents, and it is my greatest wish to bring them together in harmony and friendship. I should mention that I am here only on behalf of Miss Eustace, and have nothing to do with the gentlemen currently under arrest. She has been most dreadfully led astray by others and cannot be held to account for any doubtful proceedings, for which she is entirely blameless. It is this misunderstanding that has led to Miss Scarletti attributing to Miss Eustace the iniquity of her former associates. My mission is to see that matters are put right.'

'Miss Scarletti, would you like to comment?' asked Mr Phipps.

'I would. With respect to Miss Eustace's claims to be a spirit medium and Mr Hope's request that I sign a statement, I had wondered if it was possible to arrive at a form of words that would satisfy all parties, but now that Mr Hope has presented me with this document I can see that we are very far from that. All the evidence of my senses has proved to me beyond any doubt that Miss Eustace's supposed mediumship is a fraud. I cannot, therefore, sign a paper to attest to any other point of view, and neither will I retract any of my past statements on that subject or apologise to Miss Eustace for any of my words or actions. If a paper such as this one should emerge in the future which has my signature on it then I declare it now to be a forgery.' Mr Hope's expression was severe. 'There is one more thing. I am supposed to declare that I have not been offered any inducement. This is untrue. It has been suggested to me by Mr Hope that Miss Eustace intends to accuse Miss Whinstone of committing perjury; a very serious matter. Mr Hope intimated to me in a private conversation that if I would sign a paper sympathetic to Miss Eustace she would be willing to abandon that defence and propose only that Miss Whinstone had been mistaken and confused.'

'I deny that, of course!' thundered Hope indignantly.

'Mr Hope has recently been trying to persuade other residents of Brighton to sign similar testimonials by telling them that I have already agreed to do so.'

'I deny that also!'

'I will not sign this paper, and I confess that at present I am unable to see what Mr Hope could ask me to sign that I would find acceptable.'

'I believe you have your answer,' said Mr Phipps, 'and given Miss Scarletti's opinions on the issue I would strongly advise her not to sign, even if she had any inclination to do so, which clearly she does not.'

Hope stared at the paper, and was deep in thought. 'Very well,' he growled. 'I can see I will get no further with this. You are set against Miss Eustace, and you are also set against other celebrated mediums who you have never even met.'

'Including the Misses Bland who refuse to meet me.'

'Are they mediums?' asked Phipps.

'They purport to be. I feel sure that their defence against the charge of plagiarism will be that they dreamed the book or it was dictated to them by a spirit, or, since the writing is not theirs, that a ghost actually appeared and wrote it all down for them. Maybe Mystic Stefan's disembodied hand wrote it after visiting them by flying through a wall. They will find such claims impossible to prove; in fact, it will be hard for them not to be laughed out of court.'

'Such things do happen!' Hope insisted. 'They do! I know it! You should not ridicule what you do not understand!'

'A court of law will take a very materialistic view of the matter,' said Phipps drily.

Mr Hope was displeased but pensive. 'Supposing,' he said suddenly, 'that the Misses Bland were to agree to meet privately with Miss Scarletti. Supposing they were to offer convincing proof that they receive information from the spirit world?' He turned to Mina. 'What do you say? Is your mind closed to that possibility?'

'Not closed, of course not. Let them meet me and prove it, and I will say I am convinced.'

'Then that is decided,' said Hope, rising to his feet. 'I have nothing more to say until this event has taken place. I wish you both good day.' He departed at once and there the meeting ended.

Mina was left considering how she might best warn Enid of her danger without also warning Mr Hope, since anything the detective might achieve could do some good if it did not involve her sister.

'Enid,' she said, when they were next alone, 'please reassure me that you are not meeting with Mr Hope in a situation which might be misconstrued.'

'What is it to you what friends I have, or where I meet them?' said Enid, with a frown of annoyance.

'Well, you know what the gossips are like. However innocent it might be, if you choose to take tea with a man they will make it into something it is not. Think of what that would do to mother. I am not saying you cannot speak to him, only it might be best if you did not do so unaccompanied.'

Enid laughed. 'Do you know mother thinks he admires her? He doesn't at all, but he is kind to her because of me.'

'At least mother is single. Have you considered what Mr Inskip might think?'

'Oh, bother Mr Inskip! May he be eaten by wolves and an end of him!' Enid flounced out of the room.

Chapter Thirty-Three

'Well,' said Richard as he, Mina, Marcus Merridew and Nellie were seated around a table in a private booth at one of Brighton's smartest restaurants, 'here is another setback. I am now missing a performer. Rolly Rollason has written to say that he cannot, after all, be Napoleon in my play! He has been ornamenting the London stage to very great acclaim, where it appears that he is the only man in England, and quite possibly the world, who can play the bagpipes while riding a velocipede. The crowds have been roused to madness at the sight of him in a kilt and he has been engaged for the remainder of the season.'

The waiter arrived and Nellie ordered champagne with a nod to the company to indicate that the expense would be on her account, or to be more accurate, her husband's. 'Can he not recommend another man?'

'There is a difficulty about that, too, since those he had in mind all require to know how many performances they are to be engaged for and require fees enough to cover the train fare to Brighton and board and lodgings.'

'It is a sad fact that actors need to eat in order to perform, or the business of theatrical management would be so much simpler,' said Merridew.

'I don't suppose you could attempt it, Mina?' pleaded Richard.

'No, I could not! I think it will be quite enough of a shock for mother to see you on stage without having me appear in a breeches part. And the sword fight you plan would be very brief.'

'Might I make a suggestion?' said Mr Merridew. 'As you are all aware I am a professional actor of many years' experience. I would be willing, in return for a share in the ticket price, to perform in your play. Indeed, I do flatter myself that my name on the playbill will create some interest. You might even make a profit on the enterprise. It is not unknown.'

'Oh, that is a very kind offer and, of course, I accept!' said Richard, eagerly. The champagne arrived, as did a dish of savoury tartlets, and toasts were drunk to theatrical success.

'I also have some items of costume and wigs I could lend to you to improve the appearance of the piece — they have had some use but will look perfectly splendid from a distance — and some blunted stage swords for the fight. Many years ago I toured with a company that performed *King Lear* in the style of the court of George III, and still retain some of the ensembles, which will suit the setting of the pavilion perfectly. The play had been banned from public performance during His Majesty's unfortunate affliction, but in later years it enjoyed a considerable revival. I was Edgar. It was very affecting.'

Nellie smiled. 'I know that our work on the stage is different, but yours is a name known and held in great respect by all in the theatre. In fact, I have heard you spoken of as the handsomest man who ever trod the boards.'

'Oh, my dear,' said Merridew with a little gasp of pleasure, 'how happy it is to be remembered. Yes, I was terribly good looking as a youth. My hair, my poor long-gone hair, was the most delicate shade of auburn and fell almost to my shoulders in ringlets. It sparkled like gold in the footlights and all the ladies sighed to see it. And, oh, the many little gifts I received, the sweetmeats and nosegays, not to mention the love notes, it is astonishing that my head was not turned by the admiration.'

A large platter arrived, the very best fruits of the sea, prettily garnished, and they all fell to. More champagne was ordered, and while the ladies sipped theirs with decorum the gentlemen more than made up for their restraint. The gentlemen drank to the ladies, the ladies replied to the gentlemen and they all raised their glasses to William Shakespeare.

'There is just one little condition, if I might mention it,' said Merridew, when the platter and a third bottle of champagne were both empty. 'While I would be exceedingly happy to act in the play, I believe I would be better suited to play the Prince. I have a costume that would do very well and even with the advance of years it fits me to perfection. And my admirers do expect me to take the leading role.'

Richard looked a little disappointed for a moment, then quickly rallied. 'Well, why not? I am sure I could be Napoleon. I can speak a lot of nonsense in French.'

'In any language,' said Mina.

'After all,' said Marcus Merridew with a smile as the iced desserts were served, 'the play's the thing.'

Mina had received a note from Mr Hope confirming that she could meet the Bland sisters in a private room at the Royal Albion Hotel. She met the news with keen anticipation, but this was tinged with concern. Mr Hope knew that Lady Finsbury had been portrayed by an actress. It was not beyond his guile to present her with two impostors, ladies who were professional mediums of his acquaintance, adept in the art of illusion. Mr Hope, however, did not know that she had some useful information concerning the appearance of the sisters.

Mina arrived in good time, and after making enquiries at the reception desk, was directed to a smartly appointed meeting room, smelling strongly of polish and furnished with comfortable seating, and a side table with a vase of fresh flowers, a tray of glasses and a carafe of water. She took a seat and waited. After a few minutes there was a knock at the door and Mr Hope entered, accompanied by two ladies. Mina rose to her feet and studied the ladies carefully. Neither was of uncommon size, although one was a little taller and more slender than the other, and both had good figures, giving the impression that they were not very aged. They were well dressed, although not extravagantly so, with neat lace gloves and light bonnets, but both wore their veils forward.

'Good day to you,' said Mr Hope in a very formal manner, approaching coolness. 'Allow me to introduce Miss Ada Bland —' The taller lady inclined her head — 'and Miss Bertha Bland.' The shorter lady greeted Mina in the same fashion. 'Ladies, I would be delighted for you to make the acquaintance of Miss Mina Scarletti.' Despite his words, he looked far from delighted.

'It is my very great pleasure to meet you at last,' said Mina. She sat down and the ladies were seated side-by-side facing her. Mr Hope took a seat to one side where he could observe all of them. Mina had not anticipated that he would remain, and would have preferred it had he not been present, but felt that, as he had made all the arrangements, she could hardly insist that he withdraw.

Mina tried to see if there was anything about the Misses Bland she could recognise. Was Miss Ada, the taller of the two, the same lady she had seen outside the baths and who had fled from a meeting with her? It was possible. Mina noticed that Ada wore a thicker veil than her sister, plain and very dark so that no feature of her face could be seen. Miss Bertha's veil, however, was lace, worn more for modesty than outright concealment, although it still served to obscure her features. Unless a gross falsehood was being practised — and Mina still thought that under the circumstances it was very possible — these were the Bland sisters and the lady with the heavier veil was the one who habitually wore it to conceal some defect in her appearance.

'The purpose of this meeting, as I understand it,' said Miss Bertha Bland, 'is to enable us to make a demonstration of our small abilities. You must excuse us, as we are far from being developed in that way, but we believe that with time we may become better.' The quality of her voice and pronunciation were that of an educated young woman, but although her words were modest there was a hardness in the tone which suggested that she could not easily be confused or swayed.

'How would you describe these abilities?' asked Mina.

'We can read minds. Not all minds, but we can certainly see into each other's as we are sisters. This is something we have been able to do from a very early age. When we were children we thought nothing of it, as I suppose in our innocence we thought that all sisters could do the same. In our family it was treated as a parlour trick, and we often performed it for the amusement of visitors. It was only later that we discovered that it was something quite out of the common way.'

'Would it be possible for you to provide me with a demonstration?' said Mina. 'You would not find that my presence hinders the operation of your powers?'

'We are stronger when we read each other. If you could open your mind to the idea that we can do this, quell all negative thoughts, dismiss your doubts, then I think we can be assured of success.'

'I will do my best,' Mina promised. She glanced at Ada, who remained silent and motionless, then at Mr Hope, who was watching closely.

Miss Bertha drew a small packet from her reticule. 'It is usually done with playing cards. Please examine them. You will see that this is a normal set of cards.'

She rose to bring the cards to Mina, and as she bent to hand them over, her proximity enabled Mina to see some of the outline of the face beneath the veil. In a flash of recognition, Mina felt sure that Miss Bertha Bland was the sharp-featured lady who had attended Mystic Stefan's demonstration, and been the one person in the audience not astounded by his tricks. What, wondered Mina, was the connection? Were the two related in some way — confederates — or merely friends? Or was she simply there as a guest of Mr Hope, her reaction that of someone in the same business — the art of illusion?

Mina slid the cards from their packet and examined them. Having been assured that they were normal cards she had to wonder what an abnormal set might be. Was there some trick by which a magician might be able to read the face of a card from a secret marking on the back? What signs should she be looking for? As far as she was able to see it was the usual full deck with all the suits, but she also glanced at the backs, and saw nothing out of the ordinary. Her fingers found both sides smooth to the touch. She went to hand them back, but the lady, who had returned to her seat, declined.

'Now, Miss Scarletti, you must draw a card from the pack, but hold it close, making quite sure that I cannot see it. I will turn my back so you can be certain that I do not know which card you drew. Remember which card it is, then hand it and the pack to my sister, who will memorise and replace it. I will then read my sister's mind and tell you which card it was.'

'Very well,' said Mina. Miss Bertha rose and moved to the side of the room, her back turned so that she faced away from both her sister and Mina. There were no mirrors in the room, but all the same Mina, to be quite sure, also rose and turned away. She was especially careful that Mr Hope should not see what she did, as she would not put it past him to be their confederate, her attention so focussed on preventing the Misses Bland from seeing the card that she did not take his presence into account. When she was satisfied that she could not be overlooked, she drew a card — the six of diamonds — laid it carefully on top of the pack, then, still ensuring that Hope could not see the card, approached Miss Ada Bland, who had also risen to her feet. Mina handed her the cards and she held them close to her veil the better to see, nodded, and replaced the exposed card in the pack. Although

Mina was close to the lady, the veil was so thick that the wearer's features could not be seen through it.

'There,' said Mina, 'it is done.'

Miss Bertha turned to face her sister, and pressed her fingers to her forehead. There were a few moments of silence, during which she appeared to be making a great effort, then she said, 'I believe I am beginning to see it. Yes, it is a red card — I am sure I am right.' No one spoke, and Mina tried not to give anything away by her expression. There was another pause. 'I can see the suit, now — it is — diamonds. And now the number — yes, I can see it all, it is the six. Am I correct?'

'You are,' said Mina.

'Do you wish for another demonstration?'

'If that would not be too much trouble.'

The trick was repeated and once again Miss Bertha identified the card.

'I suppose you would like to know how it is done. It is really quite simple — at least it is to us. My sister thinks about the card, and I then look into her thoughts, and the card appears to me as if I was seeing it myself.'

'Can you read things other than cards?' asked Mina. 'Supposing I drew a picture of something in my notebook and showed it to Miss Ada — would you be able to tell what it was? Could you draw a copy of it?'

Mr Hope leaned forward and was about to speak, but Mina held up her hand. 'If you please, I wish only Miss Bland to answer that question.' Hope looked displeased but said nothing.

'As I have said,' replied Bertha, 'our powers are not yet fully developed. I could not guarantee success.'

'I suppose that would be a far harder thing to achieve.'

'It would.'

Mina turned to Miss Ada Bland. 'Forgive me, but I am concerned that you have been silent so far.'

'Please do not ask her to speak,' said Bertha quickly. 'I say all for both of us.'

Mina looked back at Ada, who nodded her head.

'Might I ask the reason for this?'

'My dear sister has a defect in her speech. Please spare her. If she objected to anything I have said for us both so far she would have made it known.'

Ada nodded again.

'Very well,' said Mina, addressing Bertha once more. 'Can you tell me how you came to write *An Encounter*? Was it through mind-reading?'

'I do not think it was intended that you should broach that subject at this meeting,' interrupted Mr Hope.

'No?' said Mina. 'I don't recall any such agreement. In any case, I was given to understand that the purpose of this interview was for me to be presented with proof of mind-reading.'

'And have you not seen proof enough?' demanded Hope.

'I will give that question some consideration. But further information will assist me.'

'I have no objection to answering,' said Bertha. 'There is still much about that incident that we do not understand. We both dreamed about the book before the words came to us. It was as if we were there ourselves, in that extraordinary palace, which neither of us had ever visited. We always talk about our dreams, and wonder what they might mean, but we have never before experienced the identical dream on the same night. We knew at once that this must mean something, but we could not tell what it might be. We decided that in future as soon as we awoke we should write down everything we remembered of our dreams as quickly as we could. When we dreamed again, a voice came to us, asking us to listen to it and write down what it said. We didn't know what to make of it, but next day, when we were both quite wide awake, we were both suddenly seized with the desire to write, and so we did. Imagine our amazement when our pens travelled across the paper, quite undirected by either of us, and the words just came. Not only that but the writing was not in the usual hand of either of us. At last we compared notes and found that although we had not written the same thing, when we put the pages in order we had a single book.'

'Did you show it to anyone?'

'No. It was so strange we didn't know what anyone might make of it — or indeed, us.'

'Why did you decide to have it published?'

'It seemed to be the right thing to do. Why else would the story have come to us? Surely it was not intended for my sister and I alone, but for the world?'

'Despite the passages that are held to be indecent?'

'You must believe me, neither of us know which those passages might be. We have been told that there are some portions which might be read in that way, but we prefer not to enquire further.'

'How can you explain the charge of plagiarism?'

'I think you have gone far enough!' said Hope, rising to his feet.

'Mr Hope, I was afraid when you remained here that you would object to my questions, but can't you see that all these matters are part and parcel of the same thing?'

'I do not!'

'We cannot explain the charges at all,' said Bertha. 'We have no knowledge of any other book describing a similar event. As far as we are aware we have copied nothing.'

'And this is to be your defence if the case goes to court?' asked Mina.

'I doubt that it will go so far. We expect that all will be settled quietly without recourse to a public airing.'

'That is as well, since you will not be able to prove you received the book through a dream.'

'No one can prove we ever went to the Royal Pavilion or saw a similar book.'

'I think,' broke in Mr Hope firmly, rising to his feet, 'it would be advisable to end this interview now.'

'As you wish,' said Mina.

'You must be aware that the time is fast approaching when I must press you for a decision on the document. You have two days. That is all.' He conducted the Misses Bland from the room, his words ringing in Mina's ears like a declaration of war.

Chapter Thirty-Four

Next morning, once breakfast was done, Louisa and Enid went out on one of their shopping expeditions to which Mina was never invited, since it went without saying that she would inevitably hinder their progress, spoil their enjoyment and was, in any case, deemed to have no interest in fashion. The twins were left in the care of Anderson, and Richard had just risen sleepily from his bed and was exploring the kitchen for leftovers of the family breakfast. Mina tried to settle to her writing, but her thoughts kept straying to the demonstration by the Misses Bland. While she could not by her own efforts devise how they had performed their mind-reading trick she recalled that Nellie, in the guise of the Ethiopian Wonder, had achieved something very similar when assisting Monsieur Baptiste, and determined to place the question before her.

Mina had not expected Mr Hope to call so soon after the meeting for a private discussion, and was therefore surprised when the doorbell rang and Rose came to announce the visitor.

'Yes, admit him to the parlour and fetch my brother to me,' said Mina, hoping that his call meant that something at least might be resolved.

Rose looked relieved that she was not to stand duty as witness again. There was some delay while Richard, devouring a toasted muffin into which he had thrust a cold fried egg and some bacon, was apprised of the situation, carelessly flung on some halfway respectable clothes and conducted Mina to the parlour, where Mr Hope awaited them.

'Thank you for agreeing to see me,' said Hope, in a milder tone than he had adopted the day before. 'I feel I should apologise for becoming a little overwrought at the interview with the Misses Bland. It is hard when one can see so clearly the great shining light of an eternal truth and find that others who are far from ignorant and worthy of respect cannot see it and refuse even to make the attempt. Have you arrived at a conclusion?'

'All I saw was a very pretty trick with cards. It reminded me of nothing more than the mind-reading acts of stage magicians.'

'Then I hope you found it impressive? They and the stage magicians you mention are all adept at that skill. It is really quite marvellous!'

Richard was lounging in an armchair, toying with his cigar case. Mina gave him a warning look as their mother would never permit him to smoke in the parlour, and he returned it to his pocket. 'Have you ever witnessed the Ethiopian Wonder?' he asked.

401

'Indeed I have,' said Hope, enthusiastically, 'I take an interest in all practitioners of that nature. She has the most extraordinary perception. If I could only persuade her to hold a séance I feel sure the results would be astounding!'

'You see I have spoken to the lady, in fact I know her very well and she has taken me into her confidence. She has admitted to me that she has no psychic abilities and her act was all down to a clever feat of memory. Her partner, Monsieur Baptiste,' Richard explained to Mina, 'first blindfolded her, then he took items from the pockets of members of the audience and asked her to identify them. Every time, she was able to describe what object he was holding.'

'Exactly,' said Hope, 'how could she have guessed?'

'Quite easily with a little preparation. There is only a limited selection of things one might have in one's pockets, and there was a secret form of words for each. I am sure the Misses Bland have their own method of passing messages to each other.'

Hope chuckled. 'I am sorry to say that so many of our conjurors claim their work is only a trick. Some cannot recognise their abilities, which they undoubtedly have, and so they go on performing their acts and forever denying what God has given them. A few, unhappily, know exactly what it is they do and yet prefer to perform for their own advantage rather than use their gifts as they were intended to. The Misses Bland may not understand their powers, but I am pleased to say they do not deny them.'

'What about Dr Lynn, who introduced you to Mystic Stefan, is he also deluding himself?'

'Lynn is a friend, and a splendid fellow in many respects. I know that in time he will come to see the true way. He thinks he knows how he performs his wonders, but what he achieves is quite impossible without the intervention of spirits. Miss Scarletti, can you now believe on the evidence of your own eyes that the Misses Bland are genuine? Would you be prepared to certify that? You may word the certificate in any way you please.'

'My eyes told me that I saw an interesting trick, but I certainly cannot attest on that basis that I believe the Misses Bland to have spiritualistic abilities. I am also concerned that if I signed any such document it would be used to defend them against the charge of plagiarism. It might even be used in the defence of Miss Eustace in an attempt to show that I have changed my mind on the subject.'

Hope's sudden hard frown told Mina that her last surmise had hit home.

'Why do you champion that woman — she is such a transparent fraud!' demanded Richard.

Mr Hope shook his head very emphatically. 'She is no fraud! I know it! Oh, I accept that spirit mediums attract the derision of the ignorant and blinkered and they have learned to ignore such ill-judged criticism, but to threaten a virtuous lady with prison only for practising her skills for the common good is outrageous. I wish to see her freed and achieve the recognition she deserves.'

'And you will achieve this by bringing her to Brighton to conduct a séance in the Pavilion?' asked Mina.

'That is my intention.'

'You are aware, are you not, that even if Miss Eustace was acquitted, she would not be allowed to hold a séance in the Pavilion? The committee are quite against such demonstrations.'

'They cannot be, since they allowed both Dr Lynn and Mystic Stefan to demonstrate there.'

'They are not mediums, they are conjurors.'

'I beg to differ. In any case,' Hope smiled confidently, 'I think I can persuade the committee to change their minds. It is my intention to bring the Misses Bland to the Pavilion, together with Mystic Stefan and the Wondrous Ajeeb. They and the spirit of Captain Pechell will create such a confluence of power that it will no longer be denied! Right will prevail. It is only a matter of time.'

He prepared to take his leave. 'Mr Scarletti, I wish you well with your play, which promises to be the first of many successes. Perhaps when I have departed you and your sister might discuss what I have said and with a little thought I am sure you will reconsider your position. Miss Scarletti, I am sorry to press you, but I must have your decision very soon. Please let your solicitor have the statement in writing by tomorrow.'

'Well,' said Richard, when their visitor had left, 'the Bland sisters, Mystic Stefan and the Wondrous Ajeeb, I should like to have tickets for that performance! It sounds like the playbill of a music hall. This business must be costing Mr Hope a pretty penny.'

'He is undoubtedly paying Miss Eustace's law costs, as well.'

'Yet he says he takes no profit from his books or lectures. All goes to the fund to rescue Dr Livingstone. Is he very rich?'

'You know who he is?'

'Er — no.'

'He prefers to go by plain "Mr" but he is actually Viscount Hope, owner of a substantial estate in Middlesex, and from what I have heard he is not one of those impoverished noblemen barely able to maintain appearances, but a very wealthy man. His standing in society, his resources and his history, which cannot be denied, make him powerfully placed to overcome any opposition.' Mina refreshed herself with some mineral water, though Richard looked as though he wanted something stronger and she could hardly blame him. 'I am doing my best to fight him, but I don't know how much longer I can go on. I am constantly under attack, first on behalf of Miss Eustace, then on behalf of the Misses Bland, and next thing I will be asked to stand up in court and say that the Mystic Stefan is a medium and the Wondrous Ajeeb works through the power of the spirits.' Mina had deliberately not told Richard what she suspected about Enid and dreaded the prospect that Mr Hope might use the potential for a damaging scandal to blackmail her. 'Mr Phipps is trying to discover some weakness of Mr Hope's with which we can arm ourselves.'

'We all have weaknesses,' argued Richard, fingering the cigar case once more. 'Apart from mother who has none. I have a great many, I know, though I try not to let it worry me. Enid is vain, Edward is serious, you think too much, Mr Hope is gullible and Miss Eustace and her like are interested in nothing but money.'

'In that case I really can't see why Miss Eustace means to return to Brighton. She could never become rich here. Too many people remember her; she has a bad name. No one of any note would receive her and she certainly would not be allowed to hold a séance in the Pavilion.'

'I agree. Once she is free, and whatever happens at the trial she will be sooner or later, she would be far better advised to avoid Brighton altogether and make a new start with new victims somewhere else.'

'Then why come here? Whatever she is, Miss Eustace is not a fool.'

Richard laughed. 'No, if there is any fool, it is Mr Hope.'

'So maybe she has another purpose, another target, perhaps one that Mr Hope does not know about. Oh, of course!' said Mina with a sudden gasp of realisation. 'Why did I not see it! The real target is Mr Hope and his fortune. I have been too preoccupied with seeing him as the enemy to recognise that he is actually the victim. I am simply an instrument. He is the mark.'

Richard mused on this. 'I think you may be right. Of course, it would be useless to warn him.'

'Poor Mr Hope, I almost feel sorry for him, he is such an easy dupe. She works on his sympathy, presents herself as the injured party and not a criminal, and he buys her the best lawyers in the land. Once she is freed she will leech off his generosity for life. That is her scheme. Well, he will learn his lesson the hard way.'

'If he ever learns it at all. But what do you mean to do?'

Mina knew she had to take a gamble that however misguided Mr Hope might be he was not actually wicked, and if necessary she could appeal to his better nature to preserve Enid's reputation. 'I will be true to myself. Mr Hope will never have a statement from me.'

Richard hugged her.

Chapter Thirty-Five

The following morning Mina received a note from Marcus Merridew stating that it might interest her to know that the Wondrous Ajeeb had arrived in Brighton, and was currently in the process of being installed in the Pavilion where, at the express behest of Mr Hope, he would perform for a few days only. Mina, as Mr Merridew's special guest, might like to come and enjoy a private viewing. Mina was eager to see the famed automaton and presented herself at the Pavilion without delay. Mr Merridew greeted her in exuberant style and conducted her to the room usually hired for meetings of the Brighton Chess Club, where the Wondrous Ajeeb was to hold court.

As Mina was ushered into the room, leaning on Mr Merridew's arm, an attendant, who was bustling about making all the arrangements, looked up in surprise. He was a tidy looking man with a deft, fussy manner, his glossy dark hair straight to the point of perfection, and combed back over his scalp as if painted on with a wide brush.

'Mr Franklin,' said Merridew, 'I would like you to meet Miss Mina Scarletti, my very particular friend, who has come to satisfy her curiosity as to the Wondrous Ajeeb.'

'Delighted, and you are very welcome,' said Mr Franklin, who seemed from a change in expression to have made the assumption that Mina required this individual visit because she was too frail to mingle in a crowd. He stepped back so that she could enjoy a better view. The apartment was decorated in light green, and was less opulent than the other rooms of the Pavilion, quieter and more subtle. As a result the display stood out even more dramatically than it might have done in a more elaborate setting.

A screen had been arranged at the back of the room and lavishly draped with multi-coloured oriental fabrics to form a suitably exotic backdrop to the figure of the Wondrous Ajeeb. 'Is he not a great marvel?' enthused Mr Franklin. 'Have you ever seen the like?'

'Never,' said Mina. She did not ask if she might move closer, but did so, knowing that she would not be prevented. She had not expected such a large piece of machinery. The apparatus towered far above her head, and must have been in all some ten feet in height. Its base was a square wooden cabinet mounted on castors, on top of which was an octagonal plinth covered in figured velvet in a rich shade of burgundy, beautifully fringed. There, sitting cross-legged upon a tasselled cushion, was the figure of Ajeeb, fully life-size, perhaps even greater. He was, to all appearances, a Turk, since his countenance, which bore a mild expression, suggesting wisdom and concentration, was burnished brown and his long beard was fashioned somewhat exotically in a double point. He wore wide, silk, scarlet trousers and soft slippers of the same shade, with vividly striped stockings and a loose chemise of pale blue, over which was a voluminous dark red coat. His turban and the brocade sash about his waist were gold. The hands and face looked as though they were made of carved painted wood, but the right hand, its fingers curled inwards, was hinged so that the thumb might be brought to the fingers to grasp objects.

As Mina took in every detail of this extraordinary machine, Mr Franklin placed the other parts of the display in place. A hookah was positioned to the figure's left and the tube with its mouthpiece put into the wooden hand. A pedestal with a circular top was placed to its right and on this rested a chessboard. On a side table was a basket of chess pieces, and another with draughts, while a third was filled with small white counters.

Mina gazed up into the enigmatic face of the Wondrous Ajeeb and he, through heavily lidded eyes, appeared to be staring down at her. 'I don't suppose I could ask how he is operated?' she asked. 'I understand he is very adept at chess.'

'Many people ask me that,' smiled Mr Franklin, 'but it is, of course, a great secret.'

'Why surely there is a man hidden inside,' exclaimed Merridew. 'He must be underneath, in the cabinet.'

'Not at all,' said Franklin, who, from his air had heard this suggestion many times. He stepped up to the figure and opened a door in the front of the cabinet. Mina and Mr Merridew peered inside, and Merridew even got down on his knees for a closer look, but the interior was filled with a profusion of rods, cords, pulleys and wheels. There was no room for a human operator.

'Then there is a man inside the figure itself,' said Merridew, getting back to his feet. 'It is large enough!'

Franklin merely smiled again and showed that part of the chemise concealed a door in the figure's chest. This he opened to reveal that inside the breast of the great Turk was still more machinery. Another door opened in the figure's back, and it was possible to see all the way through.

Merridew took a tour about the figure, looking for some method by which a man might enter it. 'Perhaps the man is not yet inside. Ah, I know, the old theatrical trick, a trapdoor, he comes in from below.' He winked at Mina. 'The Pavilion is full of surprises.'

Mr Franklin, with some effort, moved the figure about on its castors, showing that the carpet below was entire. 'As you see, there are no trapdoors. All that is needed is this.' He took from his pocket a key of the kind used to wind up a very large clock. After returning the figure to its former position, and closing the doors in the cabinet and torso, he inserted the key into a keyhole that was hidden by the fringing of the plinth and proceeded to wind the mechanism, which made a loud grinding and clicking. 'Do you play chess?' he asked Mina.

'I am afraid I have never learnt the game,' Mina confessed.

Franklin stopped winding and stepped back, dropping the key into his pocket. 'I am sorry to hear it.' There was a creaking like the movement of hinges and metal joints, and slowly the Wondrous Ajeeb shook his wooden head from side to side. This action of the otherwise impassive figure created a strange effect, as if he was both alive and not alive at the same time. 'I think Ajeeb is sorry, too. It is the finest game in the world and an excellent occupation for the mind.' The metallic noise ground out again, as this time Ajeeb nodded his head, sagely.

Mina looked at Mr Franklin, but he was too far from the Turk to have created the movements. 'I hope that Ajeeb does not pretend to bring messages from the spirits,' she said. 'There has been too much of that in Brighton recently.'

'No, he only plays chess and draughts. Let him show you what he can do.'

Franklin fetched the basket of chess pieces, but instead of setting them out for a game, he placed only one piece on the board, a white knight, which he put in a square in the row nearest the Turk. 'The chess knight has an unusual move, unlike that of any other piece. He goes in the shape of a letter L, two squares one way, and then one at an angle, like so.' He demonstrated. 'It is possible to move the knight all about the board, but going to a different square each time, so that he visits every square on the board once and once only. Sixty-four squares, and sixty-three moves.' Franklin placed the knight back on its starting square and stepped away. 'Wondrous Ajeeb I beg you to demonstrate the knight's tour.'

Ajeeb obligingly leaned forward from the waist, an action accompanied by the sound of rotating cogwheels, and stretched out his arm. Then, grasping the knight in his right hand, he lifted it and placed it on another square. Franklin had picked up the basket of white counters, and now he came forward and placed one on the square just vacated. This sequence of actions was repeated, move-by-move, and as Mina and Merridew watched, the board began to fill with white counters, each one on a different square, until finally the knight reached the last unoccupied square and the board was full.

'Oh, bravo!' exclaimed Merridew. 'I can't say how it is done, but it is a wonder.'

Ajeeb favoured him with a polite bow, then lifted the hookah pipe to his mouth as if to say that his work was complete.

'How marvellous!' Mina agreed. 'Whether done by man or machine it is very impressive. And does Ajeeb win every game he undertakes?'

'Very nearly,' said Franklin, 'but he is gracious in defeat. The only thing that angers him is an opponent who breaks the rules, or tries to cheat. I have seen Ajeeb put an end to such games by sweeping all the pieces from the board.'

'Does he speak?'

'Alas, no, he expresses himself only through gesture.'

'Will Ajeeb be performing for the public? I have seen nothing advertised.'

'He has been brought here at very short notice, so there has not been time to advertise his visit in the newspapers. But some placards have been prepared which will be placed in the vestibule. He will entertain the paying public this evening and tomorrow afternoon, and then tomorrow evening there will be a private performance for the Mayor and aldermen and other specially invited guests.'

'My thanks to you good sir for the demonstration,' said Merridew. He glanced about him. 'Would you be so kind as to tell me where we might find Mr Mott of the Brighton Chess Club? I know he is in the Pavilion today as I saw him arrive earlier and rather fancied I might find him here.'

Franklin gave an innocent smile. 'I can't say, I am afraid. Perhaps he is having tea.'

'Or smoking a pipe,' suggested Merridew. 'Well, Miss Scarletti and I will retire to the tea room for now. I am sure we will have the opportunity of speaking to Mr Mott later. He may well join us there.'

'So you think Mr Mott was inside Ajeeb?' asked Mina once she and Merridew were on their way back to the vestibule.

'I think this is how all these things work if they do anything out of the ordinary that cannot be achieved by mere clockwork, otherwise why is it so very large? The original Turk was only a figure of a man from the waist up, and no one could have fitted inside, but it rested on a very much bigger cabinet.'

'But we looked inside the cabinet and the figure and saw only machinery.'

'Oh, I expect a great deal can be achieved with false doors and mirrors. Did you ever see the head of the Sphinx?'

'No, but I have heard of it.'

'It was a disembodied head sitting on a table, telling fortunes. There was a living man underneath, putting his head through a hole in the table-top, but his body could not be seen as there were mirrors under the table so placed that they deceived the audience into thinking they could see right through to the back of the stage.'

'Both simple and clever,' observed Mina, thinking of Mystic Stefan's miraculous disembodied arm.

'All the best tricks are.'

'Do you happen to know what kind of entertainment Mr Hope is planning to give the Mayor and aldermen? I know he has brought Ajeeb to the Pavilion with the idea of having in one place all the elements that resulted in the visions said to have happened here. On that day as described in *An Encounter* there was Ajeeb, and Dr Lynn the conjuror — who Mr Hope insists is a medium — demonstrating his

Japanese butterfly illusion. The Mystic Stefan, who performs the same miracle, will be a suitable substitute for Dr Lynn. Then there is Mr Hope's former comrade, Captain Pechell, whose presence he senses hovering over the statue, and who he seems to think of as a spirit guide. He is also bringing the Misses Bland, who do a kind of parlour trick, a mind-reading game with cards. Surely he can't imagine that the sisters might have another curious experience. Well, when I say "another" it is probable that they did not have one in the first place.'

'Did they not copy their book from another's work? That's what the newspapers say.'

'I think they did, but that is for a court to decide. Mr Hope would find it better to invite the person who wrote the plagiarised book, but no one knows who he or she is.'

'Well, the public events are not of his doing, they are under the auspices of the Pavilion. It is only the last display where he is overseeing the arrangements.'

'And I think I suspect what he might be doing. I can't prove it, of course, but it is possible that he is intending to hold a private séance under the guise of an entertainment. He has invited the Mayor and aldermen so they can witness the miracles performed, his intention being that they would then be prepared to give evidence in favour of the Misses Bland. Of course, he will not have dared to describe the event as a séance or the committee would have objected, but that is what it will be, and if Mystic Stefan is the conjuror I think he is, he will be able to produce some very convincing illusions.'

'Has he not invited you?'

'I am afraid not.'

'But you said he has been trying to convince you of spiritualism.'

'He has. And that can only lead me to one conclusion. He is deliberately excluding me in case my presence exerts a negative influence and the spirits are unable to perform. That means that he has finally given up all attempts to convert me to his way of thinking and from now on I must consider him an enemy.'

Merridew looked dismayed. 'Well, we must do something!'

'I wish I knew what. I could try and gain entry to the event and observe it, but attempting to disrupt the séance by seizing the apparitions would not be the answer.'

'I should think not!' said Merridew with a gentle smile.

'I tried doing that before with Miss Eustace, and it didn't work.'

'Oh, I see.'

'And such a desperate action would be playing right into Mr Hope's hands. He has already been making enquiries to try and prove that I am mad or hysterical.'

'But nothing could be further from the truth!'

'It will look very like the truth if I create a disturbance in front of the Mayor and aldermen. Mr Hope might be half wishing I will do so, and then I would be taken away in a strait-waistcoat before I knew it.'

'Well,' said Mr Merridew, thoughtfully, 'let us have a cup of tea and make a plan. And I feel sure that we do not need to search for Mr Mott. He will know where to find us.'

Chapter Thirty-Six

'It is a pity we do not know who wrote the original piece, the one that has been plagiarised,' said Mr Merridew, as he and Mina refreshed themselves with tea. 'I have not read it myself, but from what the *Gazette* says it was beyond reproach.'

'My feeling is that it was a story rather than a history,' said Mina, thoughtfully. 'Part of it is true. A lady visited the Pavilion in the days before there were guides and, as she explored it alone, she got lost. But then, enthralled by its air of mystery and romance, she thought what an amusing adventure it would be if she met its royal owner.'

'It is very easy to become lost and confused without a guide,' said Merridew, knowingly. 'When one thinks of the number of times the Pavilion has been enlarged and altered, and then there are doors which are not actually doors at all, and real doors that don't look like doors, and long passages that run secretly alongside the main apartments to enable servants to walk about discreetly without bothering their masters.'

'You must show me them. That might well inspire me to write a ghost story myself.'

Mr Mott appeared soon afterwards, looking a little warm, as if he had been exerting himself, and joined Mina and Mr Merridew at the tea table. He was a small man, not a great deal over five feet in height, with a narrow body and the kind of whiskers that suggested he would be better advised to be clean-shaven. If he was trying to look older and more authoritative by growing whiskers he had, thought Mina, made an all-too-common error. Nevertheless, he was pleasant and polite and greeted Mina warmly when they were introduced, saying that he was charmed to meet any intimate friend of Mr Merridew.

'I am told that you entertain a great fascination for the Wondrous Ajeeb and have seen him play chess often,' said Mina.

'Oh, yes,' exclaimed Mott with all the eagerness of a devotee, 'I have lost no opportunity to watch and learn.'

'Have you formed an opinion as to how the mechanism is able to play chess so well without the assistance of a human operator?' asked Mina, signalling the waiter to bring a fresh pot of tea.

Mott paused and licked his lips nervously. 'Ah, well, I really couldn't say. I know nothing of clockwork devices, they are a mystery to me. My expertise, such as it is, lies in the art of chess.'

'I have been told by Mr Franklin, who I am sure you must know, that there will be a special demonstration given before the Mayor and aldermen tomorrow evening. Will you be in attendance?'

Mott's expression continued to be wary and anxious. 'I think,' he ventured carefully, 'that it is very probable that I will be there, yes.'

'In that case, since I am not one of Mr Hope's guests, I must entreat your assistance in a matter of some difficulty.'

'Oh, but surely you will be there? It is all over town that Mr Hope is a very particular friend of your family.'

'The town does not know everything. I have not received an invitation, and suspect that if I asked to attend it would not be permitted. I must let you into a secret, Mr Mott. I am concerned — very much concerned — that Mr Hope, who is the guiding light behind this private display, will be attempting, quite against the rules and wishes of the Pavilion committee, to hold a séance. I have said nothing, as I have no proof, only suspicions, but if you are there I would like you to observe what happens and then report back to me. Would you be prepared to do that?'

Mott looked surprised, then he became thoughtful. 'That explains a great deal,' he said at last. 'I have noticed that ever since Ajeeb arrived there have been preparations in hand for the private event, which were markedly different from the public displays and those at his last appearance here. The conjuror Mystic Stefan has been involved in the arrangements, although I am not sure how, and a large trunk has been delivered which is locked and guarded from general view. I have also heard that Mr Hope actually asked the committee if the statue of Captain Pechell could be moved to the room where the event is to take place, but he has been told it is not possible due to its weight and the danger of damage. Instead it is agreed that a portrait of the Captain will be hung there. What all this has to do with chess I am not sure, but he is very clearly not about to present the usual demonstration.'

'None of it has anything to do with chess I am afraid,' said Mina, and explained to Mr Mott what she thought Mr Hope's intentions were.

'He believes that Ajeeb is operated by disembodied spirits?' said Mott, incredulously.

'I am afraid he does.'

'Well, now I have heard everything. There are very few persons who know precisely how the Wondrous Ajeeb performs, but all are sworn to secrecy and cannot enlighten him.'

'I doubt that he would believe them, in any case.'

The teapot arrived with a plate of scones that Mina could not recall ordering. 'My treat,' said Merridew with a wink.

Mr Mott was too troubled to eat. 'And you say that Mr Hope actually champions the Misses Bland? How could he? My sister read their dreadful book in all innocence and was so upset that she has been under treatment from her doctor ever since. And didn't they copy the work of another? They should be in prison!'

'If Mr Hope has his way they will be exonerated of all blame and will reap the financial rewards of their deceit,' said Mina.

'Well, we can't have that,' declared Mott. 'Miss Scarletti, I am extremely grateful for your warning. I shall alert the committee at once.'

'Do you think they would put a stop to the event?' asked Merridew. 'The man is a Viscount, after all. And as Miss Scarletti has said we have no actual proof of what he intends to do. If challenged, he might simply say that he is providing an entertainment to honour the memory of his late comrade in arms. Since the Misses Bland are friends of his then it would not be a matter of surprise if they were invited.'

'And I would be made to seem like a hysteric,' added Mina. 'I am far from hysterical, but Mr Hope would like to prove that I am in order to assist in the defence of Miss Eustace, who he also champions.'

Mott was horrified. 'That conniving woman! I am ashamed to admit that I actually attended one of her séances, mainly because my mother insisted I go. It was all a great deal of nonsense of course, and I was not at all surprised when she was arrested. She comes from a whole family of conjurors, you know. In fact, she was the only visitor to the Pavilion who saw at once how Ajeeb performed his feats.'

'Ah, the trained eye of the illusionist,' said Merridew.

'I suggest,' advised Mina, 'that we do not try to prevent the private demonstration from occurring. I might be wrong about it, but if I am right I would hope that the Mayor and aldermen, being men of common sense, will not be deceived. If you could simply observe and let me know what actually takes place, I would be very grateful. Then I will consider the position and think again.'

'Very well, I agree,' said Mott.

The scones were finally finished and tea-time service was ending for the day. Waiters were darting about, busily sweeping dishes from the tables, and Mr Merridew peered hopefully into the teapot to see if one last cup might remain to round things off. Mr Mott rose to depart, saying that he was going to make a close observation of that evening's public performance of the Wondrous Ajeeb. It was as he walked away that a realisation struck Mina. 'Mr Mott,' she called, leaving her seat as fast as she could, and limping after him, 'pray Mr Mott, do come back — I have something very important to ask you!'

413

He stopped and looked back at her with some surprise, as if the suggestion of hysteria was not after all so very wide of the mark, and Mr Merridew quickly appeared by her side and carefully took her arm for support.

'I may have misheard you, of course,' Mina continued, 'but did you just say that Miss Eustace was the only visitor to the Pavilion who realised how Ajeeb worked?'

'Yes, that is correct.'

'But Ajeeb has not been here since last October — or has he?'

'No, you are quite right, Miss Eustace saw him when he was here last year.'

This was a surprise to Mina. 'I had been under the impression that her arrival in the summer of this year was her first time in Brighton. I can see that she might well have made a preliminary visit to gather information about the residents to provide material for her séances, and carefully concealed that fact. But you are quite sure it was she?'

'I am, yes.' Mott hesitated and looked about him, but no one was close enough to overhear. 'I cannot say too much about the location I was in at the time that I observed her, only that I was in a position to see her but she was unable to see me.'

Mina nodded. 'I understand. You need say no more on that subject.'

'When she viewed the Wondrous Ajeeb she was very amused by him, and actually said that she could see how he performed his feats. I think she may have been accompanied by a gentleman, but I am not sure. Later that day I went to see Dr Lynn's demonstration of conjuring. He was giving an exhibition for charity and the same lady was there, I recognised her, and given her earlier comment I paid some attention to her demeanour. She watched all that Dr Lynn did with very keen attention, but not as someone might have done for the mere purpose of entertainment. She was studying him with the eye of one whose family profession was in that field. When Dr Lynn's performance was over she approached him and they had a conversation. I heard her say that her father was in that line of work, and he had a business providing materials and equipment to conjurors. She gave Dr Lynn a card. I thought, earlier this year, when Miss Eustace held her séances, that it was the same lady, but I couldn't be sure, so I said nothing at the time, but then when she was arrested it was in the newspapers and mention was made of her father's business, so I knew I must be right.'

'Mr Mott, I hope you won't be offended, but have you read *An Encounter*?'

He blushed. 'I — no — when I saw how upset my sister was I threw it on the fire.'

'Without reading it?'

'Naturally.'

'Like you, I have never read the book, but I understand from those who have that the vision seen by the sisters was supposed to have taken place on the very day that you describe, the one day that Dr Lynn and the great Ajeeb were both at the Pavilion.'

'What can that mean?' asked Mr Merridew.

'I wish I knew. Mr Mott, please could you gather for me all the information at your disposal concerning what is planned to take place before the Mayor and aldermen, and then we will meet again.'

Mina wrote to Mr Phipps to advise him of Mr Hope's ultimatum, saying that she would not under any circumstances comply. He replied stating that he agreed with her position and was watching the case for her. He had attempted to make an appointment with Mr Hope to try and reach an amicable agreement, but that gentleman was currently too busy with the arrangements for the event to be held at the Pavilion to be able to attend. Mina realised to her relief that she had a short breathing space, but she knew she was in danger and would need every ounce of her limited strength for the battle to come.

On her next visit to the baths she undertook her callisthenics class under the watchful supervision of Anna Hamid. Anna sensed a new, grimmer determination and had to quell Mina's need to push her efforts too far into areas that would harm rather than develop her. 'You are making good progress,' she said, 'but you must not go too fast. I can see that the muscles in your back and shoulders are offering improved support for your spine, and your arms are far stronger. The walking you do will also, with care, strengthen your limbs and reduce the strain of movement.' As Mina rested from her efforts Anna explored with her fingers the areas of tension in her patient's back. 'You are very troubled, I can feel it. Is this still concerning Mr Hope and those dreadful women?'

'Yes. I see I can hide nothing from you. I was recently permitted an interview with the Misses Bland, but it was very strange indeed, and Mr Hope sat and watched and interrupted if he thought my questions too searching. They performed a parlour trick with cards to try and convince me that they had the power to read minds. I am sure they could not have read my mind on that occasion, which held far from flattering thoughts, although I did make it clear that I was not converted to their cause. Throughout the interview only one of the sisters, the shorter of the two, who calls herself Bertha, spoke for both of them. Miss Ada was heavily veiled said nothing at all. If I could only conduct a private interview with her, I think I would learn a great deal.'

Anna said nothing, but simply massaged Mina's back.

'Have you received an invitation to Mr Hope's demonstration at the Pavilion tomorrow?' Mina asked.

'We have but we are not inclined to go.'

415

'I would take it as a very great favour if you could both be present and observe the proceedings. I have not been invited and I fear that is no accident.'

Anna paused. 'Very well, I will speak to my brother about it.'

'Only I think Mr Hope has some strange plans afoot.'

'Strange in what way?'

Mina sensed that much as Anna felt she wanted nothing to do with Mr Hope and his mystical demonstrations, some interest had been aroused. She explained her concerns about the proposed event, and as she did so a new idea emerged. Mr Hope was not the only person who could make strange plans.

Once Mina was dressed and about to leave, Anna, after a struggle with her conscience, said, very quietly, 'The elder Miss Bland has an appointment with me tomorrow morning at ten o'clock. My brother will be seeing patients all day and will not be in his private office when she departs, so you may sit there. I did not tell you this.'

Chapter Thirty-Seven

Next morning, and with the Pavilion event due to take place later that evening, Mina presented herself at the baths and settled herself comfortably in the ladies' salon. Miss Ada Bland arrived for her appointment punctually at ten. Mina, partly hidden from her view in the depths of a large armchair, peeped out from behind a periodical and saw the distinctive figure pass quickly by. After that, it was just a matter of waiting. Mina, who had had another interview with Mr Mott only an hour before, had a great deal to think about. The all Sussex chess champion had been very diligent following their first meeting. Given his close involvement in the planned event, a certain amount of prying had not aroused any suspicion in either Mr Hope or Mystic Stefan. Mott had told Mina that he had overheard a conference between the two, in which the conjuror had reassured his patron that he could sense that the spiritual forces were very powerful in the Pavilion, and promised to produce some remarkable manifestations. The one thing that they were both agreed upon very emphatically was that on no account must Mina be admitted. If she attempted to take a place amongst the company, she would be politely but firmly removed. If she caused a disturbance, however, then other arrangements would have to be made and she could well find herself placed under the care of doctors.

Mina knew approximately how long Miss Bland's appointment might take, and once it came near to the time, she listened for each creak of a door. Finally she was rewarded, went to the entrance of the salon, and, seeing her quarry, emerged to accost her in the corridor. There was an audible intake of breath as Miss Bland stopped, then tried to move around and past Mina.

Fortunately the passage was narrow enough for Mina to be able to interpose her slight form in the lady's path, trusting that she might be reluctant to push her over in her desperation to leave. 'Miss Bland, please don't be afraid of me. I only want to talk to you.' Miss Bland paused for a moment, then turned her thickly veiled face away, and shook her head. Once again, she made to try and move on, but Mina quickly reached out and took her by the wrist. There was a slight gasp of surprise from behind the veil. Slim little fingers used to wielding dumbbells made for a sharp grip.

'We must speak. I insist on it. For both our sakes. Let us not fight each other. There is a room private here. We will not be overheard or interrupted. Please.' Firmly but insistently Mina drew Miss Bland to Dr Hamid's office. The lady was reluctant, but as another patient appeared in the corridor, she capitulated rather than make a scene. They both entered the office, and were seated facing each other uncomfortably across the desk.

'I do hope that we can be open and completely truthful with each other,' Mina began. 'I do not know what it is that afflicts you, but all the same I think we two might understand each other better than most. I cannot and do not attempt to hide what I am, neither do I conceal myself from the world. My life is a good one and I am my own woman. I speak my mind; I do not allow others to speak it for me.'

Miss Bland uttered a miserable sigh. 'It is … hard for me to speak,' she said in a slurred breathy whisper.

'For both of us, each day is one of testing and tribulation, but we must meet it and make the best of it.'

'Your body is your burden. Mine … is different.' Miss Bland paused. 'I would not show this to everyone.' Slowly, hesitantly, she raised her veil.

One side of her face was almost no face at all. It was without shape, and the surface was scarred, furrowed and reddened. Tight folds of flesh hung over one eye so that she could barely see through it, the nose was flattened, and twisted cords of skin pulled at one side of her mouth, further distorting her appearance. The other side was quite normal, and not unattractive. 'I was a child when it happened,' she said with an effort, through tightened constricted lips. 'I fainted and fell with my face against a hot stove. I was burned almost to the bone. I nearly died. Sometimes I wish I had.'

'My spine is twisted,' said Mina, 'pulled first one way and then the other. It reduces me to the size and shape you see. Too much movement can pain me. I live with the danger that my own skeleton may one day crush my heart and lungs. I will probably not have a long life. I will never marry or bear children. But we must both of us make what we can of our lives. There are respectable paths of fulfilment. I beg you, do not seek it by condoning a lie!'

The good side of the damaged mouth rose in a travesty of a smile. 'Then I am more fortunate than you. I am fulfilled in ways you can never be. I am married. And there is no reason why, God willing, I cannot in time become a mother.'

Mina found it impossible to hide her surprise at this revelation. 'My congratulations,' said Mina at last. 'I had been given to understand that you and your sister led very retiring lives. Who is your husband? How did you meet him?'

'He is — a man of business — a customer of my father's.'

Mina recalled what she had been told of the Bland sisters' father, information she was not supposed to know, and also what had been printed in *An Encounter*. 'Oh? That is a strange way of putting it. According to your infamous book your father is a clergyman. Clergymen do not, as a rule, have customers. But I have heard it rumoured that your father is an undertaker and cabinet maker. Is that true?'

Miss Bland was aware that she had made a slip. 'It is,' she said defensively. 'We were obliged to provide a *nom de plume* and a false history in order to preserve our anonymity.'

'And also provide your efforts with a gloss of respectability. How long have you been married?'

'Just three months, but he has been courting me these two years. Oh, I assure you, nothing has been hidden from him. He has seen past the veil and he does not recoil. He is young — handsome — he finds beauty in my soul. He kisses my hands.' She raised her hands, which were very white, like those of a marble statue. She wore dainty lace mittens and the fingers that peeped from them were long, slender and delicate. In a life dominated by her disfigurement, Miss Ada Bland was clearly very proud of her sole claim to womanly beauty. Seeing Mina's fascinated glance she performed a kind of ballet with the arms, which curved like the necks of two swans in a tender embrace.

Mina was powerfully reminded of another arm she had seen, one equally as white and graceful. 'Was it you — the disembodied hand at the Pavilion? Of course! I see it now. Your sister was there in the audience, but you were not because you were assisting the conjuror! And — Mystic Stefan, or whatever his real name is — is he your husband?'

The one sided smile again, and a soft throaty laugh. 'I will not deny it.'

'And now I think I understand the connection. It is not the undertaker's, but the cabinet maker's services he employs. Is part of your father's business the construction of the kind of special cabinets used by stage magicians? Like the one the Davenport brothers take on their travels?'

Miss Bland said nothing, but she didn't need to.

Mina thought again. The father of both Miss Eustace and her acolyte the dreadful Mr Clee was in the business of supplying equipment for the stage. There were few enough businesses of that kind in London. Were the Misses Bland a part of the Clee family, or friends with them? 'Is your father a Mr Benjamin Clee or a relative of his?' Mina demanded. 'Is Mr James Clee your brother or cousin?'

Miss Bland was undeniably shocked. 'No, he is — no!'

'But you know him, do you not?'

Miss Bland was silent, but she put her veil back in place and rose to her feet. 'That is enough. I regret that I agreed to this.'

'I have never met Mr Benjamin Clee, who may be a perfectly respectable gentleman for all I know, but I have encountered his son, who is an unmitigated scoundrel.'

Miss Bland was about to make for the door but turned back to face Mina with a little gasp of anger. 'That is not true! How dare you!'

'Then what is he to you that you defend him?'

Miss Bland did not reply but the fingertips of her right hand touched the knuckle of her left. From under the lace there was the thin soft gleam of a ring.

'Heaven help you woman, do not say that he is your husband!' Mina paused. 'But no, that can't be so — James Clee cannot be masquerading as Mystic Stefan, he is in prison awaiting trial. Unless of course he can fly through walls like Mrs Guppy. That is just as well for you, for had you married him you would still be single and he a bigamist.'

'What do you mean?' said Miss Bland faintly.

'Mr Clee made a scandalous marriage here last June.'

'June?' There was a long silence. 'You are lying to me.'

'Why would I do such a thing? If you don't believe me you have only to go to the Town Hall and see the evidence for yourself.'

'But …' Miss Bland suddenly sat down again, rather more heavily than she had done before.

'Yes?'

'Are you … certain of it?'

'Quite certain. They parted soon afterwards under circumstances that were reported in the newspapers. You can check that for yourself, too. There has not been time for him to regain his freedom to marry again.'

Miss Bland uttered a sob. She took a handkerchief from her reticule and applied it under the veil.

Mina took pity on her, poured a glass of the restorative water from the supply that Dr Hamid always had to hand, and limped around the desk, proffering it to the unhappy woman. Gradually, in small sips then great anguished gulps, the liquid disappeared. Mina removed the empty glass and took Ada's hand in her own. 'Tell me the truth, please. I am very much afraid that you and your sister have been led astray by a criminal.'

It was some time before Miss Bland could speak. 'He did say at first that there was an obstacle to our marrying, but when I insisted, he said that he thought he could remove it, and only a day later he told me that by some quirk in the law he was free and we could be united.' She wiped her face with an increasingly damp handkerchief. 'Very well, I will tell you all, but if you have lied to me, Mr Hope will hear of it.'

'Mr Hope will hear of this very soon in any case.' There was a crucifix on the wall behind Dr Hamid's chair, and Mina crossed the room to place her hand on it. 'I swear by all that is most holy that I am telling you the truth.'

Ada nodded. 'My husband is Mr James Clee. After his arrest last summer he was refused bail, but I begged my father to stand surety for him. He applied again and this time it was granted.'

420

Mina understood. 'And somehow that later hearing was never reported in the newspapers, so I wasn't aware of his release. When were you married?'

'July,' she sighed.

'Oh dear. So Mr Clee, who we all thought was safely in gaol, has been a free man these three months.'

'But he does love me!' Miss Bland insisted. 'He has been true to me! If he parted from that other woman, he cannot love her at all.'

'I am quite sure he does not,' said Mina, a comment that the unhappy Miss Bland appeared to find comforting. 'I suppose — I don't mean to be cruel — but before your marriage you had money of your own?'

'Some, but not a very great fortune as you seem to imagine. Of course, it is now his, as a husband's right — except — he may not be my husband at all, and I —' She sobbed again.

Mina gave her some time to recover. 'Miss Bland — who wrote *An Encounter*? It wasn't you or your sister. Was it Mr Clee?'

'I don't know. I don't think so. James brought us the manuscript. He didn't say who had written it, but it wasn't in his hand, only he said he needed it printed to make some money. What with the fraud case the family had a lot of expenses and a stop had been placed on their finances which were assumed to be the profits of crime and which might have to be restored. Many of their possessions were in the hands of the police to be used in evidence at the trial. So my sister and I agreed to act for him. He wanted to borrow the money from me to pay for the work, but I put my foot down. I said he could have the money not as a creditor, but as the rightful property of a husband. And so we were married. After all, as a wife I would have the benefit of his protection.' She shook her head in disbelief. 'I feel sure that there has been some mistake! Perhaps he has been led astray by others. James is no criminal; he has always sought to earn a living by legitimate means. The book and the conjuring are not his only business ventures.'

'Really?' queried Mina trying to keep the frank scepticism from her voice. 'What other businesses does he have?'

'He is in the export trade. And before you ask, he needed no funds from me to launch it. I suppose he used the profits from the book. In the last weeks it has been very lucrative, far more so than his other businesses, it brings in a great deal of money.'

'You surprise me. What is the name of this business? Where is his office?'

'I — don't know. I don't really trouble myself with matters of commerce. That is his affair.'

'Has he visited his office in all the time he has been in Brighton?'

'I don't think so.'

'What does he export?'

'All manner of things.'

'Where to?'

'I don't know — or at least — I did ask him once and he said he mainly sends goods to Africa, only I don't know if that was really the case or just his joke.'

'I think it was a joke,' said Mina, 'and I can guess who the butt of it was. I suppose he ordered you to have nothing to do with me?'

'Yes, and I can see why.' Her voice trembled and she applied the handkerchief to her face again. 'I can't help thinking that this is all a mistake. Perhaps James really thought he was free to marry me. The law is such a strange thing. Perhaps once he is properly free we can be married in church. I must see him.' She rose to leave.

'Miss Bland, please take my advice. First satisfy yourself that everything I have said is true. You will see that he is a villain beyond redemption and nothing can excuse his actions. Then consult a solicitor.'

'I suppose you mean to see James convicted?' she said accusingly.

'That will take care of itself. I have another matter in hand.'

Chapter Thirty-Eight

It was a fine but gusty evening as the Lord Mayor of Brighton, his aldermen and their wives arrived at the Pavilion for Mr Hope's special demonstration. Mr Hope himself conducted them into the chess room, promising them a very remarkable entertainment. The screens, with their delicate oriental traceries, were draped even more lavishly than before in brightly coloured silken shawls and in front of them, the Wondrous Ajeeb's devoted attendant, Mr Franklin, was fussing about the towering figure of the automaton, ensuring that it was beautifully presented, the chess board fully laid out ready for a game. On the wall there hung an engraved portrait of the statue of Captain Pechell, and a photograph of the man himself on the battlefield, together with some of his men of the 77th Foot. In addition, and what the visitors might have found slightly more interesting, a side table had been furnished with bottles of wine and glasses, with water for the more abstemiously inclined. A lady, demurely dressed, was standing near the table, eyeing the refreshments with anticipation.

'Before we begin,' announced Mr Hope to the assembled notables, 'there is someone I would very much like you to meet, a lady who I believe will one day be feted worldwide as a great visionary and seeker after the truth. Allow me to introduce Miss Bertha Bland.' Mr Hope offered his hand to the demurely dressed lady and brought her forward to present her to the distinguished company.

The Lord Mayor, aldermen and their wives were understandably startled to be confronted by so controversial a figure, but after a moment's hesitation, made the best of it so as not to offend their host or his guest. Cool greetings were exchanged.

'As you know,' continued Mr Hope cheerfully, 'Miss Bland and her sister have been the objects of some unwarranted publicity and vile allegations which have no foundation whatsoever in fact. Proof of this will be provided very soon, and their accusers will live to regret their words. One day we will all feel most privileged to have made the acquaintance of the Misses Bland.'

The Lord Mayor, aldermen and most especially their wives looked unconvinced, but did not comment.

'I am afraid,' Hope went on, 'that I must apologise for the absence of Miss Ada Bland, who is unfortunately indisposed. But have no fear, Miss Bertha Bland reassures me that such is the intimacy of her mind's connection with that of her beloved sister that she can achieve all that is necessary during tonight's entertainment through her very remarkable skills.'

'I hope there will be none of this psychic trickery,' said the Mayor, with a worried look.

'There will be no trickery at all,' Mr Hope reassured him.

Dr Hamid and Anna arrived, both looking rather uncomfortable at being there, and Mr Hope, leaving the dignitaries to further acquaint themselves with Miss Bland, went to greet them. Anna, after the briefest possible acknowledgement of their host, excused herself and went to pour a glass of water. 'My dear Doctor,' said Hope, unabashed, 'it is always a pleasure to see a respected man of science at my gatherings. I believe that most of the eminent men of Brighton are now present in this very room!'

'But not all of the eminent ladies,' Dr Hamid observed. 'I would have expected you to invite Miss Scarletti.'

Hope had the good grace to look slightly embarrassed at this question and did not try to evade it. 'To be perfectly honest, Dr Hamid, I believe that Miss Scarletti's presence here would not assist in the success of the demonstration. It was my choice that she should not be invited, and if she attempts to gain entry she will not be admitted. In fact, I have increasingly suspected of late that she might not be altogether in her right mind. I have consulted a London specialist on the subject, who agrees with me.'

'What is the name of this specialist?'

Hope smiled. 'We must talk about this on another occasion.'

'Indeed we must,' said Dr Hamid with a frown. Mr Hope returned to the side of Miss Bland, who was eagerly telling an alderman's wife about her wonderful ability to read what was in her sister's thoughts and know exactly where she was at all times. At present her dear Ada had a slight cold and cough, and, claimed Bertha, she could actually see the poor invalid in her mind's eye, resting before a warm fire, with a bottle of physic by her side, reading an improving and moral volume by that wonderful Brightonian author, Mr Tainsh.

The Lord Mayor was standing before the figure of the mighty Turk gazing up at the calm wooden face. 'I came here to see him demonstrate last year, and even challenged him to a game,' he told one of the aldermen. 'I was most soundly beaten, though I am no beginner at chess. But Mr Hope promises we will see something even more extraordinary tonight.'

There was a metallic grinding sound and very slowly the wondrous Ajeeb bowed his head. The Mayor was disconcerted for a moment, then chuckled. 'He is certainly a respectful fellow. One might almost imagine him to be alive.' He turned to Mr Franklin. 'How does he work?'

'By clockwork, sir,' said Franklin, with a worried look, 'although I don't remember winding the key this evening.' Ajeeb turned his head creakily to look at him and nodded.

The Mayor laughed, 'Well, it seems you did and forgot.'

Mr Franklin did not laugh.

'If you will kindly take your seats, ladies and gentlemen,' announced Mr Hope, 'the demonstration is about to begin.' Everyone complied, and Hope surveyed the distinguished company with great satisfaction. 'I would like to start with a short prayer. Let us give thanks for the lives of those noted citizens of Brighton who have gone before us across the great veil. I most especially pray for eternal blessings on the soul of Captain Pechell whose portraits grace this apartment. He was my comrade and my friend, a brave soldier and a fine example to all who knew him.'

With the brief homily done, Hope turned to Mr Franklin. 'It is time to turn the key so we may view the great mysteries of the Wondrous Ajeeb.'

'I am not sure, sir, if he has not already been wound,' said Franklin, but he tried the key and found it turned easily, which further puzzled him. He continued to wind until the mechanism was fully primed. 'We are ready now, sir. Ajeeb will be pleased to challenge any gentleman present to a game of chess.'

To his astonishment, however, Ajeeb shook his head, and the onlookers laughed. 'Is he too tired to play chess today?' joked one of the aldermen. 'That is a fine thing from a machine.'

'Ajeeb, will you not play chess?' asked Franklin, mystified. Once again the wooden head indicated he would not. 'Would you prefer draughts? I will put the pieces in place.' Franklin hurried to get the basket of draughts, but again Ajeeb declined.

'What is happening?' asked Hope.

'I don't know, sir, I don't understand it, he has never done this before.'

Hope gave a grunt of impatience, which was not improved by the amusement of the audience.

'Your Turk is misbehaving tonight,' chortled the Mayor.

Hope faced the giant figure. 'Ajeeb!' he cried commandingly, 'I order you to play chess for the Lord Mayor and aldermen of Brighton!'

Ajeeb's reply was swift. With a sweep of his arm the chess pieces were knocked from the board and tumbled across the floor. 'Franklin, deal with this!' demanded Hope.

'I'm really very sorry, sir,' said Franklin, with growing concern. He picked up the chess pieces and tried to replace them on the board, but the insistent Turk merely swept them away again, and he had to back away to avoid being struck by the mechanical hand.

'Is there nothing you can do, man?'

'I don't know,' said Franklin helplessly. 'Once it has been wound I cannot unwind it, one must just let the clockwork run down and that could take several hours, but then I didn't think it was wound before and it still moved.'

'Well, if this is all a part of the show it is very entertaining,' said the Mayor. 'I must say we had not expected a comedy.'

Franklin tried to approach his charge once more, but was defeated as Ajeeb's body began turning from side to side, both his wooden arms waving with increasing wildness. It almost looked as if the giant form was preparing to leave his plinth and wreak havoc amongst the onlookers, whose exclamations started to tell more of alarm than amusement.

'This has gone far enough,' said one of the aldermen at last, getting to his feet. 'Your machine is frightening the ladies! Make it stop!'

Franklin ran his hands through his hair distractedly. 'Mr Mott! Mr Mott!' he cried. 'Stop this at once, I beg of you!'

At the back of the room Mr Mott rose to his feet. 'Might I assist you, Mr Franklin?'

Franklin turned and stared aghast at the chess champion of all Sussex. 'But, but — who — I mean how —'

'Stop the thing now!' shouted Hope, coming forward and receiving a blow on the forehead from a thrashing mechanical hand.

'It's alive, it's alive!' wailed Franklin, his hair in a state of unaccustomed dishevelment, flopping alarmingly over his forehead.

'It is possessed!' cried Miss Bland dramatically, rising to her feet.

As if in response Ajeeb turned and, making a large gesture with one arm, struck the draped screen, which teetered and collapsed in folds, revealing the figure of Mystic Stefan crouching behind it. He was clearly unprepared for this exposure, since he was holding some images of the Prince Regent and Mrs Fitzherbert, which had been fastened to poles and draped in transparent veils.

All the invited dignities now roared with laughter.

Stefan quickly dropped the poles on the floor and rushed to tackle the Turk, which struck him across the face. As he stood dazed and surprised, Ajeeb seized hold of the dark wig and tugged it off, revealing a more natural looking set of Byronic curls. The conjuror clapped his hands to his head in dismay, then tried to retrieve the wig, which was being waved in the air like a dead rat, but the mechanical arm flung the hairpiece across the room and, turning back, began tugging at the false beard, which led the previously mute magician to cry 'Ouch! Stop!' in a very un-Hungarian accent.

'Wait — I recognise that scoundrel!' exclaimed an alderman. 'He is Mr Clee, who was arrested here only a matter of months ago, and a most contemptible fellow. I thought he was in prison.'

Clee, his beard now half hanging from his face, looked wildly about him, then quickly pushed Mr Franklin out of his path and made a rush for the door, where Mr Mott and Dr Hamid barred his way and smartly apprehended him.

The Mayor turned to a thunderstruck Hope. 'What is the meaning of this? I am shocked and amazed that you have anything to do with this villain, and have the effrontery to invite us and our lady wives here to see some fakery which you have no doubt cooked up between you. This is the grossest possible insult. Gentlemen, ladies, we will see no more of this farrago.'

The Mayor, aldermen and their wives all prepared to depart in a body, with Hope vainly begging them to remain, protesting that there had been a terrible misunderstanding, but before they could reach the door it burst open and Miss Ada Bland marched in accompanied by two constables and waving some documents. She pointed to Mr Clee, who was being held very firmly by the arms. 'There! That is the monster who deceived me, the vile criminal who took my honour and my money too. I see you have been unmasked at last you horrid fiend,' she shrieked. 'I wish I could mark you as I am marked, so you could never again work your wiles on a trusting woman.' For a moment it looked as though she might launch herself at him and make good her threat, but her sister hurried to her side and embraced her and she dissolved into sobs of anguish.

'Disgraceful!' said the Mayor's wife as the dignitaries all left. Mr Hope, speechless, sank into a chair and buried his face in his hands as the constables took Mr Clee away and the Bland sisters quickly departed.

'Well done, Miss Scarletti,' said Mr Mott, 'you astonish me, you really do.'

Mr Hope's head jerked up. He turned around and saw an unexpected tableau — the towering figure of the wondrous Ajeeb, now stilled, the maniacally giggling Mr Franklin, and beside them, the unmistakable diminutive, lopsided form of Mina. Anna Hamid had already run forward to envelop her patient in a cloak since Mina had no desire to appear in public wearing her callisthenics costume. 'But — how can that be? Where did you come from?'

'Really, Mr Hope; use your intelligence; where do you *think* I came from?' Mina gasped from exertion and dabbed her brow with a handkerchief. Anna quickly assisted her into a seat and Dr Hamid brought her a glass of water.

'I see the exercises have been of benefit,' he said dryly, 'but now I insist you rest.'

Hope, with the obvious staring him in the face, stood and turned about as if searching for another way into the room. 'But that is impossible unless — unless Miss Scarletti is a second Mrs Guppy. Of course! I knew it! I always knew it!'

'No, Mr Hope,' sighed Mina. 'I am no medium, no psychic, no seer, and I cannot fly through the air or pass through walls. All I have is common sense. You have been duped by a clever trickster, who seeks out the gullible and the credulous. You are not a fool; you are just too willing to believe. Does Mr Clee claim to be able to move objects through the ether? Has he told you he is sending needful supplies to Africa for the succour of Dr Livingstone?'

'How could you possibly know that?' demanded Hope, turning pale.

'Well, it wasn't by reading minds. I didn't need to. Clee and his accomplice in crime, Miss Eustace, see people's weaknesses and use them to extort money. I won't ask how much he has taken from you. If this scheme is ever revealed in court you would, I am afraid, become a public laughing stock. Perhaps, Mr Hope, from now on no more will be said of my having to sign any papers, neither will you pay some London doctor to declare me insane, or work your wiles on my family. Do I have your promise before these witnesses?'

Confronted by Dr Hamid, Anna and the all Sussex chess champion, none of whom from their expressions looked inclined to accept a refusal, Mr Hope promised.

Chapter Thirty-Nine

Against all Mina's expectations, Richard's play had survived its many setbacks and was due to be performed in the Pavilion as planned. The fracas at Ajeeb's demonstration, which might have prevented it by the loss of Mr Hope's sponsorship, had not done so. The cost of the room hire, which, Mina suspected, Hope would have withdrawn had he been able to, had already been paid and could not be unpaid. Whether he had ever made good on his promise to buy ten tickets she did not know. Even had he chosen to raise an objection to the performance, his protests would not have been listened to, since the Lord Mayor and aldermen of Brighton and the Pavilion management committee were of one mind on the subject of Mr Hope. Like the fabled Emperor who had paraded in supposedly invisible garments that only the wise were able to see, he had been revealed in his naked obsession and was now acknowledged to be a well-meaning, but sadly flawed man. Worse still, an ugly rumour was busily circulating in town that Mr Hope had, during his residence, been conducting an intrigue with a married woman. This last allegation was too much for Enid and Louisa, both of whom emphatically refused to believe it. Mina was anxious to know what Mr Phipps had discovered, but dared not show her hand by questioning him. Word had it that the tainted hero was preparing to leave Brighton, and might already have left.

One of the fruits of Mr Hope's patronage was a set of nicely printed handbills, which Mr Merridew had volunteered to design. Decorated with a pretty border, they read:

The Famed Exponent of Shakespeare
Who has appeared before Royalty
MR MARCUS MERRIDEW
Will grace the Pavilion in a leading role
in

THE COURTLY PRINCE
a diversion
by
Richard Scarletti

On seeing the handbills, Richard had been slightly taken aback by the fact that it was the actor and not the writer who was so prominently featured, however, Mr Merridew explained to him that the audience always came to see the actors, and never took any note of the author, and that his wording would undoubtedly sell more tickets. So it was to prove.

Louisa was impressed to learn that Richard had penned a play that was to be performed by a famed professional actor, but she had not appreciated, and had certainly not been informed, that he also planned to appear in it. She was aware that her dear Henry had written some of the stories he published, and then there were Mina's little homilies for children, and, of course, the late Mr Dickens had been a good and charitable person by all accounts, and very rich. Louisa had therefore convinced herself that the business of playwrighting was a good one, and perfectly respectable, as long as the writer did not have anything to do with the performers. This entertainment, she felt assured, was only the start of Richard's new career, which would lead to fortune and fame. She had been busy calling on all her friends insisting that they buy tickets and accepting no refusals. Several, who recalled Marcus Merridew in his heyday as the darling of the ladies, needed no persuasion. As a result, the performance, which was to take place before a potential audience of some fifty persons, which was as much seating as the apartment could accommodate, was quickly sold out.

The space available for the actors was not large and there was no furniture or properties of any sort, but Mr Merridew had taken great care in arranging the room, and it looked very elegant. Two of the ornate pillars, delicate looking yet strong, which supported the roof of the music room gallery served to mark the boundary of the acting space, framing it like the feet of a gilded proscenium arch in a London theatre, while the deep drapery of the window curtains formed an opulent backdrop. Chinese screens had been placed discreetly to the right and the left to act as wings.

Mina anticipated the event with some apprehension, but felt that she ought to be there if only to deal with any upset that might result. She made sure to carry a good supply of handkerchiefs and a smelling bottle. All the seats were filled, with the Scarletti family accorded places on the front row. Louisa was proud and excited, but Enid still wore the sour expression that had been her most prominent feature since Mr Hope's fall from popularity. As they waited for the production to begin, still more ladies crammed into the room, chattering with excitement at having bought last-minute tickets for standing room only, almost doubling the size of the audience. Most of them, Mina noticed, were of her mother's age or older, and many were holding little posies.

The tinkling of a bell announced the start of the performance and the audience, after the last trills of laughter and excitement had died down, fell silent. After a certain amount of whispering from behind one of the screens, there burst upon the stage an alarming figure. It was Richard, wearing a blue frockcoat too large for him, with ragged epaulettes very much tarnished, and an enormous bicorne hat that threatened to fall over his eyes. He was waving what Mina knew to be a blunt sword but which looked dangerously real.

'Aha!' he exclaimed, striding to the front of the space and striking a fierce pose, one hand on his hip, the other pointing the sword skywards, chest thrust out. 'Aha, aha!' he added, either for greater effect or to give himself time to think. 'I am ze great Emperor Napoleon! *Mais oui, ma foi, zut alors, sacre bleu!*' He made some wild passes with the sword, which caused the ladies in the front row to sway back in alarm. 'And my greatest enemy is George, Prince of Wales, regent of England! 'E is tall, 'e is 'andsome, and 'e 'as everysing I most desire! *Comme il faut! Consommé du jour!*' Richard strode about the stage waving the sword. Mina glanced quickly at her mother, who had clapped a palm over her mouth, her eyes wide open.

Richard took up his heroic pose again. 'Yes, 'e 'as ze srone of England, but 'e also 'as ze 'and of ze lady I love! Ze incomparable, ze beautiful Mrs Fitz'erbert. *Mon coeur! La choucroute farci!* I am determined! It is farewell to Josephine! None but Maria will be my Empress!'

There were a few titters from the audience. Undismayed, Richard paraded about in a circle once more before facing the increasingly amused assembly.

'Ah, you English, you sink that I, Napoleon, am not a tall man. But it is ze madness of love that 'as brought me low!' Here Richard fell to his knees, and his hat slipped over his eyes, requiring him to make some adjustment. 'I 'ear you ask, *quelle horreur!* What will I do to achieve my desires. I will tell you! I dare all! I will invade England wiz all of my navy. *En avance, mes amis! A l'eau, ces't l'heure!*' Richard made another circle about the stage, only this time on his knees, an art which he had not sufficiently practised. If his intention was to make the former French Emperor appear ridiculous, he was succeeding.

'And now 'ere I am *en Angleterre*, ze land I mean to rule! But where oh where is my great love, *ah mon ange! Mon petit poisson! Chacun a son gout!* My 'eart beats only for Maria Fitz'erbert. Where is she?' He placed a hand behind one ear. 'Wait, I 'ear 'er dainty feet approach, I will 'ide and learn if she returns my love.'

As Richard shuffled behind a screen, Mina braved another look at her mother. Louisa now had her face buried in her handkerchief, but whether she was laughing, crying or simply hiding, it was hard to tell.

There was a brief pause, carefully studied so as to produce the maximum anticipation in the audience, then Nellie made her entrance. Magnificently gowned in the fashion of the day, her hair shining, her skin aglow, her eyes bright and beguiling, there was no mystery as to why an Emperor should invade another country to make her his own.

She approached the front of the little stage, smiling with the knowledge that every eye was upon her. 'Ladies, gentlemen all, I beg you not to blame me for my unusual mode of life,' she said, allowing a lacy fan to flutter modestly. 'I was an honourable widow when I first became acquainted with the Prince of Wales, and he fell most passionately in love with me. For years he pursued me to attain his heart's desire, but I am a respectable lady and would never consent to an improper connection, even at the entreaties of a Prince. At last we were married, and though the law of the land will not recognise me as his true wife, I am content that our love has been sanctified by God. My dear Prince, beloved husband, my own darling George, how can I not love you and be true forever to you and you alone!'

Nellie took an elegant tour about the stage so that everyone could feast their eyes on her ensemble. As she passed by one of the side screens, Richard, still on his knees, made a lunge, probably to try and kiss the hem of her garment, and fell flat on his face, his hat tumbling off and rolling across the stage. He stood up, dusted off his knees, retrieved the hat and jammed it firmly back on his head.

'Aha!' he exclaimed. 'It is ze beautiful Maria, ze angel 'oo rules my 'eart! *Veuve Clicqot*! *Coup de foudre*! Oh, *mon amour*, say you will be mine; be my bride and I will make you Empress of *la belle* France!'

'But sir,' said Nellie, turning away bashfully, 'that cannot be, I am the wife of George, Prince of Wales, and he alone has my heart.'

'*Tonnere*! Zen I will slay 'im!' Richard waved the sword about his head in a manner that probably endangered himself more than anyone else. 'Where is my 'ated rival? I will seek 'im out and take 'is life, zen England and Mrs Fitz'erbert will both be mine!'

He rushed back behind a screen, and Nellie took the audience into her confidence. 'Little does the Frenchman know that my husband is as brave as he is handsome. He will not fear to fight, either for his country, or for me!' She moved aside in a swirl of silk and waited by the screen, her fan beating like a dove's wing, her eyes gazing from above the snowy lace.

Marcus Merridew now made his appearance. He glided rather than walked, advancing in true dignified fashion, elegant of gesture and precise of step. By the art of the actor he had turned back time, and though Mina knew he was near her mother's years, everything about him suggested a man hardly more than thirty. He was clad after the style of Beau Brummell in breeches and boots, with a buttoned long-tailed coat, and the wig he wore framed his face in a cluster of golden brown curls. Those ladies in the audience who had seen him shine as Hamlet many years ago were not disappointed, and there were many sighs of appreciation and some enthusiastic clapping of mittened hands.

Mr Merridew greeted his admirers with a gracious smile and, advancing to the fore, bowed to them several times before taking up a position, one hand pressed passionately to his heart. The audience quickly hushed with anticipation and when he spoke, his voice was rich and mellow, effortlessly filling the room. 'Ah, what a rogue and peasant slave is that Napoleon who seeks to rob me of my love! But I will defy him, take arms against a sea of troubles, and by opposing, end them. I have had word from my dear wife that the tyrant is even now on our shores and seeks to murder me. What will it be, will he, like the coward he is, pour poison into the porches of mine ears as I sleep, or stab me with a bare bodkin? But I mean to face him like a man, I will be as Hyperion to a satyr.' He looked to the side and saw Nellie. 'Soft you now, the fair Maria. How I wish to make her my lawful bride and my Queen, but the King my father would never condone it. My will is not my own, I am subject to my birth.'

He crossed the space to Nellie, who advanced to meet him. 'My dearest Maria, my eternal love, the wife of my heart.' He reached out his hand and gently clasped her fingers, then made an extravagantly stylish obeisance.

There was a strangled cry from the audience. Mrs Peasgood, in a state of great agitation, had risen to her feet. 'I can be silent no longer! It is he, or his spirit, the very he who appeared before me, he whose ghost walked through the wall dressed just so and bowed to me, he who danced with the lady in the room with the red wallpaper. Is he a ghost or a demon?'

Mrs Mowbray rose up and tried to comfort her sister, who was trembling violently. 'Oh, my dear, please sit down and calm yourself!'

'How can I when a spirit walks in the shape of a man? What does it mean?'

Several ladies waved at Mrs Peasgood and urged her to keep quiet.

Merridew turned to the gathering with an arched eyebrow. 'The lady doth protest too much methinks.'

It was left to Mrs Mowbray to remove her almost hysterical sister from the room, which, with profuse apologies, she did. The most likely place to console her was the ladies' retiring room, and Mina feared that the sight of the red dragon wallpaper would bring on another more serious fit, but there was little she could do.

After this interruption order was restored and the play proceeded. Marcus and Nellie conducted a courtly dance of matchless elegance and refinement after which the Prince, on bended knee, declared his undying love for his Maria. Richard rushed back on stage and exhausted his entire fund of repeatable French phrases, and a few others that ought never to have been uttered. Finally there was the sword fight, which was conducted with more dash than skill by Richard and with consummate skill by Mr Merridew. Napoleon duly met his Waterloo on the point of the Prince's sword and spent ten minutes expiring noisily, clawing the carpet. There was rapturous applause after which Mr Merridew was prevailed upon, an exercise that took barely moments to achieve, to entertain his admiring public with some of the great classical speeches in his repertoire, after which he was lavishly pelted with flowers by weeping matrons.

By the time it was all over Mrs Peasgood and Mrs Mowbray had long departed, and Louisa took her daughters and the entire cast for dinner. Since Mrs Peasgood's outburst had been highly embarrassing, no one chose to mention it.

The wine was poured and *hors d'oeuvres* brought to the table. 'It was a perfectly splendid evening,' said Louisa, raising her glass, 'but Richard —'

'Yes, mother?'

'You must never do that again.'

'No, mother.'

'Mr Merridew, I must compliment you on your costume,' said Mina.

'Thank you dear lady; it is the very one I wore when appearing in the Regency gloss on *King Lear*. As you saw,' he added modestly, 'it still fits me to perfection.'

'Have you ever worn it in the Pavilion before?'

'As a matter of fact I have, but not for a performance. When the Pavilion was first opened for inspection some of our little troupe made the tour in costume — it was amusing and we hoped to attract some interest in our play.'

'Do you recall if you entered the music room on your tour?'

'I expect so, but it is hard to remember exactly where we went. We did march along what I now know to be the servants' corridors and then we executed a pretty little dance.' He looked suddenly thoughtful. 'You don't think that could have anything to do with —' He shook his head, 'but no, that cannot be, it was over twenty years ago and it was all in the best possible taste.'

When Mina was home once more she again studied her guidebook to the Pavilion, and was now quite sure of the train of events. She sent a note to Mrs Peasgood, saying she hoped very much that she was well, and wished to speak to her on a matter that she felt sure would set her mind at rest.

Chapter Forty

Mina was not at all sure if Mrs Peasgood would consent to see her and half expected to receive either no reply or a letter from Mrs Mowbray with a polite refusal. To her surprise, however, a note was delivered inviting her to call. Neither Louisa nor Enid were disposed to visit Mrs Peasgood until they felt reassured that her sudden malady was not catching, and it was only to Richard, who was still exuberant from his theatrical triumph, that Mina revealed the true reason for her proposed visit.

'Mrs Peasgood knows you too well, Mina,' said Richard, 'you would have secured an interview with her sooner or later and she has decided to accept the inevitable.'

'I hope I can bring her some peace. Poor lady, it has been a long time coming.'

In Mrs Peasgood's quiet parlour Mina was greeted by the lady herself, who seemed to have recovered much of her accustomed composure and now appeared merely sad. She was attended with care and sympathy by Mrs Mowbray.

'I think,' said Mrs Peasgood, once refreshments were brought and the maid had departed, 'that you and possibly you alone, apart from my sister, understand some of the reasons for my agitation yesterday.'

'I do,' said Mina, 'and that is mainly because I was probably the only person present at my brother's play who had made a recent study of *Some Confidential Observations by a Lady of Quality*, the pamphlet you wrote in 1850.'

Mrs Peasgood's hand trembled and her sister rescued a teacup from potential disaster. 'How, pray, did you obtain a copy?'

'It was in the library. It is a part of their collection of works on the history of Brighton.'

Mrs Peasgood frowned. 'I sincerely hope it is not on open display.'

'No, it is stored in a box with a host of other pamphlets.'

'Then I don't understand. Was it just by chance that you found it?'

Mina explained how she had searched for the pamphlet when all she had was a clue that it might exist at all.

'Well that is quite astonishing,' said Mrs Peasgood. 'I compliment you on your insight and diligence.'

'I have also read an account in the *Gazette* of the occasion when the Pavilion was first opened for viewing by the public, the time you must have gone there with your father. There were no official guides as there are now, people simply walked from room to room, and given the nature of the building, and how many times it

435

has been altered and enlarged, some visitors did get lost and confused. I expect that that is what happened to you.'

'Yes, I do recall that. But I wrote a true and honest account of my visit, not the despicable and indecent invention of that horrid book.'

'Then it was not, as I had initially supposed, intended to be a work of fiction?'

'No, not at all.'

'I take it that you have not visited the Pavilion since then?'

'I dared not! I wanted no repetition of that experience. Before last night I had not stepped through its doors in over twenty years. It was only with the passage of time, and your mother being so insistent, that I consented to go again.'

'Mr Merridew, the actor who played the Prince of Wales, has been an attendant at the Pavilion for many years, and knows the building well. He told me that he and a theatrical troupe, which included some musicians, had in 1850 been performing a play costumed in the style of the court of King George III. They decided for their amusement and also to stimulate interest in the play to visit the Pavilion in costume. I believe that it was they you saw.'

'Are you sure? I heard the music very distinctly before I even saw them; it seemed to come through the walls.'

'It did come through the walls. There are long corridors for the use of servants which run alongside the main rooms. The musicians walked along them with violin and flute.'

'But how did the gentleman come into the room when the doors could not be opened?'

Mina opened the guidebook and showed Mrs Peasgood the page describing the music room. 'I think this is where you were standing when you saw him. The music room has four doors but two of them are false to give the appearance of symmetry. There is, however, another door for the use of servants covered in the same paper as the walls. The room was ill lit when you were there and you would not have noticed it. I think that is how Mr Merridew entered when your back was turned.'

Mrs Peasgood took the guidebook and spent several minutes studying it. 'So there was not, after all, a ghost,' she said at last.

'There was not.'

'I confess that that is something of a relief to me.'

'Knowing this, and being able to connect your pamphlet with the recent sensational volume, will greatly strengthen the plagiarism case.'

'I am sure it will,' said Mrs Peasgood, but she did not seem comfortable with the prospect.

'There is nothing to give offence in your pamphlet, and it is very nicely written. You could have it printed again, as a story, rather than a history. I think it would do very well.'

'Really? Well I am not sure about that.' Nevertheless she looked flattered.

'I have my suspicions as to who wrote *An Encounter*, but there are some pieces of the puzzle I am missing, although I think you might be able to enlighten me.'

The two sisters exchanged glances and Mrs Peasgood patted Mrs Mowbray's hand. 'Caroline has confessed all to me and I have forgiven her. Miss Scarletti, I am grateful to you for all you have done, and I am therefore prepared to tell you all I know.'

'I too,' said Mrs Mowbray, 'although I have much to be ashamed of. It was at one of those séances with Miss Eustace, last summer. Mr Clee was there, only none of us knew at the time that he was in league with her. There was some conversation afterwards and he was asking if there were any legends in Brighton about hauntings, so —' She uttered a despondent sigh — 'I regret to say that I mentioned the business in the Pavilion. I know I shouldn't have but it just seemed to come out. I'd never told anyone else before or since.'

Mrs Peasgood gave a faint smile. 'The young gentleman was very persuasive. After my marriage, which took place in 1851, I decided to put all that business behind me and Caroline promised to say nothing. Truth to tell I wished it had never happened at all, as I thought it made me appear rather foolish. I was not eager for it to be broadcast, and most especially I did not wish Mr Peasgood to know.'

'As soon as I told Mr Clee about it I regretted my betrayal,' Mrs Mowbray continued, 'but he kept on and on asking me more about it and he was very charming as you know, and so I told him it was in a book, and then he wanted to know where he could get a copy. I didn't know there was one in the library.'

'Nor I,' said Mrs Peasgood. 'I suppose the printers must have sent them one.'

'Well, in the end I lent him mine, thinking that would put an end to the matter. But then he said he wanted to meet the lady who had written it, so I told him the lady was dead long ago and had no family. I'm so sorry, Mattie, I didn't want you to know I'd broken my promise.'

'So, of course, he then believed that there was no one who might notice the pirating of the work, and thought he could copy it with impunity,' said Mina. 'I doubt that he was expecting it to be such a sensation.'

'That was quite a shock,' said Mrs Mowbray, 'especially after what he had done with it. It was disgusting. When he came back to Brighton recently he asked to see me saying that he had found out that the writer was alive. We met in secret a number of times, but he never wore that disguise when I saw him. He was very insistent that I tell him who the author was — I think he suspected that it was really me — he kept on asking, but I wouldn't say. He told me I must tell no one that I had given him the book and I promised him I wouldn't. He even offered to share some of the profits of *An Encounter* if I could get the action for plagiarism stopped. Do you think it will all come out in court? I will look like such a silly woman.'

'Not as silly as I will look,' said Mrs Peasgood grimly. 'I do hope that with good advice we can settle it without recourse to a public hearing. Who knows if the culprits can even pay the damages? I fear that after my public outburst it may become common knowledge, but if it does not feature in a trial which is reported in the newspapers it may, I hope, be more quickly and quietly forgotten.'

'I promise that I will not reveal the confidences you have granted me today,' said Mina. 'I do, however, have one request.'

'Oh?'

'As the matter proceeds through the usual legal channels you will undoubtedly learn more, and I should very much like, for my own curiosity, to hear the whole story.'

Mr Peasgood did not hesitate. 'You deserve no less. I agree.'

Chapter Forty-One

Mrs Peasgood was true to her word. During the next few weeks the full sequence of events was uncovered, and Mina was in receipt of much confidential information that she promised not to reveal. The plagiarism case against the Misses Bland had initially been pursued by Mr Laidlaw, of Phipps, Laidlaw and Phipps, but then, quite abruptly, he decided to retire from practice, and he and his wife left Brighton to reside in a small Scottish estate owned by his family. The reasons for his decision and the suddenness of it were never disclosed, although there was a suspicion that pretty Mrs Laidlaw and Mr Arthur Wallace Hope, as well as a certain private detective, could, had they wished, have solved the mystery. Young Mr Ronald Phipps swiftly and smoothly took up the reins of the enquiry and it was thought that the date on which a third Phipps would be added to the partnership had been considerably advanced.

Mr Phipps had established beyond doubt that *An Encounter* had been written by Miss Eustace during her summer residence in Brighton. It had been composed with the intention not only of making money, but also of creating more interest in her séances. The text, based on Mrs Peasgood's pamphlet, a history of the Pavilion, the author's recollection of her own visit, and a lurid imagination, had been completed shortly before she and her accomplices were arrested. With legal expenses mounting and the proceeds of their fraudulent activities having been seized, when Mr Clee was released on bail it was decided to use the book to raise funds. He had known the Misses Bland's family for some years and was well aware of the stricken older sister's attraction to him. He had made use of her weakness before to borrow money when business had not been successful, and approached her once again for a loan to pay the printer, only to find that he had gone to the well once too often. This time, her price had been marriage.

Thereafter he had stayed in touch with his 'wife' by letter in order that she could send him the profits of the enterprise. When Mr Hope, a wealthy and influential spiritualist, had come to Brighton to lecture, Mr Clee had spotted a chance. The friendship of Hope and Dr Lynn was common knowledge amongst magicians, and Lynn, after receiving the business card of Benjamin Clee, purveyor of theatrical supplies, from Miss Eustace, had become a customer. Letters from Dr Lynn placing orders had provided enough examples of his writing to enable Clee to forge a convincing letter of introduction to Mr Hope, and launch a new career as Mystic Stefan.

All was going well for Mr Clee until the shock accusation of plagiarism. The Misses Bland, equally unprepared for the allegation and the predicament they found themselves in, had fled to Brighton to confront him. He had been alarmed to see them at first, as he did not want his real identity revealed, but also saw that their presence in Brighton could be made to work to his advantage. He told the sisters that as far as he was aware the author of *Confidential Observations* was deceased and that they should if challenged say that they had received the book through the spirits. He also instructed that on no account should they tell anyone of his masquerade as Mystic Stefan, and above all they must not speak to Miss Scarletti, the crippled lady, as she was his enemy and the reason he was in his current difficulty.

Clee had strongly recommended that the Misses Bland approach Mr Hope for assistance, as he would undoubtedly be sympathetic. The sisters were very adept at the 'willing game', as they had since childhood employed a system of secret signals to communicate the answers, and Clee believed that this would easily fool Mr Hope into accepting them as mediums and earn his loyalty to their cause. As predicted, when the sisters came to Mr Hope with their story and performed their mind-reading trick, he was delighted with it and became a fervent believer. Hope had told the Misses Bland that while he could not personally intervene in the plagiarism case at present, although he would look for every opportunity of doing so, he could help promote them in Brighton as psychics which would assist in their defence. Clee had also become aware of Hope's obsession with finding Dr Livingstone, and was able to convince him that, while lacking sufficient power to transport the good doctor home, he could through the energy of the spirits send the beleaguered explorer comforting messages, and much needed food and medicines. It was a service that came at a price, but it was a price Mr Hope could afford and was willing to pay.

Mr Clee's one remaining difficulty was Mrs Mowbray and he had done everything short of promising marriage to extract more information from her, but the situation had finally concluded with an uneasy truce in which both parties had agreed to be silent about their involvement.

The trial of Miss Eustace and her confederates duly took place at Lewes Assizes and Mina made sure to be present. A statement was read from Dr Lynn, who was currently away on tour, saying that he had never met Mr Clee or Mystic Stefan, and had not written either of them a letter of introduction to Mr Hope. It was also revealed that Miss Eustace had never intended to return to Brighton and appear at the Pavilion. Mr Clee, anticipating an acquittal, had been making plans for them to leave for America and had secured the services of an agent there who would obtain bookings for séances and theatrical performances.

Miss Whinstone gave her evidence with as much courage as she could summon, and Mr Jellico, with tears of pride in his eyes, sat urging her on with smiles and nods. She barely faltered. Miss Eustace's counsel offered the defence that Miss

Whinstone had lied to the magistrates and was now lying to judge and jury, but in view of the other revelations this rang hollow, and was in itself a further proof of the scurrilous depths to which the prisoners would sink.

The accused were duly found guilty of obtaining money by deception, and in view of the substantial sums involved, the suggestion that there were numerous victims, and a previous conviction for the same offence, were sentenced to terms of five years in prison. Mr Clee, in a separate hearing, was found guilty on an additional charge of bigamy. As he was removed to the cells, Clee loudly derided Mr Hope as a fool, saying that he had never duped anyone as easily. Hope, he said, had even been taken in by a tawdry glass bead that came from a theatrical costume shop. Mina surmised from this outburst that the Viscount, who was not in court, had withdrawn all financial assistance from the conspirators.

Mr Hope was long gone from Brighton by that time, but Mina did hear that he still believed in the Misses Bland, who had been absolved of all blame concerning the plagiarism, and was launching them on a career as mediums and mindreaders. There was a newspaper report that he had asked Mrs Guppy to apport Dr Livingstone to one of her séances. So far she had not been successful.

Richard had decided to abandon the stage as a career. He said that he had enjoyed the experience enormously and had even made money on the ticket sales, but thought that it was too hard work to be a regular thing. Mina was obliged to remind him that his profit had mainly resulted from the fact that the venue and advertising had all been paid for by Mr Hope, which was not a source he could rely upon in future, and Richard was obliged to admit that this was true. His early return to London was precipitated by the fact that both the twins had started teething. Before he left he promised Mina to accept their brother Edward's offer of a position as a clerk. She implored him to try and make a success of it, but was concerned that it would not keep him out of trouble for long.

Following his magnificent success in *The Courtly Prince*, Mr Marcus Merridew enjoyed a well-deserved revival of his theatrical career. While continuing his work at the Pavilion, which he would never have given up as he found it very pleasurable, he was able to combine this with a sudden demand for his services as an actor and raconteur. He was soon engaged for a series of public lectures on the history of the legitimate theatre and readings from Shakespeare, and was positively begged by Brighton Theatre's stock company to ornament their stage in the leading role of his choice.

Meanwhile, fashion in Brighton changed with the wind, and there was no more talk of ghosts in the Pavilion, although there were visitors aplenty.

Enid continued to pine for the company of Mr Hope and sat wanly at meals, eating very little and making the occasional suggestion that it would be charming to visit Middlesex as there were so many fine country estates there. She seemed unable to accept that Mr Hope's attentions had not been genuine. One morning she was absent from the breakfast table and Mina was worried that she might have fled to join her admirer.

'Enid is in her room,' Louisa explained. 'She received a letter this morning from Mr Inskip. It seems that his business with the Carpathian Count has been completed earlier than expected and he should be home before winter if the weather holds. Enid was quite overcome by the news and has been bilious ever since.'

BOOK THREE: AN UNQUIET GHOST

Prologue

Lincoln, 1851

Thomas Fernwood was dying, and it was not the death he had been expecting. A man should die aged, peaceful, content, surrounded by his loving family, his soul slipping away sweetly from the prison of the flesh to join his ancestors in a higher, better place. At fifty-eight he had prided himself on his heartiness and vigour and thought he had many more years to enjoy, but it was not to be. Something deadly was tearing at his insides, eating him away. It was as if hot irons had been thrust down his throat deep into his stomach, and his bowels were molten. For hours he had retched in agony bringing up nothing but searing acid, a river of pain. Now, weak as a child, he was unable even to rise from his bed.

A face hovered above him, grim and anxious, and he recognised with some relief the heavy jowls and grey side whiskers of his physician, Dr Sperley. Thomas struggled through cracked lips to say what he feared might be his final message, but his throat was burned raw, and the words would not come.

'Don't try to speak,' said Sperley, gruffly. 'I know you've taken poison. I've done all I can.'

Only the desperation of the dying could force the mouth to move and what emerged was the merest whisper. 'Mur ... der ...' then Thomas coughed and retched again, a sour dry straining, so fierce he thought his ribs would break. His body had almost nothing left to reject. He felt a cool damp cloth pressed to his forehead, a little water wetting his parched lips. Finally, the spasm passed. Sperley's face loomed closer, furrowed with concern. 'Do you know who has done this? Nod your head if you do.'

The stricken man groaned deeply and nodded. Slowly, a hand that had been clutching the coverlet, opened, and one trembling finger moved on its surface as if he was trying to spell out a word. Sperley understood. 'I'll fetch pencil and paper.' The doctor turned to go, but in that moment Thomas's mouth suddenly bubbled with green bile and he started to choke, his body racked with convulsions so violent that he was almost thrown to the floor, and Sperley had to return and steady him, hold him to the bed by main force. Thomas gasped for air, his chest pumping rapidly, eyes wild with panic, but he gasped in vain. There was anger, frustration, despair, sorrow, acceptance, and finally a blinding light that faded away to nothing.

Chapter One

Brighton, 1871

'The land of the dead' wrote Mina Scarletti, 'is like a mysterious, unknowable sea. It has no horizon; we cannot see where it begins or where it ends, if indeed, it does either. It has no floor, but its shadowy depths go on forever, and sometimes, there arise from the silent deep strange monsters.' She laid the end of her pen against her lips and paused for thought.

Mina's busy imagination was peopled with ghosts and demons. They lived in her dreams and on the pages of her stories, but not in her daily anxieties. Other worlds, she felt, must take care of themselves while she concerned herself with more immediate problems; her mother's changeable moods, her sister Enid's unhappy marriage and her younger brother Richard's inability to find a respectable career. At that very moment, however, Mina was luxuriating in the absence of any demands on her time.

Winter in Brighton was, for those who liked to stay by their own fireside and avoid the centre of town, a season of the most beautiful peace. The oft-deplored Sunday excursion trains, which brought noisy crowds to the streets, had ceased to run at the end of October. November 5th had, as was usual, come and gone without any noticeable disturbances beyond the odd mischievously dropped squib, since the annual drunken dances around roaring bonfires took place several miles away in Lewes.

The professional gentlemen and their families had taken their autumnal holidays and were long gone, and the idle fashionables were arriving. Glittering convocations, balls and suppers that were wont to go on into the small hours of the morning and disturb nearby residents with the rattle of carriages and cabriolets were held far from Mina's home in Montpelier Road, and would not trouble her. More to the point, she had the house almost to herself since her mother was in London trying to soothe Enid, whose twin boys were teething with extraordinary vigour. Richard was also in the capital, lodging with their older brother Edward, after reluctantly, and almost certainly briefly, accepting work as a clerk in the Scarletti publishing company.

Rain pattered on glass like insistently tapping fingers, but Mina had no wish to heed this dangerous call. In the cold street beyond her heavily curtained windows breezes that carried the salt sting of the sea tore mercilessly at the cloaks of passers-by, and a steel sky clouded the sun. Mina's small fragile body did not do well in inclement weather, and she tried not to go out too often in the winter because of the danger of catching a chill in her cramped lungs. The recent charitable bazaar in aid of the children's hospital presided over by illustrious patronesses and held at the Dome had not tempted her, since the crowded conditions were fumed with coughs and agues. She had contented herself with making a personal donation by post. Neither had she gone to see the much talked about panorama of Paris, depicted both in its old grandeur and the conflagrations that had spelled the end of the recent violent disturbances.

Once a week, carefully wrapped against the cold, she took a cab to Dr Daniel Hamid's medicated Indian herbal baths where, enveloped in hot towels, she bathed in scented vapour that opened her airways and eased her chest. Afterwards, the doctor's sister, Anna, a skilled masseuse, used fragrant oils to dispel the strains arising from Mina's twisted spine, and taught her exercises to develop the muscles of her back so as to better support that obstinately distorted column of bones. Mina had last visited the baths only the day before and consequently was almost free from pain.

Mina's bedroom on the first floor of the house was her haven, where she sat at her writing desk, one hip supported by a special wedge shaped cushion that enabled her to sit upright, and created her dark tales. The dumbbells she used for her daily exercises were hidden at the bottom of her wardrobe. Even as she reflected on the quiet she was enjoying she feared that it was only a matter of time before the house was in some kind of ferment not of her making, which she would be obliged to address, and then her back and neck would start to pinch again, but on that blissful evening, with the fire crackling in the grate, her new composition begun, and a nice little fowl roasting for her dinner, all was well.

There was a knock at her door, and Rose, the general servant, appeared holding an envelope. Rose was a sturdy, serious girl who worked hard and uncomplainingly, trudging up and down the flights of stairs that linked the basement kitchen with three upper floors, keeping winter fires burning, running errands in all weathers, and coping with the petulant demands of Mina's mother and the turmoil that usually resulted from Richard's unannounced visits. 'I'm sorry to disturb you, Miss, but it's one of those letters. Shall I put it on the fire?'

Mina hesitated, but she had reached a pause in her work, and a moment more would make no difference. She laid down her pen. 'Thank you, Rose, let me see it first.'

From time to time letters would arrive in a variety of hands that Mina did not recognise, addressed to 'Miss Scarletti, Brighton'. The authors had read in the newspapers of her appearance to give evidence at the recent trial of the mediumistic fraud Miss Eustace and her confederates in crime, which had resulted in those persons being committed to prison for extortion. The unknown correspondents had guessed that due to Mina's unusual surname, letters with such an apparently insufficient address would be safely delivered, and so, all too often, they were. Since the trial had featured prominently in both *The Times* and the *Illustrated Police News*, these letters came from every corner of the kingdom.

Some correspondents believed that they could persuade Mina of the great truth of spiritualism, and wrote earnestly and at great length on the subject, declaring their fervent belief in such miscreants as D. D. Home, the celebrated medium who had tried to cheat an elderly lady out of her fortune, and Mrs Guppy, a lady of substantial dimensions who claimed be able to fly using the power of the spirits, and pass through solid walls without making a hole. Others wanted to engage Mina's services to investigate a fraudulent practitioner, distance of travel not being seen as any obstacle, on the assumption that she would be glad to pay her own way for the fame it would bring. There were also those who declared that she was undoubtedly a medium herself who would or could not acknowledge it, and offered to 'develop' her in that skill. It was with weary trepidation therefore that Mina opened the envelope, with the object of briefly reviewing the contents before they were consigned to the fire.

She found a single sheet of folded notepaper, printed with the name and address of Fernwood Groceries in Haywards Heath, a Sussex village not far from Brighton. 'Quality! Freshness! Wholesomeness!' she was promised, this notion being enhanced by an engraving of a plump, smiling child clutching a rusk. The letter, however, was not on the subject of foodstuffs.

Dear Miss Scarletti,

Please forgive me, a complete stranger, for writing to you, but I would not presume to do so unless I believed that you are able to assist me in a matter of great importance and delicacy. Please be assured that all I wish to humbly beg of you is your advice on a subject of which, I have been told, you have considerable knowledge.

My name is George Fernwood, and I recently became betrothed to a Miss Mary Clifton. We wish to marry in the spring. There is, however, a matter of grave concern to us, which I will not describe in this letter, but which we both feel should be resolved before we take that joyful step.

I hope you will permit us to call on you at whatever time would be most convenient to yourself.

Assuring you of my sincere and honest intentions,

Yours faithfully,

G. Fernwood.

'Dinner in half an hour, Miss,' said Rose, tonelessly. 'Do you want boiled potatoes or boiled rice?'

Mina had eaten savoury rice when dining with Dr Hamid and his sister and knew how it ought to look and taste. 'Potatoes, please,' she said, absently, staring at the letter. 'And when I have written a reply to this, you must take it to the post box.'

'Yes, Miss.' Rose's face betrayed nothing of her thoughts, but there was something in the tilt of her head and a slight movement of her shoulders that said 'I suppose you know your own business best.'

When the maid had returned downstairs, Mina read the letter again, considering why it was that she had decided to respond to Mr Fernwood's plea. His words were polite and respectful, that much appealed to her, and his object, a warmly anticipated wedding, was commendable. Mina could not see how she might help the couple achieve happiness, but the letter hinted that there might be a mystery to be solved, and she thought that in that quiet November time, such a project might stimulate her mind. As she penned a reply, she did however wonder if she was once more about to explore the dusty veil that lay between the living and the dead.

Chapter Two

Two days later George Fernwood and Mary Clifton were in Mina's parlour. It was a cheery room, warmed by a bright fire, furnished for comfort, and made attractive with framed portraits and ornaments that commemorated family events.

The pleasing cosiness of the room was not, however, something the visitors seemed able to absorb. They were a reserved, polite, diffident pair, and just little nervous. Even though there had been a description of Mina in the newspapers, neither of them could conceal a certain curiosity at her appearance, and gazed at her as if wondering how someone so small and twisted out of the usual shape could actually be alive.

George Fernwood was aged about thirty, with large worried eyes, his dark hair standing up around the perimeter of his scalp in a fluff of short curls which made Mina suspect that he was concealing an incipient bald patch on his crown. He made a stumbling expression of gratitude for being granted the interview, which Miss Clifton echoed, and brought a gift; a package neatly wrapped in clean brown paper and tied about with string. 'Do please accept these, they are the very best currant biscuits,' he assured Mina.

Miss Clifton was perhaps a little younger, her plain square face softened by the affectionate glances she directed at her betrothed. Both, like their offering, were respectably and demurely clad, suggesting that Fernwood Groceries was a thriving business serving the middle classes of Haywards Heath.

Rose brought a laden tray, poured the tea, unwrapped the biscuits and arranged them on a plate. They did look very good, but Mr Fernwood and Miss Clifton could only gaze at the tempting sight with expressions of deep gloom. Rose stared at the couple suspiciously and was more than content to be allowed to leave.

There was a strained silence. Neither of the visitors had an appetite, but held their teacups and sipped carefully as if delaying the dreadful moment when they would be obliged to tell Mina why they had come. Mina decided not to waste time by introducing some subject such as the weather, or the fashionable entertainment of the season, and simply waited for them to speak. At length, Fernwood heaved a deep sigh and placed his cup and saucer carefully on the table.

'I am the grandson of the late Thomas Fernwood, a grocer who conducted the family business in Lincoln. My dear Mary is his great niece, so we are cousins twice removed. We have known each other since we were children.' Miss Clifton said nothing but favoured him with a tender smile. Fernwood suddenly clasped his hands together tightly as if trying to prevent them from shaking, and Miss Clifton, her brow creasing with sympathy, placed a light encouraging touch on his arm.

'Go on, George. We must, really we must, or we will never know the answer.'

He looked at her, patted her fingertips and nodded. 'I know. But it is so hard to actually speak the words, to talk of something that our family has not discussed for many a year, even amongst ourselves.' He braced himself to continue, and faced Mina once more. 'Twenty years ago, my grandfather was murdered.'

Mina hardly knew what to say. She had expected to be told of a death, but not something of that nature. 'That must have been a terribly distressing time,' she said at last.

'I was ten years old then, and Mary just eight, so we children were sheltered from the actuality, we were merely told that he had been taken very ill and passed away. It wasn't until quite some years later that we finally learned the truth.' Fernwood, despite the warmth in the room, shivered. 'He had swallowed poison and died in great agony.'

Mina didn't want to seem to be prying, but since her visitor was having some difficulty in recounting the story he had clearly come expressly to tell her, and she did not wish the interview to last through to dinner, she decided to enquire further. 'I do hope the culprit was caught and punished.'

'No,' said Fernwood, unable to keep the anguish from his voice. 'To this day no-one other than the guilty party knows who was responsible.'

His lips began to tremble, and he pulled a handkerchief from his pocket and pressed it to his eyes, shoulders heaving with emotion. It was some moments before he was able to continue. Miss Clifton held his hand, and Mina politely averted her eyes. At last he calmed himself and went on.

'When my grandfather lay on his deathbed he told his doctor that he was a murdered man and tried to say who it was who had poisoned him, but he died before he could reveal the name. His death has been a dreadful shadow over our family ever since. My grandmother forbade anyone to speak of it and it was only after her death ten years later that my sisters dared to tell me what had really happened.'

Mina refreshed the teacups. 'Someone must have been suspected, surely? Was there a servant who had been scolded for bad behaviour? Or was there a business rival perhaps, who called at the house?'

Fernwood gave a pained smile. 'That is the thing, you see. Every person in the house at the time the poisoning took place, every suspect, was a member of the family, even the servants.'

'Oh?' said Mina, surprised.

'That is unusual, I know, but I am sorry to say that my grandfather was noted for his miserly ways. My mother kept house and cooked; my sisters were given the simplest schooling required by law and were otherwise treated as unpaid servants. After the death of Mary's father, her mother Mrs Dorothy Clifton appealed to my grandfather for assistance. She was especially anxious that Mary's brother, Peter, should be able to complete his education. My grandfather agreed that they could come and live with us — the house was large enough — but only on the condition that Mary's mother should act as cook, housekeeper and nurse to my grandmother. Mary, even though so very young, she was only six years of age at the time, was obliged to help my sisters with domestic duties. There was no respite for my mother. She was sent to work in the grocery shop. All of us in the house were related by blood. And one of us is a murderer.'

'And you want to resolve this question before you marry?'

'We have agreed,' said Miss Clifton, 'that because we are cousins we will not marry until we know the truth.' She lowered her eyes, modestly. 'At least, not for very many years.'

Mina, looking at the stricken faces of the young couple, thought she understood. 'You are concerned that there is a family weakness?'

'Exactly,' said Fernwood, looking relieved that he had not had to explain it.

'But do you have any indication that this is so? Has it shown itself subsequently? Forgive me for asking, but has any member of your family committed a crime or any kind of misdemeanour?'

Fernwood didn't look offended. 'Not to my knowledge, no, and I would not suspect it of any of them. We all live very quietly. But I fear that it is possible that the taint might still lie there, just waiting to appear, if not in this generation, then the next.'

Miss Clifton was close to tears as she pressed her betrothed's hand. 'I have sometimes felt that George's sisters share our concern, although they have never spoken of it. They have never married, or wished to be. My brother Peter, too, is single. George and I have been fond of each other all our lives. We had not spoken of marriage until recently, when we found ourselves unable to deny our true affection for each other. What if there is something in our blood, something that we ourselves are not aware of, but which might be made stronger if the two of us were to marry and pass it to our children?'

Mina sipped her tea thoughtfully. 'What does your family think? Have they offered any opinion on your betrothal?'

There was an exchange of glances. 'To be honest, Miss Scarletti, you are the first person we have told,' Fernwood admitted. 'Mary and I have been brought up so closely and have always been fond of each other. Our family thinks that our affection is more akin to that of brother and sister, and have not remarked on it. In fact, until we can resolve our dilemma we prefer not to make any announcement, and I trust that you will keep our confidence.'

'Of course I will,' said Mina, still not seeing why it was that they had chosen to consult her. 'I think that the question of whether such a trait can be inherited may be one which a medical man might answer. Have you spoken to a doctor?'

Fernwood nodded. 'I have. He said it was impossible for him, or indeed anyone, to predict what might be the outcome if we were to be blessed with a family, and could offer no assurances that our concerns were without foundation. Medical science can give us no answers as yet.'

'That is a very difficult dilemma, I agree,' said Mina, sympathetically; thinking all the while that the Fernwood tragedy would make a wonderful premise for a murder story. 'I suppose after all this time it is very unlikely that the poisoner will confess.'

'If we could only establish that it was some dreadful mistake, and not an act of evil,' exclaimed Fernwood, 'then it would set our minds at rest. But whoever carried out that horrible deed, even if it was in error, has been too afraid all these years to admit to it. After all, how can one prove it was not deliberate and avoid prosecution and scandal? The police might think the years of silence speak for themselves.'

Mina nodded, wondering if the couple had assumed that she was a clairvoyant or a detective. She would have to disabuse them of both notions, but not just yet as she rather wanted to learn more.

'Of course, there was one person who both knew the identity of the culprit and was unafraid to reveal it,' said Miss Clifton. 'That was my great uncle Thomas. But his illness took away his voice. So, when I saw in the newspapers about these spiritualists — well — I began to wonder. What if it was possible to contact my great uncle from beyond the grave, and somehow ask him? George and I have talked about it. I don't think he was happy with the idea at first, but I think I might have convinced him.'

Fernwood looked undeniably awkward. 'I've never been one for mediums and such, and if truth be told, Mary once thought even less of them than I do. What really opened my eyes was reading all about Miss Eustace and her kind. They're just criminals, really, making money from cheating people like us. The trial was most revealing; showing how she went about her work, making enquiries, getting information about folk and then coming up with it at a séance so it looked like she'd heard it from the spirits.'

'But that is only the case when the medium is a charlatan,' said Miss Clifton, gently. 'There has been so much in the newspapers of late about wonders that no-one, even the men of science, can explain. It made me think — yes, there are frauds, but surely there must be genuine people, too, if one can find them? And, of course, anyone residing in Sussex could not play the tricks Miss Eustace did, since they would know nothing of my great uncle's death in Lincoln.'

Fernwood remained sceptical. 'As to genuine, I don't know. But yes, no-one here has ever heard of our family troubles. It was twenty years ago. There was never a trial, and as far as we know, the inquest was only reported in Lincolnshire, and certainly not in Sussex.'

'That is why we wish to consult you, Miss Scarletti,' said Miss Clifton. 'You know so much more than we do about such things. Is there a genuine medium you could recommend to us? I do think that if someone could pass on information that only we knew about then even George would be persuaded.'

Fernwood did not look as easily convinced as Miss Clifton hoped, but he merely gave her a soft smile. 'We have not told any of our family about this quest. I am not sure what they would think. I rather imagine that they would disapprove and try to dissuade us, as it is never talked of or even alluded to. They think the past is best forgotten. But we need to know.'

'Can you help us?' begged Miss Clifton. 'Oh, please say you will!'

Mina chose her words carefully. 'I am sorry to say that so far all the mediums I have encountered personally or read about have been frauds. That is not to say that genuine mediums do not exist, only that I do not know of any. There are several here in Brighton who advertise in the *Gazette*, but I have never visited them, and I don't know anyone who has, so I am unable to offer an opinion. I can, however, give you some advice.'

'We would be most grateful to hear it,' said Miss Clifton, warmly.

Mina glanced at George Fernwood, who looked politely resigned. 'First of all, please avoid mediums who insist they can only work in darkness. Whatever the reason they put forward for this practice, it is really only a cover for cheating.' Mina was better informed than most on this point as she had been advised by her brother Richard's former mistress Nellie, who had once been a conjuror's assistant, and knew some tricks of her own.

'That is good advice,' said Fernwood, gratefully. 'We did go to one such séance, and there was a very unconvincing apparition whose wig fell off. Then we attended a large assembly, where a medium pretended to give messages to people in the audience. We were not granted a message, and I had my doubts about the ones that some of the people received and claimed to be accurate. I think the medium had friends in the room.'

'Now you can't know that for sure,' said Miss Clifton. 'And there was a message from Uncle Thomas, you know.'

Fernwood grunted. 'There was a message from someone who called himself Thomas, which is not an uncommon name, and all it said was that he was happy and living with the spirits. If he had specified brandy as the spirit in question it would have been nearer the mark.'

'As you say, there are many Thomases, and it was most probably a guess,' said Mina. 'Guesses will be right some of the time, and people will remember the things they want to hear and forget what was incorrect. Then they tell all their friends that the medium had wonderful insight.'

'There were three people in the room who thought the message was for them,' said Fernwood. 'We didn't go back. No, I think what Mary is looking for is someone who could give a reading just for the two of us. Do you think that is advisable?'

Mina offered the plate again. This time, Fernwood took a biscuit, and ate it in a distracted manner, while Miss Clifton, who had become more at her ease during the interview, also availed herself of one. 'There are mediums who provide private readings, but they do tend to charge a substantial fee for such a service. Do beware of anyone who makes unusually high demands. I have known people pay sums as large as £30 for a single evening. Worse than that, once the medium knows the client will part with that kind of money they continue to draw on their victim's funds for as long as possible, making ever more extravagant promises, until they have taken all their fortune.'

Fernwood, who had paled visibly at the prospect of his hard-earned profits being drained in that fashion, shook his head. 'I will be sure not to be caught by such a villain.'

Mina smiled. 'There is another test. You could mention my name to those mediums you intend to visit and see how they react. The frauds will not allow me near them for fear that I will expose them. They will tell you that I negate the spiritual energy and claim that their séances will not produce results if I am there.'

'What nonsense!' Fernwood exclaimed.

'Have you heard of a Miss Athene Brendel?' asked Miss Clifton. 'I am told she is very good and sincere. She and her mother have taken a house in Brighton and have invited those who wish to come to her "mystical readings" as she calls them. I am not sure she charges any fee.'

'I have seen something of the sort in the *Gazette*,' Mina admitted, 'but I have not thought to visit her.'

'And then there is a Mr Castlehouse. He is very new and has a slate on which the spirits write messages in chalk while no-one is near. I have heard several good reports, and we are very hopeful of him.'

Mina, who had had quite enough of knockings and rappings and table tiltings and mediums who swathed themselves in phosphorescent draperies and pretended to be ghosts, had to admit that Mr Castlehouse offered something a little different. She recalled reading about the cheating Davenport brothers who had once toured England with their cabinet of wonders. They had pretended to produce a portrait of an angel drawn by spirits on a previously blank sheet of paper. A sceptical visitor had demonstrated that the picture had been drawn before the séance and hidden inside a folded sheet. Such general devices, which were usually pious in nature, meant to reassure sitters that the spirits came from above and not below, could easily be conjured into existence by clever trickery, but the kind of message Mr Fernwood and Miss Clifton hoped for was of quite another order.

'If you do decide to go,' said Mina cautiously, 'I would recommend that you do not give your real names, and neither should you ask questions or say why you have come. One can never know if the medium might have heard of you, or use what you tell them to make a good guess. And I have another warning. If you go for a reading in a small gathering, or more dangerously still, undertake a personal meeting, you will find it extremely hard not to give away your feelings about what you are being told, and provide some valuable clues.'

'We will do our best to heed your advice, and then we can be assured of learning the truth,' said Miss Clifton with approval.

'I hope that I have been able to help you in some measure, and that you will find the answers you seek,' said Mina. 'Would you care for more tea? These are excellent biscuits.'

Fernwood and Miss Clifton glanced at each other once more. 'There is another favour I would like to ask you,' said Fernwood. 'We would be most grateful if you would consent to accompany us when we visit Miss Brendel and Mr Castlehouse. We would arrange for your travel and pay all your expenses, of course. You have seen so much that is fraudulent that I know you would be able to tell us at once if they are genuine or not.'

'Oh, please say you will!' exclaimed Miss Clifton, before Mina could even consider the request. 'For my part I would like to make an appointment to see Miss Brendel first, as she is said to be quite fascinating.'

Mina hesitated, as while she was familiar with many mediumistic tricks she was far from expert on seeing when sleight of hand was being employed. Nevertheless, the conundrum did interest her. 'Very well, but if you make an appointment for any medium on my behalf, make sure to give my real name. If you are refused it will save you a wasted visit. But I do have one concern. Supposing we attended a séance and you receive messages, how am I to judge whether or not they are true? I know you will say that you would know, but I have seen so many instances of people believing something because it is what they want to believe, that I fear that however much you guard against it, it may still happen.'

'I have thought of that, and I agree,' said Fernwood. He put his hand in his pocket and drew out a small package. 'We found these amongst my grandmother's papers after her death. We didn't even know she had kept them. They are the newspaper reports of the death of my grandfather and the inquest. All are from Lincolnshire newspapers. I have also enclosed some documents I have prepared which will provide you with details of my family. And if there are any further questions you might like to ask before we consult a medium, do write to me and I will answer them all honestly. You will then be armed with as much information as we have. We trust you to keep this confidential, as we do.'

It was irresistible. Mina took the package.

Chapter Three

Once her visitors had departed, their sadness unabated but now coloured with relief and fresh hope, Mina took the package of papers to her room and laid out the contents on her desk. An unsealed envelope contained neatly folded cuttings from several Lincolnshire newspapers, giving full accounts of the inquest on Thomas Fernwood, together with a small clipping of the death announcement, some correspondence from chemists and medical men regarding the risks of using poisons in the home, and a paragraph describing the funeral. No item in the newspapers was subsequent to the date of that event, from which Mina assumed that after Thomas Fernwood's burial his death held no further interest for the press. There were two sheets of notepaper written in George Fernwood's hand, one of which listed the members of the family who had been living in the house at Lincoln at the time of the murder, the other related the history of the family after Thomas Fernwood's death. Mina asked Rose to bring her a light supper and tend the fire, and then she settled down to read.

At the time of his death in 1851, fifty-eight-year-old Thomas Fernwood was master of a large, rambling, dilapidated house in the centre of Lincoln, and owner of a grocery business in a busy double-fronted shop not far from his home. On the death of his father in 1839, Thomas had inherited both house and business. He was a strict master, supervising the family trade with a firm unbending eye, arriving each morning to check that all was in order, and snap out instructions. Twelve years later, however, the main work in the shop and storeroom was carried out by his son, thirty-five-year-old William, with the assistance of his wife Margery. Thomas still liked to think he was the authority, but in recent years his grip had relaxed, and he had taken to arriving later in the morning and leaving before the shop closed.

Thomas's wife, Jane, who was some seven years his senior, was troubled with pains in her legs and back and consequently spent a great deal of her time in bed being looked after by her granddaughters, Ada and Ellen, who, in 1851 were aged fifteen and thirteen. The girls' brother, ten-year-old George, attended a local school. Thomas and Jane Fernwood's only other children had died in infancy; therefore William Fernwood and his mother were Thomas's principal heirs. At the time of Thomas's death his exact worth was unknown, but it was assumed to be a substantial sum, since his chief fault, as agreed by all who knew him, was his extreme parsimony. His only indulgence, one that had, over the years, encroached into a greater proportion of his time, was cheap brandy, of which he sometimes consumed sufficient of an evening to leave him dull and unwell.

Dorothy Clifton was the only daughter of Thomas's late brother. Her marriage to a tea merchant had been happy but short and, on his death in 1849, she had discovered financial irregularities that left her, and her children, Peter and Mary, destitute. When she appealed to Thomas Fernwood for help he had agreed to give them a home and board, and arrange for the education of the son, but only in return for unpaid domestic duties. Dorothy, with the workhouse looming, had been more than grateful to accept. When Thomas Fernwood died, she had been his housekeeper for two years and Peter and Mary were aged ten and eight.

Early on the morning of Friday 5 December 1851 Dorothy had, as she did every day, made a cup of tea for Thomas and brought it up to his bedroom. He and his wife Jane slept in separate rooms, since his movement at night often disturbed her. When Dorothy entered the bedroom, Thomas was still asleep and snoring loudly, having imbibed a substantial amount of brandy the night before. She knew better than to wake him and risk his ill temper, so she placed the cup on the night table beside the bed within easy reach, and slipped away.

It was some half an hour later that the household was disturbed by loud cries of distress coming from Thomas' bedroom. Ada, who had been in the kitchen helping to prepare the breakfasts, rushed upstairs to see what the matter was, then hurried back down to tell Dorothy that her grandfather was very unwell. Dorothy went to help and found Thomas still in his bed, writhing in pain and vomiting a thin, bloodstained liquid. It was naturally assumed that he was suffering the consequences of his over indulgence the evening before, either that or it was a bad consignment of brandy, or some insect had got into the bottle. No-one else had drunk any of the brandy and no other member of the household was affected. As the day wore on, however, Thomas's agonies only increased, and eventually the family physician, Dr Simon Sperley was summoned. He listened carefully to the family's account of Thomas's illness, administered medicines that were rapidly rejected, attempted washings of the stomach with milk and water, and removed the bottle of brandy for examination. Thomas died that evening.

On the following day Dr Sperley visited the house, where the body had been laid out in preparation for burial. He asked the adult members of the family to assemble in Jane Fernwood's bedroom, since she was unable to leave her bed, and informed them that the cause of Thomas's death could not be ascertained, and it would be necessary to order a post mortem examination. He thought, however, that Thomas had not died from a disease such as cholera, but as a result of something he had eaten or drunk, which he had consumed most probably less than half an hour before being taken ill. Sperley asked for a description of what everyone in the house had prepared and eaten for breakfast. Thomas was the only member of the family not to have had breakfast, but it was well known that he expected a cup of tea to be brought to him in bed each morning. Dorothy confirmed that she had carried out this duty, but had not seen him drink it, as he had been asleep when she entered the room. He had not awoken when she placed the cup on the night table, and she had returned to the kitchen immediately. At that time, all the other members of the household were awake and either in the breakfast room or the kitchen, apart from Jane Fernwood, who was in bed, Ada having taken her a tray. Soon afterwards, William and Margery left to open up the shop, Peter and George walked to school and the women and girls of the house went about their domestic duties, until they were alerted by Thomas's cries.

The post mortem examination revealed that Thomas Fernwood had died from the effects of a corrosive poison that had attacked the lining of his stomach. Dr Sperley had been careful to conserve samples of vomit, which on testing revealed what he had suspected all along. Thomas had been poisoned with arsenic. The contents of the brandy bottle were examined and revealed no trace of arsenic, but Dr Sperley had already expected that, since had there been poison in the bottle, it would have taken effect far sooner. It followed that unless Thomas had consumed something that no-one else knew about the poison must have been put in his tea. Thomas would not have noticed any taste but within minutes he would have felt violently sick, with burning pain from the destructive effects of the poison.

All the family had drunk tea at breakfast made from water boiled in the same kettle, and brewed in the same teapot used to make Thomas's tea without any ill-effects, so it followed that the poison must have been introduced directly into his cup. No-one had seen anyone tampering with the cup, but it had been left unattended beside the sleeping man long enough to give everyone in the house the opportunity to slip poison into the tea. Unfortunately, due to the consternation in the house at Thomas's illness and the early assumption that the brandy was to blame, no-one could recall if Thomas had drunk any of his tea, and the cup, one of several similar ones in the house, had been taken away and scoured with the other breakfast things.

The source of the arsenic was not a mystery. In a kitchen drawer was a paper packet labelled 'Mouse powder. POISON' which was used to kill vermin by sprinkling it on bread and butter and distributing fragments in places where mice had been seen about the house. Everyone knew about this practice and had been warned that the little pieces of bread should not be touched. The contents of the packet were pure white arsenic supplied from the stock of the grocery shop. Earlier that year it had been made illegal by Act of Parliament to sell arsenic without some form of colouring matter, in order to avoid the kind of fatal mistakes so often reported in the newspapers, but the packet in the Fernwoods' kitchen pre-dated that requirement. At the inquest Dr Sperley told the coroner's jury that although arsenic did not dissolve well in cold water, it was certainly possible for a fatal dose, perhaps as little as three grains, to dissolve in hot tea if it was stirred well in. Had the cup been available for examination, some undissolved powder would undoubtedly have been visible at the bottom, if one knew what to look for, but this could well have been missed in the usual process of rinsing.

The coroner summed up the evidence. Judging by Thomas's dying statement, it did not appear that he had poisoned himself. There was no suggestion of insanity or thoughts of suicide, no reason for the healthy and successful man to take his own life. Since he took his tea without sugar, and did not use it for the administration of a medicine, it could not have been contaminated with arsenic by mistake. If suicide and accident were ruled out, then it followed that he had been murdered. The one question exercising the coroner's mind was how had Thomas Fernwood known who had poisoned him? One theory was that the deceased must have seen his killer stirring his tea, and assumed that it was done for an innocent purpose, perhaps to cool it. As regards the identity of the killer, it was apparent that during the time between the making of the tea and the deceased drinking it, every member of the family was in the house. None of the witnesses recalled having seen anyone go to Thomas Fernwood's room between his being brought the tea by Mrs Clifton, and being taken ill. During his illness he had been looked after by Dorothy, Ada and Ellen, and visited by his son and daughter-in-law, but none had been able to understand his attempts to speak through an acid-torn throat, and none could offer a clue as to what he had been trying to impart.

The coroner's jury had no difficulty in reaching the verdict that Thomas Fernwood had died from arsenical poisoning, that poison being administered by another person or persons unknown. It was a case of murder, but the culprit was never identified.

Chapter Four

Having learned all she could from the newspapers and George Fernwood's own account, Mina went on to study the history of the family following the murder.

There were no surprises in the will. Thomas's widow, Jane inherited the family home and its contents, and received an annuity, while their son William became sole owner of the grocery business. There were small legacies for Dorothy Clifton, the grandchildren, nephew and niece, which the minors would receive on their majority.

The Fernwoods and the Cliftons continued to live in the old house. It had been much neglected due to Thomas's parsimony, but under its new ownership, it was cleaned, freshened, painted, varnished, better lit and equipped, carpets replaced and the garden made pleasant. Jane Fernwood, who had become very attached to Dorothy, asked her to stay on as her companion, appointing a cook/housekeeper and maidservants to do the domestic work so that Ada, Ellen and Mary could be afforded the education they merited. George had shown an early aptitude for the grocery trade, and on leaving school, became a valued assistant to his father. Peter was less able, but also joined the business in a more junior capacity, and was content with his position.

On the death of Jane Fernwood in 1861, her son William inherited the family home. It soon became apparent that it was only Jane who had kept the family together. Within weeks of her death, the business was sold, and the house converted into apartments and let. All the family wanted to get away from the house of death with its terrible memories. William and Margery Fernwood retired to a pleasant villa on the coast where they lived comfortably from rents and investments. They were generous to the family with their legacy. Ada and Ellen, neither of whom had married, were able to purchase a small cottage in Dorset where they lived simply and quietly on the proceeds of annuities. George purchased a grocery business in Haywards Heath, which he ran together with his cousins, Peter and Mary, and his aunt Dorothy. The Fernwoods and the Cliftons were as comfortable and content as it was possible to be, but the shadow of suspicion remained.

Now that Mina knew that the murderer could only be a member of the family, there was one question she did not think she could bring herself to ask, and that was, who did George and Mary suspect? They had behaved as if they were mystified by the puzzle, but they would not have been human if they had not had their doubts about at least one person. The most obvious suspect was George's father William, because he had benefitted the most, but that was hardly proof.

Mina returned to the newspaper report of Thomas Fernwood's funeral. There had been a brief ceremony, attended only by his son and daughter-in-law. Friends and business connections were notable by their absence. Mina was struck by what the account did not say, the gaps between sentences, pauses filled by silent insinuation that the dead man was disliked and everyone was relieved to see him dead. In one way or another, and to a varying degree, all the members of the family had improved their situation following the death of Thomas Fernwood, and it would not be pleasant for George and Mary to point an accusing finger.

Mina, having made a name for herself as an enemy of fraudulent mediums, did not anticipate being admitted to the spiritual circle of Miss Athene Brendel, however, curiosity led her to consider the reasons why that lady had attracted such interest in town.

Three months earlier the society page of the *Brighton Gazette* had carried a notice stating that Mrs Hermione Brendel and her daughter Miss Athene Brendel were newly arrived in town, and they and their retinue were to make their home in Brighton for a twelvemonth. Those residents of Brighton who liked to follow the dazzling lives of fashionable visitors were soon deep in discussion about these ladies of fortune and mystery, and rumour spread its tendrils throughout the town like a particularly insistent vine, probing its way into every corner. Mina, while waiting for her appointments with Anna Hamid in the ladies' salon of the vapour baths, did not generally engage in gossip, but it went on all around her, and was hard to ignore.

Mrs Brendel was a handsome and elegantly dressed lady of about forty-five, with a tall figure and an imperious manner. Without giving any warning as to her arrival or her intentions, she had swept up in a carriage in front of a lodging house advertised as available furnished throughout, demanded to see the landlady, and after a brief inspection of the premises declared it to be perfectly suited to her needs, and offered to rent the entire house at a cost of 180 guineas a year, paying a quarter in advance. On the very same day she and her daughter took possession of the property.

Their new home was in Oriental Place, a street lined on both sides with terraces of superior five storey apartment buildings and hotels, which ran north from the seafront close by and parallel to Montpelier Road. Mrs Brendel, it was believed, was something of importance in society and was a well-known and highly respected figure at gatherings in the greater houses in the country. Mr Brendel had not yet been seen but his fortune was said to be in mines and he was therefore obliged to spend much of his time in the north of England where his interests were located.

The daughter, who was twenty, exhibited a delicate and refined beauty, and many rare accomplishments, having been carefully educated in all the necessary arts that would attract a gentleman's interest in such an enchanting maiden. Her most charming skill was said to be her ability to coax delicious music from a piano. An only child, she was the pampered darling of her parents' eyes, and held the promise of a substantial marriage portion, but only if a gentleman could be found to match her in both fortune and temperament.

No sooner had the ladies and their luggage arrived when a visit had been made to Potts and Co, the town's leading musical instrument emporium and soon afterwards a magnificent piano was delivered to Oriental Place. There was, however, so the whispers went, much more to the delightful Miss Brendel than mere music. She was reputed to be a medium of extraordinary sensitivity. While she did not promise to converse with the dead, produce glowing spectres or tell the future, she was able, through an inner eye, to actually see the spirits, not only of deceased persons, but also of those who lived but were far distant. These presences clustered about her, and while others in the same room, but without her gifts, were unable to see them, the psychic energy she gathered to herself enhanced the perceptions of her visitors. Those who consulted her had claimed to receive reassuring news of loved ones whom they feared might be in danger in a foreign land, or messages of comfort from those who had passed over.

If Miss Brendel had hoped to become the sensation of Brighton, she would have been disappointed. That might have been the result had she arrived much earlier in the year, but in recent months, following the downfall of Miss Eustace and her co-conspirators, even the dedicated spiritualists of Brighton had grown wary, and did not make their beliefs public for fear of the inevitable torrent of ridicule that would fall upon their heads. It was with considerable caution, therefore, that only a few adventurous persons approached the shy Miss Athene Brendel and asked to consult her.

Mrs Brendel, however, made bold with any cavillers, and was quick to declare that she and her daughter had nothing to hide. When asked about Miss Brendel's unusual gifts she pointed out that all the séances were conducted in full light, and not cloaked in suspiciously concealing darkness. Miss Brendel did not fly into the air or make flowers appear from nowhere. There were no glowing apparitions, bells or trumpets. Tables did not tip, and there were no knockings on walls. Such cheap, coarse trickery, said Mrs Brendel, was beneath contempt.

Miss Brendel's fame might have flourished as briefly as a late blossoming flower and then faded into the winter of obscurity, but for one remarkable incident. In a sitting attended by several of her most devoted adherents, she had revealed that she saw a man in the room, one who shook his head as if it pained him, and appeared very distraught, wringing his hands and moving about in a distracted manner. She did not know who the man might be, or why he had come, but she felt very strongly that either he had recently passed over, or would very soon do so in highly unpleasant circumstances. It was later learned that a Mr Hay, a Scottish wine merchant who occupied an apartment in Oriental Place, had recently taken his own life by cutting his throat. At the inquest on the unhappy gentleman it was revealed that some years earlier he had suffered a serious injury to his head in a railway accident, and since then had been plagued by pain, despondency and the wholly unwarranted delusion that he was guilty of a terrible crime.

Mina, sitting in the flower-scented salon of Dr Hamid's establishment, had overheard the other ladies discussing Mr Hay's wretched and hideous demise, and the sensational news that the tragedy had been foretold by Miss Athene Brendel. There was even a letter to one of the Sussex county papers to that effect, a piece of information concerning which the editor had declined to comment.

Mina had instructed Mr Fernwood and Miss Clifton that when making their appointment to see Miss Brendel they should not conceal the fact that she was to accompany them; in fact they must make a point of giving her name. She anticipated either that the young couple would be admitted only on the condition that Mina would not be of their party, or all three would be very politely declined with some unconvincing excuse. It was to her considerable surprise, therefore, that she received a letter from George Fernwood advising her that the appointment was made and they would all be very welcome. He and Miss Clifton would arrive in Brighton by train and hire a cab to collect Mina and convey them all to Oriental Place.

Chapter Five

Mina was at her desk considering this news when she heard voices from the hallway below, her brother Richard's strident declamatory tones and, unusually, a titter from Rose. Mina left her papers and proceeded down the stairs as quickly as was safe, carefully clasping the bannister with both hands to avoid a dangerous tumble as her slight form rocked inelegantly from side to side. A stout greatcoat with a heavy shoulder cape was hanging on the hallstand, topped with a tweed travelling cap, its earflaps dangling. Mina had never seen her brother wearing such an ensemble before, but thought it an unusually sensible one. Richard was leaning against the wall, head in the air, gesturing artistically as if reciting a poem, while Rose, her cheeks flushed, was stifling bursts of laughter with her apron.

Richard, with his slender effortless elegance, untidy blond curls and far more charm than was good for him, was a cheerful scamp who could make even carelessness attractive. A constant source of anxiety when Mina was not keeping an eye on him, she realised with a pang how dreadfully she missed him when he was away, and how his unexpected and usually unannounced visits enlivened her days. As ever he had brought only a small and shamefully battered leather bag, since a room and some necessaries were always kept ready for him.

'Darling Mina!' exclaimed Richard, seeing her swaying approach, and Rose looked up, went even redder than before, and scurried away. Richard bounded eagerly up the stairs to his sister, and enveloped her in a warm hug.

'I hope you have not been teasing Rose,' said Mina, trying her best to be severe with him, which was always difficult.

'Not at all. I merely bring a little much needed light into the girl's life, with the occasional quip or *bon mot*. She has just informed me that cook is making a boiled pudding for dinner, which is just the thing in this nasty weather, and if I am very well-behaved there be will jam on it.'

They descended the stairs together arm in arm. 'I hope you are not too dull all alone here, my dear,' said Richard, fondly. 'How terribly you must miss Mother!'

'I keep myself occupied,' she reassured him.

'Ah, those little tales for children that flow so easily from your pen! I am quite envious of your industry. I think, you know, that I do have it in me to be a great author, only whenever I put pen to paper I can't think what to write.' Mina felt somewhat guilty at deceiving her family as to the true nature of her tales, but reflected that if her mother found out she would never hear the end of it, and Richard was as incapable of keeping a secret as he was of doing a day's work. The only person who knew that she was the author under the *nom de plume* Robert Neil of such titles as *The Ghost's Revenge*, *A Tale of Blood* and *The Castle of Grim Horrors*, was Mr Greville, her late father's business partner, who managed the popular fiction department of the Scarletti publishing house.

As they reached the last step, Richard swept Mina off her feet as he would a child, and placed her gently and lovingly on the floor beside him. 'You are in good health? I do hope so! And I swear you may even be a little plumper than you were.'

'Dr Hamid says that I am in the very best of health, and the baths and massages do me good.' Mina was aware that she was a trifle heavier than she had been some months ago, but that was not due to putting on fat. Anna Hamid had been teaching her exercises to help support her spine. Mina's form, while still slender, and far from robust, was developing a protective shell of muscle, which, it was hoped, would prevent any further distortion of her shape and constriction of the lungs. She was becoming like the crab that moved oddly and carried its skeleton on the outside.

Richard rubbed his hands together briskly. 'I know there will be a good fire in the parlour, and Rose will be bringing us hot coffee so let us make ourselves comfortable!' He pushed open the parlour door, sighed with appreciation of the cosy interior, and proceeded to place himself at his ease, slouching in a chair in a manner that his mother would have deplored.

Mina sat by the fireside and gazed at him affectionately. 'Richard dear, I am always pleased to see you, as you know, but I can't help but feel concerned at the reasons for your visit. I hope your employment with Edward is going well?'

Richard pulled a case of small cigars from his pocket, and glanced at Mina in what he hoped was an appealing fashion. She shook her head. 'No, Dr Hamid has expressly forbidden me to go anywhere near tobacco smoke.'

'Ah, yes. Very sensible I suppose.' Richard swallowed his disappointment, returned the case to his pocket and warmed his hands before the fire. 'Edward has not dismissed me, if that is what you are thinking. I thought he might, several times, and I wouldn't have blamed him. Really, the work is so dashed tedious, and if a fellow has been out late in town then where is one to sleep if not at one's desk?'

Mina smiled. 'As I am sure you are aware, sleeping is something you are expected to do in your own time and not the company's.'

'So I was told. But I would never have any time to myself if I had to work all the while. I don't know how Edward manages it. He seems to do little else now that he is betrothed to the bewitching Miss Hooper, his divine Agatha, who promises to be a very expensive wife. Anyhow, I did get most terribly bored by it all. Do you know, Edward insisted that I learned how to spell! What use is spelling to anyone? Then he told me to cut pieces out of newspapers; I have no idea why. So I used my idle moments to amuse myself by drawing little sketches. Just faces, mainly. Well, would you believe it, when Edward saw them, he said how good they were, and next thing, he asked me to do more.'

'For publication in the paper, you mean?'

'I think so, yes. He showed me some photographs of public figures — ugly fellows with big moustaches and little eyes — and asked me if I could copy them and I did.'

'So you may have found your *métier* at last! I am very pleased for you!' Mina tried to sound encouraging, even optimistic. Richard was forever looking for some method of becoming rich without the necessity of working, and had launched and abandoned several hopeless schemes, usually on funds borrowed from his doting mother. Honest work was a new adventure for him, and Mina hoped that this time he would succeed.

Richard did not share Mina's enthusiasm. 'A low paid one, I am afraid. But then, I thought, why should I not find a wealthy patron, someone who will pay well for a flattering portrait? Edward said that newspapers want pictures to be as close to the original as possible, so people who can't see the real thing can at least know what they look like. But those ugly gents and old ladies like to think they are handsomer than they really are, so that is what I will draw. I did try my hand at oil painting, but the wretched stuff takes an age to dry. I managed a halfway decent self-portrait but I don't think I mixed the paint right; the colours ran and it looked hideous. I put it in the attic — I might come back to it later.'

'You will not do any painting here, I hope,' said Mina, knowing that it would be impossible for Richard to confine the inevitable mess to one room.

'No, drawings are far quicker. I can finish one almost before I am bored with it.'

'Does Edward know you are here?' It was a natural question, given Richard's usual habit of acting on a whim.

'Of course he does. I borrowed his hat and coat after all. I suggested that I should come to Brighton for the season, and draw ladies in the high life and write about how they spend their husbands' money. He's about to start a ladies' newspaper, and they like that kind of thing. *The Society Journal*. It will be like *The Queen*, only different. He has even appointed a lady editor, a Mrs Caldecott, who, I understand, knows everyone and everything — if they are worth knowing, that is. She used to write society gossip for one of the London papers.'

'Do you know anyone in Brighton who might effect introductions in the right circles?'

'That's a bit of a poser, because I don't yet. Although Nellie might have moved up in the world by now.' He sighed. 'How is dear Nellie? I do miss her, you know. None of the London girls are half as much fun.'

Richard and Nellie had parted as lovers, although they still retained a warm regard for each other. She had married a Mr Jordan, a partner in Jordan and

Conroy, dealers in high-class ladies and gentlemen's clothing and accessories. She was now a walking advertisement for the business, lavished with all her husband could afford and Richard could not.

'Nellie is as lovely as ever. I see her often and she assures me that her life is all she would wish it to be. She and her husband have just taken possession of a new home, where they mean to entertain prodigiously. Their drawing room will be a sea of French fashion.'

'Then I shall go there and bathe in silk. The ladies will clamour for my sketches, and if I am in luck I will meet a rich widow who will fall madly in love with me.'

Mina could only feel grateful that her value in the marriage market was so low. She did not broadcast her monetary worth, the comfortable annuity she had inherited from her father nicely augmented by the income from her stories, and since no man looked past her appearance she had never had the occasion to disappoint a suitor. Many years ago, as she was emerging into womanhood, and the twist in her spine had first become noticeable, a doctor had told her that she ought never to marry and she had learned to be content with that. The more she saw bargains being made based on money and breeding the more she prized her friendships.

Rose arrived with a tray. Either it was warm in the kitchen or she was still blushing after Richard's jokes. She set a large pot of hot coffee on the table, with cups, milk, sugar and a dish of little cakes.

'Oh, my favourites!' exclaimed Richard.

'Were those not for teatime?' asked Mina.

'I'll ask cook to make some more, Miss,' said Rose, and almost ran back to the kitchen.

Mina poured the coffee. 'Have you seen Enid recently? I do worry about her.'

Richard took a large bite of cake. 'Not as much as Mother does, I can assure you.'

Their sister Enid's troubled married life had been far happier in the summer due to the extended absence of her husband, solicitor Mr Inskip, who was abroad conducting property business with a foreign Count. She had been still more cheerful when visiting Brighton that autumn, after plunging into a highly indiscreet flirtation. The object of her admiration was Mr Arthur Wallace Hope; Viscount, war hero, explorer, lecturer, author and passionate advocate of spiritualism. Mina had no idea how far the indiscretion had gone, but it was clear to her why it had occurred. Mr Inskip was a dull fellow, with a slinking gait, wan complexion and eyes like a dead newt. By contrast, Mr Hope's robust masculine physique and impressive history of narrow escapes from death made Inskip seem to be merely a pale shadow of a man. That unwise affair, if affair it had been, had ended abruptly when Hope had left Brighton to avoid exposure in a scandal involving another lady, and Enid's health had been poor ever since. Her condition had worsened substantially on receiving a letter advising her that Mr Inskip was planning to be home before the winter set in.

'I hope she is no thinner,' said Mina anxiously, since it was Enid's habit to eat almost nothing and lace tightly.

Richard looked gloomy. 'Mother says there is no danger of that. She is being dosed on pennyroyal and Widow Welch's Pills which claim to be able to remove obstructions from the female system. But the obstruction is still there, it seems, and may be so for some time. Mother thinks it will not be relieved for six months at least.'

'Oh,' said Mina, understanding his meaning. 'I hope when Mr Inskip returns he will not be dismayed by her condition. He is an educated man and can do arithmetic.'

'I am told that no further correspondence has been received from Mr Inskip. In fact, no-one quite knows where he is. Perhaps he is lost like Dr Livingstone, or he may suddenly appear on Enid's doorstep, groaning and rattling his chains. Enid hopes he has been killed in an avalanche while traversing the Carpathians. He might be more entertaining as a ghost than he ever was as a living man.'

'When did he set out for home?'

'I'm really not sure.'

'I had assumed he was simply delayed by business. Well, I shall write to Mother and Edward to let them know that you have arrived safely. Maybe they will have more news. And I will make sure to tell Edward that you have his coat and hat, just in case you forgot to mention that you were borrowing them, and he has had someone arrested for their disappearance.'

'And write to Nellie, for me, won't you?'

'I will.'

Richard washed down his third cake with a gulp of coffee. 'We had such fun last summer, didn't we? Nellie pretending to be a medium, and you showing up Miss Eustace and her tricks! And then all that business at the Pavilion. That was a bit near the mark, wasn't it? I suppose Brighton is free of hauntings nowadays?'

'So I understand. But there are still mediums plying their trade. A Miss Brendel who has visions and a Mr Castlehouse with a slate that writes by itself. I have decided to visit them both.'

Richard laughed. 'Goodness! They must be shaking in their shoes! I rather thought you had determined not to visit mediums again. Unless these be the most abominable villains, and you must have them put in prison for the public safety.'

'That remains to be seen. But they do have the attraction of novelty.'

'If you should need any assistance I am your man!' He ate the last cake. 'When is luncheon?'

'In half an hour as I am sure you know.'

'Splendid! And afterwards, while I am waiting for an invitation to Nellie's fashionable *salon*, I will go about Brighton looking for pretty ladies to draw. One must suffer for one's art, you know.'

Mina wondered how much, if anything, Mr Jordan knew about her brother's former association with his wife, and what kind of reception Richard might receive if he decided to call on her. In the past Richard's visits to his former *inamorata* had tended to coincide with those times when her husband was not at home, and preferably abroad on business.

Soon after luncheon, and newly spruced, Richard donned his coat and hat, borrowed a guinea from Mina, and went out. Despite the promise of boiled pudding, he did not return until well after Mina had gone to bed.

Chapter Six

Dear Nellie,

I trust that this finds you in the very best of health and Mr Jordan likewise. I do hope that the removal to your new home proceeded as well as these things possibly can. As I write this I am recalling my family's move to Brighton, which was not achieved without a certain amount of quarrelling, hysteria and broken china. I am sure you have managed it more successfully. I know you have great plans and I look forward to hearing all about them.

I do not go out a great deal in the present season as I am under strict orders from Dr Hamid to spend the entire winter closely blanketed like a baby and existing on a diet of nothing but beef tea, coddled eggs and sherry. But I do go to the baths, of course, where the herbal vapour affords me great relief, and Miss Hamid's ministrations drive any discomfort from my shoulders.

My brother Edward has sent Richard to Brighton on business. He is to make sketches of fashionable visitors and residents for a new society journal. If you could think of some way to obtain commissions for him to advance his career without his actually getting into any trouble, I would be eternally grateful.

Kindest wishes,
Mina

Dear Mina,

I know how trying the winter must be for you, so I am delighted to hear that you are well and taking great care of yourself.

My new home will, once properly furnished, be a wonder to behold, and I look forward to you seeing it in all its glory. Yes, there will be gatherings and entertainments galore! I have such plans!

So Richard is to be an artist? How exciting! I promise to devise something very special in his honour, and I know he will be greatly in demand.

Kindest wishes,
Nellie

Dear Mother,

I hope this finds you well. The weather here is cold but I am pleased to see from the newspapers that you are enjoying better conditions in London.

Richard has just arrived. At Edward's suggestion he is developing his talent as an artist, and will be preparing some sketches for a fashionable society journal. He has every confidence that one day he will be a great name, and much in demand in the very highest circles.

Do send me news of Enid. I trust that her health is improving. Has anything more been heard from Mr Inskip? I do hope his business abroad has prospered and he will be safely by his own fireside very soon.

Please kiss the twins for me.
Fondest love,
Mina

Dear Mina,

It is impossible to describe the dreadful situation here, which has made me as miserable as I have ever been in my life. There is a terrible epidemic of bronchitis and other even more horrid things in town, and I hardly dare stir from the house, so there is no entertainment to be had even if I felt strong enough to endure it, which I do not. You must not come to London at any cost; it would be the death of you.

Enid is in a state of distraction. The twins are strong and well grown, but their gums are so red and swollen that I fear for their very lives. Their cries are piteous and give me the most terrible pain in my poor head so I can hardly think. I try to comfort Enid as best I can but there is no helping her. She is not permitted to go out, and exists in the very depths of melancholy. I fear it will be many months before there is any prospect of recovery.

There is no news of Mr Inskip. We cannot discover if he is alive or dead, and in view of his long silence must fear that he is no more. Enid is so distressed that she cannot even bear to hear his name spoken, the very thought of his fate sends her into paroxysms, so we do not speak of him at all now. Edward came to see us, saying he wanted to help, but as soon as he started explaining things to me, I knew it was useless to listen to him. There are some papers in the house but I can do nothing with them, I am far too ill. Perhaps he can make sense of them.

Richard is my only comfort. He is a dear good boy and will make something very fine of himself one day.

Your unhappy
Mama

Dear Edward,

I trust that you and Miss Hooper are both well, and that the business flourishes.

First of all, the news here. Richard, you will be pleased to know, has arrived safely, thanks to your kindness in lending him your warmest coat and hat. He is very eager to start making sketches of the fashionables in town, of whom there will shortly be very many as they are even now arriving for the season. He has already been busy seeking admission to the best houses and gatherings. He is working so hard that I have scarcely seen him since he arrived.

Please let me know the news concerning the whereabouts of Mr Inskip. Richard tells me there have been no letters from him for some time. I hope Enid is not suffering too much anxiety on that account. How is Mother bearing up under the strain of caring for Enid and the twins?

Fondest love,
Mina

Dear Mina,

The good news is that I am pleased that scallywag Richard is actually consenting to do some work and I hope something will come of it, but you will understand that I have my doubts. Tell him not to damage or lose my best warm coat and hat, or I will have to take the cost from his wages.

I suppose Richard has told you about Enid's indisposition. It is very irritating but there is nothing I can do, the foolish girl must take the consequences. It is pointless to remonstrate with her. I tried to question her about Mr Inskip, to discover whether he left any instructions before he went away but she laughed so hard she became hysterical and had to be given a soporific to calm her. She really tries my patience.

Mother is Mother as always. I now find myself obliged to spend some considerable time going through Mr Inskip's papers, as Mother, despite having so much time on her hands refuses to take any practical action, so it has all been left to me. It is very hard when I have the business to attend to as well. To be blunt, it was a relief to dispatch Richard to Brighton as he takes up more time in the office than he saves. Fortunately my dearest Agatha has been very patient and understanding. I have made sure not to trouble her with our family woes.

I will write again if I learn anything,

In haste,

Affect'ly,

Edward

Chapter Seven

'We have given our names as Mr Wood and Miss Clive,' said George Fernwood, as he and Miss Clifton arrived by cab to convey Mina to Oriental Place for the séance with Miss Brendel. 'As you asked, I gave your full name to Mrs Brendel when securing our places, and she raised no objections.'

'Perhaps, as she is only recently arrived in Brighton she knows nothing of me?' suggested Mina. She knew she should not have felt a little disappointment at this, but could not avoid it.

Fernwood smiled. 'She knows you very well by name, since others who have consulted Miss Brendel have mentioned you and your history. You are seen by some as a violent opponent of all things psychic. They have even recommended that she invite you to meet her daughter as they feel that such an encounter would change your views on spiritualism.'

'I have no views on spiritualism, so it would be hard to change them,' said Mina. 'I have very strong views on people who extort money from the bereaved under false pretences.'

'I understand,' said Miss Clifton, warmly, 'and believe me, we are of a like mind on that subject. These false practitioners should be rooted out and punished. How else can we reach the great truth?'

The wind was brisk, with a hint of approaching frost. Mina, who had no wish to encounter the great truth any sooner than was necessary, was grateful that the journey would be a short one, grateful too that she had spent more money than her mother would have approved of on a deeply lined cloak. Rose had made sure she was carefully wrapped with a heavy veil and a thick muffler to protect her face, so that she should not draw the cold air directly into her lungs. There was a small flask of hot water for her to clasp in her hands, and Dr Hamid had provided some herbal sachets that gave out a scent that was very comforting to inhale. It was a great deal of trouble for a ride lasting just a few minutes, but it was time well spent. Fernwood opened the cab door and entered first, then reaching out, he took both Mina's hands and drew her inside, ensuring that she moved at her own pace, and had all the support she needed. The driver, one whom Mina recognised, as he liked to wear a tartan muffler in the winter, watched the process, and she knew that had she required it, he would have jumped down and lent a hand as he had often done in the past.

At last they were all comfortably settled, and the cab moved off. On the way, Mina faced her companions and found herself considering them as a stranger might on a first meeting. What, if anything, could Miss Brendel deduce from their appearance? Their good state of health and robust serviceable clothing suggested a comfortable life in the middle portion of society, but not the more elevated echelons of the gilded idle, where garments were as much a matter of displaying position as practicality. There was no hint of mourning about either, not so much as a ribbon, locket or edge of a handkerchief, which at once told any onlooker that neither had been recently bereaved. If Miss Athene Brendel was to offer this information and tried to suggest that it came from the spirits, Mina would be less than impressed. She also had to consider their voices, touched with a gentle accent that might well suggest they were born and bred north of Sussex, but not so distinctive that their origins could be traced to Lincoln.

The cab drew to a halt outside their destination, a double-fronted house, rising to a full five storeys above ground, its exterior painted cream and garnished by carved scallop shells, with spider-black railings around the basement area and first floor balconies. Mina wondered how many occupied the residence, as it seemed large for a family of two, and the landladies of these superior properties did not take kindly to unauthorised subletting. Perhaps Mrs Brendel meant to entertain. Perhaps she just wanted to inform the town of her correct place in society.

Mr Fernwood assisted Mina down the steps of the carriage as if she was a piece of bone china that might break if dropped. The muffler slipped down from her face, and she quickly pulled it back into position. The air was as cold as a knife blade, as the wind, travelling from the surface of the chilly sea, swept up the narrow channel of the street to disperse itself in the alleys and byways of the middle of town.

The street was almost deserted apart from a youth clad too thinly for the weather, who was walking past rather more slowly than was advisable if he wished his movement to keep him warm. To Mina's surprise, as they advanced towards the house, he suddenly changed direction and darted around the carriage as if intending to cross to the other side of the street. This, however, he did not do, neither did he enter the carriage. She gained the impression that he was lurking behind the vehicle to hide from view. She glanced at her companions but neither appeared to recognise him or consider his strange behaviour to be of any note. Was he hiding from the new arrivals, or the house they were visiting? There were only two shallow steps up from the pavement and Mina and Miss Clifton mounted them arm in arm, while George Fernwood hurried ahead up the pathway to ring the doorbell. As Mina heard the cab draw away she looked back and saw the lone young man move quickly to cower behind a nearby gatepost.

They were met at the door by a maid, who, Mina thought, must have come with the house like the hall furniture, as she was not in her first decades of her life, and rather wooden but well-polished. 'Party for Miss Brendel?' asked the maid.

'Yes, Mr Wood, Miss Clive and Miss Scarletti,' said Fernwood.

The maid glanced up the street, from right to left, then looked the visitors over, her eyes lingering on Mina for a moment, before she nodded. 'This way.'

Once cloaks and bonnets and mufflers had been dealt with they were led along the hall. It was a little cooler than Mina liked her home to be, and she was pleased to have brought a warm shawl. The maid knocked on a door and opened it to announce the arrivals, then stood back for them to enter.

'How delightful!' exclaimed the lady who rose from her chair and came to greet them. 'I am always so happy to make new acquaintances in town. I am Hermione Brendel. Do please come in and make yourselves at home.'

Mrs Brendel, while no longer young was nevertheless both elegant of figure and quick of movement, giving the impression of an almost girlish vivacity, although Mina sensed that her air of good cheer rested lightly and transparently on a steely determination. The drawing room was of a good size for entertaining, well-lit and with a bright fire burning in the grate. Mina, expecting a séance, made a careful study of her surroundings, but saw none of the usual arrangements. There was no curtained recess, no rows of seating for the faithful, no table surrounded by a close circle of chairs, for the practice of tipping for messages. Since the house was let furnished it was not possible to come to any conclusion about the family from its interior, which was nicely appointed although not brand new. One item did stand out, however, a pianoforte in figured walnut with fretwork ornamentation. Potts and Co had been advertising them in the *Gazette* as the very latest thing.

'Allow me to introduce my daughter, Miss Athene Brendel. Athene, we have new members for our little gatherings, Mr Wood, Miss Clive and Miss Scarletti.'

The young woman who was the only other occupant of the room had been seated with her head slightly bowed, but on the arrival of the visitors she slowly looked up and gazed on them evenly and without emotion. She was as light and frail as a fairy with large, bright, pale violet eyes. Her skin was almost white, her hair, like that of her mother was dark and abundant, further accentuating her almost unnatural ghost-like pallor.

While neither she nor her mother could be described as beautiful there was something very striking about the appearance of both that demanded attention. In the mother it was her energy, and the searching expression in her eyes, and in the daughter the transparency of her form, like a fading picture. Mina, recalling her father and sister Marianne, both of whom had died far too young, was obliged to wonder if Miss Brendel carried within her the seeds of consumption that would shorten her life.

'I am so very pleased to meet you,' said the young woman, softly, moving one hand in a welcoming gesture. Her wrist bones stood out as bony knobs beneath lace cuffs, and her fingernails were like cloudy pearls.

Mrs Brendel motioned the visitors to sit down. 'We are expecting some more to our little gathering, who I am sure will be here directly. Mr Wood and Miss Clive, are you newly arrived in Brighton?'

'Ah, we are here just for a brief visit,' said Fernwood.

'And Miss Scarletti — your fame precedes you,' the lady beamed. 'So much so that I am given to understand you have quite frightened away those practitioners of deceit who have plagued Brighton of late.'

'So I am told,' said Mina, 'I can't say how true that might be.'

'Oh, I do so hope it is. You cannot imagine how mortifying it is for those who are genuine mediums to see charlatans using their tricks and wiles, and demanding payment, which we never do, and giving the art a bad name.'

'I hope you don't mind my commenting,' said Mina, 'but I have been to a number of séances, and your room is not prepared in the way I had expected. Can you advise me how the evening is to be conducted? How do you expect the spirits to address us?'

'Oh, there will be no scratchings or knockings, you may be quite sure of that. It is simplicity itself. Think of tonight only as a gathering of acquaintances. There may be spirit visitors, and there may not. If there are, Athene, with her special gifts, will be able to see them. Most people, I have found, are not so gifted. We cannot be sure that Athene will see anything of note, but should she do so, then she will describe her visions to us. We will then concentrate on what she imparts and her insights will in many cases open up our minds so we will achieve clarity.'

Mina thought this very clever. Miss Athene promised nothing, and asked for nothing. If she received any impressions, since no-one else could see them, she could not be contradicted or exposed. Anything the guests might gain from the exercise was solely due to their own efforts. Under the circumstances it could prove impossible to determine if the medium was genuine or a cheat, and as Mina waited for the séance to begin, she feared that she was due to have a very dull time.

Chapter Eight

A gentleman arrived dressed in mourning clothes, and was introduced to the company as Mr Harold Conroy. Mina had never met him, but she knew his name, since he was the younger brother of Frank Conroy, the business partner of Nellie's husband. He was aged about thirty-five, and, like his brother, was very portly with every sign that this robust demonstration of prosperity would increase over the years. His face was florid, and his extravagant auburn side-whiskers failed to conceal the sagging throat or the neck that had begun to bulge over his collar. Mina recalled that he conducted a successful business manufacturing uniforms for the army and navy. He had been widowed in the previous year, and was the father of four children all less than ten years of age.

The next arrivals were an elderly couple, both clad in deepest black, who were introduced as Mr and Mrs Myles. They walked together arm in arm for mutual comfort, creeping along with small shuffling steps. Conducted by their hostess to a sofa, they sat together like a dark mound of misery. Everything about them announced a recent bereavement, but Mina found herself wondering if this was true. The Queen herself, after all, had been in mourning for ten years with no sign of it abating. This couple wore their grief like a mantle that they were unable to remove, and who could tell how long ago they had put it on?

A gentleman of about sixty was next to appear, tall and spare of figure, very upright in his posture, and faultlessly dressed, with white hair expertly coiffed, and a smartly pointed beard. He was introduced as Mr Honeyacre. He was not clad in black, but wore both a wedding ring and a small mourning ring, which suggested that he had been widowed some years before.

The next visitors were a Mrs Tasker, a lady of mature years and figure, with her son, a youth in his twenties, who showed by his sulky expression that there were very many other places he would rather be, and was accompanying his mother under sufferance. Neither was in mourning, but a locket worn by the lady suggested that she was there in remembrance of a close family member. Young Mr Tasker both walked and sat with a miserable slouch, which his mother repeatedly corrected by tapping his arm with an insistent finger. Each time this happened, he scowled, and straightened his shoulders unwillingly, then let them slump again almost at once. Mrs Tasker gave elaborate greetings to both Mrs and Miss Brendel, and pushed her son into doing the same. He barely recognised the presence of other persons in the room, but the one thing that did attract his interest was the piano, and as they took their seats he fastened his attention on it to the exclusion of all else.

The gathering was completed by a Mr Quinley a man in his middle years, who said nothing about himself, but greeted everyone briefly with an ingratiating smile, sat down, and remained determinedly silent.

A tray was brought with a large pot of tea, and all the company was served with the exception of Miss Brendel. There was a delicate china cup on the same tray, one with pretty flowers painted around the rim. It was filled from a smaller pot and handed to Miss Brendel by her mother without the addition of either sugar or milk. Mina was too far away to see what was in the cup, but wondered if it was something medicinal in nature.

Slowly, gasping with the strain, Mina rose to her feet and rubbed her shoulder. 'I hope you don't mind, Mrs Brendel, but my poor back aches so when I remain idle. Might I take a brief turn about the room? If I do, I will be well again directly.'

'Oh, please do,' said Mrs Brendel.

'May I assist you?' asked Fernwood, leaping to his feet.

'Yes, thank you,' said Mina, gratefully, 'if you could just let me lean on your arm.'

They made slow progress about the room, watched with anxiety by the other occupants, and Mina made sure that her path took her close enough to Miss Brendel to see the contents of her teacup, a brew so pale that it could hardly be flavoured at all, and had no very strong aroma.

Once all were back in their places, and it was established that Mina was quite restored by her walk, Mrs Brendel gazed happily about her. 'How pleasant it is to see so many familiar faces, and also some new ones. Some of you may already know Miss Scarletti, by reputation at least. She is held in great regard here in Brighton.' Those who had thus far been too polite to stare at Mina now took the opportunity to do so.

George Fernwood coughed gently. 'As this is the first time we have come here, I would be very obliged if we could be told when the proceedings are about to start.'

'Oh, there is no start,' said Mrs Brendel, with a smile. 'Neither is there any end. Athene's gifts cannot come and go as a candle is lit or extinguished. Athene sees what she sees at any moment. She may see something tonight or she may not.'

Athene's large brilliant eyes turned about the room. 'I do see,' she said. 'I see the figure of a man. His eyes are open, as one who lives, he gazes far away, but he does not move.'

Mrs Myles uttered a loud sob. Her husband patted her arm. 'Can you describe him?'

'He is young. His face is much sunken, the expression melancholy.'

'Where is he?'

'He is standing behind your chair.'

Inevitably the other occupants of the room, apart from the surly Mr Tasker, looked to where Miss Brendel indicated. There was nothing to be seen.

'Please! Address him! Does he have a message for us?' begged Mr Myles.

Miss Athene smiled indulgently, from which Mina supposed that it was an entreaty she had heard before. 'Sir,' she said, to the vacant air beside Mr Myles, 'if you are able to speak, please do so. Say whatever you will.'

There was a long pause, silent except for the sound of breathing, which as far as Mina could make out was produced only by the living occupants of the room. 'Oh, do tell me what he says!' asked Mr Myles at last. 'That may be our dear boy, our darling Jack, who we laid to rest ten years ago.'

Miss Brendel shook her head. 'I cannot tell. He is gone. But I have seen him before. I think he will come again. Perhaps next time, he will have a message for you. Be patient.'

Mrs Myles choked back a paroxysm that threatened to close her throat.

'Oh, that is our poor son, I know it!' exclaimed Mr Myles. 'Come to bear witness to his place in Heaven!' He pulled a large handkerchief from his pocket; white with the broadest edge of black Mina had ever seen, pressed it to his face and sighed into its depths.

'Do you see anyone by me?' asked Mrs Tasker, impatiently.

Athene sighed and shook her head. 'No, but my art is not certain. I do see a gentleman standing by Miss Scarletti. I have not seen him before. He is neither young nor very old. He seems troubled. That is all I can say.'

George Fernwood and Miss Clifton glanced at each other.

'How is he troubled?' asked Mina. 'It is an affliction of the mind or the body?' Despite herself she could only think of her father, and realised how easily one could be drawn into hope and belief.

'It is hard to tell. He is walking about the room. He does not see any of us.'

'I hear no footfall.'

'Nor do I,' said Miss Brendel. 'That is one way I know that the people I see are apparitions. I see them walk, they seem to be present, but their feet make no sound.'

'Do you know if this is someone living or one who has passed?' asked Mr Honeyacre. He spoke not as someone who thought he might know the apparition, but from simple curiosity.

'I cannot say. Both the living and the dead appear before me, but I can only distinguish between them if they are known to me. The gentleman is gone now. But there are several more persons, who have appeared, some close, some distant. Both ladies and gentlemen. I can't see their faces. They move back and forth as if passing each other in the street. They stop, and greet each other, then walk on. Some have bright clothes, others are dull as if the colours have faded.' Athene closed her eyes, and raised a skeletal hand to her forehead. 'I must rest for a while.'

Mrs Brendel fetched a carafe of water from a side table and poured a small glassful, which she pressed into her daughter's hands. Athene looked weary, and sipped very carefully.

'Are you quite well?' asked Mr Honeyacre, gently.

Athene favoured him with a kind smile. 'I am, only so many visions are an unusual exertion and I must rest from time to time. I will be recovered in a moment.'

'Can you tell me if the figures you see appear to be as real and solid as actual persons or if they are more like shadows or mist,' asked Mina.

'For the most part when they first appear they are like actual persons. If you were to see one, you would assume it was a living being and address it as such. I can see the colour of the skin and hair and clothing quite distinctly, and they move and walk like real persons in every way. But they are not aware of me, or at least they do not seem to be, and after a while they start to fade and become transparent, like a painting on glass. I can see the room through them. And then they vanish.'

'Do they make any sound at all? Do they speak?'

'There is no sound. Sometimes I can see their lips moving, some of them even converse with each other, but I cannot always distinguish what they say.'

'Have you ever approached one to touch it?'

'I have. I once saw my father at a time when I knew he was far from home. He walked about the room and smoked his pipe, but I could not smell the tobacco. Then he sat in his favourite armchair, and I went to touch him, indeed I made to sit in his lap. But there was nothing there and he vanished immediately.' She set her glass down, and her eyes took on that dreamy look, a distant gaze that suggested that a vision had appeared.

'What do you see?' asked Mr Conroy, hopefully. 'Is it a lady?'

'Yes, I see a lady; she is very aged, dressed all in black. She has white hair.'

Mr Conroy looked disappointed.

'My grandmother, perhaps?' said Mrs Tasker, hopefully. 'She passed away seven years ago. Perhaps she has a message for me? Or for Geoffrey? He was always her favourite. How might I receive a message?'

'Close your eyes and think of her. If it is she, it may be that her words will come to you.'

Mrs Tasker obediently closed her eyes and smiled. 'Ah, yes, I think I can hear her now. Her voice was so — distinctive. She has a message about Geoffrey.' She patted her son's arm, reassuringly. 'All will be well.' Geoffrey shrugged off his mother's touch.

Mina wondered if like she, he was unconvinced that the message came from anywhere other than his mother's wishes. Mrs Tasker had some very definite motives for bringing her son to the séance. Whatever the underlying intention, and that was not clear to Mina, she obviously wanted her own wishes to be amplified by sage advice from one who had passed and therefore could be said to have divine understanding.

Miss Brendel was obliged to rest once more, and after a whispered conversation with her mother, it was announced that the sitting was over, although the guests might remain for light refreshments if they so wished. Miss Brendel rose and guided by her mother's hand, left the room. Mina wondered if her ghosts accompanied her or remained. There was no way of knowing.

Mr and Mrs Myles decided to take their leave, as did the Taskers. Mr Quinley stayed and said nothing, but watched the company as if they were simply visions of his own, and therefore not to be disturbed.

Mr Honeyacre rose and went to speak quietly to Mrs Brendel. Mina observed the conversation though it was conducted in tones too low for her to hear. Mrs Brendel listened, and nodded and he seemed pleased with that response.

Mr Conroy, deep in thought, approached Mina, and sat by her. 'Miss Scarletti, we have not met before, but your name is known to me; you are a great friend of Mrs Jordan.'

'Yes, we often take tea or, in clement weather, we like to drive about the town.'

'You are new to this circle. But I think I can guess your mission. You hope to find some fault with Miss Brendel, uncover plots to show her to the world as a fraud. But I can tell you now that you will fail.'

'Oh? How interesting! Please tell me how you have come to that conclusion.'

'I have attended four meetings, and the lady is undoubtedly sincere. She does not, as the cheats do, ask for payment or gifts. She has a rare ability and she uses it selflessly to bring comfort to others who are in sore need of it.'

'Have you ever seen the visions she describes?'

'No, and I would not expect to. I do not have her gifts.'

'Has she ever seen a vision which, from her description, is of someone known to you?'

Conroy paused. 'The first time I was here, I thought, yes. I expect you know I have been widowed for almost a year. All my tender thoughts since then have been of the fine wife I have lost. Otherwise I have distracted myself with my family and business matters. But —' There was a long silence, and he puffed out his cheeks like a man who dared not say more. He pulled his watch from his pocket. 'I'm sorry. I have an appointment and must go at once. I can see you are a sceptic, but in my estimation, Miss Brendel will confound all criticism.' He rose to his feet and bowed. 'Good evening.' After briefly taking his leave of the hostess who was still conversing quietly with Mr Honeyacre, he hurried away.

'I wonder what that was about?' said Fernwood.

'Oh, but can't you see?' said Miss Clifton with a knowing smile. 'He was distracting himself from his grief, but then he comes here and finds Miss Brendel more of a distraction. In six months we may hear of an engagement.'

Fernwood raised his eyebrows. 'Is it the lady or her fortune that tempts him, I wonder? Probably the latter.'

'And what do you think of Miss Brendel?' asked Miss Clifton turning to Mina. 'Is she true or false? We both thought the vision of the gentleman might have been my great uncle Thomas.'

'There was little enough description,' said Mina. 'How many families have a gentleman of that age, or an old lady with white hair? But I saw no sign of conjuring, and there could have been none. She merely states what she sees and cannot be contradicted. She does not even pass on messages but leaves it to us to gather what we wish for.'

'But does she believe in it herself?' asked Fernwood. 'She could be a deliberate deceiver, or subject to delusions, or genuine. She may have some fault with her eyes. How can we know which one she is?'

'As to her eyesight, there is a doctor who might be able to advise me on that point.'

'That is very kind of you,' said Miss Clifton. 'Once we know more we can decide if we should pay her another visit. For myself, I feel that she shows great promise, and I would very much like to see her again.' Fernwood said nothing but Mina saw from his expression that he did not share Miss Clifton's optimism.

Moments later, Mr Honeyacre also made to leave, but as he departed, there was a small careful movement, in which he produced an envelope from his pocket and slipped it into his hostess's hands. Mina glanced about but her companions were gazing at each other and had not noticed, and Mr Quinley if he had noticed was not about to reveal that he had.

'I do have one question,' said Mina quietly to George Fernwood. 'As we walked about the room, did you happen to see what it was in Miss Brendel's teacup?'

'Some variety of tisane, but without being able to smell it, I could not say which one.'

'We must find out what it is. It could be innocent, or it could just be the key to what we need to know.'

Chapter Nine

Mina made sure to be warmly wrapped against the sharp weather before she emerged with her companions onto Oriental Place. As they descended the steps she was surprised to see, cowering in the shadows thrown by the yellow glow of the gas lamps, the same youth who had been outside the house before they went in. He looked chilled, and she realised that he might well have been lurking there the whole time.

'Ladies,' said Fernwood, 'please remain here by the gate where there is some shelter from the wind, and I am sure there will be a cab in moments.' He strode purposefully up the street. Before long a vehicle approached and he quickly hailed it.

To Mina's surprise, once the maid had withdrawn into the house and the front door was closed, the youth emerged from his hiding place and crept shyly forward to speak to her and Miss Clifton. He was clad in a greatcoat too thin and mean to be adequate for the cold weather, and he was clutching his arms about his chest in the vain hope that they might lend him some warmth. His face, which bore an expression of extreme meekness, was stark white, pinched with blue. There was nothing threatening in his manner, neither did he look like someone about to beg alms, nevertheless it was an unusual thing to do. Mina glanced anxiously at Mr Fernwood, who having seen what was occurring, was hurrying back to their side.

'Please excuse me, ladies,' began the youth, 'I don't mean to alarm you, and I know I should not address you in this way, but I beg you to hear me out. I assume you have been to one of Miss Brendel's séances?'

Fernwood reached them. 'We have,' he said suspiciously. 'What is it to you?'

'I was wondering if you could tell me if the lady is in good health? I am concerned that she is in some dreadful decline.'

'I am afraid that none of us have met the lady previously and so cannot judge if her health is any better or worse than previously,' said Mina.

'But did she look well? Was she weary?'

'I am sorry,' said Fernwood, brusquely, 'but we cannot have this conversation in the open street. The ladies may catch a chill.' The cab had drawn up and he went to open the door.

'I agree,' said Mina, but her curiosity had been piqued. 'Let us all enter the cab and talk there.'

Fernwood looked surprised, but reluctantly agreed, and before long they were all four settled and comfortable.

'My name is Ernest Dawson,' said the youth. 'I am twenty-one and I live with my mother and two sisters on Upper North Street. I am employed by Potts and Co, the music emporium on King's Road, and work on the counter selling sheet music. Some three months ago Mrs and Miss Brendel came to the shop and purchased a piano, which was delivered to their lodgings in Oriental Place. Miss Brendel is very adept at the piano — I heard her play and it was delightful — and she also purchased some music. I — I must confess,' he added bashfully, 'that I found her extremely interesting. On a later occasion when she came to purchase more music, we conversed for some while, and I think — in fact I am sure — that she returned my regard. I did go to the house to attend one of the séances, but really my true reason in doing so was to see Miss Brendel again. When I went a second time I enquired of Mrs Brendel whether her daughter had a sweetheart, and if she did not, I asked if I might be permitted to call upon her. This Mrs Brendel absolutely refused. She was not unkind at first, but became harsher as I continued to entreat her. It was made very clear to me that my fortunes were insufficient, and I must not entertain any tender feelings for Miss Brendel. I do, of course, I cannot repress my feelings, but now I know I must be content only to be the lady's sincere and concerned friend. It is in that capacity that I ask for your assistance.'

'What do you expect us to do?' asked Mina.

'I am very worried indeed about Miss Brendel's state of health. Even in the few times I have seen her I have noticed a decline. I cannot discover if she is being attended by a medical man — I have never seen one enter the house. Neither Mrs Brendel nor the maid will speak to me. The maid, Jessie, I think is not unsympathetic but she is governed by her mistress. Miss Brendel rarely goes out nowadays, so I cannot think that she is consulting anyone. I fear for her, I really do! I wonder — would you be so kind as to deliver a message to her from me the next time you visit? Her mother has forbidden me to call again, and I am sure she would intercept any letters.'

Mr Fernwood and Miss Clifton looked at each other, but Mina spoke sternly before they could respond. 'Mr Dawson, if you have any sense at all, you will know we cannot do this. The mother's word, whether or not you agree with it, is law. If she has forbidden you the house and ordered you not to pay court to her daughter I cannot intervene in this underhand fashion.'

'Even at the cost of a life?' he pleaded.

'Is she really in such danger? How can you know for sure? You are not a medical man.' Even as she spoke, Mina had to admit that she too, had concerns for Miss Brendel's health, but at the same time, was hardly in a position to advise.

485

'I know what I see, and,' he shivered, 'I have still graver suspicions.'

'Go on, do.'

'I think that Miss Brendel's visions may well be produced either by her declining health, or something she consumes — a herb or medicine. Mrs Brendel is using her daughter's special gifts to achieve fame and position, but in doing so I very much fear that she is administering some poisonous substance, which may if she is incautious, kill her.'

'Do you have any proof of this?' asked Fernwood. 'It is a serious allegation.'

Dawson shook his head. 'No, or I would have told the police.'

'Then I doubt that there is anything you could do.'

'I have no funds to engage a professional man to see her, and even if I did her mother would not allow it. I thought, if I could get a message to her, and find out if she is well and happy ...' His shoulders slumped miserably. 'In the meantime, all I can do is watch the house whenever I can.'

'Miss Scarletti is right,' said Fernwood. 'We cannot interfere between mother and daughter without good reason.'

Mina suddenly recalled a remark that Dr Hamid had made to her some months ago. Some of his patients at the baths had reported seeing the ghosts of the recently departed. He had been mystified as to the reasons for this, but perhaps he might now have further observations to share as to the likely causes of this phenomenon. He might even be tempted to go and see Miss Brendel out of curiosity. 'Mr Dawson, do you have a card?'

All the other occupants of the cab looked startled by the question. 'Er — no, but I have a card of Potts and Co.'

'Then let me have it and write your address on it. I have a card of my family publishing company and you may have it with my address. I will make some enquiries. I have a medical friend who might be able to advise me. But I make no promises.'

'Oh, I am so very grateful!' he exclaimed. 'Any hope at all is better than none! Tell me, was there a fellow there by the name of Quinley?'

'Yes, there was.'

'I thought so. He is not a guest but a solicitor, he manages all Mr Brendel's affairs.'

'How do you know this? He gave no clue when I saw him. In fact, he said nothing at all.'

'I know because of the purchase of the piano. Mrs Brendel's bills are paid by the husband through Mr Quinley. In Brighton he is the wife's watchdog. He chases away impecunious suitors, even the noble ones. No lordling need think he can trade his title for settlement of his gambling debts.'

The cards were exchanged, and after Mina was taken home, it was agreed that young Mr Dawson could be taken to his apartments before George Fernwood and Miss Clifton travelled on to the railway station. As Mina turned the key in her front door a thought struck her. All the arrivals at the Brendel séance had been preceded by the doorbell. All but one, Mr Quinley. Which suggested that he was already in the house.

Chapter Ten

Before she retired for the night, Mina started to plan another tale. In this story there was a witch who only used her powers for evil. She was jealous of a much younger witch who only used her powers for good. The wicked witch kidnapped the good witch and cast a spell on her, so that the good witch believed she was the wicked witch's daughter. Out of daughterly duty the good witch did everything her supposed mother told her. Thus, the wicked witch made use of the good witch's powers for her own purposes.

Mina thought this was a promising start, but wasn't sure how to end the story. It was too easy to have a handsome prince arrive unexpectedly and fall in love with the good witch and set her free. Far better for the good witch to fight her way out of her predicament using her own resources. But how? A magical amulet she just happened to have forgotten she had, or even discovered by chance? No. Mina did not like to bring more coincidence into a tale than was necessary. What if the good witch had a dream about her real mother and realised she had been practised upon, and that broke the spell? Better. That at least had the attraction of greater possibility.

Or maybe, thought Mina, the good witch just wasn't the docile creature the wicked witch had taken her to be, and every so often she wanted to be very naughty and disobey her mother? Yes.

Mina scribbled happily for so long that she even heard Richard creeping in late.

Young Mr Dawson's distress had given Mina substantial cause for thought, and the following morning she considered the mysterious Brendels, and what action she might reasonably take. Mrs Brendel, who had arrived in Brighton in the autumn season knowing no-one of any position, was, she felt sure, trying to attract the kind of attention that would provide her with an invitation to fashionable circles, not merely for herself but for her pretty, accomplished, unusual and oh-so-eligible daughter. Miss Athene Brendel was undoubtedly a little strange and a trifle delicate-looking for many men's tastes, but a large marriage portion would soon overcome any hesitation.

It occurred to Mina that apart from watchful Mr Quinley, the deeply mourning Mr and Mrs Myles, and her own party, those present at the séance — she could hardly think of it as anything else — were widowed Mr Conroy, an unmarried youth and his mother, and a veteran who was almost certainly a widower, too, Mr Honeyacre. All these gentlemen were therefore potential suitors for Miss Brendel. Mina was consumed with curiosity as to what was in the envelope Mr Honeyacre had passed to Mrs Brendel. Money? An invitation? A letter? A proposal of marriage? It was obvious that whatever the nature of Miss Brendel's peculiar ability, she was, in the best of traditions in moneyed families, being displayed as a valuable commodity by her mother. The presence of a solicitor, as advisor and protector, was understandable.

Mina was obliged to remind herself that there was no reason for her to interfere in Mrs Brendel's plans, apart from the mischievous pleasure it would bring her, as well as providing fuel for her stories. Had the séance been the kind of performance she was accustomed to seeing, with glowing apparitions and trumpets that played by themselves and similar chicanery, she would have had no difficulty in telling her companions that Miss Brendel was a fraud to be avoided, but this was altogether different and she didn't know what to make of it. She needed sensible expert advice, and there was no-one she could rely upon more than Dr Hamid.

The truly important issue in Mina's mind, and the one that might require some action by an outside party, was the state of Miss Brendel's health. Was she, as Mr Dawson suspected, being poisoned by her mother, either deliberately or unintentionally, and was this the source of her visions — or was she subject to a wasting illness, one, perhaps, that had gone unnoticed by her family and for which she was receiving no treatment? Or was Mr Dawson simply a susceptible young man, being led astray by his anxiety and Miss Brendel's undoubted attractions? Mina recognised that she was not equipped to answer these questions, but she knew a man who was.

It did occur to her, however, that as Dr Hamid was a widower with a thriving business, a circumstance that could well earn him a warm welcome from Mrs Brendel, she ought to issue a gentle warning to him. Once his period of mourning was over, society would consider him highly eligible and ripe for remarriage. The doctor was undoubtedly a fine-looking gentleman, his interesting complexion a tribute to his Bengali father, a well-respected man of medicine in his own right, who had married a Scottish lady and settled in Brighton. He was also clever, well-mannered, and anxious to do good in the world. A friend of Mina's mother, Mrs Mowbray, an ample and mature widow, had long admired Dr Hamid in a manner wholly obvious to everyone, with the exception of the doctor himself, who was oblivious to the passion he had inspired. His loving devotion, with which he was well supplied, was not addressed to any ladies other than his sister Anna, his daughter, and the memory of those who had passed from the world.

When Mina wished to consult Dr Hamid in fine weather she simply took a pleasant ride to the baths, but on this occasion she sent him a note, in which, so as not to cause alarm, she reassured him that she was in good health, but wished to speak to him on another matter involving the health of another individual. He quickly replied saying that he would be able to call on her after his last appointment of the day, and Mina instructed Rose to arrange suitable refreshment. She might have included Richard in the interview, but she discovered that he had gone out, having failed to inform anyone of where he was going or when he was to be expected back.

There had been no mention in Mina's letter that she was once again delving into the world of the psychic, but when Dr Hamid arrived, his expression told her that his suspicions had already been aroused.

'How is your sister?' he asked, as they made themselves comfortable in the parlour before a roaring fire with a jug of hot cocoa and toasted and buttered currant cakes.

'She is in delicate health, but my mother is attending to her, and is confident that all will be well in time.'

'And your mother?'

'She will outlive Methuselah I am sure, for all her protestations. Edward's business thrives, and he is looking forward to his wedding to Miss Hooper next year. Richard is back in Brighton, and he is the same as ever.'

He nodded. 'So it is not a family member you are concerned about?'

'No,' said Mina cautiously. He gave her a wary look. 'Have you heard of a Miss Athene Brendel? Is she perhaps a patient of yours?'

'She is not, but the name is familiar.' It took a moment's thought for him to recall it. 'The lady claiming to see ghosts? I have read about her in the newspaper, and some of my patients have mentioned her. She is in Brighton with her mother. How have you come to know her?'

Mina chose her words carefully. 'I was asked to attend a séance on behalf of an acquaintance who wanted my opinion as to whether or not she is genuine. On the basis of what occurred I was unable to form any opinion.' Mina described her evening at Oriental Place, with particular reference to Miss Brendel's appearance and manner. Dr Hamid listened to the story with mounting disquiet.

'You believe that Miss Brendel is in poor health?'

'Yes, she seems very delicate. Of course, I have only seen her once, so I have no means of knowing if this is her usual appearance. As my friends and I were leaving the house, however, we were accosted by a young man, a Mr Dawson who works at Potts and Co, the music emporium. He was very anxious about Miss Brendel, and undoubtedly has tender feelings for her, but her mother has refused to allow him to pay court to her daughter, as he has no fortune. He told me that he thought Miss Brendel's health was in danger, possibly even her life, and that her mother was not making the efforts to care for her that she ought. In fact, he even suggested that Mrs Brendel was quite unintentionally giving her daughter something that was harming her. Of course, he may be wrong, but everything I have seen suggests to me that there might well be cause for concern. I noticed especially that Mrs Brendel gives her daughter a drink, some kind of tisane, which she does not serve to others. Who knows what it is?'

'I am not sure what you wish me to say,' said Dr Hamid, cautiously. 'I can understand the reasons for your disquiet, but you do appreciate that if Miss Brendel is already being attended by a doctor then, leaving aside a sudden emergency, there is nothing another man can do unless he is consulted?'

Dr Hamid had often given in to Mina's requests for help, even when he had felt them to be somewhat beneath the dignity of a practitioner of medicine, but this time his tone and expression told her that here was a path he would not cross.

'There would be no harm in an informal enquiry, surely? I seem to recall our first meeting when you asked if I would be willing to consult you.'

'But on that occasion you had already advised me, quite forcibly as I remember, that you distrusted doctors, so I felt safe in assuming that you were not already under treatment. I am glad that you have spoken to me about Miss Brendel, as the information could well be of value if I am ever asked to attend her, but I am not sure what you wish me to do at present.'

'I only seek an opinion. But there are two issues here. I feel they may be connected but I am not qualified to determine if they are, I can only observe. Yes, I know that strictly speaking none of it is any of my business, since neither I nor a member of my family is involved.'

'Why do I think that will not stop you?' said Dr Hamid, dryly.

Mina waited for him to raise an objection, but as he made no protest she continued. 'The most important thing is Miss Brendel's safety. If she is in danger and I know about it, I can hardly stay silent. Then there are the visions. She may, of course, be merely playing a role, but I felt, and I could be mistaken, that she genuinely saw something, although the nature of what she saw no-one can tell. I think you know more about these things than most men, in fact more than most doctors. I remember you once told me that some of your patients had reported seeing ghosts. You said that these patients appeared to be sincere and not delusional. So you have encountered others who have made similar claims to Miss Brendel. You would know if there was some reason relating to their state of health that might produce such visions. And I feel certain that you have some curiosity about this condition.'

He smiled. 'As to the explanation for the visions, I am not sure if I have one, but you are right about the curiosity.'

Mina did not mention it, but in one of his more confiding moments he had confessed to her how he wished he possessed the ability to see images of those who had passed; not simply as a picture in his mind, but something outside himself, so he could sit at home and look on the faces of his late and much-loved wife, Jane, who was ever in his thoughts, and his dear sister Eliza, both of whom who had died that year.

'Can you tell me more about your patients? What did they see? How did they explain it?'

There was a long pause for thought, partly occasioned by the buttering of a teacake, partly, Mina felt sure, by Dr Hamid considering what, without betraying the confidence of his patients, he could safely say. 'There were two. I cannot name them, of course. One was a gentleman, who was suffering from anxiety, mainly concerning his business. He was in constant discomfort from indigestion. He told me, not without some hesitation, that he had begun to see the figures of men and women in his house, people he knew were not actually there. Of those he recognised, some were deceased and some living, others he did not know. He attributed the visions to a disturbance of the brain, and was afraid that he was losing his mind. His own doctor advised sea bathing and also recommended that he consult me.'

'The gentleman did not think he saw the spirits of the dead, or living phantoms?'

'No, not at any point. Once he had established that the figures were not actually present, he was quite sure that the visions emanated from his mind and were not real.'

'Did he speak to the figures or try to touch them?'

'He did at first, but they took no notice of him, and if he attempted to approach them either they vanished altogether before he reached them, or his hand passed through them and then they faded away.'

'Does he still see them?'

'No. His health improved with a regimen of vapour baths and massage. His digestion returned to its normal robust condition. Also, he very sensibly retired from business and decided to go and live abroad. Just before he left he told me that the visions had decreased as his circumstances improved and he had not seen one in some time.'

'And what of your other patient?'

'A lady of advanced years who was much afflicted with a cancer in her intestines. Her illness was progressing rapidly and she knew there was no hope, but she came to me for an easing of her pain. She told me that she saw animals and birds in her house, which no-one else could see. She received only two treatments and passed away not long afterwards.'

'Did she believe she saw ghosts?'

'She liked to think so, and never attempted to question the reality of what she saw. She was very fond of animals, and the visions comforted her.' He looked wistful.

'Miss Brendel and your patients cannot be the only people in the world who have seen such apparitions. Can you explain how these visions occur? Where do they originate? How are they formed?'

'I am not convinced that the visions had any origin other than in the mind of the person seeing them. But I find it hard to conceive how a thought can become so real that one actually sees it outside oneself as a solid person. Neither of my patients was insane. Anxious, yes, unwell, yes, but both were in full possession of their senses.'

Mina refilled his cocoa cup. 'I have a favour to ask you.'

'I had feared as much. As long as I am not expected to creep about spying on people. I am no detective.'

Mina had once asked him to do this for her when there had been no alternative. He had found it highly embarrassing and she had promised never to ask him to do so again.

'No, I wish to draw on your special knowledge. Would you be prepared to visit the Brendels for one of their evening gatherings? It occurred to me that Mrs Brendel might not have seen or recognised the signs of illness in her daughter. Since she sees her daughter every day she might not have noticed any slow changes. After all, my mother never noticed the trouble with my spine until the dressmaker pointed it out. Might there be something very specific to which you could draw her attention?'

He considered this. 'It is certainly possible, but if Mrs Brendel does not choose to consult me there is nothing practical I can do.'

'A gentle hint might be all that is required. Enough to make her think of what she might not have seen, that a trained eye has noticed. Enough to suggest that she consults a doctor. Otherwise I am afraid that Mr Dawson will try and effect a cure by taking Miss Brendel away from her mother and removing her to Gretna Green.'

'Would he do so?'

'He seems very devoted. But you will go?' She offered another currant cake, which he took.

'If only to prevent a misguided elopement, yes. But I am no great expert on the eye and its connection with the brain. I have had another thought, however. There are a number of oculists in Brighton with whom I have a slight acquaintance. They have made the special studies I have not and might be able to offer some insights into the nature of illusions. Would you like me to make enquiries? I am happy to do so as it would help me if I was to encounter any further cases in my practice.'

'Please do. If you find an oculist who can enlighten me I should like to meet him. Perhaps he might be willing to call on Miss Brendel? But before we make such an arrangement I would first need to know if he is a married man.'

Dr Hamid looked a little shocked at the question. 'Why is that of importance?'

'I do not ask on my own account. I ask because Mrs Brendel seems to be favouring eligible gentlemen for her guests. I think she is hoping to marry her daughter into the moneyed classes, someone who will match the father's fortune and not squander it. A professional man, perhaps, one with a thriving business.' She allowed a meaningful pause to follow.

Dr Hamid nodded and it was only gradually that realisation dawned and he looked alarmed. 'Oh! No! I have no intention of marrying again. Not now, or ever.'

'Then you should be immune to Mrs Brendel's wiles. But you can be assured of a warm welcome in her house.'

Dr Hamid did not meet this information with any pleasure.

'On that subject, are you acquainted with an elderly couple, a Mr and Mrs Myles? They were there that night. Also a Mrs Tasker and her son, and a Mr Honeyacre.'

'Well, none of them are patients of mine. Honeyacre, hmm, that name does sound familiar. I'll give it some thought.'

Mina very much wanted to ask Dr Hamid about the prospect of criminal tendencies being inherited; whether they lay dormant only to emerge several generations later, and if they could be multiplied by the marriage of cousins, but she decided to remain silent. George Fernwood and Mary Clifton had already consulted a medical man, without result. It seemed unlikely that Dr Hamid would have a better answer and all she would have done was arouse his suspicions and betray the confidence with which she had been entrusted.

'If you can let me know what days are convenient for you I will write to Mrs Brendel and arrange a visit for us both.'

'I knew you would have your way. And let me consider what I might reasonably do concerning Miss Brendel. If I do not overstep the accepted bounds I might venture some simple questions, but I will take no action which would be unprofessional.'

Mina nodded. Dr Hamid's firm and careful manner was a steadying influence. He was a source of calm and thoughtful advice, which was always welcome. If, on the other hand, action needed to be taken that was both foolhardy and dangerous, and which no man in his right mind ought to attempt, she knew that Richard would do it without being asked.

Chapter Eleven

Once Dr Hamid had departed Mina quickly made notes of a new idea for a story that had just occurred to her.

An impoverished but noble-minded young man was in love with a beautiful maiden who possessed a fortune. Mina hesitated over the word 'beautiful'. This would imply that the young man was shallow enough to admire the maiden only for her outward appearance. It was, however, an inevitable part of popular stories that a heroine who was much loved and sought after should always be beautiful. Surely, Mina thought, those who were not so favoured could be loved as well? And could only beautiful women have adventures in storybooks? It seemed so. Mina gave the question further thought and crossed out the word 'beautiful.' No doubt her readers would simply assume it was there in any case. This, however, presented a new difficulty since it now appeared that the youth was not in love with the maiden at all, but only wooed her for her fortune, which was not at all the idea that Mina wished to convey. She began again.

An impoverished but noble-minded young man was in love with a virtuous maiden, who although not rich, was in herself a priceless jewel and deserving of his devotion. She loved the youth in return, and they had promised each other that one day they would marry. There was, unfortunately, an obstacle to their happiness. The honest maiden of indeterminate appearance and meagre dowry was being pursued in marriage by an elderly rich gentleman, and although she did not care for him, her avaricious mother had agreed to the match. The interest of the old gentleman in a bride who was one third of his age, even if she was neither beautiful nor rich, did not, Mina thought, need to be explained. The wedding to the aged suitor took place much against the daughter's will and she was immediately carried off to her new husband's castle. Meanwhile the youthful admirer had discovered that the elderly gentleman had been married many times before, always to very young wives who died soon afterwards, sometimes on the wedding night. He hurried to the castle, arriving just in time to rescue his beloved from a grisly fate. The elderly husband, seeing that he was about to suffer for his catalogue of dreadful crimes, threw himself from the battlements and perished. The tale ended with the wedding of the maiden to her deserving swain.

There were a few details to be smoothed out. Since the youth was poor he would not own a horse, and therefore could not pursue the newly married couple in their wedding coach and arrive in time to avert disaster. A youth of such impeccable character would, however, be bound to have a loyal friend who would happily lend him a steed. Mina would also have to insert a scene in which the hero braved death to save his love — always popular with the reader. Once the wicked husband had plunged to his death, the maiden bride, now a widow, was wonderfully wealthy, thus satisfying her mother's avarice. After the wedding, the dutiful daughter rewarded her mother with the gift of a fine house with servants — at some considerable distance from the castle.

Richard was not yet home when Mina retired to bed, but next morning he arrived at the breakfast table, late, dishevelled, dull of eye and thirsty for strong coffee. She knew better than to question him about where he had been and with whom. Rose brought him a dish of bacon and kidneys, which he smothered in Brighton sauce and fell to as if he had not eaten in a week, while Mina, studying the morning post, contented herself with a boiled egg and a toasted muffin. 'It is a good thing Mother is not here to see you with your collar in that state,' she observed.

'Oh, Mother has more things to worry about than my collars,' said Richard, pouring his third cup of coffee. 'But you are doing duty for her, I see.'

'Someone has to. I have received a letter this morning from Edward. He says I must make sure you don't misbehave yourself and you are to work hard. I would like you to manage at least one of those, but preferably both. He wants you to post back a sketch to him every day.'

Richard looked appalled, and almost choked on his coffee. 'Every day? Surely not!' he spluttered.

'That is what he has asked for. Well, you did say you could complete them quickly, and I am sure he knows it, so the request is not unreasonable. How many sketches have you completed since you arrived?'

He wiped his mouth with a napkin and shrugged. 'Not many. These things take time. I have to settle myself to it properly before I can begin. Get my surroundings just so; be in the right artistic frame of mind. You understand, don't you? It must be like that when you do your writing.'

'No. So I assume you have done nothing, which means you had better make a start. And Edward says that each sketch must have a story attached to it.'

Richard groaned and knuckled his eyes. 'But where am I supposed to find these stories? They don't just lie in the street to be picked up.'

Mina took pity on him, and opened the newspaper. 'Look here. The papers are full of them. Town gossip is awash with stories, and some of them are even true. The *Gazette* has a whole page, sometimes more, about the society events taking place in the season. You've missed the panorama of Paris in flames, I'm afraid, which was a very popular attraction, but the County Hospital Ball is tonight. There will be carriages all around the Pavilion and the Dome. Everyone will be there. And Mr Burrows was elected Mayor last week, for the third time. That is a very notable event. You could offer to sketch him. Oh, and look here — Dickinson's Gallery on

King's Road is displaying a new portrait of the Queen. Every fashionable person in town is sure to be there to see it.'

Richard picked up the paper and stared at it, but the prospects of work it offered did not cheer him.

'And this is only the beginning. Next week the whole town will be preparing for Christmas.'

'Already? But it's not even December yet.'

'No, but people like to start early.' She reached out and squeezed his hand. 'Richard, let me help you. If you can do the sketches, and tell me who they portray I will write a few words to accompany them. Is that not a reasonable offer?'

Richard's despondent moods never lasted long. A smile brushed his face like sunshine, and he patted her hand, so tiny that it vanished beneath his like a child's. 'You are the very best sister a man could have. Dearest Mina — I don't suppose — ?'

'But I won't lend you any more money.'

Dear Mr Fernwood,

I have recently consulted a medical man of my acquaintance who has some experience of patients who see apparitions. In his opinion the question of what such visions mean and how they come about is one that should be addressed to someone who has made a special study of the eye and its connection to the brain. He may well know of a suitable individual to approach, and I hope to be able to advise you further in due course.

In the meantime, I am pleased to say that he has consented to pay a call on Miss Brendel and consider if there is any foundation to the unusual anxieties of Mr Dawson.

Yours,
Mina Scarletti

Dear Miss Scarletti

Mary and I are most grateful for all you have done on our behalf and your continued interest in our difficult position. We anticipate your next communication with interest. As soon as time permits we will return to Brighton and see Miss Brendel again, as we feel there may be more to learn there.

We have decided to pay a brief visit to Lincoln, in the hope of reviving old memories of the place. We intend to look once again on the house where we lived as children and also ensure that my grandfather's grave has been properly tended. Who knows but that his shade might rise up and tell us what we wish to know and then he will confer his blessing on our union? At least that is what Mary hopes, and for her sake I would like to think so, too.

I will write again on our return,
Yours,
George Fernwood

Chapter Twelve

As Mina had anticipated when she applied for two invitations to the next séance, there was no difficulty in Dr Hamid being welcomed to the Brendels' home. He hired a cab and called for her, taking great care before he would even allow her to leave the house, to satisfy himself that her health would stand the exertion. The weather, he warned, had taken another wintry turn, and he supervised Rose as she prepared Mina for the outdoors, instructing her to use every means possible to protect her mistress against the cold air.

While this was in progress, Mina, as she had done with George Fernwood and Miss Clifton, studied Dr Hamid's appearance for clues that he would provide to a medium. He wore the usual signs of mourning; the black gloves and the band around his hat and sleeve. His wife had died the previous March and it would therefore be several months before it would be acceptable to make some variation to this attire; indeed, he might, as the Queen seemed to be doing, decide to make it a permanent state. This was valuable information to a fraudster, but since Hamid's vapour baths were well known in the town, Mina thought it was very likely that the Brendels already knew something of Dr Hamid or had found out his history in anticipation of his visit. Like Mina, he could hardly disguise his appearance since he was quite probably the only gentleman of Anglo-Indian descent in Brighton. Apart from those obvious considerations, there was, she thought, nothing else that could be learned.

By the time Mina had been enveloped in shawls, cloak, hood, veil, mittens and a muff, she felt ready, with the addition of a good ship, some dogs, a sled, and a team of native guides, to undertake a mission to find the North Pole, where, so a recent expedition had informed the press, there was thought to be a sea swarming with whales. Horrible as the North Pole must surely be, she thought she could understand its allure for the adventurous. Not only was it a challenge to both body and spirit, offering the thrill of discovery, and the opportunity of claiming new territory for one's nation, even if it should only prove to be a useless drift of ice, but it was also an escape from what might be the even greater cares of civilisation. No-one at the North Pole had to organise Christmas for a family whose members had scattered itself to the four winds in upset and disarray.

It occurred to Mina that one never saw a whale in the sea at Brighton. She supposed that the climate did not suit them. Of course, anything might happen in a story. She made a quick jotting in the little book she always carried with her to record ideas.

The transfer from doorstep to cab was done as quickly as possible. The driver was so heavily wrapped in multiple shawls that only his eyes were visible through the narrow slit between the folds of material and his hat. The interior of the cab was chill, but at least they were sheltered from the cutting wind, and Mina, clasping her flask of hot water, held it up before her face to warm the air.

Dr Hamid turned up the heavy collar of his greatcoat, and thrust gloved hands into his pockets. 'Of course, moments after we last spoke I recalled where I had heard the name Honeyacre. I found it in our record books. The gentleman was not a patient of mine, but his late wife suffered from an affliction that all the skills of medicine could not cure. They lived in the country, quite close to Brighton, and from time to time she was brought here to the baths, where her visits afforded her great relief. I later learned that she had passed away peacefully and without pain, which was the best outcome that could have been hoped for.'

'How long has Mr Honeyacre been widowed?'

'About five years. After that I think he went travelling abroad for a while. I don't know when he returned. I mentioned his name to Anna, and she informed me that he is now resident in Brighton where he has recently been paying court to a spinster of his own age, a Miss Macready. An engagement has yet to be announced, but is believed to be imminent.' He smiled. 'I am sure you know that Anna is not one for gossip of that sort, but ladies like to talk about the news of the town while she is treating them.'

'So, from what you say, he is neither a recent widower nor a suitor for Miss Brendel's hand?'

'That would appear to be the case.'

'You surprise me. Those are the very two reasons for which I would expect him to have attended the séance. Is he wealthy?'

'I believe so. He owns a number of estates in the county and amuses himself by collecting art and antiquities.'

'Perhaps the Brendels hope he can introduce them to the cream of Brighton society?'

'He is more likely to introduce them to the Brighton Antiquarian Society.'

Mina was mystified. What was the reason for Mr Honeyacre's visit to the Brendels, and what was in the envelope he had passed to his hostess? If it had been any other medium Mina would have assumed that the envelope contained money, but Mrs Brendel had been adamant that she did not require payment for the evening, neither had there been the slightest hint that a little gift would be appreciated. The answers to those questions might well provide some insight into Miss Athene's vaunted abilities, and deliver a firm answer as to whether she was genuine, a fraud or a victim of her own illusions.

On their arrival at Oriental Place it was no great surprise to find young Mr Dawson pacing back and forth outside the house, stamping his feet, blowing on his fingers, and making the most out of a thin muffler. 'Miss Scarletti!' he exclaimed, advancing towards her as she descended from the cab, then broke into a fit of coughing.

'Young man!' said Dr Hamid, severely, placing himself between Mina and Dawson. 'Keep your distance! You are a danger to the lady's health and a danger to your own if you persist in this behaviour! I know who you are, Miss Scarletti has told me all about you. You cannot help Miss Brendel by making yourself ill. Go home and warm yourself by the fire. If there is anything you can usefully do, we will inform you.'

Mr Dawson had the good grace to look ashamed. 'I meant no harm,' he wheezed.

Dr Hamid might have pointed out that the man who had carried an infection into his home that had killed his sister Eliza had also meant no harm, but the words lay unspoken on his lips. He could not, thought Mina, be so unkind. 'I know,' he said, more gently. Then he took a card from his pocket and handed it to the youth. 'You need a herbal bath to ease your lungs. Have one, gratis, if you present this. Then you will be of some use.'

Dawson took the card, croaked his thanks, and with a polite nod to Mina, began to walk away, coughing.

'Oh, please take the cab!' said Mina, signalling the driver to remain.

Dawson hesitated, and she realised that he did not have the fare and was unwilling to accept money. 'I'll walk home,' he said. 'The fresh air will do me good.' He stifled a cough as he hurried away.

'Come, let us go indoors quickly,' said Dr Hamid, offering Mina his arm.

'Poor young man!' Mina exclaimed. 'I hope he takes your advice.'

500

Chapter Thirteen

They were not the first to arrive. Mina was especially delighted to see her friend Nellie Jordan, who greeted them both with her usual sparkling good humour. Nellie was resplendent in the newest winter ensemble, her shapely form coddled in dark blue velvet with deep sleeves heavily trimmed in fur and all accessories to match, a costume she carried off in perfect style, and which probably weighed as much as Mina did.

Although Mina had not seen any hints of conjuring or sleight of hand in Miss Brendel's performance, she thought that Nellie's expert eye on the evening's events could prove invaluable. She suspected, however, that Nellie's presence in Oriental Place was more to display the latest Paris fashion acquired by her husband's business than any interest in the proceedings. It was very noticeable that Mrs Brendel eyed Nellie's gown and its trimmings very closely, as if calculating their cost and how they might enhance her own standing.

The other persons who assembled around the fireside were young Mr Conroy, Mr and Mrs Myles, the Taskers, Mr Quinley, as watchful as ever, and Mr Ronald Phipps, a junior partner in one of Brighton's most prestigious firms of solicitors, together with his elderly spinster aunt. Miss Phipps' presence was not altogether surprising, as she liked to be taken to every new entertainment in town, where she would drink a cup of tea and then fall contentedly asleep. She relied on her youthful relative to squire her safely there and back, and he managed this very well, hardly ever appearing to be either bored or discomfited by the arrangements. Mina wondered if Mrs Brendel knew that Mr Phipps had been of assistance to her before, providing the information and advice that had enabled her to unmask the frauds that had tried to cheat her mother and friends. Perhaps Mrs Brendel, confident in her daughter's abilities, did not see Mr Phipps as a threat, in the same way that she had welcomed Mina's visits. There was also the fact that Mr Phipps, a young professional and single gentleman, with a sound future, must in the mother's eyes, be a possible match for Miss Athene. Whether or not Mr Phipps was aware of this, only time would tell.

On being introduced, Mr Phipps acknowledged Mina with a polite inclination of the head, but took care not to reveal that they were already well acquainted. Given her previous activities in investigating tricksters and cheats, Mina surmised that he was thinking that she was present for the same purpose, and was therefore wary of revealing more than he thought she wanted Mrs Brendel to know. Miss Phipps was less reliable in the area of confidentiality, but since she gave every impression of being asleep almost as soon as she sat down, this was not a great worry. After seeing that his aunt was comfortable, Mr Phipps looked about him very carefully, trying not to make his inspection of the room appear to be any more than polite interest. He was probably, thought Mina, searching for the paraphernalia of the dark séance, as she too had done on her fist visit, but as she already knew, there was none, neither was there an obvious start or end to the sitting.

Mina had hoped that Mr Honeyacre would be present, as Dr Hamid would then be able to converse with him, and she might learn something useful, but disappointingly, he did not appear.

Mrs Brendel greeted Dr Hamid with an acquisitive gleam in her eye and extravagantly welcoming gestures, commenting that she knew him both by name and reputation. It was only now that Mina noticed that Mrs Brendel had a peculiar way of addressing her gentleman guests. She had been misled on her first visit by her hostess's undisguised interest in herself, but now saw that her manner to the gentlemen was different in quality. It was as if she was weighing them, like a commodity, viewing them as one might a row of plump fishes lying on a slab in the market. One could almost imagine her saying 'yes, he will do, I will have that one.' Was there a scale, Mina wondered, a balance in which the ambitious Mrs Brendel set one man against another? And what was she using for weights? Dr Hamid, having been forewarned as to how he might be regarded, was cool courtesy personified.

Miss Athene, her dress a drift of light grey silk, her complexion little better, was no thinner or paler than she had been before. Young Mr Tasker, who remained impervious to the lady's personal charms, was instead irresistibly drawn to the piano and asked Mrs Brendel, almost in a whisper, if he might hear Miss Brendel play. The mother agreed at once, and taking her daughter's hand, spoke briefly to her, then led her to the piano. She sat before it like a ghostly presence, her slender fingers seeming barely strong enough to turn back the lid and expose the keys. She laid a light touch on the music sheet, then began to play. The sound flowed like the gentlest of wavelets, very soft and sweet. Mrs Tasker, seeing her son stand by Miss Brendel so devotedly, made no secret of the pleasure this sight afforded her.

'I want to play as well,' said Mr Tasker, and although his manner was abrupt, no sooner had the words left his mouth than another seat was brought and he and Miss Brendel sat side by side and caressed the keys. Both mothers looked on appreciatively at this development, and exchanged meaningful glances.

When the tune was done, everyone settled comfortably for the séance, and the maidservant brought a tray with tea, once again serving Miss Brendel with a different brew.

'I hope you don't mind,' said Dr Hamid, 'but I do not customarily drink tea at so late an hour. Perhaps some of that delicious smelling tisane if there is enough for another person?'

'Of course, I quite understand,' said Mrs Brendel, nodding to the maid, who poured some of the contents of the smaller pot into Dr Hamid's cup. Mina was near enough to appreciate a delicate flowery scent rising from the golden fluid.

'Do you find it pleasant living in Brighton?' she asked, sociably.

'We do indeed,' said Mrs Brendel. 'Our home in Yorkshire is not nearly as comfortable in the winter, and Athene far prefers the climate in the southern regions.'

'What part of Yorkshire do you hail from?'

'We live in the environs of Wakefield.'

'I have never travelled so far north. Will we see Mr Brendel here in Brighton for the season?'

'I think not. Aloysius dislikes society, in fact it would be true to say he detests it; not only that but he fears to be away from his business concerns for too long. But he is happy for me to travel with Athene and make new friends.'

Mrs Myles sniffled into a black lace bordered kerchief but it was not clear why. The noise did have the effect of drawing attention away from Mina, which might have been the desired result. 'Are you quite comfortable, my dear Mrs Myles?' asked Mrs Brendel, kindly.

Mrs Myles nodded wordlessly.

'Miss Brendel, if I might be permitted to ask you a question?' began Dr Hamid, who had been sipping his golden tea with every sign of enjoyment.

'Of course,' whispered Miss Brendel with a shy smile that spread over her face like a dream.

'How long have you been able to see things that others around you cannot?'

It was not a contentious question since Miss Brendel did not even glance at her mother before she replied. 'I think the first occasion was about six or seven months ago.'

'That must have been very frightening for you.'

'It was unsettling, certainly.' She stroked her thin teacup and its painted flowers with the tips of her fingers. 'I was sitting in the library, and my father came into the room. I was surprised to see him, as I knew he was away on business, and was not due to return until the next day. I made some comment to him to the effect that he had come home early, but it was obvious that he had not heard me. He walked about the room, and even stood by the fire as he usually did. I questioned him again, still without receiving any response, but then I saw that his clothes were more faded than usual, as if some of the colour had been washed from them. As I looked on, the colour became still fainter, until it was gone, and all I could see was his form like a cloud tinted in grey and white. Then he vanished altogether. My chief fear at the time was that I had seen some premonition of an accident befalling him. I told Mother about it, of course, and I am sure that she did not believe me.'

Athene cast a glance at Mrs Brendel, who acknowledged that this had been the case. 'The next day my father returned home in good health, and indeed he remains so to this day.'

'Were you especially anxious about him before he went away?'

'No more than usual. I had no reason to be. I missed him, of course.'

'But you also see forms of the deceased,' interrupted Mr Conroy, his heavy face flushed and furrowed with thought.

'I do. There was poor Mr Hay, the gentleman who made away with himself recently. I had sometimes seen him walking about the street holding his head as if it pained him. He appeared before me in this very room, making the same gesture. I have also seen others whom I do not know, but who are recognised by my visitors as relatives they have lost. There is a lady sitting in that chair now.' Athene indicted a small armchair, which to the eyes of everyone in the room was empty. 'She is very distinct but I can tell, since she was not there a moment ago, that she is a spirit. She is reading a book.'

'Can you describe her?' asked Dr Hamid, unable despite himself to disguise a slight catch in his voice. His late sister Eliza had been an avid reader.

Miss Brendel turned her large bright eyes towards him. 'I can only say what I see. She wears spectacles. Her hair is grey and her features are regular, her expression is content.'

Mina saw Dr Hamid struggling with himself. He wanted to ask if the lady was of a complexion similar to his own, he wanted to ask if she was misshapen due to scoliosis even more advanced than Mina's, but he knew that such questions would be a mistake. Charlatans, as he had already learned to his sorrow, could take those hints and use them to convince the sceptical. They could bend facts to their own uses — suggest for example that if the ghost had a straight spine then although twisted in life it had been healed in the spirit world.

'My late sister was a great reader,' said Mr Myles, eagerly. 'It must be she. What book does she hold? Is it a work by Mr Dickens?' He turned to the empty chair. 'Amelia? Is that you?'

'She turns the pages,' said Athene. 'It makes no sound. Her lips are moving, but I cannot hear her voice.'

'Can she hear me?' asked Mr Myles, becoming increasingly agitated. All eyes were now on the chair, and it seemed that everyone was straining to see, but only Miss Brendel was calm and serene.

'She fades — she is gone.'

Mr Myles groaned. 'If I could be granted just one word! It is Amelia, I know it!' His wife sobbed noisily, and he patted her hands.

'Miss Brendel,' said Dr Hamid. 'Is it possible for you to teach another person your skill?'

'I have never tried to,' she said. 'But I doubt that I could since I don't know myself how it comes about.'

'But when it first started, was there any special circumstance you can recall? Was the weather warm or cold, for example? Had you just dined or were you about to?'

Mina could see what Dr Hamid was attempting to do. While carefully moving about the margins of the subject, he was trying to discover without direct questioning if the visions had their origins in an illness suffered by Miss Brendel.

Miss Brendel opened her mouth to reply, but was prevented by the interruption of her mother, which was a little too sharp for courtesy. 'There was nothing of any significance as I recall.'

'Forgive my questions which come naturally from scientific curiosity,' said Dr Hamid. 'If we can rule out circumstances such as the weather or a disturbance in the balance of the constitution, it may simply be, although I am not an expert in this area, that Miss Brendel has better than usual eyesight and can see what most others cannot. Has any examination taken place?'

'Athene places her gifts before society to do with them what it wills,' said Mrs Brendel, firmly. 'We do not question, or examine; we do not attempt to explain. I will not under any circumstances allow my daughter to be treated as a medical curiosity.'

'Certainly not!' said Mr Conroy, glancing harshly at Dr Hamid for his temerity.

Mrs Tasker looked thoughtful. 'Your daughter does seem very delicate,' she observed. 'Is she quite well?' She leaned forward and stared at Miss Brendel. 'You are not about to faint, are you my dear?'

'Athene is in excellent health,' said Mrs Brendel, although this time the chilly severity of her tone was directed at Mrs Tasker. 'The ladies of our family always appear frail but we often live to be a hundred. Appearances can be most deceptive.'

'Then I am reassured,' said Dr Hamid, quickly. 'I am sorry if I gave any offence, and in recompense I would like to invite you both to partake of the facilities of the steam baths, which are most refreshing and without the dangers that may attend sea bathing in the winter months.' He handed Mrs Brendel a card. 'The ladies' salon is very select and patronised by the best of Brighton society.'

Mrs Brendel looked willing to forgive, although Mina wondered if she would take up the invitation and risk submitting her daughter to the doctor's closer scrutiny.

The evening was completed with less controversial conversation, music, and some more gossamer visions, which from Miss Brendel's description might have been anyone, but which Mr and Mrs Myles were convinced were departed relatives.

'What is that strange tea?' asked Mina, in the cab home. 'It is not China.'

'Camomile,' said Dr Hamid. 'It has many benefits, and is more soothing to the system in the evenings than the usual teas. I often have it myself.'

'Then it is not responsible for Miss Brendel's visions?'

'I very much doubt it.'

'What was your impression of Miss Brendel?'

'She certainly appears frail, but it is hard to say more without an examination. I could not take her pulse or listen to her heart, or look into her throat. But I did not see any of the obvious signs of poison as insinuated by Mr Dawson. She has a youthful constitution, but I do feel that there is something that is holding her back, not allowing her to achieve her best. I don't know what it is, and I would very much like to. However, we must thank Mrs Tasker for alerting Mrs Brendel to the fact that some of her visitors have doubts about the daughter's health and this may make her send for a doctor. I have done all I can.'

'Have you heard from the oculists you have consulted?'

He took a deep breath before replying. 'Some, yes, and their general opinion is that what ails Miss Brendel is not a disease of the eyes but the brain, and her mother ought to send her to an insane asylum for her own safety.'

Mina was shocked, though not entirely surprised. 'Surely that is not what you believe? I seem to recall when I was first examined for scoliosis several doctors told me it was all my own fault, and accused me of standing on one leg or carrying heavy weights on one side, and when I denied it they refused to believe me. Is everyone mad or harming themselves when they have a disease that doctors cannot explain?' Mina found it hard to keep the anger out of her voice.

'Now I hope you exclude me from that accusation,' said Dr Hamid, mildly.

'I do, of course I do, or I would not be attending the baths.' Mina had avoided doctors as soon as she was old enough to follow her own inclinations, and had often been urged by friends to take the vapour bath 'cure' long before she ever met Dr Hamid and finally found in him a man she could trust.

'There might, however, be some hope. I have been told of a Mr Marriott, an oculist who has made a special study of patients who report visions. I will find out where he practises and write to him. But what do *you* think of Miss Brendel?'

'I don't know what to think of her. There is no pattern to her visions. She does not pander to the wishes of her visitors, as she would do if she was simply a deceiver. But that may just be her subtle ways. I do not rule out deliberate deception as an explanation. However, I have only seen her when presented on a stage for admiration, as it were. I am sure the maidservant sees and knows more than any of us will ever know.'

'I doubt that the maid would consent to be interviewed, and Mrs Brendel would never allow it, if that is what you are planning,' said Dr Hamid.

'Oh, I had a quite different plan,' said Mina.

Chapter Fourteen

'This is proving harder than I had imagined,' said Richard at the breakfast table next morning. 'I called on Mr Burrows as you suggested, but while he was very polite he said he has no need for a sketch as there is a very fine portrait in oils of him already which is on display in a gallery, and he is thinking of commissioning an engraving of it. I have seen engravers at work in London and how they do it I really don't know. But while I was speaking to him I was able to note his appearance. I did a drawing of him from memory afterwards, and must hope he will not sue.' He showed Mina a pencil sketch and while she was obliged to admit that it was not of the first quality it did capture quite recognisably the intelligent and dignified features of the new Lord Mayor.

'I think Edward would welcome this for his new journal, and I promise to append some words to explain its significance. And if Mr Burrows has not yet commissioned his engraving you will have the advantage of showing your picture to the public first. Priority is very important, and not everyone will have seen the painting.'

'That is something I suppose,' admitted Richard reluctantly, 'but I receive nothing for it. I was thinking of presenting it to him, but I have been told that he does not have a daughter so there is no advantage in that. So I might as well send it to Edward. That will content him for a day at least, and maybe he will send me a few pennies out of charity.' Richard, digging into a large platter of eggs and bacon, gave Mina a piteous look, but if he was trying to resemble a needy orphan he failed.

'I may have good news for you,' said Mina, briskly, 'I have found a marvellous subject for a sketch, and the work would be both profitable and a diversion, as well as useful to me.'

Richard was alerted at once. 'Oh, Mina my dear, you are up to something, I can tell!'

'I won't deny it,' she said, and described her visit to the Brendels, emphasising the fact that the mother was ambitious for a place in society. 'Miss Brendel has very unusual gifts, but I cannot establish how they have come about; whether she is genuine or feigning or if they are caused by some disturbance in her system. There is something very strange about that household and I would like to know what it is, but it is something I would never, as a guest, be permitted to see. If, however, you were to gain a commission to sketch Miss Brendel, offering to publish her portrait in a fashionable magazine, you would be very well placed to observe her.'

'Is she young, pretty and rich?' demanded Richard.

'She is all three.'

507

'Then I will call on her immediately!' He began disposing of the bacon and eggs at speed.

Mina held up a warning hand. 'It might be as well to wait a short while. If you were to reveal that you are as yet a humble clerk, even one connected to the Scarletti family, you might be suspected of being a fortune hunter and be shown the door by the Brendels' solicitor Mr Quinley, who acts as their protector. There is a poor young gentleman, a Mr Dawson, who admires the lady and wishes to court her, and he has been refused admission to the house for precisely that reason. What you need is proper business credentials. Leave that to me. I will write to request a letter of introduction.'

Richard, never cheered by the prospect of having to wait for anything, grunted with disappointment and helped himself to toast and coffee. 'If I must. Of course, if this Quinley is a suspicious type who thinks the worst of everyone, he will think I am your spy. Which, of course, I am.'

'That is a good point. It would not do to call yourself Richard Scarletti, or you would be most unlikely to learn any secrets. Very well, I will ask for the letter in the name of Richard Henry,' said Mina, Henry being the name of their late father as well as Richard's middle name. 'And it had best not be on Scarletti company notepaper.'

Mina found that her brother had finished the coffee and rang for more. 'It might take a while,' said Richard. 'Rose is cleaning a wine stain out of my coat. She's a good girl.'

'Edward's coat,' Mina reminded him.

Richard shrugged. 'He'll get it back. So, what am I expected to do apart from sketching the lady? Do I have to marry her? I am sure I could win her over. What of the mother? Married or widow?'

'Married,' said Mina, unsure how much of a difference that made to Richard. 'But you are not required to woo anyone. In fact, I absolutely forbid it.'

'Not even a little?' he pleaded.

'Not at all. You are going there to get information. I have a feeling that the Brendels' maid, Jessie, might know something, but I have not had the opportunity of speaking to her alone. You might do better. In fact, I would like to discover a great deal more about the Brendels. If they are as rich as they claim, then surely your editor, the lady who knows everybody of note, might be able to tell us all about them.'

'Yes, Mrs Caldecott, the fount of all society wisdom,' said Richard. 'After all, we know almost nothing of Mr Brendel, in fact, since no-one in Brighton has ever seen him, we do not know for certain if there *is* a Mr Brendel, or even if there ever was a Mr Brendel. We only know that there is a Miss Brendel, and that could mean anything at all.'

Mina duly wrote to her late father's former business partner, Mr Greville, who managed all her publications at the Scarletti publishing house, asking him to supply the required letter for Richard, mentioning that a Mrs and Miss Brendel had created a stir in Brighton society and might well consent to him drawing the eligible maiden for the company's new journal. She added that any information that Mrs Caldecott could provide about the Brendel family might well prove to be the deciding factor in her brother gaining this important commission.

For Mina, the warmest and most deliciously comfortable place in Brighton was Dr Hamid's baths, where she could exist for a blissful hour enveloped in scented vapour, with fragrant herbs easing her lungs. When this was done, hot towels continued to soothe her aches, as she lay on a softly draped table, while Anna Hamid applied the Indian medicated 'shampoo' or 'massage' as it was also called. In the months that Mina had been attending the baths, Anna's skilled hands had learned every twist and knot of strained muscle, as it fought against Mina's distorted spine, which tilted her ribs and hip. Anna also noticed changes from week to week, and it was always apparent to her when Mina's mind was troubled.

'I see your brother is visiting again,' she commented.

Mina smiled. 'Is it so obvious?'

'There is a kind of strain that crosses your shoulders when he is about. He is a good soul, but with an instinct that leads him astray.'

'At least his current activities seem not to have involved him in impropriety or crime. As far as I know, that is. It's the part I don't know about that worries me.'

'I understand from my brother that you have been dabbling in the spirits again,' Anna continued, her skilled fingers giving the impression that she was endowed with more than the usual number of hands. Her quiet almost unemotional tone was nevertheless insufficient to conceal her disapproval.

'I am not seeking to expose a fraud, since the lady concerned asks for no payment. I am making enquiries simply to satisfy the curiosity of some acquaintances. I didn't mean to draw Dr Hamid into that aspect of the Brendels' séances, but there are medical concerns, one of which I know he finds especially pertinent, since it relates to symptoms reported by some of his patients. But, I have to admit it, Miss Brendel is very interesting and I am not at all sure what she might do next. Have Mrs Brendel and her daughter attended the baths? Your brother gave them his card, but I rather think they will not come.'

'He has described them to me, and I can only agree.'

'Do you happen to recall a Mrs Honeyacre? Her husband has visited the Brendels. The lady passed away some five years ago, but she was a patient here for a while.'

Anna anointed her hands with fresh, warm oil and her fingers explored the hollow under Mina's shoulder blades, working on the protesting muscles there. 'I do recall her. She was suffering from a painful illness, which could not be cured, only relieved. I did what I could for her. She was very courageous; she knew what the future held. I remember her husband, too, he was very kind and attentive. Nothing was too much trouble for him. Her only fear was that he would be lonely once she was gone.'

'They had no family?'

'I believe not.'

'A Mrs Myles is not a patient of yours, is she?'

'I don't know the name. Is she another of Miss Brendel's adherents?'

'She is, and her husband, too. Then there is a Mrs Tasker and her son.'

'Ah, yes. Mrs Tasker comes here often and speaks of nothing but her son to all who will listen and many who prefer not to. He is her only child and she says he is a great trial to her, although her devotion to him is absolute.'

'He is a skilled pianist, that much I know.'

'Mrs Tasker acknowledges this, and says it is a worthy accomplishment, but she feels a man of twenty-five should have another interest in life and he does not. He prefers objects to people and music to everything else. His one desire is to learn by heart every piece of piano music ever written and he is apparently a fair way to achieving this.' Anna transferred her attention to the long muscles on either side of Mina's suffering spine, curved and stretched and pulled out of all reasonable shape.

'I think Mrs Tasker may be hoping her son will marry Miss Brendel, as they have a fondness for music in common, but having observed him, I think all his desires are directed towards the piano.'

Anna gave the smallest sigh of regret. 'One cannot command inclination in another, or even in oneself. But that will not stop mothers from trying to do so in their children.'

Mina did not think she had any inclinations, or if she had, she had so stifled them that they never troubled her. Were these feelings really so hard to control? She thought of Enid and her unwisely precipitate marriage and the illicit passion that had been aroused by Mr Arthur Wallace Hope, and wondered just how much her sister really was to blame.

Later that day, seated at her writing desk, Mina tried to write a sympathetic letter to Enid, but no matter how hard she tried, she could not find any words which her beleaguered sister would not interpret as a cruel reminder of her own unhappiness.

Dear Edward,

I hope this finds you in good health. Poor Mother, she must be sorely tried. I would come to offer some assistance but Mother believes that the London air would do me no good and I think she may be right. Please let Enid know that I wish her well and think of her and her dear boys every day.

I believe I may have found some suitable subjects for Richard to draw, and you may expect some sketches from him soon.

I send my regards to Miss Hooper, and look forward to knowing her better.

Fondest love,

Mina

Chapter Fifteen

Mina was eager to discuss her recent visit to Miss Brendel with Nellie and a note soon brought that lady to Montpelier Road, riding up in her smart little carriage that was hardly large enough to contain both her and her new winter ensemble.

Had Mina been anticipating a visit from any of her mother's friends, there would have been a thick sponge cake and custard tarts to eat. Dr Hamid and Anna preferred sandwiches, buns and almond biscuits. Mina had nothing to tempt Nellie's appetite that she herself could not obtain at home or in the gilded teashops she frequented, and cook, while a capable hand with short paste and pound cake, would have been highly surprised to be asked to bake French fancies. Mina therefore ordered only tea, and sent Rose to the best pastry-cook's to purchase a tray of those delicate little sweetmeats that Nellie loved so much.

What Mina always had in store, which she knew would draw Nellie to her fireside, was the promise of interesting conversation, and the ladies settled down in the warm bright parlour to a fragrant brew, tempting confectionary and appetising gossip.

'I am fascinated to know the reason for your visit to Miss Brendel,' said Nellie. 'Mine must have been very clear to you, but I am sure you did not wish to consult the lady and her imaginary ghosts. Is this another of your adventures? I do hope so! You know I will assist if I can.' She bit into a crisp iced biscuit the size of a penny, topped with a sugared violet.

Mina did habitually take Nellie into her confidence as to her activities, however on this occasion she felt obliged to adhere to the promise she had made to George Fernwood and Miss Clifton. She sipped her tea and chose her words carefully. 'Miss Brendel has been described in the newspapers as a gifted spiritualist, and friends have also mentioned her to me. I went there to observe her and judge for myself if her claims are genuine. Dr Hamid attended out of professional curiosity. But given what took place, it was beyond both our abilities to come to any definite conclusion. I was very pleased to see you there as I always value your opinions on these subjects.'

Nellie smiled and pressed a napkin to her lips. 'I observed her most carefully, too. I may be a respectable wife nowadays, but the theatre is in my blood and always will be. My opinion is that if Miss Brendel hopes to commence a career as a stage illusionist she would be best advised not to think of it. She has nothing to offer beyond her face, figure and manners, and that is not sufficient. She has no skills that I could detect. There was nothing to draw the eye; nothing to deceive the eye. We are simply asked to believe that she sees the visions she describes. The entire performance is dependent on an atmosphere of expectation in which the guests are receptive to anything she says, interpreting her visions as best suits them. Of course, with many people, that will be highly effective. But it is a parlour game, not a profession.'

'I was surprised that they seemed perfectly happy enough to admit me, despite knowing that I have exposed frauds in the past. In fact, they welcomed me, and decried the cheats and charlatans.'

'That was most probably because they knew that there was nothing for you to question, no conjuring, no trickery. And since they make no charge, they can never be accused of taking money under false pretences, so they cannot be prosecuted. And there is more, perhaps,' Nellie added thoughtfully. 'Your very presence there, the fact that you have exposed others but cannot expose them is something that they can make use of. They gain from it; it is a mark of approval which will weigh with the public they hope to attract.' Nellie's tone suggested that for her, that was the final word required on the matter. She selected a glazed almond and nibbled at it, her white teeth crunching through the coating.

Mina considered these comments, especially the uncomfortable conclusion that her interest had only enhanced the fame of the medium. 'You are right. Miss Brendel is safe from criticism because she does not employ illusions or sleight of hand. But what I cannot determine on the basis of my visits, because I have been to see her on a previous occasion, too, is whether she genuinely sees apparitions, is a deliberate deceiver, or is simply deluded.'

Nellie paused in surprise, her teacup halfway to her lips. 'Is that of importance to you? In the past you have only concerned yourself with dissemblers who extorted money. Miss Brendel provides an unusual evening's diversion at no charge. Yet you have made two visits to her. Why so?'

Mina could see how strange that must look and thought quickly. 'It is true that she may ask for nothing now, but she might do so in future, once she has a great assembly of the faithful.'

Nellie did not appear convinced by that argument. 'Yet the family is reputed to be wealthy. Surely she has no need? Unless the father is mean with his allowance.'

Mina decided not to comment on that point, as it would show she knew more than she might be expected to.

'As to whether or not she is a cheat,' Nellie continued, 'she might not know it herself. Even those who start out as blatant deceivers can come in time to believe their own lies.' Nellie's fingers hovered over the tray of delicacies once more, but withdrew without making a selection. 'They are so tempting, but I must be prudent. Have you considered that Miss Brendel might do more good than harm? She gives comfort to the bereaved.'

'But no real answers to those who seek them. There are a Mr and Mrs Myles, for example, they are hoping for something, but I don't know precisely what it is. They seem to grasp at anything that might have some meaning for them, but they take no comfort from it. And when I was there before, a Mr Honeyacre received nothing of any note and did not call again.'

'The mind is a strange thing. It denies the truth, deceives the eyes. If it did not, there would be no magicians. Perhaps Mr Honeyacre did receive something but you were unaware of it. Something that only he could recognise, because it was already there, waiting for him.'

Mina was thoughtful. 'Are you saying that people look for answers when they already know them? But the answers are hidden from them in some way, and just need to emerge?'

'Possibly. If people receive answers to their questions after consulting with Miss Brendel, and if her visions have no existence in reality, then there is only one place those answers could be. They lie within the questioner, and are brought out when Miss Brendel quite unwittingly helps her visitors to concentrate their minds. A magician often asks his audience to direct their thoughts and attention in a particular way. Of course, it is the way that suits the illusion. But people can deceive themselves quite well without the need for a conjuror, and all it needs is for them to engage their minds in the right way to reveal the truth.'

'So, even if Miss Brendel is deluding herself, she can still help people, but not in the way she imagines.' Mina finished her tea and poured another cup for them both. 'Do you know anything of a Mr Castlehouse? He too has been mentioned in the newspapers, and I am thinking of visiting him. He persuades the spirits to write on slates for him.'

'What, with ghostly glowing hands?' said Nellie with a teasing laugh.

'I'm not sure. It would be a sight to see, even if he did charge a shilling for it.'

'You must watch him carefully and then tell me everything about him.'

'Have you ever seen a slate-writer at work?'

'No, but I have heard about them. Their tricks are not very mysterious to those who know what to look for. In fact, many conjurors do something very similar, as part of a performance in which they ask someone to think of an object and the words appear on a slate. They do not, however, pretend to be receiving messages from the deceased.'

'Then these slate-writing mediums are all charlatans?'

'So I have been told. Even the most famous of them have been caught cheating.'

Mina had no great objection to someone providing an evening's diversion for a shilling, and would not on that account have devoted herself to the exposure of Mr Castlehouse, but she had agreed to see him and provide her opinion to Mr Fernwood and Miss Clifton. There was always, she reminded herself, the possibility that the slate-writer was secretly demanding much larger sums from the vulnerable for private sittings, and if he was, then the young couple might well be in a position to advise her if this was taking place.

'If you like we can go to see him together, you and I,' said Nellie. 'But not quite yet as I have a scheme in mind to help Richard's new career, and that is engaging all my energies.' She succumbed to another glazed almond.

'I hope you succeed. He talks incessantly about drawing and how it will gain him fame and fortune, but so far he has done very little actual work. That is always the way with him, as you know. At least this scheme will not place him in the bankruptcy court, or prison, or even worse — disappoint Mother.'

'I will tell you my grand plan. I will host a *salon*, to which I will invite Richard, and yourself, of course, and as many people as I can muster to view his work. He did a sketch of me recently and while I am no great expert on art, I did think that he has ability.'

'I would like to see that.'

Nellie's smile told Mina that the drawing in question was not for public display. 'I have been buying paintings for my new home from Mr Dorry's gallery in town, so I am hoping that he will come to my *salon* and bring some of his customers, too. If he likes Richard's work he might even purchase a sketch or two. He is known for encouraging young talented artists. I am sure that I can persuade him at the very least to exhibit some of Richard's drawings at the gallery, where they may well attract attention. Also, an old friend of mine is coming to stay in Brighton soon, Miss Kitty Betts. She has a season at the music hall in New Road where she will perform as Princess Kirabampu, the only lady contortionist in the world.'

Mina knew better than to ask if this claim was true.

'She would be a wonderful subject for a portrait,' Nellie continued. 'Kitty's performance, I promise you, is the height of elegance, grace and good taste, delighting the gentlemen without shocking the ladies. What is not permissible in an Englishwoman may be tolerated and even admired in a foreigner, especially if she is from the Far East and knows no better. I have thought it would be an interesting novelty if I were to place an easel in the drawing room and have Richard sketch Kitty as we watch. She would be fully dressed, of course, and I would make her promise not to place her feet behind her ears, as the company might find it alarming. Oh, do say you will come.'

'I would be delighted. I ought to mention that Richard now draws under the name Richard Henry, not Scarletti.'

'So he has informed me.' Nellie leaned forward and pressed Mina's hand, confidingly. 'Mina, my dear, I can guess that there is something you cannot tell me, and I am sure that you must have the best of reasons for it. I am not offended. We all have our secrets, and many of them should remain so.'

515

While accepting that Miss Brendel and her mysterious visions could benefit those visitors who were looking for general comfort or whose answers were locked within, Mina wondered if was possible for her to help in the very peculiar circumstances of Mr Fernwood and Miss Clifton. At first glance it seemed she could not, which meant that Mina should advise them not to continue their visits. But, she reminded herself, both those individuals had been in the house at the time of Thomas Fernwood's murder. As children they had naturally been shielded from sights of suffering and death, but it was possible that either or both held a memory of some apparently trivial incident that seemed to have no bearing on the tragedy and was therefore long forgotten, but which was in actuality, the vital clue needed to reveal what had occurred.

Mina reflected that chance comments or circumstances could sometimes bring to the forefront of her mind events from long ago, that she had not thought of since they happened. There was no reason to suppose that she was unique in that respect. Perhaps further visits to Miss Brendel by Mr Fernwood and Miss Clifton might lead them to the truth.

Mina decided to write to George Fernwood, and to word her letter very carefully. She wanted to encourage him to continue visiting Miss Brendel, but without putting into his mind any expectation of what might be achieved by it that might add false colour to any recollection.

Dear Mr Fernwood,

I do hope your visit to Lincoln is productive, and look forward to hearing from you further.

I have paid a second visit to Miss Brendel, which was conducted in the same way as the one you attended. In view of the fact that Miss Brendel does not produce any apparitions or sounds that her visitors can detect, it is not possible for me to determine whether or not she has genuine abilities. On the other hand, I cannot, on the evidence of what I have seen, declare her to be a fraud. I therefore suggest that you continue to attend her demonstrations as long as you feel there is the possibility of some benefit.

Yours faithfully,

M. Scarletti

Chapter Sixteen

Dear Mina,

Thank you for your recent letter. As you requested I assured Enid of your concern for her welfare. She received this information entirely in the manner that you might imagine, and she and Mother quarrelled over it. I am not sure which one of us was deemed to be more to blame.

I have now completed my examination of Mr Inskip's papers; several days of painstaking work for which I cannot expect to be thanked. Mother and Enid are impossible to talk to on the subject, so I must address my findings to you, as you appear to be the only other sensible person in this family. What Agatha must think of us! My darling girl is a saint!

I have very little to report for my efforts. I have found notes of Inskip's travel plans, although whether he actually followed those plans or was diverted from them by circumstances is, of course, unknown. My only useful discovery is that since travel in that dreadful part of the world is so primitive, there are not multitudes of different routes or means of conveyance for me to investigate.

If Inskip's last letter from Carpathia is anything to go by he had intended to depart for home in the first week of October, the weather in the mountain regions being so very inclement in the winter months, something he wished to avoid. His journey home would undoubtedly have commenced by coach, obliging him to follow some very indifferent roads. He would have been entirely at the mercy of the climate, the horses, the drivers, the vehicle and the terrain, none of which inspire me with any confidence. I have no means of knowing the prevalence of accidents in that region, but I would not be surprised if they were frequent. Gangs of robbers composed of desperate cutthroats are far from unknown. If all these dangers can be avoided, it would take the coach two days to traverse the mountain pass, and reach a civilised town from where it would be possible to catch a train. Even the worst locomotive would reach the coast of France in four days from where he would have boarded the next steamer. He should, therefore, have been home in little more than a week. Inskip was usually meticulous about advising family and colleagues of the progress of his journeys, and would surely have sent a telegram on the way. The fact that none has been received is a great cause for concern.

I have written to the telegraph, railway and steamer companies to discover if there is any news. I have also written to the Carpathian count, but even if my letter were to reach him I would not expect a reply for at least two weeks.

On other matters, I have received a sketch from Richard, which might well do for the Journal. The accompanying notes, I judge from the spelling, must have been written by you. Please don't indulge him too much. He has not returned my coat and hat, and I dread to think what state they will be in when I next see them.

Affect'ly,
Edward

In the same post was an invitation to Nellie's select *salon* for lovers of fine art.

Richard, finding himself obliged to produce some work to display at that occasion, had retired to his room with a plateful of boiled eggs and buttered muffins, and a pot of coffee. Mina found him sitting at his desk, hunched over a sketchbook with a pencil grasped in his fist, his face contorted in an expression of agony. As she entered he quickly flipped the cover of the book to close it so she could not see what he was drawing.

'It isn't finished yet,' he said. 'And I don't know if it ever will be. It's not just about eyes and nose and mouth and the shape of the head, it's about — oh, I don't know — something else. Whatever it is, I don't think I can do it.' He clutched distractedly at his hair until uncombed curls threatened to stand up straight from his scalp.

'Perhaps all you need is practice,' said Mina. 'I am sure the best artists doubted themselves from time to time.' She showed him the invitation, and he looked at it despondently. 'It is very kind of Nellie to host a *salon* to show off your work.'

'Yes, and she is a darling girl, but I am to have at least six pictures done beforehand. Why has it all become so dashed hard? It was jolly fun when I used to do little drawings in the office.'

'That was because you were drawing instead of working. Now the drawing *is* work. But do your best and you may find a patron yet.'

Richard did not look hopeful, and Mina, although offering words of encouragement, did not anticipate any great success from this new venture. She saw Edward's coat and hat draped across the bed, liberally spattered with mud. Leaving Richard to his labours she told Rose to send up another pot of coffee and rescue the garments from disaster.

Chapter Seventeen

Mina was looking forward to seeing Nellie's new home, a townhouse not far from the Marine Parade, which must have cost her husband a small fortune to purchase and another one to furnish. Mr Jordan, when a single man, had been content to conserve his pennies by residing in an apartment above the fashionable emporium he commanded, attended by just one servant, but soon after the wedding he was informed by his lovely bride that this would no longer do. His married life, in which he was able to display Nellie as a great prize to the envy of half of Brighton, also involved acceding to her every wish, and he seemed to be content with that arrangement.

Mina's home was run by Rose and the cook, with regular visits from a charlady, all supervised by Mina, and this was sufficient for their needs. Since her marriage, Nellie had found that it was impossible to do without a general maid, a lady's maid, a scullery maid, a charlady, a washerwoman, and a cook/housekeeper. Additional servants were to be brought in for the evening *salon* to ensure that her guests were comfortable and had every article of food and drink they required. Mina wondered how many servants Nellie had had to wait on her when, in her former life as assistant to Monsieur Baptiste the conjuror, she had existed in a series of theatrical lodgings, and rather suspected that there had been none.

The pride of Nellie's home, and the space to which all the guests were ushered, was the drawing room in which, at her insistence, every item was brand new. The seating had been carefully selected to ensure that the ladies dresses were not crushed but could be displayed to their full advantage, and while the ornamentation was expensive, there was a quality of restrained luxury, so that the surroundings could not outshine the occupants. It was like a stage, where the curtain, scenery and furniture should never appear more important or eye-catching than the performers.

The paintings that Nellie had chosen to decorate the walls with were bucolic scenes in which hearty sons of the soil gathered harvests while buxom wives stirred puddings for a feast and trees waved in the distance across a vista of golden cornfields. Several of Richard's sketches were on display, and these were exclusively pencil portraits of ladies. One, Mina realised, with some surprise, was of herself. She rarely gave much thought to whether her appearance would please anyone or not, since so few troubled to look beyond her twisted back to appreciate her face, but Richard had brought out the expression in her watchful eyes, the shape of her pretty chin and sweet smile. Had her spine been straight she might have attracted some attention. She realised that it must have been this picture he had hidden so quickly when she had walked into his room. Mina tried to look at her brother's work in an unbiased fashion, and concluded that the portrait of herself was the most successful of his drawings, most probably because he knew the subject and could convey character as well as outward appearance.

The one thing Mina was unable to judge was whether Richard had talent enough to make an appreciable living from his work. As the guests strolled about the room, sipping wine from chilled glasses and nibbling warm savoury tartlets brought to them by footmen bearing silver trays, she noticed a tall and extremely broad gentleman staring at the sketches though an eyeglass with more than the usual degree of curiosity.

'Who is that gentleman?' she asked Nellie, hoping that his interest might result in a sale.

'Ah, that is the famous Mr Dorry, who owns the art gallery in St James's Street where we purchased our paintings. Come, I shall introduce you.'

'Do remember it is a great secret that Richard Henry the artist is really Richard Scarletti. Can Mr Jordan be trusted not to reveal it?'

Mina glanced across to where Nellie's husband stood at the edge of the room, neither mingling nor circulating, but in close conversation with his business partner, the elder Mr Conroy, and casting the occasional hard glance at Richard. For all that they took any notice of the art it might not have been in the room.

'He would not have agreed for Richard's sake but he would never risk offending you,' said Nellie with a smile. She took Mina's arm and led her to where Mr Dorry was still examining one of Richard's sketches. 'Mr Dorry, I would like you to meet Miss Mina Scarletti, my very particular friend.'

The gentleman turned to face them, revealing a physique of substantial dimensions, and a magnificent expanse of floral brocade waistcoat. Such was the volume of his figure that it was hard to determine whether his tailor was more troubled by his height, his width or the extent to which his abdomen preceded the rest of him. His complexion was as florid and pitted as a blood orange, his hair and whiskers abundant, and of a reddish shade like a sunset worked in paint. There was a moment or two before he realised he had to adjust his gaze downwards to take in Mina's tiny form. She recognised the look of uncertainty that appeared on the faces of so many persons on first meeting her, while they decided on the best manner of address. 'It is a great pleasure to make the acquaintance of any friend of Mrs Jordan,' he said at last, in a voice that purred resonantly from his throat.

'I am delighted to meet you,' said Mina. 'I have heard your name mentioned as a great expert in the art world.'

'Oh, what flattery!' he laughed, with a toss of his leonine head. 'But I do have some experience in these things, having bought and sold art for many years.'

'I would be interested to know your opinion of these sketches. I believe they represent friends of Mrs Jordan's.'

'Yes, and Mrs Jordan has directed me to look at them most particularly.' Dorry pursed his lips, his expression less than enthusiastic. 'They are quite good, the artist has some skill, but I am afraid they are not very much out of the common way.'

Nellie had left them, crossing the room to find Richard, and Mina felt pleased that neither had been near enough to hear this less than glowing appreciation. When Nellie returned to Mina, she was leading Richard by the arm. Mr Jordan's eyes flashed darts from the other side of the room at the sight of that touch.

'Mr Dorry,' announced Nellie, 'allow me to introduce Richard Henry, who is the talented hand behind the sketches.'

'I do hope you like my little pictures,' said Richard, with his most engaging smile.

Mr Dorry gazed at Richard. He studied him as he might have done a portrait, and seemed to like what he saw. 'Indeed. Very attractive; very desirable. My compliments to you, sir.'

'Thank you. It is so hard to judge one's own work, but I believe I have some talent in drawing beautiful ladies in a way that will delight them.'

'Ah, yes, beautiful ladies, what gentleman of taste does not admire them!' Dorry took a glass from the tray of a passing footman, raised it in a toast and drained it at a gulp.

'Mrs Jordan has asked me to sketch a friend of hers tonight, so you will be able to see me at work,' Richard continued.

'Oh, that will be a fine treat. I should like to see that very much. But what we have here,' said Dorry, with a sweep of his plump hand to indicate all of Richard's work, 'is the art of the pencil. Oh, don't mistake me, delicacy has its place, but I also like something deeper, more robust. Have you ever worked in oils, Mr Henry?'

'Very little, I'm afraid, I think that sketches are my forte. Would that prevent me advancing in my career?' Richard added anxiously.

Dorry waved aside the slight inconvenience. 'Not necessarily; some of my customers do prefer the refinement of a drawing to the richness of oil. Are you a married man?'

Richard blinked in surprise. 'Um — no, I am not.'

'Betrothed?'

'No. Does that matter?'

Dorry smiled and patted Richard's cheek playfully. 'Oh, it is good. Very good indeed. All the young gentlemen I promote are of the single persuasion. No artist should ever be married; it is too much of a distraction. And then there is the expense!'

'Are artists not very rich men?' asked Richard, innocently.

Mr Dorry permitted himself another laugh. 'Not as a rule. For the most part they suffer the most terrible privations, driven by their art, and expire tragically young in a cold cheerless attic in which there is no food, since they have spent their last shilling in the world on paint.'

'Oh dear!' said Richard, since this was clearly not the future he had in mind.

'But you, sir,' said Dorry, taking Richard warmly by the shoulder and speaking to him as if he was imparting a confidence, 'you may be the exception, if you are able to work quickly, and allow yourself to be guided by me.'

'We are ready for you now,' said Nellie, indicating the easel, sketchbook and pencils that had been brought by a servant. 'And here is your model. I would like to introduce Miss Kitty Betts. Kitty this is Mr Henry, the artist, Mr Dorry who is a great expert in all matters artistic, and my dear friend Miss Scarletti.'

Kitty Betts, also known as Princess Kirabampu, the exotic contortionist, was a lady of about thirty in a scarlet gown. She was not beautiful in any meaning of the term, but possessed a fine figure, and a lively manner that only just stopped short of being dangerously enticing. She greeted all her new acquaintances with friendly eyes and a smile that indicated she could derive excitement and pleasure from almost anything.

'My dearest Nellie, I am overwhelmed with delight! Such surroundings! Such company! And your husband is so handsome and charming! Oh, do show me where I must sit. I can hardly wait!' She approached Richard, tilting her face up to him. 'Mr Henry, may I take your arm? You must advise me how I might best display myself to your eye.'

Richard complied all too willingly and offered his arm, which Kitty, unblushingly, took. A velvet-upholstered armchair had been placed ready, and Kitty settled herself into it like syrup that had just been poured into a sauceboat and was reaching its natural level. She released Richard's arm with a noticeable sigh of reluctance. Mina might have felt a little concerned at this had she not received the impression that Kitty had the ability to make any man feel he was the object of her undivided attention, and Richard was not of any special regard to her other than as an artist. As she might have predicted, once Richard had moved behind the easel, he no longer interested Kitty, who, now he was not in view, behaved as if he had ceased to exist, and passed her gaze about the room to see what other gentlemen she could charm.

'Miss Scarletti, what a pleasure it is to meet you again so soon,' said a voice beside Mina, as the assembled company gathered in a circle about the artist and his model to watch the process of sketching.

Mina looked around and recognised Mr Honeyacre, who, she quickly recalled, was a collector of art and antiquities. 'Do you have a special interest in art?' he went on.

'I am interested in many things, although on this occasion I have been invited here by Mrs Jordan who is a friend of mine.'

'I am here at the suggestion of Mr Dorry, whose gallery I frequent. He has been offered a display by a new artist, whose work is said to be very interesting.' Mr Honeyacre shook his head in a manner that did not promise well for Richard's future. 'I am sorry to say that the sketches I have seen do not encourage me. But allow me to introduce Miss Macready who is a dear friend.'

Miss Macready was a stern-faced lady in her late fifties, very plainly dressed in a gown of dark green. The plainness was not, Mina thought, a matter of expense, since the material was thick and luxurious, and she concluded that it must be in accordance with the wearer's taste. Miss Macready greeted Mina very formally, with no change in expression.

'Miss Scarletti and I met recently when attending the sitting given by Miss Brendel,' Mr Honeyacre explained.

'But of course,' said Miss Macready, 'your name is known to me from that dreadful affair over Miss Eustace. If ever a woman deserved to be in prison it is that one. You have done a good service to all right-thinking persons.'

'Thank you,' said Mina.

'But what do you think of Miss Brendel? Is she, too, a dreadful fraud? I suspect she is, but Mr Honeyacre thinks she may not be.'

Mina chose her words carefully as this was not the occasion to offend either the gentleman or the lady. 'It is hard for me to tell since she does not produce apparitions or claim to fly through walls. Had she done either I would have had no hesitation in agreeing with you. In fact, she seems to do very little, so little that I am unable to make any judgment. Do you intend to go and see her for yourself?'

'Oh no,' said Miss Macready in a tone of fierce determination. 'I do not wish to attend any occasion in which spirits are invited. The very idea makes me shudder. Either Miss Brendel is a fraud and should be stopped, or she is genuine, and may therefore by chance or ineptitude call up something that should have been left where it was. The dangers cannot be calculated.'

'So, you do believe that the living can communicate with spirits?' asked Mina.

'I am sure we can, but I do not think it is always advisable. I certainly do not approve of tempting fate by meddling with things we do not understand. My mother was a great believer. She was especially devoted to table tipping, which she indulged in whenever she could. It became her passion and made her quite deranged. No table in our house was safe from her. Unfortunately, she believed everything she was told, so was often gravely misled. She gave a great deal of money to people who were later found out to be scoundrels. I would not be at all surprised if the spirits stay away from such people out of sheer disgust. Once all the conjurors have gone then we will look to find a higher, purer art, but not before. My belief is that if the spirits wish to speak to the living then they will do so of their own accord, through dreams and visitations. They do not need to be called up or made to appear.'

'Is it not possible,' said Mr Honeyacre gently, 'that some spirits are not able to reach the living without some assistance, however much they might wish to? Surely that is the task of the medium, to be the channel through which the spirits can convey their messages.'

Miss Macready's attitude failed to soften. 'I cannot say that I am convinced of that.'

'Will you be visiting Miss Brendel again?' Mina asked Mr Honeyacre.

'I rather think that one visit was enough,' snapped Miss Macready, before Honeyacre could reply.

The gentleman looked pained. 'I will not attend another séance, although I would very much like to invite Mrs and Miss Brendel to a supper with myself and Miss Macready at my lodgings.' He glanced at Miss Macready with an expression of earnest appeal, tinged with apprehension. She remained unmoved. 'Miss Brendel is a modest and refined young lady, with the most beautiful manners and there is nothing at all to be afraid of.'

'Is there not?' queried Miss Macready. 'You have told me that the lady is frail, and it may be that the visions are consuming what little strength she has. If that is the case, even if she has so far been a channel for benevolent spirits, her weakness might open the way for a different kind of spirit from another place entirely. If that should occur I wish to be nowhere near it.'

'She does look frail,' agreed Honeyacre, 'and I think her mother may protect her a little too much. She needs to move in society, make new acquaintances, marry.'

'When she is a respectable wife and no longer concerning herself with things she can neither understand nor control, I will sup with her, but not before,' said Miss Macready.

Mr Honeyacre wisely declined to debate the matter with her further, and made an effort to change the subject. 'But look, we have a sketch nearing completion,' he commented brightly, nodding towards the easel.

While they had been talking, Richard's pencil had been at work, and something was taking shape on the paper that might have been a face. It was not promising to be his best work, and he was looking a little flustered at being stared at by so many people. 'How long can it take to draw a picture?' said Miss Macready, severely. 'That young man is far too slow. Can there be anything duller than watching a man draw?' She moved away to where a fresh tray of savouries was awaiting attention and attacked it with relish.

Mina felt more emboldened in her questioning of Mr Honeyacre. 'Do you really believe that Miss Brendel is genuine? Only, you can probably guess why I was there but I was not sure about your reasons. Of course, if it is a matter you find too painful to discuss, you must tell me to mind my own business and you will hear no more of it.'

He smiled. 'Miss Brendel has an unusual gift, and there is no doubt in my mind that she is sincere. As you have observed, Miss Macready is somewhat scathing of the spiritualists who have been working in Brighton of late, and in many cases, with good reason. But she is so blinded by prejudice that she cannot see that lying amongst the dross there is much that is good and pure and holy. Spiritualism is something that I have never previously explored, but in recent years it has come to interest me deeply, and I want to know more. In fact, I mean to make a study of it; a serious study. I want to discuss it with men of learning and assist them in experiments to reach the truth of the matter. Have you read *The Brighton Hauntings* by Mr Arthur Wallace Hope? It is a recent publication. I have just procured a copy and it promises to be very interesting.'

Mina was disturbed by the fact that the noted explorer and seducer of her own sister had sought to record the spiritualistic scandal of the previous autumn in a book that elevated the work of charlatans into a supernatural mystery. Her last meeting with Mr Hope had been a tempestuous one, and he had not come out of it well. 'I will make sure to obtain a copy,' she said.

'I would not take my interest any further, however, without the approval of Miss Macready. I therefore wish to introduce Miss Macready to Miss Brendel so she can see for herself that a medium may be a virtuous individual, and the spirits that appear through her are benevolent.'

'I can see that Miss Macready's opinion is of great importance to you.'

'It is.'

Mina did not say it, but if the rumours were true and Mr Honeyacre wished to marry Miss Macready, then their differences of opinion on spiritualism would be a major obstacle to her accepting his proposal. The supper he planned was of mutual benefit. If Miss Brendel could reassure Miss Macready of the purity of spiritualism, then Mr Honeyacre would achieve his bride and there would be harmony in the marital home. Miss Brendel and her mother would gain Mr Honeyacre's approval, which for them could be a further step into the more elevated areas of Brighton society. However much money the Brendels might have, it would always be tarnished by the dark dirty whiff of the coalmine.

'Until a few years ago,' Mr Honeyacre continued, 'I lived with my dear late wife Eleanor on an estate just outside Brighton, but our home was too small to accommodate my growing art collection, so I purchased a manor house in Ditchling Hollow, meaning to restore it to its former elegance. Eleanor fell in love with the old house, and we looked forward to making it our home. The work had hardly begun when Eleanor fell very ill and despite all the care I could give there was no hope. She suffered very much at the end. She was a good, brave, generous, kind-hearted lady and I will never meet her like again. After she passed away I closed up the house and travelled a great deal. It was only last year that I returned to Sussex. I now live in apartments in Brighton. It was here some months ago that I first met Miss Macready. It is now my intention to complete the work on the manor house and make it my home. My servants are delighted, as they also loved the old house. The cleaning and restoration has already commenced. But I am sorry to say that when I told Miss Macready my intentions she declared very firmly that she will not set foot in it.'

The statement was left hanging in the air for Mina to make of it what she would.

'I think I understand. The purpose of your visit to Miss Brendel was not to consult her as a medium, but to assure yourself that she is a suitable person to convince Miss Macready of your point of view?'

'How perceptive. Yes, it was.'

'You were not anticipating that Miss Brendel would enable you to converse with the spirit of your late wife?'

'No, and she did not.'

'Does Miss Macready fear encountering your wife's spirit at the manor house?'

'If she does, she has not said so. But that can hardly be. A spirit that haunts a house is a troubled soul. Eleanor is at rest and content to await me in heaven, of that I am quite sure.'

'Have you asked Mrs Brendel if she and her daughter will take supper with you?'

'I have and they were delighted to accept. But thus far, Miss Macready has refused to meet them.' A sudden thought struck him. 'But I think I know how I might persuade her. It is clear that she holds you in some esteem. You have exposed the frauds she so despises. If you would be kind enough to join us she might yet agree. Would you be willing to attend?'

'If my evening is free, which it almost certainly will be, and the winter holds off a little more, yes, I would.'

'Then I will make the arrangements.' Mr Honeyacre provided his card and Mina responded with hers.

'There!' announced Richard, standing back from the easel. 'It is complete!'

'Oh bravo!' said Nellie. 'Well done! It is an excellent likeness.'

'Please may I see?' enquired Kitty, although she did not wait for permission but bounced from the chair as if ejected by a spring, and twirled around like a dancer to see the drawing.

Just for one heartfelt moment Mina knew that she would have given up all the little beauty of face she possessed to Kitty just to have her supple spine. She saw at once that this was a foolish and unworthy thought and pushed it away, hoping that it would never emerge to trouble her again.

'It is very fine, I agree,' said Kitty. 'What lady would not wish Mr Henry to draw her so elegantly!' She smiled up at Richard admiringly.

Mr Dorry examined the picture through his glass, but looked less enthusiastic.

Mr Jordan had sidled up, still directing a hard look at Richard. 'What do you think of it?' he asked Dorry. 'I am no judge of art. I leave all that to my wife.'

'Hmm,' said Dorry, thoughtfully. 'It is well enough, but I do not think the artist has fully developed his talent, which may lie in quite another direction.'

'Well, I'm glad I have talent, at least,' said Richard.

'A word in your ear.' Dorry linked his arm comfortably through Richard's and drew him away from the other guests, who crowded around the portrait while Kitty uttered bursts of laughter like the chirping of tiny birds. Mina slipped away after her brother, and was able to lurk nearby unnoticed. 'Tell me,' said Dorry, 'have you ever tried the art of the landscape?'

'What trees and that kind of thing? Well, no, I haven't. I'm not sure I could draw a tree. All those leaves and branches. I don't know why they're so complicated. And grass. That's even worse. Grass must be impossible.'

'What about the sea? It is a very sought after subject in my gallery.'

'Is it? I can't imagine why. I'd much rather look at a pretty lady.'

Mr Dorry handed Richard a business card. 'Why don't you try your hand at it? Just a simple sketch. Put in a ship if you like, and then show it to me.'

Richard took the card but looked dubious.

'Make it a stormy sea so it will be more interesting. Big waves, cloudy sky. A steamer in danger of sinking. Can you do that?'

'I can try, yes.'

Mr Dorry leaned closer to Richard, and spoke so confidingly that Mina was hard put to make out his words. 'I make no bones about it, sir, I am interested in buying sketches of that nature and I think you can draw them. When you have completed your sketch, come and see me at the gallery, and I will show you a book with illustrations of the kind of thing I am looking for. If you can achieve something in a similar style it would be to your advantage.'

'What about my own work? My portraits?'

Mr Dorry chuckled and patted Richard's arm. 'Take it from me, sir, there is no originality in your work; no individual style at all. It is empty. You are a blank paper, which, in the world of art that I inhabit, can be a much better thing.'

Chapter Eighteen

Mina had received a letter from George Fernwood to say that he and Miss Clifton had returned from their brief stay in Lincoln, and an arrangement was soon made for them to visit.

Mina wished she could have discussed Mr Fernwood and Miss Clifton's difficulty with another individual. Had she been allowed to speak freely she would have placed the position before Dr Hamid who could be relied upon for common sense and caution. As she awaited the couple's arrival she was therefore obliged to delve into her own thoughts to consider how best they might solve their dilemma.

There was no doubt that they were an affectionate pair who very much wished to marry, and hoped to welcome children. If they did not succeed in resolving their question, she feared that they might well feel doomed to remain single until such a time as it was impossible for their union to produce offspring. Both were young and the wait would be a long one; a severe test of their devotion. Were they equal to it? Mina thought they were, but it was hardly the preferred solution, and what an unhappy marriage that barren partnership would be.

What were their prospects of success in their quest? Mina examined the possibilities. What if they were unable to find a genuine medium who might help them discover the truth? Mina, though she had never met such a person, would not go so far as to say that this rarity did not exist, but since she had encountered or read about so many frauds, she felt it was far more likely that they would unwittingly fall into the hands of a charlatan who would be able to convince them of his or her genuineness. Here at least, she might be able to assist them.

The next question, however, was whether or not being duped by a skilled fraud was a bad thing. Could such a person, even though unacquainted with their question, provide quite by chance, an answer that might satisfy them? In Mina's experience, spirit messages passed on by charlatans were always soothing and reassuring since this was what their clients wanted to hear. They were especially anxious to reinforce the notion constantly promulgated by adherents of spiritualism that mediums always acted in a pure and devout manner. It was further asserted that anything indelicate or irreligious in a message should be attributed to malevolent spirits masquerading as the deceased. Mina concluded that there was little likelihood of a charlatan providing a message containing an accusation of murder, especially against a named living person who might reasonably object.

Given the ages of Mr Fernwood and Miss Clifton, it would require no great skill for a medium to guess that there was a deceased grandparent. In the absence of any clues, the most probable kind of communication they were likely to receive was something suggesting that their ancestor was content in his life in the spirit. If they could be led to believe that the message was from Thomas Fernwood, it might be all they needed to put an end to their quest and marry with confidence. Under such circumstances, Mina would have no hesitation in advising them to marry. If the spirit was content, she would argue, then it must feel that all its troubles were over and they should likewise be content. She would not say this to them, but she thought that their mutual affection and determination to raise happy carefree children would be sufficient to overcome any unwelcome family tendencies.

Mina found herself obliged to consider next what might occur if they actually succeeded in contacting the unquiet ghost of the murdered man. Supposing the spirit named the person who had killed him; the answer could be either satisfying or devastating. But what if Thomas Fernwood, lying on his bed of pain, had been mistaken? What if he had simply seen someone stirring his tea for some innocent purpose? Had his mind and eyesight been fuddled by the brandy he had consumed, and the pain of his final agonies? One granddaughter, seen through clouded vision might well resemble the other. This raised another question. Did the dead have all the truth revealed to them after they had passed, or were they as ignorant as they had been on earth?

Mina realised that beyond the facts that Thomas Fernwood was authoritative, careful with his money, and over-fond of the brandy bottle, she knew almost nothing about him. Was he a truthful person? Was he motivated by prudence, honour, or malice? And did people, whether good or bad, undergo a change of character after death? Could spirits lie? Might Thomas Fernwood accuse an innocent person from beyond the grave, simply to get some revenge he had long harboured when alive? This quest for the truth was, now she had given it so much thought, a highly dangerous business.

Before the comforting crackle of the parlour fire, Mina once again entertained the young couple to tea. It was very apparent from their demeanour that the journey to their old home had brought them no comfort, no resolution.

'I am sorry to say that our visit was a great disappointment,' said Miss Clifton, sadly. 'I had hoped so much that going to the place where my uncle was born and raised and lived all of his life we might get closer to him. But I felt — nothing. I am certain that if Uncle Thomas was able to speak he would tell us at once what he had tried so hard to impart on his deathbed. I can only conclude that there is some special gift in speaking to those who have passed which neither George nor I possess. How must my poor uncle feel, to be unheard all this time with never the chance to accuse the person responsible for his death, or to absolve us all from blame by admitting that there had been a mistake. If he can look down and see us now, and how the uncertainty mars our chances of happiness, I know he would want to help us if he could. It would be a mercy to him, too, to let him say what he holds hidden, and bring his spirit peace.'

'He cannot be the only person in spirit who is afflicted in such a way,' said Mina. 'We often hear stories of apparitions who cannot rest easy but must haunt the living with unfinished business on earth that must be completed before they can find contentment.'

She decided not to mention that she herself had written several stories with that theme. It was an old device but one that readers never seemed to tire of.

'We visited his grave; we even stood by it and called upon him, but he did not appear to us there,' said Fernwood. 'We went to the house where our family had once lived, and asked the present occupants if they had seen him, or had any communication from a spirit but they said they had not.'

'They may do so in future, of course,' said Mina, feeling only pity for the current tenants, who might not previously have been aware that a murder had been committed in their home. 'What I cannot understand is why, if he is so restless as you believe, he has not spoken before? There have been twenty years of silence on the subject. There is no lack of mediums. Any one might do. Why has he not haunted the perpetrator of the crime to force an admission, either as a spirit or in dreams? In fact, what prevents his spirit from acting as he might have done had he survived the poison? Rather than make his complaint through a medium he could take it to a justice, who would be the proper person to deal with it.'

Fernwood shook his head. 'I cannot fathom how those in spirit can act. They may have ways mysterious to us, their own rules of what they can and cannot do.'

'Perhaps he has left messages with mediums who could not interpret them,' said Miss Clifton. 'And he might well be haunting his murderer. If that person has any conscience at all they will be unable to rest easy at night, but will not dare to reveal what ails them.'

'Can you tell me more about Thomas Fernwood?' Mina asked. 'I have gathered that he had a firm manner, was careful with money, and enjoyed his brandy, but I know very little more about him. Was he loved by his family? Did he treat them well? His son? His daughter in law, his other grandchildren? What about in business? Was he honest? Did he have rivals? Friends?'

George Fernwood and Miss Clifton glanced at each other. 'Most of what we know we learned after he died,' said Fernwood. 'But he and my grandmother spent very little time in each other's company, especially as she was an invalid, and she would not speak against him. Yes, he was strict. He had always been so, even with himself, which was why he owned a successful business. In recent years, however, he had left most of the labour to my parents, and indulged himself more with the brandy bottle. He expected all the family to do his bidding without question and work hard, whether at school, in the house or the shop. He chastised us when he felt it necessary, and I never knew him to be kind. But there are many men like that, and it is hardly a reason to commit murder.'

'He took almost no notice of the girls,' said Miss Clifton. 'We were his blood relations but he regarded us only as servants. I don't think he ever spoke to me other than to give orders. But had he not taken in my mother and brother and myself I don't know what would have happened to us. We were grateful to have somewhere respectable to live and food to eat.'

'Was there no-one he disliked or quarrelled with?'

'Not especially,' said Fernwood. 'Why do you ask?'

'I just feel that I need to know as much as I can so I can judge whatever messages you might receive in a séance. I was wondering about asking another member of your family for any details that could provide enlightenment, but if as you say, everyone is a suspect, that would not be for the best. Have you still not told them of your betrothal?'

'We have not. My grandfather's death is a subject we avoid discussing at all times. Mary and I have explained our absences from the business by saying that we are visiting old friends or finding new suppliers for the shop.'

'Was your grandfather a truthful man? If you do receive messages that you feel confident are from him, how can you be sure that he is telling the truth?'

'Can a spirit lie?' asked Fernwood.

'We don't know. Or he could simply have been mistaken in whatever he saw.'

'Even if he was mistaken in life he would surely know the truth of it now,' said Miss Clifton, confidently.

'And there is another question,' Mina went on. 'We only have one witness, Dr Sperley, to say that your grandfather even suspected that he had been deliberately poisoned, and knew the identity of the culprit. He might have been unable or unwilling to tell anyone else earlier, or perhaps he only realised the truth as he lay dying. But I need to consider if Dr Sperley was telling the truth. Is he trustworthy?'

'Eminently so, I would say,' replied Fernwood, obviously shocked by the question. 'He continued to attend my grandmother up to her death, and I had the opportunity of getting to know him well. I would respect and believe anything he had to say.'

'Oh, but Miss Scarletti is right to question everything,' said Miss Clifton. 'What if Dr Sperley gave my uncle the wrong medicine by mistake after he became ill from the brandy and then invented this story to conceal his error? Even the best of doctors can make mistakes sometimes.'

'I refuse to believe that of him,' said Fernwood, resolutely, 'convenient as it would be to do so. He was an honourable man. Surely he would have admitted a mistake. To invent a story that threw suspicion on the family he had attended for over twenty years! He would not have made us suffer so. No, I am convinced that he spoke the truth.'

Mina knew too well that doctors prized their professional reputations above all else, and it was almost impossible to get them to admit to an error, especially one that had proved fatal to a patient. If Dr Sperley had indeed made a mistake that had killed Thomas Fernwood, and wanted to avoid blame, then the most likely person he would have pointed to was the dead man himself, suggesting perhaps that he had taken something in error that had been left in the sick room to kill vermin.

'I suppose you have had no correspondence with Dr Sperley recently?' said Mina. 'Would you object if I wrote to him?'

'I'm sad to say he passed away six months ago or we would have paid him a visit when we were in Lincoln,' said Fernwood. 'Poor man, he was in decline and his wife nursed him as if he had been a child.' There was a long pause during which a thought hovered in the air that a deceased Dr Sperley might still be capable of providing some information.

'What will you do next?' asked Mina.

'George wishes to continue to visit Miss Brendel in the hope that she can help,' said Miss Clifton, 'but I would like to go and see what Mr Castlehouse can do. Have you been to see him?'

'I have not.'

'He actually receives proper messages written on slates, and that sounds very interesting.'

'I agree. We should arrange to go very soon.'

Mina's study of the newspapers had told her that Mr Castlehouse was a recent arrival in Brighton, where he had taken lodgings. His first advertisements in the *Gazette* were to the effect that he would be holding slate-writing demonstrations at his address once a week. Admission was one shilling per person, payment to be made at the door. There followed another advertisement only two weeks later to the effect that due to the popularity of the demonstrations and the demand for admissions, they would now be held twice a week. Soon afterwards this was increased to five times and to avoid disappointment tickets, which were now priced at two shillings, should be purchased in advance from the larger bookshops. Mina showed a recent advertisement to Miss Clifton who said that she would buy the tickets and call to collect Mina on the following Wednesday.

By this arrangement, none of the attendees would have to give a name, which was all very well for Miss Clifton, however Mina could hardly disguise herself. She would have to take the chance that Mr Castlehouse had not been warned to avoid a lady who was four feet eight inches tall with a twisted spine, who had a reputation for disrupting séances and sending mediums to prison. Even if he had been so warned he might believe himself immune to Mina's observation, either because he thought his art to be true or he had some means of avoiding being detected in fraud. Mina had to remind herself that there was always a chance that Mr Castlehouse might prove to be the genuine article. Nellie had decried all slate-writers as frauds, but she did not know them all.

Chapter Nineteen

Later that day, Richard returned home, shaking rain from the thick tweed of his coat. Rose ran up quickly and took the rumpled garment from him to be brushed, together with the travelling cap that had water dripping from its peak.

'Have you been to see Mr Dorry?' asked Mina, as Richard slumped before the parlour fire, dragging his fingers through the wet curls on his forehead.

'I have, and showed him my drawing of the sea, which he thought promising. He does not intend to buy any of my pictures of ladies, which is a great shame, because I think they are the best of my work, but he showed me some books with pictures in by famous men and asked me to try and copy one. I did, there and then, and he seemed pleased with it, so he has sent me away to do some of my own. They need to be very like, but not exactly like, the ones in the book.'

'How unusual. I always thought artists drew their own favourite subjects unless commissioned for a portrait. Is there much demand for these kinds of pictures?'

'Yes, well, he explained it all to me. There are some artists who are very popular indeed, whatever they draw or paint, and their pictures sell for high prices, only they are dead so there is no more work to come from them, but people still want their work or something as like as makes almost no difference. So, if I can make copies that are "in the style of" as Dorry put it, people will buy them and hang them up and their visitors will be very impressed, and only the buyer will know they are not the real thing.'

'I hope you are not going to make a great mess with paint. Or is it just drawings he wants?'

'Just the drawings for now. Paint is such a bore. But I shall still want to draw pretty ladies — for my own amusement, you understand. I — er — I don't suppose I could borrow a little something from you? Just until I sell a picture or two.'

Mina looked stern. 'I have lent you money before. I am not a bank. In fact, no bank would lend to you on the same principle, that you never pay it back. Doesn't Edward pay you a salary?'

'It's a pittance!' Richard protested. 'No-one could live decently on a clerk's wages! And have you seen the price of pencils? We artists can't use just any kind of pencil, you know.'

'Then I shall buy you a big box of them as a Christmas present.'

Richard took no cheer from the promise, although he brightened when Rose brought hot cocoa and biscuits. She also had a letter for Mina.

Mr Greville was manager of the Scarletti Library of Romance, the division of the publishing house that produced the horror tales written by Mina under the *nom de plume* Robert Neil. He had received far stranger requests from Mina than her recent one for a letter of introduction for Richard under a *nom de crayon*. It was therefore no surprise when she opened the envelope to find that he had readily obliged with a formally composed letter, recommending artist Richard Henry, on notepaper printed with the name of the *Society Journal*. In the covering letter to Mina he did not trouble to ask why the name Scarletti was not to be mentioned. Given her previous activities in investigating psychics, he no doubt thought this to be a superfluous enquiry.

'This is the letter of introduction which we hope will admit you to the presence of the fair Miss Brendel,' said Mina, handing the document to Richard. 'And I have a note here from Mr Greville. He has discussed the Brendels with Mrs Caldecott but all she could tell him is that Mr Aloysius Brendel hails from Yorkshire, and is something in mining. He is of common stock, and chooses not to mix in society, but devotes all his energy to making money, of which he is said to have a great pile. I suggest,' she continued, seeing Richard's eyes light up at the prospect of piles of money, 'that you exercise considerable caution. Start by sending a note to Mrs Brendel, asking her permission to call. If she is the woman I think she is, there should be no difficulty. After that, I leave it to your charm to gain an entry to the house and will pray for some good sense to ensure that you are not ejected. Be polite and respectful, and find out what you can without exciting suspicion as to your real motives.'

'That should be no trouble at all, and with the added pleasure of spending time in the company of a pretty young heiress. To add to my fame I can show them Mr Dorry's business card.'

Richard was looking more cheerful, and hurried away to write the note to the Brendels, and make a start on new drawings for Mr Dorry. It was an unusual level of industry for him, but in both cases there was the prospect of glittering rewards.

The following morning, Richard received a reply from Mrs Brendel, saying how delighted she would be to see a portrait of her daughter gracing the pages of the *Society Journal*, and an appointment was made for him to call. Richard had completed the drawings requested by Mr Dorry, and took them to the gallery. He returned in time for luncheon with more good news.

'He was very pleased indeed with what I have done and has engaged me to draw pictures of the sea at Brighton, which he says is an especially popular subject. In the current climate I shall not have to use my imagination for the storm, and there is an old toy ship of mine that will be shown battling the waves in fine style.'

'What will he pay you for the work?'

'That is to be determined when I deliver the drawings. He has every confidence that they will sell, if not in Brighton, then in London, where he also has a gallery. And would you believe, Edward was delighted with my sketch of Miss Kitty Betts, and has actually sent me some wages. After luncheon I shall go to Jordan and Conroy's and purchase a new cravat the better to impress the Brendels.'

Chapter Twenty

When Mina waited in the ladies' salon at Dr Hamid's baths for her weekly appointment with Anna, she often saw groups of gossips who dropped their voices and spoke very quietly from behind lace-clad fingers, after first glancing in her direction to ensure that she was far enough away not to hear them. Mina had learned to ignore this, as there was hardly anything they might be saying which she had not heard before, often far more offensively worded, and shouted at her in the street by children. She was used to pity and rudeness, and they rolled from her like drops of winter rain leaving no trace.

Recently, however, she had overheard the start of a lively conversation on the subject of Mr Castlehouse, who was thought to be very mysterious, and this was far too interesting to be ignored. One lady had remarked that he was such a funny little man that she could hardly look at him without laughing. She was quickly hushed by her companions who indicated with glances and flickering eyebrows that Mina was in the room. That aspect of the conversation was quickly dropped, but it went on to the effect that the gentleman did produce very convincing spirit messages, and had become all the rage. There followed another glance at Mina and rapid whispers punctuated by giggles, from which she could only gather that the gossips had concluded that she and Mr Castlehouse were deemed by their strangeness to be an ideal match for each other.

There was one lady amongst them, young, with a nervous look like a startled fawn, who, while listening but not contributing to the unkind chatter, had the good grace to feel ashamed of her companions' sly remarks about Mina. Once or twice she glanced at Mina, with an expression of regret, and when their eyes met, her lips moved to say 'I am sorry' and Mina smiled to show that she was not offended.

When Miss Clifton next called on Mina, having purchased the tickets for Mr Castlehouse's séance, it was detectable that the visitor was in a state of breathless anticipation. 'I know that Miss Brendel has achieved great things,' she said, 'and George will continue to see her and be a witness in case she has anything of value to say to us, but since we last spoke I have been making some enquiries about Mr Castlehouse, and all those who have seen him have been *so* impressed.' She gave a little gasp of excitement that was almost a squeal and looked ready to bounce out of her chair like a balloon inflated with the heady gas of optimism. 'I am really very hopeful indeed.'

Mina saw danger signs in the lady's manner and spoke to her calmly and evenly. 'Miss Clifton, might I make an observation?'

'Yes, yes, of course. Please do. You know how much we value your experience in these matters.'

'I recall that at our first meeting Mr Fernwood mentioned that you were once a non-believer in the work of sprit mediums.'

Miss Clifton dismissed the comment with a laugh and a little shrug. 'I know, but that was before I began to look into it properly. I have learned so much more about it and I am sure that if we consult the right person we will have our answer. I have been trying to convince George, but he is too inclined only to believe in what he can actually see.'

Mina was not reassured. 'Then I beg you most earnestly to beware.'

'Oh? Of what must I beware?' said Miss Clifton, startled. 'If you mean false spirits and demons, of course I know they might come, but I am armed by my faith, and will resist them.'

'That is not what I meant. A convert to a cause can be as ardent in its favour as he or she was once against it. Do not allow your natural enthusiasm to mislead you; do not be too willing to believe. We need calm heads and common sense.'

Miss Clifton looked at Mina with reproachful eyes, her antipathy slowly melting into acceptance, her tightly tensed posture settling.

'You are right, of course. But I so much want to believe that either Mr Castlehouse or Miss Brendel, or some other medium who we have not yet seen, will have the answer that we are hoping for. That is why George and I have been so careful to say nothing about our purpose, to say not one word about our dreadful past or even give our real names. But even if Mr Castlehouse can tell us nothing, perhaps he can at least demonstrate that it is possible to communicate with the spirit world. That would be some comfort.'

'Be cautious, that is all I ask. And if Mr Castlehouse should ever approach you privately suggesting a special reading at a high price, you must let me know at once.'

Miss Clifton promised, although it was all too obvious that the prospect of a special private reading interested her, and was not in her estimation the warning sign that it was in Mina's.

It was time to depart and there was a cab ready waiting. There were the usual wrappings to see to, and Rose fussed over Mina like a nursemaid with a delicate child in her care. Both ladies were thankful for a pleasant turn in the weather that had lessened the ferocity of the sea breezes.

Mr Castlehouse's lodgings were in a well-kept family house, near Queens Park, respectable, but too plain and too far from the sea to be fashionable. They approached the door, tickets in hand, and were met by the maid, a tall woman of advanced age and gaunt features who seemed better suited to managing a house of mourning. She studied the tickets, looked piercingly at Mina as if she was a performing animal that ought to be on a chain, and finally ushered them in, with every appearance of reluctance.

They were shown to a spacious and well-lit apartment on the first floor, where rows of chairs had been assembled to seat about twenty persons in close proximity. Many of the chairs were already occupied, and the majority of those in attendance were ladies. Mina was relieved to note that none of her mother's friends were there, having already been alerted to the deceiving ways of mediums by the example of Miss Eustace. One of those present, she noticed was the timid individual she had seen in the ladies' salon at the baths, sitting very quietly alone. Others were more communicative, and a hush of whispered conversation told Mina that many of them had attended these demonstrations before and were anticipating this one with barely repressed eagerness.

At one end of the room and facing the seated gathering, was a sideboard, on which lay a pile of slates of the kind typical of the schoolroom, a dish of coloured chalks, several dusters, a length of cord, a bowl of water and a sponge. In front of it was a table with two side flaps, both down, and three dining chairs of the usual kind.

'Shall we take a look at the slates?' asked Miss Clifton. 'Are we supposed to? Do you think it is allowed?'

'If we were not meant to examine them then they would not have been left out unguarded,' said Mina. 'Let us do so by all means.'

'I feel quite nervous,' Miss Clifton confided. She took Mina's arm. 'Do come with me.' She and Mina went to the sideboard and together they examined the slates, dusters, chalks and sponge, finding nothing unusual. Most of the slates were single sheets in wooden frames, but there were also some of the double folding type, which hinged in the middle and closed like a book. Mina could not be sure if the items were as innocent as they seemed or if there was something she should have noticed but had not. On reflection, however, and recalling what Nellie had said about the conjuror's art, she decided that anything on open display must be innocuous and if there was deception it must lie elsewhere.

The door opened again and admitted the deeply mourning couple who had attended Miss Brendel's séance, Mr and Mrs Myles. As before, they appeared enclosed within themselves, and hardly looked about them as they crept to two empty seats, but in doing so, Mr Myles chanced to notice Mina and nodded in recognition. Mina wondered if the couple, swaddled in grief, had been going to every medium in Brighton, looking for a solace that they had not yet received. Moving as quickly as she could, Mina was able to take the seat by Mrs Myles, and Miss Clifton trotted after her.

'Good evening,' said Mina.

'Oh!' said Mrs Myles, gloomily. 'Yes, yes indeed, I trust it will be.' She crushed a black-edged handkerchief in her hand, and Mina saw she wore a mourning ring, an onyx dome with a lonely seed pearl at its centre like a teardrop.

'Have you attended a sitting with Mr Castlehouse before? This is my first visit.'

'Yes, we have seen him several times.'

'Has he provided messages for you?' asked Miss Clifton, hopefully.

'There have been communications,' said Mrs Myles, although this circumstance seemed not to have brought her any joy. 'Many of them highly evidential.'

'The sittings are not always successful, so you must persevere,' said Mr Myles. 'Sometimes the spirits do not come. The atmosphere can impede them. You might need several visits before you achieve success.'

'Atmosphere?' queried Mina. 'Please do explain.'

'I refer to the weather. It may be cloudy or stormy, and then, I am not sure why, they find it hard to come through. But today has been a little milder and I feel we will be fortunate.'

Miss Clifton opened her mouth to speak again, but Mina quickly shook her head, as a signal to be silent in case she revealed too much. Miss Clifton realised her potential error, nodded and said nothing.

Mr Conroy the younger was next to arrive, and seeing so many places taken, looked about him with a worried expression on his heavy features, and finally secured a seat at the edge of the company.

After a few more minutes during which further visitors filled the room to capacity, the maid entered, looked about to see that all was ready, and withdrew. At last, the door opened to admit Mr Castlehouse. He was a short man, barely five feet in height, which was mainly due to greatly bowed legs that gave him a waddling gait. He was aged about forty, with piercing dark eyes, a full head of glossy black hair, worn rather long, and a luxuriant moustache, very full in the middle and coming to fine waxed points at either end. To compensate for the reduced size of his legs, his arms looked too large for his body, the hands highly expressive with long slender fingers.

He smiled at the assembly, as well he might as they were paying two shillings apiece, and bowed. 'My dear friends,' he announced, in a voice that sang from his chest, 'I am very happy to see that so many of you have returned to me again, and happy too, to greet newcomers. All are welcome. I cannot, of course, promise you what will transpire this evening. That much is in the hands of the almighty —' He made a dramatic gesture to the ceiling — 'and to the spirits he commands. But let us begin.'

Mr Castlehouse now made himself busy, lifting up one of the end flaps of the table, and securing it in place, then drawing up three of the dining chairs. He next picked up a slate from the pile on the sideboard, in a casual manner that suggested it was a chance selection, held it up so all could see it was clean, and turned it about to display the other side. Despite his curious gait there was something tidy, deft and practised in every movement.

'As you see, nothing is written on the slate, but to make quite certain of it, I will ask any person here present to pass a wetted sponge over its surface to ensure that nothing at all is there, no hidden marks, no paint, no pencil. Quite clean. Would anyone like to do so?'

Miss Clifton rose immediately and came forward. Mina was anxious at first in case she gave anything away but reflected that it would be useful to learn her impressions later on. Mr Castlehouse bowed respectfully, and handed over the slate and sponge. Miss Clifton carefully applied the sponge to both sides of the slate, showing by the energy in her shoulder and dexterity of her action that she was no stranger to scouring surfaces, then took it to one of the gas lamps to examine it more closely. 'It is perfectly clean,' she announced, and handed it back to Mr Castlehouse.

'Excellent. You may now return to your seat.' She looked disappointed but complied.

He placed the slate on the edge of the raised flap of the table, then selected a white chalk, broke a small piece from the end of it and dropped it on the surface of the slate. Mina watched, unsure if she was about to see the fragment of chalk move by itself, propelled by a ghostly hand, but was not so rewarded. 'I would like to ask two members of the company to come forward and sit at the table.'

Miss Clifton glanced at Mina as if to suggest that she might like to go, but Mina suspected that if there was any trickery about to take place it was those closest to Mr Castlehouse who might be the most deceived. Mr Myles and another gentleman came forward and, at the medium's invitation, sat facing each other across the table, the seat by the raised flap remaining unoccupied. Both the sitters glanced at the slate but neither appeared to notice anything unusual. Mr Castlehouse now took the third seat nearest to the slate, and requested the gentleman on his left to take hold of his hand. With his right hand, he lifted the slate, and proceeded to slide it carefully under the table as if it was a drawer, keeping it perfectly flat and in contact with the underside as he did so. His thumb remained on the tabletop, although his fingers were now out of sight. 'Gentlemen, I would be obliged if you would both hold the slate with one hand as I am doing, keeping it pressed firmly against the table. There must be no gap between the edges of the slate and the table.' Mr Myles and the other sitter complied, Myles resting his free hand on the tabletop where it could be clearly seen by everyone. 'I am sure we are all agreed that in its current position no human agency can write on the upper surface of the slate.'

Mr Myles nodded emphatically. 'Oh yes, I can attest to that.'

Mr Castlehouse inclined his head with a smile. 'I thank you, sir. If you have a question to ask the spirits, please do so.'

Mr Myles directed an anxious glance at his wife, who was sitting with her head bowed, then turned back to address not Mr Castlehouse, but some more lofty place, his face tilted upwards as if hoping his words would fly through the ceiling and the rooftop, and find the heavenly regions. 'I would like to ask if Jack is happy.'

'That is a good question,' said Mr Castlehouse, approvingly. 'Ladies and gentlemen, you may speak amongst yourselves if you so desire, and we will wait to see what transpires.'

There was a clock on the mantelpiece, a heavy dark timepiece with a loud deep tick like a wooden hammer striking something hollow. Mina knew that in séances things usually did not occur immediately in order to build anticipation amongst the sitters and make them more receptive. She glanced at the clock, which showed some fifteen minutes past the hour and resolved to memorise how long it took before Mr Myles received his answer. As they sat, Mr Castlehouse appeared to tremble a little, and breathe more rapidly, then he grew calm. Time passed, and the sitters began conversing in whispers.

'Is it usual to wait so long?' Mina asked Mrs Myles.

'It is, yes. The spirits must pass through the ether to reach us.'

'I suppose it must be a long way,' said Mina. 'I did not know they were subject to such requirements.'

'There is so much we do not know about the spirit world,' said Mrs Myles, and it was hard to tell from her voice whether she was unhappy at the general state of ignorance or hopeful of finding out more in the near future.

'Why does the slate need to be under the table?'

'The spirits require darkness to perform.'

'Ah. I understand.' Mina was familiar with séances that were conducted in almost complete darkness, affording maximum chances for trickery. Here, where the séance was performed in the light, only the slate was hidden from view. The wooden frame of the slate meant that a space a small fraction of an inch in depth existed between the underside of the table and the writing surface, and that crucial space was in darkness.

Mina glanced at the clock. Ten minutes had passed.

'Shall we see if there is any message?' asked Mr Castlehouse, and with the agreement of Mr Myles and the other gentleman the slate was carefully withdrawn from under the table for inspection. All three gentlemen seated at the table gazed at it, but it was clear from their expressions that it remained clean. Mr Castlehouse asked the second gentleman to fetch the cloth and then employed it to rub the surface.

'Let us try once again,' he said, replacing the tiny chip of chalk, and the process of sliding the slate under the table was repeated with Mr Myles being particularly exhorted to hold it securely against the underside of the table, and think deeply of his question. 'And if there are other questions, from anyone here present, please state them now, speak them aloud, it will encourage the spirits to come.'

'I would like to know if the spirit of my late wife is here,' said the second gentleman, and other voices chimed in.

'Can the spirits advise if I should sell my house?'

'What are you called?'

'Write the name of my mother.'

'Does the sun shine in heaven?'

'What is the name of the last book I read?'

'Is there a message for me?' asked Miss Clifton.

'Let us all think of the spirits of our departed loved ones, that they can be strengthened on their path to us,' said Mr Castlehouse.

The clock ticked, Mr Castlehouse trembled again, and the sitters were now quiet in thought. Everyone was listening. At last, a tiny noise, high and clear, brought gasps of appreciation. It was the sound of scratching, the noise made by chalk moving on a slate. Mrs Myles uttered a sob.

'I swear,' gulped Mr Myles, 'the slate is being held against the wood as firm as firm can be! No human hand can write on it!'

The scratching noise lasted for only a minute then ceased. Everyone waited in case it should come again, but after a few moments, there were three loud taps that made several people start in surprise.

'That is a sign that the message is complete,' said Mr Castlehouse. 'Let us see.'

Once again, the slate was slid out from beneath the table. On its upper surface were two lines of writing. 'Can you read what it says?' he asked, handing the slate to Mr Myles.

'Oh yes, yes I can!' exclaimed Myles, with some emotion. 'It says — "I am in heaven with the angels. I am happy. Jack."' His shoulders shook, and he pressed a handkerchief to his eyes.

Mr Castlehouse, after permitting the other gentleman to see what was there, held up the slate for all the sitters to see, and Mina noticed something surprising. Had the writing been made by a spirit or prepared by the medium in advance, she might have expected it to start either near the top of the slate, or in the middle. If Mr Castlehouse had been able by some manipulation to slide his fingers between the slate and the table and write the words himself with that tiny fragment of chalk, then the lines of writing would have been placed at the edge of the slate nearest his hand, the tops of the letters furthest from him. When Mr Myles was handed the slate by Mr Castlehouse, he would therefore have been obliged to turn it around to

543

read from it. Instead, the writing was at the edge furthest from the medium's hand, with the tops of the letters towards Mr Castlehouse, and Mr Myles had not needed to turn the slate about. Castlehouse, with his thumb in clear sight on the tabletop, could not have stretched even his long slim fingers to reach the far edge of the slate. Had he been able to do so, he would have then been obliged to write upside down, not a simple skill. Either way, any secret writing carried out by Mr Castlehouse would have had to be performed without the other two gentlemen holding the slate noticing that it had been tilted away from the underside of the table to enable the medium to introduce his fingers, or with both of them being in collusion with him. The only other possibility that occurred to Mina was that either Mr Myles or the other gentleman had written on the slate, but to do so they would still have needed to tilt the slate without losing the little crumb of chalk, and write in a sideways style. The only interesting thing about the writing itself, as far as she could observe, was that it was uneven in size, and not keeping to a straight line, as if it had been produced by someone unable to see what he was doing.

'Tell me,' whispered Mina to Mrs Myles, 'is it always the same two gentlemen Mr Castlehouse selects to sit with him?'

'Oh no, it is different persons on each occasion. This is the first time Mr Myles has been chosen.' Mina glanced about the room, but could not imagine that everyone there was a confederate of Mr Castlehouse.

'Thank you, gentlemen,' said Mr Castlehouse. Mr Myles and the second gentleman returned to their seats. Mina thought that if more persons were wanted she would try next, but on Mr Castlehouse asking for two more, in the time it took her to rise from her seat she was forestalled by Mr Conroy and a stout lady who was so determined that she might have elbowed her aside had she made the attempt.

Mr Castlehouse returned the slate to the table and rubbed it well with a cloth, and then Mr Conroy inspected the surface minutely before it was once again slid underneath. Ten minutes elapsed before the scratching sound made itself known. Mina watched carefully, slipping down in her seat as far as she dared, trying not to make it too obvious that she was attempting to peer underneath the table, but she was not able to deduce anything. After the three taps were heard, Mr Castlehouse withdrew the slate. This time the message for their consideration was 'Heaven is a beautiful place.'

Other messages followed and Mina tried to memorise as many as she could. They were in the nature of 'I cannot advise you now' — 'all good souls go to heaven' — 'be comforted, the future will become clear' — 'there will be a wedding soon' — 'you are looked upon with love' — 'you will know great happiness' — 'I am here,' and finally 'you are blessed by the spirits.'

Mr Conroy and the stout lady returned to their places, and Mr Castlehouse laid aside the slate and took up a set of hinged slates from the sideboard. He placed it on the table, then with a smile, beckoned forward a lady from the company. It was the timid lady, who, after looking about her, and making sure that it was indeed she whom he had chosen, rose and came forward very slowly. She was asked to clean the slates thoroughly with the sponge and dry them with a duster. Mr Castlehouse showed the company that the slates were clean and unmarked, then placed a fragment of chalk on one slate, closed the pair, took a length of cord from the sideboard and tied the closed slates shut. The slates were then placed on the table.

'Please be seated at the table,' he said, ushering the lady to a chair. 'Now, I would like you to place your hand on the slates. Do not remove your hand at any time. There is nothing to be frightened of.' She complied, and he too, laid a hand on the slates. 'I now call upon any spirit here present to write a message if the conditions are favourable.'

There was a pause, but soon the familiar scratching sounded again. The lady jumped with fright, and almost withdrew her hand from the slates, but Mr Castlehouse smiled and encouraged her to keep her hand in place and lean forward to press her ear against the top slate so she could confirm that writing was taking place. As she did so, her eyes opened wide in amazement. 'I feel the movements most distinctly,' she said.

At length the scratching noise stopped and the three taps sounded. Mr Castlehouse withdrew his hand from the slates and asked the lady to untie the cords and open them up for everyone to see. It was a long message this time, not in the untidy scrawl of the previous ones, but neatly written in a bold flowing easily legible hand. 'Please read it aloud,' said Mr Castlehouse.

The lady took the slates. 'The conditions are favourable. I will do my best for you, although at the cost of great effort. There are many persons here present who are mediums but are not aware of it. They have the power within if they could develop it. My advice is take the trouble to sit often and it will come. You must be patient. The result will be great happiness. The power is fading. Good-night.'

Mr Castlehouse rose and faced his audience. 'Ladies and gentlemen, I fear that the spirits have become exhausted by so many communications. That is all we will have tonight, but once their powers have been restored, we shall hear from them again.'

Chapter Twenty-One

A cab was ordered to take Mina home before going on to convey Miss Clifton to the railway station. Miss Clifton, who had been required to keep firm control of her excitement and very nearly succeeded, was now visibly trembling as her emotions threatened to overflow. 'Well? What do you think? Was it not marvellous?'

'I have never seen anything like it,' said Mina, truthfully.

'I am as certain as it is possible to be that no human agency can write on a slate when it is pressed against the underside of the table. I tried very hard to see how it was being done, but all the time the chalk was writing the slate didn't move at all. And Mr Castlehouse didn't move, either. And the double slate tied with a cord was actually lying on the table in plain sight when the spirit wrote on it. If anything had been done by trickery the other ladies and gentlemen who were holding the slates would have noticed.'

'Not necessarily,' said Mina. 'I have seen conjuring performed in front of my eyes which I knew to be conjuring, but I still could not see how it was done.'

'But we were both looking to see if there was any trickery,' said Miss Clifton. 'And from some of the questions that were asked I think we were not the only ones. Yet not one person stood up and accused Mr Castlehouse of cheating. If the slate had been moved or tilted so someone could write on it, would people not have seen?'

'I am not sure,' said Mina. 'But I know I cannot explain what I saw.'

'And I received a very clear message, which gave me great hope for the future!'

'You did?' queried Mina.

'Oh yes, didn't you hear?'

'I — don't know — there were so many. Was there something you might have recognised which I did not perhaps?'

'I was very careful as you advised — I gave no clues. The message said, "there will be a wedding soon," you must recall it.'

'Oh, yes, I think I do. And you are quite sure it was for you?'

'I am sure — I hope it was. Oh dear! Do you think it was for someone else?'

'I too hope that it was for you,' said Mina soothingly. 'Who else could have received the answer with such pleasure? The question we must ask is who wrote it?'

Once she was home, Mina went straight to her writing desk and recorded to the best of her memory, a full account of the events of that evening. When she tried to remember all the questions and answers she realised that it was not possible after the first question to be sure whether the subsequent ones had actually been answered, since the replies were very general and could have applied to more than one question or even to some that had not been asked. It was also apparent that while some of the questions were seriously meant, since they were directed at the spirits of the departed, others seemed to be aimed at no more than testing whether or not an answer could be given on the slate.

Eager to discuss her visit to Mr Castlehouse, Mina wrote to Nellie asking if she could call, and sent Rose out to obtain *macarons* and wafers, offering her the loan of her warm cloak.

Richard, looking handsomer than ever in his new cravat, was abundantly cheerful at supper. 'I have just spent a delightful hour drawing the beauteous maiden, looked upon very sternly all the while by the maid, Jessie, in case an improper syllable should leave my lips. But I shall win her over, have no fear. I think I have half done so already. The girl, however, says almost nothing. She sits staring into a far distant place where saner people cannot, and most probably should not go. The man who wins her hand will live forever on the edge of damnation, and will have to weigh up whether or not the reward is worth it. The mother, who is a far handsomer creature, and has an unforgiving spirit that I can only admire, comes in from time to time, to measure with her eyes the distance that lies between me and her precious jewel of a daughter. At least five feet is the minimum. We must not be able to touch fingertips. If anything is required in the matter of arrangement of the charming model, then Jessie is to carry it out at my direction. There were no refreshments offered, apart from a curious smelling tea which Miss Brendel sipped and the maid declined.'

'Camomile, I believe,' said Mina. 'Dr Hamid has told me it is beneficial. Did you learn anything else?'

'The mother seems very anxious to know about the new *Journal*. She asked me how many society people read it and when her daughter's portrait would appear. I didn't know the answers so I made them up. And she questioned me very closely about Mr Dorry. She wanted to know if he was a wealthy and prominent man in town, and whether he was married. I had to say that he was rich, and very prominent indeed, and almost certainly a bachelor, but my feeling was that he was not the marrying kind of gentleman. But I have not disgraced myself, and I am to call again.'

'Was Mr Quinley there?'

'Yes, he looked in once, and gave me a very hard stare. I think it was a warning. Then he left the room and I heard some discussion in the hallway with Mrs Brendel about some papers that needed to be examined, and they moved away. It was all business and no endearments, but —' he shrugged — 'who can tell?'

547

Chapter Twenty-Two

Mr Honeyacre had finally prevailed upon Miss Macready to attend a supper with the Brendels, as evidenced by the charming little printed invitation Mina received to join them, accompanied by a notelet expressing his gratitude. After enjoying her weekly steam bath and massage she decided to discuss the forthcoming gathering with Dr Hamid, and found him in his office where he was grateful to find an excuse to put aside his paperwork.

'You are looking very well,' he observed.

'I feel very well,' said Mina. 'Miss Hamid knows how to frighten away the demons that tug at my back.'

He brought two glasses and poured out drinks of the herb and fruit mineral water produced especially for customers of the baths. 'I have not reached any further conclusions concerning Miss Brendel, I am afraid.'

'Ah, but I am hoping to have some new information for you soon.'

As Mina mentioned the supper invitation, which would afford her the opportunity to make a further study of the young medium, Dr Hamid bent his head in concern and folded his arms across his body. 'You are venturing out quite frequently and you know how cold and wet it has been of late. The newspapers have just reported a substantial increase in cases of bronchitis, many of which have proved fatal. See how unwell the Price of Wales has been, and still is.'

Mina nodded meekly. The Prince, a robust man of thirty was dangerously ill with typhoid, a condition that Mina knew she would be unlikely to survive. She could only hope that the sanitary arrangements of Brighton would prevent an outbreak closer to home.

'I must be very firm with you about this,' Dr Hamid continued. 'Take no unnecessary risks. In the daytime, if the weather is mild, a little excursion for fresh air may be beneficial. After sunset, or in inclement weather you must take great care. If you suspect for a moment that anyone at an event you are attending is suffering from a cough or fever or shortness of breath, you must leave at once. Do not breathe in cold air. Do not breathe in infected exhalations.'

Mina could not resist a smile. 'I am permitted to breathe?'

'Please do, for as long as possible.'

He fetched a stethoscope and listened carefully to her lungs, an expression of intense concentration gradually mellowing to relief. 'Well, it all seems sound. Had it not been I would have forbidden you to go out for at least a week. But remember my instructions.'

'I will do my best,' said Mina.

'This gathering at Mr Honeyacre's, what is its purpose? The guest list suggests to me that he has some scheme in mind. A séance, perhaps?'

'Mr Honeyacre has recently taken a keen interest in spiritualism and wishes to pursue a study of it. He is, so I have been led to believe, intending to offer marriage to a Miss Macready, who has grave doubts as to the safety of conjuring spirits. He has been anxious to convince his intended bride of the purity of spiritualism, but the lady has so far been resistant to the idea. So, as you have detected, there is a scheme. He will introduce her to Miss Brendel at a convivial supper, in the hope that this will have the desired effect. But Miss Macready was loath to break bread with Miss Brendel and would not have consented to attend the supper unless I was present.'

'Miss Macready must be a sensible woman. If Mr Honeyacre is fortunate he will be the one persuaded of his foolishness. Very well, I will allow you to go. Write to me afterwards describing the event and also the appearance of Miss Brendel, whose health is, I agree, a matter of concern. And if you feel unwell, send for me at once.'

'Did young Mr Dawson attend the baths?'

'He did, as it was gratis, and I doubt that he will return, but I can report that his lungs have cleared, and he is well again. He is young but does not look after himself properly. He tried to extract information from me concerning Miss Brendel, but I could tell him no more than I told you. Then he begged me to intervene but I said I had done all I could. And finally, would you believe, he asked me to go and see her again and carry a message from him, to be delivered secretly and out of sight of the mother. Of course, I said I would do nothing of the sort. He departed in a very bad state of mind.'

'I hope he will not do anything unwise.'

'He has been unwise enough already. There are no medicines to cure that, I am afraid. I wish there were. I tried to talk sense into him, but I doubt that he listened.'

'Poor young man,' said Mina. 'After the supper I will write to him and reassure him that Miss Brendel is well, but that is all I can do.'

'I do have some good news for you, however. I have today received a letter from Mr Marriott, the oculist, who has confirmed that he has a special interest in the phenomenon of apparitions, and has himself been consulted by several people who have been afflicted in that way. He would be very happy to meet us both and share his knowledge. If you agree I will arrange a meeting at your home.' He wagged a warning finger. 'No more of this unnecessary travelling about!'

Nellie, sipping her preferred China tea in Mina's parlour was eagerly anticipating her account of the visit to Mr Castlehouse. 'Tell me all,' she said. 'Was it a success? Did you receive a visit from chalk-writing spirits?'

Mina described, as well as she could, everything that had occurred, using the notes she had made on the same evening. As she did so she saw how valuable it had been to write everything down so soon afterwards. She did not think she could have recalled as much or so well, without having done so.

'What interested me particularly was that the séance was conducted in the light. However, where the actual effect was taking place, the space between the surface of the slate and the table, or between two slates, was in the dark. I was told, as one so often is, that the spirits needed darkness in order to work, but why that should be was not explained. I was simply expected to accept it, as many do, but, of course, I do not. After all, if the spirits descend from the heavenly regions to write on Mr Castlehouse's slates they must pass through areas of light in order to do so. But I decided not to mention this to Mr Castlehouse, as I don't know how he deals with criticism. If badly, that would have been an end of the demonstration which would have been considered a failure, and then the fault would have been laid at my door.'

'From what you tell me the messages were of a very general nature, and given that there were so many people present each reply could have satisfied more than one of the sitters.'

'I agree,' said Mina. 'The only reply that actually supplied a name was the one given to Mr Myles, and he had already spoken the name aloud, so that was not a great surprise. He received words of comfort, but there was nothing to prove that the reply came from a spirit. But there remains the question of how the writing was done on a slate that was pressed against the table.'

Nellie bit thoughtfully into the crisp edge of a wafer. 'I recall some years ago, when the interest in slate-writing first began, there was a man in London who made a great deal of money from it. Some of his dupes were simply gullible people hoping to find hidden knowledge about the world. Others, I am sorry to say, were grieving for lost relations, and willing to pay him any amount for a message from beyond. Ellison, I believe his name was, and he became very rich. Stage magicians, who never pretend to provide anything other than entertainment, regarded him with distaste. Then a conjuror by the name of Angelo decided to expose Ellison's tricks, and went to a number of his séances incognito. He later wrote an account of his campaign and it was very instructive. The first time he went, he was quite mystified as to how the effect had been brought about, and, as he freely admitted, was very nearly convinced that he had actually seen something marvellous. But he went again, and the second time he began to see just a little of how it was done. He continued his visits, so often that Ellison must have hoped he had a new devotee he could draw into his net, little thinking that he had met more than his match. Each time Angelo went, he was able to observe more, and, finally, not only could he conclude how the illusion was done, but he then taught himself how to reproduce it. He went on to demonstrate the trick to a number of people in a mock séance, and fooled them all, before he revealed to them how it had been achieved. The result was that Ellison fell out of favour and there was even a suggestion that he should be arrested. I think he went abroad; at least he has not been heard of since.'

'I suppose,' said Mina, 'that the difference between a conjuror and a false medium is that a conjuror's audience knows they are being misled and enjoys the spectacle. The medium's audience wants to believe that what they see is real. But what of those people who go to mediums in order to study them to see if they are genuine? There are a few such, and I wish there were more. Some are convinced, others are not, but they all see the same thing.'

'They do see the same thing, but they may not recall the same thing. Some may miss details that others see. Some might even recall seeing something that did not in fact occur.'

Mina refilled the teacups. 'I shall be speaking to an oculist soon and will ask him about that. The eye is such a miraculous thing, how can it be so deceived?'

'Our eyes play tricks on us all the time. We are confident that our eyes tell us the truth, but they are the most easily deceived of all the organs of sensation. Every conjuror knows that. It is how he makes his living.'

'But it is not only the eye, itself. What of the mind that interprets what the eye sees? Can that be fooled?'

'Oh, indeed. Have you never seen a shadow and thought it was the figure of a person?'

Mina nodded. 'Yes, fears and fancy can delude us.'

Nellie selected a *macaron*, tasted it, and smiled. 'The art of the conjuror is to ensure that the audience sees what he wants them to see and does not see what must remain hidden if the illusion is to work. This does not always mean that things are concealed; it may only require that they are misinterpreted. To achieve this, he must lead the onlookers' attention away from what is important and direct it to matters that are not. Events that are seen but appear to be trivial and may even be forgotten by observers may be crucial to the entire proceeding. Now, you told me that you were watching very carefully when you heard the sound of the pencil on the slate.'

'Yes, I think everyone was. Mr Castlehouse's thumb was on the table, and did not move, and Mr Myles and the other gentleman who held the slate seemed quite unable to detect what was happening.'

'That is because nothing *was* happening. I suspect that the sound was produced not by chalk on a slate, but by Mr Castlehouse scratching a fingernail on the table.'

'So, when were the messages written?'

'Angelo, when he exposed Mr Ellison, stated that it was quite possible for messages to be written on a slate without making any sound at all, and without the

551

other man holding it to be aware of it. All it needed was for the medium to make some trembling movements to suggest that some great power was passing through his body, and that would be enough to conceal what he was doing.'

Mina cast her mind back to the event. 'I think Mr Castlehouse did do something of the sort. But not when we heard the sound of writing. Well — the sound we all took to be writing. So, the message was written — when — before the sound?'

'You said that the slate was held under the table for ten minutes without result.'

'Yes, and then he brought it out and showed it to us. It was blank.'

'On both sides?'

Mina paused for thought. 'I assumed so. But now you ask, I am not sure.'

'Half the people there will swear on the bible that they saw both sides blank. Some will say they were only shown the side that was against the table, the side where the piece of chalk was laid, while others remain unsure. I would be willing to wager that you were only shown the side that was uppermost.'

'Are you saying he wrote on the underside? But there was no chalk there. The chalk was between the slate and the table.'

'That was not the chalk he used to write. It is easy enough to conceal a piece of chalk in the fingernail. He might even have a tailor's thimble with a piece of chalk glued to it in his pocket, that he slips on his finger before he places the slate under the table.'

'So,' said Mina, thinking it through. 'He places the slate under the table and writes on the underside. Then, he draws out the slate for the first inspection, and shows us only the blank side?'

'Yes.'

'But when he next withdrew it, the writing was on the upper side. So — he must have turned it over before he replaced it?'

'Yes.'

'Can he do that without anyone noticing?'

'Oh yes, it is easily done if he is dexterous enough.'

'But the writing — and I am sure of this, because I paid particular attention to it — was at the far end of the slate from his hand, a place he could not have reached while his thumb was on the table.'

'Did he perform any action as he took the slate out to look at it the first time?'

'I don't think so. No. Well, he rubbed it with a cloth. Oh! Oh I see. Or at least I didn't see. The cloth was a cover for some action he performed. Now I understand! The use of the cloth seemed to have one purpose but actually it had another. He used it as a cover so he could turn the slate around before he replaced it.'

'Now, I can't prove that is how it was done, but that is my guess. I would not expose the methods of a conjuror, but Mr Ellison denied conjuring and said he received messages from the spirits. What we have discussed is what Angelo said was the method by which Mr Ellison worked his frauds, and he made his conclusions public.'

Mina sipped her tea, thoughtfully. 'I can see now that Mr Castlehouse could have written the short messages himself, but what about the message on the hinged slate? That was a long piece, covering most of the slate. It must have been prepared before, but I examined all the slates very carefully.'

'If you were free to examine them that was quite deliberate. And there would have been nothing unusual about them. Were they all of the same type?'

'Yes, I think so.'

'I am sure they were. He would have had an identical set of slates already prepared, kept hidden, perhaps under his coat, and there are a multitude of ways he could have distracted his audience so as to make the substitution. A skilled man could do it in moments and never be suspected.'

'The other people who attended were convinced he was genuine. Even those who were not sure of him at the start were won over by the end. How could I convince someone that he is a mere conjuror? I am not a magician, or ever likely to be. And if someone receives a message that comforts them, they will be most unwilling to doubt it.'

'Is he demanding large sums, like Ellison?'

'Not as far as I know. Not yet. Two shillings a performance, and he gets as many as he can crowd into his rooms.'

'Would you like to test him?' Nellie smiled mischievously.

'How might I do that?'

'You could try taking along your own slate for him to use. A double slate hinged in the middle is best, as you can then tie it closed with a cord. It must be a type different to the ones Castlehouse uses. It is unlikely that he will have something identical that he can substitute for yours. But all the same, do take the precaution of marking it in some secret way so there is no doubt that it is yours. Place the piece of chalk there yourself, then close and tie it securely. You must do your best to observe it constantly, in fact try not to let go of it even for a moment.'

'Do you think he would agree to this?'

'I think he would. After all, it would not reflect well on him if he refused in front of so many people. He might even see it as an advantage to have you test him in that way, as your attention would then be fastened on your own slates and not on his. If he is the trickster we suspect him to be, then he will obtain results from his own slates, but not with yours, and he will then make some excuse, perhaps claim that the spirits are not active.'

Mina nodded. 'That is a good test, but a believer would accept his explanation.'

'Oh, do not think you can expose him in a single visit. Tell him that you would like to return and bring your own slates once more. He may then decide to trick you. If he asks you to make a second trial, do so. He will in the meantime try to obtain a set of slates that could pass for yours, and if he succeeds, then he will prepare them before the demonstration with a message, and using some means of distracting your attention, substitute his own. But his slates will not have your secret mark, and you can then point this out.' Nellie took another *macaron*. 'Are you prepared to do this?'

'I have done far worse. Will you be able to come with me? It would be so much better to have your eye on the proceedings.'

'I should like nothing better, but Mr Jordan and I are going to London for a fortnight where he means to display me to a host of dull men who speak only of profit, and their duller wives who speak of nothing at all, often at great length. I shall miss our conversations.'

'I expect you will miss Richard also,' said Mina with just a hint of potential mischief in her voice.

'He is such delightful company, but I am sorry to say that Mr Jordan cannot abide him, and only permits him in the house when part of a large company so he may safely ignore him without appearing to be openly impolite.'

Mina wondered if Mr Jordan's decision to remove his wife from Brighton and introduce her to London's commercial society had anything to do with Richard's recent appearance. 'I feel you are not happy,' she ventured.

'One does not marry for happiness in this world,' said Nellie. 'And certainly not for love, not of the romantic kind at any rate. Love may grow, even on barren ground, but once it has bloomed it can only fade, and lead to disappointment. Marriage is woman's only real business and she must make a profit from it. I will not always look as I do now, but I must make sure to do so for as long as possible.' She stretched out her hand for another *macaron*, but thought better of it.

Chapter Twenty-Three

That evening Mr Honeyacre had been kind enough to engage a cab and send it to collect Mina so she could be conveyed to his home with the minimum of trouble. He currently lodged in a superior apartment far from the low-lying centre of Brighton and the damp collections of mists that settled there. He favoured the elevated eastern part with its bracing air, although sufficiently distant from the sea to avoid the glare of the winter sun from the steel grey water.

The visitors were entertained in a large drawing room, furnished for peaceful repose, with a substantial fire blazing in a brass-fronted grate that amplified the golden flames. There were armchairs and sofas replete with deep comfortable cushions, and thick-fringed draperies everywhere to prevent draughts. Gas lamps glowed from cut-glass lanterns like so many full moons, and paintings in elaborate frames hung from panelled walls. On the sideboard was a large tureen from which a delicious savoury scent emanated, and there were soup cups and plates piled with thin slices of bread and butter, as well as pies, tarts, salads, roast meats and relishes. A tower of small plates accompanied by dessert forks held the promise of another course.

Mr Honeyacre, with a hopeful smile fastened to his face, greeted his guests as they arrived, while Miss Macready, standing by his side like a monolith, looked on with features of stone.

Mrs Brendel, proudly displaying a new winter ensemble in dark red, remarkably like the blue one that Nellie had worn to the séance, swept into the room like a fighting ship, with her daughter, a reluctant ghost dressed in pale violet, trailing after her. Mina, while not warming to Mrs Brendel's company, could quite see why Richard admired the older woman's energy more than the insipid attractions of Miss Athene.

'Mrs Brendel, Miss Brendel, it is my great honour to introduce you to my dear friend, Miss Macready,' said Mr Honeyacre in a voice that shook just a little.

'Delighted to make your acquaintance!' gushed Mrs Brendel.

'Likewise,' said Miss Macready, but her eyes said something else.

Mr Honeyacre's manservant, Gillespie, a tall fellow, dignified and impeccable, ushered the visitors to seats and placed side tables within convenient reach. 'What a charming apartment!' exclaimed Mrs Brendel, carefully ensuring that her daughter took the place closest to herself. 'How lovely this must be in the summer!'

'Brighton has its charms at any time of the year,' said Mr Honeyacre, 'although I shall not make it my home for much longer, as I plan to live in the country.'

'But I can hardly believe you mean to remove from such a delightful location.'

'Oh, I shall still frequent the coast and enjoy the sea air, the galleries, museums and concerts, that is for certain, but I am determined to open up my manor house in Ditchling Hollow, which is not far from town, and entertain there. It has lain empty for too long.'

'A manor house?' Mrs Brendel could hardly have appeared more pleased if it had been hers. 'But is it entirely closed up at present?'

'No, my housekeeper and her husband live in the servants' quarters and look after the house and grounds for me, or it would undoubtedly have fallen into dangerous disrepair. When I told them of my intention to return they were delighted. The entire property is now being cleaned and restored. I even mean to engage my former cook who has not been entirely happy in her new situation since I went abroad and would be very pleased to come and manage my kitchen again.'

'Is it not a very ancient property?' said Miss Macready. 'I am not sure that such a house can be made entirely comfortable. Are there no horrid draughts, and what of the noise of the wind in chimneys and creaking boards keeping everyone awake at night?'

'I do not recall it being so inhospitable before,' said Mr Honeyacre. 'And I am sure that any defects, if there be such, can be corrected. If you would only agree to view the house I am sure you would see how it can be made very comfortable indeed.'

Miss Macready did not look convinced.

'Perhaps it is haunted?' ventured Mrs Brendel. 'I believe so many of these old houses are.'

'I have never experienced anything to suggest it, and neither have my servants,' said Mr Honeyacre. 'I wonder if Miss Scarletti might venture an opinion. Have you ever seen a ghost?'

'I have not,' said Mina. 'I do not say that I will never see one, only that I have not yet done so.'

'Neither have I,' said Miss Macready, in a voice that would have dismissed a dozen inquisitive ghosts, 'and I have no wish to. I am sorry to say it in this company, but I feel that no good can come of calling up spirits.'

'Ah, but I hope you do not think that my daughter does so?' said Mrs Brendel. 'The spirits come to her, she does not call them and has no means of dismissing them.'

Miss Brendel had been sitting silently in her drift of violet silk, like a drowning woman in a river waiting for her skirts to drag her down. 'I do not call them, I assure you,' she said softly. 'I have often wished them not to come, and when they do, I have asked them to leave me, but they do not, they will go only in their own good time.'

556

'Well, let us have some delicious soup before it cools,' said Mr Honeyacre, cheerily. 'Gillespie, please serve our guests.'

The manservant ladled the soup deftly into cups and brought it to the guests with a serving of bread and butter. It was a concoction of boiled fowl and leeks, a very grateful drink on a winter's day. Athene took a cup, but her mother, while accepting bread and butter for herself, declined it on her daughter's behalf. There was much appreciative sipping and complimentary comments.

Miss Macready drained her cup, and beckoned Gillespie to serve her a second portion. 'Miss Brendel, I do not mean to insult you, or call into question what you claim, but I must ask you this; how can you be certain that the spirits you see are really who they purport to be?'

Athene allowed the tip of her tongue to savour the last drop of soup on her lips, and put the cup down. 'All I can tell you is that I have never seen anything that has frightened me, and no-one who has attended the evenings has ever felt alarmed or upset.'

'Only benevolent spirits reach out to my dear daughter,' said Mrs Brendel. 'She has been most carefully brought up, and properly instructed in the scriptures. Her likeness will shortly grace the pages of a society journal of the most elevated character!' Mrs Brendel glanced about her as if to imply that neither of the other ladies present had any chance of being so honoured.

'But what I don't understand,' persisted Miss Macready, 'is that some of the spirits are of those who have not yet passed?'

'Yes, sometimes they are,' said Miss Brendel.

'There was that business with poor Mr Hay that was in the newspapers.' Miss Macready turned to Mina. 'He was the unfortunate Scotch gentleman who made away with himself. Now that was a troubled spirit.' She put two thin slices of bread and butter together and ate them as one.

'Did he appear to you before or after he passed away?' asked Mina.

'I — I don't really know,' said Miss Brendel. 'I only know that I saw him.'

Mrs Brendel interrupted in a very determined manner. 'I believe you will find that he appeared before Athene at the very second he passed.' She seemed so confident in this assertion that no-one sought to contradict her, although Mina thought there were any number of reasons to question this statement.

'Well, I only hope we shall have no such things as that tonight!' said Miss Macready.

Once the soup cups were cleared the guests were invited to help themselves from the plates on the sideboard with the deferential assistance of Mr Gillespie. Mina selected a slice of savoury pie and salad, Mrs Brendel served herself with pie, tart and relishes, and placed some slices of lean meat on another dish which she brought to her daughter, and Miss Macready piled a plate high with some of

557

everything. Gillespie, who clearly knew what his master liked, brought him a slice of tart, although he looked too distracted to eat it.

Miss Brendel picked listlessly at the meat with her fork. Her mother spoke to her quietly and gently, but Mina was unable to hear the words, and the room then fell into the soft sounds that people made when trying to eat politely.

Miss Brendel had been staring at her plate, but daring to glance up while lifting some shreds of meat to her mouth, looked sorrowful, paused, and slowly put the fork down, the food untasted. 'I see a lady,' she said faintly.

'You mean — a lady in spirit?' asked Mr Honeyacre, hopefully.

Miss Macready made a sharp intake of breath and placed a hand over her face as if shielding herself from contamination.

'Yes, I am sure she is. She sits peacefully, but she does not move. I'm not sure why that is. I cannot say whether or not she has passed.'

'Where is she?' asked Mina.

Miss Brendel hesitated, and appeared for once curiously unwilling to reveal this information. At last she said, 'She is there, sitting on the sofa beside Mr Honeyacre.'

'Oh!' exclaimed Honeyacre glancing at the empty place at his side. 'Does she speak?'

'No. Her lips do not move, her eyes do not blink, but her form is very clear.'

'Describe her, please, I beg you!'

Miss Brendel laid her plate aside, and studied what no-one else could see. 'The lady has a round face, her hair is grey, and there are little curls at her temples. Still she says nothing, does nothing. There is a cameo brooch at her throat and on her lap a puppy dog. Her hand rests on its back, like so...' Miss Brendel gestured with her fingers, held as if curling affectionately around the cherished animal. 'There is a portrait behind her, not one in this room, but somewhere else. An old portrait, the man wears a ruff and has a pointed beard.'

During this speech Miss Macready's protective hand had gradually dropped to her side, and she stared at Miss Brendel with an expression that combined astonishment with outrage.

'Why, you describe my dear Eleanor and her favourite pet, also a portrait she much admired,' said Mr Honeyacre, joyfully. 'That is marvellous, all the more so because I know you can never have met her, but your description — it can be none other! Are you sure she does not speak?' he continued. 'Is she happy? Is she at peace? Does she smile? What message does she have for me?'

Miss Brendel looked blank, then alarmed. She shook her head as if trying to dislodge an unwelcome thought.

'Oh, but I think I can guess what she is saying,' cried Mr Honeyacre enthusiastically. 'She wishes me well in all my future endeavours, does she not?'

Miss Brendel appeared to be struggling with a conflict between her ideas and what she could see. She looked away from the vision. 'I — don't know. I am not sure.'

'But you must be!' he insisted.

'Mr Honeyacre,' said Mrs Brendel firmly, 'if my daughter cannot hear the message then she cannot hear it.'

'She smiles, though, does she not? Eleanor smiles? Please say she does!'

Mrs Brendel took her daughter's hand and patted it. 'There, my dear. Don't strain yourself. Just rest and take a deep breath and open your eyes so you can see properly. It's a simple question. Does the lady smile, or does she frown?' Was it imagination or did Mina see Mrs Brendel give her daughter's hand a squeeze on the final word.

Miss Brendel stared at her mother. 'She frowns. Yes. She frowns.'

'No! Surely not!' exclaimed Mr Honeyacre. 'It can't be! Eleanor would be happy for me, I know it.'

'Oh, I have heard enough of this!' said Miss Macready, putting aside her plate with a loud bang on the table that made everyone start, and rising to her feet in a fury. 'What is happening here? Is it a play? Is it a pantomime? Perhaps a comedy to be given at the music hall. Will the lady float up into the air? Will the puppy dog do tricks?'

Mr Honeyacre rose quickly from his chair. 'Miss Macready, I am sure nothing is wrong. Miss Brendel, as you see, is sincere.'

'A sincere fraud!' bellowed Miss Macready. 'It is outrageous; I will not be played upon in this way! There has been some confederacy between you, I know it!'

Athene started to weep. 'Please! I don't know anything about it, I only say what I see!'

'Miss Macready, I merely want you to understand that there is no danger in communicating with the world of the spirit,' pleaded Mr Honeyacre.

The lady uttered a derisive laugh. 'If that is indeed what is happening, which I somehow doubt.' She turned to Mina. 'And what of you, Miss Scarletti? What part did you play in all this?'

'None at all,' said Mina, bemused at being suddenly taken to task in that way.

'I am not so sure of that,' Miss Macready hissed with a curl of her lip.

'But my dear —' protested Mr Honeyacre.

Miss Macready rounded on him. 'Enough! I forbid you to address me so! I am appalled and insulted at being treated in this fashion. Do you think I am so foolish as to be taken in by such a sham? I am leaving this house now, and I have no intention of returning. Have your man call me a cab.'

'But —'

'Not another word! Now do as I say, or you will regret it! I am something in Brighton society, as you well know. If I have my way your reputation will not survive this!'

Mr Honeyacre looked defeated. He nodded and signalled to Gillespie, who, without a change in expression, went to fetch Miss Macready's cloak. The lady was gone within minutes, declining to take her leave of the company either by word or gesture.

Mr Honeyacre sat down heavily, silent and shocked, unable even to glance at his other guests. Mrs Brendel stayed beside her distressed daughter, stroking her hands. Miss Brendel turned to her with a tearful face. 'Did I say something wrong?'

'No, my dear, of course not. You cannot help what you see. You are not to blame if the truth is rejected or ill understood.'

Mina was not sure what to do. It was an embarrassing situation but she felt that if she was to learn anything she ought to remain at least until it was suggested the guests should go. Nothing more was said for a time, but whether that was because there was nothing that could properly be said, or Mr Honeyacre and the Brendels did not wish to discuss what had occurred with someone else present, Mina could not decide.

Gillespie returned. 'I secured a cab, and have seen Miss Macready safely on her way. Will there be anything more, sir?'

'It is time we were going,' said Mrs Brendel. 'Athene needs her rest. These events always take so much out of her.'

Mr Honeyacre sighed. 'I am so sorry it has come to this. Of course, Miss Brendel must be our first concern, and I will see that you are both conveyed home at once. Miss Scarletti — I cannot say how upsetting this has been and I am deeply ashamed that you have been obliged to witness it.'

Mina decided not to say that it had been a more than usually interesting evening. 'One can never predict how these things will turn out,' she said.

He gestured to the laden sideboard. 'Please, everyone, select anything you wish to complete your supper. Gillespie will make up a parcel.'

This was soon done, and before long the Brendels and Mina had both departed, sharing a cab since their homes were so close.

Miss Brendel was a mere wraith of herself. She didn't speak, but sat beside her mother, who held her in her arms and rested the girl's head on her shoulder. 'My poor dear,' she said soothingly, 'we will go home and you will have some of your lovely tisane, and then you will rest and you will be as good as new in the morning. That dreadful woman was quite deranged. It wouldn't surprise me if Mr Honeyacre never spoke to her again. And to think it was rumoured that he was intending to marry her. If you ask me, he has had a lucky escape. He is such a very good man, and deserves far better.'

Mina said nothing, but thought back to what Mr Honeyacre had said when he had invited her to supper. His declared intention in introducing Miss Macready to the Brendels was to allay her doubts about spiritualism by showing that a medium could be respectable. Mina was now beginning to think that he had only told her half the story, and had been planning far more than just a sociable encounter. What could not be in doubt was that the evening had, from his point of view, been a disaster. Far from strengthening the attachment to Miss Macready, the debacle had parted him from her, perhaps forever. The question arose whether the turn of fate had occurred by chance, or if, unknown to Mr Honeyacre, it had been engineered by Mrs Brendel.

The motive was all too clear. Although Mr Honeyacre was the oldest of Miss Brendel's single male visitors, he was also the most promising. Young Mr Tasker, for all his interest in music, did not warm to the lady. Mr Conroy had four small children who needed mothering, a task for which Miss Brendel was ill suited. Mr Phipps was not yet something in the world. Dr Hamid was too recently widowed to be seriously thought of. Mr Dawson was ardent but had no fortune. Mr Fernwood's dress marked him indelibly as trade. Mr Honeyacre, however, was wealthy, eager to marry and had no dependents.

There was nothing Mina could do in the face of these frauds and delusions. She could voice her ideas, but there was no proof. She thought it unlikely, when Mr Honeyacre had made his arrangement with Mrs Brendel, that any money had changed hands. The only thing that had changed hands was an envelope, and Mina was beginning to suspect what had been in it.

Chapter Twenty-Four

Next morning, with the breakfast table groaning with Mr Honeyacre's discarded pies and tarts, Mina was surprised to receive a note from Miss Macready asking if she might call. Since Mina's last conversation with this lady had ended with an accusation of deceit, she was not sure what to make of the request except that the interview promised to be more interesting than most. The note revealed that Miss Macready lived in a highly desirable apartment building in Kemp Town, which confirmed Mina's opinion that she was not without means. Mina said nothing about the proposed call to Richard, and decided also not to describe the turbulent end to the supper, saying only that the previous evening had been one of good food and conversation. He was due to sketch Miss Brendel again, and she did not want him to accidentally reveal that he had learned about Mr Honeyacre's private gathering and its outcome, or the Brendels might suspect a connection. Instead she wrote to Dr Hamid saying that she had had a very instructive evening which she would describe when they next met, and replied to Miss Macready saying that she would be delighted to receive her.

After a hearty luncheon in which Richard was able to demolish much of the excess foodstuffs, he departed with the intention of drawing the chain pier and then proceeding to Mr Dorry's gallery.

Miss Macready arrived soon afterwards. She was conducted into the parlour, where Mina greeted her politely, offered her a comfortable chair, faced her with equanimity, and waited to hear what she had to say. It was clear from her expression that Miss Macready's anger of the previous evening had evaporated very little considering that many hours, a night's sleep and two meals had intervened. Nevertheless, she was calmer and did not look at Mina with the same ferocity.

'I have given a great deal of thought to the events of last night. I recall that in my annoyance, which I am sure you will agree was perfectly natural under the circumstances, I suggested that you might have had a hand in the atrocious deception that was practised on me. You denied it, and I can now inform you that on further consideration, I accept that denial.'

'Thank you,' said Mina, realising that this was the nearest thing to an apology she was likely to hear.

'Of course, your reputation in this town is one of uncovering fraud and deception, not of promoting it. Therefore, it is most improbable that you conspired against me. In fact, your part in the affair has now become clear. You could not have known it, but you were invited there as one who inspires trust, to be a witness to a deception, and to be deceived yourself.'

'I was invited because Mr Honeyacre hoped that you would consent to meet Miss Brendel and he thought you would not do so unless I was present.'

'In that he was correct.'

'He places considerable value on your good opinion. I believe that he hoped to allay your concerns about spiritualism, and so smooth the way to a closer association. What transpired was as much a surprise to him and to me as it was to you.'

'That much was apparent. Well, at least you have not disappointed me. But you have seen this young person's performances before. What do you think of them?'

'I have doubts about Miss Brendel's claims to be a medium, but thus far I have not been able to explain her visions. She may be feigning, of course, but somehow I don't think she is, or her descriptions would have more purpose, and appear to be designed. I think she really is seeing what she says she does, but how that comes about, I can't tell. Perhaps she has some disease of the eye. Usually she sees very clear images of people she knows, such as her father, but there are also vaguer descriptions of others, perhaps people she has just seen in passing. But last night was different. She saw a lady who she was able to describe in considerable detail, such that Mr Honeyacre was able to identify her as his late wife, yet Miss Brendel cannot have met her.'

Miss Macready laughed. It was a grating noise at the back of her throat, with no hint of humour. 'As to that, there is no mystery to me, and I am sure you will be interested to have an explanation. You cannot have failed to notice that the image Miss Brendel claimed to see was of a lady seated in front of a portrait, and not moving or speaking, a lady with a puppy dog in her lap.'

'Yes, and again that was different to her previous visions. She usually sees people walking about, or even if seated they are moving in some way. This was more like —'

'Like she was describing a painting, or a photograph?'

Mina was pleased that the suggestion came from another. She was feeling surer of her conclusion. 'Yes.'

'I do not know whether to be angry with her or offer my sympathy. Personally, I think the mother is the one to blame. What Miss Brendel saw, or claimed to see was not the late Mrs Honeyacre at all, but a portrait of her. It was a *carte de visite* made about two years before her death. I know because I have seen it. She is seated with her pet dog on her lap, in front of a painting. There are a number of these cards in an album. She liked to collect them. I expect Mr Honeyacre forgot that I had looked through the album or did not realise how well I had noted the portrait. Either that or he was not aware that Miss Brendel would describe it in such detail.'

'Then Miss Brendel must have seen the portrait in question.'

'She must, and there is only one reasonable way she could have done so, if Mr Honeyacre himself provided her with a copy.'

'I am sure you are right.'

Miss Macready shook her head with an expression of grim distaste. 'What a dreadful business this is! Not only does he have no understanding of what he is meddling with, but he hopes to draw me into it with fraud and trickery. Outrageous!'

'He may not have seen it as defrauding you, since he sincerely wants you to believe what he himself believes.'

Mina's attempt to soothe the bad feelings between Mr Honeyacre and his intended fell on unsympathetic ears. 'Do not speak for him; he is a scoundrel, a deceiver! He tried to manoeuvre me in a most underhand way. That is an action I shall never forgive. He wants me to condone his dangerous and foolhardy pursuit of spiritualism, something he knows full well I will have no truck with.'

She made a dismissive gesture. 'But let him do as he wants. I care nothing about him anymore. He has been hinting for some while that he will offer me marriage and I had thought I might accept him, but that will not happen now. I am done with Mr Honeyacre. I have more than enough money of my own, and I have no wish to see my fortune turned over to him so he can spend it on mediums conjuring who knows what, and restoring that horrid old ruin of a house in the middle of nowhere. I much prefer to live in Brighton as he is well aware.'

'Have you spoken to him since yesterday evening?'

'No. He has sent me several notes and I have returned them all unopened.'

'Would you like me to speak to him?'

'On my behalf? That is quite unnecessary. I have nothing more to I wish to communicate, and there is nothing I wish to hear from him.'

Mina could see that Miss Macready was the kind of lady who once her mind was thoroughly made up, would not relent, and there was little point in her pleading Mr Honeyacre's case any further.

Her visitor rose to depart. 'I wish you well Miss Scarletti. I shall seek contentment in my own way and not depend on another for it. We may meet again; I would not object to that.'

Soon after Miss Macready's departure a note arrived from Mr Honeyacre requesting Mina's permission to call, to which she replied in the affirmative. He arrived soon afterwards, bearing a posy of hothouse flowers, which he proffered as one might a hopeful addition to an altar. He was miserable and desperately apologetic, with the strained look of a man who had been without sleep. It was probably only the ministrations of his manservant that had sent him out in his customary state of good grooming.

'I am so terribly sorry for what occurred last night,' he said, rubbing chilled hands before the parlour fire. 'I know you will have concluded that the upset was all my fault, which indeed it was, and I have suffered mightily for my dreadful mistake. But you must believe me, I never intended that it should happen in that way, which only shows the unpredictable nature of spirits, I suppose. One may not command them to do one's bidding as one might a servant. I called on Mrs Brendel this morning and spoke to her at some length. She was very kind, far kinder than I deserved, and has explained everything to me.'

'And now I hope you will explain it to me,' said Mina.

'Yes, yes of course. You merit no less.' He took a deep breath of preparation. 'You may have heard, because I know it is gossiped about in Brighton, that it is my hope to one day make Miss Macready my wife. That is true, but unfortunately there are certain obstacles in the way, such that I have not yet dared to ask the question. The chief of those is my close interest in spiritualism, which she perceives as dangerous, and, of course, in the wrong hands it might be. But I cannot persuade her that it is entirely safe provided one only uses the most devout and respectable practitioners. I also believe that she might be afraid that Eleanor's presence is still influencing my life and that she would disapprove of a successor. That may well be at the root of her concerns about living in the manor house, which Eleanor had so loved and wanted to make our home. I had hoped that Miss Brendel with her gentleness and modesty would easily overcome the first of those objections. There was also, to my mind, a very strong possibility that she might be able to pass on a message from Eleanor to the effect that she was content with my choice. I asked Mrs Brendel if that could be achieved and she said she thought it could. But somehow, it all went counter to the way I had anticipated. I really don't understand it,' he concluded sadly.

'You gave Mrs Brendel a copy of a photograph of your late wife,' said Mina.

He had been staring into the fire, but looked up, startled. 'How do you know that?'

'It was obvious. Both to me and to Miss Macready.'

'But is that not a commonly done thing — to supply a picture of the subject one wishes to contact? The medium uses it as a focus for her energy.'

'Is that what Mrs Brendel said?'

'Yes. I have consulted other mediums and many of them ask for something similar.'

'And do they then produce apparitions of the deceased?'

'Indeed they do,' said Honeyacre, missing the implications of Mina's comment. 'But I can see that you are not willing to be convinced of this,' he added, regretfully.

'My mind remains open, but it has not yet been satisfied.'

'I am always disappointed when a person of keen perception cannot see the truth. One day, I am sure you will. But that is not the reason I am here — I was hoping that you might agree to intercede with Miss Macready on my behalf. She is angry with me and has returned all my messages, but I am sure that if she would just allow me to see her and explain my intentions, I could make amends. I know she said some hard words to you, but that is just her way. She undoubtedly respects your opinion.'

'It so happens that I spoke to her earlier today.'

'You have? How come?'

'She called on me. I did attempt to calm the troubled waters that lie between you, but I am sorry to say that she was adamant that she no longer wishes to be friends with you. If you are looking for a wife then I suggest you abandon all thoughts of Miss Macready and make an offer to Miss Brendel.'

His eyes opened wide in astonishment. 'But I have no interest in Miss Brendel! None whatsoever! Whatever gave you that idea?'

'Oh dear. Mrs Brendel will be very upset to know that, as she went to such great pains to chase away Miss Macready.'

Honeyacre struggled to understand. 'Chase away? Whatever do you mean?'

'Mrs Brendel wishes to marry her daughter to a gentleman of fortune. You are a gentleman of fortune. The only obstacle to the match, as far as she was aware, was Miss Macready. You must have suggested to Mrs Brendel that you hoped to receive a message that would encourage Miss Macready to believe that your late wife approved of your intentions. What she actually and quite deliberately arranged was the exact opposite. She must have shown her daughter the portrait you provided and asked her to describe it as if it was a vision. She also prompted her daughter to suggest that your late wife disapproved of your intentions. But Miss Macready had already seen the portrait in an album and recognised Miss Brendel's detailed description of it, so exposing the deception.'

Mr Honeyacre gasped and ground the heels of his hands into his eyes. It was some moments before he could speak. 'That dreadful conniving woman! Have I been taken for such a fool?'

'It seems so,' said Mina, softly.

'But Miss Brendel's powers are genuine, I am sure of it!'

'I cannot say if she simply memorised the picture or if studying it actually produced a vision. That is a matter for a doctor or an oculist to advise on.'

Mr Honeyacre sat in a welter of unhappiness. 'Well, you will think me such a silly old man.'

'Not at all. Please, may I offer you some refreshment?'

'No, thank you, I have no appetite.' He stared into the fire again, and there was a long reflective silence. 'The truth is,' he said at last, 'I lead such a solitary existence.

I have wealth, I have comfort, I have friends, I have all the beautiful things I have collected over the years, but no companionship. What I seek is a respectable, sensible, intelligent lady to share my life, one with whom I can converse on subjects such as art and literature.' A thought struck him, and he turned to Mina. 'Miss Scarletti, I don't suppose you might do me the honour of considering —?'

'No.'

'But if you would just take a little time and give it some thought —'

Mina was about to refuse him a second time, when the parlour door burst open, admitting Richard, impetuously tousled. 'Mina, my darling, I have just come from Mr Dorry's and he has actually advanced me some funds on the drawings!'

Mr Honeyacre sprang to his feet in a state of confusion. 'I am so sorry!' he gasped. 'My apologies for anything I might have said. I have taken up too much of your time already. Please don't trouble the maid, I will see myself out.'

He dashed past Richard without even a glance at him, and moments later there was the sound of the front door opening and closing.

'Well, how very peculiar!' exclaimed Richard. 'What was that all about?'

Mina smiled. 'Mr Honeyacre has just proposed marriage to me, and I refused him, but since he is now under the impression that I am your mistress, I will not need to refuse him again.'

Richard laughed. 'So, he's seen off the old dragon, has he? Well done! He's not a bad sort, and pretty well heeled. You might do a lot worse. I'll go after him and explain, shall I?'

'Please don't. I doubt that he will be spreading my shame all over Brighton, and if he did, no-one would believe it. In any case, I have no wish to marry Mr Honeyacre or anyone else. Wait until you are done pretending to be Mr Henry and then you may set the record straight.'

Richard seemed happy with that arrangement, and flung himself into a chair. 'Is there any tea on its way?'

Mina rang to summon Rose. 'When are you due to visit Miss Brendel again?'

'This very evening.'

'Has anything been said about payment for your sketch?'

'Not yet, but I have promised them the original when it is done. That ought to be worth something, surely.'

'I am pleased you have some payment from Mr Dorry.'

'Yes, two guineas. He wants six more pictures, though.' Richard looked unenthusiastic at the prospect.

'I assume you are signing them as Richard Henry?'

'No, I'm not signing them at all.'

'Oh? But why? I thought pictures ought to be signed.'

'Mr Dorry has explained to me that at present it is better not to. A picture that is not signed attracts more interest because there is a mystery about it.'

Mina thought this a little strange, but as she was not well versed in the art world, was unable to question it. The one person who might have been able to advise her, Mr Honeyacre, was unlikely to welcome her company.

Chapter Twenty-Five

Mina peered out of her window at passers-by battling through showers of needle-like rain, driven by eddying gales, and saw the baleful threat of approaching December. She thought of Richard spending his days trying to draw the sea and was thankful he had a warm coat and hat. Mina loved looking at the sea, but in winter she dared not venture to the promenade on foot. One thunderous wave, one blast of wind, could sweep her to that eternity where all her questions would be answered. She could be patient. There were too many challenges, too many concerns in her earthly life to give her time to think about the one to come.

Dr Hamid arrived, eager to hear about the supper with Mr Honeyacre and to reassure himself that Mina had come to no harm from her risky expedition. On learning about the debacle and subsequent visits of Miss Macready and Mr Honeyacre, he became concerned. 'We now have a strong indication of the ways in which the mother is both controlling and exploiting her daughter, who is in fragile health. I am sorry to say that I fear this will not end well.'

'Is there really nothing you can do?'

'There is no proof that she is actually ill-treating the girl. You said that she was all tenderness and care towards her. The tea is a calming and beneficial brew. I could see no obvious symptoms of disease, but concerns about Miss Brendel's health have already been expressed and dismissed. If you should learn anything that suggests Mrs Brendel is harming her daughter, let me know and I will act at once. But we may have answers to some of our questions when we see Mr Marriott. He will be here tomorrow afternoon at three.'

Dear Edward,

I trust that everyone is as well as can be expected. I wait anxiously for news of Mr Inskip. This uncertainty as to his whereabouts must be extremely distressing.

There is good news about Richard, who now has a patron for his artwork, a Mr Dorry who has a gallery in Brighton, and is reputedly very important.

Fondest love,

Mina

Dear Mina,

I am no further forward, and I feel we must consider Mr Inskip lost, although I dare not say so to Mother or Enid. Agatha's father is pressing me to name a day for the wedding, but I feel it will be hard to do so if this matter is not resolved one way or another. Indeed Mother has hinted in the most obvious manner that she would be quite unable to think of attending a happy occasion while her thoughts are with Enid's plight. My wishes are not to be considered, of course, and I must be patient until June at least.

I have now heard from the various railway, telegraph and steamer companies, and can confirm that Mr Inskip has not dispatched a telegram for several weeks, neither has he travelled by train or steamer in the last two months, or even so much as purchased a ticket. I then thought to make enquiries about the weather in that ungodly part of the world, and it was as I feared. Winter arrived early this year with unusual severity and there were heavy snows and avalanches on the Borgo Pass, wherever that is. The area was blocked, and no coaches have been able to get through in either direction. Anyone trapped there and unable to reach shelter would be unlikely to be found alive. There are two possible hopes, one is that the snow descended before Mr Inskip's coach entered the pass, in which case he might have been able to return to the castle of his client, and is safe, but unable to travel or send messages. The other is that although trapped, he might have been able to reach an inn. The men of that harsh region seem to subsist on the vilest of foodstuffs, but at least they know how to survive the winter. In either case he will be obliged to remain where he is until the weather clears and we will hear nothing from him until next spring.

I decided to inform Enid of this, as she has a right to know, but took care to tell her in the gentlest possible way that she must prepare herself for bad news. Her distress was so profound that, at first, she seemed unable to react at all. She did ask me how long it would be before Mr Inskip could be presumed dead, and I was obliged to inform her that the law requires seven years since he was last heard from. At this she flew into a tirade in which she was almost incoherent. I know she suffers but I wonder why she is obliged to do so at such great volume.

So, Richard has a patron? How extraordinary! I have heard of Mr Dorry who has a gallery in London, too. Perhaps there is more to my brother than I thought. Please make sure he continues to send sketches for the Journal. One a day ought not to tax his energies, surely.

The weather continues cold here. If Richard can send me back my coat and hat that would be appreciated.

Affct'ly,
Edward

Dear Mina,

The news that Richard has a rich patron for his art has brought a little light into my unhappy existence here. I always knew I could rely upon him. Please make sure he has everything he requires in the way of nourishment, a warm and pleasant place in which he can draw, and peace and quiet. I am sending him a few guineas so he cannot want for paint or whatever it is he uses. Really Edward is so mean with his wages, and I cannot persuade him even to indulge his own brother, it is positively cruel. He has complained so much about Richard borrowing his coat and hat that it has made my head spin. It would be very nice if Richard could write to me and say how he progresses, but I suppose he must be very busy, and perhaps I oughtn't to trouble him.

Enid and I are not to stir from the house or it might kill us both. London is awash with the most terrible diseases, and everyone thinks the Prince of Wales will die. The poor Queen, I know how she suffers!

There is no news of Mr Inskip. I don't know what Edward is doing, if anything, he tells me nothing at all. If he was interested in soothing my anguish he would go out there and look for himself, but he makes no attempt to do so, pleading business duties, which may just be an excuse. All he seems to talk about is Miss Hooper, or Agatha as I am expected to call her now, as we are almost related. I cannot see what he finds attractive in her, she is so very quiet and reserved, and says so little, but I suppose I must make the best of it. She has no interests at all apart from making pressed flowers, and that is of limited usefulness to a wife. At least there is money in the family.

Your beleaguered,

Mama

Mr Marriott was an oculist with a practice on the Old Steine. In addition to attending to his patients, he had made a great study of unusual conditions of the eye, and was consequently in demand for lectures on the subject. It was with keen anticipation, therefore, that Mina awaited his arrival together with Dr Hamid. Rose had been ordered to provide generous refreshments, and Richard was strictly enjoined not to interrupt their conference. He looked sulky for a moment when she told him this, but when she explained that it was a discussion on scientific matters, declared that it would probably have sent him to sleep in any case. He donned his coat and hat, which were looking in need of a good brushing, and took up his sketchbook and pencils. 'Now for something to draw! I still have to send sketches to Edward, more's the pity. What a slave driver he is! What do you suggest? Is the aquarium completed yet?'

'There is no hope of that until the contractor and the company have settled their differences in court. We are promised grand archways and gothic structures as well as gigantic fish, but all we have so far is a new sea wall and promenade by the East Cliff. You could try sketching fashionable persons visiting the Pavilion or the Dome.'

'Mr Dorry wants me to draw waves breaking against the end of the chain pier with a view of the Pavilion behind it.'

'Really?' Mina tried to imagine this. 'Can one see the Pavilion from the pier?'

'Not very well, but he said that didn't matter. Artists are allowed to move entire buildings if it makes for a better picture. Dashed cold work, though. I'm glad of this good coat!'

Mina didn't have the heart to ask him to return it.

Chapter Twenty-Six

Dr Hamid arrived promptly at 3pm, together with the distinguished oculist. The gentlemen were ushered into Mina's parlour, which had been made warm and welcoming. All three gathered about the table and Rose brought a tray of refreshments.

Mr Marriott was a tidy-looking individual, aged about fifty, his face adorned with neat gold-rimmed spectacles. He carried a little leather case, which he placed carefully on the floor beside him, and smiled as Mina gazed at it with interest. 'I like to make visual demonstrations to illustrate my words,' he said. 'All will be revealed.'

'I have already advised Mr Marriott of the reasons for this discussion,' said Dr Hamid. 'We are principally concerned with the phenomenon whereby a man or woman, who is apparently quite sane, sees apparitions. There are many questions to consider. Is this a natural process relating to the power of eyesight? Are such people sensitives who can see the souls of both the living and dead? Or is it the result of disease?'

Marriott nodded at each point as Dr Hamid spoke. 'These are not new questions; they have occupied the minds of men of science for almost a hundred years. In earlier times, it was rarely doubted that apparitions were due to some supernatural agency, especially if the person who saw them did not seem to be disordered in the mind. Have you by chance read the works of Sir David Brewster? His *Letters on Natural Magic*, especially.'

'I regret that I have not, but I will amend that fault,' said Dr Hamid, and Mina wrote the information in her notebook.

Marriott leaned back in his chair with a smile and laced his fingers. 'Brewster once wrote, "The human mind is at all times fond of the marvellous". He knew all too well that where a phenomenon may be explained either by a mundane truth or a more fantastical supposition, many persons would far prefer the latter; more than that, they will be irresistibly drawn to it, so it will be their very first conclusion. Now then —' he went on, raising a warning eyebrow — 'before I say any more, I have a word of caution. I speak only of our modern world, in which we may explain certain occurrences by means of scientific principles, which show that they do not bear the supernatural character often ascribed to them. I make no such claims for what is recorded in the Holy Scriptures and believed to be attributable to divine agency. That is something which I am sure we can agree is a quite different matter.'

'Leaving that aside, of course,' said Dr Hamid. 'Now, I appreciate that there are many instances where the organs of perception do not perform their proper function and mistakes will occur, but two of my patients who had otherwise good eyesight nevertheless reported phenomena which I found quite mystifying. They told me that they had seen ghosts of both the living and the dead; men, women and even animals. If this is due to a disease, is it the eye or the mind that is affected, or both? Or must we suppose that ghosts are real and some persons have unusually acute perception?'

'We must accept, however,' said Mina, 'that some people who claim to see ghosts are simply practising a deception. Both Dr Hamid and I have recently observed a Miss Brendel who claims to be a spirit medium and says she has visions of people both living and dead. I really don't know what to make of her.'

'Not all persons who claim to see visions are practising fraud,' said Marriott. 'There are many things to consider, not only the eye and the mind, but the feelings and beliefs and the state of health of the individual.'

'Ah, yes,' said Dr Hamid, thoughtfully.

'You have said that you believe your patients to have been of sound mind?'

'I do, and having observed Miss Brendel, I saw about her nothing to suggest mania or hysteria. I think she may have a weak constitution, but she seemed perfectly composed and sane. Neither was there anything to suggest feverishness. I am sure she was not under the influence of a drug. Since I am not her doctor and cannot examine her, I am unable to say more. Even my most sensitive questioning was greatly resented by her mother, who declared her daughter to be in good health, and said that every appearance to the contrary was misleading. I did wonder if Miss Brendel has a disease of the eye, which can so easily be missed.'

Marriott nodded sagely. 'Perhaps, but not necessarily. Even where there is no detectable fault, either in the eye or the brain, it can happen in certain states of bodily disturbance that are not located in either organ, that impressions which have their origins in the mind will determine what the eye sees. There are, of course, many instances which are well known to oculists where even in a person who enjoys perfect health, the eye can play tricks on the mind.'

Mina recalled how not long ago she had witnessed a conjuror's illusion in which it appeared that a disembodied hand was able to write, a trick created by the use of mirrors, and Nellie had once demonstrated that she was an adept at sleight of hand, making a card seem to disappear and reappear.

'The human eye is a truly marvellous thing,' enthused Mr Marriott, 'so singular, so exquisite, capable of such power and variety of movement. Compare sight with all the other senses — touch and taste may be exercised only by contact with our bodies, smell in close proximity, hearing at a further but measurable distance. The eye, however, can look to the heavens and see the stars. It is like a small *camera obscura.*'

He opened his leather case, selected a booklet entitled 'The Anatomy of the Eye' and opened it. 'Here you see a diagram of a section through the eye. It shows how light from external objects passes through the front of the eye and falls on the retina, this surface here at the back of the eye, and the impression is then conveyed via the optic nerve, which travels from the retina to the brain. Only then do we truly see.'

'But as you say, our eyes may be deceived,' said Mina. 'Conjurors do it all the time, they rely on it.'

'Indeed they can and most profoundly,' said Marriott. 'Either from the inner working of the mind, or from the dexterity and artistry of others, which persuade us that we have seen something impossible, '

'But the eye, even in full health, is not a perfect organ,' said Dr Hamid. 'Is it not true that in the place where the optic nerve leaves the eye, no image can be detected?'

'That is true,' said Marriott 'and it can be demonstrated very simply.' He removed a piece of card from his case. It was black apart from two white circles side by side and a few inches apart. 'Now then, if Miss Scarletti would be so kind, I will hold this card before her eyes.'

'Oh, please do,' said Mina eagerly.

He held up the card. 'Do you see the two white circles?'

'Yes, very clearly.'

'Now, if you would be so good, place your hand over your right eye, and direct your gaze to the circle on the left.'

Mina did so, and to her surprise the right hand circle had disappeared.

'Is the circle on the right visible?' asked Marriott.

'No. I can see only the one on the left.'

'Please don't be concerned, that is quite usual. Now, if you would cover your left eye and gaze on the right hand circle.'

Mina complied. 'The one on the left is not visible now.'

'Exactly. That is no trick; I do not have the skill of a conjuror. It merely shows that a small part of your retina, where the optic nerve leaves the eye, is insensible to light. When one has two eyes working together, this slight inconvenience is not noticeable. Another curious illusion is that when the eyes stare fixedly at an object, other objects which are seen indirectly nearby may seem to disappear and then reappear. It is a phenomenon which is especially powerful in semi-darkness.'

'And that is the condition under which most séances are conducted,' said Mina. 'In fact, I believe that people are far more likely to report seeing ghosts in the dark than the light.'

Marriott smiled. 'They are, and I believe the phenomenon may account for many tales of apparitions, and also for the fact that spectres are usually white. They are

574

white because in near darkness, no colours can be seen. Inanimate objects when seen by moonlight or the glow of a candle, especially ones of irregular shape, may have different parts that reflect light differently and might appear to change in form and even move. A figure might seem to vanish altogether.'

'Yet people commonly say that "seeing is believing",' Mina observed.

'They do, and often cannot or even refuse to accept how easily they can be deceived. If they see something they are unable to explain, and believe in ghosts and apparitions then their imaginations will do the rest. And remember, I speak only of the eye in full health.'

Mina pondered this statement. 'I have watched Miss Brendel very carefully, and listened to how she described her visions. At no time did she see something the rest of us saw and place a different interpretation on it. She claimed to see persons in the room that no-one else present could see. She said that they appeared to her to be quite real and moved as real people do. The only exception was when she claimed to see a vision of a lady who did not move, but she had previously only ever seen that lady in a portrait. My question is, were these pictures produced by the eye or the mind?'

'I have never met Miss Brendel, so it would be hard to say,' observed Marriott, cautiously. 'There are people who see visions produced by an overheated mind, and they often believe that demons are tormenting them. But what you describe as the very particular case of Miss Brendel does not smack of such disturbed behaviour. You think she is quite comfortable with her visions?'

'She is, yes, at least she has no fear of them.'

'Many doctors believe that seeing an object which is not present is evidence of a weak or troubled mind, or a disease of the eye, and that may sometimes be the case, but not, I think, always. You know, of course, that if you stare at a bright object then turn your eyes to look at something dark, the shape of that object will appear before you still, and will take some time to fade. It has long been known that the eye will retain the impression of an object for a time even after it is gone from view. That is a normal effect in the healthy eye.'

He took something new from his bag, a disc of painted card. The disc had two perforations on opposite edges, and a cord had been threaded through each hole. 'This delightful toy is the thaumatrope. There are two images, the one on this side — ' he held it up — 'is a beautiful bird. But the bird alas, is not in its cage. The cage — ' He reversed the card to reveal a drawing of a birdcage — 'is on the other side. The puzzle is, how can we put the bird in the cage so it will not fly away? I can do so by using the ability of your eyes to retain a picture.' He wound the strings on either side so that they were twisted. 'Now, when I pull the strings, the card will rotate, and it will be made to appear that the two scenes have become one.' He did as promised and while the images were not as clear as before, they had become

575

combined, so the bird seemed to be in the cage. When the movement stopped, Marriott once again showed that the two pictures were on opposite sides of the disc. 'Now this retention of the image lasts a very short time indeed, but many people believe that in some cases images may be remembered and appear a long time after they were initially seen. Sir Isaac Newton that great man of science, experimented on himself, by staring at the sun, and he found that the effect lasted for some months, if indeed it ever disappeared.'

'I know that the mind can retain pictures,' said Mina. 'If I think about someone, my dear late father, for example, I can see him in my mind. But that is not the same thing as seeing his ghost standing in the room.'

'Quite,' said Marriott. 'So, before we consider what it is that Miss Brendel and Dr Hamid's patients were actually experiencing, let us define what it is we are talking about. We all know that there are those who practise deception, or mistake something natural for a ghostly apparition, and then there are ghost stories told purely to entertain, such as Mr Dickens's *A Christmas Carol*. But think of this — if no-one had ever seen a ghost, would there be ghost stories? Would people imagine that a curtain flapping in the breeze was a ghost, and run away in terror? I don't think so.

'Tales have been told of people confronting the spirits of the dead since antiquity. I find it impossible, therefore, to believe that these reports have no foundation in actual experience. So, the question we need to resolve first, before we even consider how people see apparitions is, what is a ghost? I will not consider here those situations where someone has seen a patch of mist or a shadow and persuaded themselves that they are in the presence of spirits. Only those cases where a human or animal form has been clearly observed deserve our attention.'

Mina and Dr Hamid glanced at each other. Both were concerned but also stimulated by the turn of the conversation, which had veered away from mere consideration of eyesight.

'Nowadays,' said Mina, 'people generally suppose that a ghost is the spirit of a deceased person. That is why in séances the mediums strive to demonstrate that there is some intelligence behind the communication.'

Marriott nodded agreement. 'That belief has its roots in ancient times. The Egyptians, the Romans, the Greeks, all believed that ghosts were spirits returned from the mansions of the dead to impart important information and issue dire warnings, even prophesy doom. They were rarely a sight to be welcomed, and I do not think they were often encouraged to appear. But that is only one hypothesis; there have been many others. Some philosophers suggested that ghosts were composed of thin films of ash and salts sloughed off from bodies, fermenting in the earth and rising up to form the shape of the deceased, but I think that idea has been long abandoned. Others believe they are what is called the astral body, something said to lie between the physical body and the soul, a part of the individual quite separate from the gross form which is laid in the ground. None of these theories, however, explain why apparitions are normally seen clothed, as they would have been in life, although we must be grateful that this is the case. Another explanation is that ghosts are created by the imagination, and given colour by fear and superstition. Still another, is that there is a derangement of the mind which renders it incapable of differentiating between ideas and reality. Demonologists naturally suggest that ghosts are actually agents of Satan sent to torment the minds of men.'

Marriott looked at the rapt faces of Mina and Dr Hamid and smiled. 'But there is another view and it is the one preferred by men of science. This is not a new thing; there have been papers on this subject going back many years. It is the idea to which I personally subscribe. Ghosts are simply true images preserved in and recollected by the mind, which for some reason have become as vivid as reality.'

'So, they are memories made flesh, as it were?' asked Mina.

'Appearing to be flesh, yes.'

'Which would mean that a ghost could only ever be of an individual that the person who sees it has previously seen?'

'Yes, although the acquaintance might be very brief. The clearest visions are of persons well known. As you observed earlier,' said Mr Marriott, 'when you think of your father, you can easily recall his picture to your mind, yet you are well aware that this is an image only in the mind and not before you. Supposing, however, there is some way in which that image can appear to be real, corporeal, and seem to lie outside yourself? Then you might be persuaded that you have seen a ghost.'

'Is that possible in a sane person?' asked Dr Hamid, wonderingly.

'It is, and there are many cases on record. The mechanism is far from being understood. It was Sir David Brewster's belief that in certain states of health, the mind, which has retained a memory of what the eye has seen, can produce those images again, but in the form of spectral illusions. In many cases, the person subject to these illusions simply assumes that they are of supernatural origin and does not question them. I am sure that there are many who choose not to speak of them in case they are considered insane. In a few cases, however, they have been studied scientifically. There was a German gentleman called Nicolai whose case is well known. He was a bookseller and writer, a thinking man, who had strained his resources due to overwork. Startled on seeing a vision of a deceased person, which others present could not see, he soon realised that the image was not of external origin. He recorded his experiences, and gave a paper to a learned society on the subject. Sir David Brewster studied the case of a lady who suffered from a disorder of the digestion, and experienced both visual and auditory illusions.

'A Dr Hibbert made an extensive study of the phenomenon. He was convinced that these spectral images are ideas or memories produced by the mind when the individual is indisposed. They may be extremely vivid and convincing. Indeed, the mind's eye may produce a greater impression than the eye of the body. His work and that of Brewster have had a powerful influence on scientific thought.'

'That is most encouraging,' said Mina, writing down the name 'Dr Hibbert'. 'One does need a healthy antidote to the claims of the spiritualists who try to delude the public into parting with their fortunes.'

'Oh, I doubt that the charlatans will take any note of men of science,' said Dr Hamid. 'They prefer the unscientific, the mysterious, the unprovable.'

'Might it be possible to meet Sir David Brewster and Dr Hibbert?' asked Mina. 'I should like to speak to them, or correspond at the very least.'

Mr Marriott paused. 'Not unless the mediums are correct after all. The gentlemen are both deceased.'

Mina frowned. 'When did they publish their theories on illusions? And what of Mr Nicolai?'

'Oh, Nicolai's paper was some seventy years ago. Hibbert, if my memory serves me correctly, wrote on the subject in the 1820s, and Brewster not long afterwards.'

Mina was astounded. 'I had not realised that illusions had been studied and explained before the advent of spirit mediums.' She fell silent in thought.

'But if someone was to see what they believed to be a spectre,' asked Dr Hamid, 'how would they know if it was a genuine ghost with an existence external to themselves, or simply an illusion created by the mind?'

'An excellent question. You know that you can strain the eyes in such a way as to make objects appear double? In doing so, any external object would be doubled, but one produced by the mind would not be. Also, many persons who have experienced these illusions soon learn to notice the difference; they report that they are paler, fainter than real persons, move soundlessly, and will often simply vanish.'

'Like ghosts.'

'Yes. Although sometimes they will still be seen when the eyes are shut.'

'You have mentioned the state of health of the individual as a factor,' said Dr Hamid. 'Is this something that only occurs to a person who is unwell?'

'In the examples that have been studied the bodily health of the individual was disordered. Many diseases will create conditions in the body that can affect vision; the pressure in the blood vessels, for example, with which the eye is provided, may be affected by an affliction in another part of the body such as the stomach. In a balanced system if these illusions do occur they are weak and will never appear more prominent than genuine objects. I also believe that grief, such as follows the loss of a loved one can bring about something very similar.'

'Miss Scarletti has been very thoughtful,' commented Dr Hamid. 'In fact, there was a point in the conversation when she became quite lost in her own thoughts. I should inform you, Mr Marriott, that that is the moment when men of good sense should be on their guard.'

'Would you be willing to share your thoughts?' asked Mr Marriott.

Mina roused herself to speak. 'I was thinking about how long ago Dr Hibbert and Sir David Brewster did their work. And then there was Mr Nicolai before them. So, scientists believed they knew the cause of spectral apparitions long ago, yet now, it is as if their work had never taken place. All about us are stories of ghosts, and charlatans taking people's money to practise deceptions on them. People want to believe they can speak to the dead, and receive messages from them. They want to be reassured of the existence of the immortal soul. I really think that no amount of scientific endeavour will ever shake the belief in psychics. Yet the bible teaches us that after we die we sleep to awaken only at the Day of Judgment. Our spirits do not wander about waiting to be called up so our relatives can ask us if we are happy or where we buried our treasure.'

'For that belief we must thank the writers of ghost tales,' said Mr Marriott.

'But the stories are only meant to amuse and they often have a moral,' Mina protested. 'They are not meant to be received as truth.'

The idea troubled her, however. Would she one day hear someone relate one of her own tales back to her as if it had really occurred? Would a believer in the work of mediums choose to deny that her work was fiction at all? Mina glanced at Dr Hamid but he said nothing. Mina had given copies of some of her tales to his sister Eliza, although she had been careful to select only the lighter ones, and spared her the more blood-curdling efforts, which, now she thought about it, were the ones that sold the best. Dr Hamid and his sister Anna, to whom Eliza had enthused about the stories, were the only persons apart from Mina's publishers who were aware that she did not exclusively write for children.

'They have another purpose,' said Marriott. 'They keep superstition alive as the counterbalance to science. For some they are a more acceptable truth. To my mind it is possible for science and religion to co-exist, but many church leaders have felt concerned at the rise of materialism, and have striven to maintain belief in the wonderful, something beyond what is found in the bible. Witches, prophecies, demons, ghosts. Stories not of ancient times, but in this modern age.'

'But this opens the door for criminals to practise on people's credulity,' said Mina. 'The church is welcoming and offers comfort, but it should not tolerate false mediums making a fortune by cheating the bereaved.'

'I am sure that sensible persons will be able to tell the difference between the words of the bible and stories of haunted houses,' said Dr Hamid. 'And as for charlatans it is for science to show them up for what they are.'

Mr Marriott was due for another appointment, and took his leave, but Dr Hamid, seeing that Mina was anxious to speak further, remained, especially as cook had made some of her excellent sandwiches.

'That was a most enlightening interview,' said Dr Hamid. 'The most important thing I have learned is that the individuals who experience these illusions all appear to have one thing in common, a failing in their health, either through disordered digestion, or the stress brought about by overwork or grief. Since the latter does not appear to apply to Miss Brendel the answer to her situation might well lie in her stomach.'

'Is it possible,' Mina wondered, 'that Mrs Brendel is more aware of the situation than we have supposed? She wants her daughter to make an advantageous marriage and may be deliberately concealing any weakness from potential suitors. Could the camomile tea be of importance here?'

'I have read further on the properties of camomile tea, and there is nothing that causes me any concern.'

'Perhaps Miss Brendel has an unusual sensitivity to it. She drinks it during the day as well as in the evening.'

'She does? How do you know?'

'Richard has been going there to sketch her for a society journal. He has observed the arrangements in her house, and is trying to win the confidence of the maid.'

'Is that wise? I mean your brother going there?'

'The visits are carefully chaperoned. All he has told me so far is that Mrs Brendel places a careful guard on her daughter.'

'A precaution of which I strongly approve. This was your idea, I suppose?'

'It was, yes, and I hope we will learn something by it.' Mina was thoughtful. 'Do you think ghost stories by their nature lead people into the clutches of frauds? Have I been guilty of the very thing I despise?'

'Your stories are designed to entertain, not mislead. They deal with the battle between the forces of good and evil; they have a moral. If someone is not wise enough to tell the difference between a fiction and what is real, then they will be at the mercy of every kind of fraud and not just the false mediums.'

Despite this reassurance, Mina remained concerned.

Chapter Twenty-Seven

Richard returned late, and a heavy gloom had descended on him. It was a state that he rarely remained in for long, but this time there was a cloud of unhappiness in his eyes, and Mina was obliged to hug him.

'Would you believe, Mr Jordan has gone and taken Nellie to London?' he complained. 'If I didn't think better I would imagine he was deliberately stopping me from seeing her. She is a good friend, and I ought to be able to see her whenever I please. I know she likes my company.'

'Mr Jordan might think she prefers your company to his,' hinted Mina.

'Oh, he doesn't think so, he *knows* so. After all, who would not?'

'She'll be back in Brighton soon enough. In the meantime, now that you have less to distract you, you will be able to concentrate your mind on your drawings.'

'All I can think about drawing is Nellie, not the sea and ships and rusty old piers. She would inspire anyone. Is that bad of me? If I was rich I would have married her in an instant. And now that I am to be a great artist and make a lot of money it is too late.'

'Are you continuing your visits to Miss Brendel?'

'Yes, I have been a second time, but I'm not sure if I can make many more excuses to call again, or the mother might suspect me of wooing her daughter.'

'Does she still drink the camomile tea?'

'Yes, I can't think why. I wouldn't touch it. Smells like some nasty medicine.'

'Medicine?' said Mina, in surprise. 'But camomile has a light flowery scent. It's quite pleasant.'

He pulled a face. 'Not this kind.'

'Richard — did you get a glimpse of it? Was it pale yellow?'

'No, it was more of a green colour, and I can promise you there was nothing flowery about it. Nothing of the sort.'

'How interesting! Of course, it might be nothing, it might be another harmless beverage or some beneficial infusion Mrs Brendel is giving her daughter, but it just might be the cause of what ails her. Richard, I know this might be difficult without arousing suspicion, but do you think you could obtain some of it next time you visit? If you could, I will send some to Dr Hamid. He knows so much about herbs and is bound to be able to say what it is.'

'Hmm, well, I might be able to help you there. I was trying to ingratiate myself with the charming Jessie by helping her with the teacups and I think I got some of the blessed stuff on my shirt cuff. If Rose hasn't sent the laundry out yet, you might just rescue it.'

By the time Rose had retrieved Richard's shirt from the laundry basket, he had gone out. Mina examined the cuff with its pale green stain, and had to admit it was like no tea she had ever known. On the question of scent she could only agree with Richard. It was certainly not camomile. She wrapped the shirt in brown paper, wrote a note to Dr Hamid, and told Rose to ensure that it was delivered without delay.

She was gratified when later that day she received a note from the doctor thanking her, with the comment that some investigation would be needed to determine the composition of the strange brew.

When Miss Clifton next called on Mina, she reported that there had been an unexpected incident at one of Miss Brendel's séances that Mr Fernwood had attended. Once again, the séance had not produced anything he regarded as being of significance to their concerns, although events had taken a remarkable turn.

'You recall a Mrs Tasker and her son who were there before?' said Miss Clifton, full of amusement at her story.

'I do, and the son looked most unwilling to attend at first, but then he saw the piano and seemed more content. He plays very well. I believe music is his chief passion in life.'

'George said that he and his mother looked to be on the verge of a falling out almost from the moment they arrived, and it became still worse when Mr Tasker determined that he would do nothing but play all evening. He went straight to the piano, and sat there and opened it without even asking permission. It was terribly impolite, and you could see that his mother was mortified by his behaviour. And then he started to play so loudly that no-one could hold a conversation. Both Mrs Brendel and Mrs Tasker told him to desist, and he became very angry, almost violent, so much so that he alarmed all the ladies. Mr Quinley and Mr Conroy were obliged to intervene, and George had to go and help them, because it really looked like Mr Tasker would overthrow them both. There was a horrid struggle and a great deal of noise before his mother managed to calm him.

'Of course, Mrs Brendel told the Taskers she could not tolerate such a dreadful display of bad manners and they were not to come again. There were high words spoken on both sides before they left. Then Mr Conroy said that he was most unhappy with the proceedings and he would go too. A Miss Landwick was there and she was so upset by the scene that she also decided to leave.'

'Was that the end of the séance?' asked Mina, regretting that she had not been there.

'No, George still remained, and Mr and Mrs Myles were there, and they all wanted to continue if Miss Brendel felt able. So, Mrs Brendel sent for some tea to bring a little calm, and when everyone was more composed, Mrs Myles was told of a vision which she felt sure was that of a deceased relative and took great comfort from it.'

'Does Mr Fernwood intend to go again?'

'He says he will. He has not learned anything so far, but while the visions continue and other sitters do receive good evidence there is still hope that we might. Also, he feels great sympathy for Miss Brendel, who is hardly more than a child. Her mother imposes on her too much and is in danger of draining her of any little strength she may still possess. That young fellow who accosted us in the street, Mr Dawson; I fear he was right about one thing. George went to see him at Potts Music Emporium, and under the pretence of an interest in purchasing an instrument, they conversed privately. They both agreed that Miss Brendel was being paraded before some unworthy suitors, and might be forced into marriage, but there was nothing they could do about that. George does not, however, believe that the young lady is being poisoned.'

'No. Her mother gives her herbal tisanes, camomile, which is soothing to the mind and one other, I believe. She may benefit from them. I hope Mr Dawson did not try and persuade Mr Fernwood to pass Miss Brendel a note?'

Miss Clifton gave a little sigh of regret. 'I am sorry to say he did, and begged most piteously, but, of course, George refused. Since Mr Dawson is still barred from the house he implored George to go again, and come back to tell him how Miss Brendel does, and he has agreed to do that much.'

'I do have some further information which may affect your confidence in Miss Brendel. I have consulted an expert gentleman, an oculist, who told me of other people who have had similar visions to Miss Brendel's when their constitutions were disturbed. He felt that something similar might lie behind her situation. One can only hope that she will recover her health, and then she may be cured of these apparitions, which she does not especially welcome.'

Miss Clifton seemed reluctant to accept this explanation. 'But, whatever the cause, her visions can still be real. They can still be messages from those who have passed. Mr and Mrs Myles are quite convinced of it.'

'If I have the chance, I will speak to them and discover more about why they are so sure that they have been in touch with the spirits. But I also have something to say about Mr Castlehouse. An acquaintance of mine knows about the art of slate-writing, and told me that many of the tricks done by Mr Castlehouse have been performed by other mediums, all of whom have later been exposed as frauds.'

'That does not mean that Mr Castlehouse is a fraud,' said Miss Clifton, a trifle petulantly.

'Of course not, only that it is possible to do all the things he does by means of conjuring. He might be writing on a slate himself, or he could, by distracting the attention of his audience, be substituting a slate he has already written upon for one that is blank.'

'I don't see how that can be. I was watching him very carefully. We both were. We didn't see anything of that sort.'

'Neither of us is expert enough to see through a conjuror's skills. Just consider — if a conjuror stood on a stage and did exactly the same as Mr Castlehouse does, you would not for a moment entertain the idea that he was summoning spirits. However, we do have a way of determining whether he is genuine or cheating. If he is a cheat it will be harder for him to produce his results if he is not able to use his own slates, especially if they are sealed. So, this is my suggestion. We purchase a set of folding slates, of a type sufficiently different from the ones he uses that no substitution is possible. We then place a secret mark on them so there can be no mistake, and ask him to use them.'

Miss Clifton considered this. 'I don't know. We shall look as if we do not trust him.'

'I am sure we will, but I doubt that it will be the first time he has been asked such a thing. The worst that can happen is that there will be no result.'

'But that will prove nothing,' objected Miss Clifton. 'There are many reasons why there might not be a result. Sometimes the spirits just don't have enough power, or the conditions may not be right.'

The visitor was hard to convince, but Mina persisted. 'That is one explanation, but if we see that Mr Castlehouse consistently only achieves results when he is in full control of the circumstances, which means using his own slates, and never when we test him, that will be a very good reason to suspect him of deceit. After all, if the writings are genuinely produced by the spirits then what does it matter to them whose slate they write upon?'

'I suppose you are right, as ever,' said Miss Clifton with noticeable reluctance. 'But I do want to believe so very much! And he may pass our test, which would be a wonderful thing. If he does not, and proves to be a cheat, then there must be others we can test until we find one who will prove true.'

Mina fixed her visitor with an intense and determined stare. 'We must be strong; we cannot allow ourselves to be led astray. In a matter of such importance it is essential that we are sure of our ground. Remember, the answer could mean life or death to someone.'

Miss Clifton wavered, then acknowledged the force of Mina's statement. 'You put it so well, Miss Scarletti. I will take your advice, and we will do as you suggest. I will buy tickets for us both to see Mr Castlehouse next Wednesday and call for you with a cab. And I will purchase a set of slates as well, as different as possible from the ones Mr Castlehouse uses, and mark them secretly. If he is a scamp, which I hope he is not, then at least we will know the worst.'

Chapter Twenty-Eight

Later that day, Mina received a much-anticipated visit from Dr Hamid. He brought a neatly-wrapped parcel which contained Richard's shirt, nicely laundered.

'Now tell me,' said Mina, eagerly, 'is Mrs Brendel poisoning her daughter?'

He smiled. 'Not at all. The infusion, judging by its scent is composed of a number of commonly used medicinal herbs. None of them is poisonous in the quantities used in that way, and none are known to produce illusions. Many ladies like to rely on regular doses of their preferred medication, not always wisely, but if this is the worst thing Mrs Brendel gives her daughter I would not interfere.'

Mina, while relieved that Mrs Brendel was not, after all, doing harm to her daughter, was disappointed that she was still no nearer an answer. 'But what is the purpose of her giving it?'

'I really can't say. Half the persons who take medicines that are not prescribed by their doctor could not tell you why, or even what ailment they think they are treating. They might have read in the newspapers that it is good, or seen an advertisement, or a neighbour recommended it, or it helped their aunt and they think it might help them too.'

'Well, if it is harmless as you say, then Mrs Brendel should be asked what it is and why she gives it, and should not object to replying.'

'That is true. Are you still going there?'

'No, but an acquaintance of mine is. Perhaps a general enquiry on the benefits of herbal tisanes might stimulate a conversation on the subject without arousing suspicion.'

'Let me know if you should learn anything more. And now it is I who have a favour to ask you.'

'Please do.'

'I am thinking of writing a little memoir. An account of the medicated vapour baths and the other treatments provided. There are very few establishments of this nature in England, and I think it would be of some interest.'

'I am sure it would. Do you want me to recommend it to Edward? The Scarletti publishing house does issue works which are not children's stories or sensational fiction.'

'Oh, that would be so much appreciated. But,' he hesitated and Mina detected a slight embarrassment, 'the work is not yet written. It is barely started. In fact, every time I attempt it, I find that writing is not my forte. I know what I wish to convey but perhaps my sentences are not very elegantly formed. And to be truthful my spelling is a little weak. I hoped, if I could write a chapter or two, would you look at it and advise me? I am sure any publisher would regard the work more kindly if it was readable.'

'I would be delighted to help,' said Mina. A sudden thought struck her. 'Tell me, is it very common for doctors to write a memoir of this kind?'

'Not all do so by any means. A doctor might have a specialist practice, or work in a location that is of interest, or have observations on unusual cases. Then he might well believe that he has something to impart to his fellow doctors or to the public, and publish a memoir.'

Mina thought carefully before asking her next question. 'Supposing a doctor was called to a case in which murder was suspected, a poisoning, perhaps? Might he write about it?'

Dr Hamid smiled knowingly. 'I can see that you are planning another of your stories.'

Mina saw her opportunity and seized it. 'I am. How did you guess? I was thinking of writing a tale in which it is believed that a man has been murdered, but there is a great mystery attached to it. No-one knows who the culprit is. It is easy enough to think up a mystery, of course. The hard part is how to solve it. The detective who is examining the case can't simply dream the answer, there have to be clues for him to find, or the story would not be interesting. You have just suggested how he might proceed. Perhaps the doctor who attended the man suspected a certain individual but did not have enough proof to make an accusation. He might have written a memoir and the detective finds it. The doctor would not have openly denounced someone, but perhaps, hidden in his words — there might be a clue. Does a doctor who writes his memoirs ever mention his patients by name?'

'I certainly don't plan to. I suppose it might just be permissible if the patient is deceased but one has to consider the feelings of the family. In the circumstances you describe I very much doubt that the writer would actually name his suspect, or he would risk prosecution for libel. But someone who knew the family might be able to guess to whom he was alluding. It sounds like an interesting story; I look forward to reading it. If you need any medical advice, you have only to ask.'

'And this time, I promise, there will be no ghosts,' said Mina. 'I do have another question for you. I don't suppose you know anything about art?'

'I'm afraid not. Is this for another story?'

'No. It is just that Richard has been engaged by Mr Dorry of the new gallery in town to do some drawings for him. I am very pleased about it, as it seems a respectable enough career, but Richard tells me that Mr Dorry has asked him not to sign them. I always thought pictures were more valuable when signed, but Mr Dorry has said not.'

'I would have thought the same, but, of course, Mr Dorry is the expert on such things.'

Mina rose and peered out of the window. 'I think, if the weather permits, I would like to visit the gallery and see for myself how Mr Dorry is displaying Richard's work. Is that permitted?'

'I'm not sure. You really ought not to go alone. Perhaps you might consult a doctor on that point.'

'Would you take me there? Rose can call a cab and the gallery is still open.'

'Not tonight. It is late, and there is a threat of frost. Tomorrow morning, if the wind drops, I will call for you at ten o' clock. Can you still your impatience until then?'

Dear Edward,

I trust that the situation in London is not too trying for you, and hope that everyone is as well as possible.

I am writing on another matter. I know that the company has recently been publishing some historical and biographical works. Would you be interested in a medical memoir? Dr Hamid, who is very famous here in Brighton and owns a fashionable establishment that provides an Indian herbal vapour bath and medicated 'shampoo', is composing an account of his work, which should prove very interesting. I hope you will consider it when it is complete.

Dr Hamid informs me that many medical men publish memoirs that can be very useful to their fellow practitioners. I was wondering how one might discover whether or not a leading medical man has ever published? The gentleman in question is a Dr Simon Sperley of Lincoln.

Fondest love,

Mina

Mina hoped that her careful wording had made it appear that the enquiry regarding Dr Sperley's possible memoir was not on her own behalf, but that of Dr Hamid. It was as Mina put the finishing touches to the letter that she realised that something had been at the back of her mind, troubling her like a slight itch. She had tried to ignore it as something trivial, but now she understood what it was. It was probably meaningless but she needed to resolve it.

Chapter Twenty-Nine

Next morning, Mina looked out of her bedroom window with some anxiety, since she knew that severe weather would inevitably result in the arrival of a short note from Dr Hamid postponing their excursion, and she was not sure she wanted to wait to see Mr Dorry's gallery until the following spring. Fortunately, there was no more than the usual sea breeze, and a heavy layer of grey cloud even suggested a slight rise in the thermometer. The note did not arrive, but at 10 am a cab drew up bringing Dr Hamid.

With an engaging diffidence he proffered a small package of papers, which he said comprised the introduction and commencement of the first chapter of his volume. 'If you would be so kind...'

'I will study it with interest.'

'Richard is not accompanying us?'

Earlier that morning Mina had gone to find Richard when he had not appeared at breakfast and found him slumped across his writing desk, pencil in hand, snoring loudly. A drawing of doubtful delicacy portraying Nellie was lying before him. Mina had decided not to disturb him.

'No, he is hard at work on a new commission. And, in any case, I would like to speak to Mr Dorry without my brother being present. He is drawing under the *nom de crayon* of Richard Henry, and I don't think Mr Dorry knows he is my brother. He will be more open with me if he does not.'

Dr Hamid smiled, appreciatively. 'I think your idea of writing about a detective is a good one. You have the mind for it.'

Mr Dorry's gallery was on St James's Street, just north of Old Steine. Their ride took them past the entrance to the new West Pier, which was crowded with visitors during the warmer months, but now afforded a walk and a view of the surging waves only for those very determined to brave the winter weather. Ahead, she caught a glimpse of the old chain pier, which was falling out of fashion as it had fewer attractions than its more modern rival. The sea was whipping it without mercy, as if determined to erase it altogether. Part of what had once been a handsome frontage including an esplanade and a tollhouse had been taken over by the new sea wall and promenade necessitated by the proposed aquarium, leaving the old pier with a narrower and less inviting entrance. Mina was sorry to see the chain pier being squeezed out of existence, as she liked its calmer atmosphere, and feared that it was only a matter of time before it was dismantled and forgotten.

St James's Street had long been a centre of fashion in Brighton. Its residents had money to spend and this was reflected in the jewellers, hatters, furniture dealers, confectioners, hairdressers and purveyors of fancy goods who thrived there. Mr Dorry's gallery was a recent arrival and occupied a single-fronted premises. The window display was a marvel of taste and restraint, since it was composed of two easels, on each of which rested a landscape painting. A sign at the very front of the window proclaimed in bold lettering that that Mr E Dorry, who was connected with several of the great art houses of London, was interested in buying collections or single items of merit. He would also, for a fee, examine works of art, offer his expert opinion of authenticity and provide a certificate of valuation. Mention was made that a larger selection of highly sought-after pieces was held at his London gallery.

'This is very impressive,' said Dr Hamid, with some surprise. 'If your brother has attracted Mr Dorry as a patron he has done well.'

'Yes, I must admit, this was not quite what I had been expecting,' Mina confessed. 'In fact, I am not at all sure what I was expecting.' She didn't say it, but she had feared that Mr Dorry might be one of those cheats who made money from the labour of others and failed to pay their bills when due. Of course, that could still be the case.

Dr Hamid pushed open the glassed and gilded door, which was very heavy, and they entered. They were met by a subtle aroma of old paper, wood and varnish, with a hint of something floral. Although the premises were not large and the items on display were few they were presented with great care, offering the promise that further treasures could well be available.

In the centre of the gallery was a marble statue on a plinth of a handsome youth in classical Greek style, since he was in a state of undress that might have been quite disturbing had his loins not been draped with a silken scarf. A card read 'Adonis. Not For Sale.'

At the back of the gallery was a separate display counter for artists' materials, and a schedule of costs for framing works of art, which to Mina's scant knowledge seemed extraordinarily expensive. A svelte young man stood behind the counter, showing boxes of paints to a man whose entire wardrobe was probably worth less than a single tube of colour.

Most of the pictures that hung about the walls were oils, with a few watercolours, but there was small section of pencil and ink drawings, and Mina noticed that one of Richard's works was included, enclosed in a very simple wooden frame. She went to examine it. It was a view of the chain pier being inundated with ferocious waves, and threatened by lowering clouds. Far out to sea, she recognised Richard's favourite penny toy ship, struggling manfully to stay afloat, while on the shoreline the Royal Pavilion had managed to creep forward from its usual position until it occupied a prominent position on the Marine Parade. The drawing was labelled 'The Chain Pier, Brighton. Unknown artist, in the style of J. M. W. Turner.'

'Is this your brother's work?' asked Dr Hamid.

'Yes, and unsigned as he said.'

'I am no judge of art, but it does have its merits.' He peered more closely and pointed. 'Should the Pavilion be there?'

'Richard said that didn't matter.'

'Really? If I was a stranger to Brighton and saw this picture I would be quite mystified when I paid a visit and found the Pavilion not where I thought it ought to be.'

'So, if you had studied the picture it would have become more real to you than the actuality?'

'It might have, at that.'

Mina glanced about but there was no sign of Mr Dorry.

The customer left the shop, a small paper bag clutched in his hand indicating a humble purchase. Almost instantly the svelte young man appeared by their side, as if conjured into existence by a spell. 'Good morning, Sir, Madam,' he said, with a polite inclination of his sleek head and an ingratiating smile. 'Does this picture interest you?'

'It might do,' said Dr Hamid, cautiously.

'Perhaps you could tell us something about it?' asked Mina.

'But, of course.' The young man made a graceful gesture towards the work. 'It has been recently acquired, but is already attracting considerable interest from collectors. Notice the charming, almost primitive style, the deceptively careless way in which the pencil has been used. The pier has been well rendered, the little storm-tossed ship is quite delightful, evoking the vulnerability of life when man is at the mercy of the sea, while the texture of the waves shows a young artist still exploring his skills.'

'I don't think the position of the Pavilion can be quite right,' said Dr Hamid.

'Ah, but that is where the eye of the artist places it,' said the young man with an indulgent smile. 'In his mind it achieves such a measure of importance that he perceives it as larger and closer than it really is in that view, and so gives it the same prominence in his work that it has in his imagination.'

Dr Hamid did not look convinced by that argument.

'The drawing does not appear to be signed,' said Mina. 'What is the name of the artist?'

'I regret that I am unable to say. But it is very common with works such as this one for there to be no signature. It was probably never intended for sale at the time it was composed, perhaps merely as a study for a major work in oil. But these sketches are now becoming very sought after in their own right. If you are interested you could see Mr Dorry and discuss a price. But I cannot see him letting it go for under ten guineas, and it could well fetch much more at auction. We have only a few examples of the artist's work, which are quite rare.'

'Might we have a moment to consider?' asked Dr Hamid.

'Of course, Sir, Madam.' The young man bowed and withdrew.

'I suspect,' said Dr Hamid, 'that Mr Dorry is hoping to make a very large profit from your brother's work, by paying him a pittance. I fear, however, that he is in no position to bargain at present, but if the drawings do sell, then he should ask for an account of what they fetch and in future demand a fair portion of the sale price.'

'I will make sure to advise him.'

'Have you seen all you need? I have an appointment with a patient soon. I can take you home and then I must return to the baths.'

Mina was about to assent to this, when Mr Dorry hove into view, like a leviathan risen from the deep.

'Why, good afternoon Miss Scarletti. What brings you here?'

'I had never visited your gallery and was curious to see the display. Mr Dorry, allow me to introduce Dr Hamid.'

Dr Hamid proffered his card.

'Ah, a steam bath! Just the thing.' Mr Dorry pressed a hand to the small of his back, which was doing extremely well to support such a very large front. 'I might well avail myself of your services. Do you collect art, Dr Hamid?'

'Not at present.'

'Well, if you see anything that attracts you, just let me know.'

'In fact, I must depart now, as my work calls.'

'I think I would like to remain a little longer,' said Mina.

Her companion gave her a look that told her he knew she had some plan in mind, but he could not very well discuss it with Mr Dorry present. 'Very well, I will send the cab back here to bring you home. And do take care.' Dr Hamid took his leave.

'So, he is your personal physician?' asked Mr Dorry.

'Yes, the treatments I have received at Dr Hamid's baths have been very beneficial. But do tell me something about this drawing. I see it is unsigned and described as being by an unknown artist.'

'It is.'

'And yet, as I look at it, it is plain to me who the artist is, and I am sure it is plain to you, too.'

Dorry looked down at her, and one enormous eyebrow rose until it resembled an arched rustic bower. 'Oh?'

'Yes. I recognise the style of Mr Richard Henry, the young man who was sketching Miss Kitty Betts at Mrs Jordan's salon. Please don't deny it, it is very plain. The manner of rendering the sea is so like the lady's coiffure.'

Mina could see he was debating whether or not to contradict her; finally he conceded with a little smile. 'How very acute of you, Miss Scarletti. What an eye you have!'

'Then perhaps you could explain to me why the drawing is described as being by an unknown artist?'

Mr Dorry chuckled, a noise that thundered deep in his throat to which the rest of his vast form vibrated in sympathy. 'Ah, now I understand your query. Allow me to explain. When we in the art business say "unknown artist" it does not mean that we do not know the identity of the artist only that he is not a known name in the world of art.'

Mina wasn't sure if this was true but she could hardly dispute it without more information. 'He might gain a name if he signed his work.'

'Be assured by me, at this early stage in his career it is better if he does not. It lends an air of mystery and is more likely to stimulate discussion and attract interest.'

'The picture has similarities to the work of another artist.'

'Exactly. As it says on the card, in the style of Mr J. M. W. Turner. Very highly regarded.'

'Forgive my ignorance, but when copying a style is it necessary to consult the artist one is copying?'

'Not at all, as long as one labels the work correctly. And in any case Mr Turner is deceased.'

'I hope your customers don't imagine this drawing is by Mr Turner?'

'If they do, they do not say so. Also, the drawing is not priced as a Turner. It has a low price, a humble price. Not the price a Turner would command.'

'But is there not a danger, since the work is unsigned, that the buyer might delude himself into believing that he has seen a bargain.'

Mr Dorry was disconcerted for a moment. He glanced about, but there was no other customer in sight, and he took on a more confiding tone. 'He might, but what he believes is his own business, surely? Suppose he sees what he thinks, or suspects might just be an undiscovered Turner, not one of his finest, of course, an early work, perhaps a study for a future painting, something he himself discarded as unworthy and therefore quite deliberately did not sign. Is the customer going to reveal his suspicions, and say to me, "Oh, Mr Dorry, you have found a rare thing here and are offering it so cheaply!" No, of course not. He hopes that he has seen what I have not. He hopes to secure something valuable at a low price. He knows that if he alerted me to his suspicions, then I would put up the price and that would never do. So, he stays silent, and buys the drawing for more than he would pay for an unknown artist. Part of the price is the picture, and the rest is for that hope, the chance of a bigger prize, a hope I never gave him.'

'What you are saying is that you are not cheating them, they are in effect cheating themselves.'

'Precisely. I cannot know what the man is thinking. I do not tell him it is Turner. If he was to ask me outright is it Turner I would say no, it is not, it is in that style. You see the card; all it attests to is the style. Everything else is in the eye and the mind. If the customer flatters himself that he is cleverer and more observant than I am, if he hopes for a handsome profit, then he might see what he wishes to see. But I do not put the thought there.'

Mina could only wonder at how vulnerable people were to their own deeply held desires. Mr Dorry pandered to greed, while Mr Castlehouse, who performed the same feats as a conjuror, promised more than just diversion. The slate-writer's sitters felt they had been gifted with an insight into the greatest mystery that life had to offer, received a special, deeply personal and secret knowledge, an advantage over others not so blessed. The svelte assistant saw artistic merit in a deliberate artifice, and persuaded not only collectors, but himself, also, that it was the expression of a unique imagination. Both Mr Dorry's and Mr Castlehouse's customers accepted all that their deceived eyes told them, all that they profoundly wished to believe.

'Oh, Mr Dorry!' said the young man, moving lithely towards them like an eel slipping through greasy water. 'There is a cab waiting outside, the driver says he is for Miss Scarletti.'

'Then I must depart,' said Mina. 'I hope we may meet again, and I wish Mr Henry every success.'

The door was opened for her, and Mina peered out cautiously, but the weather remained mild and the east-west orientation of the narrow street protected her from any dangerously inclement gusts. 'Good morning, Miss,' said the cab driver. 'Am I to take you to Montpelier Road?'

'Not yet. I would like to go to the offices of Phipps and Co solicitors.'

Chapter Thirty

'I felt sure it was only a matter of time before you came to see me again,' said young Mr Phipps, permitting himself one of his rare smiles, as he ushered Mina to the chair that faced his across his desk. Mr Phipps had a newer, less humble office than the one he had occupied the last time Mina consulted him. Still only the most junior Phipps in the firm, he nevertheless merited a fractionally larger carpet than previously and a slightly bigger desk, the better to accommodate the increased amount of work he was expected to do. As he moved up the Phipps ladder towards the top rung, so the workload would grow until he reached the midpoint then it would start to decrease as some of it tumbled from his desk and fell to land on the desks of younger iterations of Phippses.

'I assume this is concerning poor Miss Brendel. All I can say about her is that the unfortunate young lady is the puppet of her mother, who commands when she shall breathe in and when out again.'

'I have visited them a second time, and friends of mine have also, but I have found no evidence that the Brendels are asking for payment for their sittings,' said Mina. 'Have you discovered anything?'

'No, nothing. I simply attended on that occasion to accompany my aunt, who maintains a lively curiosity in such things. But the young lady is an heiress and there are single gentlemen clustered about her like flies around a honey jar. I think that is the real interest.'

'Did *you* find her interesting?' asked Mina, teasingly.

Mr Phipps actually reddened a little, and neatened some papers on his desk, an action that was quite unnecessary. 'I — no. In fact, following my visit, I did receive a little note from Mrs Brendel inviting me to take tea with them. I expect she has heard of my recent admission to the partnership and deems me eligible. But I have declined the invitation due to extreme pressure of work. When I marry, as I hope to do one day, my wife will be a sensible woman, and most definitely not one who has visions.'

'Are you acquainted with Mr Quinley?'

'No, ought I to be?'

'He is not a visitor, but Mr Brendel's solicitor, staying in Brighton as consultant and protector to the wife and daughter.'

'I have not heard of him, but then there are very many solicitors.'

'But the Brendels are not the subject of my call.'

'Oh?'

'I happened to visit Mr Dorry's art gallery in St James' Street earlier today. He claims to have a lifetime of experience in the art world and I have been told he has another gallery in London. There was a picture being offered for sale — a pencil drawing which was described as being in the style of a Mr Turner, a deceased artist whose work is very much admired. The thing is, I happen to know who the artist is, and the picture is not by Mr Turner.'

Mr Phipps gave a deep frown of concern. 'It is not being described as by Turner, I hope?'

'No.'

'Is it signed by the artist?'

'It is unsigned, and labelled as being by an unknown artist.'

'Does Mr Dorry know who the artist is?'

'He does, because it is he who commissions them. But a buyer might imagine that they are early works by Turner.'

'But there is nothing in writing to suggest it?'

'No.'

Mr Phipps plunged into further thought. 'What of the buyers who make enquiries? Are they in any way, even by a hint, being led to believe the picture is by Turner?'

'No, and Mr Dorry says that if openly asked he would reply truthfully. But he is hoping that buyers suspect they have seen something he has missed, in which case they would not ask him for fear of having the price increased, and so miss securing a bargain.'

'I see. And you want to know if this activity is breaking the law?'

'I think that Mr Dorry, who knows his business, is being very careful to avoid something openly fraudulent. He never tells an outright untruth but leaves it to the inclinations of his customers to supply the conclusions he hopes for. I did point out that his card described the picture as being by an unknown artist, which is not true as he knows who the artist is. He tried to persuade me that the expression simply means one who has not made a name for himself. I do not know if that is true or not.'

'Neither do I. He does not invoke the spectre of Mr Turner to bolster his sales?'

'Only in the manner of style,' said Mina, suddenly realising that Mr Phipps had made a humorous reference to her previous activities. 'I believe that the artist is quite innocent of the somewhat dubious way in which his work is being presented.'

'Your concern is for the artist.'

'It is.'

'Perhaps I ought not to ask you if you know the artist.'

'I would be grateful if you did not.'

'I can only supply an opinion on what I know so far, but I feel that if the artist has created the works in good faith, and sold them to a dealer, then he cannot bear responsibility for how they are sold once he has parted with them. If, however, he receives some of the fruits of Mr Dorry's underhand measures, then he may unwittingly be making a profit from duplicity, and might find it hard to convince the authorities that he knew nothing of the scheme. It would be as well if you were to warn him of any potential dangers. In the meantime, I promise I will keep my eyes open for any news of Mr Dorry.'

On her way home Mina called in at Mr Smith's bookshop and reluctantly parted with five shillings for a copy of *The Brighton Hauntings* by Mr Arthur Wallace Hope. Mr Smith did not carry any of the works of Sir David Brewster or Dr Hibbert and suggested that in view of the age of those publications she might try an antiquarian bookseller. She returned home disappointed. Richard had gone out, but she resolved to speak to him on the subject of Mr Dorry as soon as possible, although it was always hard to get anything useful from him on the subject of money. There was a letter from Edward and she opened it hoping for good news.

Dear Mina,

Little has changed here. I visit Mother and Enid almost every day, as they make poor company for each other, but nothing I do is appreciated. The twins continue to thrive, if the noise they make is anything to judge by. Would it be too much trouble for Richard to write a few lines? Mother is actually sending him money, so the least he could do is thank her.

If a memoir such as you describe had been published then a copy would be held by the British Museum Library. One of my authors is often in that library, so I asked him to look for any record of such a volume. He has just reported to me that as far as can be determined, Dr Sperley did not write a memoir, since there is no mention of that author's name in the catalogue.

As you are a great reader with a penchant for history, I should mention that the author to whom I referred is writing an account of notable executions at the Tower of London. I have to confess that I am somewhat concerned about publishing something in such dubious taste, and would welcome your opinion on the matter. To my mind, it is of the same unpleasant ilk as the tales of supernatural entities and horrible disasters that Greville will insist on presenting to the less discerning portion of the public. He assures me, however, that these alarming stories are a useful source of income, so I suppose I must tolerate it. Their author, a Mr Neil, is certainly a person of doubtful mental stability and you should avoid reading his works.

At least the book I have commissioned is English history and there is no getting away from that, even if it is an aspect I would not personally wish to dwell upon. I would far rather publish nobler and more elevated forms of literature, and I hope that may come in future. A medical memoir would be something I might consider, and you must ask Dr Hamid to send it to me when it is complete.

Greville tells me that your stories for children are well received, and I am glad that you have something interesting to occupy you. Mother worries constantly that you are still risking your health by spending time with spirit mediums. I have reassured her that that particular concern is a thing of the past, but I am not sure she listens to me.

Affect'ly,

Edward

Mina, disappointed that there was no memoir written by Dr Sperley, spent the afternoon composing a new story about a whale, which having made the long journey from the North Pole, unexpectedly appeared cavorting in the sea at Brighton. Even amongst whales, which were naturally large, this one was a veritable monster of its kind, its shining body hung about with ribbons of bright red seaweed, and assiduously groomed by a battalion of fawning eels. The unusual sight naturally created great excitement in the town, and both population and visitors came to the promenade and walked along the pebbled beach in droves to see the spectacle, only to find to their horror that the whale was able to come on shore and cause mayhem. The huge creature of massive girth would rise up to a terrifying height, before allowing its weight to fall, crushing unsuspecting onlookers to death before returning to the sea with a flip of its tail. Boats set to sea to try and conquer it, but they and their crews were eaten at a gulp. The danger was finally averted by the hungry beast swallowing an abandoned torpedo, resulting in an explosion that scattered evil smelling blood-stained debris over half the town. Once the mess had been cleared, however, Brighton was well supplied with whalebone, meat and oil for some months to come.

Mina laid aside her pen and examined the writings of Dr Hamid. The proposed title was *The Indian Medicated Herbal Vapour Bath and Shampoo: Methods and Benefits*. It did not have quite the immediacy of *Attack of the Killer Whale*, but it did undoubtedly describe the subject of the book. The introduction gave some of Dr Hamid's history; his father making his way as a doctor in a foreign land, the tribulations of his sister Eliza, afflicted from childhood with advanced scoliosis, his determination to study medicine with particular attention to conditions affecting the spine, and his struggle to establish a practice in Brighton. The first chapter was an overview of the many conditions that would benefit from the treatments offered by Dr Hamid's practice. That was all he had written so far and there followed notes as to the subjects of the remaining chapters — how the treatments were applied — the value of herbs and spices in medicine — some examples of patients cured or improved. Mina, bearing in mind that his readership was likely to be different to hers, decided to concentrate on faulty spelling, and punctuation and grammar, which were occasionally highly eccentric.

This did lead Mina to think further about Dr Sperley. True, he had never published a memoir, but he might have left notes and diaries, not in a publishable form, which could cast further light on the mystery. Mina returned to the package of newspaper cuttings supplied by George Fernwood. It included a letter to the press from Dr Sperley, on the subject of how great caution was to be used in the employment of arsenic as a vermin killer, as accidents had been known to occur. Was this a clue? Did Dr Sperley believe that the poisoning of Thomas Fernwood had been an accident? If so, why had he not said so at the inquest? Or was he merely doing his duty as a doctor? The letter was signed 'S. Sperley, M. D., Newland House, Lincoln'.

Mina took up her pen.

To: Mrs Sperley
Newland House
Lincoln
Dear Mrs Sperley,
I am writing to you on behalf of the Scarletti Publishing House. We are looking for suitable memoirs written by noted medical practitioners. While we cannot guarantee publication we are interested in seeing anything of promise. Can you advise us if your late husband kept any notes, perhaps for a memoir he was intending to offer for publication?
I hope very much to hear from you.
Yours faithfully,
M. Scarletti
Montpelier Road
Brighton

Mina enclosed a Scarletti Publishing business card to establish her bona fides, and sealed the letter.

Richard returned in time for dinner but, unusually, with little appetite. 'The sea is such a bore!' he said. 'I had been hoping for a good shipwreck but there has been no such luck.'

'Richard dear, can you enlighten me as to the nature of your arrangement with Mr Dorry? Does he pay you an agreed price for each of your drawings, or do you receive payment only when he sells one to a customer?'

Richard looked mystified. 'Arrangement? I don't know. I draw what he asks for and he says I will be very successful one day. He has made some small advances of funds, but that is all.'

'You have nothing from him in writing?'

'No. Is that usual? I mean, Dorry must know his business. He's done well enough out of it, after all.'

'Do you know if any of your drawings been sold?'

Richard began to look uncomfortable with the questioning. 'He hasn't mentioned it. I think he has sent some to his London gallery. He says the exposure to the public there will advance my career.'

'Well, if something does sell, it would be very interesting to know how much it fetches.'

The only answer Mina received was a shrug and silence, and she knew she would learn no more.

She retired to her room to read Mr Hope's *The Brighton Hauntings*. It was a book written by a true believer, a man who on hearing an unexplained noise thought it to be the sound of a spirit knocking without ever considering a thousand other more natural causes. His book provided a colourful account of the sensational sightings said to have taken place in the Royal Pavilion earlier that year, declaring his absolute belief in them. It was Mina's actions that had exposed the deception, something he appeared to have either forgotten or swept aside as a delusion. He had taken great care, however, not to name her. He knew she was a writer and part of the Scarletti publishing family, and could not impugn her honesty without fear of a legal reprisal. What he had written was, however, far worse. 'There is,' he concluded, 'a person now residing in Brighton who I know is destined to become one of the greatest and most celebrated spirit mediums of our age. For the present those eyes remain firmly closed to the truth, but I am as certain as I see the sun rise every day that they will open, and open soon. When the world is threatened with catastrophe, it is to this individual we will turn to lead us to the light. One day I will stand in that wonderful faerie aura again, and this humble being with a mighty soul will be ready at last to acknowledge the power that lies within.'

To Mina this could only mean one thing. Mr Hope, confident that she would read his words, was sending her a warning. He had not forgotten her. He was still her enemy.

Chapter Thirty-One

That evening, Mina and Miss Clifton were to make their first test of the veracity of Mr Castlehouse. Miss Clifton called at the appointed time, bringing with her as promised, a set of folding slates in a brown paper parcel tied with cord. She pulled back the paper to show that the slates were in a light-coloured wooden frame. 'These are quite unlike the ones Mr Castlehouse uses, where I recall that the wood is darker. And look, I used my needlework scissors to make a little scratch in one corner. So even if by chance he had something similar, we would know this set from any other.'

Mina examined all the surfaces of the slates with great care, and, satisfied that they were clean and smooth, pronounced them ideal for their purpose, re-wrapped them in the paper and tied the cord.

'I have been wondering about how best to introduce them,' said Miss Clifton.

'We should be bold with him from the start — no whispering in corners — the others in the room should all be aware of what we are asking. That will make it harder for him to refuse us. I also think, if it is at all possible, that we should not allow Mr Castlehouse to handle the slates.'

'Would he permit that?'

'We shall see.'

'But it would be a sign in his favour if he did, surely?'

'Only if we saw any result. We must make certain to show them to everyone present so they can satisfy themselves that all the surfaces are perfectly clean. And it should be one of us who dusts them and then ties them up in the cord.'

Miss Clifton nodded emphatically. 'You have thought of everything.'

'Even if he can open a set of slates and write on them by sleight of hand without people noticing I doubt that he will be able to untie them quickly if we make very secure knots. He might want to take them from us, but we have to resist that.'

It was early evening, and there was a fresh bite of winter in the air. Darkness had spread like ink over a cloudless sky that offered no shelter from the wind. The cab waited outside, and the driver with the tartan muffler, knowing that some assistance would be needed, had already descended to hand the ladies into the comparative comfort of the interior.

'There is one small matter that I was wondering about,' said Mina, as they proceeded on their way. 'When I last spoke to Mr Fernwood, it was soon after your return from Lincoln. Am I correct in thinking that neither of you has been there since the family moved away?'

'That is correct,' said Miss Clifton.

'When I asked if you had visited Dr Sperley, Mr Fernwood replied that you would have done, if he had not passed away six months ago, and he spoke very movingly of the doctor's last days. If he had not visited, how could he have known?'

Miss Clifton was unembarrassed by the question. 'George corresponds with a friend in Lincoln whose family was also attended by Dr Sperley and they exchange news.'

'Ah, I see. I recall that Mr Fernwood placed great trust in Dr Sperley and would not hear a word spoken against him, but I know you have another view. Even if Dr Sperley was blameless, do you think he knew anything about your great uncle's death; I mean, something he didn't say at the inquest?'

Miss Clifton needed no time for consideration. 'If he did, I don't know what it might have been. He certainly never confided in me.'

Mr Castlehouse's séance was as well attended as before. The usual pile of slates was on the sideboard, and included a number of double slates that Mina was careful to examine. She was quickly able to establish to her satisfaction that none of them could be mistaken for the set Miss Clifton had brought. There was a new addition to the sideboard, a row of books bound in dark brown leather, which comprised the volumes of a dictionary of the English language, with additional notes on grammar. Rather more attractive was a copy of *The Pickwick Papers*, prettily bound in maroon and stamped with gold. There were also some slips of paper, pencils and envelopes.

Young Mr Conroy was present, as was the timid lady, and Mina inclined her head to both in greeting. The lady was accompanied by a gentleman Mina did not recognise.

Mr Conroy looked reluctant to approach Mina, but after a few moments, decided to do so. 'Good evening,' he said and Mina introduced him to Miss Clifton but giving her companion's name as Miss Clive. 'I see that you too have abandoned the Brendels' salon for what we must hope will be a calmer place,' he commented. 'Did you hear of what occurred there lately?'

'There were rumours of a disturbance.'

'Indeed. I was present at that event, which was highly unpleasant, but at least it served to open my eyes. Mrs Brendel has finally shown herself in her true colours. She may be the wife of a wealthy man but she has the manners of — well — something quite different. I will admit that I entertained great hopes that the daughter was genuine, and for all I know she may be, but now I have seen in her mother what she may become in future. I will not go there again.'

'Miss Scarletti,' whispered the timid lady, making a cautious approach, 'we have not been introduced, but we have encountered each other before. I am Ethel Landwick and this is my brother, Charles.'

'I am delighted to make your better acquaintance, Miss Landwick,' said Mina warmly, 'and pleased to meet you, sir. Allow me to introduce Miss Clive and Mr Conroy.'

'Miss Landwick and I are already acquainted,' said Mr Conroy, and his expression suggested that he thought this circumstance to be no very bad thing.

'I was also at the last séance of Miss Brendel's,' explained Miss Landwick, 'and it is thanks to Mr Conroy that it ended as peaceably as it did. I thought young Mr Tasker was about to lose control and have to be restrained. It is a wonder the police were not called.'

'I am sorry I was not there to witness it,' said Mr Landwick, stiffly. 'Not that I place any value on Miss Brendel's visions, which may have their origins in another kind of spirit altogether. But I am sorry to have missed the opportunity of correcting a man who has no idea how to behave in the company of ladies.'

'We must hope that the chastisement of his mother will be more than sufficient punishment,' said Mina. 'Do you hope for better fortune from Mr Castlehouse?' This was a question for both the Landwicks and Mr Conroy.

Miss Landwick looked unsure and glanced at her brother for guidance, but he only grunted.

'I have been unable to explain what he does by any other means but that he is in touch with the spirits,' said Conroy, 'so yes, I am hopeful.'

'Perhaps you might volunteer when he asks for someone to come forward,' said Miss Landwick. 'Or you, Miss Scarletti.'

Mina smiled. 'Oh, I do have a plan for this evening which I hope will add to the interest of the occasion.'

The gaunt-looking maid entered the room, and in sepulchral tones urged the company to be seated. When everyone was comfortably settled, Mr Castlehouse appeared, as dapper as ever, and smilingly introduced himself. He took a number of the single slates from the sideboard, and scattered them on the table in a casual manner that suggested their precise arrangement was of no importance. 'I would like a lady or gentleman to select from these slates any two that they would like to use today, and examine them carefully to show that they are blank.'

A lady from the front row jumped up at once, and almost ran forward in her eagerness. After careful study, she picked out two slates. At Mr Castlehouse's request these were minutely examined on both sides, washed with a sponge, dried with a cloth, and placed side by side on the table.

'Now then,' said Mr Castlehouse, picking up a small box, 'I have here a number of chalks of different colours. In a moment I will place pieces of six different ones on the slate. If the lady would be so kind as to look at what colours we have, and think, but do not state out loud, three colours in which she would like to receive messages.'

The lady peered at the box of chalks and spent what seemed to Mina to be a wholly unnecessary amount of time making her selection. After her conversation with Nellie, Mina was aware that any choices made by the sitters that were under Mr Castlehouse's control would have no effect on any result. Was there, however, another motive? The lady's attention had been distracted from the slates on the table, and more to the point, the sitters were probably watching her rather than Mr Castlehouse.

'Have you made your choice?'

'Yes, I have!'

Mr Castlehouse held up one long warning finger. 'Do not say what it is just yet. I now take one piece of each colour and place them on the slate, like so. Next, I take up the second slate and use it to cover the first. They now lie in the middle of the table, with the six chalks between them. I will no longer touch them.' He stepped back gesturing with both hands open and arms held wide. 'Now you must put your hand on the slates to ensure that they do not move.'

The lady, a little timorously, since she knew that the slates might be visited by spirits, placed her hand on them.

'And, at last, you can tell us all, which colours did you select?'

'Oh — er — white, and red, and green. I think it was green.'

'Notice,' said Mr Castlehouse to the onlookers, 'that I am standing well away from these slates. I cannot influence anything that might occur.' He took a deep breath, his eyelids fluttering closed. 'I call upon the spirits to announce their presence and write messages for us in the three colours selected. Is there a spirit here?'

There was a silent pause, and then Mr Castlehouse extended one hand, directing the palm towards the slates, making circles before him like the mystic passes of a wizard of old, his head thrown back, his body trembling. A minute or two elapsed, then a sound broke the expectant quiet, the rasp of a chalk scratching on slate, and the lady cried, 'Oh! I can hear it! I can hear it!'

'Are your powers strong tonight?' demanded Mr Castlehouse to the air.

There was the sound of further scratching. Mina tried not to gaze at Mr Castlehouse's theatrical one-handed gesture, but tried to see how his other hand was employed. It appeared to be behind his back.

'What message do you have for us, oh spirit!' he called.

There was a further outbreak of busy scratching followed by three taps.

Mr Castlehouse opened his eyes. 'Now, dear lady, I think the spirit has done all it can for tonight. Please lift the top slate.'

The lady reached forward and did so. There on the slate were three messages, one in each of three colours. There was certainly a red and a white but it was hard to determine in the lamplight whether the third was green or blue.

'Please read out the messages.'

The first message was 'yes', the second was 'the power is strong' and the third was 'those who listen to the spirits will prosper.'

Once the messages had been read, and subjected to much wonderment and admiration, Mr Castlehouse took charge of the slates and chalk, and by means of a courteous bow dismissed the lady back to her place.

Mina took the opportunity afforded by this pause in the proceedings to rise to her feet. 'Mr Castlehouse, if you would be so good?' she called out in a voice that pervaded every corner of the room.

He turned towards her in surprise. 'How might I assist you?'

Mina had untied the cord around the parcel and she now unwrapped the purchased slates. 'I have brought my own set of slates. I assume it would be no more difficult for the spirits to write on these than it would using the ones provided by you?'

'Their ability to write depends on the spiritual power and not on any earthly means,' he said, but there was a wariness behind the geniality.

'That is very good to know. So, you will have no objection to employing these?'

'None whatsoever.' Mr Castlehouse reached out for them but Mina simply smiled.

'If you don't mind, it would be such an interesting thing for me to display them to the company. Please do indulge me.'

A knowing smile told Mina that he was well aware that he was being tested. He inclined his head briefly. 'Of course. Nothing could give me greater pleasure.'

Mina turned and faced the assembled company, who were all attention, and opened up the hinged slates to reveal that they were blank. She then took up the duster and passed it over the surfaces of the slates in view of the onlookers. Next, she selected a fragment of chalk from the box, placed it on one of the slates and closed the pair. Finally, she used the cord that had tied the parcel to bind around the slates, securing it with a number of firm knots.

Once again, Mr Castlehouse offered to take the slates from her but at the risk of being impolite, Mina shook her head and placed them on the table herself. He maintained his good humour. 'You take great care, but I am not offended. The spirits will come if they please.'

He picked up the duster. Mina thought he was about to replace it on the sideboard but instead he whirled it deftly around like a miniature cloak and covered the slates with it. 'And now, while we wait, I would be obliged with your assistance on another matter.'

Mina had been making her way back to her seat, but stopped. 'Of course.'

'If you would come and look at the books I have displayed here.'

Mina obliged.

'Take a slip of paper and an envelope. Select any book you please, but not just yet. When you have done so, open the book, choose the number of a page, the line and position of a word. You will have three numbers. Write these numbers on the paper and place it in the envelope and seal it. Take another slip, write down the word and put it in your pocket. So you may be assured that I cannot possibly see what has been written, I will leave the room for a minute or two. Please, while I am absent, no-one must disturb the covered slates or we will have no result from them.' He bowed, and departed.

Mina was half tempted to pick a dictionary, which would lead to the word 'fraud' but did not want to antagonise Mr Castlehouse. He was clearly assuming that she would select the book with the attractive cover and not one of the dingy volumes that flanked it. She pulled out a volume at random, found the word 'Story', recorded the page, line and word number on the sheet, sealed it in an envelope and noted the word on a second slip. As she regained her seat Mr Castlehouse returned. He paused only to direct a sharp glance at the books on the shelf, but Mina had been careful and no clue remained as to which one had been selected.

He then turned and stood a little back from the table, gazing down at the set of covered slates but made no attempt to come near enough to touch them. 'I would like everyone to concentrate on calling the spirits here present to give us a message.' He stretched both his arms forward palms down, and moved his hands in slow circles like a lazy swimmer.

There was a long expectant silence, in which ears were alert for any sound of chalk on slate. Mina stared at the duster on the table and wondered if it had been touched or disturbed in any way while her attention was elsewhere. Had that been the purpose of the exercise? Had Mr Castlehouse somehow managed to put a message on one of the bound slates before leaving the room, while she had been distracted contemplating the books? It seemed impossible, for if he had done so, then the others in the room must have seen him, and no-one had spoken out. Time passed, five, perhaps ten minutes, and Mr Castlehouse, still making mysterious movements of his hands was shaking his head in disappointment and looked to be about to announce the experiment a failure when there was the unmistakable sound of writing. Everyone stared at the cloth on the table. The noise lasted only a minute, and then there were three loud taps.

Mr Castlehouse, looking exhausted, allowed his arms to drop to his sides. Still he made no attempt to touch the slates, but glanced at Mina. 'I would be grateful, since these are your slates if you could come and look inside and confirm that they are the same ones you brought.'

Mina crossed over to the table and lifted the cloth. The slates certainly looked the same, and they were still tied with a cord. Mina untied them, and opened them up, and as she did so, the fragment of chalk dropped to the table. To her astonishment a message was written on one of the inner faces of the slates. She made a quick examination to see if the tell-tale scratch Miss Clifton had made was there, and it was.

'Please read the message,' said Mr Castlehouse.

Mina held up the slates. She was trembling, not so much because of the appearance of the message but its contents, and what it would mean to Miss Clifton and Mr Fernwood.

'I am to blame. I thought only to stop him drinking. J,' she read.

'Does that mean anything to you?' he asked.

'I am not at liberty to say,' replied Mina. She looked at Miss Clifton who, her eyes wide and frightened, had clasped both her hands over her mouth as if unable to trust herself with what words might emerge. Mina returned to her chair with the slates, and showed them wordlessly to Miss Clifton so she could see the scratch mark. Her companion could only nod.

The room was enlivened by an outbreak of whispers, in tones of awe and admiration. Mina caught the word 'evidential', being the highest accolade any medium might desire. Mr Castlehouse had provided what so many devotees of the supernatural had been earnestly seeking — a phenomenon considered tantamount to scientific proof of communication with the deceased.

Mr Castlehouse did nothing to still the conversation. 'I accept that some messages might be of a highly confidential nature, and I will not press you for details. Perhaps you can now supply the envelope you prepared before?'

Mina had almost forgotten it, but it still lay in her pocket, and she passed it to Mr Castlehouse while Miss Clifton stared at the slates on her lap.

Mr Castlehouse called up another sitter who was prepared to place the envelope between two slates and assist in holding them under the table. Mina barely observed what was happening and Miss Clifton was too distracted to watch at all. The result after several minutes was only the words 'We can write no more. Good-night.'

'It appears that the power of the spirits is exhausted tonight,' said Mr Castlehouse. 'We will hear no more from them.'

Miss Clifton carefully closed the slates, without disturbing the message, wrapped them in their paper and bound them in cord. 'I must show this to George,' she said.

'I trust that you are not too distressed?' said Mr Castlehouse, approaching them, as the other sitters dispersed. 'We do not always receive the messages we expect.'

'It was a surprise, to be sure,' said Miss Clifton. 'But not unwelcome.'

'Let me summon you a cab,' he offered.

'That would be very kind, thank you.'

He looked on them both very kindly. 'Do please call again. The spirits are powerful in your presence, and we receive good results. I would not be surprised if you are both mediums.'

'I have been told so before,' said Mina, although she did not add that those persons who had said so were now residing in prison.

Chapter Thirty-Two

The cab driver was instructed to take Mina home then to go on to the railway station with Miss Clifton. Mina hardly knew what to say as her companion sat absorbed in her thoughts, the wrapped slates clasped to her bosom.

'Miss Clifton,' she ventured at last, 'I know you were watching very closely when I was not in a position to do so. Did Mr Castlehouse touch the slates at any time after I tied them?'

'He did not; I can assure you of that. And how could he have untied them and written on them and tied them up again all in plain sight of everyone in the room?'

Mina agreed. There had been a brief moment when the duster had been whirled about, and then again as she had turned her back to return to her seat, but her companion had been a second pair of eyes, and there had simply not been enough time for the deception to be carried out.

'What do you make of the message?'

'J can only be my aunt Jane.'

'But she was confined to her bed, was she not?'

'She was able to walk a little. And the message explains everything; it is an answer we had never thought of. I think Aunt Jane must have given arsenic to my uncle Thomas, not meaning to kill him but with good intentions. It was only to make him a little unwell so he would forswear the brandy. Do you see what this means? It means that no member of the family had murder in his or her heart and George and I may marry with confidence.'

Her eyes were glittering with unshed tears, and Mina decided that this was not the moment to cast any doubts on the result. If the message was a genuine one then it could only mean happiness for the couple. Even if it was a fraud, and a member of the family was indeed a murderer, no doctor could confirm that this constituted a risk to the next generation. The chance might be small or not exist at all. Mr and Mrs George Fernwood would make good parents. That must count for a great deal.

The cab brought Mina to her door and the driver was kind enough to descend and help her down the steps. 'You take care now, Miss, it's mighty cold out,' he said. 'There'll be ice about soon.'

Before long Mina was sitting by the fire with a bowl of hot broth, wondering about what she had just witnessed. Did spirits really write on slates with pieces of chalk? And if they did why did the slates have to be closed shut or held underneath a table? Why did the power not work in the open? She would have thought it easier to move chalk on an uncovered slate than between two close surfaces. It was not as if the spirits had anything to hide. In fact, the only person who had anything he might want to hide was Mr Castlehouse. If he was a conjuror, he had every reason to conceal how the writing was done.

She finished her broth, and went to her desk, taking out a sheet of paper, pen and ink. She needed to write down all she could recall of what had occurred that evening. It was not, she realised, an easy task. In what order had events occurred? Where had Mr Castlehouse been standing? What movements had he made? She did not know the identity of the lady who had selected the two slates for the first sitting, and tried to recall how many slates had been on the table. Several, she thought. The slates had been washed and dried with the duster, and the chalks laid on them before they were placed together. Mina realised that she had simply assumed that it was the same two slates, but what about the others on the table? Could Mr Castlehouse by sleight of hand, have substituted an already written slate for one of the blank ones? It was possible. The messages were innocuous enough. He had, however, successfully predicted the chalk colours that would be chosen. Even that was not too hard. Red, white and blue might be an obvious choice, and it was hard to see whether one of the chalks was blue or green. Even if he had been wrong about one colour, or two, or all three, it was still a convincing demonstration.

Mina had kept a hold of her set of slates right up to the moment they were laid on the table. Miss Clifton was right, they could not have been interfered with in front of so many people in so short a time. Mina looked at her notes and realised that she had concentrated on her own actions, but had omitted one vital fact. When she had been told to make a note of a chosen word from the book, Mr Castlehouse, saying that he did not want to be accused of being able to see what she was writing, had actually left the room, and been absent for some two minutes. Could he, while appearing to place a duster over the slates, have quickly substituted another one and left the room with Mina's slates hidden under his coat? A conjuror could certainly do such a thing. While she was engaged in selecting a book and recording her chosen word and its location, he was untying the cords, opening the slate, writing the message and re-tying the cord. Had he had the opportunity to restore the slates to their place under the duster? Mina could not be so sure of that. Her back had been turned as she went back to her seat and Miss Clifton was sure he had not tampered with anything, but a moment's inattention was all a conjuror needed.

Mere suspicion was not enough, however, and Mina was loath to declare Mr Castlehouse a fraud without proof, especially as the results were so favourable. Interestingly the message not only removed the fear of an inheritable taint, it placed the guilt of the murder on the one member of the family who was deceased, thus ensuring that there could be no further grief to the Fernwoods and Cliftons. This was all very well as it stood, but what the young couple sought was the truth behind Thomas Fernwood's death. The message would only suit their purpose if it was a genuine solution to the mystery. Supposing Mina could show that Mr Castlehouse, imagining that he was providing what was wanted, had invented the message, then all their fears would be restored. Under the circumstances she might be best advised to leave well alone, but there was still her own curiosity to satisfy, even if she then decided not to communicate her doubts to another person.

Mina could deduce that conjuring could have produced the writing, but how had the medium come up with the contents of the message? How likely was it that he had by pure chance devised something that appeared to solve the dilemma of George Fernwood and Mary Clifton? Mina could not believe this. Either the message was genuine and came from a spirit or somehow Mr Castlehouse knew about the Fernwood case. If he did know, then his motive in creating the message was obvious enough — any medium who appeared to have knowledge of something he could not reasonably have known had made a strong claim to being in contact with the spirits. Producing the message in the presence of a person who recognised its import was crucial to this. The impact on the other sitters had been immediate.

Both George Fernwood and Mary Clifton had been adamant that they had told no-one in Brighton of their family tragedy. Was it possible, however, that one or other of them had incautiously let something slip that had led Mr Castlehouse to make further enquiries and discover the true reasons for their visits?

They might, thought Mina, have talked to visitors at other séances, the ones they had attended before consulting her. Miss Clifton, despite her eagerness, had not been incautious in the séances she had attended with Mina, she had always been careful not to supply her real name, and to make only the most general comments. George Fernwood, however, had continued to visit the Brendels, and these were séances at which Mina had not been present. Mr and Mrs Myles, she recalled, had attended both Miss Brendel's and Mr Castlehouse's séances. Mrs Myles was a sad, suffering creature that anyone might have taken pity on and there could have been an exchange of comforting words. Mr Conroy, too, had visited both mediums, and there must be others who Mina did not know about.

The thought struck her that if the Brendels and Mr Castlehouse were in collusion, exchanging information about their clients, then although she had not given her name to Mr Castlehouse he might still know precisely who she was and was acting accordingly.

But there was some distance between a carelessly dropped word and a message that revealed greater knowledge. What other sources of information were available to Mr Castlehouse? Mina's past experience had taught her that mediums cast their nets wider than most people imagined, and gathered news from all available places, sometimes exchanging titbits that could be brought out to astonish sitters. Some had vast collections of material, newspaper cuttings, notes made from gravestones or gossip. Did Mr Castlehouse or Mrs Brendel know people who had visited Lincoln and were familiar with the Fernwood case? Mrs Brendel, Mina reminded herself, was only recently arrived in Brighton, and had previously resided in Wakefield. This was near enough to Lincoln that she might well have seen some northern editions of the newspapers, and therefore know the story behind the Fernwood mystery.

The other possibility, Mina was obliged to remind herself, was that Mr Castlehouse, for all his theatrical methods, was a genuine medium and he really had received a message from the late Jane Fernwood.

Chapter Thirty-Three

Mina was hoping that the library would be able to furnish her with the volumes recommended by Mr Marriott, so when going out for her weekly trip to the baths, she departed rather earlier than usual to make one journey serve for two. On making enquiries about books by Sir David Brewster and Dr Hibbert, however, she was informed that their works of scholarship were not held. She contented herself with a volume entitled *Traditional Ghost Tales of Olde England*, something she would not have borrowed if her mother had been at home. The reading room was well supplied with newspapers and periodicals, and she took the opportunity to examine them in case there was anything more she might learn about Miss Brendel and Mr Castlehouse, but there was not.

She had also hoped she might encounter either Mr Castlehouse or Mrs Brendel there, since the reading room was a useful source of local information that might well be patronised by those purporting to be mediums in order to gather material that they could then reveal at a séance. Miss Eustace and her confederates had used it and they had also attended Dr Hamid's and Brill's Baths, where the ladies and gentlemen's lounges were formidable gossip exchanges. Mina, enjoying the warmth and the quiet of the library, decided to remain as long as she could, in case her two suspects made an appearance, but neither did.

Disappointed, she was about to leave, when a sudden, unusually sharp movement caught her eye. A veiled lady who had entered the reading room had stopped and quickly turned her head aside. She was too short to be Mrs Brendel, too stout to be the daughter, yet there was something in the abrupt way she had turned that suggested she had done so to avoid someone's notice. Could it be Mina she did not wish to meet, or someone else? The lady hurriedly picked up a journal, placed it on a reading stand and bent over it, examining the pages in a manner that suggested keen interest in its contents. To do so, she was obliged to slightly lift her veil.

Mina decided to walk about the room towards the stand where the periodicals were displayed, her path taking her past the intent reader. As she neared, the lady, who seemed to be disturbed in case Mina was coming to speak to her, shot a brief glance in her direction, then, as Mina continued to walk on in the direction of the periodicals, quickly fastened her gaze onto the page before her.

Mina had now glimpsed enough of the face to feel that it looked a little familiar, but there was nothing about the clothing that she recognised. If the lady had not acted as she had Mina might have assumed that there was simply a resemblance to someone she knew, and departed, but her suspicions had been aroused. She opened a journal on the subject of notable buildings of Sussex, and gave the question some thought. The reader was not a maidservant sent on an errand, being better dressed than a servant, and in any case she did not resemble either in face or form the Brendels' or Mr Castlehouse's maid. Mina dared another quick look, and realised that the lady bore a close resemblance to Mrs Myles, who was grey haired and normally to be seen in deepest mourning, but now had brown hair and was wearing a mustard coloured ensemble with a matching bonnet. Ladies did dye their hair, so that was not altogether unusual. They did emerge from their weeds but not so abruptly as this. And if they knew the secret of shedding twenty years in age they would not need to visit public reading rooms.

Mina put down the journal and turned to the lady. 'Mrs Myles? What brings you here?'

'Oh,' said the lady, dropping her veil, and holding a gloved hand in front of her face. 'I think you are in error. That is not my name, but I am often addressed in that way since I bear a remarkable resemblance to another person called Myles. Please excuse me.' She closed the journal and made to return it to its stand.

'I am sorry for my mistake,' said Mina, but as the lady replaced the journal she saw, through the lace of the right glove, a mourning ring of domed onyx, with a single pearl. Mina hurried to her side as fast as she was able. 'There is no mistake. You are Mrs Myles, who attended the séances of Miss Brendel and Mr Castlehouse. We spoke, and I remember you distinctly, although you were not dressed as you are now, which did confuse me initially, or I would have known you at once. And I think you must have been wearing a wig. Come, now, what do you mean by this masquerade?'

'Do not speak so loud!' hissed the lady, who Mina was now quite sure was Mrs Myles.

'I promise to keep my voice down, but only if you agree to explain yourself.'

'Very well,' said Mrs Myles reluctantly, 'but let us go out as people are beginning to stare at us.'

'I have no fear of that, people always stare at me. But we will go only as far as the entrance hall. We may talk there. Do not run away from me. That will have consequences.'

They retired to the entrance hall, and found a location where they would not impede anyone coming and going. Mina, despite her warning, took care to place herself between Mrs Myles and the door. 'Well? What do you have to say?'

Mrs Myles, recovering from her initial discomfiture, drew herself up to her full height, lifted her veil, and squared her shoulders with pride. Her dissimulation had been a good one, since Mina did not think the lady could be much over thirty-five. 'Myles is not our real name, but Mr Myles is my husband and we have been theatrical artists for some years. We provide a service. It is an ancient and honourable profession. Similar to that of mourners. We do that too, but we are particularly in demand by mediums.'

'So — let me understand this — you pretend to be bereaved persons; you attend séances and claim to have received communications from the dead when you have not?'

Mrs Myles seemed perfectly satisfied with that description of her activities. 'That is a part of what we do. We will also ask certain questions when required to. What most people do not appreciate,' she went on, speaking indulgently, as if explaining to a child, 'is that the art of the medium is not something that may be lit or unlit like a lamp. Sometimes it blazes brightly and at other times it does not. But the medium does not know when that will be. Each séance is a journey into the unknown.'

'Do you mean that there might be unbelievers at a séance emitting negative energy which will stifle the medium's powers, or the atmospheric conditions might prevent the spirits from getting through?'

'I am so glad you understand,' said Mrs Myles with some relief, failing to appreciate the satirical nature of Mina's tone. 'And that is why our particular skills are needed. The public, in their ignorance, expect to receive results every time, especially if they have paid. So, in order to satisfy them we attend to make sure that there is some activity at least. It is a comfort to the bereaved.'

Mina did her best to control her annoyance. 'You see nothing dishonest in what you do?'

'No, of course not. We are actors playing on a stage. We like to vary the characterisations; sometimes we are an elderly couple in deep mourning, other times we are younger and searching for a lost child. For much of the year we are in London and then we come to Brighton for the winter. We did especially well last year when so many lives were lost in the sinking of the *Captain*, and the relatives of the drowned men were wanting to speak to them. All the best mediums employ us.'

'I have no doubt of it,' said Mina. 'You are very convincing. If I might be permitted to ask an impertinent question, do you receive a percentage of what they take, or a fee?'

'Oh, that depends on the nature of the event.'

'What of Mrs Brendel, since she does not charge for her séances?'

'We have asked for nothing as yet. We agreed to attend gratis three times as a demonstration and hope for business in future.'

'And Mr Castlehouse?'

She gave a simpering smile. 'Now that would be saying. But the public is not being cheated; they get a good performance for their money. We are actors, after all. If we stepped on stage and said we were Anthony and Cleopatra it would be the same thing.'

'But that is not what the public go to a séance for. They hope to receive the truth.'

Mrs Myles waved away the objection airily. 'Oh, who can tell what the truth is?'

'Do you perform other services for mediums? I mean, do you collect information about sitters and pass it on?'

'We are not specifically engaged to do so, but then we are artistes, not detectives. We do converse with the other sitters, and the mediums ask us afterwards if we have learned anything of interest. This is because the knowledge will assist the spirits in coming through to the right persons.'

Mina could not trust herself to comment on this. 'If you believe there is nothing wrong in what you are doing, why did you try and escape from me just now? Why did you deny who you were?'

'Because your opinions are well known in Brighton. We have been warned about you. I feared that you would spoil the illusion.'

'Then you admit that everything at the Brendels and Mr Castlehouse's is an illusion?'

Mrs Myles hesitated, glanced about to see that no-one was approaching, then stepped closer and spoke more softly. 'Well, to be frank with you, Miss Scarletti, what I said to you just before, about the art of the medium, that is what they would have us believe. But I see now that you are more astute than that. Of course it is all an illusion. I have never been to a séance that was not. But most sensible people know that, don't they?'

'One would hope so. I notice you wear a mourning ring.'

'Ah yes, my grandmother's.'

'That is how I was so certain it was you. So, in all the séances you have ever attended, and I assume it is a considerable number, you have never received a genuine communication?'

'Why no.' She glanced at the ring. 'I had better be more careful of this in future.' She smiled contentedly. 'It has been a pleasure to make your acquaintance, Miss Scarletti. I do hope you will attend the Theatre Royal to see the grand Christmas pantomime, *Goody Two-Shoes and her Queen Anne's Farthing*. We are understudies for King Counterfeit and Fairy Spiteful, and it promises to be excellent.'

Mrs Myles exited stage right, and Mina was left wondering what to do if she should encounter the lady and her husband at a future séance. They were instrumental in promoting deceit but denouncing them would most probably lead to an unpleasant scene, and rebound on Mina who would then be branded as someone who had made distressing accusations against a bereaved couple. Such consummate thespians would have no difficulty in remaining in character and retaining the upper hand.

Chapter Thirty-Four

Mina was pondering this problem on her way to the baths where she once again encountered her new acquaintance, Miss Landwick. The lady's previous companions, who enjoyed their cosy gatherings in the salon where they could descant on the deformities of others, were astounded to see her greet Mina as a friend, and move apart from them to talk to her. There was much whispering behind hands.

'Your companions disapprove of me, I think,' said Mina.

'No matter,' said Miss Landwick. 'I disapprove of them, and was only in their company before to have someone to speak to, but such empty-headed conversation I never knew.'

'I have just had the most remarkable encounter,' said Mina. 'Mrs Myles, fashionably dressed and looking twenty years younger than she had at the séances she attended. I challenged her, and she admitted with no trace of shame, that she and her husband are actors, paid by persons such as Mr Castlehouse to pretend to receive messages from the spirits.'

Miss Landwick was suitably shocked. 'Oh my word, whatever next! So Mr Castlehouse is a fraud?'

'I am sure of it, although mediums will always claim that they only cheat occasionally when the spirits are reluctant or unable to appear, so as not to disappoint sitters who are in need of comfort. It is very hard to prove that they cheat all the time. Your brother seems confident that he could do so, however.'

'Oh, he is,' said Miss Landwick, eagerly. 'From the first moment he ever saw a conjuror, when quite a small child, Charles has wanted to do conjuring tricks and he has amused himself with this interest ever since. He entertains us all after dinner, and really he is marvellously adept, good enough to take to the stage, though he would never do so, of course. When I first went to see Mr Castlehouse I was very impressed by him and told Charles what I had seen, but he pooh-poohed the whole thing and said he could do the same thing perfectly easily without any spirits being involved.'

'I am less mystified about the manner of writing on the slates than the content of the message,' said Mina. 'If your brother could explain that to me, I would be extremely grateful.'

'I will be sure to ask him. In fact, you may ask him yourself, as he is coming here to meet me and you may share our cab.' Miss Landwick paused. 'Miss Scarletti — perhaps you could inform me of something. Mr Conroy — is he by any chance connected with Jordan and Conroy, the garment emporium?'

'He is the younger brother of the Mr Conroy in question.'

'Oh, I see.'

'He has his own business manufacturing military uniforms. A highly successful one, I understand.'

'And he is in mourning — is he a widower?'

'He is. I believe his wife passed away about a year ago.'

Miss Landwick did not comment but absorbed the information.

'And there are four small children.'

Miss Landwick smiled. 'How comforting for him. I am so very fond of children.'

When Miss Landwick and Mina were ready to depart, they boarded the cab hired by the lady's brother and all three proceeded together.

'I would be interested to hear your opinion of Mr Castlehouse's performance,' said Mina to Mr Landwick.

'As I anticipated,' said the gentleman, with a grunt of derision, 'the entire evening was an illusion. The man is no more than a stage conjuror pretending to be a medium. He uses sleight of hand to change a blank slate with one he has written on before. I know about these things because I do a little myself and I know what to look for.'

'But Miss Scarletti, you brought your own slates did you not? How could he trick you?' said Miss Landwick. 'I can see that he might have changed like with like using his own slates, but he didn't have another set like yours. And they were tied up with a cord.'

'I have given that some thought,' said Mina, 'and I believe that when he covered my slates with the duster he quickly substituted a set of his own, just so that it would look as though mine were still there, and then he slipped mine under his coat.'

Mr Landwick nodded. 'I thought at the time that there was some trick with the duster.'

'Then he distracted me by asking me to choose a word from a book, and left the room, taking my slates with him. He said his purpose was to ensure that he could not see what I was writing but I think that while he was out of the room he untied the slates, wrote a message, and re-tied them. When he came back I didn't notice him at first, and he might have done anything behind my back. I think he must have lifted the duster on the pretext that he just wanted to look at the slates, apparently an innocent movement, but he used it to perform more sleight of hand, and substituted my slates for his. Were you watching him? Did he do something of that sort?'

'I was looking very carefully,' said the gentleman, 'in fact I followed him with my eyes as soon as he re-entered the room. I remember thinking that as you had

617

brought your own slates, there would be no result unless he could somehow abstract them and write on them, so I was watching for the moment that might provide the opportunity, even if he could do it too quickly for my eyes to detect the movement. I agree with you thus far, he might have taken the slates, certainly, but when he returned to the room, he did not go near the table at all. I saw him cast a glance at the books on the sideboard, and thought to myself he is trying to see which one you chose. Then we heard the sound of scratching, which I know he must have made himself. Perhaps with something in his pocket, or with his foot. But at no time before you uncovered he slates was he within arm's reach of them. I must confess that my initial thought on seeing the message was that you were in collusion with him, and the slate was a trick slate of some sort.'

'I can understand why you must have thought that, but I can assure you that the slates were of quite the usual kind, and so far from being in collusion with Mr Castlehouse I was trying to test him. If you can offer any suggestions as to how he achieved the trick, I would be very grateful.'

'Well, I might be able to help you, there,' said Landwick. 'I attend exhibitions of conjuring quite often and am acquainted with several of its best practitioners. I will make some enquiries and see what I can discover. I am not of their fraternity, but they approve my interest and admit that I have some ability. I am sure Mr Castlehouse is no mystery to them.'

'I would be extremely grateful to hear from you on that matter,' said Mina, and cards were duly exchanged.

'Perhaps Mr and Mrs Myles helped with the trick,' said Miss Landwick. 'I saw them there, but Miss Scarletti has just told me they are confederates of Mr Castlehouse paid to pretend they receive messages.'

'Outrageous!' said Landwick.

'But the message you received!' exclaimed the lady turning to Mina. 'How extraordinary! What did it mean? I could see that you were very shocked by it.'

'Yes, I was, but I regret I am not at liberty to reveal why.'

'Oh, I promise I will tell no-one, it will be our secret!'

Mr Landwick rolled his eyes.

'I would tell you if I could, and one day if I am permitted, I might. But not today.'

There were two quite separate puzzles engaging Mina's mind. How had Mr Castlehouse written on the marked slate? And how did he know what to write? The answer to the Fernwood mystery, now Mina thought about it, was too simple, too pat. If Jane Fernwood had really wanted to confess to murder from beyond the grave why had she not done so long before and saved her family years of miserable uncertainty? If she had been too ashamed or fearful to confess it, why had she not left a sealed letter of confession to be opened after her death? Mina was not at all convinced that the message was genuine but it was exactly what suited the needs of the young couple. As to how Mr Castlehouse had written on the slate, who knew how he had done so if he had not taken it from the room? Perhaps he had some dexterous ability to abstract the slate, hold it behind his back, untie the knots, write the message with one hand and re-tie it, then replace it when the sitters' attention was distracted elsewhere. Most men could not do so, but a conjuror might be trained in that art. Now that Mina thought about it there had been something unusual about the slate when she had untied it. She had been so eager, in fact far too eager, to untie the cord and look inside, that she had not especially taken note of how it had been tied. If she had had her wits more about her she would have sealed the knots with wax. But now she recalled that although the slates had been tied as before, in the common style of a parcel, the ends of the cord were shorter than she remembered. Either it was a different piece of cord, or more likely the same piece re-tied more loosely, as it might have been if only one hand was employed. Was that the answer?

Mina determined to ask Nellie about this the next time they met. There only remained the more complicated question of the message. It seemed so very remote a chance that Mr Castlehouse had ever resided in Lincoln and was therefore acquainted with the Fernwood tragedy, or even that he knew someone who recalled it. He had been given no clues that Miss Clifton had any connection with the event. Dr Sperley, even if he had written a memoir had never published it.

This speculation, Mina told herself, was idle. Mediums were adept at providing information that their dupes were convinced it was impossible for them to know, but once all was revealed, the trick was seen to be simple enough. The only person who knew the secret was Mr Castlehouse.

Chapter Thirty-Five

Dear Mr Scarletti,

Thank you for your letter. I have been trying to go through my late husband's papers, but it has been something of a trial to me as my old eyes are just not what they were and his handwriting is very hard to read at the best of times. I enclose some notebooks, which appear to be a journal of some sort. If you can make anything of them it would be such a boon to me, as it would relieve me of a difficult task. There may be more, but I cannot lay my hands on them at present.

Yours truly,

Sophia Sperley

Newland House

Lincoln

Enclosed with Mrs Sperley's letter were about two dozen notebooks, all closely written. Mina quickly replied to the sender to confirm that they had been safely received and she would take great care of them. Then she sat down to read.

As she had been warned, the writing was small, and it took a while to acquaint herself with the style so she could make out the words.

Most of the notebooks were appointment diaries covering the period from about 1840 to 1862 when Dr Sperley had retired from practice. Others were a series of observations on patients, and fortunately, these were dated. Mina found a number of entries concerning the Fernwoods and the Cliftons. Mrs Jane Fernwood featured often as the doctor visited her regularly to attend to her back and legs. Privately, however, he thought that the lady preferred to be thought of as an invalid, and was better able to move about than she liked to pretend. He had tried to encourage her to make more of an effort to walk regularly as it would do her good.

The boys, cousins Peter and George, had never required the attention of a doctor, and neither had Mrs Clifton and her daughter. Mrs Clifton was skilled in home remedies and did what was needed for colds and coughs and the scraped knees from boyish games. Ada and Ellen, Thomas Fernwood's granddaughters had received occasional treatment for the usual female complaints. Fernwood himself had been told repeatedly that he drank more than was good for him, and had taken this advice with very ill humour. It had changed his behaviour not one whit.

Sperley had recorded in detail the events of Thomas Fernwood's death; the appalling symptoms, the suspicions of poisoning from the outset, Fernwood's last communication that he had been murdered and knew the culprit, his death before he could divulge the information, the post mortem examination carried out by four doctors, of whom the writer had been one, the many indications that proved beyond any doubt that death was due to arsenic, and the inquest. Mina read it all with great attention, but there was nothing further to be learned.

In 1861 Mrs Jane Fernwood had died peacefully from heart failure with her loving family at her bedside.

The final entry in the last journal was in the smallest writing Mina had ever seen.

Today I was informed by William Fernwood that the family will be removing from Lincoln. I had attended them for more than twenty years and have seen them at their best and worst. I was aware from the very beginning of my acquaintance with them that theirs was a desperately unhappy household, and this was due to a single cause, Thomas Fernwood, whose bad temper, meanness and ill treatment of his family cast a shadow over the lives of all who shared his home.

Following Thomas Fernwood's death, the darkness that had shrouded the Fernwoods and Cliftons largely dispersed. I say 'largely' because there are some things that are so terrible they can never be undone.

I have no doubt at all, although I cannot prove it, that Thomas Fernwood was murdered by a member of his own family. Of course, I suspect who that individual is, but I must not put a name to that suspicion, as I might be mistaken. Better to stay silent unless I have proof. I have no wish to add to this family's unhappiness.

It is true that every member of the family benefitted by Thomas Fernwood's death. I am not referring only to money, although that is one factor. Mrs Fernwood was undoubtedly a far happier woman for the loss of her tyrannical husband. She was able to stir from her bed of pain, walk about more than she had done before and have some pleasure in life. She enjoyed the companionship of Mrs Clifton, and the two became great friends. I believe that her previous insistence that she was an invalid was largely due to a desire to be ignored by her husband as far as was possible, and in that she was successful. Her son, Mr William Fernwood inherited the bulk of the property, and he and his wife were able to enjoy a more comfortable life free from excessive hours of labour.

The three girls, Ada, Ellen and Mary, were no longer treated as unpaid drudges, and were sent to good schools to complete their education.

As to the boys, I am sorry to say that Thomas Fernwood had been in the habit of using severe corporal punishment on them if they failed to do well at school. Both Peter and George were beaten in a manner that far exceeded what even an advocate of that kind of chastisement would think acceptable. George was much the better scholar and so suffered less, but Peter, who was a little slow for his age, was beaten often and hard, in a manner that caused great distress to Mrs Clifton, who begged Fernwood not to hurt her son. I am convinced that it was only the threat of the workhouse for Mrs Clifton and her son and daughter that kept them in the house.

There is only one person who I know for certain did not commit the murder, and that was Mrs Jane Fernwood, not because she did not have a motive, but because she had suffered a fall the day before, and in addition to her painful back and legs she had twisted her ankle which was very swollen and would not bear her weight. She was therefore quite unable to walk unassisted. To go

621

downstairs and get the arsenic and put it in her husband's tea, however much she might have wished to, was beyond her capabilities.

I can say no more. The murderer will be punished one day, if not in this life then the next.

Mina was still wondering what it was that Thomas Fernwood had seen which had so convinced him that he had been deliberately poisoned. If he had noticed someone putting something in his tea and thought it suspicious, then surely he would not have drunk it. Perhaps the poisoner had told him it was sugar being added or it was being stirred simply to cool it, and he had only found out differently when the corrosive savaged his throat and intestines.

Mrs Clifton, Mary's mother, was an obvious suspect since she had made the tea and bought it to him. She, Mina reasoned, would have put the poison in the tea when it was made, and not added it later, at the bedside, unless there was a potential witness in the kitchen or on the stairs. Once again, she studied the inquest report. No-one else had said they were in the kitchen when the Thomas Fernwood's tea was being made, and no-one had seen Mrs Clifton take it up to his bedroom. Mina began to wonder if Fernwood had not, after all, seen anything suspicious, but had simply assumed that it was Mrs Clifton who had poisoned the tea.

If it was not she, then the poison must have been stirred into the tea after it was made. Mrs Clifton had not left the cup unobserved at any time right up to the moment it was placed beside Thomas Fernwood's bed. There was then a clear ten or fifteen minutes for the deed to be done. William Fernwood, as his father's main heir, was an obvious suspect although his wife Margery might have carried out the actual poisoning at his behest.

Did Peter, though only ten, poison his great uncle to avoid more beatings? But would Peter have even known where the arsenic was kept in the house? It was in a kitchen drawer to which he was unlikely to have gone. Also, the inquest evidence suggested that all the children were at the breakfast table at the crucial time.

And yet, Mina thought, memory being what it was, no-one would have been paying attention from moment to moment where everyone in the house actually was. The only record of it was in recollections too fallible to trust. Anyone might have absented themselves from a room for a minute or two, an incident so trivial that the others might not have remembered or even noticed it.

Mina was obliged to remind herself that fascinating as the puzzle was, it was none of her business who had killed Thomas Fernwood, but she needed to consider the question if only to judge how truthful or possible any messages from mediums might be. If Dr Sperley's notes were correct, then Jane Fernwood was innocent, and Mr Castlehouse's message did not apply to the Fernwood case at all, although Miss Clifton was understandably convinced it was.

And now Mina had a terrible dilemma. Should she tell George Fernwood and Miss Clifton what was in Dr Sperley's notes? The message on the slate had taken away their fears and would enable them to marry with a clear conscience. Perhaps, Mina thought, she ought to leave strictly alone.

Chapter Thirty-Six

Dear Mina,

I am returning to Brighton at once as I have some very exciting news, which I can't wait to share with you! I will call on you tomorrow afternoon, at 3 and tell all. Oh, do say you will be at home!

Yours,

Nellie

Mina wondered if Nellie, several months married, was anticipating an addition to her domestic scene, but suspected that news which many women would have met with great happiness was not something which would bring Nellie so much satisfaction. She dispatched a note to say that she would be at home and would be delighted to receive a visit.

'Well!' said Nellie, her face glowing, as she kissed Mina on both cheeks. 'It is the most wonderful thing I have to tell you! I do hope you have a beautiful gown as you will be required to wear it!'

'Dare I ask for what event?' asked Mina, adding cautiously, as they made themselves comfortable before the glow of the parlour fire. 'From the tone of your letter, I had suspected a christening.'

Nellie's eyes opened very wide, then she laughed. 'Oh, no, nothing of that kind, not if I am concerned. That will never be.'

'Never? Does Mr Jordan know that?'

'Not yet.' Nellie placed a hand flat to her waist, which was as trim as it had always been. 'Mina, my dear,' she said confidingly, 'you and I, we are not made to be mothers. I did think, when I was with M. Baptiste, that there was a danger it might happen, but instead, I learned that it never could.' Her voice softened and her face became solemn as she went on. 'Believe me, we two are better off that way, I am sure of it.' A bright smile jumped into life, bringing fresh warmth to her features. 'Well, enough of that. No, the news concerns my dear friend Kitty Betts, the miraculous Princess Kirabampu, who Richard drew so beautifully at my *salon*. Would you believe, she is to be married! And before the year is out!'

Rose brought the tea tray, and cook's attempt at almond biscuits, which were more icing than biscuit and topped with roughly chopped almonds. 'Thank you Rose,' said Mina, kindly, and the maid withdrew.

'Richard has flattered cook into attempting confectionary but she is a little heavy handed at present. Still, we hope for improvement with practice.' Mina poured the tea. 'I didn't know Miss Betts was betrothed.'

'Well, that is what is so surprising,' said Nellie, selecting a biscuit, examining it to see if it was edible, and taking a careful bite. 'When you met her at my house she wasn't. It was all so sudden. And to think it was actually my doing, as she first met her future husband on that very evening. It seems that soon afterwards she was shopping in St James' Street and chanced to meet the gentleman again, and they started to converse. There could not have been more romance in the air if it had been spring blossom time. They agreed to meet again and it was all settled in days. The license has been applied for and they will be married before Christmas.'

'St James' Street?' Mina recalled that this was the location of the art gallery. 'She is not marrying Mr Dorry, is she?'

'Mr Dorry? Oh, goodness me, no, Mr Dorry will never marry unless the law is amended so one can wed a statue. Did you not know? He is in love with a beautiful Adonis, all in marble, and quite nude. No, Kitty is to marry Mr Honeyacre.'

Mina was so astounded she nearly dropped her teacup, and for a moment thought she had actually misheard. The last time she had seen Mr Honeyacre he had assured her in perfect seriousness that his ideal life companion was a respectable lady of culture and good sense, and he was now about to marry a flirtatious contortionist. Once again, she felt thankful that men and marriage were things with which she did not need to concern herself.

'I am to be matron of honour,' Nellie continued, placing the uneaten half of her biscuit on her plate, where Mina felt sure it would remain, 'and tomorrow night there will be a delightful supper to celebrate the betrothal, which you must attend.' Nellie handed Mina an invitation.

Mina felt obliged to mention the recent misunderstanding between herself and Mr Honeyacre and Nellie laughed until tears started in her eyes and then assured Mina that she would see things put right. 'And now I must hurry away as there is so much to do. Kitty is choosing her trousseau and her going away gowns, all from Jordan and Conroy, of course, and I am to advise her. No expense will be spared. The wedding breakfast will be held in the assembly room at the Grand Hotel, and the entertainment will be second to none. Kitty's mother is a Red Indian and will be sawn in half, her father is a Chinese sword-swallower, and her brothers are Greek acrobats. It will be the wedding of the year.'

'I have spoken to Nellie,' said Richard, as he and Mina ate luncheon the following day. 'We met at a coffee room, suitably chaperoned by Miss Kitty Betts and Mr Honeyacre, who has quite forgiven me for being your secret *amour*. The private detective who was watching us from the next table will be able to report that there was no unseemly behaviour. I am given to understand that I am not to attend the little celebratory gathering tonight, as Mr Jordan prefers not to sit across a table from me unless it is very much wider than the Grand Hotel can accommodate. No matter, I can do without his presence, which would quite put me off my food. He has a stare that would curdle milk. He hopes it will curdle my blood but it does no such thing.'

'Poor Richard, I hope you will be at the wedding.'

'Oh yes, Miss Betts wants me for an usher, and has asked me to sketch the event.' He served himself a large helping of trifle, which was mainly composed of custard and leftover almond biscuits. 'Tonight, however, I will take my busy pencil to the theatre, where that shining star of the Brighton stage, Mr Marcus Merridew, will personating all the great heroes of Shakespeare with a dozen changes of costume and twice as many wigs, after which there will be champagne and laughter.' Once luncheon was over, he departed in far better humour than Mina had feared.

For that evening's select gathering Mr Honeyacre had secured a table in a private portion of the restaurant attached to the Grand Hotel. As Mina awaited the cab he had ordered, Rose, who must have received a schedule of instructions from Dr Hamid, loaded her in enough layers of clothing to promote heat rash and escorted her down the front steps.

'Where too, Miss?' asked the cabdriver with the tartan scarf. He had already climbed down and opened the door for his passenger. 'Will it be Mr Castlehouse's again?'

'Not today,' said Mina with a smile. 'Is Mr Castlehouse's a very popular destination?'

'Oh, he is, yes, Miss. I take a great many people there, both ladies and gentlemen. They tell me all about it, too. Very strange it is, and all. Some of them even come straight from the railway station so they have come a long way special to see him. One lady even went there twice in one day.'

Mina, leaning on his arm, was about to step into the cab but she paused. Was this the evidence she had been looking for, that Mr Castlehouse conducted private séances at high prices?

'Two sittings in one day?' she exclaimed. 'How extraordinary. He only advertises one in the newspapers. Are you certain?'

'Well, not for a sitting, as she wasn't there above ten minutes the first time. That was the same lady you travelled with.'

Mina was so astonished by this news it made her shiver. 'Twice in one day? The lady I travelled with went to Mr Castlehouse twice on the same day? Tell me more.'

The driver was a little taken aback by her intensity but did his best to remember. 'Well I took her from the station to Mr Castlehouse's lodgings. She told me to wait for a few minutes, and then she came out again and straight after that I took her to you. Then I took both of you to Mr Castlehouse.'

Mina had been to Mr Castlehouse's twice, both times in the company of Miss Clifton. 'Do you recall what day this was?'

He scratched his head. 'Not rightly, no.'

'Was the lady carrying a parcel?'

He thought hard. 'Yes. Something. Two parcels, I think. Yes, that's right, she had two, and she left one with Mr Castlehouse and then she took the other one to you.'

Mina hardly dared ask the next question. 'Two parcels the same size and shape?'

'Yes.'

'Tied with cord,' said Mina, faintly, though it was less of a question than a statement.

'Both of them, yes, I think so. Are you alright Miss?'

Mina nodded, speechlessly.

'May I help you, Miss?' He offered his arm and assisted her into the cab.

Mina wanted to stay at home. She wanted to sit quietly alone by her own fireside with hot soup and bread and a glass of sherry and think about what she had just learned. Instead she was obliged to go to the shine and bustle of the Grand Hotel, and pretend that all was well.

Miss Betts and Nellie chattered away the evening, and Mr Honeyacre, after attempting to apologise to Mina for his rapid departure at their last meeting without actually saying why it had occurred, sat bemusedly gazing on his vivacious betrothed. If Mina said less than was usual, it was scarcely noticed. She did take the opportunity to ask about the expression 'unknown artist' and Mr Honeyacre replied that in his experience it referred to the fact that no-one knew who had created a work. He could not say why lack of a signature could ever be thought a good thing.

Once home, Mina wrote a letter to Miss Clifton, saying that she would like to speak to her when she was next in Brighton, as she had something of great significance to impart.

Chapter Thirty-Seven

Miss Clifton was able to call on Mina in two days' time, and arrived in tremendous good humour. 'I am so very excited to hear what you have to say! Why could you not have put it in a letter instead of making me wait so?' she teased. 'Have you been to Miss Brendel again? Or Mr Castlehouse? Or is it another medium? But I must tell you, George was so astonished when I showed him the slates. He is almost convinced, now, I am sure of it. We are planning to go to Mr Castlehouse together as soon as possible, and this time I am certain we will receive proof that even George cannot dismiss!'

'Miss Clifton,' said Mina, quietly, 'I am sorry to have to say this to you, but I have discovered that you have deceived me. I have chosen to speak to you alone because I do not as yet know whether you have also deceived Mr Fernwood, or whether the two of you were working together, or if the deception was actually his and you were merely his agent.'

Miss Clifton looked shocked, and as she recovered from her initial surprise, a host of emotions flickered across her face. Mina watched this procession carefully. Since she had been careful not to reveal what she knew, her visitor had been plunged into a state of uncertainty. She could guess what Miss Clifton must be thinking. What, precisely, did Mina know? How much could be denied or safely revealed? 'I am sure I don't know what you mean,' said Miss Clifton at last, with a fragile defiance that sounded doomed from the start not to last.

Mina continued. 'What I am not yet sure of is if you intended to deceive me from the very beginning or turned to the scheme afterwards. Either way, it is clear that I cannot assist you further. I do have some passing interest in your motives, but if you choose to tell me nothing that is your affair. I regret that after today we cannot meet again. You may say whatever you wish to Mr Fernwood. That is your business.'

Miss Clifton looked as if she was about to say more, but remained silent.

Mina reached for the bell to summon Rose. 'If there is no more to discuss, then I bid you good-day.'

'Please!' said Miss Clifton, impulsively. 'I am so sorry, but I believe I have done nothing very wrong. I only wish to be married before I am middle aged. That is every woman's desire — a husband — children.' She paused and blushed suddenly, recalling that this was an ambition to which Mina could not aspire.

Mina stayed her hand. 'And you thought you could achieve that by consulting a medium? Even though at one time you had no belief in them?'

'I had never visited a medium before, I only knew what I had heard and read, but George and I were desperate for an answer, and it seemed the only way. But when we went to our first séances I concluded that as I had originally thought, these people were charlatans intent on making money from unhappy people. The replies they gave us were so general, so vague they could have applied to anyone. The other sitters — I felt so sorry for them, grasping at little hints they thought were meant for them. They wanted to believe, but if I ever had any faith in such a thing, it soon vanished.'

'And yet you went on. In fact, you gave me every impression that you were a devoted believer, whereas Mr Fernwood doubted that any result was possible.'

Miss Clifton chewed her lip and moved her hands convulsively. 'You must understand, Miss Scarletti. When George and I consulted our doctor as to whether it was advisable for us to marry and have a family, he said he thought that the dangers were slight, but he could not reassure us that there were none. I was willing to take the chance. I know I can be a good mother and lead my children along the paths of honesty, but George said he could not accept even a small risk of what terrible things might ensue from the mixing of the same blood. I thought that if there was some answer that would satisfy him we might yet marry, but he said that it was hopeless as the only person who knew the answer was uncle Thomas. George always thought that Dr Sperley had his suspicions, but he had passed away not long before. Then I read in the newspapers about the trial of Miss Eustace and her confederates, and the evidence you gave in that affair, and it gave me the idea of consulting you to see if there was a genuine medium who could help.'

Mina was not placated, and her manner did not waver. 'But it was more than that. Perhaps you did entertain the possibility of finding a genuine medium, but you must have thought it far more probable that you would find another clever and convincing cheat like Miss Eustace. My feeling is that you never became a believer; you began as a sceptic and continued as one, and remain one still. You pretended to believe solely in order to persuade Mr Fernwood to visit mediums. In fact, I will go further; you were never really looking for a genuine medium at all, were you? You were looking for one who was capable of providing evidence that would convince Mr Fernwood, and could be bribed into doing so. Am I correct?'

Miss Clifton began to look afraid.

'You told Mr Castlehouse what to write on the slate, didn't you? You made it up.'

Miss Clifton nodded.

'You bought two identical sets of folding slates, and made the same secret mark on them both, one of which you gave to Mr Castlehouse before the séance.'

'How do you know that?'

'Let it remain a mystery. So, am I correct that Mr Fernwood knows nothing of your deception?'

629

'You are. But I beg you not to tell him!'

'That is really none of my business. As a matter of curiosity, do you think your solution was the correct one? Your great aunt was an invalid and might not have been able to commit the crime. What if she was unable to stir from her bed?'

'She could walk better than she liked to admit. But I don't mind or care if it is right or not. It is the answer we need in order to live our lives. The past is past, and we can't change it, we must accept that and look to the future. If we dwell forever in the past we will have no future. All I want is to marry George and help him with the shop and have a family. Is that really too much to ask?'

Mina's annoyance with Miss Clifton began to soften. 'No, it is very natural. But I think under the circumstances I have done all I can, and more. I now leave it to you to convince Mr Fernwood that he has nothing to be anxious about, and I wish you both every happiness for the future.'

It was a formal parting of the ways. Once Miss Clifton had left, Mina gave further thought to the question of Thomas Fernwood's death. It was possible that the children did not know about Jane Fernwood's twisted ankle. A visit from Dr Sperley to attend her was a regular event and would not have invited curiosity. Even if Dr Sperley was correct, however, and Jane Fernwood could not have left her bed to poison her husband's tea, it was, Mina realised, still possible that Miss Clifton had stumbled on the right answer, and her aunt was the guiding intelligence behind the murder. The unhappy Mrs Fernwood had been tended by Mrs Clifton and granddaughters, Ada and Ellen, and her own son and daughter in law must also have visited her. She could have suggested to any one of them the idea of curing Thomas Fernwood's fondness for the bottle with a little medicinal arsenic. His death could still have been due to an accidental overdose, or maybe his drinking had weakened his stomach and made him more likely to die from a dose that would not have killed a healthier man. Whoever had actually added it to the tea had been horrified by the unplanned death, and understandably chosen to remain silent. There was still, to Mina, the puzzle of how Thomas Fernwood had known the identity of his poisoner. It was something she was now sure she would never know.

It was done. Mina had no intention of seeing either Miss Clifton or Mr Fernwood again. Neither did she wish to visit Miss Brendel or Mr Castlehouse. What she needed was an hour at the baths, surrounded by scented vapour and then the delicious ease of perfumed oils being gentled into her skin. The baths were her haven, where no-one could demand she do anything or deliver complaining letters. She could let her thoughts glide through the ether and pick up the story ideas that swam there. She would write a story about a magic herb, whose vapours made bad people good and discontented people happy, that took away pain and selfishness, and anxiety. The more she thought about it the more she saw that such an invention would only bring chaos to the world.

Once her treatment was over, she thought of going to see Dr Hamid to tell him how things had transpired, but on learning that he was busy with a patient, she decided not to wait, and ordered a cab home.

Mina was just descending from the cab when she heard a rapid tapping of footsteps, and was advanced upon at speed by Mrs Brendel who had clearly been lying in wait for her.

'At last!' exclaimed that lady with a face of fury. 'Your maid was very rude to me just now, she absolutely refused to allow me to come in and wait for you!'

'I am very sorry,' said Mina, mystified, wondering how Mrs Brendel had obtained her address. 'That is so unlike Rose to behave in that way. I will be sure to reprimand her.'

'But you cannot escape me now! You will not!' Mrs Brendel waved a determined fist from which a forefinger emerged like the claw of a savage bird. 'I demand to know where my daughter is!'

Mina had been about in invite Mrs Brendel in, but in view of the ferocity of her manner, hesitated. She wasn't at all sure if Richard was at home, and was not happy to deal with this potentially violent situation alone.

'Mrs Brendel,' she said, trying to speak calmly, 'I am very sorry that you are upset, but I am afraid I can't help you. I don't know where your daughter is. I have not seen her since the supper at Mr Honeyacre's. Why do you think I would know?'

Mrs Brendel stamped her foot in annoyance. 'Because she has run away from home, and I know the culprit, it is that horrid Mr Dawson from the music shop who has tempted her to elope with him. He has been sending the most disgusting love notes to my daughter, and I suspect that you were his agent in this.'

'I can assure you, I was not.'

The agitated mother threw up her hands and paced back and forth, her cloak rippling in the wind. Mina wanted to make for her front door but knew that she could not reach it before Mrs Brendel, and did not want the distracted woman forcing her way into the house in that state. 'I was only from home for a short while!' wailed Mrs Brendel. 'Mr Quinley, who watches our affairs, is away on business, and a villain has taken advantage of that and abducted my daughter, my poor innocent girl! She will be ruined!' Mrs Brendel pulled a handkerchief from her pocket and pressed it to her eyes. 'I thought it was safe to go out and leave Athene under Jessie's care, but on my return just now, I found a note to the effect that the maid had been called away as she was needed for some emergency. I am convinced that this was a ruse by Mr Dawson, a forged appeal to lure Jessie from the house and leave Athene alone and unprotected.' She wiped her eyes and gulped, a new burst of fury overtaking her distress. 'I went to see him at Potts Music Emporium and the scoundrel denied everything, but then I made him turn out his pockets in front of the manager, and found a note he was intending to send to Athene making plans for her to run away with him. He is even now being questioned by the police. And I found one other thing — a card with your address on it.' She glared at Mina. 'You must be his confederate.'

'I am not his confederate,' said Mina, beginning to tremble with cold, and pulling her cloak more closely about her. 'When I first paid you a visit Mr Dawson approached me outside your house and expressed his concern for your daughter's health. I suppose I took pity on him and we exchanged cards, but nothing more.'

'Where is Athene?' demanded Mrs Brendel. 'Have you lodged her somewhere?'

'Mrs Brendel, please believe me, I don't know where she is. I did not even know she was from home until you told me just now.'

Mrs Brendel was not a lady who gave up easily. 'Is she in your house?'

Mina knew she could not stay outside much longer or all the good of the vapour bath would be undone, and even reversed. There was only one thing she could do. She mounted the front steps, with Mrs Brendel running after and overtaking her, unlocked the door and pushed it open. 'Come in, Mrs Brendel, do. You may search my house from attic to basement, every room there is. Question the servants if you must, examine my private papers. I give you complete freedom. I promise you will not find your daughter here.'

Mrs Brendel hesitated.

'Well? What are you waiting for? Search to your heart's content. Under the beds, in the wardrobes, everywhere.'

Even Mrs Brendel declined to commit that outrage. She shook her head. 'Very well,' she said reluctantly, 'I accept your assurance. There are other places for me to look. But Dawson is the villain and he will not get away with this!' She shook her fist again, and strode away.

Mina thankfully entered the comparative warmth of her hallway and closed the front door. Moments later Richard opened the door of the front parlour and peered out.

'Has she gone? She was making a dreadful fuss earlier. I had Rose send her away, and tell her no-one was at home. Why did she come here?'

'She thinks I have connived with Mr Dawson to steal away her daughter. As if I would do such a thing!'

'No, of course you would not. But do come into the parlour, and warm yourself by the fire. There is cocoa and sandwiches. And I have some good news for you. You are going to be very pleased with me. I have found out all the secrets of the Brendels!'

632

Chapter Thirty-Eight

'You never cease to surprise me,' said Mina, hoping that her brother had not done anything foolhardy or indelicate. She removed her cloak, bonnet and muffler, and followed Richard into the parlour where she was astonished to see the Brendels' maid Jessie, sitting at the table. There was the promised jug of cocoa and a plate of sandwiches, and every sign that both Richard and Jessie had been enjoying an early supper. The maid, on seeing Mina, looked highly embarrassed to be there at all, and immediately got to her feet and curtseyed.

'Oh, please, do sit,' said Mina, and poured some cocoa for herself. It was very welcome, and she hoped it might just stave off a nasty chill. Jessie had a half-consumed sandwich on a tea plate before her, but was reluctant to eat above stairs with Mina present, and let it lie there.

'I will tell you everything that has happened,' said Richard, cheerfully, as Jessie remained nervously silent. 'Earlier today, I was sketching Miss Brendel, as I have been doing this last week, and Jessie here was sitting by as chaperone, as was all good and proper, when quite suddenly, the poor young lady came over faint, and had to be revived with her tisane. While this was being done, Jessie quick-mindedly took the opportunity to tell me all her worries and very pleased I am that she did. Jessie, I want you to tell Miss Scarletti what you told me.'

Jessie gave a little cough to clear her throat. 'Yes, well, I've been very worried for quite some while. It's a good place as places go, but there is something strange happening in that house and I don't know how to account for it.'

'Have you been there long?' asked Mina.

'No, only a few months. I was engaged by the landlady, Mrs Fazackerly, as general maid. There were three tenants in it before, and then Mrs Brendel came and took the whole house on a quarterly rent. She is very particular about how things are done, not that there's anything wrong in that. Only, I'm concerned about Miss Brendel, as I can see she is very delicate. She told me once that she had been in good health until her stomach turned bad and she lost her appetite. That was when her visions began. Very peculiar they are, too. She sees all sorts; men, women, children, animals, even carriages. She doesn't like to see them, but she can't make them stop. But her mother; she thought it was all very interesting and ever since then the poor girl has been kept on short commons. Just fed enough to keep body and soul together. If she feels hungry I'm under orders to give her nothing except her tea. It isn't right. The poor thing hasn't had a proper square meal in six months.'

Mina was appalled. 'So you are saying that her mother starves her in the belief that if she feeds her properly the visions will stop?'

'That's what I think, yes.'

'This is monstrous! Someone should send for the girl's father. I'm sure he would have something to say about it. What about Mr Quinley, the solicitor? I thought he was there to look after the welfare of the family on behalf of Mr Brendel. Does he say nothing?'

'No, he's been at the beck and call of Mrs Brendel. But only until recently. He's gone now.'

'Gone? Not for good, surely?'

'Oh, I don't know about that. Last week Mrs Brendel had a letter — from Mr Brendel it was. At least, I think it was from him because it was from Wakefield where he lives. I didn't see what was in it but when she read it there was a big upset, and Mrs Brendel and Mr Quinley had a long talk about it. I had the feeling it was about money. Then Mr Quinley said that he would go straight up to Wakefield and see Mr Brendel and make it all right, because he didn't think it could be mended in a letter. Then he ordered his bag to be packed. He left the same day.'

'And has he made it right?'

'I don't know. I don't think so. He hasn't sent a letter. There's nothing at all come from Wakefield. Mrs Brendel has looked very unhappy ever since.'

Richard helped himself to more cocoa and sandwiches, content to allow Mina to ask the questions.

'You say that you have been worried about Miss Brendel's health. Has her mother been worried? In all the time that they have been in Brighton, has Miss Brendel ever been examined by a doctor?'

'No, there's no doctor come to see her, that I am sure of. I did once mention to Mrs Brendel how thin her daughter was, but her mother just said that gentlemen liked a lady with a trim waist, so that was all to the good. I didn't dare say anything about it again.'

'Scandalous, isn't it,' exclaimed Richard. 'I am sure that the reason the mother would never allow her daughter to be seen by a doctor is because that would reveal her cruel treatment. So I have taken the liberty of summoning Dr Hamid. I sent him a note just before you arrived.'

'You have summoned him?' queried Mina. 'Where to?'

'Why here, of course.' Richard bit into a sandwich.

'But Miss Brendel is not here.'

'Mmm. Yes she is. I gave her some tea and now she is lying down to rest upstairs.'

Mina was astounded. 'Richard! I can scarcely believe what I am hearing! You abducted her?'

'Not at all. She came of her own accord.'

'But her mother doesn't know where she is!'

He laughed. 'I certainly hope not.'

Mina was aghast at the situation, and its potential for hideous embarrassment. 'I have just told Mrs Brendel that her daughter is not here. I invited her in to search the house and prove it to herself.'

'Just as well she did not.'

'She is beside herself with worry!'

Richard shrugged. 'I don't know why. Miss Brendel penned a little note to say that she was safe and happy.'

'Little enough comfort for her mother, I fear. She is determined that her daughter has run away and is being hidden somewhere by Mr Dawson, the young man who wants to marry her. In fact, she has had him arrested, on the strength of some love notes he had intended to deliver. Richard, please tell me you have not been delivering Mr Dawson's love notes for him.'

'I'm not sure I have ever met Mr Dawson, and I know I haven't delivered any notes. Jessie can attest to that.'

Mina looked sharply at Jessie. 'Oh, no, Miss, I've not delivered any notes to Miss Brendel, I promise.'

Richard finished his sandwich. 'Dear me. Poor Mr Dawson. I suppose Miss Brendel had better write another note to say she isn't with him.'

'If such a note would be believed,' said Mina.

'True. But we should try. Shall I see it written? Rose can deliver it. Of course, even if Dawson is exonerated Mrs Brendel might still think her daughter has run away with an unsuitable man.'

'She has,' said Mina drily. She thought quickly. 'Very well, I agree that it would be no bad thing if a doctor was to see her and learn how she has been treated, but immediately that has been done we should return Miss Brendel to her mother who will, we must hope, accept sound advice from Dr Hamid as to how her daughter ought to be looked after.'

'But she doesn't want to go back,' Richard objected.

'I doubt that she will have any choice. She can't stay here. Sooner or later when Mrs Brendel does not find her daughter she will return. How come she does not suspect Mr Richard Henry of being her abductor?'

'Ah,' said Richard, 'now that was where I was very clever. Miss Brendel didn't leave with me. I left the house this afternoon, after the sketch was completed, and then Jessie here made all the arrangements, and later on I sent a cab round and when Mrs Brendel went to do her shopping, they crept out.'

'The only reason I stayed on was to look after Miss Brendel,' said Jessie. 'I've sent a note to Mrs Fazackerly and left one for Mrs Brendel to say I've been called away urgently to look after a sick lady, but to be truthful I don't want to go back. I don't know what to do.'

'We'll think of something!' said Richard, confidently. 'In the meantime, will you stay here to look after Miss Brendel until she is restored to health?'

'I'd like to, yes.'

'There we are!' said Richard. 'That is all arranged.'

The doorbell prevented Mina from further comment and Dr Hamid was admitted.

'I was called to a serious case,' said Dr Hamid, as he came in, looking quickly about him at the occupants of the parlour. 'Please tell me what is wrong.'

'Yes, it is Miss Brendel, who was visiting with her maid, and I am sorry to say arrived in a state of collapse,' Mina explained. 'Jessie, could you show Dr Hamid to where Miss Brendel is resting?'

'Has her mother been sent for?'

'Mrs Brendel was out, but a message has been left for her,' said Richard.

Fortunately, Dr Hamid required no further information and hurried upstairs with Jessie to see the patient.

'What were you thinking of?' demanded Mina when she and Richard were alone.

'The lady's health, of course. What should I have done?'

Mina had nothing to suggest. 'I only hope the matter is settled before Mrs Brendel sends the police here. Thank goodness Mother is away.'

Richard munched on another sandwich, while Mina wondered what to do, and decided that she would take no action until she had consulted Dr Hamid.

He returned shortly. 'You did right to call me. I understand that Miss Brendel has been deliberately kept short of food by her mother. The maid, Jessie, has been very helpful. She assisted Mrs Brendel in the composition of the tisane and has given me a precise list of what it contained. I have been extremely foolish not to notice before what I now perceive. All the herbs used, while essentially harmless, and with some beneficial effects, do have one thing in common. They all suppress the appetite. Mrs Brendel's actions have seriously endangered her daughter's health and may well amount to a criminal offence. I have no alternative but to notify the police of my findings. I shall also write to the father and suggest that as soon as Miss Brendel is strong enough to travel, he comes and takes her home. In the meantime, I have advised that Miss Brendel should rest, and be given what nourishment she can manage. I will prescribe a tonic, and have written full instructions as to her care and feeding. Would it inconvenience you if she was to remain here for a few days?'

'Not at all,' said Richard. 'She has her maid to attend her.'

'What if Mrs Brendel should discover where her daughter is, and comes to take her back?' asked Mina.

'Say that she is not to be moved on my orders. I take full responsibility. Other than that, I trust you are all well here?' he asked, glancing at Mina particularly.

'Yes, thank you,' said Mina.

'All we need to do,' said Richard, once Dr Hamid had departed, 'is keep Miss Brendel away from her dreadful mother until her father comes.'

'I think that is for the best,' said Mina, 'although I am hoping to resolve this without a great commotion in the street and a paragraph in the *Gazette*.'

'And now, as we have two more mouths to feed, I suggest you order an extra large breakfast for tomorrow morning. Oh, and I will need a little loan. I spent my last money on the cab for Miss Brendel and Jessie. And I am not sure of being paid for my sketch work now.'

Chapter Thirty-Nine

Next morning, Miss Brendel, having enjoyed a restful night, appeared at the breakfast table, looking petulant.

'I am supposed to be dosed with this tonic three times a day!' she exclaimed, peering at the label on a brown glass bottle. 'It tastes very nasty. I prefer my tea.'

'Dr Hamid has left strict orders that you are to have Indian or China tea in the daytime from now on, and camomile at night, but not the green brew your mother gave you,' said Mina. 'I know she meant it for the best, but it was disagreeing with you, and making you unwell.'

'Let me help you to some breakfast,' said Richard, waving a serving spoon over a laden sideboard. 'We have scrambled eggs and bacon, and kidneys, and toast and muffins, and marmalade, and honey, and once you have eaten all those then you can go around to the start and eat it all again.'

'Oh, just a little dry toast, please,' said Miss Brendel. Richard brought the toast rack to the table. She took the smallest piece and nibbled a corner. 'Mother says my digestion is very delicate and I will upset my stomach if I eat too much.'

Richard piled his plate high with food and sat down. 'When was the last time you ate too much?'

She frowned. 'I can't remember.'

'You know, that toast will be too dry to swallow easily unless you put a little scrambled egg on it.'

Miss Brendel paused and looked at the toast, then put it down on her plate and Richard spooned some scrambled egg on top. She picked up her knife and fork, and sawed off a tiny piece, then lifted it to her mouth and chewed thoughtfully.

'Can you tell us about your visions?' he asked. 'How did they start? When did they start?'

'Oh, it was last spring. I ate something that upset my digestion, which is why it has been so poor of late. Fish, I think it was. I didn't eat a morsel of food for a whole week. And that was when the visions came. I started off only seeing Father at first. Mother said it was caused by my worry at his being away, and it wouldn't happen again once he was home. Then one morning, as I opened my eyes, I saw them, standing at the foot of my bed.' She took a larger bite of toast and egg.

'Who were they?'

'I wasn't sure. Just people, ladies and gentlemen, as one sees in the street or the shops. I was frightened at first. I wondered why they were in my bedroom. I called out for Mother, but by the time she came, they had disappeared.' There was a pause and some loud munching as Miss Brendel cleared her plate, then she took a good gulp of tea. 'It was strange, to see them grow paler and paler until they vanished like mist. Mother insisted I had had a dream, but I knew I was awake.' She dabbed her lips with a napkin.

'A little more, perhaps?' Richard suggested. 'The bacon is very good.'

'Oh, I have not eaten bacon for so long. Just one slice. And I think I could manage another piece of toast.'

After breakfast, Miss Brendel, afraid to go out lest she should encounter her mother, returned to her room to hide behind the pages of a book, and Jessie agreed to sit with her.

Soon afterwards, a letter for Mina was delivered in an envelope embellished with the address of Phipps and Co. Mina opened it with trepidation and the contents were far worse than she could have imagined.

Dear Miss Scarletti,

I hope this finds you well.

As we discussed recently, I have been keeping my eyes and ears open for any news of Mr Dorry. I chanced to read in today's Telegraph *that his gallery in London has been suddenly closed down, amidst some controversy, and I have made some further enquiries to discover the circumstances. All I have been able to glean is that it was in connection with a recent exhibition of signed early sketches by J. M. W. Turner. I will let you know at once if I should hear any more.*

I would advise any artist to be very cautious about carrying out work for Mr Dorry.

Yours faithfully,

G. Phipps

Mina went up to Richard's room, to find him stretched out on the bed like the dying hero of a tragic novel.

She sat beside him and stroked his tumbled blond curls. 'Are you well, my dear?'

'Oh,' he groaned, 'as well as a man can be whose life is one of boredom and disappointment and penury.'

'Are you really so poor? Has Mr Dorry not paid you anything more, or were those two guineas the sum total?'

'Yes, that was all so far. And I had to spend most of it on materials in his shop. Art paper is deucedly expensive, you know!' He made an effort and struggled into a sitting position. 'You couldn't lend me a spot of cash? Just until I sell some pictures?'

'No, Richard, I could not. Tell me, how many sketches have you done for Mr Dorry?'

'Oh, about twenty I think. I have five more I am supposed to be taking to him today. Perhaps I shall ask him for something on account.'

'That might be an idea. Richard — I know you told me that you had not signed any of the sketches you did for Mr Dorry. Is that still the case? Has he asked you to put a signature on any of the recent ones? Your name or — another, perhaps? I know they are in the style of Mr Turner. Did you write Mr Turner's name on them?'

'No. He did once ask me if I could copy Mr Turner's hand, just as an exercise, you understand, and he showed me how it was done, and I tried but I couldn't get it right. He was much better at it.'

Richard, with the prospect of money in mind, eventually stirred himself, put his new sketches in a portfolio case and went out.

Mina sat at her writing desk and composed a new idea for a story about an evil sorceress who created a potion that deluded people into believing that blank sheets of paper were valuable works of art, which they bought at high prices. They were so proud of their purchases, that they hired a gallery for an exhibition and invited the press. The sorceress attempted to fool the visitors by serving them with her potion, but one of the pressmen distrusted the strange looking drink. When he argued that the papers were blank, the buyers all saw that they had been duped, and demanded their money back. The sorceress fled with the angry men in hot pursuit, and tried to escape them by taking wing from the edge of a cliff. But the creation of the potion had depleted her powers and she plunged into the sea and drowned.

Richard returned two hours later and came into Mina's room without knocking. He was even more despondent than he had been when he had set out, and was still carrying the sketches. He sat down heavily on the bed. 'Well, here's a thing. I go all the way to St James' Street only to find that Mr Dorry's gallery is closed down. There isn't even a sign to say when it will open again, or where customers are to go in the meantime.'

'Is the shop empty?' asked Mina.

'It could not be emptier if it had been burgled. All the pictures are gone, including mine, and the statue, and the man himself is gone too, and no-one knows where, although it is rumoured that he is on his way to Italy. And his assistant has vanished as if he had been conjured away. It's too bad, Dorry is nothing more than a thief.'

Mina came and sat beside him and gave him a hug.

'So I thought, well, I still have all these pictures to sell, and someone else might want to buy them, so I went to Dickinson's gallery on the Kings Road; you know, where they are exhibiting the new portrait of the Queen. And they have some very good watercolours of fine ladies. I'm not sure I could do anything nearly as good. So I showed the proprietor my drawings and asked him if he would buy them, or display and sell them for me, and do you know, he became quite annoyed. I don't know why. He even said that if I didn't leave at once he would call the police. Now what do you think of that?'

'I think,' said Mina, concluding that Richard had probably had a lucky escape, 'that it is time you gave up doing sketches of the sea and went back to your original plan of illustrating articles for the new journal. At least that way you will meet pretty ladies.'

'True,' said Richard, 'I was getting rather tired of the sea. Do you ever tire of it? I mean, you look at it more than I do.'

'It's never the same twice,' said Mina. Now she thought about it, so many of her stories were inspired by the sea. She loved its mysteries, its power, even its sinister invitation, promising pleasure but concealing a lurking threat of danger. In fine weather, its sounds soothed her, and the constant changes of colour and form refreshed her eyes and mind. How easy it was, she thought, to see dead faces in the water, fingers rising up like ghostly wave tips, all to be swept away in a heartbeat. But Richard could never be refreshed by the sea; his senses demanded something more.

Richard looked through his portfolio of sketches and threw them to the floor disconsolately. 'And now I have to hope that Mother doesn't get to hear about Mr Dorry being such a cheat. But if I don't tell her, she will think I still have a patron and expect me to be doing well. I'm sure Edward will hear of it in any case and have a joke at my expense.'

'Perhaps,' suggested Mina, 'you could make a sketch of Mr Dorry?'

Richard pulled a face. 'That scoundrel! Why would I want to draw him?'

'Because he is a scoundrel. And you need not think to flatter him, make it an honest portrait. If he is the villain we think he is, the newspapers will be clamouring for an image of him. And the police might find it very useful indeed.'

Richard, who had been slumped in misery, suddenly sat up straight. 'Ah, I understand! They will need the likeness to help them find him. And I would be instrumental in his capture!'

'You would.'

He leaped off the bed with renewed energy. 'I'll do it now!'

Dear Edward,

I hope the family is in as good health as is possible in this dreadful weather. You are very kind to take so much care of them, and I am grateful for everything you do.

You may have read in the newspapers that Mr Dorry's London gallery has closed, and as it so happens his Brighton premises has met a similar and sudden fate. It might be best if Mother was protected from this news until such time as Richard's standing improves.

We are all well here.

Fondest love, Mina

With Richard busy, and her story complete, Mina looked in on their unexpected houseguests. Jessie was making herself useful with some mending while Miss Brendel was sitting up in bed with a glass of milk, a plate of biscuits and *Traditional Ghost Tales of Olde England*, all three of which were absorbing her attention. She glanced up at Mina and brushed crumbs from her lips. 'When is luncheon?'

Chapter Forty

Luncheon an hour later was minced beef turnovers with mushrooms, which Miss Brendel attacked with relish, and Mina was pleased to see Richard arriving at the table more cheerful than he had been earlier. 'I have made a portrait of Mr Dorry in which he looks like a large hirsute frog. It is an excellent likeness and I shall take it to the police this afternoon.'

When the plates were empty, which took very little time, Rose cleared them away and brought bottled fruit, sponge cake, and two letters for Mina, one of which was in the printed envelope of Scarletti Publishing. 'A cheque, I hope?' said Richard.

'No,' said Mina. 'A letter, from Mrs Caldecott.'

Dear Miss Scarletti,

Your recent questions concerning the Wakefield mine-owner Mr Brendel piqued my interest, and I have made some further enquiries with acquaintances who are prominent in the best Yorkshire society. The have advised me that Mr Aloysius Brendel is a widower with two sons, and does not, as far as they are aware, have a daughter. He is expected very shortly to announce his betrothal to Miss Araminta Cartwright, eldest daughter of Sir Wilfrid and Lady Margaret Cartwright of Dundersby Hall near Harrogate. The ladies residing in Brighton calling themselves Mrs and Miss Brendel are undoubtedly imposters. While Mr Brendel does not care to move in society, the Cartwrights do. Friends of theirs who knew of the impending announcement are in Brighton for the season, and on learning of the situation, were impelled to advise both the Cartwrights and Mr Brendel, who will be taking appropriate action.

Yours,

E. Caldecott (Mrs)

The second letter was from Dr Hamid, and there was an enclosure.

Dear Miss Scarletti,

As you know, I wrote to Mr Brendel, advising him that his daughter was recuperating at your house, and requesting that he should, at his earliest convenience, call to take her home. I have today received a letter from him which astonished me and which I enclose.

I trust that Miss Brendel is recovering her strength, and I will be informed should a second visit be required.

Yours faithfully,

D. Hamid, M.D.

643

Dear Sir,

I thank you for advising me that a young woman calling herself Athene Brendel is staying at a respectable house in Brighton. It has recently been drawn to my attention that a female who I feel sure from the description is Mrs Martha Jones, a former housekeeper of mine, has been staying in Brighton with her daughter masquerading under the name of Mrs Brendel, and claiming to be my wife.

Earlier this year, I had agreed, in view of Mrs Jones's long and loyal service to my house, to meet some of her expenses, but I certainly did not authorise her to use my name, to which she has no entitlement. This outrageous imposture, which has caused me no little inconvenience, renders that agreement void, and she will receive nothing more from me. Miss Athene is, so I have always been told, Mrs Jones's daughter, but her paternity is something no-one can determine, and I am under no obligation to keep her. I will not, therefore, call to remove her to my home, and she and her mother may do as they please.

Yours faithfully,
Aloysius Brendel
Westgate House
Wakefield

Mina undoubtedly held in her hands the reasons behind the sudden upset in the household at Oriental Place and Mr Quinley's abrupt departure. But the letters could not, she thought, contain the whole story. Would Mr Brendel really have agreed to the generous support of a former housekeeper and her daughter, of whose parentage he could not be certain, a daughter he had brought up and educated so carefully? On that evidence alone, Mr Brendel was in no doubt at all concerning the identity of the young lady's father.

Mina could only guess as to the reasons why Mrs Jones, as she must now be known, had left Mr Brendel's employ, but a strong possibility was that the housekeeper, mother to her employer's natural daughter, to whom he had been very generous, had demanded that Mr Brendel marry her and legitimise Miss Athene, only to be thwarted when the radiant Miss Cartwright, a younger, well-connected rival had appeared. Mr Brendel, wanting to keep peace with all parties, had agreed to support his former housekeeper and her daughter, imagining that she would be content with that arrangement. He had not reckoned with the lady's effrontery which had led her to adopt the name she thought was due to her, an action which must inevitably have threatened his marriage plans. Under the circumstances he had seen no alternative but to withdraw funds and deny any blood connection with the daughter.

As for Mr Quinley, who must have been a confederate of Mrs Jones in her career of deception, he had left Brighton in a hurry with not the slightest intention of returning, and was probably now in Wakefield assuring his client that he knew nothing about her scheme.

'Miss Brendel,' said Mina hesitantly, 'if that is your name...'

Miss Brendel's eyes opened wide. She was devouring a hearty portion of pudding, and hardly paused. 'Of course it is my name.'

'And you are the daughter of mine-owner Aloysius Brendel of Wakefield?'

'Yes, I am.'

'And the lady you lately resided with is your mother?'

'She is. I don't understand; why are you asking me this?'

'And your mother is Mrs Brendel, wife of Mr Brendel?'

There was a long silence.

'I see we have finally reached the point where the lies begin,' said Mina.

'Well,' said Richard, 'my sister is as full of surprises as ever. What do you say, Miss Brendel? Is that your name?'

Miss Brendel looked surly, and curled a defiant lip. 'Yes. It is the name I have always been called by. I admit that Mother and Father are — not exactly married. But it was intended they should be. They are as good as. Mother has kept house for Father for more than twenty years. He has been a widower for a long time, but all he thought of was business. He was too busy to think about marrying again. She did keep reminding him, but...'

'But he would not?' asked Mina. 'Perhaps she pressed him too hard? Or maybe he never meant to?'

'I don't know. Mother tells me very little. But I know things were very friendly between them and then suddenly it all went cold. Perhaps that is why we left Wakefield.'

Mina held up Mrs Caldecott's letter. 'I have just received news that Mr Brendel is on the point of announcing his betrothal to another lady. A Miss Cartwright. Do you know her?'

Miss Brendel affected a look of supreme disdain. 'Yes. She is very plain, and has no figure at all, but her father has money and likes to think of himself as gentry.'

'Mr Brendel has been told by friends of the Cartwrights that your mother has been passing herself off as his wife. This at a time when he is about to become betrothed. Her actions have naturally excited his displeasure.'

Miss Brendel was so startled she put down her spoon. 'Oh dear. That would explain...'

'Yes?'

'Mother received a letter from father a week ago. She wouldn't tell me what was in it, but she and Mr Quinley had a long talk and then Mr Quinley said he would go to see father and smooth things over. He left the same day, and promised that he would write as soon as he got there, but we have heard nothing since. And Mother is very upset because there are bills to be paid, and nothing to pay them with.'

'Mr Brendel was paying your bills in Brighton?'

'Yes, through Mr Quinley. Mother said that if we didn't hear from him soon we would have to go back to Wakefield. But I don't want to go back to Wakefield. I like it here. I'll be twenty-one soon and then I'll be able to live where I please.' She picked up the spoon, and attacked her pudding again.

'Do you have any income of your own?'

'No. Not as such. Father has made a settlement on me. When I am twenty-one I will have a hundred pounds a year.'

'We must hope he does not revoke it,' said Mina, 'or you will be cast adrift in the world. Your mother will be obliged to find employment, and you will have to make what you can playing the piano and holding séances.'

'Oh, I don't get the visions anymore,' said Miss Brendel airily. 'I hated them. I'm glad they have gone.'

'You could always marry Mr Dawson.'

To Mina's surprise, Miss Brendel laughed. 'Oh, I'm not interested in him.'

'Is that so? He thought you liked him.'

She shrugged. 'I don't know why.' She scraped her dish clean with the spoon.

'I doubt that he could afford to keep you, in any case. When is your birthday?'

'In two weeks.' She licked the spoon. 'Do you have any cheese?'

Mina was left wondering how the difficulty could be settled. She could hardly keep her unwanted guest indefinitely. If the worst came to the worst, she decided, Miss Brendel would have to be sent to Wakefield with Jessie, at Mina's expense, in the hope that her father would relent and take her in.

Chapter Forty-One

Once luncheon was over, Richard went to take his sketch of Mr Dorry to the police station, and Miss Brendel explored the kitchen in search of cheese. Jessie had proved to be a useful addition to the household, as she knew a recipe that would improve cook's handling of pastry, and Mina was hoping for fancies that a hungry bird would not have refused.

The doorbell rang, and soon afterwards, Rose appeared at Mina's door. 'There's a Mrs Fazackerly wants to see you. I don't know her. She did ask for you by name.'

Mina remembered that this was the name of the landlady of the house in Oriental Place, and wondered how she had obtained her address and what had brought her to her door. She could only hope that Mrs Fazackerly would not be troublesome. 'Show her into the parlour, and tend to the fire. I will come down.'

Mrs Fazackerly, Mina was pleased to see, did not look as if she was about to make trouble, rather she was deeply concerned. She was a widow in middle life, very neat about her person, her face framed in a black bonnet that only emphasised her anxious pallor.

'Oh, Miss Scarletti,' she gasped, as Mina entered, 'it is so kind of you to see me without warning!'

'Not at all, what may I do for you?'

'I am the landlady of a property in Oriental Place, which I believe you have visited.'

'That is true,' said Mina, 'although I have not done so recently.'

'I should explain. Mrs Brendel, who took the house, has not paid her quarterly rent, which has come due. I called on her again this morning, to ask about the rent, but to my great surprise, I found the house locked up. The maid has been away of late, as she was sent for to deal with a sudden illness, but I thought she would have been back by now. Of course, I have a key, and when I let myself in, I found that no-one was in residence and all of Mrs Brendel's boxes were gone. I had half a mind to sell her piano to pay the debt, but while I was there some men came from Potts Music Emporium and took it away. They said it was only on hire and she had paid the first quarter and not the second. Then the police came, saying they wanted to talk to the tenant as there had been a complaint made, and they had been trying to find her. They asked me where she was, but I knew no more than they did. It was all very upsetting. It is a very superior residence, as you will have seen, and I am used to having respectable tenants. I went home, not knowing what to do, and next thing I received a letter from a solicitor, a Mr Quinley who wrote on Mr Brendel's behalf.'

'Where was he writing from?'

'Wakefield, that is where Mr Brendel lives. He told me that the woman who took the house who calls herself Mrs Brendel is not Mrs Brendel at all but a Mrs Jones. His client had been paying her expenses out of an old friendship, but he had not given her permission to make free with his name. He had just found out what she had done, and as a result there would be no more funds forthcoming. So now I have all the trouble of cleaning the house and finding a new tenant, and I am still owed for the quarter. If Mrs Jones is a married lady then I must find her husband and ask him to pay my rent and expenses. If she is not a married lady then I must seek the money directly from her, but she is nowhere to be found, and neither is her daughter. I searched the house and found some papers, which included names and addresses of visitors, and have been calling on them to discover if they know my former tenant's whereabouts. So far, no-one has been able to help me. This morning I discovered the carrier who took her boxes and was told that she went with them to the railway station. But where she went from there I don't know.'

'It is some days since I last saw the lady and she did not then inform me that she was about to leave her lodgings,' said Mina. 'But if I was to hazard a guess, I would say that she has realised her mistake in angering Mr Brendel, and has gone to Wakefield to plead with him.'

'I don't suppose you know his address?' said Mrs Fazackerly, hopefully.

'As a matter of fact, I do.' Mina went to fetch Mr Brendel's letter and her grateful visitor made a note.

When Mrs Fazackerly had departed, Mina felt obliged to inform Miss Brendel that her mother had vacated the house in Oriental Place and had almost certainly fled Brighton. Miss Brendel might have asked Mina where her mother had gone, but she did not, in fact she seemed not to care.

On the face of it, Mrs Jones's actions since leaving Wakefield had seemed foolhardy, but, thought Mina, the housekeeper, knowing Mr Brendel's habits so very well, had gambled on the fact that he did not take an interest in society and was therefore unlikely to hear of her deception. She had tried to arrange a fashionable wedding for her daughter to afford her the security of wealth and position that Mr Brendel had promised but not provided. Perhaps she hoped that her daughter's advancement would persuade Mr Brendel to relent from his decision not to marry her. Mrs Jones had not, however, reckoned with the aspirations of the Cartwrights, which had proved her undoing.

Mrs Jones, thought Mina, was not a foolish woman. At present, she might seem powerless in the face of Mr Brendel's fortune, but she would use every weapon at her disposal to retrieve the situation. She might plead her old alliance with Mr Brendel, and the future prospects of their daughter. And there was one other path she would surely explore. On the evidence of his letter to Mrs Fazackerly, Mr

Quinley was in Wakefield and was still being entrusted with Mr Brendel's affairs. For that to be the case he must have told his client that he had no knowledge of the masquerade. If Mrs Jones was the woman Mina thought she was, she would have kept any documents which would demonstrate that when Mr Quinley had paid her bills he knew full well that he was paying them on behalf of a woman calling herself Mrs Brendel. Her silence on that point could be a winning card.

Chapter Forty-Two

The next day, a small package arrived for Mina from Lincoln. On opening it she found a letter from Mrs Sperley, and an envelope. The envelope was inscribed with one word: 'Fernwood' and it was in Dr Sperley's handwriting.

Dear Mrs Scarletti,

I have made another search of my late husband's writing desk, and found a great clutter of rubbish. I chanced to find a compartment whose existence I had not even suspected, containing this envelope, and as the name is written clearly I was able to make it out. It refers to a strange medical case that my husband knew of many years ago. I know it troubled him and he would never speak of it to me. Perhaps it might interest you?

Yours truly,

Sophia Sperley

Newland House

Lincoln

Mina stared at the envelope, which had once been sealed, but the gum had dried and cracked and it was possible to open the flap and extract the contents. She hesitated. The name Fernwood might mean that it was intended for someone of that name, but if that had been the case there would have been a Christian name, or at the very least an initial. No, she told herself, Fernwood was not the intended recipient, but the subject matter.

Mina opened the envelope and removed some closely written sheets also in Dr Sperley's hand. The first words struck her with apprehension, so much so that she informed Rose that she did not wish to be disturbed until further notice, retired to her room, and sat at her desk before continuing to read.

It is with a heavy heart that I commit these words to paper. Indeed, it is a secret I would have kept hidden within my breast if it had not been for the fact that it might one day save a life. I have advised Mr Grundy, my solicitor, that should anyone be charged with the murder of my former patient, Thomas Fernwood, who died after being poisoned with arsenic in 1851, this letter should be opened and passed to the police. Its existence and place of concealment is known only to Grundy. I hope that it never sees the light of day! I take upon myself the entire responsibility of keeping this secret. I am an old man, and nothing can be done to me now.

Just two weeks after the death of Thomas Fernwood, with the man barely cold in his grave, I was called to the Fernwood house once more. My first thought was that I would be shown to the bedside of Mrs Jane Fernwood, the only member of the family to be in poor general health. To my surprise, Mrs Fernwood, whose twisted ankle had healed, was up and about and doing well. It pains me to record it, but her health and spirits had greatly improved following the death of her husband, indeed, it is not too much to say that the improvement came as a result of his death. Her only anxiety was the health of her granddaughter, Miss Ada Fernwood, who had been suffering from fits, and was in considerable pain. Despite this, Miss Ada had begged her not to summon me, but such was the young lady's torment that Mrs Fernwood had ignored that entreaty. I was deeply concerned, as Miss Ada had never shown signs of hysteria before, rather she was a quiet and modest person. My greatest fear was that I was about to be confronted with another poison victim.

On examining Miss Fernwood, however, I was soon reassured that she had not been poisoned, and it was at first very hard for me to account for her sudden distressing indisposition until unmistakable signs supervened, and I realised that she was miscarrying a foetus, which I judged to be no more than four months from gestation. The misery of this young lady, who was at the time just fifteen years of age, can only be imagined. Soon afterwards she was seized by a fever that rendered her delirious and for some days her condition hovered between life and death, with little indication as to what the final result might be.

One evening, which she honestly thought to be her last on earth, Miss Fernwood begged to be allowed to tell me all her story, assuring me that she was lucid and knew the difference between truth and imagination. I could not deny her, but I might almost wish that I had, as she told such a tale of horror as one could never think might take place in an apparently respectable home.

Miss Ada revealed that the father of the child she had been carrying was none other than her grandfather Thomas Fernwood, and this was not the first time she had miscarried as a result of his assaults on her person, although on the previous occasion, which I deemed from her account to have been at a far earlier stage, she had managed to conceal her plight from her family. She denounced Thomas Fernwood as a thoroughly evil man, who had ruled his family like a tyrant, controlling them through his unyielding hold on the purse strings. His son and daughter in law loathed him for his drunkenness and foul language. His wife, due to her condition as an invalid, had suffered the least, as he had mainly ignored her, but the boys, his grandson George and nephew Peter, had been beaten savagely, often for no reason, and had learned to avoid him as much as possible. Ada had been subject to his disgusting advances since the age of ten, as had her sister Ellen, and even little Mary had found her great uncle frightening, although she could hardly express why, and had begged not to be left alone with him.

Finally, Miss Ada, with what she believed to be her dying breath, confessed to killing her grandfather in order to save her family from torment. Soon afterwards, her fever broke, and within a day it could be seen that she was on the mend.

When she was well again, I took care to reassure her that in view of her terrible sufferings her secret was safe with me. To my surprise, she only smiled enigmatically and said that she had nothing with which to reproach herself. It then occurred to me most forcibly that she had not committed the murder after all, she had confessed to it when she believed herself to be dying only to save the real culprit from suspicion, and relieve the family from the stress of not knowing the full *story. I am ashamed to say that I was overcome by curiosity, and demanded to know the truth from her. I pointed out that if the wrong person was ever to be charged then her silence could lead to an innocent being condemned. She only said that she would never allow that to happen. I asked if the reason for this was that the culprit was a relative, something that had always been apparent. She was silent but she did not deny it. And then I saw how dreadfully naïve I had been. I had imagined that it was only I to whom Thomas Fernwood had voiced his plea, his insistence that he had been murdered, and attempted to name his murderer. How foolish to have flattered myself in that way! During the early stages of his illness, before the acid had corroded his throat and he was better able to speak, he had been tended to by his granddaughters Ada and Ellen, and sister-in-law Mrs Clifton. Mr William Fernwood had made a visit to the bedside, as had his wife, Margery. Had I really imagined that the dying man had not also attempted to tell at least one of these persons what he knew? And succeeded? Yet all of them had been adamant that they could not cast any light on the mystery. Horrible thought — that at least one member of the family probably knows the identity of the culprit and is prepared to take the secret to the grave.*

The letter was dated just two months after the conclusion of the inquest on Thomas Fernwood.

Mina sat for some time drowned in the horror of this terrible letter. Although she had never met Ada and Ellen, how piercingly she felt for those terrified girls. George Fernwood had almost certainly never been told what his sisters had endured. It had been easy for him to assume that their aversion to marriage was due to the fear of an inherited taint, but now she saw it ran far deeper than that. The lives of the sisters had been rendered sterile and joyless, and they could only achieve some small measure of peace in each other's company. The only good thing she had learned from the letter was that Mary had been spared the ultimate insult.

Mina spent an hour or more wondering what she should do with this devastating information. Would it be right for her to tell Miss Clifton and Mr Fernwood that Dr Sperley had believed that at least one family member held the secret they had been so desperately seeking? Important as it was, Mina hesitated to reveal what she knew. She reminded herself that all she had been asked to do was help them assess whether or not the mediums they visited were genuine. She had not been given any authority to delve into their family affairs, beyond the details they themselves had provided, and they might not thank her for doing so. Through Mr Castlehouse's slate-writing demonstrations they had found an answer to their dilemma. It might not be the right one, but it was one that satisfied them, and brought both consolation and the chance of happiness. Did it really matter whether the solution written on the slate was the right one or not? Why cause them unnecessary distress? Once again, Mina decided that her best course of action was to leave well alone.

Chapter Forty-Three

Two days later, Mina received a note from Miss Landwick.

Dear Miss Scarletti,
Have you see the recent edition of the Sussex Times*?*
My brother is triumphant as he has effected Mr Castlehouse's downfall!
Yours,
E. Landwick.

Mina had not seen the journal in question and sent Rose out to obtain a copy. In between the announcement of a fat stock show and the market preparations for Christmas was a letter.

To the Editor;
I am sorry to say that Brighton has once again taken leave of its senses and been subject to yet another outrageous display of duplicity. For some years past I have been entertaining my family and friends with conjuring and legerdemain, in which I flatter myself I have some small skill. I have learned a great deal from studying the performances of some of the most accomplished stage magicians in the country, and while it is not possible to know all their secrets I am confident that I can tell when an apparently impossible effect is being produced by clever manipulation.

I am therefore in a position to announce to the world that Mr Castlehouse, who claims to invoke the spirits to write on his slates with chalk, is nothing more than a conjuror, who finds he can make a better living from fraud than he can from honest performances. It astonishes me that his method of producing writing on a slate which he holds underneath a table has succeeded in mystifying any observer other than the youngest child. The trick whereby he substitutes a blank slate with one on which he has already written is too well known to be worth describing here. Worse than that, after making some enquiries, I have it on good authority that Mr Castlehouse is none other than the same man who once performed as Angelo, and was the very conjuror who exposed the scandalous frauds of Ellison, who so narrowly escaped prison only last year.

I advise Mr Castlehouse to pack up his chalks and slates and leave Brighton before he suffers a worse fate. If he does he should go in the company of Mr and Mrs Myles who are his puppets.

I take full responsibility for the assertions in this letter and if Mr Castlehouse presumes to sue me he is free to do so, but he will not profit by it, and may only increase his woes. I therefore have no hesitation is signing myself,
Charles Landwick

Mina knew too well that Mr Castlehouse would not pack up his slates and chalks on the basis of that challenge. It took much harder work than a single letter to the press to dislodge devoted adherents from a fraud. Those who needed to believe would still cling to their beliefs, and the next week's papers would be awash with their letters all loading insults onto the head of Mr Landwick, who would be declared either grossly ignorant of the subject or himself a medium without knowing it. Mr Castlehouse would bask in still greater fame, and perhaps come up with novel tricks with which to astonish and enthral his audiences. If he was indeed the magician Angelo than he would have many at the tips of his long agile fingers.

Mina wondered if George Fernwood and Miss Clifton had paid a joint visit to the slate-writer and if so, what messages had they received? More worryingly, did Mr Fernwood read the *Sussex Times*, and if he did, what now remained of any belief that his dilemma had finally been resolved?

Mina had heard nothing from either George Fernwood or Miss Clifton for a while, and expected not to see either of them again, however a brief note arrived from George Fernwood. It was on the same notepaper as his very first letter to her, but the handwriting, although recognisably his, was different in quality. What had previously been a measured copperplate had become unsteady and undisciplined, with little flicks of ink that revealed a slight tremor. The message itself was unexceptional. He wanted to pay Mina a visit to retrieve the package of papers he had left with her. He preferred not to have them consigned to the post but wished to collect them in person. Mina replied to make the appointment.

With Mrs Jones, the housekeeper formerly known as Brendel, now absent from Brighton, there was no reason for her daughter not to dare go out on the town. Athene became so insistent about this, that Richard, who was beginning to find her demands tiresome, nevertheless agreed to take her and Jessie out for a ride in a carriage, something to which Miss Brendel agreed, making the condition that their excursion should include a visit to a cake shop and the purchase of cheese. Mina was naturally expected to pay for this, but she thought it worth the expenditure it if only to have some peace in which to write. She wanted to complete her latest story before Mr Fernwood's visit that afternoon.

She was busy at her desk anticipating a nice brew of hot coffee, when an unexpected visitor was announced, Mr Ernest Dawson. She went downstairs and found him shivering by the parlour fire. 'Please don't be anxious, I am well,' he said, 'but even the walk here did not warm me.'

Mina sent Rose to fetch the coffee. 'I understand that Mrs Brendel caused you some embarrassment recently. But you need not fear her any more as she is no longer in Brighton.'

He looked relieved. 'That is the best news I have had in an age. Did you know she dared to come storming into Potts, making a terrible commotion, disturbing all the customers, and accusing me of abducting her daughter? The manager ordered her to leave and when she would not, he was obliged to call the police. In the event we were both taken to the station. Of course, I had no idea where Miss Brendel was, and when it was proved that I had actually been at work at the time she left the house, the police soon saw that there was no truth in the accusation, and let me go. But I came very near to losing my position.'

'Mrs Brendel came here afterwards. She actually accosted me in the street and accused me of being your confederate.'

'Did she? How extraordinary! The woman is quite deranged.'

'She told me that you had been searched and my card was found in your pocket, together with a love note you intended to deliver to Miss Brendel. Is that true?'

Dawson looked guilty. The coffee arrived and was poured and he warmed his hands on the cup. 'That is true, yes. But why shouldn't I? It was all perfectly proper.'

'Mrs Brendel claimed that you had been planning an elopement. Was that the subject of your love note?'

'I — well —' He gulped the coffee, gratefully, 'I admit it was a plan that had crossed my mind, but there was nothing of that sort in the note, well, not precisely, only a sincere declaration of affection, and the hope that we might be married one day.'

'Who passed the notes for you?'

There was a moment of reluctance, and then a shrug. 'Oh, I suppose there is no harm in telling you, now, but you must promise not to say anything. It was a young fellow by the name of Tasker. I knew him because he bought sheet music, and I had seen him being almost pulled into the house in Oriental Place by his mother. He told me he didn't want to go there, as his mother was going to make him marry Miss Brendel and he didn't want to. So I said I could help him, if he helped me. If he could deliver notes to Miss Brendel when he visited, then I would be able to marry her and he wouldn't have to. He seemed very happy to do it.'

'I see. Well, he will not be visiting Miss Brendel again. But how might I assist you? I assume that is the reason you have called?'

'Yes, if you would be so kind. The thing is — my manager told me that if I wanted to keep my employment I must not go near Oriental Place again, and I have tried really hard to comply, but this morning I just couldn't help it, so I went there again, and the house was empty. It has a letting sign outside. A neighbour told me that the Brendels had gone away but no-one knew where. You have just told me that Mrs Brendel has left Brighton. But what of Athene? Is she still here or is she with her mother? Do you know where she is?'

Mina hesitated, since Miss Brendel was still a few days shy of her twenty-first birthday. 'At this moment I am afraid that I cannot say with any precision where either of them might be. The one thing I do know is that Mr Quinley has returned to Wakefield.'

Dawson looked downcast at this evaporation of his hopes. 'I suppose it is pointless for me to write to him. If I only knew that the dear girl was safe and well!'

Mina took pity on him. 'All I can say on that point is that the last time I set eyes on Miss Brendel she did look very much better than previously. Her appetite has returned, and she also informed me that she no longer has the visions.'

'Where did you —' Dawson stopped, with a shocked expression. 'No visions?'

'Yes. It seems that they were produced by something she ate which disagreed with her. Fish, I think it was.'

'Fish,' said Dawson, blankly as if the concept was new to him.

'Yes. I think that as long as she is careful not to eat fish or at least to make sure of its absolute freshness, she may be assured of not being troubled with the visions in future.'

Dawson continued to look dumbfounded. 'That is — quite — extraordinary.'

Mina sensed that this was a piece of news he was less than happy to hear, and she should test him further.

'The other thing I should mention, and that may be partly to blame for Mrs Brendel's distracted state when you last encountered her, is that she is not actually Mrs Brendel.'

'I beg your pardon?' said Dawson, incredulously.

'Yes. She is actually a Mrs Martha Jones, Mr Brendel's former housekeeper, and has no real call upon him at all.'

'But that can't be so!' Dawson protested. 'He paid her bills! I have seen them myself!'

'I suspect that he did so out of old affection and duty to Miss Athene, who I believe may well be his daughter, but that, I am sorry to say, no longer concerns him, as he was very annoyed when he discovered that his housekeeper was pretending to be his wife, especially as he was courting another lady. As a result, he has ceased to support them.'

Dawson took a little while to come to terms with this information. He was still clutching the coffee cup, but put it down, the drink unfinished. 'I am — somewhat confused by all this. You say that Miss Brendel is Mr Brendel's natural daughter, not lawful?'

'Yes. But she has been well brought up and given every advantage.'

'I thought —' he paused. 'I was told that she was his only daughter and I assumed his only child, since no brothers were mentioned.'

'Oh no. He has two sons by his late wife.'

Mr Dawson looked undeniably dismayed. 'That explains a great deal. The quarterly hire for the piano has not been paid, and the instrument has been returned to the shop. I had imagined it was due to some delay on Mr Brendel's part, but now you say he is no longer paying her bills.'

'So it appears. And he has chosen no longer to acknowledge Miss Brendel as his daughter, which must be very painful for her. But I do have some good news for you.'

'You do?' said Dawson, hopefully.

Mina favoured him with a smile of pure delight. 'I do. You will be pleased to know that Miss Brendel — as she still continues to call herself — will be twenty-one very soon, and will be able to follow the dictates of her heart.'

Mr Dawson was now looking distinctly alarmed. 'Oh. That is — I am sure that will be a wonderful thing for her.'

'If I should chance to encounter her again, is there any message you would like me to give her?'

'I — thank you, I will give that some thought and let you know.' He rose to his feet.

'I can always pass a note to you at the music shop.'

'Indeed. I must take my leave of you now. Thank you for all your assistance and advice.' Mr Dawson departed with rather more haste than Mina thought strictly necessary. It was as if he had arrived in the hope of finding Miss Brendel, and left in fear that he might do so.

Chapter Forty-Four

When George Fernwood arrived, the parcel of papers was wrapped ready for him to collect and a nice pot of hot fresh tea was ordered. He was not, Mina saw at once, the same man he had been on his first visit. Then he had seemed worried, anxious, and uncomfortable. He was now in pain.

Mina poured the tea. 'Mr Fernwood, forgive me for mentioning it but you do not look at all well. Is there something I can obtain for you? Or I could summon a doctor. You only have to say the word.'

He clutched the parcel with an expression of sheer misery. 'Thank you. I am in bodily health, and need no medicine, but you are right, I am suffering.'

'Perhaps a small glass of brandy?'

He shook his head. 'No. No! I shall never touch that wretched drink again. It was the curse of our family. It would have to be forced down my throat. It would choke me.' He took a large handkerchief from his pocket. 'I'm sorry, I think I might have a chill after all.' He wiped his eyes, and eventually gave up all pretence and sobbed, noisily.

Mina could do nothing but wait until he was recovered.

He blew his nose. 'My apologies for this unseemly and embarrassing display. What you must think of me!'

'I do not judge you. I only wish I could help.'

'There is one thing you can advise me about. The last séance you attended of that villain Castlehouse. Tell me your impressions. Did you think he was a fraud then?'

'I suspected it, but I had no proof. My difficulty was that the result made Miss Clifton so very happy, I did not have the heart to express a contrary opinion without being sure of my ground. I could see that the performance might have been one of a conjuror, but I was quite unable to explain the content of the message.'

'Yet, you later accused Mary of deceit. And in that, as I now know to my cost, you were quite right. She has confessed it to me.'

'I did so as a result of information I received subsequent to the visit. Miss Clifton had obtained duplicate slates, given them to Mr Castlehouse and told him what to write on them. Sleight of hand did the rest. She explained her motives to me, which were the natural ones of achieving contentment. What should I have done? Written to you and destroyed your chances of happiness? I reckoned without Mr Landwick, however. I asked him to report his conclusions to me, but instead he could not resist announcing them to the world.'

'Yes, Mr Landwick,' said Fernwood, miserably. 'You see, after the séance, Mary showed me the slates, and said that neither she nor you could explain the message by any other means except that it was a communication from my grandmother. As you say, she was happy, she said that it was all the reassurance we needed. I wasn't so certain, so she persuaded me to go and see Mr Castlehouse. We went together. We took our slates with us. At the séance we received a message from my grandmother begging our forgiveness and wishing us happiness. And so — I allowed myself to be convinced. It was the easy way, I suppose.

'We went home and told Aunt Dorothy and my cousin Peter that we intended to announce our engagement, and marry in the spring. I also explained the reasons for our initial hesitation and gave them the good news that the concerns about our family tragedy could now be laid to rest. We showed them the slates as proof. Now that I look back on it, Aunt Dorothy reacted very strangely, almost as if she was not pleased at all, and I think she had to work hard to conceal her real thoughts.

'I wrote to my parents, and to my sisters, Ada and Ellen to tell them our happy news. We agreed on a wedding day. Mary began to plan her trousseau. And then,' he groaned like a man whose heart was being twisted savagely in his chest, 'Mr Landwick wrote his horrible letter to the *Sussex Times*. I had to show it to Mary, of course. She tried her best to defend Mr Castlehouse, saying that he was really a medium, but I knew something was wrong. In fact, I think I knew it before, when I saw the expression on my aunt's face, and I had been denying it to myself ever since. So I told Mary that I would go and see Mr Castlehouse and make him tell me the truth, even if we came to blows. Mary begged me not to, and at last she was forced to admit how she had practised on all of us. Until that moment I had no idea that she could even contemplate dishonesty.'

'You told me, at our very first meeting in fact, that Miss Clifton was at one time even more sceptical of mediums than you.'

'That is true, yes.'

'Yet she came to me that day as a believer. I know people can go from doubt to belief when they see something that convinces them, especially if it meets what they wish to believe, so I didn't question it at the time. But now I see that I should have done. I only had to assume that Miss Clifton had never changed her beliefs about mediums, but simply appeared to do so, and the real purpose of her actions became clear. She was not searching for the truth, whatever that might be. She was looking for a medium who was a convincing fraud whom she could bribe into providing the answer she needed in order to put an end to the doubts over your grandfather's death. But she did it from the best of intentions. She did it for the future happiness of you both.'

Fernwood shook his head. 'And look what it has brought.'

'What will you do?' asked Mina.

'Do?' He threw up his hands in despair. 'I can do nothing. There will be no wedding, not now or ever. Mary has packed a box and left. I don't know where she has gone, and even if I did, I shan't go after her.'

'That seems very extreme. What did you say to her? I know it was a disturbing thing to do, but considering her motives, could you not have forgiven her?'

Fernwood looked on the verge of another flood of tears. 'Mary did not leave because of anything I said. It was to avoid what she knew must follow once matters were being spoken of openly again. The day after she left Ada and Ellen and my parents all came to see us. We sat down as a family and talked about what had happened in Lincoln for the first time in many years. Peter and I spoke of the whippings we had been subjected to, but it was only then — only then that we learned that for the girls, my grandfather had a worse fate, something I cannot name. Then Aunt Dorothy tried to take the blame for Grandfather's death on herself, saying that she had put the arsenic in the tea, and she had done it to save the girls, but Ada put her hand so lightly on her arm and soothed her and said she knew it wasn't she. She knew that my aunt had lied at the inquest when she said she had taken the tea up to my grandfather that morning. Ada knew who had really killed Grandfather, really carried up the teacup, really added that fatal pinch of arsenic and stirred it well in. Ada had seen who came down the stairs carrying the empty cup and laughing at what she had done. Perhaps Grandfather heard that laugh also, too late, after he had drunk the tea, and realised that he had been poisoned.' New tears streaked George Fernwood's face. 'She was only eight years old.'

It took a moment for Mina to understand whom he meant. 'Mary?'

He gulped and nodded.

'Perhaps she didn't know what she did,' said Mina. 'She would have been too young to understand. Perhaps, as in the message she devised, there was no intention to murder.'

'Oh, she knew,' said Fernwood bitterly, 'yes, she knew. Even so young she knew the difference between alive and dead. Ada told me that Mary used to sprinkle arsenic on the bread and butter and put it down for the mice. That old house, it was a nest of vermin. We used to find the little bodies twitching in agony. Ada said that Mary used to like watching them die, and as she watched, she laughed. "They won't bother us again" she used to say. That's almost what she said when she came downstairs bringing Grandfather's teacup. "He won't bother us again".' Fernwood wiped his face. 'My grandfather knew it was Mary. He didn't see her put the poison in the cup but he heard her laugh after he had drunk from it. He knew. And he told Ada and Ellen what he knew, but they said nothing to anyone.'

There was a long silence of contemplation. 'Do you mean to accuse her?' asked Mina.

'No. Even if we could find her, it would be pointless. I cannot imagine Ada or Ellen or my aunt giving evidence against her. No court could convict her. No, I must go home and stand in my shop and run my business, and make the best of things.'

'Might I ask you one more question?'

'Yes?'

'When you heard of Dr Sperley's death, was that just before or after you and Miss Clifton decided you wished to marry?'

He pondered this for a while. 'I think — yes I am sure. It was just before. I recall Mary saying how sad it was that we would not be able to give him the happy news.' He paled. 'Of course. Sperley must have suspected something. I wonder if he ever spoke to her, or gave away perhaps by a look or a gesture that he knew the truth. So it wasn't until after his death that she felt truly safe.'

He was about to leave when the door opened and Miss Brendel peered in. The cold wind had stung her cheeks so they glowed red, and her eyelashes were damp with mist.

George Fernwood started in amazement. He saw before him a new Miss Brendel, no longer a fading flower on a stem that looked ready to break, but a young beauty in full bloom, with hair that shone and skin like that of a chubby child advertising good health.

'I thought I heard a familiar voice,' she said, brightly. 'Mr Wood, is it?'

'Ah, yes.' He scrambled to his feet and stared at her. 'Miss Brendel. If you don't mind my saying so, you are looking remarkably well.'

She smiled. 'I thank you. It seems that my malady was all down to eating some bad fish, and I am now quite cured!'

'I am glad to hear it. Wholesome food is so important to health. If you are ever in Haywards Heath, you must call in at my business, Fernwood Grocery, where purity and cleanliness are held in the highest regard.' He handed her his card.

She studied it with approval. 'Do you sell cheese?'

661

Chapter Forty-Five

Dear Mina,

I am not sure if I will be able to come and see you over the festive season, as there is just too much to do in London, most of it trying to keep Mother and Enid from the madhouse.

I see Richard has covered himself in glory once again. Very well, I promise not to mention Mr Dorry's downfall to Mother, and see what fiction Richard can dream up to conceal the truth from her. He did send me a portrait of the renowned antiquarian Mr Honeyacre together with his betrothed, Miss Kitty Betts. It is a good picture, but I am not sure whether this should go in the society column or be classed as humour.

He has also sent me a great many sketches of the sea, which are not at all interesting. Please tell him to stop.

Affect'ly,
Edward

The missing Mr Elmer Dorry got as far as Marseilles before he found that a man of his impressive waistcoatage could not go unnoticed forever, especially if his portrait was in all the leading newspapers and he was accompanied by a life-sized marble statue of a nude Adonis. He was arrested on charges of fraud and forgery that had arisen in six different countries. The only thing remaining to be decided was where he was to stand trial.

Dear Mina,

Did you know that one of Richard's drawings has been published in the Telegraph*? My darling boy has been so very clever! I actually had a letter from him explaining everything, and as he writes so rarely I will treasure it especially. All this time he has been working in secret for the authorities helping them catch the most dreadful criminal. I hope he did not take any risks, and am so greatly relieved to hear that the police now have their man. What a cruel place the world is, and how fortunate to have clever people like my son to put things right! Who would have thought he could turn detective? But it is a dangerous profession and he should not go on with it.*

Richard's success has brought me a little ease. The twins are over the worst with their teeth, and the house is more peaceful now, which is a mercy, as I don't think my poor head could have stood any more.

Enid is a trial, but at least her bilious attacks have ceased, and she complains less than she did, which means only about every ten minutes instead of every five. I can't imagine who she takes after, she can be so difficult at times.

Edward is no further forward in discovering the fate of Mr Inskip, and we have all but given him up as lost. He has complained so bitterly about Richard borrowing his warm coat and hat that I have bought him new ones.

Your sorely tried,

Mama

As the season of merriment and goodwill approached, and Great Britain breathed a sigh of relief at the recovery of the Prince of Wales from typhoid, it appeared that romance was all around.

Young Mr Conroy finally shed his mourning and invited Miss Landwick to accompany him to a concert at the Dome.

George Fernwood continued to visit Brighton, where he made every possible excuse to call upon Miss Brendel. Whether it was the result of the pleadings of her mother or Mr Quinley was unknown, but Mr Brendel relented from his determination not to support his daughter further, and she did receive her annuity on her twenty first birthday. Soon afterwards she left Brighton to take up a post on the cheese counter at Fernwood's Grocery store, sharing a lodging with Mrs Clifton. A month later Mr Fernwood and Miss Brendel announced their engagement. The event met with the approval of the bride-to-be's mother, who had in the meantime exacted her full revenge on Mr Quinley by marrying him.

Mr and Mrs Myles were not seen in Brighton again, although a Mr and Mrs Morton who bore a strong resemblance to that couple, presented a season of dramatic and tender dialogues from the classical repertoire at the best Brighton hotels, with afternoon tea and biscuits.

Mr Castlehouse continued to practice slate-writing, although he was not as popular as he had once been, as Brightonians in search of something more appropriate to the season turned to other entertainments. Declining business obliged him to leave Brighton. Almost immediately, Angelo the magician made a re-appearance in London, thrilling audiences in the best theatres, where he created brilliant illusions. The best part of his performance, as everyone agreed, was causing his new lady wife to disappear from a locked cabinet and reappear in a sack, to the wonderment of all. Mrs Angelo, dressed in a spangled costume that revealed shapely limbs, bore it very well, though there was a hint in her expression that this was far beneath her dignity and not at all the life she had imagined for herself. One of Mr Angelo's most mystifying tricks involved making writing appear on sealed slates. These were first given an expert cleaning by his wife, who showed by the energy in her shoulder and the dexterity of her action that she was no stranger to scouring surfaces.

Shortly before Christmas, Mr Honeyacre and Kitty Betts were married in a grand and unusually spectacular occasion, and the happy groom bundled his blushing bride into a carriage and swept her away to his manor house, which had finally been restored to its old fashioned glory.

Mina had half expected to spend Christmas alone, as Richard was wondering whether to return to London and Edward's hospitality, but so it was not to prove so. On the day after the Honeyacre wedding their mother arrived in Brighton, leaving Enid and the twins in the care of a stern and capable nurse. She was overjoyed to see Richard and listened with maternal pride to his tales of how he had caught a master criminal. Thereafter she declared herself too exhausted to plan the family celebrations and left it to Mina to make all the arrangements.

Dear Mina,

Much as I would like to come to Brighton for Christmas, I fear it will not be possible this year. I am to dine with the Hoopers who have been heroically patient about the time I have spent with Enid and Mother. Mr Greville has also been very kind allowing me to deal with our family upheavals but now I must buckle down and catch up with my work.

Please tell Richard he may keep my best caped coat and tweed travelling cap. If he is to go about pretending to be a detective he should at least be dressed warmly for it.

I was just about to close this letter to you when I unexpectedly received two communications concerning Mr Inskip. They are not from him but from his client in Carpathia, the first dated October and the second only two weeks ago. The weather has been too poor to allow any post to either reach or leave that dreadful region until now. It appears that Mr Inskip was preparing to depart for home when he was suddenly taken very ill. He has spent the last few weeks in a state of delirium, but has been well cared for in the nobleman's castle, where some holy sisters skilled in medicine have tended him, and they are hopeful of his eventual recovery.

Enid has begged me to reply at once reassuring Mr Inskip that he is not to even think of stirring until he is entirely well. There is no danger of that since I am told that he is not yet strong enough to travel home, and may well remain where he is for some months. I have not mentioned this to Enid, but I am told that when she next sees him, he may not be quite the man he was.

Affect'ly,

Edward

***

Enjoyed The Mina Scarletti Series Boxset? Join the Sapere Books mailing list for the latest releases, eBook deals, author news, and much, much more!

<u>**SIGN UP HERE**</u>

HISTORICAL NOTES

MR SCARLETTI'S GHOST

Brighton's Royal Suspension Chain Pier was built in 1823. It has been represented in paintings by both J M W Turner and John Constable. By 1871, when this novel is set, it was falling out of fashion, as it had competition from the West Pier, which was opened in 1866. The Chain Pier was destroyed in a storm in 1896. The West Pier closed in 1975. Since then, it has been ravaged by storms and fire, and today its skeletal remains are considered to be beyond restoration.

Sake Dean Mohamed (1759-1851) was born in Patna, India. He and his British wife settled in London where he opened the capital's first ever Indian restaurant, the Hindoostanee Coffee House, in George Street. The site is now commemorated by a plaque. He later moved to Brighton, where he established his Indian Medicated Vapour bath in 1821. The business attracted high society visitors and he was granted a Royal Warrant and became known as 'Dr Brighton'.

Brill's Baths was a popular sea-water bathing and leisure establishment which opened on East Street, Brighton, in 1869. An earlier establishment, because of its shape and protrusion onto the seafront, was nicknamed 'Brill's bunion.'

Christ Church with its tall slender spire was built in Montpelier Road, Brighton in 1838. In 1871, when Mina and her family worshipped there, services were taken by Reverend James Vaughan. The church was badly damaged by fire in 1978 and the ruins were finally removed in 1983.

The Ghost Club was founded in 1862, and Charles Dickens is known to have been a member. Twice dissolved and revived, it exists today and its members hold regular meetings and conduct investigations into paranormal phenomena.

Daniel Dunglas Home (1833-1886) was one of the most acclaimed mediums of his day, who attracted many wealthy patrons. The case of Lyon vs. Home, in which Home was obliged to repay the substantial funds he had obtained from an elderly widow, is documented in Bar Reports, volume VII, 1868, pp. 451-457. Robert Browning's poem, 'Mr Sludge the Medium', first published in his *Dramatis Personae* in 1864, was an attack on spiritualism, and Sludge was based on Home. Mrs Browning believed in Home, and her comments regarding Home being both morally worthless and a true medium are from a letter she wrote in 1856. See *The Browning's Correspondence*, no. 3742. Vol 22, pp. 138-140.

Modern spiritualism was effectively founded in 1848 when sisters Kate Fox (1837-1892) and Margaret Fox (1833-1893) then living in Hydesville New York, claimed to be in touch with spirits that made clicking and rapping noises. Their fame spread and they embarked on a successful career as mediums, appearing before large audiences. In 1888, Margaret made a public confession of trickery, saying that the noises had been made with their joints, although she retracted her statement in the following year.

Sir David Brewster (1781-1868) was a scientist especially noted for his pioneering work on optics.

William Crookes (1842-1919) was a chemist and physicist, editor of the *Quarterly Journal of Science* from 1864 to 1878. Following the death of his younger brother from yellow fever at the age of twenty-one, Crookes became interested in spiritualism, and conducted scientific experiments with noted mediums including D.D. Home. Many of his contemporaries thought that he was too uncritical and easily duped by frauds. He later became president of the Society for Psychical Research and the Ghost Club.

In 1825 Dr Frederick Struve of Saxony opened a German Spa in Brighton, selling his mineral waters. It was enormously popular for several years, but fell out of fashion and was closed by 1850. The company continued to produce the bottled waters until 1891 when it merged with another.

The London Dialectical Society was a professional association established in 1867, which in 1869 formed a committee to investigate spiritual phenomena. A report was produced in July 1870, but the methods of investigation were criticised as unscientific. When the Society declined to publish it, it was published by the committee in 1871. One member of the committee, Dr James Edmunds, attended a seance held by the Davenport brothers, Ira Erastus Davenport (1839-1911) and his brother William Henry (1841-1877), American stage illusionists who toured Britain in 1868. The Davenports claimed that their effects were produced by spirit power, but Edmunds wrote of his exposure of their trick with the supposed spirit drawing. The Davenports were best known for the cabinet in which they were placed, tied up, with musical instruments, which would then be heard to play. They were frequently denounced as frauds, most famously by magician John Neville Maskelyne, (1829-1917) who had a similar cabinet constructed and demonstrated in public how their tricks were achieved.

Mrs Agnes Guppy (later Guppy-Volckman) (1838-1917) was a popular spirit medium noted for producing apports such as fresh flowers. In June 1871, she claimed to have been transported almost instantaneously from her home to a house three miles away. The claim was ridiculed in the press.

The M Houdin mentioned by Richard was the legendary French magician and father of the modern art of conjuring and illusions, Jean-Eugène Robert-Houdin (1805 –1871).

Women were admitted to study medicine at Edinburgh University in 1869, but faced considerable hostility, and were not permitted to graduate. Davina Hamid would later have been able to obtain her medical qualification at the London School of Medicine for Women which was founded in 1874.

John Henry Pepper (1821-1900) was an analytical chemist and lecturer who developed the method devised by engineer Henry Dircks (1806-1873) in which a ghost-like image of an actor was projected onto a stage. Dubbed 'Pepper's Ghost' it was first demonstrated in 1862.

Lawyer Edward William Cox (1809-1879) was a member of the Dialectical Society, and served on the committee that investigated spiritualism. He assisted William Crookes in his experiments and coined the term 'psychic force.'

The New Oxford Music Hall in New Street, Brighton, was opened on 6 August 1868.

THE ROYAL GHOST

The principal inspiration for this book was *An Adventure*, first published in 1911 by Miss Charlotte Anne Elizabeth Moberly and her companion Miss Eleanor Frances Jourdain, under the pseudonyms Elizabeth Morison and Frances Lamont. The ladies had visited Versailles in 1901, and, after comparing notes and conducting extensive research, became convinced that while there they had entered a time-slip and seen Marie Antoinette and members of her court.

In the summer of 1871 the sensation of Brighton was Christiana Edmunds, a spinster who had attempted to poison the wife of a Dr Beard, for whom she had an obsessive admiration. She tried to deflect suspicion from herself by distributing poisoned food, resulting in the death of a four-year-old child. The police issued a warning notice and newspapers reported that people were talking of the 'days of the Borgias' returning. At her later trial she was declared insane and sent to Broadmoor.

Dr Hamid must have read about the plagiarism case of Pike *v.* Nicholas, which was reported in *The Times* on 25 May and 25 November 1869.

Wondrous Ajeeb the chess automaton was built in 1865 by Charles Hopper, a Bristol cabinet maker. Ajeeb would have been inspired by Wolfgang von Kempelen's more famous Turk, which was destroyed in a fire in 1854. Ajeeb, like the Turk, was controlled by a hidden operator. From 1868 to 1876 it was exhibited at London's Crystal Palace, but performed at the Royal Pavilion in October 1870. It was later taken to the United States, where it was destroyed by a fire in 1929.

Captain William Henry Cecil George Pechell was the son of Vice-Admiral Sir George Brooke Pechell, Bt, Member of Parliament for Brighton. Pechell, a Captain in Her Majesty's 77th Middlesex Regiment of Foot, was twenty-five when he was killed at the siege of Sebastopol on 3 September 1855. A statue was commissioned by public subscription and placed in the vestibule of the Royal Pavilion in 1859. It remained there until about 1940 when it was placed in Brighton's Stanmer Park, where it stood neglected until 2015. It was rescued and at the time of writing it stands near 22 Waterloo Street, Hove, and can be viewed on Google street view.

An article about the public viewing of the Royal Pavilion can be found on p. 5 of the *Brighton Gazette* of 24 January 1850. No one seems to have reported seeing any ghosts.

The 'willing game' was a popular Victorian parlour game played as described in these pages.

Hugh Washington Simmons (1831–1899) was a stage magician who toured the world performing under the name Dr H.S. Lynn. One of his specialities was the Japanese butterfly illusion, which he claimed to have seen in Japan, and first introduced it to the West in 1864. On 17 October 1870 he gave a performance in the Royal Pavilion, Brighton for the benefit of the families of the men lost on HMS *Captain* that sank on 7 September with the loss of about 480 lives. This performance is described on p. 5 of the *Brighton Gazette* of 20 October.

Edward Campbell Tainsh (1835–1919) was a Professor of Literature and author of morally uplifting novels, who disapproved strongly of sensational fiction.

A paper device that answers 'yes' or 'no' is described in *Houdini's Paper Magic*, by Harry Houdini, (E.P. Dutton, New York, 1922). Mystic Stefan must have used an earlier version.

The 'floating arm' and Sphinx's head were both Victorian stage illusions.

Dr Livingstone was discovered by Henry Morton Stanley in November 1871, although the news did not reach Britain until the following year.

William John Smith, bookseller, traded from 41–43 North Street from 1865 to 1913.

Mrs Guppy did indeed claim to have flown through a wall as described. For more information see *Mrs Guppy Takes a Flight* by Molly Whittington-Egan (Neil Wilson Publishing, Castle Douglas, 2015).

Mr Arthur Wallace Hope is a fictional character but his beliefs as described in this book were held by many educated men and women of his day and have not been exaggerated for the purpose of fiction.

AN UNQUIET GHOST

The books for which Mina searched unsuccessfully in the library and bookshop were:

Letters on Natural Magic, addressed to Sir Walter Scott, by Sir David Brewster, (London, John Murray, 1832)

Sketches of the philosophy of apparitions; or, an attempt to trace such illusions to their physical causes, by Samuel Hibbert, (Edinburgh, Oliver & Boyd, 1825). Both these books may be viewed for free on the splendid website www.archive.org.

Sir David Brewster (1781-1868) was a noted scientist and author, especially renowned for his contributions to optics.

Samuel Hibbert, MD, FRSE (1782-1848) was a geologist and antiquarian.

Christoph Friedrich Nicolai (1733-1811) was a German author, editor and bookseller, who wrote about his experience of spectral illusions in 1799.

The originator of slate-writing séances was American medium Henry Slade, (1836-1905) who is thought to have devised them around 1860. He was later copied by other mediums. He visited Britain in 1876, was exposed as a fraud, and prosecuted for obtaining money under false pretences. Found guilty, the verdict was later reversed on appeal and he left the country. Slate-writing soon fell out of fashion. All its proponents have been shown to be frauds.

Pennyroyal (*mentha pulegium*) was once used as a culinary and medicinal herb, but is now known to be toxic. In the nineteenth century it was sometimes used to try and procure an abortion and occasionally proved fatal.

Widow Welch's Pills, first manufactured in 1787, were a popular remedy for all female disorders including what the advertisements described as 'obstructions in the Female System.'

Potts and Co was a prominent dealer in musical instruments at 167 North Street, Brighton.

Brighton sauce was a popular relish for meat.

On Tuesday 7 November 1871 a 39-year-old Scottish wine merchant Athole Peter Hay was found dying in his apartments in Oriental Place Brighton, having cut his throat. A surgeon was called but by the time he arrived the man had died. Hay had been badly injured in a railway accident in April 1866 in which he had suffered a concussion. Since then he had been troubled with weakness, depression and partial paralysis, and the delusion that he was guilty of a crime for which he felt great remorse. (Reported in the *Hastings and St Leonards Observer* 11 and 18 November 1871)

The story of Mrs Brendel is partly inspired by a Mrs Henrietta Bradshaw, a fraudster who took a house in Oriental Place Brighton and ran up considerable debts. See the *Brighton Gazette* 3 November 1870.

In November 1871 the panorama of 'Paris in its grandeur and in flames', including many scenes connected with the late war was exhibiting at the concert hall West Street, Brighton, and was so popular it prolonged its stay to Saturday 19.

The annual bazaar for the children's hospital was held at the Dome in November

1871, and attracted over 8,500 people.

The County Hospital ball, "recognised as the official start of the Brighton fashionable season, was held on 22 November 1871. Dancing commenced shortly after 10pm to the band of the nineteenth hussars, and carriages did not depart until the early hours of the morning.

Lowes Cato Dickinson was a portrait painter who with his brothers established the business of Dickinson Brothers in Brighton and London. In 1871 Dickinson's gallery at 107 King's Road Brighton was exhibiting a new portrait of the queen in her robes and jewels of state, while in the adjoining gallery there were watercolour portraits of ladies of the British aristocracy.

John (later Sir John) Cordy Burrows was elected Mayor of Brighton for the third time in November 1871.

The Times of 21 October 1871 reported on a recent German expedition to the North Pole. Dispatches confirmed the discovery of an ice-free North Pole sea, swarming with whales.

The 1871 Christmas pantomime at Brighton Theatre Royal was *Goody Two-Shoes and her Queen Anne's Farthing*. Leading characters were King Counterfeit and Fairy Spiteful. Mr and Mrs Myles were not called upon to perform.

In 1824 J.M.W. Turner painted the chain pier from the sea, with the Pavilion in the distance. He rotated the Pavilion by about 90 degrees in order to show the whole of the east front.
http://brightonmuseums.org.uk/discover/2016/04/15/stormy-weather-turners-sublime-vision-of-brighton-in-1824/

In September 1870 *HMS Captain* capsized with the loss of nearly 500 lives.

A NOTE TO THE READER

Dear Reader,

Thank you for taking the time to read this collection of the adventures of the indomitable Mina Scarletti. I hope you had as much fun reading them as I did writing them and will want to see what she and her family and friends do next! I love exploring the stranger and more colourful areas of Victorian life and beliefs, and it has been a great pleasure researching the spiritualists; their histories, techniques, believers and antagonists. For more details of the actual persons and places mentioned in the book, see my Historical Notes below.

Reviews are so important to authors, and if you enjoyed the collection I would be grateful if you could spare a few minutes to post a review on **Amazon** and **Goodreads**. I love hearing from readers, and you can connect with me online, **on Facebook**, **Twitter**, and **Instagram**.

You can also stay up to date with all my news via **my website** and by signing up to **my newsletter**.

Linda Stratmann

lindastratmann.com

Sapere Books is an exciting new publisher of brilliant fiction and popular history.

To find out more about our latest releases and our monthly bargain books visit our website:
saperebooks.com

Printed in Poland
by Amazon Fulfillment
Poland Sp. z o.o., Wrocław

53830859R00397